Robert Fleming Rankin was ███████████████████ was educated at Grange Infant████████████████ ████ Ealing, Horsenden Secondary, Greenford, and Ealing School of Art. His hobbies range from the study of the occult and the paranormal to the mastery of blowlamp technique and the science of loft insulation. He was for two years Writer in Residence at Watermans Art Centre, where he founded the Brentford Poets Circle, wrote and produced two plays, *The Golden Gryphon* and *Armageddon, The Musical*, and frequented the bar whenever possible. He is the nephew of Edmund Crispin, the crime novelist, but never actually met him. He now lives in Brighton and still does all his own decorating. His fourth novel, *The Sprouts of Wrath*, is also published in Abacus.

Robert Rankin

THE BRENTFORD TRILOGY

The Antipope
The Brentford Triangle
East of Ealing

SPHERE BOOKS LTD

Published by the Penguin Group
27 Wrights Lane, London w8 5TZ, England
Viking Penguin Inc., 40 West 23rd Street, New York, New York 10010, USA
Penguin Books Australia Ltd, Ringwood, Victoria, Australia
Penguin Books Canada Ltd., 2801 John Street, Markham, Ontario, Canada L3R 1B4
Penguin Books (NZ) Ltd, 182–190 Wairau Road, Auckland 10, New Zealand

Penguin Books Ltd, Registered Offices: Harmondsworth, Middlesex, England

The Antipope was first published in Great Britain by Pan Books Ltd 1981
The Brentford Triangle was first published in Great Britain by Pan Books Ltd 1982
East of Ealing was first published in Great Britain by Pan Books Ltd 1984
This omnibus edition first published in Abacus by Sphere Books Ltd 1988

Printed and bound in Great Britain by
Richard Clay Ltd, Bungay, Suffolk

For my three sons, Robert, Alex and William

THE BRENTFORD TRILOGY

CONTENTS

THE ANTIPOPE

PROLOGUE

A long finger of early spring sunshine poked down between the flatblocks and reached through the dusty panes of the Flying Swan's saloon-bar window, glistening off a pint beer glass and into the eye of Neville the part-time barman.

Neville held the glass at arm's length and examined it with his good eye. It was very clean, small rainbows ran about its rim. It was a good shape too, gently rising to fill the hand with an engagingly feminine bulge. Very nice. There was a lot of joy to be had in the contemplation of a pint glass; in terms of plain reality of course, there was a deal more to be had in the draining of one.

The battered Guinness clock above the bar struck a silent eleven o'clock. Once its chimes had cut like a butcher's knife through the merry converse of the Swan's patrons. But it had been silent now these three long years, since Jim Pooley had muted it with a well-aimed pint pot. These days its lame thuds went unheeded, and Neville was forced to more radical methods for clearing the bar come closing. Even the most drunken of revellers could understand a blow to the skull from the knobkerry he kept below the bar counter.

At the last thud of the Guinness clock Neville replaced the dazzling glass. Lifting the hinged bar top, he sidled towards the saloon-bar door. The Brentford sun glinted upon his Brylcreemed scalp as he stood nobly framed in that famous portal, softly sniffing the air. Buses came and went in the morning haze, bound for exotic destinations west of London. An unfragrant miasma drifted from the Star of Bombay Curry Garden, sparrows along the telephone lines sang the songs their parents had taught them. The day seemed dreamy and calm.

Neville twitched his sensitive nostrils. He had a sudden strange premonition that today was not going to be like any other.

He was dead right.

3

I

Jim Pooley, that despoiler of pub clocks, sat in the Memorial Library, pawing over ancient tomes in a never-ending search for the cosmic truths which might lead a man along the narrow winding pathway towards self-fulfilment and ultimate enlightenment. 'Looking up form and keeping out of the rain' was what the Head Librarian called it. 'Mr Pooley,' she said, in those hushed yet urgent tones affected by those of her station. 'Mr Pooley, why don't you take your paper around to the bookie's and there study in an atmosphere which must surely be more conducive to your purposes?'

Pooley, eyes fixed upon his paper as if in a trance, mouthed, 'You have a wonderful body on you there, Mrs Naylor.'

Mrs Naylor, who lip-read every word, as she had done upon a thousand other such occasions, reddened slightly but maintained her dignity. 'Why can't you look at the books once in a while just to keep up appearances?'

'I have books of my own,' said Jim silently, 'but I come here to absorb the atmosphere of this noble edifice and to feast my eyes upon your supple limbs.'

'You haven't even a ticket, Mr Pooley.'

'Give us a French kiss,' said Jim loudly.

Mrs Naylor fled back to her desk and Pooley was left to his own devices. His eyes swept over the endless columns of racehorses. Somewhere, he knew, amid this vast assortment, existed six horses which would win today at good odds, and if placed in a Yankee accumulator would gross two hundred and fifty thousand pounds at the very least. Such knowledge, of course, is generalized, and it is the subtle particularities of knowing which horses to choose that make the thing difficult.

5

Pooley licked the end of his Biro, especially blessed by Father Moity for the purpose. He held it up to the shaft of sunlight which had suddenly and unexpectedly appeared through an upper window. Nearly spent, more than half of its black life-fluid ebbed away, and upon what? Upon ill-considered betting-slips, that was upon what. Pooley sighed, his concentration gone. The delicate balance had been upset, and all through Mrs Naylor's chatter.

Oh well, thought Pooley, the sun is now over the yardarm. He rose from his seat, evoking a screech from the rubber-soled chair legs which cut Mrs Naylor like a rapier's edge. He strode purposefully towards the door, and on reaching it turned upon his heel. 'I shall be around then this evening directly your husband has departed for his night shift,' he announced.

Mrs Naylor fainted.

As Neville stood in the door of the Flying Swan, musing upon the day's peculiarity, a beggar of dreadful aspect and sorry footwear shuffled towards him from the direction of Sprite Street and the Dock. He noted quite without thinking that an air of darkness and foreboding accompanied this lone wanderer.

'Ugh,' said Neville. He felt twin shudders originate within his monogrammed carpet-slippers, wriggle up the hairs of his legs, and meet in the small of his back, where as one united shudder they continued upwards, finally (although all this took but a second or two) travelling out of the top of his head leaving several strands of Brylcreem defying gravity. Neville felt a sudden need to cross himself, and performed that function with somewhat startled embarrassment.

He returned to the bar to await the arrival of the solitary traveller. Time passed, however, and no such shadow darkened the Swan's doorway. Neville sloped over to the door and gazed cautiously up the street. Of ill-omened tramps the street was empty.

Neville scratched his magnificent nostrils with a nicotined finger and shrugged grandiloquently. 'Now there's a thing,' he said to himself.

'Could I have a glass of water, please?' said a voice at his elbow.

Neville controlled his bladder only by the merest of lucky chances. 'Lord save me,' he gasped, turning in shock to the quizzical face of the materialized tramp.

'Sorry, did I startle you?' asked the creature with what seemed to be a voice of genuine concern. 'It's a bad habit of mine, I really must control it.'

By this time Neville was back behind the bar, the top bolted shut, and his shaking hands about glass and whisky optic. 'What do you want?'

'A glass of water, if I may.'

'This isn't a municipal bloody drinking fountain,' said Neville gruffly. 'This is an alehouse.'

'My apologies,' said the tramp. 'We have I think got off to a rather poor start. Perhaps I might have a pint of something.'

Neville downed his large whisky with a practised flick of the wrist and indicated the row of enamel silver-tipped beer pumps. 'State your preference,' he said, and here a note of pride entered his voice. 'We have a selection of eight ales on pump. A selection which exceeds Jack Lane's by four and the New Inn by three. I think you will find it a hard business to out-rival the Swan in this respect.'

The tramp seemed fascinated by this intelligence. 'Eight, eh?' He walked slowly the length of the bar past the eight gleaming enamel sentinels. His right forefinger ran along the brass rim of the bar top and to Neville's horror deftly removed the polish, leaving in its place a trail like that of a slug. Halting at the end he became suddenly aware of Neville's eyes and that the barman was involuntarily clenching and unclenching his fists.

'Sorry,' he said, raising his finger and examining it with distaste, 'again I have blotted my copybook.'

Neville was about to reach for his knobkerry when the friendly and reassuringly familiar figure of Jim Pooley appeared through the bar door, whistling a tuneless lament and tapping his right knee with his racing paper. Jim mounted his very favourite bar stool with time-worn ease and addressed Neville with a cheery, 'Mine will be a pint of Large please, Neville, and good morning.'

The part-time barman dragged his gaze from the unsightly tramp and drew Jim Pooley a fine glass of the true water.

'Ah,' said Jim, having drained half in a single draught, 'the first one is always the finest.' Pushing the exact amount across the bar top for fear that prices might have risen overnight, he sought anew the inspiration, his by divine right, that had so recently been denied him in the Memorial Library. 'I feel a winner coming on,' he said softly. This was occasionally a means of getting a free top-up at this hour of the day.

7

Neville made no reply.

'I think this might well be the Big One,' continued Jim.

Neville maintained a stony silence. He did not appear to be breathing.

'I wouldn't be at all surprised if . . .' At this point Jim Pooley looked up from his paper and caught sight of the part-time barman's ghastly aspect. 'Whatever's up, Neville?'

Neville clutched at his breath. 'Did you see him leave?' he stuttered.

'Who leave? I didn't see anybody.'

'He . . .' Neville peered over the bar top at the brass rim. It shone as unsullied and pristine as it had done when he had polished it not fifteen minutes previous.

'A tramp.'

'What tramp?'

Neville decanted himself another large scotch and threw it down his throat.

'Well I never noticed any tramp,' said Jim Pooley, 'although, and you'll think this ridiculous when I tell you –'

'What?' said Neville shakily.

'Well, when I came in here just now I felt the strangest of compunctions. I felt as if I wanted to cross myself.'

Neville did not reply.

A scratch of the bell, a screech of brakes, a rattle of front wheel against kerb, and a hearty 'Hi-ho Silver', and John Omally had arrived at the Flying Swan. 'You stay here and enjoy the sun, I'll be out later,' he told his bike, and with a jovial 'God save all here and mine's a pint of Large please, Neville,' he entered the bar.

Neville watched his approach closely, and noted to his satisfaction that Omally showed no inclination whatever towards crossing himself. Neville pulled the Irishman a pint and smiled contentedly to himself as Omally pushed the exact amount of change across the counter.

'How's yourself then, Jim?' said Omally.

'I feel a winner coming on,' Pooley confided loudly.

'Now is that a fact, then it's lucky you are to be sure.' Omally accepted his pint and drained half in three gulps.

'You are late today,' said Pooley, by way of conversation.

'I had a bit of bike trouble over on the allotment, Marchant and I were not seeing eye to eye.'

8

Pooley nodded. 'Your bike Marchant would be all the better for the occasional squirt of Three-in-One and possibly a visit to a specialist once in a while.'

'Certainly the old lad is not what he was. I had to threaten him with premature burial before I could get it out that he needed new front brake blocks and a patch on his back tyre.'

'Bikes are not what they were,' said Jim. He finished his pint. 'This one's done for,' he said sadly.

'Seems so,' said John Omally.

'Whose shout is it?' said Jim.

'Whose was it last time?' said John.

Jim Pooley scratched his head. 'There you have me,' said himself.

'I think you were both buying your own,' said Neville, who had heard such discussions as these go on for upwards of an hour before one of these stalwarts cracked under the pressure.

'Lend me a pound John,' said Jim Pooley.

'Away into the night boy,' the other replied.

'We'll call it ten bob then.'

'We'll call it a good try and forget about it.'

Jim Pooley grudgingly patted his pockets. To the amazement of all present including himself he withdrew a pound note. Neville pulled Jim Pooley another pint, and taking the pound note with both hands he carried it reverently to the till, where he laid it as a corpse to rest. Jim Pooley counted and recounted his change. The terrible knowledge that Jim had the price of two more pints within his very pockets made Omally more companionable than ever.

'So how's tricks, then, Jim?' asked the Irishman, although his eyes were unable to tear themselves away from Pooley's waistcoat pocket.

'I have been experiencing a slight cash-flow problem,' said Pooley. 'In fact, I am on my way now to pay several important and pressing debts which if payment was deferred by even minutes might spell doom to certain widely-known political figures.'

'Ah, you were always a man of strong social conscience, Jim.'

Pooley nodded sagely. 'You yourself are a man of extraordinary perception at times, John.'

'I know how to call a spade,' said John Omally.

'That you do.'

Whilst this fascinating conversation was in progress Neville, who

9

had now become convinced that the ill-favoured tramp had never left the Flying Swan but was hiding somewhere within awaiting closing time to riffle the till, was bobbing to and fro about the bar, squinting into dark and obscure corners and straining his eyes about the upper portions of the room. He suddenly became aware that he was being observed.

'I'll just go and check the pumps,' he muttered, and vanished down the cellar steps.

Pooley and Omally drank a moment in silence. 'He has been having visions,' said Jim.

'Has he?' said John. 'An uncle of m'... used to have visions. Said that a gigantic pig called Black Tony used to creep up on him and jog his arm when he was filling in his betting-slips – blamed that pig for many a poor day's sport, did my uncle.'

'It's tramps with Neville,' Jim confided.

'What, nudging his arm and that?'

'No, just appearing like.'

'Oh.'

The two prepared to drink again in silence but found their glasses empty. With perplexity they faced each other.

'It's time I was away about my business,' said Jim, rising to his feet.

'Will you not be staying to have one more before you go?' John asked. Neville, rising like a titan from the cellar depths, caught this remark; being a publican, he was inured against most forms of sudden shock.

'Same again, lads?' he asked.

'Two of similar,' said John.

Jim eyed him with open suspicion.

'Ten and six,' said Neville, pulling two more pints.

'Jim,' said John.

'John?' said Jim.

'I don't quite know how to put this, Jim.'

Jim raised his right hand as in benediction; Neville thought for one ghastly moment that he was going to cross himself. 'John,' said Jim, 'John, I know what you are going to say, you are going to say that you wish to buy me a drink, that in fact it would be an honour for you to buy me a drink and that such would give you a pleasure that, like good friendship, is a jewel without price. You are going to say all this to me, John, because you have said it all before, then

10

when you have made these eloquent and endearing remarks you will begin to bewail your lot, to curse the fates that treat you in so shabby a manner, that harass and misuse you, that push you to the very limits of your endurance, and which by their metaphysical and devious means deprive you of your hard and honestly earned pennies, and having done so you will confess supreme embarrassment, implore the very ground to swallow you up, and possibly shed the occasional deeply felt tear. Then and only then you will beg, impeach, implore and with supreme dignity of stature approach me for the loan of the very ten shillings and sixpence most recently mentioned by our esteemed barlord here.

'I am conscious that this request for funds will be made in the most polite and eloquent fashion and that the wretchedness you will feel will be a profound and poignant thing to behold and so considering all this and considering that Neville is not a man well-known for offering credit and that you are my noblest friend and that to attempt to drink and run as it were would bring down a social stigma upon both our heads I will gladly pay for this round.'

Omally stood, head bowed, during this touching oration. No more words were spoken and Neville received the ten and sixpence in a duly respectful manner. The two drained their glasses and Jim excused himself quietly and vanished off into the direction of the bookie's shop.

Neville pushed Jim's glass into the washer and spoke softly to the pensive Omally. 'You have a good friend there in that Jim Pooley,' he said.

John nodded. 'God moves in mysterious circles,' he said.

'How so?'

'Well' – and here John Omally drained his pint glass to the bottom – 'I was touched to my very soul by Jim's remarks over the purchase of these drinks but strange as the man is he mistook the remark that I made to him completely.'

'Oh?' said Neville.

'Yes,' said John. 'I had no intention of borrowing the price of a drink whatever.'

'What then?' said Neville.

'I merely thought to mention to him in as discreet a manner as possible that his flies were undone, but I shan't bother now.'

John Omally offered Neville all his best for the time of day and left the bar.

2

Archroy had rented the section of allotment land nearest to the viaduct ever since it had been bequeathed to him five years before by a half-forgotten uncle. Each night during the season he would come from his shift at the wiper works and sit in the doorway of his hut, smoking his pipe and musing about the doings of the day. Omally owned two adjacent strips, having won one of them from Peg's husband at the papershop, and old Pete had a further one. Over in the corner was the untouched plot that had once belonged to Raymond, who in a previous episode had been snatched away into outer space by the invisible star creatures from Alpha Centauri. You could see a lot of life on an allotment.

This particular warm spring evening Archroy lazed upon an orange-box, smoking the blend of his taste and thinking that the world would be a better place if there was a bounty put upon the heads of gypsy car-dealers. Not that he had anything against them in general, but in particular he was very resentful. Archroy was not only the tenant of an allotment, he was also a man of marriage. Archroy's marriage was a nebulous affair; he working day shifts and his wife working nights. Their paths rarely crossed. Omally thought this was the ideal state of wedded bliss and prayed for a woman who might wed him, then take a job overseas.

Archroy accepted the acclaim of his fellows for choosing so wisely, but privately he was ill at ease. Certainly he saw little of his wife, but of her workings and machinations the catalogue was endless. Archroy kept coming home to find new furniture and carpets; one day he stuck his head up in the roof and discovered that his loft had been insulated. Strangely, Archroy was never asked by his wife to contribute to any of these extravagant ventures. Possibly because he rarely saw the woman, but mainly he suspected, because an alien hand was at work in his stuccoed semi-detached. He suspected that his wife had a lover, in fact not one lover but many. Archroy had an inkling that his wife was putting it about a bit.

He had found five minutes one evening just as they were changing shifts to interview his suspect spouse. Archroy had noticed that his old Morris Minor, which his wife described as 'an eyesore', was no longer upon its blocks in the garage but seemed to have cried 'horse and hattock' and been carried away by the fairies.

'Woman,' he addressed his wife, for he had quite forgotten her name, 'woman, where is my car?'

'Gone,' said she, straightening her headscarf in the mock rococo hall-mirror. 'I have sold your car, and if you will pardon me saying so I have made a handsome profit.'

Archroy stiffened in his shirt-sleeves. 'But I was working on that car, it needed but an engine and a few wheels and I would have had it working!'

'A truck came and took it away,' said his wife.

Archroy pulled at his hair. 'Where's my car gone to? Who took it?'

'It was a gypsy,' said his wife.

'A gypsy? You part with my priceless car to a damned gyppo?'

'I got a good price.'

Archroy blew tobacco smoke down his nose and made himself cough.

'It's on the mantelpiece in a brown envelope,' said his wife, smearing gaudy red lipstick about her upper lip.

Archroy tore into the front-room and tore open the envelope. Pouring the contents into his hand he found five brown beans.

'What? What?' Archroy began to foam at the mouth. 'Beans?'

'He assured me that they were magic beans,' his wife said, slamming the door behind her.

Thus it was that Archroy sat this particular evening in the doorway of his allotment shed, bewailing his lot and cursing not only car-dealers, but untrue wives and all those born of Romany extraction. 'Magic beans.' He grimaced as he turned the offenders over in his palm. 'Magic bloody beans, I'll bet he gave her more than just magic bloody beans.'

The six-twenty steamed over the viaduct and told Archroy that now would be as good a time as ever to repair to the Swan to see what the lads were up to. He was about to pocket his magic beans and rise from his orange-box when a stark black shadow fell upon him and sent an involuntary shudder up the wee lad's back.

'Might I have a look at those beans you have there, mister?' The voice came from a disreputable tramp of dreadful aspect and sorry footwear. 'Sorry, did I startle you?' asked the creature with what seemed to be a voice of genuine concern. 'It's a bad habit of mine, I really must control it.'

'What do you want here?' snarled Archroy, outraged at this trespass upon his thoughts and land.

'About the beans?' the tramp said.

Archroy pocketed his beans. 'Clear off!' he said, climbing to his feet. The tramp raised his right hand and made a strange gesture. Archroy slumped back on to his orange-box, suddenly weak at the knees.

'Those beans,' said the tramp. Archroy felt about in his pocket and handed the tramp the five magic beans.

'Ah.' The tramp held one between thumb and forefinger. 'As I thought, most interesting. You say that your wife received them in payment for your old Morris Minor?'

Archroy didn't remember saying anything of the kind but he nodded bleakly.

'They are beans of great singularity,' said the tramp. 'I have seen beans and I have seen beans.' He returned the articles to Archroy's still-extended hand. 'These are beans indeed!'

'But, magic?' said Archroy.

The tramp stroked the stubble of his chin with an ill-washed knuckle. 'Ah,' he said, 'magic, is it? Well that is a question. Let us say that they have certain *outré* qualities.'

'Oh,' said Archroy. He felt a little better about the beans now; the loss of his trusty Morris Minor seemed less important than possessing something with *outré* qualities, whatever *outré* might mean. 'What are you doing on my allotment?' Archroy asked in a polite tone.

The tramp described a runic symbol in the dust at Archroy's feet with the toecap of his sorry right shoe. 'You might say that I am here to meet someone,' he said, 'and there again you might not. If you were to say here is a man upon a mission, you would be correct, but also at the same time you would be mistaken. There is much about my presence here that is anomalous, much that is straightforward, much that . . .'

'I must be on my way now,' said Archroy, attempting to rise and feeling at his knees. They offered him no support. 'I am incapacitated,' he announced.

'. . . Much that will be known, much that will remain unexplained,' continued the tramp.

Archroy wondered if he had eaten something untoward, toadstools in his hotpot, or slug pellets in his Thermos flask. He had read of strange distillations from the Amazon which administered upon the head of a pin could paralyze a bull elephant. There were also forms of nerve gas that might find their way into the sucking section of a fellow's Briar'.

The tramp meanwhile had ceased speaking. Now he stared about the allotment in an interested fashion. 'And you say that Omally won one of those plots from Peg's husband at the papershop?'

Archroy was certain he had not. 'The one over in the corner with the chimney,' he said. 'That one there is the property of Old Pete. It has been in his family for three generations and he has made an arrangement with the council to be buried there upon his demise. Blot the Schoolkeeper runs the one to the west backing on to the girls' school, it is better not to ask what goes on in his shed.'

Archroy rose to point out the plot but to his amazement discovered that the old tramp had gone. 'Well I never,' said Archroy, crossing himself. 'Well I never did.'

3

No one could ever accuse Peg's husband from the papershop of being dull. His wife, when inquired of by customers as to her husband's latest venture, would cup her hands upon her outlandish hips and say, 'There's never a dull moment is there?' This rhetorical question left most in doubt as to a reply, so the kindly soul would add, 'You've got to laugh haven't you?', which occasionally got a response, or 'It's a great old life if you don't weaken', which didn't.

Her husband, however, shunned such platitudes, and preferred, during moments of acute brain activity, to deal exclusively in the proverb. On the occasion of his bike going missing for the thirteenth time from its appointed rack at the Rubber Factory he was heard to mutter, 'Time is a great healer.' And during that particularly hot summer when someone set fire to his runner beans, 'Every cloud has a silver lining.'

Norman's proverbs never quite matched up to the situation to which they were applied, yet seemed in some bizarre way to aid him to the solution of extremely obtuse problems. This lent him the air of a mystic, which made him regularly sought after by drunks in need of advice. His 'ventures', as they were termed, were never devoid of interest. 'Wading to France', for example, which began, as so many tales have a tendency to do, one lunchtime in the saloon-bar of the Flying Swan.

'There is much talk lately of these Channel swimmers,' John Omally had said by way of conversation, as he perused his copy of the *Brentford Mercury*. 'They do say that the dear fellows lose the better part of three stone from the swimming.' There was an informed nodding as Omally continued, 'There's a king's ransom to be had in that game if a fellow has the way of it.'

Norman, who had been listening and was currently between

16

ventures, felt a sudden surge of regret that he had never learned to swim. 'It never rains but it pours,' he said, which gave most to suspect that he was having an idea.

'You don't swim at all do you, Norman?' asked the astute Omally, sensing money in the air.

'Sadly no,' said Norman, 'but I wade.' With these portentous words he left the saloon-bar.

Little was heard of Norman for some weeks, and his wife answered Omally's repeated inquiries with the encouraging, 'You certainly see some sights' and 'It takes all sorts to make a world doesn't it?'

The Irishman was pretty much at his wits' end when his eye caught a tiny paragraph on an inside page of the *Brentford Mercury*: 'Local Man to Wade Channel'. Omally read the short paragraph once, then again slowly; then, thinking that he must have misread it, he gave the thing a careful word-for-word scrutiny.

Norman Hartnell, local Rubberware Foreman (not to be confused with the other Norman Hartnell), stated yesterday in an exclusive interview with the *Mercury* that it was his intention within the forseeable future to have constructed certain marine apparatus which will make it possible for him to become the first man to wade to France from England. Mr Hartnell (not to be confused with the other Norman Hartnell) told the *Mercury* in this exclusive interview when asked his reason for this attempt that 'Kind words butter no parsnips.' Mr Hartnell is 43.

'What other Norman Hartnell?' queried John Omally, whose only claim to fashion-consciousness was tucking his shirt in all the way round even when wearing a jacket. There was still no word from Norman, and Omally even took to phoning the offices of the *Brentford Mercury* daily for news. He was not a man to be cheated of his pennies, and the more time passed the more he became convinced that whatever plans were hatching in Norman's obtuse cranium, he, Omally, was due at least part of any income deriving from their fruition. 'It was me reading about the Channel swimming that started it all, was it not?' he asked. Those present at the bar nodded gravely.

'You have a moral right,' said Neville.

'You should get a contract drawn up,' said Jim Pooley.

'He owes you,' said Archroy.

That Saturday the *Brentford Mercury*, which had for some days been refusing to accept John Omally's reverse-charge calls, announced in large and impressive type: BRENTFORD CHANNEL WADER NAMES THE DAY. Omally read this startling headline over the shoulder of the paper's owner and gasped in disbelief. 'He's naming the day and he still hasn't brought me in on it.'

'Pardon?' said the stranger.

'Fares please,' said the bus conductor.

Omally, who had in his palm a number of pennies exactly equal either to his bus fare or to the price of a copy of the *Brentford Mercury*, shouted, 'Stop that dog,' and leapt off the bus at the next set of traffic lights.

On the well-worn bench afront the Memorial Library he studied the newspaper. There were the headlines, below them a photograph of Norman smiling hideously, with the caption: 'All roads lead to Rome, says plucky Brentonian.'

Omally read paragraph after paragraph, desperately trying to pluck out something substantial enough to merit legal action. Yes, the plucky Brentonian had been working for some months now upon certain marine apparatus suitable to his requirements. He had made several unsuccessful tests with these (Omally raised his eyebrows at this intelligence). He had gauged his exact course through careful study of coastal topography and undersea mappings loaned to him by the Royal Maritime Museum. He had allowed for spring tides, onshore drift, wind variations, and even shoals of fish that might be encountered en route. He was certain of success. He had been given the go-ahead by the Royal Navy, who had agreed to escort him with helicopter and motor torpedo boat and keep in contact with him by certain sophisticated pieces of top-secret equipment which Norman had kindly agreed to test for them during the walk over.

It was believed that this crossing would herald a new era in international travel. A veritable golden age was about to dawn, and without a doubt the patent holder of this aquatic legware was sitting on (or more rightly in) a proverbial goldmine, not to mention a piece of history. Omally groaned. 'Proverbial goldmine, he'll love that.' The more he read, the less he liked what he read, and the less he liked it the more cheated he felt and the more furious he became. The cross-Channel walk was scheduled for the following Saturday; it was to be covered by both television channels and shown live on *World of Sport*. Norman was to appear that very evening on the Russell Harty Show.

Omally tore the newspaper to ribbons and flung the pieces to the four winds.

It is not a long walk from the library to Peg's papershop; one simply turns right down Braemar Road, right at the bottom past the football ground, left into Mafeking Avenue, and left again up Albany Road into Ealing Road. John Omally covered this distance in a time that would have made Roger Bannister hang up his spikes in defeat. Panting, he stood in the doorway attempting to compose himself.

Two pensioners came out of the shop. 'Proverbial goldmine,' said one. 'Place in history,' said the other.

Omally made an attempt to enter, but found to his amazement that the usually empty and dust-hung place of business bore a sprightly and jubilant appearance, and was going great guns in the customer stakes. Bunting hung about the door and 'Good Luck Norman', emblazoned upon lengths of coloured toilet-roll, festooned the front window – which, suddenly bereft of its timeless Woodbine display, now blazed with photographs of Royal Navy cruisers and postcards of Captain Webb, 'Souvenir Channel Trews on Sale Now' said a card. 'Bottled Channel Water' said another. Below this was a display of seashells and a number of jam-jars apparently filled with seawater 'Bottled by the Wader Himself', and priced at a quid a time.

Omally made another attempt to enter but again found his way barred, this time by a number of schoolgirls wearing 'Norman Wades OK' t-shirts.

'What is the meaning of all this?' muttered the Irishman as he edged his way forward. Over the heads of the crowd he could see that Peg had taken on two extra salesgirls. Peg's gargantuan frame, sporting a 'Norman Wades OK' t-shirt the size of a bell-tent, could be made out swinging bundles of the *Brentford Mercury* on to the counter and dispensing souvenir windmills and flags to all comers. The cash register was ringing like a fire alarm. Of Norman, however, there was no sign. Omally edged his way nearer to the counter and made some attempt to draw Peg's attention.

'The Norman action dolls are four pounds, love,' he heard her say. 'Yes, that's right, three for a tenner.'

Omally clutched at the counter for support. 'Peg,' he stammered, 'Peg I say.' Peg finally caught sight of the swaying Irishman. 'Hold on John love, and I'll be with you,' she said. 'Yes love, the Bottled Channel Water can be made available for bulk export purchase.'

The proverbial light at the end of the dark corridor, to which no doubt Norman had previously alluded in some moment of irrelevance, was beginning to appear before Omally's bloodshot eyes. 'Could I have a word with Norman, please Peg?' he asked.

'He's at present in conference with members of the press, prior to an enforced period of lamaic meditation necessary for him to attune himself to the correct cosmic state of awareness required for his walk,' said the suddenly lucid Peg.

Omally nodded thoughtfully. 'No doubt then he will neither reveal himself nor the now legendary legwear prior to the great event.'

'It's unlikely, love,' said Peg, then, 'excuse me a moment. Yes, I can do you a gross of the "Wade Against the Nazis" beanie hats at cost if you are willing to do a deal on the film rights.'

Omally slid quietly away from the shop and along the road to the Flying Swan. He ignored the 'Wade for Britain' banner which hung above the bar, and also the Disabled War Wounded Waders Fund tin that Pooley rattled beneath his nose. He ordered a pint of Large. 'I have been cheated of my place in history,' he told Neville.

'Do you want a regular Large or Wader's Jubilee Ale?' asked the part-time barman. 'Only the brewery seem to have overestimated demand and I've got rather a lot going begging as it were.' One look at Omally's fearful countenance set Neville straight. He drew Omally a pint of the usual and drew the Irishman's attention to a figure in a white coat who was tampering with the antique jukebox. 'The brewery sent him down too, said we needed a few topical tunes to set the scene as it were, said that with all the extra trade the pub would be attracting some attempt on our part to join in the festivities would be appreciated.'

Omally cocked a quizzical eyebrow at the aged machine. 'You mean that it actually works? I thought it was broken beyond repair.'

'I suspect that it will not take him long to discover that it is only lacking a fuse in its plug.'

Omally's face took on a strangely guilty expression.

'I have seen the selection he proposes to substitute,' said Neville gravely. 'And I fear that it is even grimmer than the one you have for so long protected our ears against.'

'It has a nautical feel to it, I suspect.'

'There is more than a hint of the shanty.'

'HMS Pinafore?'

'And that.'

'I suppose,' said Omally, hardly wishing to continue the conversation, or possibly even to draw breath, 'that there would not be a number or two upon that jukebox by the Norman Hartnell Singers or Norm and the Waders?'

'You are certainly given to moments of rare psychic presentiment,' said the part-time barman.

At this point there occurred an event of surpassing unreality, still talked of at the Flying Swan. John Omally, resident drinker at that establishment for fifteen long years, rose from his stool and left undrunk an entire pint of the brewery's finest, bought and paid for by himself. Not a mere drip in the bottom you understand, nor an unfortunate, cigar-filled, post darts-match casualty, but an entire complete, untouched, pristine one-pint glass of that wholesome and lifegiving beverage, so beloved of the inebriate throughout five counties.

Some say that during the following month John Omally joined an order of Trappist monks, others that he swore temporary allegiance to the Foreign Legion. Others still hint that the Irishman had learned through the agency of previous generations a form of suspended animation, much favoured by the ancients for purposes of imposed hibernation in times of famine. Whatever the case may be, Mr Omally vanished from Brentford, leaving a vacuum that nobody could fill. His loss was a sorry thing to behold within the portals of the Flying Swan, time seemed to stand still within those walls. Pooley took on the look of a gargoyle standing alone at the bar, drinking in silence, his only movements those born of necessity.

But what of Norman Hartnell (not to be confused with the other Norman Hartnell)? Certainly Norman's ventures had, as has been noted, tended to verge upon the weird. This one in particular had transcended bounds of normality. When Peg made grandiose statements about her husband's press conferences and tendencies towards lamaic meditation it may be said without fear of contradiction that the fat woman was shooting a line through her metaphorical titfer. Norman, who by nature was a harmless, if verbally extravagant, eccentric, had finally played directly into the hands of that volatile and conniving fat woman. She had watched him night after night experiment with inflatable rubber footwear, buoyant under-garments, and stilted appliances. She had watched him vanish beneath the murky waters of the Grand Union Canal time after time, only to re-emerge with still more enthusiasm for the project. Only on his last semi-fatal attempt had she realized the futility of his quest; if any money was to be made out of it, then she'd have to do it.

Since she was somewhat more than twice her husband's weight it had been a simple matter one dark night to subdue him and install him in the coal cellar, where, other than for continual cramps and the worrisome attention of curious rodents, he was ideally situated for lamaic meditation, should he so wish.

The long-standing and quite fornicatious relationship that she was having with the editor of the *Brentford Mercury* was enough to seal poor Norman's fate. When the police, having received many phone calls from simple souls during the week, inquiring after their daily papers and packets of Woodbines, broke into Peg's papershop they found the bound and gagged figure of the erstwhile Channel Wader. Blinking in the sunlight, he had seemed quite unable to answer the inquisitions by various television companies, newspaper combines and foreign press agencies, each of whom had paid large cash sums for exclusive rights to the Channel Wade. Many questions were asked, but few answered.

Peg had upped and awayed it with her pressman stud, never to be heard of again. Norman simply shrugged his shoulders and remarked, 'A rolling stone gathers no moss yet many hands make light work.' These proverbial cosmic truths meant little to the scores of creditors who daily besieged his papershop, but as Norman had no legal responsibility, his wife having signed all the contracts, little could be done.

A few pennies were made by others than Peg and her paramour; Jim Pooley had successfully rattled his tin under enough noses to buy Omally several pints of consolation upon his return.

Neville had a hard job of it to sell the Wader's Jubilee Ale, which was only purchased by those of perverse humour and loud voice. It was only a chance event, that of a night of heavy rain, which saved the day, washing as it did the Jubilee labels from the bottles to reveal that they contained nothing more than standard brown ale.

Norman seemed strangely unmoved by the whole business, con-sidering that his wife had left him penniless. Perhaps the fact that his wife had also left him wifeless had something to do with it. Possibly he still secretly harboured the wish to wade to France, but principle alone would have forbidden him to relay this information to another soul. Still, as Jim Pooley said, 'Time and tide wait for Norman.'

4

If there was one ideal spot in Brentford for the poet to stand whilst seeking inspiration, or for the artist to set up his three-legged easel, then it would certainly not be the Canal Bridge on the Hounslow Road, which marks the lower left-hand point of the mysterious Brentford Triangle. Even potential suicides shun the place, feeling that an unsuccessful attempt might result in all sorts of nasty poisonings and unsavoury disease.

Leo Felix, Brentonian and Rastafarian, runs a used-car business from the canal's western shore. Here the cream of the snips come to stand wing to wing, gleaming with touch-up spray and plastic filler, their milometers professionally readjusted, and their 'only one owners' inevitably proving to be either members of the clergy or little old ladies.

Norman had never owned a motor car, although there had been times when he had considered building one or even constructing a more efficient substitute for the internal combustion engine, possibly fuelled upon beer-bottle tops or defunct filter-tips. His wife had viewed these flights of fancy with her traditional cynicism, guffawing hideously, and slapping her preposterous thighs with hands like one-pound packets of pork sausages.

Norman squinted thoughtfully down into the murky waters, finding in the rainbow swirls a dark beauty; he was well rid of that one, and that was a fact. He was at least his own master now, and with his wife gone he had left his job at the Rubber Factory to work full time in the papershop. It's not a bad old life if you don't weaken, he thought to himself. A trouble shared is a trouble halved.

'And it is a long straight road that has no turning,' said a voice at Norman's elbow.

Norman nodded. 'The thought had recently crossed my mind,'

he said dreamily. Suddenly he turned to stare full into the face of a shabby-looking tramp of dreadful aspect and sorry footwear.

'Sorry, did I startle you?' asked the creature with what seemed to be a voice of genuine concern. 'It's a bad habit of mine, I really must control it.'

'Oh no,' said Norman. 'It is just that on a Wednesday afternoon, which is my early-closing day, I often come down here for an hour or two of quiet solitude, and rarely expect to see another soul.'

The tramp smiled respectfully. 'There are times when a man must be alone,' he said.

'Exactly,' said Norman. The two gazed reflectively into the filthy waters for a moment or two. Norman's thoughts were soft, wavering things, whose limits were easily containable within the acceptable norms of local behaviour.

The tramp's, however, hovered in a spectrum that encompassed such dark and unfathomable colours that even to briefly contemplate their grim hues would be to trespass upon territories so ghastly and macabre that the very prospect would spell doom in any one of a dozen popular dialects.

'Can I treat you to a cup of tea along at the Plume?' the tramp asked.

Norman felt no affinity towards the tramp, but he felt strangely compelled to nod at this unexpected invitation. The two left the canal bridge and strolled up the Brentford High Street towards the Plume Café. This establishment, which stands at a point not twenty yards from the junction of Ealing Road and the High Street, can be said at times to play host to as many Brentonians as the Flying Swan itself. Those times being, of course, those when the Swan is closed.

The Plume is presided over by an emormous blonde of Peg-like proportions known to all Brentford as Lily Marlene. Why Lily Marlene is uncertain, since the sign above the door says 'Proprietor: Mrs Veronica Smith'. Lily presides over all with the air of a brothel madam, her expansive bosoms moving in and out of the shadows behind the counter like twin dirigibles. Whatever happened to Mr Veronica Smith no one has ever dared ask.

Norman swung open the shattered-glass door and entered the Plume Café followed by a sinister tramp. In the gloom behind the counter, unseen by human eye, Lily Marlene made a shadowy sign of the cross.

'What will it be?' Norman asked the tramp, who had seated

25

himself beside the window and showed no inclination whatever to do any buying.

'I shall have one of Lily's surprising coffees, I think,' the creature replied.

Norman strode to the counter. 'Two coffees please, Lil,' he requested of the hovering bosoms, which withdrew into the darkness of their hangar and returned in the company of a pair of arms. These generous appendages bore at their fingers' end a brace of coffees in the traditional glass cups. Norman paid up and carried the steaming cups back to the table.

'Cheers,' said the tramp, holding his cup up to the light and peering into its bottom.

'What are looking for?' queried Norman.

'Aha,' the tramp said, tapping his nose significantly. 'Now you are asking me a question.'

'I am,' said Norman.

'And I shall answer you,' said the tramp, 'with a short tale which, although brief, is informative and morally satisfying.'

Norman said, 'Many a mickle makes a muckle,' and it was clear that his thoughts were elsewhere.

'A friend of mine used to drink coffee – I say used to; for all I know he still does, but as I have heard neither hide nor hair of him for five years I must remain uncertain upon this point –'

Norman yawned. 'Sorry,' he said, 'I had a rough night.'

The tramp continued unabashed. 'This friend of mine used to drink coffee in a glass cup not dissimilar to this, and one day as he finished a cup do you know what he found had been slipped into it?'

'The King's Shilling,' said Norman, 'I've heard this story.'

'The King's Shilling,' said the tramp, who was plainly ignoring Norman's remarks. 'He tipped it into his hand and said the fatal "Look at this lads", and within a trice the pressmen were upon him –'

'I've had some dealings with the press myself,' said Norman.

'The pressmen were upon him and he was dragged away screaming to a waiting bungboat and thence to who knows where.'

The tramp made this last statement with such an air of sombre authenticity that his voice echoed as if coming from some dark and evil dungeon. Norman, who was lining up another sarcastic comment, held his counsel.

'You said just now that you had heard the story,' said the tramp in a leaden tone.

'Did I?' said Norman, perspiring freely about the brow. 'I don't think I did.'

'You did.'

'OK.'

'Then let me put you straight on this, Norman.' Norman did not recall telling the tramp his name, and this added to his growing unease. 'Let it be known to you that this story, which although brief was in its way informative and morally satisfying, was a true and authentic tale involving a personal acquaintance of mine and let no other man, be he living, dead or whatever, say otherwise!'

Norman fingered his collar, which had grown suddenly tight. 'I wouldn't,' he said in a voice of tortured conviction. 'Not me.'

'Good,' said the tramp. Leaning forward across the table he stared hard into Norman's eyes much in the manner of a cobra mesmerizing a rabbit. Norman prepared his nostrils to receive the ghastly reek of dereliction and wretchedness generally associated with the ill-washed brotherhood of the highway. Strangely, no such stench assailed his delicate nasal apparatus, rather a soft yet strangely haunting odour, one that Norman could not quite put a name or place to. The scent touched a nerve of recollection somewhere in his past, and he felt a cold shudder creeping up his backbone.

Norman became transfixed. The tramp's eyes, two red dots, seemed to swell and expand, filling all the Plume Café, engulfing even Lily's giant breasts. Two huge red suns, glittering and glowing, gleaming with strange and hideous fires. Awesome and horrendous, they devoured Norman, scorching him and shrivelling him to a blackened crisp. He could feel his clothes crackling in the heat, the skin blistering from his hands, and the nails peeling back to reveal blackening stumps of bone. The glass melted from his wristwatch and Mickey's face puckered and vanished in the all-consuming furnace. Norman knew that he was dead, that his life had slipped from his grasp, and that he was far, far away, watching this destruction of his human form from some place of safety. Yet he was also there, there in that blazing skeleton, there inside the warped and shrinking skull, watching and watching.

'Are you going to drink these coffees or shall I pour them down the sink?' said Lily Marlene.

Norman shook himself awake with a start. The tramp had gone

and the two coffees were cold and undrunk. He looked at his watch; Mickey's head nodded to and fro as it always had. It was nearing five-thirty p.m. An hour had passed since he had entered the Plume.

'Where did the tramp go?' asked Norman.

'I don't know anything about any tramp,' said Lily. 'All I know is you buy two cups of coffee then fall asleep and let them go cold. Reckon if you want to sleep it off you can do it as well in your own bed as here, so bugger off home, will you Norman?'

Norman rose shakily from his seat. 'I think I shall go round to the Flying Swan instead,' he said. 'For still waters run deep, you know.'

'And it never rains but it bloody buckets down,' Lily called facetiously after the receding figure.

Neville the part-time barman drew the bolts upon the saloon-bar door and swung it open. Nervously, he stuck his head out and sniffed the early evening air; it smelt pretty much as it always did. He sniffed it a few more times for good measure. Neville believed strongly that a lot more went on in the air than was generally understood by man. 'Dogs have the way of it,' he had often said. 'Dogs and a few gifted men.' 'It is more than just pee on a post,' he had told Omally. 'Dogs sense with their noses rather than simply smell with them.'

This line of conversation was a bit out of Omally's range, but he thought he recalled a joke about a dog with no nose. 'A dog is a wise animal, that much I know,' said the Irishman. 'Back in the old country few men would venture out of doors of a night without a dog at their heels. The faithful fellow would sit at his master's elbow the evening, and if in the course of conversation the master felt the need for a bit of support he would nudge his dog, and the animal, who would have been following every word, would assist him.'

It was always remarkable to Neville that at times when Omally was stuck for something to say he would simply resort to the first thing that came into his head, no matter how thoroughly absurd it might be. 'You are saying that the dog would advise his master, then?' said the long-suffering part-time barman.

'Heavens no,' said Omally. 'The dear creature would simply go for the other fellow's throat, thus cutting short any chance of his master losing the argument.'

28

As Neville stood in the pub doorway, sniffing the air and thinking to discern the possibility of snow, his eyes were treated to a spectacle which spelt dread.

Norman was stumbling towards the Flying Swan, crossing himself wildly and reciting the rosary.

'Oh no,' groaned the part-time barman. He dropped the notice that he had painted that very afternoon, fled behind the counter, and lunged at the whisky optic. Norman entered the Flying Swan at a trot and tripped immediately upon a newly-painted notice which read NO TRAMPS. Picking this up in the trembling fingers he too said, 'Oh no!'

Neville anticipated the shopman's request and thrust another glass beneath the optic. 'Evening Norman,' he said in a restrained voice, 'how are things with you?'

'Did you paint this sign, Neville?' Norman demanded. Neville nodded. 'Give me a . . .' Neville pushed the glass across the counter. 'Oh yes, that's the one.'

Norman drained the glass with one gulp. Pausing to feel the life-giving liquid flowing down and about his insides, Norman said slowly, 'You know, don't you?'

'Know?' said Neville, with some degree of hesitation.

'About the tramp, you've seen him too, haven't you?' Neville nodded again. 'Thank God,' Norman said, 'I thought I was going mad.'

The part-time barman drew off two more scotches and the two men drank in silence, one either side of the bar. 'I was up on the canal bridge,' said Norman, and began to relate his story. Neville listened carefully as the tale unfolded, only nodding thoughtfully here and there and making the occasional remark such as 'The King's Shilling, eh?' and 'Strange and pungent odour, eh?' by way of punctuation.

Norman paused to take another gulp of whisky. Neville was taking careful stock of how many were being drunk and would shortly call the shopkeeper to account. 'And the next thing, you looked up and he was gone,' prompted the part-time barman.

Norman nodded. 'Gone without a by your leave or kiss my ankle. I wonder who on earth he might be?'

'Who who might be?' The voice belonged to James Pooley, whose carefully calculated betting system had until five minutes previous been putting the wind up the local bookie.

'How did the afternoon go for you, Jim?' asked Neville. Pooley shook his head dismally. 'I was doing another six-horse special and was up to a hundred and fifty thousand pounds by the fifth and what do you know?'

Neville said, 'Your sixth horse chose to go the pretty way round?'

'Tis true,' said the blighted knight of the turf.

Neville pulled a pint of Large, and Jim pushed the exact amount in odd pennies and halfpennies across the bar top. Neville scooped this up and tossed it without counting into the till. This was an error on his part, for the exact amount this time included three metal tokens from the New Inn's fruit machine and an old washer Jim had been trying to pass for the last six months.

Jim watched his money vanish into the till with some degree of surprise – things must be pretty bad with Neville, he thought. Suddenly he caught sight of the NO TRAMPS sign lying upon the bar top. 'Don't tell me,' he said. 'Your tramp has returned.'

Neville threw an alarmed and involuntary glance from the sign to the open door. 'He has not,' said the barman, 'but Norman has also had an encounter with the wretch.'

'And Archroy,' said Jim.

'What?' said Neville and Norman together.

'On his allotment last night; quizzed him over some lucky beans his evil wife took in exchange for his Morris Minor.'

'Ah,' said Norman, 'I saw that same Morris Minor on Leo's forecourt this very afternoon.'

'All roads lead to Rome,' said Jim, which Norman found most infuriating.

'About the tramp,' said Neville, 'what did Archroy say about him?'

'Seemed he was interested in Omally's allotment patch.'

'There is certainly something more than odd about this tramp,' said Norman, 'I wonder if anybody else has seen him?'

Pooley stroked his chin. If there was one thing he liked, it was a really good mystery. Not of the Agatha Christie variety you understand; Jim's love was for the cosmic mystery. Many of the more famous ones he had solved with very little difficulty. Regarding the tramp, he had already come to a conclusion. 'He is the Wandering Jew,' he said.

'Are you serious?' said Norman.

'Certainly,' said Pooley. 'And Omally who is by his birth a

Catholic will back me up on this – the Wandering Jew was said to have spat upon Our Lord at the time of the Passion and been cursed to wander the planet for ever awaiting Christ's return, at which time he would be given a chance to apologize.'

'And you think that this Jew is currently doing his wandering through Brentford?'

'Why not? In two thousand years he must have covered most of the globe, he's bound to turn up here sooner or later.'

'Why doesn't he come forward to authenticate the Turin Shroud then?' said Neville.

The other two turned cynical eyes on him. 'Would you?'

'Do you realize then,' said Neville, who was suddenly warming to the idea, 'that if he is the Wandering Jew, well, we have met a man who once stared upon Jesus?'

There was a reverent silence, each man momentarily alone with his thoughts. Norman and Neville both recalled how they had felt the need to cross themselves; this seemed to reinforce their conviction that Jim Pooley might have struck the nail firmly upon the proverbial head. It was a staggering proposition. Norman was the first to find his voice. 'No,' he said shortly, 'those eyes never looked upon Christ, although they may certainly have looked upon . . .'

'God save all here,' said John Omally, striding into the Swan. Somehow the talkers at the bar had formed themselves into what appeared to be a conspiratorial huddle. 'Hello,' said John, 'plotting the downfall of the English is it I hope?'

'We were discussing the Wandering Jew,' said Pooley.

'Gracious,' said John 'and were you now? Certainly there'd be a penny or two to be made in the meeting up with that fellow.' The shifting eyes put Omally upon the alert. 'He's not been in and I've bloody well missed him?'

'Not exactly,' said Neville.

'Not exactly is it? Well let me tell you my dear fellow that if you see him lurking hereabouts you tell him that John Vincent Omally of Moby Dick Terrace would like a word in his kosher shell-like.'

Neville pulled Omally a pint of Large and accepted the exact coinage from the Irishman; upon cashing up the sum he discovered Jim's washer. Jim, observing this, excused himself and went to the toilet. Shrugging hopelessly, the part-time barman took up his NO TRAMPS sign and crossed the bar. Before the open door he hesitated. His mind was performing rapid calculations.

31

If this tramp was the Wandering Jew maybe he could be persuaded to ... well some business proposition? He would most
certainly have seen a few rare old sights, a walking history book.
Why a man with a literary leaning, himself for instance, could
come to some arrangement. This Jew might have personal remi-
niscences of, well, Shakespeare, Napoleon, Beethoven? He might
have strolled around the Great Exhibition of Eighteen fifty-one,
rubbed shoulders with Queen Victoria, met Atilla the Hun (not at
the Great Exhibition, of course); the list was endless, there would
surely be a great many pennies to be had, as Omally said. Neville
fingered the painted sign. The tramp certainly carried with him an
aura of great evil. Maybe if he was the Jew he would kill anyone
who suspected him? He had nothing to lose. Christ's Second
Coming might be centuries off, what were a few corpses along the
way? Maybe he didn't want redemption anyway, maybe ... But it
was all too much, Neville gritted his teeth and hung the sign up at
the saloon-bar door. Jew or no Jew, he wanted no part whatever of
the mystery tramp.

Alone in the privacy of the gents, Jim Pooley's head harboured
similar thoughts to those of Neville's; Jim, however, had not had
personal contact with the tramp, and could feel only a good healthy
yearning to make a few pennies out of what was after all *his* theory.
It would be necessary, however, to divert Omally's thoughts from
this; in fact it would be best for one and all if the Irishman never
got to hear about the tramp at all. After all, Omally was a little
greedy when it came to the making of pennies and he might not
share whatever knowledge came his way. Pooley would make a few
discreet inquiries round and about; others must have seen the tramp.
He could quiz Archroy more thoroughly, he'd be there now on his
allotment.

Pooley left the gents and rejoined Norman at the bar. 'Where is
John Omally?' he asked, eyeing the Irishman's empty glass.

'I was telling him about the tramp,' said Norman, 'and he left in
a hurry to speak to Archroy.'

'Damn,' said Jim Pooley, 'I mean, oh really? Well I think I'll take
a stroll down that way myself and sniff the air.'

'There's a great deal more to sniffing the air than one might
realize,' said Neville, informatively.

But Jim Pooley had left the bar and naught was to be seen of his
passing but foam sliding down a hastily-emptied pint glass and a

pub door that swung silently to and fro upon its hinge. A pub door that now lacked a NO TRAMPS sign.

'If our man the Jew is wandering hereabouts,' said Jim to himself upon spying it, 'there is no point in discouraging the arrival of the goose that may just be about to lay the proverbial golden egg.'

Norman would have cried if he'd heard that one.

Archroy stood alone upon his allotment patch, pipe jammed firmly between his teeth and grey swirls of smoke escaping the bowl at regulated intervals. His thumbs were clasped into his waistcoat pockets and there was a purposeful set to his features. Archroy was lost in thought. The sun sinking behind the chemical factory painted his features with a ruddy hue, the naturally anaemic Archroy appearing for once to look in the peak of health. Sighing heavily, he withdrew from his pockets the five magic beans. Turning them again and again in his hand he wondered at their appearance.

They certainly were – how had the tramp put it? – beans of great singularity. Of their shape, it could be said that they were irregular. Certainly, but for their hue and texture, they presented few similarities. There was a tropical look to them; they seemed also, if held in certain lights, to show some slight signs of luminescence.

Yes they were singular beans indeed, but magic? The tramp had hinted that the term was somewhat open-ended to say the least. Beanstalk material perhaps? That was too obvious, thought Archroy. Some other magic quality then? Could these beans cure leprosy, impassion virgins, bestow immortality? Could beans such as these unburden a man of a suspect spouse?

Archroy held up the largest of the beans and squinted at it in perplexity. Surely it was slightly larger, slightly better-formed than it had been upon his last inspection. He knelt down and placed the beans in a row upon the top of his tobacco tin. 'Well I never did,' said Archroy. 'Now there is a thing.'

Suddenly Archroy remembered a science fiction film he had seen on the television at the New Inn. These seed pods came down from outer space and grew into people, then while you were asleep they took over your mind. He had never understood what had happened to the real people when their duplicates took over. Still, it had been a good film and it made him feel rather uneasy. He examined each bean in turn. None resembled him in the least, except for one that had a bit on it that looked a little like the lobe of his right ear. 'Good Lord,' said Archroy, 'say it isn't true.'

'It's not true,' said John Omally, who was developing a useful knack of sneaking up on folk.

'John,' said Archroy, who had seen Omally coming, 'how much would you give me for five magic beans?'

Omally took up one of the suspect items and turned it on his palm. 'Have you as yet discovered in what way their magic properties manifest themselves?'

'Sadly no,' said Archroy. 'I fear that I may not have the time to develop the proposition to any satisfactory extent, being an individual solely put upon by the fates to the degree that I have hardly a minute to myself nowadays.'

'That is a great shame,' said John, who knew a rat when somebody thrust one up his nose for a sniff. 'Their value I feel would be greatly enhanced if their use could be determined. In their present state I doubt that they are worth more than the price of a pint.'

Archroy sniffed disdainfully; his trusty Morris Minor exchanged for the price of a pint, the injustice of it. 'I have a feeling that large things may be expected of these beans, great oaks from little acorns as it were.'

'There is little of the acorn in these beans,' said Omally. 'More of the mango, I think, or possibly the Amazonian sprout.'

'Exotic fruit and veg are always at a premium,' said Archroy. 'Especially when home-grown, on an allotment such as this perhaps.'

Omally nodded thoughtfully. 'I will tell you what I will do Archroy,' said he. 'We will go down to my plot, select a likely spot and there, under your supervision, we shall plant one of these magic beans. We will nurture it with loving care, water it when we think fit, and generally pamper its growth until we see what develops. We will both take this moment a solemn vow that neither of us will uproot it or tamper with it in any way and that whatever should appear will be split fifty-fifty should it prove profitable.'

Archroy said, 'I feel that you will have the better half of the deal, Omally, although I am sure that this is unintentional upon your part and that you act purely out of a spirit of friendship and camaraderie.'

'The beans are certainly worthless at this moment,' said Omally, ingeniously. 'And the responsibility of what grows upon an allotment is solely that of the tenant. What for instance if your beans prove to be the seeds of some forbidden and illegal drug or some poison cactus? Will you take half the responsibility then?'

Archroy thought for a moment. 'Let us not talk of such depressing things, rather let us enter into this venture with the spirit of enterprise and the hope of fine things to come.'

Omally shook his companion by the hand and the two swore a great covenant that fell only slightly short of blood brotherhood. Without further ado they strode to Omally's plot, selected a space which they marked with a bean pole, and planted the magic bean.

'We shall water it tomorrow night,' said Omally, 'then together watch its progress. This project must be maintained in total secrecy,' he added, tapping his nose significantly. 'Come now, let us adjourn to my rooms and drink a toast to our success. There is something I should like to discuss with you in private.'

Jim Pooley watched the two botanical conspirators vanish into the distance from his nest in the long grass. Emerging stiffly, stretching his legs and twisting his neck, he drew himself erect. With many furtive sideways glances, stealthily he stole over to Omally's plot and dug up the magic bean, which he wiped clean of dirt and secreted in his coat pocket. With devious care he selected a seed potato from the sack at Omally's shed door and planted this in the place of the bean, erasing all traces of his treachery with a practised hand.

Then with a melodramatic chuckle and light feet Jim Pooley departed the St Mary's Allotments.

5

Professor Slocombe lived in a large rambling Georgian house on Brentford's Butts Estate. The house had been the property of the Slocombes through numerous generations, and the Professor's ancestry could be traced back to Brentford's earliest inhabitants. Therefore the Professor, whose string of doctorates, Master's degrees, and obscure testimonials ran in letters after his name like some Einsteinian calculation, had a deep and profound love for the place. He had produced privately a vast tome entitled:

THE COMPLETE AND ABSOLUTE HISTORY OF BRENT-FORD: Being a study of the various unusual and extradictionary circumstances that have prevailed throughout History and which have in their way contributed to the unique visual and aesthetic aspects inherent in both landscape and people of this locality. Giving also especial reference to religious dogma, racial type, ethnic groupings, and vegetation indigenous to the area.

The Professor was constantly revising this mighty volume. His researches had of late taken him into uncharted regions of the occult and the esoteric. Most of the Professor's time was spent in his study, his private library rivalling that of the Bodleian. Show cases packed with strange objects lined the walls, working models of da Vinciesque flying machines, stuffed beasts of mythical origin, brass astrolabes, charts of the heavens, rows of apothecary jars, picked homunculi, and dried mandragora lined each available inch of shelf space and spilled off into every corner, nook, and cranny. The whole effect was one to summon up visions of medieval alchemists bent over their seething cauldrons in search of the philosopher's stone. The Professor himself was white-haired and decrepit, walking only with the aid of an ivory-topped cane. His eyes, however, glittered with a fierce and vibrant energy.

Fulfilling as he did the role of ornamental hermit, the Professor made one daily appearance upon the streets of Brentford. This ritual was accompanied by much ceremony and involved him making a slow perambulation about Brentford's boundaries. Clad on even the warmest of days in a striking black coat with astrakhan collar, his white hair streaming behind him, this venerable gentleman trod his weary morning path, never a pace out of step with that of the day previous.

Jim Pooley said that should this phenomenon cease, like the ravens leaving the Tower of London, it would spell doom and no good whatever to this sceptred isle. Jim was a regular visitor to the Professor, acting as he did as self-appointed gardener, and held the aged person in great reverence.

He had once taught the Professor to play darts, reasoning that excellence in this particular form of pub sport was entirely the product of skill and much practice, both of which Jim had to a high degree. He had explained the rules and handed the Professor a set of darts. The old man had taken one or two wild throws at the board with little success. Then, pausing for a moment, he took several snippings from the flights with a pair of nail scissors, licked the points, and proceeded to beat Jim Pooley, one of the Swan's most eminent darts players, to the tune of ten pounds. Pooley assumed that he had either become subject to some subtle form of hypnosis or that the Professor was a master of telekinesis. Whatever the case the Professor earned Jim's undying admiration. He did not even resent the loss of the ten pounds, because he was never a man to undervalue education.

This particular warm spring evening the Professor sat at his desk examining a crumbling copy of the *Necronomicon* through an over-sized magnifying glass. A soft breeze rustled amongst the honey-suckle which encircled the open French windows, and from not far off the Memorial Library clock struck eight o'clock.

The Professor made several jottings in a school exercise book and without looking up said, 'Are you going to skulk about out there all evening, Jim Pooley, or will you join me for a small sherry?'

'I will join you for a sherry,' said Jim, who showed no surprise whatever at the Professor's uncanny perception, 'but as to a small one, that is a matter I suggest we discuss.'

The Professor rang a tiny Indian brass bell that lay half hidden among the crowded papers upon his desk. There was a knock and the study door swung open to reveal an elderly retainer, if anything even more white-haired and ancient than the Professor himself.

'Would it be the sherry, sir?' said the ancient, proffering a silver tray upon which rested a filled crystal decanter and two minuscule glasses.

'It would indeed, Gammon. Leave it there if you would.' The Professor indicated a delicately-carved Siamese table beside the white marble fireplace. The elderly retainer did as he was bidden and silently departed.

The Professor decanted two glasses of sherry and handed one to Jim. 'So,' said he, 'and to what do I owe this pleasure then, Jim?'

'It is this way,' Pooley began. 'It is well-known hereabouts and in particular to myself that you are a man of extensive knowledge, widely travelled and well-versed in certain matters that remain to the man in the street inexplicable conundra.'

The Professor raised an eyebrow. 'Indeed?' said he.

'Well,' Jim continued, 'I have recently had come into my possession an object which causes me some degree of perplexity.'

The Professor said 'Indeed' once more.

'Yes,' said Jim. 'How I came by it is irrelevant, but I think that you as a learned and scholarly man might find it of some interest.'

The Professor nodded thoughtfully and replaced his glass upon the tray. 'Well now, Jim,' he said. 'Firstly, I must say that I am always pleased to see you; your visits are rarely devoid of interest, your conversation is generally stimulating, and it is often a challenge to match wits with you over some of your more extravagant theories. Secondly, I must say now that whatever it is you have with you is no doubt something of great singularity but that should it be anything short of the philosopher's stone or one of the hydra's teeth I do not wish to purchase it.'

Pooley's face took on a wounded expression.

'So, if we understand each other completely I will gladly examine the object which you have in your possession and give you whatever information I can regarding it, should the thing prove to be genuine.'

Pooley nodded and withdrew from his pocket the magic bean, which had been carefully wrapped in his despicable handkerchief.

'Only the object,' said the Professor, eyeing Pooley's hankie with disgust, 'I have no wish to contract some deadly virus from that hideous rag.'

38

Pooley unwrapped the bean and handed it to the Professor. Jim noticed that it seemed slightly larger than upon previous inspection and he also noticed the unusual expression that had crossed the Professor's face. The usually benign countenance had become distorted, the colour, what little there was of it, had drained from his face, and a blue tinge had crept across his lips. This grotesque manifestation lasted only for a moment or two before the Professor regained his composure.

'Put it over there on to that marble base,' he said with a quavering voice. Pooley, shaken by the Professor's terrifying reaction, obeyed without hesitation.

'Put that glass dome over it,' the Professor said. Pooley did so.

'Are you all right, Professor?' he asked in a voice of some concern, 'Can I get you a glass of water or anything?'

'No,' said the Professor, 'no, no, I'll be all right, it's just that, well,' he looked Pooley squarely in the eye, 'where did you get that thing?'

'I found it,' said Pooley, who had no intention of giving very much away.

'Where though? Where did you find it?'

Pooley stroked his chin. Clearly the bean had well-rattled the old gentleman, clearly it was more than just any old bean, it was indeed a bean of great singularity, therefore possibly a bean of great value. He would not mention that Archroy had four more of them. 'It is valuable then?' he asked nonchalantly.

'Where did you find it?' the Professor repeated, in a voice of grave concern.

'I dug it up,' said Jim.

The Professor gripped Pooley's lapels in his sinewy fingers and made some attempt to shake him vigorously. The effort, however, exhausted him and he sank back into the armchair. 'Jim,' he said in a tone of such sincerity that Pooley realized that something was about to happen which would not be to his advantage. 'Jim, you have there —' he indicated the bean beneath the glass dome — 'something, if I am not mistaken, and I sadly fear that I am not, something so heinous that it is best not spoken of. I only hope that you have not had it in your possession long enough to become contaminated by it.'

'Contaminated!' Pooley yanked his handkerchief out of his pocket and hurled it into the fire which blazed away in the hearth no matter what the season. 'What is it?' said Pooley, a worried sweat breaking out on his brow. 'Is it poison then?'

'Worse than that, I fear.'

Worse than poison? Pooley's mind turned several somersaults. What could be worse than poison in a bean?

'Help me up if you please.' Pooley aided the Professor to one of the massive bookcases flanking the study door. 'That green volume with the gold lettering, hand me that down if you will.' Pooley obliged and the Professor placed the great book upon his desk and leafed slowly through the pages.

'My glass, if you would.' Pooley handed him the magnifier and peered over the ancient's shoulder. To his dismay the book was written in Latin. There was, however, on a facing page covered by a slip of tissue paper, an illustration in fading colours of a bean apparently identical to that which now rested beneath the dome. The Professor ran his glass to and fro across the page, raising his eye occasionally to take in both bean and illustration. Then, sitting back in his chair with a sigh, he said, 'You've certainly pulled off the big one this time, Jim.'

Pooley, uncertain whether or not this was meant as a compliment, remained silent.

'Phaseolus Satanicus,' the Professor said, 'Phaseolus being in general the genus of the ever-popular and edible bean, Satanicus being quite another matter. Now this book –' he tapped at the vellum page with his exquisite fingertip '– this book is the work of one James Murrell, known as the Hadleigh Seer, who enumerated and copied the masterworks, astrological charts and almanacs of previous and largely-forgotten magi and minor wizards. Little remains of his work, but I have through means that I care not to divulge come into the possession of this one volume. It is a book entirely dedicated to the detailed study of what you might term magical herbs, spices, seeds, and beans. It lists the pharmaceutical, thaumaturgical, and metaphysical uses of these, and includes within its skin bindings certain notes upon plants and seedlings which the ancients referred to as sacred. Either because of their mindbending qualities when distilled or because they possessed certain characteristics which were outside the scope of normal explanation.'

'So there are magical properties adherent to this particular bean then?' said Pooley.

'I should not care to call them magical,' said the Professor, 'but let me tell you that this bean of yours pays allegiance to the powers of darkness to a point that it is better not thought of, let alone mentioned in the public-bar of the Flying Swan.'

'I prefer to patronize the saloon-bar actually,' said Pooley, 'but pray continue, I find your monologue fascinating.'

'I shall read to you directly from the book,' said the Professor, 'then when I have finished we shall see if you still find my monologue fascinating.'

Pooley poured himself yet another sherry and wondered whether he might interest the Professor in a home-brew lager kit.

'"Phaseolus Satanicus",' the Professor read once more. 'This first passage is a loose translation from the Greek: "And when the casket was opened and when the evil one set his burning hoof upon the plains of earth, then did Pandora weep those five bitter tears. And where those tears fell on to the fields of men there did they take root and flourish withal. And Ephimetheus seeing the ill work that his wife had performed snatched forth those five dark saplings and cast them into the places of absolute night from whence should man go onward to seek them then surely he should never more return."'

'That's all very well,' said Jim Pooley.

'The next quotation comes from Jean-François Champollion, 1790–1832, the man who originally deciphered the Egyptian hiero-glyphic system: "Anubis stared upon the manchild that had come before him and questioned him over his possessions and the pharaoh did answer saying I bear seventeen oxen, fifteen caskets of gold and precious stones, carvings and set tableaux of rich embellishment and the five that dwell within the sacred house where none may tread. And Anubis took fright, even he that stands guardian over the realms of the beyond was afeared and he turned back the manchild that stood before the sacred river saying never shall you cross until your weight is above the holy balance. Which never can it be for the five set the scales heavily against you."'

Pooley reached for the sherry decanter but found to his dismay that it was empty. 'This five whatever they are sound somewhat sinister,' said he, 'but the threat seems also a trifle nebulous.'

The Professor looked up from his antique tome. 'This book was handwritten some three centuries ago,' said he, 'not by some casual dilettante of the occult but by a mage of the first order. I have given you two quotations which he sought out, neither of which seem to impress you very much. Now I shall read to you what James Murrell wrote in his own hand regarding the five beans which had at the time of his writing come by means unfathomable into his possession: "I am plagued this evening as I write with thoughts of the five I have here before me. Their echoes are strong and their power terrific. My ears take in strange cries that come not from an earthly throat and visions dance before my eyes whose very nature and habit appal me and fill my soul with dark horror. I know now what these may be and what, if they were to receive the touch of the dark one, they might become. It is my intention to destroy them by fire and by water and by the power of the mother church. Would that I had never set eyes upon them for no more will sleep come unto me a blessed healer."' The Professor slammed shut the book. 'The illustration of the bean is still clear in Murrell's hand, there can be no mistake.'

Pooley was silent. The Professor's voice had induced in him a state of semi-hypnosis. What it all meant was still unclear but that there was a distinctly unsavoury taint to the beans was certain.

'Where are the other four?' said the Professor.

'Archroy has them,' said Pooley promptly.

'I do not fully understand the implications myself,' said the Professor. 'These beans, it would seem, are objects of grim omen – their appearance at various intervals in history always precede times of great ill, plague, war, famine, and the like. On each occasion a dark figure to whom in some inexplicable way these five beans appear to owe some allegiance is always mentioned – what his ultimate purpose may be I shudder to think.' The Professor crossed himself.

Upon the verandah, shielded by the trelliswork of honeysuckle, a tramp of hideous aspect and sorry footwear watched the Professor with eyes that glowed faintly in the late twilight. He ran a nicotine-stained finger across a cultivated rose and watched in silence as the petals withered beneath his touch. Mouthing something in a long-dead tongue he slipped away down the garden path and melted into the gathering darkness.

Jim Pooley sat upon his favourite seat before the Memorial Library, deep in thought. It was nearing midnight and growing decidedly cold. Above him a proud full moon swam amongst shredded clouds and the stars came and went, wormholes in the wooden floor of heaven. Jim turned up the collar of his tweed jacket and sat, shoulders hunched and hands lost in his bottomless trouser pockets.

All this bean business had become a little too much for him. After all, he'd only gone around to the Professor to get the damn thing identified. This was Brentford in the twentieth century, not some superstitious medieval village in the grip of witch mania. Pandora's box indeed! Jim searched about for his tobacco tin, and the clock struck twelve. The search proved fruitless and Pooley recalled placing the tin upon the Professor's mantelpiece while he was asking the old man for a refill of the sherry decanter.

Jim sighed dismally. It had not been a very successful night, all things considered. His tobacco growing dry on the fireplace, whilst his bean lay valueless in its glass prison. Pooley thought back over all that the Professor had said. Could the old boy be pulling a fast one? Jim had left the bean there after all, and no money had changed hands. Possibly the Professor had instantly recognized the bean as an object of great value and dragged up all this Phaseolus Satanicus stuff simply to put the wind up him. Jim scratched the stubble upon his chin.

No, that couldn't be it; the Professor had been genuinely shocked when he saw the bean and it was most certainly the same as the illustration in the ancient book. No one could make up stories like that on the spur of the moment, could they? And he had known of the existence of the four others. All this intense thinking coupled with the intake of two pints of fine sherry was beginning to give Jim a headache. Better to forget the bean then, let the Professor do what he pleased with it.

Pooley rose and stretched his arms. Another thought suddenly crossed his mind. 'If these beans are dangerous,' the thought said, 'then it would be best to inform Archroy of this fact as the four he carries with him may possibly do him harm.' Jim sat down again upon the bench.

'But if you tell him,' said another thought, 'then he will ask how you know all this and you will have to confess to the abduction of the bean from Omally's allotment.'

This thought did not please Pooley whatsoever.

'But he is your friend,' said the first thought in an angelic voice, 'and you would feel very guilty should any ill befall him that you are empowered to prevent.' Pooley nodded and rose once more to his feet.

'Better not to get involved,' said the second thought. 'Who is to say that the Professor's suppositions are correct?' Pooley bit his lip. It was all a terrible dilemma. He let the angelic thought have the final word upon the matter.

'If the Professor had told you that the bean was that of a plant which bears gold doubloons upon its boughs each spring you would have believed him. You went there to take advantage of his boundless knowledge, did you not?' Pooley nodded meekly. 'So if the Professor says that the beans are evil and must be destroyed, you would do well to follow his advice.' Pooley seemed satisfied by this and took some steps into the direction of home. Then as if jerked to a standstill by a rope he stopped.

'But then I must somehow get those four other beans from Archroy,' he said. 'And in some way that I will not implicate myself in any duplicity.' Jim Pooley wished with all his might that he had never set eyes upon any beans whatever, be they baked, curried, buttered, soya, or magic to the slightest degree.

A new thought came to Pooley, one whose voice he did not recognize but one which was so sound in logic that Pooley felt very grateful that it had chosen his head to come into. 'Why don't you go around to Archroy's now, while he is away on the night shift, gain entrance to his house and remove the four magic beans?' The angelic thought had some doubts about this but was finally cowed into submission.

'I do this deed for Archroy,' said Jim Pooley. 'A noble venture for which I expect to receive no thanks, as by its very nature the perpetrator of the deed must remain anonymous.'

Jim girded up his loins and strode purposefully in the direction of Archroy's house. It was seldom indeed that a noble thought entered his head and the entry of this one filled Jim with reckless confidence. He would climb on to Archroy's garage and pull down the aluminium ladder, then go round and try all the upper windows, one of which must surely have been left open. Once inside, if the beans were there, he would most certainly find them.

Having checked that there were no late-night revellers returning to their haunts, or policemen out upon their lonely beats, Pooley slid away down the side-alley beside Archroy's garage. His stealth and silence were there sadly impaired, however, by a noisy collision with Omally's bicycle Marchant, which was resting against the garage wall lost in the shadows. Jim and Marchant crashed noisily to the ground, Marchant ringing his bell in protest at his rude awakening, and Jim swearing great oaths upon every form of two-wheeled conveyance known to mankind.

With much shooshing and hand-flapping, Jim rose to his feet, flat cap cocked over one eye and trouser turnup firmly in the grip of Marchant's back brake. Amid more cursing and the distinctive sound of tearing tweed, Jim fought his way free of the bicycle's evil grasp and limped on up the alley.

He stopped suddenly in his tracks and gazed up in amazement, but there, propped up against the side-wall and leading directly to an open upstairs window, was Archroy's extendable aluminium ladder. 'Luck indeed,' said Jim Pooley, gripping it delightedly and testing its footings for safety.

He was all of five rungs up when a small clear voice in his head said, 'Pooley, why do you think that there would be a ladder resting so conveniently against Archroy's wall and leading directly to an open upstairs window?'

Pooley arrested his ascent and thought for a moment or two. Perhaps Archroy was cleaning his windows and forgot to remove the ladder? The small voice said, 'Come now, Pooley.'

'I'll just shin up and have a quick shufty in through the window,' Pooley told the voice. He accomplished the ascent with admirable dexterity, considering that the effects of the Professor's sherry seemed to be increasing by the minute. The full moon shone down through the bedroom window, flooding the room with its septic light. Pooley's head rose cautiously above the window-sill and came to rest, his nose hooked over it in the manner of the legendary Chad. As his eyes took in the situation the words that escaped his lips in an amazed whisper were generally of a sort totally unprintable.

There upon the continental quilt, bouncing and gyrating in a frenzy of sexual abandonment, was Archroy's wife. Locked in passionate congress with this insatiable female was none other than John Vincent Omally, bachelor of this parish.

'Bastard,' mouthed Jim Pooley, which was at least in the Oxford Dictionary. 'The conniving treacherous . . .' his mind sought about for an adjective suitable to the expression of his displeasure. It was during the search that Pooley's eyes alighted upon the very objects which had led him to the unexpected viewing of this lewd and certainly X-certificate performance.

There they lay, glowing with a faint luminescence, upon the dressing-table inches away from the window. Pooley spied them with great satisfaction, feeling that his noble quest had been justly rewarded by instantaneous success achieved with only the minimum of physical exertion and with next to no danger to life or limb. This feeling of well-being was, however, almost immediately succeeded by one of disgust. For although the beans lay in attitudes suggestive of lifelessness, it was obvious to Jim from where he clung to his airy perch that they were very much on the alert. They were quite definitely watching and apparently thoroughly enjoying the erotic spectacle. They exuded such a sense of dark evil and inhuman nastiness that Jim was hard put to it to subdue the disgust which rose within him like an out-of-season vindaloo.

Taking a deep yet silent breath, he thrust his hand through the window and snatched up the sinister beans from their grandstand seats on the dressing-table. Omally's bum, glowing ivory in the moonlight, rose and fell undeterred. Pooley thrust the beans into his coat pocket and made haste down the ladder.

Here he transferred the beans into a drawstring bag sanctified by the Professor for the purpose. 'Another job jobbed,' said Pooley with some relief. The operations had been a remarkable success, handled with alacrity, diligence, dexterity, and skill. High upon Olympus, hosts of ancient Pooleys opened a bottle of champagne and toasted their descendant.

Pooley strode down the alley with a jaunty spring to his step. He had not gone but three yards, however, when the vengeful left pedal of Marchant caught him by the sound trouser-cuff and upended him into the muddy gloom.

'You swine,' growled Pooley, lashing out with his boots in as many directions as possible.

'Who's there?' said a voice from an upper window.

Jim edged along the side-wall of the house, gained the street, and took to his heels. In the darkened alleyway Omally's bike chuckled mechanically to its iron self and rang its bell in delight. On High Olympus the Pooleys sought other amusements.

6

Captain Carson stood upon the porch of the Seamen's Mission, taking in the fresh morning air. The Mission was situated on the Butts Estate not a stone's throw from Professor Slocombe's house. It was a fine Victorian building, built in an era when craftsmen took a pride in their work and knew nothing of time and a half and guaranteed Sunday working. Now the once-proud structure had fallen into bitter disrepair; its chimney-pots leaned at crazy angles, its roof lacked many essential tiles, paint peeled from the carved gables. That which the tireless assault of wind and weather had not achieved without, had been amply accomplished within by woodworm and a multifarious variety of fungi, dry rot, and deathwatch beetle.

The Captain stood framed in the doorway, master of his landbound ship. Thirty years he had been at the helm. The Mission, bequeathed to the borough by a long dead Victorian benefactor and maintained by a substantial foundation, was the Captain's pride. A fine figure of a man, still erect and dignified although now the graveyard side of seventy, the Captain took a pull upon his cherrywood pipe and let escape a blue swirl of seaman's smoke. His white hair and tabby beard, the faded blue of his rollneck sweater, the bellbottom trousers and yachting sandals, all bespoke in him a man who lived and breathed for nothing but the salt winds of the briny deep and the roar of the shore-bound breakers.

Sad to say, the Captain had never seen the sea. He had taken the job at the Mission at a time when jobs were few and far between and one took what one could. The only stipulation given had been that the applicant must be a man of nautical bent with a love of the sea who would maintain the Mission to the highest ideals and qualities of His Majesty's Fleet.

47

Togging up at a theatrical outfitter's with his last few pennies, Horatio B. Carson applied for the post. His characterization must have been as convincing as that of Charles Laughton in *Mutiny on the Bounty*, because 'Captain' Carson was immediately accepted for the job.

His duties were not arduous. Few if any sailors had ever honoured the Mission with their visits. However, a proliferation of down-and-outs, ne'er-do-wells, roguish knights of the road, shoelace pedlars, and grimy individuals smelling strongly of meths and cheap sherry had soon appeared upon the doorstep. The Captain welcomed each in turn, extending to them the utmost courtesy, carrying their sorry bundles and opening doors before them.

'Here is your room, sir,' he would say, drawing their attention to the luxuriance of the pillows and the fine quality of the bedcoverings. 'Our last lodger had to leave in something of a hurry,' he would explain. 'He, like your good self, was a sea-faring man and the doctors at the isolation hospital said that there would have been some hope of saving his life had they been able to identify the crippling and particularly virulent form of disease to which he so sadly succeeded. I haven't had a chance to fumigate the room yet, but I am sure that your travels must by now have made you immune to most sicknesses, even of the horrendously disfiguring and painful variety which so sorrowfully took him from us.'

At this point the Captain would remove his hat, place it over his heart and look skyward. The tramp to which he was addressing this tragic monologue would follow the direction of his eyes then make his exit, often at astonishing speed, with talk of 'pressing engagements' and 'business elsewhere'.

In the thirty long years of the Captain's residence, no visitor, no matter how apparent his need or dire his circumstance, be his tale one to raise a tear in a glass eyeball, no visitor had ever spent a single night within the Seamen's Mission.

On this particular morning as the Captain stood upon the porch his thoughts dwelt mainly upon money, the strange ways of fate and the scourge of homosexuality. He knew that he could not expect many more years within the Mission and that his days were most definitely numbered. The job supplied no pension, and with the swelling list of forged signatures speaking of the enormous physical effort required of one man to maintain the Mission there had been talk of employing a younger person. The yearly meeting between

48

himself and the Foundation's trustees had been but a week before and he, the Captain, had handed over his tailored accounts and spoken modestly of his good works. But a new face had appeared upon the Committee this year, a young and eager face. During the previous twelve months one of the Trustees had died and the lot had fallen for his nephew to succeed him.

Young Brian Crowley had no love for elderly sea-captains. His distaste for such patriarchs was only exceeded by his out-and-out hatred for tramps, loafers, down-and-outs, gypsies, foreigners, and women. The limp-wristed Brian cared little for anybody other than an Italian waiter who worked at the Adelaide Tea Rooms. He had promised to set Mario up in his own restaurant, the dago waiter being a veritable 'wizard-de-cuisine' and exceptionally well-hung into the bargain.

The fates, which had conspired to arrange the sad demise of his dear uncle and Brian's succession to the Foundation committee, had also decreed that this year the Council would raise their annual offer for the purchase of the Mission to a more than adequate sum.

The Captain sucked again upon his pipe. He could read faces well-enough, and young Brian's had been an open book. It might well be the time to shape up and ship out. His nestegg was by now pretty substantial, enough for a small cottage somewhere, possibly by the sea. It might be nice to actually see the waves breaking on a beach. 'I wonder if they make a lot of noise?' he said to himself.

Suddenly, far up the road a flicker of movement caught his eye. He watched with passing interest as a ragged figure turned the corner beside the Memorial Library and shambled towards him with an odd yet purposeful gait.

It was the figure of a tramp. The Captain raised his nautical glass to view the apparition. A swift glance was enough. 'Ugh!' said the Captain.

The tramp plodded nearer and nearer, and the Captain rummaged about in his vast mental storehouse for a tale of woe suitable to the occasion. Strangely, none seemed readily available. The tramp trod closer, his big floppy boots stomping down into the ground. The captain began to whistle an uneasy version of the famous shanty 'Orange Claw Hammer'.

The tramp was crossing the road towards the Mission. He stopped. The Captain ceased his whistling. The birds were silent and the Captain could no longer smell the fragrant scent of

49

honeysuckle. He felt cold, and even though the early summer sun breathed down upon him, a shiver arose at the base of his spine. The Captain held his breath. Of a sudden the wretch turned upon his heel and stalked away down a side-turning. As if at a signal the birds burst forth again into a cascade of song and the Captain regained the use of his nostrils. He let free a sigh of utmost relief and reached into his sleeve for his matches.

'Could I trouble you for a glass of water, please?' said a voice at his elbow.

The Captain turned in horror, spilling his matches to the ground. Beside him stood a tramp of hideous aspect. 'Sorry, did I startle you?' said the creature with what seemed to be a voice of genuine concern. 'It's a bad habit of mine, I really must control it.'

'Damn you, sir,' swore the Captain. 'Creepin' up on a fella.'

'My apologies,' said the tramp, removing the battered relic which served him as hat, and bowing to the ground. 'But if you would be so kind, a glass of water would serve well at this time.'

The Captain muttered a terse 'Come in then,' and led his unspeakable visitor into the Mission. 'You caught me at a bad moment,' he said.

The tramp found no cause to reply.

'I was just having a moment or two's fresh air before I continue my search.' The Captain drew the tramp a glass of water. The tramp received it with a great show of gratitude. 'My thanks,' said he.

'Yes,' the Captain continued, 'my search.'

The tramp seemed uninterested in the Captain's search but he nodded politely.

'Yes, carelessly I have upset my case of deadly scorpions, I fear that they have gone to earth in the sleeping quarters.'

'Scorpions indeed?' said the tramp. 'I have some experience in such matters, I will help you search.'

The Captain eyed his visitor with suspicion. 'That will not be necessary. I should not like there to be an unfortunate accident, these fellows are wantonly vicious in their attitude towards any but myself.'

'If you are on such good terms, possibly you should just put out some milk and give them a call,' said the tramp helpfully.

The Captain sucked strongly upon his pipe. 'I fear that would prove futile,' he said. 'Devious fellows, scorpions, and mine I believe to be deaf.'

'Devious indeed,' said the tramp. 'Have you seen this trick?' He held the glass of water out at arm's length and stared into it with a fixed and steady gaze. The Captain watched in puzzlement, his eyes flickering between the glass and the tramp's glaring red pupils, which now began to glitter with a strange and sinister light.

Bubbles began to appear in the glass; one by one they popped to the surface, growing in force, one upon another they burst upwards; steam began to rise.

The Captain said, 'It's boiling, be damned!'

The tramp handed the churning glass to the Captain, who gingerly received it. 'I should like a room for the night,' said the tramp.

'The water is cold,' said the Captain, dumbfounded.

'A trick, no more. About the room?'

'The scorpions!'

The tramp said, 'I don't think we need worry about the scorpions, I have here in my pocket a trained cobra that will easily seek out any scorpions lounging about.'

'Hold there,' said the Captain. 'That surely will not be necessary I think that the warm sun may well have drawn any errant insects beyond the bounds of the Mission.'

'That is good to hear,' said the tramp. 'Now, about the room?'

'This room is vacant.' The Captain swung open a door to reveal a neatly-dressed cubicle. 'It is sad that it carries such a dreadful reputation.'

'Indeed?' The tramp prodded the bed and turned back the woollen coverlet.

'Yes, no soul has ever stayed a full night in it, none reveal what horrors take hold of them, but of those who attempted to remain, one committed suicide and three more are even now residents at St Bernard's Asylum, hopeless lunatics.'

'Indeed?' The tramp sat down upon the bed and bounced soundlessly upon the steady springs.

'Gibbering they were,' said the Captain. 'I have sailed the seven seas and seen sights that would blast the sanity from a lesser man, but I can tell you I was shaken when I saw the looks upon the faces of those unlucky fellows.'

The tramp shook his head slowly. 'My word,' was all he would say. The Captain had an uneasy feeling that Brian Crowley had a hand in this. 'The hospitality of the Mission is well-known,' said the tramp. 'Only last week I bumped into Alfredo Beranti and Roger Kilharric, both joyfully extolling the virtues of your beneficient establishment.'

The Captain scratched at his head. The names seemed strangely familiar. 'And Dennis Cunningham,' the tramp continued, 'forever praising the *haute-cuisine*.' The Captain became suddenly weak about the knees; he knew those names well enough, they were three of the cast of imaginary tramps with which he peopled the pages of his yearly accounts.

'And Old Wainwright McCarthy,' the tramp said, 'and . . .'

'No, no,' screamed the Captain in an unnatural voice, 'enough, enough!'

'What time is dinner to be served?'

'Dinner?'

'Knobby Giltrap spoke highly of the shepherd's pie.'

'Six o'clock,' said the Captain.

'A little early, perhaps?'

'Seven then,' said the Captain, 'or eight if you please.'

'Seven will be fine,' smiled the tramp, 'now I think I shall take a brief nap. Pray awaken me at six-thirty.'

With that the Captain was ushered from the cubicle and out into the corridor, where he stood in the semi-darkness, chewing upon the stem of his pipe, his breath coming and going in rapid grunts.

'And don't over-season my veg,' came a voice through the panelled cubicle door.

The tramp sat back in the Captain's chair and eased open the lower buttons of his waistcoat. 'Very palatable,' said he.

The Captain had watched with set features whilst the tramp devoured two bowls of soup, all the shepherd's pie, a plate of potatoes, two double helpings of peas, a bowl of custard and a large slice of chocolate gâteau.

'Is there anything to follow?' asked the tramp politely.

'To follow?'

'Well, brandy, a cigar, or even a fill for my pipe?'

The Captain rose to his feet, pulling away the napkin from his rollneck. 'Now see here!' he roared.

'Gaffer Tim Garney was telling me of your generosity with the navy plug?'

52

The Captain flung the tramp his tobacco pouch. 'Shag,' said he, slumping into a chair.

'Shag then, my thanks again.' The tramp took to filling his pipe, his glittering eyes wandering towards the Captain's brandy bottle.

'I expect you'll be wanting to make an early start tomorrow?' said the Captain.

The tramp said, 'Excuse me?'

'Well,' the Captain replied, 'I know you fellows, can't keep you cooped up under a roof for very long. Life of freedom, eh? Knights of the road, the sky above, the earth below.'

The tramp scratched his head, raising small clouds of blue dust. 'There I am afraid you are mistaken. Please do not construe from my appearance that I incline towards the life of the casual wanderer. On the contrary, my every movement is guided towards inevitable consequence. I follow my kharma as all must.'

'Indeed?' said the Captain. 'Well, far be it from me to hinder you in your search for the ultimate truth.'

'I feel that our paths have not crossed out of idle chance,' said the tramp, 'in fact, I will go so far as to say that destiny has pointed me to your door with a straight and unwavering digit.'

'Possibly this same destiny will point you in yet another direction tomorrow?'

'I doubt that,' said the tramp, with a note of finality. 'Now, about this brandy?'

The Captain rose early the next morning. He had lain sleeplessly upon his bunk, chewing at his knuckles and muttering nautical curses into the early hours. The ghastly truth that he was no longer alone beneath the Mission-roof gnawed at his hermitical soul like a rat at a leper's foot. By dawn he had run himself dry of profanity and fallen into an uneasy sleep.

Now he stalked to and fro along the verandah, emitting thick clouds of seaman's shag and grumbling to himself. Somehow he must rid himself of this unwelcome visitor, but if Brian Crowley was at the bottom of it he must be on his guard. He would just have to treat the hideous stranger with politeness while hinting with firm conviction that the traveller might fare better in distant and sunnier climes. He looked up at the sky and was appalled to see that it was likely to be another beautiful day.

53

Suddenly a voice at his elbow said, 'I see you like to make an early start to the day, Captain.'

Colour drained from the Captain's face and he dropped his tobacco pouch, spilling its contents to the verandah floor. 'Must you always come damn well creeping up?' he coughed, as he took a great gust of smoke up his nostrils.

'I must say that I slept very well,' said the tramp. 'What is on the menu for breakfast?'

The Captain folded his brow into a look of intense perplexity. 'You seem exceedingly spry for a man who demolished an entire bottle of brandy and better part of an ounce of shag in a single evening.'

'And very nice too,' said the tramp. 'Now as to breakfast?'

'I make it a rule never to over-eat at this time of the day,' the Captain explained. 'Makes a man sluggish, impairs the limbs, corrodes the arteries. A simple bowl of bran and a glass of salt water serve as my early morning repast.'

'I should kindly prefer double eggs, bacon, sausages, beans, mushrooms, tomato, and a fried slice. Possibly, as I have no wish to lessen your resolve, you would prefer to eat alone,' said the tramp.

The Captain pulled upon his lower lip. 'Possibly that would be impolite of me, it is always wise to eat well before travel.' Here he looked at the tramp from the corner of his eye. 'Thus we shall have a hearty meal of it before your departure.'

The tramp smiled. 'Have no fear upon that account, I have no intention of moving on within the foreseeable future.'

The Captain frowned furiously and stalked away to the kitchen. The tramp scooped up the fallen pouch and proceeded to refill his pipe.

7

As founder and sole member of the Brentford and West London Hollow Earth Society Soap Distant thought it about time to put matters firmly into perspective. 'There have been many words spoken and much local controversy over the arrival of a certain extraordinary being upon our streets of late,' he announced to the Saturday evening crowd in the Swan's saloon-bar.

Neville nodded thoughtfully. The tramp had been pretty much the sole topic of conversation in the borough for nearly a month, although his last sighting was more than a fortnight ago.

'I know that you all understand to whom I refer,' said Soap.

Those who did nodded. Those who did, but had no wish to listen to yet another of Soap's endless diatribes upon the denizens of the inner world, took a sudden interest in the bottoms of their pint glasses.

'Speculation has been rife,' Soap continued, 'and up until now I have kept my counsel whilst the false prophets among you have battled one another to a standstill. Now and only now I am ready to impart to you the sole and unimpeachably cosmic truth.'

Omally groaned. 'I had an uncle once,' said he, hoping to change the subject, 'who swallowed a golf ball thinking it to be a plover's egg.'

'Really,' said Old Pete, who hated Soap Distant and his 'bloody silly notions'. 'And what happened to your uncle, how was he?'

'A little under par,' said the Irishman.

'There are none so deaf as those who will not hear,' said Soap.

'Here, steady on,' said Norman.

'How many times have I propounded my theories regarding the lands beneath and their interterrestial occupants, and how many times have I offered irrefutable proof as to their existence, only to

55

be scoffed at and ridiculed by those pseudo-intellectuals who nestle in seats of authority having sprung up like mildewed fungi upon the rotting corpse of this present society?'

'Many times,' said Omally. 'A great many times.'

'Listen.' Soap rattled his pint glass upon the bar top in agitation. 'I know all about your views on the subject, you are a Philistine.'

'I resent that,' said John, 'I am from the South.'

'Beneath the surface of the globe,' said Soap in a reverent tone, 'is the vast and beautiful land of Agharta, and in that sunken realm at the very centre of the planet, Shamballah, capital city of Earth. Here in unimaginable splendour dwells Rigdenjyepo, King of the World, whose emissaries, the subterranean monks of black habit, weave their ways through the endless network of ink-dark corridors which link the capital cities of the ancient world.'

'Such is the popular Buddhist doctrine,' said Omally.

'Rigdenjyepo is in constant contact with the Dalai Lama,' said Soap.

'The Dalai rarely drinks in these parts,' said John.

Soap threw up his arms in dismay. 'When the great day comes and the portals are opened then the smile will flee your face like a rat from a sinking ship.'

Omally brought his smile into full prominence. 'I have always found it to be the case,' said he ingeniously, 'that most ships, especially those sailing under the colours of the Esoteric Line, generally sink due to a surfeit of rats weighing heavily upon the bows.'

'Holes in the Poles,' said Soap, thrusting the Irishman aside and stalking away to the gents'.

'I think you may have offended him,' said Neville.

Omally shrugged. 'He'll be back. Give me another of the same please, Neville. And pray take one for yourself. And what is the explanation of that poster in your window?'

Neville, somewhat taken aback at the Irishman's generosity, reddened about the cheeks upon the mention of the poster. He pulled two pints in silence. 'Poster?' he said, finally. Omally accepted his pint.

'The poster displayed upon your window which reads, and I quote from memory, "Thursday Night is Cowboy Night at the Flying Swan, Yahoo, Barbeque, Country Music, Best-Dressed Cowboy Comp, Big Prizes, Fancy Dress Optional."'

Neville hung his head in shame. 'The brewery,' he said. 'After

56

the Channel wading business the brewery seem to have been taking an indecent interest in the Swan's affairs.'

Omally drew deeply upon his pint. 'A sad business,' said he.

'I have been issued with an outfit,' said Neville in a hushed tone.

'Outfit?'

'Cowboy, chaps and all that.'

'Good God.'

'There are prizes for the best-dressed cowboy, a bottle of scotch, two hundred cigarettes, and a voucher which enables you to dine at one of the brewery's licensed eating-houses.'

Omally raised his bristling eyebrows. 'A bottle of scotch, eh?' His voice was one of casual unconcern. 'Has Pooley been in today?'

Neville shook his head. Omally gestured to Neville with a motion which counselled secrecy and discretion. 'It is better,' said he, 'that we do not cause any great rumpus over this cowboy thing. The regulars might become somewhat incensed, the Swan being an establishment renowned for its conservatism.' Omally pulled at his lower eyelid suggestively.

Neville nodded thoughtfully. 'I can sympathize with your feelings, John,' said he, 'but you must understand that the brewery pull the strings as it were and I must comply with their wishes, no matter how unseemly they might appear.'

'Unseemly is hardly the word. And what's all this about a barbeque?'

'I've had one built on the patio of the beer-garden.'

'Beer-garden?' Omally leant forward across the bar and fixed Neville with a baleful stare. 'I have partaken of alcoholic beverage in this establishment man and boy these fifteen years. Possibly I suffer from some strange aberration of the optical apparatus which deprives my sight of beer-gardens and patios thereupon, but if you might be referring to the tiny strip of back yard behind the gents' where you stack the empties then I might suggest that you reconsider your terminology.'

'The brewery have done a conversion,' said Neville.

'Oh, a conversion is it? Would this conversion by any chance have been carried out by those two master builders known locally as Jungle John and Hairy Dave?' The part-time barman nodded. 'And this patio has been built with the bricks and mortar we were led to believe were to be used in the restructuring of the bog roof?'

Neville hung his head in shame. He had led the deception, it was true. 'It was meant to be a nice surprise,' said he, in a wounded tone.

'Might we view this nice surprise?' the Irishman asked.

'Not until Thursday,' said the barman, 'and Omally, I might beg you not to cause anything in the way of a scandal over this patio. A representative from the brewery will be present for the occasion and any controversy might reflect badly upon my position here.'

Omally sipped thoughtfully at his pint. 'How many are you expecting then?'

'About two hundred.'

Omally spluttered into his beer, sending a stream of froth up his nose. 'Two hundred?'

'The brewery say that such a turn-out is average, they have put some adverts in the local papers.'

'Regarding these two hundred cowboys who will shortly be descending upon the Flying Swan for a hoe-down in the ten-foot-square backyard,' said Omally. 'Can you expect to hear the crack of the mule whip, the roaring of Colt forty-fives, the rattle of wooden wheel and flap of canvas as the mighty covered wagons roll over the prairie bound for Brentford, the thunder of pony hoof upon tarmac, and the lusty vocal renderings of "Mule Skinner Blues" and "Do Not Forsake Me, Oh My Darling"?'

'There will be cheap drinking and an extension until eleven-thirty,' said Neville.

'Do Not Forsake Me, Oh My Darling,' sang John Omally, flinging an imaginary stetson into the air.

Soap Distant, who had finally returned from the gents', said, 'With a bottle of scotch as a prize, cut-price drink, and an eleven-thirty extension we can expect to see at least one Irish John Wayne impersonator swaggering through the saloon bar door toting a six-gun and asking for two fingers of redeye.'

Omally smiled indulgently. 'Possibly, Soap,' said he, 'you will be taking the opportunity to invite up a few of your chums from the inner earth. Tell me now, does old Rigdenjyepo get the likes of Laramie on his underworld twenty-inch or is the reception a bit ropey down there?'

Soap rose purposefully to his feet and stood swaying to and fro, his hand upon the bar top for support. 'You, sir, are an ignorant Irish blaggard,' quoth he, raising a shaky fist to strike Omally.

'Soap was telling me that flying saucers are manifestations of the static souls of bygone civilizations,' said Neville, who was not only pleased that the subject of Cowboy Night had been forgotten but was also a great stirrer.

'I've heard that little gem on more than one occasion,' said John, 'but you and I know that there is a logical and straightforward explanation for that particular phenomenon.'

'There is?'

'Of course. Flying saucers are in fact nothing more than the chrome-plated helmets of five-mile-high invisible fairy folk.'

The Irishman, having both sobriety and the eye for impending violence to his account, stepped swiftly out of the hollow-earther's range. Soap's fist whistled by harmlessly.

Neville was making some motion towards his knobkerry when the door swung open to reveal none other than Mr James Pooley. Jim stood framed in the opening, thumbs clasped into his belt and a liquorice-paper roll-up in the corner of his mouth. 'Howdy pardners,' he drawled.

Omally groaned and hid his face in his hands.

'Howdy Soap,' Jim continued, 'you subterranean sidewinder. You look mighty like as if yore meaning to slap leather with this here Irish hombre.'

Soap was squaring up for another shot at Omally's chin; now his fist hovered motionless in mid-air, as if freed from the powers of gravity. 'You what?' was all he could say.

Neville leant across the counter. 'Before you ask, Jim,' he said, 'I am fresh out of Buckskin bourbon, Mississippi Sippin' liquor, Kentucky rye, Redeye whiskey, or any other brand of white man's firewater.'

'I shall just have a pint of the usual then Neville.' Jim seated himself between the two combatants and withdrew from his pocket the exact change. Neville drew off a pint of his very best.

Soap placed a drunken hand upon Jim's shoulder. 'I am glad you have arrived, Jim Pooley, for now you can witness the rapid demolition of this Irish lout here.'

Pooley whistled through his teeth. 'That indeed will be a sight worth watching.'

'It will be terrible but instructive,' said Soap.

'Soap,' said Jim, 'Soap, may I ask under which grand master of the oriental arts you study?'

Soap said, 'Eh?'

'Well, I take it that you are acquainted with Mr Omally's skills in this direction?'

Soap shook his head and peered suspiciously over Jim's shoulder at the Irishman.

'You are surely aware,' Jim continued, 'that Omally here is an exponent of Dimac, the deadliest form of martial art known to mankind, and that he could instantly disable you should he so wish, his hands and feet being deadly weapons?' Soap's face took on a look of bewilderment as Jim rambled on. 'That he was personally schooled by Count Dante, dubbed by friend and foe alike as none other than the Deadliest Man on Earth. That he is a master of Poison Hand, surely the most horrendous of all the vicious crippling skills, whose maiming, mutilating, disfiguring, tearing, and rending techniques strike terror into the hearts of even the most highly-danned and darkly-belted Kung Fu, Karate, and Ju-jitsu exponents. That with little more than a deft touch he can . . .'

'Enough, enough,' said Soap, 'it was merely a difference of opin-ion, nothing more. Here, John, let us speak no more of such things, join me in a pint.'

John waggled his fingers in a movement suggestive of immense dexterity. 'I shall be pleased to,' said he, 'and possibly as our friend Jim here has acted the role of arbitrator you would wish to show your appreciation with a similar gesture of goodwill.' He clicked his knuckles noisily.

'Three pints please, Neville,' said Soap, 'and have one yourself.' With many echoes of 'Cheers' and 'Down the hatchway', the three set in for an evening's drinking.

Thus did Omally form a deep and meaningful relationship with Soap Distant. That the two held each other generally in absolute and utter contempt was no longer important. Here, as Neville ejected the dear friends into the street and pushed the bolt home, Soap Distant, Jim Pooley, and John Omally found themselves swaying along the highway, arms about each other's shoulders, engaged upon the vocal rendition of one of Pooley's own compositions, 'If there are no spots on a sugar cube then I've just put a dice in my tea.'

Omally halted to urinate into the doorway of Norman's paper-shop. 'That is for all waders to France,' he said.

'And for the exorbitant price of imported Fine Art Publications,' Pooley added, following suit.

'I have no axe to grind regarding the proprietor of this establishment,' said Soap, 'but I perform this function out of biological necessity and the spirit of pure badness!'

'Well said, Soap,' said Omally. 'I have surely misjudged you as an individual.'

'All for one and one for all,' said Jim Pooley, as three golden rapiers crossed in the moonlight. Amid much fly-zipping, in which three separate shirt-fronts were torn asunder, Soap said, 'I have maturing in my cellar several bottles of a home-produced claret which I think you gentlemen might find most pleasing.'

'If, in this newfound eloquence,' said Omally, 'you refer to that home-brewed lighter fuel which you call Chateau Distante, then we would be pleased to join you in a glass or three.'

8

Rumours abounded regarding the mysteries lurking behind the gaily-painted front door of Fifteen Sprite Street. Strange noises had been heard in the nights coming as from the bowels of the earth, weird rumblings and vibrations. Cats gave Soap's backyard a wide berth and the milkman would venture no further than the front gate. How this ordinary little house had managed to gain such notoriety had always been beyond Omally's understanding. Believing as he did that Soap was little more than a buffoon, the way in which his neighbours avoided him and even crossed over the street before reaching his house had the Irishman baffled.

Pooley, to whom most doors swung open one way or another, had never yet managed to cross the portal, although he had employed many devious devices. He could probably have persuaded even Cerberus to leave his post and go off in search of a few dog biscuits. Soap had always been impervious. Thus it came as something of a shock to find himself and Omally now standing in the tiny front garden whilst Soap shushed them into silence and felt about in his pockets for the key.

'Now,' said Soap in a voice of deadly seriousness, 'before you enter I must ask that all you may see within must never be divulged to another living soul.'

Pooley, who had been in the Scouts for a day, raised two fingers to his forehead and said, 'Dib-Dib-Dib.' Omally, who was finding it hard to keep a straight face, licked his thumb and said, 'See this wet, see this dry, cut my throat if I tell a lie.'

Soap shrugged. 'I suppose I can expect no more. Now come, step carefully because the light will not function until the front door is closed and bolted from within.' He turned the key and pushed the door open into the stygian darkness within.

'You seem somewhat security-conscious, Soap,' said Omally.

Invisibly in the darkness, Soap tapped his nose. 'One cannot be too careful when one is Keeper of the Great Mystery.'

Pooley whistled. 'The Great Mystery, eh?'

Soap threw the bolt, made several inexplicable clicking noises with what seemed to be switches, and suddenly the room was ablaze with light.

'My God,' said Omally in a voice several octaves higher than usual. As the two stood blinking in the brightness Soap studied their faces with something approaching glee. These were the first mortals other than himself ever to see his masterwork, and their awe and bewilderment were music to his eyes. 'What do you think then?'

Omally was speechless. Pooley just said, 'By the gods!'

The wall dividing the front room from the back parlour had been removed along with all the floorboards and joists on the ground floor. The section of flooring on which the three now stood was nothing more than the head of a staircase which led down and down into an enormous cavern of great depth which had been excavated obviously with elaborate care and over a long period of time. A ladder led up to the bedroom, the staircase having been long ago removed.

Omally stared down into the blackness of the mighty pit which yawned below him. 'Where does it go to?' he asked.

'Down,' said Soap. 'Always down but also around and about.'

'I must be going now,' said Pooley, 'must be up and making an early start, lots to do.'

'You've seen nothing yet,' said Soap, 'this is only the entrance.'

Omally was shaking his head in wonder. 'You dug this, then?'

'No, not just me.' Soap laughed disturbingly. 'My great-grandfather began it shortly after the house was built, the lot fell then to my grandfather and down the line to me, last of the Distants, and guardian of the Great Mystery.'

'It's madness,' said Omally, 'the whole street will collapse.'

Soap laughed again. 'No, never, my family have the know as it were. They worked upon the Thames tunnel back in the days of Brunel.'

'But that collapsed.'

'Never; that's what the authorities said. The truth was that the navigators who dug that ill-fated pit stumbled upon an entrance to

63

the worlds beneath and the tunnel had to be closed hurriedly and an excuse found to please the public.'

'You mean your old ones actually met up with these folk below?'

'Certainly. Shall we go down then?' said Soap.

Pooley said, 'I'll wait here.'

'I invited you in for a drink, and a drink you are going to have.'

'I think that I am no longer thirsty,' said Jim, 'and after this, I think that I might take a vow of abstinence.'

'God,' said Omally, 'don't say such a thing even in jest.'

'Come on then,' said Soap. 'I will lead the way, it is not far to the first chamber.'

'First chamber?'

'Oh, yes, the caverns lead down into the bowels of the earth and subsidiary tunnels reach out in all directions, some for several miles at a stretch.' Soap flicked several more switches and led the way down the long flight of steps which reached downwards into the darkness. As they descended, the way before them sprang into light and the pathway behind fell to darkness.

'Clever that, eh?' said Soap. 'An invention of my great-grand-father's, don't ask me how it works because I don't know.'

'Must save some money on the electric bill,' said Jim.

'Electric bill?' Soap gave another of his hideous laughs which boomed along the corridors and down into the pit, returning in ghostly echoes back to them. 'I'm tapped directly into the grid. I've never paid for gas or electric as long as I've lived.'

Jim shook his head in dismay. 'This is unreal,' said he. 'How can all this exist and nobody know about it? And what did you and your forefathers do with all the earth from these diggings?'

'Aha,' said Soap, having another tap at his nose, 'aha!'

At length they reached a vaulted chamber. Pooley later reckoned that it must have been about fifty yards in diameter, but it was impossible to tell for certain as the lighting was only evident at whichever spot they stood.

'Now, about this wine,' Soap said. 'The temperature here is ideal for hocks, border rosés, Rhine wines, sweet sherry, and growing mushrooms.'

From an enormous wine-rack Soap withdrew a dusty-looking bottle and, having no corkscrew readily at hand, punched in the cork with his thumb. 'Bottoms up,' he said, taking an enormous swig. He passed the bottle to Omally. 'Try it, it's a fifty-year-old vintage.'

Omally took a small indecisive sip, smacked his lips a few times, took a great swig and then one very large swig. 'It is indeed good stuff,' said he, wiping his sleeve across his mouth and passing the bottle to Jim Pooley.

Jim, who had watched the Irishman's performance with interest, needed no telling twice. He put the bottle to his lips and drew off a long and satisfying draught.

'Very shortly now,' said Soap, accepting the bottle from Pooley and finishing it off, 'very shortly now contact will be made. I may be only inches away.'

Omally nodded, his eyes wandering over the wine-rack. Soap pulled out another bottle and punched in the cork. 'Feel free,' he said.

Omally felt free.

'I have all the ancient maps, you see. My forebears knew the locations and they knew it was the work of several generations, but now I am there, the moment is close at hand, mankind stands poised upon the brink of the greatest of all discoveries, the new Golden Age, the dawn of the new tomorrow . . .'

Soap's voice was rising in pitch. John Omally took another hasty pull upon the bottle and passed it hurriedly to Jim. 'We had best get out of here old pal, I have a feeling I know what's coming,' he whispered.

Soap was stalking about the cavern, arms raised, ranting at the top of his voice. Jim and John watched in stunned silence as the haunting light followed him from place to place, eerily illuminating his frantic motions. As he drew further from them his voice faded as if absorbed into the rock; his staccato movements and dramatic gestures lent to him the appearance of some bizarre mime artiste acting out an inexplicable saga beneath a travelling spotlight.

Soap lurched over to the wine-rack and popped the cork from another bottle of wine. 'Here,' he said, 'here I'll show you, the legacy of the Distants, I'll show you.'

'We'll take your word for it,' said Omally.

'We really must be making a move now,' Jim added in a convincing tone which concealed the fact that he was having great difficulty in controlling his bladder.

'No, no! You are here, the only ones! You must be present when the Portals are unlocked, you cannot be allowed to leave!'

'That is what I thought was coming,' muttered Omally.

'This way, this way!' With the wine bottle bobbing in his hand and the eerie light shining about him, Soap made his way rapidly down a side-corridor, leaving Pooley and Omally in the darkness.

'I cannot remember by which entrance we came into this place,' said John.

'I have no idea as to that myself,' Jim replied, 'and I am beginning to feel very poorly, vintage wine and Neville's Large making a poor cocktail.'

'I fear we must follow him or stand alone in the darkness,' said John, 'for the trick of light apparently works only to his account.' Jim wondered if magnetism might play some part in the situation. But now seemed a bad time for idle speculation, so he shrugged his shoulders in the darkness and the two set off to follow the glow-worm figure of Soap Distant as it moved away in front of them.

'I estimate, although it is impossible to be certain, that we must be somewhere beneath the London Road,' said John.

'I had the same feeling myself,' Jim replied. 'But I hope you realize and will record upon some tablet or graven plaque even though it be in my own memoriam that this whole thing is utterly fantastic and totally impossible.'

'Certainly these caverns appear to be the work of no earthly spade. I think that somewhere back along the bloodline of the Distants someone must have discovered this place by chance, although as to its original purpose and its manner of excavation, that is unimaginable.'

'Come quickly now!' screamed Soap, shining up ahead. 'We are nearly there!'

Of a sudden they came to a halt, the tunnel terminating unexpectedly in what appeared to be a pair of massive iron doors.

'You see!' screamed Soap. Omally noted that beads of perspiration were rolling down his forehead and that evil lines of white foam extended from the corners of his mouth and vanished beneath his chin. 'You see. You see, the holy Portal!'

Omally approached the gigantic doors. They were obviously of great age and looked capable of holding back the force of several armies. In the ghost light he could make out the heads of enormous rivets running in columns from top to bottom, and what appeared to be a large yet intricately constructed mechanism leading from two wheels that looked like the stopcocks on some titanic plumbing system. Central to each door was a brass plaque bearing upon it a heraldic device of uncertain origin.

It was the wheels that drew Omally's attention. There was something hauntingly familiar about them, and he tried to recall where he had seen them before. As he stepped forward Soap Distant barred his way. 'No, no!' he screamed. 'You may not touch, it is for me, I, the last in the line, I who must fulfil the prophecies, I who must open the portal.'

'Soap,' said John seriously, 'Soap, I do not feel that you should open these doors, something tells me that it would be a grave mistake.'

Pooley nodded wildly. 'Best leave them eh, Soap? Can't just go unlocking every door you come to.'

Soap turned and ran his hands over the pitted surface of the iron doors. 'I think,' said John, who was fast realizing the gravity of this particular situation, 'I think Soap, that if you are adamant about this door opening business, then it would be better for you to be alone at the moment of opening, it would be wrong of us to stand around looking on. If the prophecies say that you are to open the Portal then open it you should. Alone!' Soap looked somewhat dubious, but Omally continued unabashed. 'The honour must be yours, we have no right to share it. Show us back to the foot of the staircase where we will await your glorious return.'

'Glorious return, yes.' Soap's voice was suddenly pensive. Pooley's head nodded enthusiastically while at the same time his legs crossed and recrossed themselves.

'So be it then!' Soap strode between the two men and as the light moved with him Omally took one last look at the gigantic doors, chewed upon his bottom lip a moment, then followed the receding Soap back along the death-black corridor.

Soap's will-o-the-wisp figure danced along ahead of them like a marsh phantom, weaving through the labyrinth of tunnels and finally into the huge central chamber. Peering up, Omally could make out the lights of Fifteen Sprite Street, a reassuring glow high above. Soap stood breathing heavily through his nose, his fists clenched, and his face a wax mask of sweat. Pooley was clutching desperately at his groin. Omally shifted nervously from one foot to the other.

'You wait then!' said Soap suddenly. 'Tonight is the night towards which the entire course of mankind's history has inevitably run.

Tonight the ultimate mysteries will be known! Tonight the Portal will be opened!'

'Yes, yes,' said Omally, 'we'll wait here then.'

Soap's eyes had glazed. It was clear that he no longer saw Pooley or Omally; he had become focused both mentally and physically upon some distant point. His voice boomed on, filling the caverns, washing over the black rocks like some evil sonic wave. 'Blessed be the Gods of Ancient Earth. The dark ones and dwellers of the deep places. Great Rigdenjyepo, King of the World, Lord of the Nether Regions, Guardian of the Inner Secrets!'

Omally cupped his hands about his ears and muttered the rosary beneath his breath. Pooley, whose bladder was on the point of giving up the unequal struggle, rolled his eyes desperately.

Without warning, Soap suddenly jerked forward. The two friends watched his glittering form flickering away into the darkness, his voice bouncing to and fro about the vaulted corridors, until finally the light died away and the ghastly echoing cries became only a memory.

Omally and Pooley stood a moment, faintly outlined by the light above. Slowly they turned to face one another, came to a joint decision which argued strongly for the authenticity of mental telepathy, and with one movement made for the stairs.

Minutes later on the corner of Sprite Street Omally crouched, bent double, hands upon knees, gasping for breath. Pooley did little other than sigh deeply as he relieved himself through the railings into the Memorial Park. Between the gasps, gulps, and Woodbine coughs, Omally uttered various curses, veiled blasphemies, and vows of impending violence directed solely and unswervingly towards Soap Distant.

Pooley finished his ablutions to the accompaniment of one last all-embracing sigh. Having zipped himself into respectability he withdrew from his inner pocket a bottle of Soap's fifty-year-old wine. 'Shame to leave empty-handed,' he said. 'One for the road John?'

'One indeed,' the Irishman replied. He took a great pull and swallowed deeply.

Pooley said 'What should we do? Soap is clearly mad!'

Omally wiped his mouth and passed the bottle across. The full moon shone down upon them, in the distance cars rolled over the flyover, and a late-night dog returning from some canine revelry loped across the road. All seemed so normal, so mundane, that their experience within the caverns was already taking on the nature of a bad dream. The clock on the Memorial Library struck two.

'If all that we saw was real and not some shared vision, I am truly at a loss to know what action we should take. Soap is not harming anybody, although I am certain that such an enormous maze of tunnels should be reported to the authorities, if only that they might be certified as safe. While I was down there I had the feeling that most of Brentford could have sunk easily into them, still leaving room for half of the Chiswick High Road.'

'But what about the doors?' said Jim. 'Surely one man could not open them alone, they looked pretty hefty. You don't really believe that they lead into the inner earth do you?'

Omally shook his head. 'I haven't a clue, although those crests, I've seen them before somewhere.'

All further conversation was however stifled by a low and ghastly rumble which came apparently from the lower end of Albany Road. Like a hideous subterranean clap of thunder it rolled forward. From far along the street, lights began to blink on in upstairs windows. Cats began to whine and dogs to bark.

Pooley said, 'It's an earthquake!'

Omally crossed himself.

Somewhere deep within the earth a monstrous force was stirring; great ripples ran up the paving stones of Sprite Street. A shock-wave spread across the grass of the Memorial Park, stiffening the coarse blades into regimented rows. A great gasp which issued from no human throat shuddered up from the very bowels of the earth, building to an enormous crescendo.

Omally felt inclined to run but his knees had turned to jelly. Pooley had assumed the foetal position. By now Sprite Street was a blaze of light, windows had been thrown up, front doors flung open, people issued into the street clad in ludicrous pyjamas and absurd carpet-slippers. Then, as rapidly as it had begun, the ominous rumbling ceased, seemed to pass away beneath them and fade away. The denizens of Sprite Street suddenly found themselves standing foolishly about the road in the middle of the night. Shuffling their carpet-slippers and feigning indifference to conceal their acute embarrassment they backed into their respective abodes and quietly closed their front doors.

The night was still again, the lights of Sprite Street dimmed away and Pooley rose to his feet, patting dirt from his tweeds. 'John,' said he, 'if you will excuse me I am now going home to my bed where I intend to remain for an indefinite period. I fear that the doings of this evening have forever destroyed my vitality and that I am a broken man.'

'Certainly this has been an evening I should prefer to forget,' said Omally. With that he put his arm about his companion's shoulder and the two friends wandered away into the night.

9

It was indeed a mystery. The pressmen thrust their way through the crowds of baffled onlookers and peered disbelievingly down from the bridge to the muddied track of twisted bicycle frames, old tin cans and discarded pram wheels which spread away into the distance. How an entire one-mile stretch of canal from the river lock to that of the windscreen-wiper factory could simply have vanished overnight seemed beyond anybody's conjecture.

'It couldn't have gone out through the river lock,' an old bargee explained, 'it is high water on the Thames and the river is six foot up the lock gates on that side.'

'And at the other end?'

The bargee gave his inquisitor a look of contempt. 'What, travel uphill into the next lock, do you mean?' The interviewer coloured up and sought business elsewhere.

Archroy, who was a great follower of Charles Fort, explained what had happened. 'Teleportation,' said the lad. 'The water has been teleported away by those in sore need of it, possibly inhabitants of a nearby sphere, most likely the moon.'

The pressmen, although ever-anxious to accept any solution as long as it was logical, newsworthy, or simply sensational, seemed strangely diffident towards his claims for the existence of telekinetic lunar beams.

It was certainly a most extraordinary event however. One which would no doubt catapult Brentford once more into the national headlines, and at least bring good trade to the Flying Swan. Neville was going great guns behind the bar. The cash register rang musically and the 'No Sale' sign bobbed up and down like a demented Jack-in-the-box.

'And don't forget,' said the part-time barman above the din, 'Thursday night is Cowboy Night.'

Jammed into an obscure corner and huddled over his pint, Jim Pooley watched with loathing the fat backside of an alien pressman which filled his favourite bar stool.

Omally edged through the crush with two pints of Large. 'It was only after I got home that I remembered where I'd see those crests before,' he explained as he wedged himself in beside Pooley. 'They were the coat of arms of the Grand Junction Water Works. Those doors must have been part of the floodgate system from old Brentford dock.'

Pooley sucked upon his pint, his face a sullen mask of displeasure. 'Then what of old Soap?'

A devilish smile crossed Omally's face. 'Gone, washed away.' His fingers made the appropriate motions. 'So much for old Rigdenjyepo and the burrowers beneath, eh?'

Pooley hunched closer to his pint. 'A pox on it all,' said he. 'The Swan packed full of these idiots, old Soap flushed away round the proverbial S-bend, and Cowboy Night looming up before us with about as much promise as the coming of Ragnorok!'

Omally grinned anew. 'There are many pennies to be made from an event such as this. I myself have organized several tours of the vicinity for this afternoon at a pound a throw.'

Pooley shook his head in wonder. 'You don't waste a lot of time, do you?'

'Mustn't let the grass grow under the old size-nines.'

'Tell me, John,' said Jim, 'how is it now that a man such as yourself, who possesses such an amazing gift for the making of the well-known "fast buck", has not set himself up in business long ago and since retired upon the proceeds?'

'I fear,' said John, 'that it is the regularity of "the work" which depresses me, the daily routine which saps the vital fluids and destroys a man's brain. I prefer greatly to live upon wits I have and should they ever desert me then, maybe then, I shall take to "the work" as a full-time occupation.' Omally took from his pocket a 'Book Here for Canal Tours' sign and began a 'roll up, roll up' routine.

Pooley rose from the table and excused himself. He had no wish to become involved in Omally's venture, he wished only to forget all

72

about subterranean caverns and vanishing canal water; his only thoughts on that matter were as to what might happen should they attempt to refill the stretch of canal. Was Sprite Street lower geographically than the canal? If it was, would the attempt flood the entire neighbourhood? It really didn't bear thinking about. Pooley slouched over to the bar and ordered another pint.

'Looking forward to Thursday night I'll bet, Jim,' said Neville.

Pooley did not answer. Silently he sipped at his ale and let the snippets of bar-side conversation wash disjointedly about him. 'And my old grandad is sitting by the dartboard when he threw,' came a voice, 'and the dart went straight through the lobe of his right ear.' Pooley sipped at his ale. 'And as they went to pull it out,' the voice continued, 'the old man said "No don't, it's completely cured the rheumatism in my left knee".'

Pooley yawned. Along the bar from him, huddled in their usual conspiratorial poses, were Brentford's two resident jobbing builders, Hairy Dave and Jungle John, so named for their remarkably profuse outcroppings of cerebral hair. The twin brothers were discussing what seemed to be a most complex set of plans which they had laid out before them on the bar top.

'I don't think I can quite understand all this,' said Dave.

'It's a poser for certain,' his brother replied.

'I can't see why he wants the altar to be so large.'

'I can't see why there aren't to be any pews.'

'Nor an organ.'

'Seems a funny kind of a chapel to me.'

Pooley listened with interest; surely no one in the neighbourhood could be insane enough to commission those two notorious cowboys to build a chapel?

Hairy Dave said, 'I can't see why the plans should be written in Latin.'

'Oh,' said his brother, 'it's Latin is it? I thought it was trigonometry.'

Pooley could contain his curiosity no longer, and turned to the two master builders. 'Hello lads, how's business?'

John snatched the plan from the bar top and crumpled it into his jacket. 'Ah, oh . . .' said his brother. 'Good day Jim, and how is yourself?'

'For truth,' Pooley replied, 'I am not a well man. Recently I have been party to events which have seriously damaged my health. But let us not talk of me, how is business? I hear that you are on the up and up; won a large contract I heard.'

The two brothers stared at each other and then at Pooley. 'Not us,' said one. 'Haven't had a bite in weeks,' said the other.

'My, my,' said Jim. 'My informant was certain that you had a big one up your sleeve, something of an ecclesiastical nature I think.'

John clutched the plan to his bosom. 'Haven't had a bite in weeks,' his brother reiterated. 'Been very quiet of late.' Hairy Dave shook his head, showering Pooley with dandruff. Jungle John did the same.

Neville stormed up the bar. 'Less of that you two,' said the part-time barman. 'I've warned you before about contaminating my cheese rolls.'

'Sorry Neville,' said the brothers in unison, and rising from their seats they left the bar, leaving their drinks untouched.

'Most strange,' said Pooley. 'Most astonishing.'

'Those two seem very thick together lately,' said Neville. 'It seems that almost everybody in this damn pub is plotting something.'

'Tell me Neville,' said Jim, 'did you ever see any more of our mystery tramp?'

'Thankfully no,' said the part-time barman, 'and with this canal business taking up everybody's attention, let's hope that no more will ever be said about him.'

Pooley shook his head. 'I wouldn't be too certain of that,' he said doubtfully.

Captain Carson stood upon the canal bridge, staring down into the mud and idly casting his eyes along the bank to where an official-looking Mr Omally, dressed in a crested cap and jaunty blazer, led a group of Swedish students along the rutted track towards the woodyard. The Captain's loathing for tourists almost overshadowed that which he felt for the figure standing calmly at his side, hands in pockets, and smoking seaman's shag in one of the Captain's favourite pipes. The figure was no longer distinguishable as the wretched and ill-clad monstrosity which had cast an evil shadow across his porch but two short weeks ago. Cleanly-shaven and smelling of Brylcreem, the figure was dressed in a blue rollneck sweater and a pair of the Captain's best khaki trousers, a yachting cap, and a pair of sailing shoes.

The tramp had become a kind of witches' familiar to the Captain, haunting his dreams and filling his waking hours with dread. Somehow, and the Captain was at a loss to explain how, the tramp had now permanently installed himself at the Mission. During meals he sat in the Captain's chair whilst the Captain was obliged to eat in the kitchen. No matter which way the Captain turned the tramp was always there, reclining upon the porch, smoking his cigarettes, lounging in the cosiest fireside chair, sipping rum. He had tricked the Captain, again by means that the Captain was at a loss to understand, out of his chair, his tobacco, his food, drink, and finally out of his bed.

The tramp sucked deeply upon the Captain's briar and blew out a stream of multicoloured smoke. 'There would seem to be unusual forces at work in this neighbourhood,' he observed.

The Captain surveyed his unwelcome guest with ill-concealed hatred. 'There would indeed,' he replied. Somehow, deep down in the lowest depths of his loathing for the tramp, a strange and grudging respect was beginning to stir. The Captain could, again, not fully account for these feelings, but now, clean-shaven and well-dressed as he was, the tramp seemed to exude a definite air of authority. Possibly of nobility. It was inexplicable. The aura of evil which surrounded him was almost palpable and the Captain seemed to sense his approach at all times; a kind of darkness travelled with the red-eyed man, a funereal coldness. The Captain shuddered.

'Cold?' said the tramp. 'We'd best be going back then. Don't want you coming down with any summer colds now, do we?'

The Captain followed the tramp back towards the Mission with doglike obedience. As the tramp strode on ahead of him the Captain watched the broad shoulders swing to and fro in a perfect rhythm. Surely the tramp had grown? Surely his bearing was prouder, finer than before?

No wonder, all the food he eats, thought the Captain. But who was he? His age was indeterminate, he could be anything between twenty and fifty; there was a vagueness about his features which

75

eluded definition. The Captain had gone to great lengths to draw some information from him regarding his name, family, and background, but the tramp was infuriatingly evasive. He had made only one statement upon these matters and this was, 'There are five here that know my name and when they speak it, all shall know.' As to who these five were, the Captain was unable to guess. Possibly the tramp alluded to five of the fictional names he had quoted from the Mission's yearly reports.

The tramp turned into the Mission, which he opened with his own key. The Captain followed meekly; the tramp was wearing down his resistance to a point that he no longer questioned any of his actions.

'I wish to speak to you upon a delicate matter,' said the tramp suddenly. 'It is a matter which affects both our futures and one which I know lies heavily upon your soul.' The Captain raised a bristling eyebrow. 'Possibly you will wish to open the reserve bottle of rum you keep in the locked cupboard beneath the stairs in order to fortify yourself for what I am about to say.'

The Captain humbly obeyed. The two seated themselves upon either side of the Captain's table and two large tots of rum were poured.

'It has come to my notice,' said the tramp, 'that there is one not far from here who would do us harm.'

The Captain's face showed no expression, but his mind paid silent homage to anyone who would wish ill upon his guest.

'One Brian Crowley,' said the tramp. The Captain started up in astonishment. 'It has come to my notice,' the tramp continued, 'that this man harbours the desire to close down this Mission and to dismiss you, my honourable host, without thanks or pension. You who have done so much for the poor and needy, you who have dedicated your life to the unfortunate.' The Captain shifted uneasily in his seat. 'There is, I understand, a conspiracy between this Crowley,' again he spoke the hated name, 'and a certain Councillor Wormwood, to demolish this Mission in order to extend the Butts car park.'

The Captain bit upon his lip. So that was their intention was it? How the tramp could have come by this intelligence was, of course, beyond any conjecture, but the Captain hung upon his every word. 'I have given the matter much thought,' he told the tramp. 'Night after night I have lain cursing the very name of Crowley and racking my brain for a solution, but none have I found.'

'I think that one might be relatively close at hand,' said the tramp. 'In fact, I feel its warm breath upon my neck even now.' The Captain poured two more large tots of rum. 'We shall invite these two individuals to dinner,' said the tramp.

The Captain bent double in a fit of frenzied coughing. 'Calm yourself,' said the tramp.

'I fear,' said the Captain, 'that the breath you feel upon your neck is one of severe halitosis.'

The tramp's face was without expression. He drank down his tot of rum and watched the Captain, his eyes unblinking, two drops of blood upon colourless orbs. 'Thursday night would be ideal,' said the tramp.

'But what if they won't come? After all, Crowley hates me and Wormwood will never want to expose himself in any way.'

'They will come,' said the tramp, 'and I think I can promise you a most entertaining evening.' His ghastly eyes glittered with a fierce luminosity, and the Captain tossed back his rum with a quivering hand.

Brian Crowley held up the gilt-edged invitation card to the sunlight. It presented a most extraordinary appearance, almost transparent and clearly wrought of the finest vellum. Never for one moment would he have attributed such style, taste, or elegance to the old sea-captain. The edging of the card had more the look of being worked in gold leaf than sprayed in the gilded paint of the printer's shop. The typeface was of a design that Brian did not recognize, its finely-drawn serifs and cunning arabesques seeming of almost Islamic origin. And the smell of it; something stirred within him, some recollection from his past. It was the smell of incense, church incense. He had smelt it many times before, as a choirboy at St Mary's. That was it, church incense.

While Brian's romantic imagination ran in luminous spirals about the card, the callous side to his nature gloated, for the card which had flopped through his burnished letter-box to land with the many plain brown wrappers upon the purple shagpile bore an inscription which made his heart leap for joy.

YOU ARE FORMALLY INVITED
TO A RECEPTION & BANQUET
ON THURSDAY 15TH JUNE
AT THE SEAMEN'S MISSION, BRENTFORD
IN CELEBRATION OF THAT HONORABLE
ESTABLISHMENT'S CENTENARY YEAR
AND ALSO TO HONOUR
CAPTAIN HORATIO B. CARSON
UPON THE ANNOUNCEMENT OF HIS
RETIREMENT

Black Tie   R.S.V.P.
7.30 p.m. for 8.00 p.m.   Admission by this card only

Brian sighed deeply and pressed the scented card to his lips. Things could not have been better – the Captain to announce his retirement! He had not realized that it was the Mission's centenary year, but it was clear that for the sake of appearances he must attend. The rest of the Committee would be there and his absence would not go unnoticed.

He would R.S.V.P. this very morning. At last the wheels of fortune were beginning to turn to his advantage. He could almost smell the delicious odours of Mario's cooking.

IO

As Monday turned into Tuesday and Tuesday did what was expected of it, the patrons of the Flying Swan grew increasingly uneasy. Strange changes were taking place amid the timeless décor of the saloon-bar. A grotesquely moth-eaten bison's head had materialized above the counter and traces of sawdust had begun to appear about the floor. A large painting of a rotund and pinkly-powdered female, clad only in the scantiest of ostrich-feather boas and an enticing if tobacco-stained smile, had been hung lopsidedly over the dartboard. 'A temporary inconvenience,' Neville assured the irate darts players. 'Hold on thar pardners.' But the casters of the feathered flight sought their amusements elsewhere at Jack Lane's or the New Inn.

'Son of a gun,' said Jim Pooley.

It was John Omally, a man who looked upon himself, no matter how ironically, as a guardian of the neighbourhood's morals, who was the first to notice the new selection which had found its way into the disabled jukebox. '"The Wheel of the Wagon is Broken"?' he said suddenly, his coarse accent cutting through the part-time barman's thoughts like a surgeon's scalpel. '"A Four-legged Friend"?'

Neville hung his head in shame. 'It is regrettable,' said he, 'but the brewery feel it necessary to alter the selection on that thing to keep in pace with what they think to be the vogue.'

'Come on now,' said Omally, 'surely it is the brewery who are dictating this particular vogue with their horrendous plans for a Western Barbeque and all its attendant horrors.'

'Don't forget the extension and the cheap drink,' Neville reminded his Irish customer.

Omally cocked his head thoughtfully to one side. 'It is a poor consolation for the ghastly transfiguration currently taking place in this establishment, I am thinking.'

Jim agreed. 'To think I'd see the day when three of the Swan's finest arrowmen defect to Jack Lane's.'

Neville chewed upon his lip and went back to polishing the glasses.

'I see you are still sporting your official guide's cap,' said Pooley suddenly.

Omally smiled and reverently removed the thing, turning it between his fingers. 'You would not believe the business I am doing along that stretch of dried-up canal.'

Jim shook his head. 'Although to the average man the disappearance of a canal must seem an extraordinary thing, I frankly fail to see what pleasure can be derived from paying out good money to wander up and down the bank peering into the mud. By God, I was down that way myself earlier and the smell of it is no pleasant treat to the nostrils.'

'I have devised a most fascinating programme,' the Irishman said, 'wherein I inform the visitors as to the many varied and bizarre legends associated with that stretch of canal.'

'Oh yes?' said Jim.

'We visit the very spot where Caesar encamped prior to his march upon Chiswick.'

'Really?'

'The place where the ghost of Little Nellie Tattersall, who cast away her earthly shell into the murky depths one dark and wintry Victorian night, still calls her tragic cry.'

'Calls her tragic cry?'

'And to the site of the famous Ripper murder of eighteen eighty-nine. 'It's a highly-educational tour.'

'And they believe all this drivel?'

'Whether they believe it or not is unimportant. At the current rate of business I may well shortly be having to employ an assistant to deal with the parties that are forced to queue for several hours at a stretch. There are more of them every day. There are many pennies to be made in this game,' the Irishman said, flamboyantly ordering two pints.

Pooley peered round at the crowds which swelled the Swan. Certainly they were a strange breed, with uniformly blank expressions and a kind of colourless aura surrounding them. These were the faces which one saw jammed into a tight crowd surrounding an accident victim or one fallen in a fight. Ambulance men have to force past them and little short of outright violence will budge them an inch.

Old Pete entered the bar, his half-terrier close upon his heel. 'There's a coachload of Japs out there asking for the guide,' he told Omally.

'Duty calls,' said John, leaping to his feet and thrusting his official cap on his head. 'I shall see you anon.'

Jim bid his companion farewell and with a satisfied smile settled down to tackle the two untouched pints.

'That will be ten and six please,' said Neville the part-time barman.

'Damn and blast,' said Jim Pooley.

Norman threw the door bolt and turned over the sign which informed customers that he was 'Closed Even for the Sale of Rubber Bondage Monthly'. Rubbing his hands together he strode across the shop and disappeared through the door behind the counter. The small kitchenette-cum-living-room at the rear had been allowed of late to run somewhat to seed. The sink was filled by a crazy mountain of food-besmirched crockery, now in a state long beyond reclamation. Cigarette ends spotted the linoleum like the pock-marks of some tropical disease, and great piles of newspapers, fine art publications, and scientific journals were stacked into every available corner.

'Every cloud has a silver lining,' he said. Reaching to the back-door he lifted down and donned a leather apron, welder's goggles, and a pair of rubber gloves. 'And now, the end is near,' he said profoundly, 'and so, I face the final curtain.' With a grandiloquent gesture he crossed the room and flung aside a ragged strip of cloth which curtained a corner. There, lit by the kitchenette's naked light-bulb and glowing like a rare pearl torn from its oyster shell, hung what must surely have been one of the most extraordinary suits of clothes ever viewed by mortal man. It was a stunning salmon-pink, and tailored from the best quality P V C. Its body and sleeves glittered with rhinestones and sequins worked into patterns roughly suggestive of Indian headwear and western horsemen. The trousers were similarly ornamented and ended in massive bell-bottoms edged with braid and long golden tassles. Emblazoned across the shoulders of the jacket in letters of gold, marked out with what were obviously at least a dozen sets of Christmas tree fairy lights, were the words: THE SPIRIT OF THE OLD WEST.

It was Norman's *pièce de résistance*, and it actually worked. In truth of course, no human hand, no matter how skilled, could have wrought the creation of such a costume in the short time given as notice by the Swan of the impending Cowboy Extravaganza. No, this was the work of several long years. Originally intended as THE SPIRIT OF THE JUBILEE, it had been far from completion at the time of that event and Norman had feared that its day would never dawn. It had taken him several long and sleepless nights to alter the coronation coach into a covered wagon and change the Prince of Wales feathers into the war-bonnet of an Indian chieftain. The effect, all in all, was one to bring a tear of pride into the eye of its creator.

The stetson had been a bit of a problem, as his source of PVC, a young woman customer who worked in the Rubber Factory, had been dismissed for unauthorized removal of the company's stock. He had persevered, however, and done what he could with an aged trilby and an improvised brim. This he had sprayed gold and sprinkled with glitter from the carnival shop.

The electrification of the fairy lights had been the biggest problem, and Norman's rudimentary knowledge of the workings of electricity had cost him many a scorched fingertip. He had toyed with the idea of simply running an extension lead to the nearest available wall-socket but this was too limiting to his movements. Thus Norman, through his usual system of trial and error, had perfected an efficient though weighty set of pre-charged solid-cell batteries, which were strapped about his waist very much in the nature of Batman's utility belt. A set of switches upon the buckle enabled him to alter the fluctuation and sequence of the lights in a manner both pleasing and artistic.

Happily the PVC of the suit acted as an excellent insulator, and the whole contraption was earthed through leads which ran down the backs of his trouser-legs to brass plates nailed to the heels of a pair of rented cowboy boots.

Norman tinkered happily about with screwdriver and soldering iron; here replacing a defunct bulb, here resoldering a faulty socket. Tomorrow, all Brentford would salute his creative genius. No longer would they smile indulgently and allude to his previous failed ventures with unconcealed mirth. He'd show 'em.

Norman flicked a switch upon his belt buckle. Sadly, he was not wearing the brass-heeled boots on this particular occasion and the crackle of electrical energy which snapped through his fingers crossed his eyes and rattled his upper set.

'Damn and blast,' said Norman.

Archroy sat in the doorway of his allotment shed, elbows upon knees, and chin cupped in the palms of his hands. At his feet a cup of cocoa was rapidly growing cold. His wife was up to something back at the marital home; there was a new roll of wire-netting standing ominously in the hall and a large stack of red flettons in the back-yard. She had muttered something about an aviary on the last occasion he had seen her. Also there was the affair of the beans weighing heavily upon his narrow shoulders.

Archroy sighed tragically. Why couldn't life be the straight-forward affair it had once been?

As he sat in his misery Archroy's eyes wandered idly in the direction of Omally's allotment plot. There upon the rugged patch of earth stood the solitary stake which marked out the location of the planted bean. Archroy had diligently watered the spot night after night. Omally had not been down to the site once during the last couple of weeks, and Archroy felt he had lost interest in the whole affair. He rose from his orange-box and slouched over to inspect the Irishman's dark strip of land. The stake appeared slightly crooked so he straightened it, stooping to smooth over the earth. There were no signs of life whatever, no pleasant green stripling or young plantoid raising its head to the sunlight. Nothing but the barren earth. Archroy bent his head near to the ground and squinted. This was, after all, his last bean, and if this failed he would have nothing whatever to recompense him for the tragic loss of his Morris Minor.

Perhaps if he just dug it up for a moment to check that it was all right, it couldn't do any harm? Then if it showed any signs of life he could always replace it. No, it wouldn't hurt, one quick look; he needn't mention it to Omally.

The earth was soft and damp from its daily watering. Almost at once his fingers closed about a damp and clammy object which he hastily brought to the surface. Gently laying it upon his palm he smoothed away the dark earth which clung to it – exposing to his horror the familiar outlines of a common seed potato. Archroy's expression became one of grave concern. He hurled the potato aside and flung himself to his knees. Rooting to and fro across the plot like a demented hog in search of a truffle he delved into the earth. Oblivious to the muddy destruction of his tweeds, Archroy covered every inch of the plot to a depth of some ten inches.

There was nothing; the plot was as barren as a desert, although now it would be ready to yield many varieties of vegetable, having been so thoroughly turned. Archroy rose to his feet, mud clinging to the knees and elbows of his suit; his toupe, which the manufacturers had assured him would stand up to a channel swim, had become strangely detached from its moorings and swung above him like a spinnaker.

Archroy turned his eyes to the potato. So it was treachery. No wonder the Irishman had not troubled to come down and water the plot. Why should he wish to water a seed potato?

'Damn and blast,' said Archroy.

Captain Carson watched the vehicle approach the Mission. He had never seen anything quite like it before. The enormous lorry was absolutely, unutterably black. Not a trace of colour was there upon its deathly sides, but for a single red crest emblazoned in the likeness of a bull. The vehicle moved in total silence and seemed strangely lacking in form, like some half-remembered version of the way a lorry should be. It bore neither headlights nor radiator grille, and the windscreen, if such it were, was of the same night hue as the rest of the vehicle. The doors lacked any sign of handles, nor even a crack or line to signify their location. It was a thing to inspire nightmare. Soundlessly it drew up before the Mission door, enveloping the Captain within its cold shadow. Shaking away his feeling of revulsion the Captain squared his shoulders and stalked up the short path to confront the dark vehicle.

Certainly it was a unique and striking thing. The Captain noted with interest that there was not a single sharp corner, edge, or angle to it; the surfaces flowed away from one another in curve after curve.

The Captain stretched out an inquisitive finger to touch the lorry, but withdrew it at a vastly accelerated rate. It was as if he had thrust it into a vat of liquid oxygen. 'By the gods,' he said, examining his frost-bitten digit.

As if in response to the Captain's oath there was a click near the front of the vehicle and the cab-door swung slowly open. The Captain wandered towards it upon hesitant feet. No light showed from within, it was like peering into the black void of space.

Without warning a figure appeared from the darkness, as one stepping from behind a velvet curtain. He was as black and featureless as his conveyance. Down from the cab he climbed, bearing in his gloved hand a clipboard to which was attached a sheaf of papers.

'Captain Horatio B. Carson,' he inquired in a voice of indeterminate accent. The Captain nodded slowly and without enthusiasm. 'Delivery.'

'I ordered nothing!'

'There is no cause for alarm,' said a soft voice behind and slightly above the Captain.

Turning, the Captain squinted up into the face of the tramp. 'What is all this?' he demanded.

'Kindly assist this gentleman with the removal of all the old furniture from the dining-room.'

'Old furniture? You can't do that, the furniture is the property of the Mission.'

'Kindly do as I request, all will be explained to you later.'

The Captain threw up his arms in a gesture of helplessness and led the dark figure into the Mission, where under the tramp's direction the two stripped the dining-room of its furnishings. When these had been heaped into an untidy pile in the yard, the tramp said, 'And now if you will be so kind, the new furniture is to be brought in. May I beg your caution when handling it as some pieces are of great worth and all irreplaceable.'

The Captain shook his head in bewilderment and mopped the perspiration from his brow with an oversized red gingham handkerchief. For the next half an hour his life was nothing short of nightmare. The truck's dark occupant swung open the rear doors of the mighty vehicle, exposing another fathomless void. Working without apparent effort and clearly oblivious to the great weight of some of the more ornate and heavily-gilded pieces of furniture, he and the Captain unloaded and installed in the Mission an entire suite, table, chairs, sideboard, cabinet, a pair of golden candelabra, velvet wall-hangings, and a crested coat of arms. All these items would clearly have been well at home amid the splendours of Fontainebleau. Each was the work of exquisite and painstaking

85

craftsmanship, and each bore, etched into the polished woodwork or inlaid in precious metals, the motif of the bull.

When all was installed the Captain numbly put his signature to the manifest, which was printed in a language he did not understand. The driver returned to his black cab, the door swinging closed behind him leaving no trace of its presence. The vast black vehicle departed as silently as it had arrived. The Captain leant upon the Mission porch, exhausted, breathing heavily, and clutching at his heart.

'There is one more thing to be done and you may return to your quarters,' said the tramp, looming above him.

'I can do no more,' gasped the Captain. 'Leave me here to die, I have seen enough of life, too much in fact.'

'Come now,' said the tramp, 'no need to be melodramatic, this is but a simple task.' He handed the Captain a gallon can of petrol. 'That rubbish in the garden, dispose of it.'

'What?'

'It is offensive, put it to the torch!'

The Captain took the can. Upon giddy legs he stumbled through the Mission and out into the yard to confront the mound of furniture which had served him these thirty long years.

'The torch,' ordered the tramp.

The Captain's fingers tightened around the petrol cap, he was powerless to resist. 'Damn you,' he mumbled beneath his breath. 'Damn and blast you to hell.'

II

It was Thursday. The sun shone enthusiastically down through Neville's window and twinkled upon the white cowboy suit which hung in its plastic covering upon the bedroom door. Neville raised a sleepy eyelid and yawned deeply. Today was going to be one to remember. He cast an eye towards the suit, pristine as a bridal gown. Beside it upon the chair hung the silver pistols in their studded holsters and the fringed white stetson. He put a hand beneath the pillow and withdrew the chromium sheriff's star. Squinting at it through his good eye he noted well how it caught the light and how the mirrored surfaces shone like rare jewels. Yes, he was going to look pretty dapper tonight, that was for sure.

He was still, however, harbouring some doubts regarding the coming festivities. It was always impossible to gauge exactly what the locals might do. He knew some would attend, if only for a chance at the scotch and to take advantage of the cheap drink and extended hours. But the dart players had already defected, and the seasoned drinkers were hard upon their heels, tired of being jockeyed from their time-honoured places at the bar by the continual stream of tourists and sensation-seekers currently filling the Swan. But still, thought Neville, if only a small percentage of the morbid canal viewers turned up, the evening would be far from dull.

Neville climbed out of bed, placing his star reverently upon the side-table. He stifled another yawn, straightened his shoulders and stepped to the window. From Neville's eyrie high in the upper eaves of the Swan he was afforded an excellent view of the surrounding district. With the aid of his spyglass he could see out between the flatblocks as far as the roundabout and the river. He could make out the gasometer and the piano museum and on further into the early haze where the cars were already moving dreamily across the flyover.

It was a vista which never ceased to inspire him. Neville's spirit was essentially that of the Brentonian. From this one window alone he could see five of Brentford's eighteen pubs, he could watch the larval inhabitants of the flatblocks stirring in their concrete cocoons, Andy Johnson's milkfloat rattling along the Kew Road, the paperboy standing in the shadow of the bus shelter smoking a stolen Woodbine and reading one of Norman's Fine Art Publications, destined for a discerning connoisseur in Sprite Street.

This morning, as he drew great draughts of oxygen through his nose, an ominous and hauntingly familiar perfume filled Neville's head. He had scented it vaguely upon the winds for many weeks, and had noted with growing apprehension that each day it was a little stronger, a little nearer, a little more clearly defined. What it was and what it meant he knew not, only that it was of evil portent. Neville pinched at his nostrils, shrugging away this disturbing sensation. Probably it was only nerves. He stepped into his carpet-slippers and down two flights of stairs to the bar.

The paperboy, seeing the bar lights snap on, abandoned his study of the female form and crossed the Ealing Road to deliver Neville's newspaper.

Omally was stirring from his nest. Wiping the sleep away from his eyes with a soiled pyjama sleeve the man from the Emerald Isle rose, a reluctant phoenix, from the ashes of the night before. There was little fire evident in this rare bird, and had it not been for the urgency of the day which lay before him he would surely have returned to the arms of whatever incendiary Morpheus rekindled his combustible plumage. He lit a pre-cornflake Woodbine and through the fits of terrible coughing paid his early morning respects to the statuette of Our Lady which stood noseless yet benign upon the mantelpiece.

The Irishman's suite of rooms was far from what one would describe as sumptuous. The chances of it appearing in *House and Garden*, except possibly as an example of the 'Before' school of design, were pretty remote. Upon this particular morning, however, the monotone décor was overwhelmed by an incongruous and highly-coloured object which stood upon the Fablon table-top in Omally's dining-room. It was a large and gaudy carton, bearing upon its decorative sides the logo of the carnival shop.

Within this unlikely container, which Omally had smuggled home in a potato sack, was nothing less than an accurate reproduction, correct to the smallest detail, even to the point of spurs and mask, of that well-known and much-loved mode of range-wear affected by the Lone Ranger. It was also identical in every way to the one which Jim Pooley had hired not an hour previous to the furtive Omally's entrance to the carnival shop.

For Mr Jeffreys, who ran the faltering business, it had been a day he would long remember. How he had come into the original possession of the ten identical costumes was a matter he preferred to forget. But upon this particular day that he should, within a few short hours, not only hire out these two costumes, but the other eight to boot, was quite beyond all expectation. Possibly the ancient series had returned to the small screen, bringing about a revival. Anyway, whatever the cause, he didn't care. The cash register had crashed away merrily and there would soon be enough in it to pay off the bill for the two dozen Superman costumes he had similarly ordered in error.

Neville picked up his newspaper from the welcome mat and gazed about the bar. He had been up until three in the morning arranging the finishing touches. Little remained of the Swan's original character; the entire bar now resembled to a Model T the interior of a western saloon. The sawdust which had for the last few days been getting into everybody's beer now completely smothered the floor. Wanted posters, buffalo horns, leather saddles, and items of cowboy paraphernalia lined the walls.

The shorts glasses had been piled in pyramids behind the bar and the place was gaudy with advertisements promoting 'Old Snakebelly – The Drink That Made the South Rise Again'. This doubtful beverage was the sole cause of the Swan's bizarre transformation. It was the brainchild of the brewery owner's eldest son, who had spent two weeks on a package tour of the States and had returned with a mid-Atlantic accent and a penchant for Randolph Scott impersonations. It was not the finest blend of spirits ever to grace a bar optic, and would probably have been more at home removing tar from bargees' gumboots. The old brewer, however, was not only a man indulgent of his progeny's mercurial whims but a shrewd and devious entrepreneur who knew a tax dodge when he saw one.

*

Lunchtime trade at the Flying Swan was alarmingly slack. Two sullen professional drinkers sat doggedly at the bar, glowering into their pints and picking sawdust from their teeth. Old Pete entered the bar around twelve, took one look at the decorations and made a remark much favoured by gentlemen of his advanced years. Young Chips lifted his furry leg at the sawdust floor, and the two departed, grumbling to themselves.

When Neville cashed up at three, the till had taken less than two pounds. Neville counted the small change with nervous fingers; he was certain that the ominous smell he had detected that morning was beginning to penetrate the beer-soaked atmosphere of the saloon-bar.

It all began in earnest when at three-fifteen a van from the brewery catering division drew up outside the Swan in the charge of a young man with advanced acne and a cowboy hat. This diminutive figure strutted to and fro in a pair of boots which sported what the Americans humorously call 'elevator heels'. He announced himself to be Young Master Robert and said that he would be taking over personal control of the event. Neville was horrorstruck. He'd been looking forward to it for weeks, he'd got the sheriff's star, and everything and now at the eleventh hour, this upstart . . .

To add insult to injury, the young man stepped straight behind the bar and drew himself a large scotch. Neville watched open-jawed as a parade of supplies sufficient to cater for half the British Army passed before his eyes in a steady and constant stream. There were packets of sausages, beefburgers, baconburgers, beans and baconburgers, sausage beef and baconburgers, and something round and dubious called a steakette. There were enormous catering cans of beans which the porters rolled in like beer casks. There were sacks of French rolls, jars of pickled onions, radishes, beetroots, cocktail cucumbers, and gherkins. There were hundredweight sacks of charcoal.

'I have been light on the cooking oil,' Young Master Robert announced as the slack-jawed Neville watched two porters man-oeuvring an enormous drum in through the saloon-bar door.

Young Master Robert drew himself another scotch and explained the situation. 'Now hear this,' he said, his voice a facetious parody of Aldo Ray in some incomprehensible submarine movie. 'What we have here is an on-going situation.'

'A what?'

'We have Product, that is to say Old Snakebelly.' He held up a bottle of the devil brew. 'We have location' – he indicated the surroundings – 'and we have motivation.' Here he pointed to the banner which hung above the bar, draped over the moth-eaten bison's head. It read: GRAND COWBOY EXTRAVAGANZA PRIZES PRIZES PRIZES.

Neville nodded gravely.

'I have given this a lot of thought, brain-wise,' the youth continued. 'I ran a few ideas up the flagpole and they got saluted and I mean S-A-L-U-luted!'

Neville flexed his nostrils; he didn't like the smell of this. The young man was clearly a monomaniac of the first order. A porter in a soiled leather apron, hand-rolled cigarette dripping from his lower lip, appeared in the doorway. 'Where do you want this mouthwash then, guv?' he asked, gesturing over his right shoulder.

'Ah, yes, the Product,' said Young Master Robert, thrusting his way past Neville and following the porter into the street. There were a hundred and eight crates of Old Snakebelly, and when stacked they covered exactly half the available space of the newly-built patio.

'There is nowhere else we can put it,' Neville explained. 'There's no space in the cellar, and at least if they're here whoever is cooking at the barbeque can keep an eye on them.'

Young Master Robert was inspecting the barbeque. 'Who constructed this?' he queried.

'Two local builders.'

The youth strutted about the red brick construction. 'There is something not altogether A-O-K here, design-wise.'

Neville shrugged his shoulders. He knew nothing about barbeques anyway, and had never even troubled to look at the plans the brewery had sent. 'It is identical to the plan and has the Council's seal of approval, safety-wise!' Neville lied.

Young Master Robert, who also knew nothing of barbeques but was a master of gamesmanship, nodded thoughtfully and said, 'We will see.'

'What time will the extra barstaff be getting here?' Neville asked.

'Eighteen-thirty,' said the Young Master. 'A couple of right bits of crumpet.' He had obviously not yet totally mastered the subtler points of American terminology.

*

By half past six the Young Master had still failed to light the bar-beque. The occasional fits of coughing and cries of anguish coming from the patio told the part-time barman that at least the young man was by no means a quitter.

At six forty-five by the Guinness clock there was still no sign of the extra barstaff. Neville sauntered across the bar and down the short passage to the patio door. Gingerly, he edged it open. Nothing was visible of Young Master Robert; a thick black pall of smoke utterly engulfed the yard, obscuring all vision. Neville held his nose and squinted into the murk, thinking to detect some movement amid the impenetrable fog. 'Everything going all right?' he called gaily.

'Yes, fine, fine,' came a strangled voice, 'think I've got the measure of it technique-wise.'

'Good,' said Neville. Quietly closing the door, he collapsed into a convulsion of laughter. Wiping the tears from his eyes he returned to the saloon-bar, where he found himself confronted by two young ladies of the Page Three variety, who stood looking disdainful and ill at ease. They were clad in only the scantiest of costumes and looked like escapees from some gay nineties Chicago brothel.

'You the guvnor?' said one of these lovelies, giving Neville the old fisheye. 'Only we've been 'anging about 'ere, ain't we?'

Neville pulled back his shoulders and thrust out his pigeon chest. 'Good evening,' said he in his finest Ronald Coleman. 'You are, I trust, the two young ladies sent by the brewery to assist in the proceedings?'

'You what?' said one.

'To help behind the bar?'

'Oh, yeah.'

'And may I ask your names?'

'I'm Sandra,' said Sandra.

'I'm Mandy,' said her companion.

'Neville,' said Neville, extending his hand.

Sandra tittered. Mandy said, 'It's a bit of a dump 'ere, ain't it?'

Neville returned his unshaken hand to its pocket. 'You didn't come through the streets in those costumes did you?'

'Nah,' said Mandy, 'we come in the car, didn't we?'

'And you are, I trust, acquainted with the running of a bar?'

Sandra yawned and began to polish her nails. Mandy said, 'We've worked in all the top clubs, we're 'ostesses, ain't we?'

Neville was fascinated to note that the two beauties seemed unable to form a single sentence which did not terminate in a question mark. 'Well then, I'll leave you in charge while I go up and get changed.'

'We can manage, can't we?' said Mandy.

The cowboy suit hung behind the bedroom door in its plastic covering. With great care Neville lifted it down and laid it upon the bed. Carefully parting the plastic, he pressed his nose to the fabric of the suit, savouring the bittersweet smell of the dry cleaner's craft.

Gently he put his thumbs to the pearl buttons and removed the jacket from the hanger. He sighed deeply, and with the reverence a priest accords to his ornamentum, he slipped into the jacket. The material was crisp and pure, the sleeves crackled slightly as he eased his arms into them, and the starched cuffs clamped about his wrists like loving manacles. Without further hesitation the part-time barman climbed into the trousers, clipped on the gunbelt, and tilted the hat on to his head at a rakish angle. Pinning the glittering badge of office carefully to his breast he stepped to the pitted glass of the wardrobe mirror to view the total effect.

It was, to say the least, stunning. The dazzling white of the suit made the naturally anaemic Neville appear almost suntanned. The stetson, covering his bald patch and accentuating his dark sideburns, made his face seem ruggedly handsome, the bulge of the gunbelt gave an added contour to his narrow hips, and the cut of the trousers brought certain parts of his anatomy into an unexpected and quite astonishing prominence.

'Mighty fine,' said Neville, easing his thumbs beneath the belt buckle and adopting a stance not unknown to the late and legendary 'Duke' himself. But there was something missing, some final touch. He looked down, and caught sight of his carpet-slippers; of course, the cowboy boots. A sudden sick feeling began to take hold of his stomach. He did not remember having seen any boots when the suit arrived. In fact, there were none.

Neville let out a despairing groan and slumped on to his bed, a broken man. The image in the mirror crumpled away and with it Neville's dreams; a cowboy in carpet-slippers? A tear entered Neville's good eye and crept down his cheek.

*

It was seven-thirty. The bar was still deserted. The two hostesses were huddled at a corner of the counter, sipping shandy and discussing the sex lives of their contemporaries in hushed and confidential tones. The gaudily-dressed bar had become a gloomy and haunted place. Once in a while a passer-by would cast a brief shadow upon the etched glass of the saloon-bar door, conversation would cease and the two beauties would look up in wary expectation.

Neville descended the stairs upon tiptoe. The Page Three girls saw Neville's slippers before they saw Neville. They should have laughed, nudged one another, pointed and giggled, and possibly on any other occasion they would have done just that, but as the part-time barman reached the foot of the stairs he had about him such an air of desperate tragedy that the two girls were moved beyond words.

Neville squinted around the empty bar. 'Hasn't anybody been in?' he asked.

Mandy shook her powdered head. Sandra said, 'Nah.'

'You look dead good,' said Mandy, 'suits you.'

'Like that bloke in them films you look,' said Sandra.

Neville smiled weakly. 'Thanks,' he said. Just then the sound of a muffled explosion issued from the direction of the patio. The yard door burst open, and down the short corridor staggered the blackened figure of Young Master Robert. He was accompanied by a gust of evil-smelling black smoke which made his entrance not unlike that of the Demon Prince in popular panto.

As he lurched towards the bar counter Neville stepped nimbly aside to avoid soiling his suit. The two Page Three beauties stood dumb with astonishment. Young Master Robert stumbled behind the bar. Tearing the whisky bottle from its optic, he snatched up a half-pint mug and filled it to the brim.

'Two bloody hours,' he screeched in a tortured voice. 'Two bloody hours puffing and blowing and fanning the bloody thing! Then I see it, then I bloody see it!'

'You do?' said Neville.

'The vents, man, where are the bloody vents?'

Neville shrugged. He had no idea.

'I'll tell you where the bloody vents are, I'll bloody tell you!' The line of Neville's mouth was beginning to curl itself into an awful lopsided smirk. With great difficulty he controlled it. 'On the top, that's where the bloody vents are!'

Neville said, 'Surely that can't be right.'

'Can't be right? I'll say it can't be bloody right! Some bastard has built the barbeque upside down!'

Neville clamped his hand over his mouth. Young Master Robert raised the half-pint pot in a charred fist and poured the whisky down his throat.

'What shall we do then?' asked Neville, fighting a losing battle against hilarity. 'Call it off, eh?'

'Call it off? Not on your bloody life. No, I've fixed it, fixed it proper I bloody have, gave it what it bloody needed. Proper Molotov cocktail, got vents now it has, I'll tell you.'

'Oh good,' said Neville, 'no damage done then.'

Young Master Robert turned on the part-time barman a bitter glance. 'I warn you,' he stammered, 'I bloody warn you!' It was then that he realized the bar was empty. 'Here!' he said. 'Where is everybody?'

Neville moved uneasily in his chaps. The Young Master fixed him with a manic stare. Mandy watched his fingers tightening about the handle of the half-pint pot. She stepped between the two men. 'Come on Bobby,' she said, 'let's 'ave a look at them burns, can't 'ave you getting an infection can we?' With a comforting but firm hand she led the blackened barbequeist away to the ladies'.

Neville could contain himself no longer. He clutched at his stomach, rolled his eyes, and fell into fits of laughter. Sandra was giggling behind her hand but she leant over to the part-time barman and whispered hoarsely, 'You wanna watch that little bastard, he can put the poison in for you.'

'Thank you,' said Neville, and the two of them collapsed into further convulsions. Suddenly there was a sound at the bar door. The smiles froze on their lips, for it was at this exact moment that the Lone Ranger chose to make his appearance.

He was quite a short Ranger as it happened, and somewhat stout. Neville immediately recognized the man in the mask to be none other than Wally Woods, Brentford's pre-eminent purveyor of wet fish. Wally stood a moment, magnificently framed in the doorway, considering the empty bar with a cold cod-eye of suspicion. For one terrible second Neville thought he was about to change his mind and make off into the sunset in the manner much practised in the Old West. 'What'll it be, stranger?' he said hurriedly.

Wally squared his rounded shoulders and swaggered to the bar, accompanied by the distinctive smell of halibut oil which never left

95

his person come rain, hail, or high water. 'Give me two fingers of Old Snakebelly,' he said manfully.

During the half hour that followed, the Flying Swan began slowly to fill. In dribs and drabs they came, some looking sheepish and muffled in heavy overcoats, despite the mildness of the season, others strutting through the doorway as if they had been cowboys all their lives. Three Mavericks had begun an illegal-looking game of poker at a corner-table, and no less than six gunfights had already broken out.

Neville loaded another case of old Snakebelly on to the counter. Young Master Robert returned from the ladies', a satisfied expression upon his face, which was a battleground of sticking plaster. Mandy was wearing her bustle on back to front. Two more Rangers arrived, swelling their ranks to eight. 'What is this, a bloody convention?' asked one. Old Pete arrived wearing a Superman costume. 'They were right out of Lone Rangers,' he explained.

A few stalwart professionals were sticking to their regular beverages, but most were taking advantage of the cut-price liquor and tossing back large measures of Old Snakebelly, which was proving to have the effect generally expected of white man's firewater.

The last of the Lone Rangers rounded the corners at either end of the Ealing Road and strode towards the Flying Swan. One was of Irish descent, the other a well-known local personality who had but several hours before come within one horse of winning two hundred and fifty thousand pounds. The two caught sight of one another when they were but twenty yards apiece from the saloon-bar door. Both stopped. The Lone Pooley blinked in surprise. The Lone Omally's face took on a look of perplexity. Surely, he thought, this is some trick of the light, some temperature inversion or mirror image. Possibly, by the merest of chances, he had stepped through a warp in the time-space continuum and was confronting his own *dopplegänger*. A similar thought had entered the Lone Pooley's mind.

They strode forward, each in perfect synchronization with his twin. The Lone Pooley made a motion towards his gunbelt, his double did likewise. But for these two lone figures, the street was deserted. The sun was setting behind the gasometers and the long and similar shadows of the two masked gunmen stretched out across the pavement and up the side walls of the tiny terraced houses.

It was a sight to make Zane Grey reach for his ballpoint, or

Sergio Leone send out for another fifty foot of standard eight. Closer and closer stalked the Rangers, their jaws set into attitudes of determination, and their thumbs wedged into the silver buckles of their respective gunbelts.

They stopped once more.

The street was silent but for the sounds of western jollity issuing from the saloon-bar. A flock of pigeons rippled up from their perch atop one of the flatblocks and came to rest upon the roof of the church hall. A solitary dog loped across the street and vanished into an alleyway.

The Rangers stared at one another unblinking. 'This town ain't big enough for the both of us,' said the Lone Omally.

'Slap leather, hombre,' said the Lone Pooley, reaching for his six-guns. It would be a long reach, for they were back in his rooms upon the kitchen-table where he had been polishing them. 'Oh bugger it,' said the Lone Pooley. Guffawing, the Ranger twins entered the Flying Swan.

'Cor look,' said Mandy, 'there's two more of 'em.'

'My God,' cried Pooley, 'ten Lone Rangers and not a Tonto between the lot of us.'

'Two shots of good Old Snakebelly please, Miss,' said Omally, ogling the extra barstaff. Mandy did the honours, and on accepting Omally's exact coinage pocketed it away in some impossible place in her scanty costume. 'A woman after my own heart,' smiled the man from the Emerald Isle.

Things were beginning to hot up at the Flying Swan. Old Pete was at the piano, rattling out 'I Wish I Was in Dixie' upon the moribund instrument. Young Chips was howling off-key as usual. A fight had broken out among the Mavericks and Neville was flourishing his knobkerry, yet seeming strangely reluctant to make a move from behind the bar.

Young Master Robert raised his hands to make an announcement. Being ill-acquainted with the manners and customs of Brentford he was ignored to a man.

'Ladies and gentlemen,' he bawled, the visible areas of his face turning purple, 'if I might have your attention.'

Neville brought the knobkerry down on to the polished bar counter with a resounding crash. There was a brief silence.

'Ladies and gentlemen,' roared the Young Master, his high voice echoing grotesquely about the silent bar, 'ladies and gentlemen

I. . .' but it was no good, the temporary silence was over as swiftly as it had begun, and the rumblings of half-drunken converse, the jingling chords of the complaining piano, and the general rowdiness resumed with a vengeance.

'Time gentlemen *PLEASE*!' cried Neville, which silenced them once and for all.

Young Master Robert made his announcement. 'Ladies and gentlemen, as I was saying, as a representative of the brewery' – at this point Young Chips made a rude noise which was received with general applause – 'as a representative of the brewery, may I say how impressed I am by this turnout, enthusiasm-wise.'

'Enthusiasm-wise?' queried Omally.

'As you may know, this evening has been arranged at the brewery's expense to launch a new concept in drinking pleasure.' He held up a bottle of Old Snakebelly. 'Which I am glad to see you are all enjoying. There will shortly be held a barbeque where delicacies of a western nature will be served, also at the brewery's expense. There will be a free raffle, prizes for the best-dressed cowboy . . .' As he spoke, Young Master Robert became slowly aware that the assembled company of cowboys was no longer listening; heads were beginning to turn, whispers were breaking out, elbows were nudging. The Spirit of the Old West had entered the bar.

Norman stood in the Swan's portal, his suit glittering about him. The sequins and rhinestones gleamed and twinkled. He had added four more sets of fairy lights to the arms and legs of the costume and these flashed on and off in a pulsating rhythm.

Norman came forward, his hands raised as in papal benediction. Spellbound, like the Red Sea to the wave of Moses' staff, the crowd parted before him. Turning slowly for maximum effect, Norman flicked a switch upon his belt-buckle and sent the lights dancing in a frenzied whirl. To and fro about the golden motto the lights danced, weaving pattern upon pattern, altering the contours of the suit, and highlighting hitherto unnoticed embellishments.

Here they brought into prominence the woven head-dress of an Indian chieftain, here the rhinestoned wheel of a covered wagon, here a sequinned cowboy crouched in the posture of one ready to shoot it out. To say that it was wondrous would be to say that the universe is quite a big place. As the coloured lights danced and Norman turned upon his insulated brass conductor heels the assembled company began to applaud. In ones and twos they clapped their hands together, then as the sound grew, gaining rhythm and pace, Old Pete struck up a thunderous 'Oh Them Golden Slippers' upon the piano.

The cowboys cheered and flung their hats into the air, Lone Rangers of every colour linked arms like a chorus line and Hi-ho Silvered till they were all uniformly blue in the face. Pooley and Omally threw themselves into an improvised and high-stepping barn dance, and the Spirit of the Old West capered about in the midst of it all like an animated lighthouse. Then a most extraordinary thing happened.

The sawdust began to rise from the floor towards Norman's suit. First it thickened about his feet, smothering his polished boots, then crept upwards like some evil parasitic fungus, gathering about his legs and then swathing his entire body.

'It's the static electricity,' gasped Omally, ceasing his dance in mid kick. 'He's charged himself up like a capacitor.'

Norman was so overcome by his reception that it was not until he found himself unable to move, coughing and spluttering, and wiping sawdust from his ears and eyes, that an inkling dawned upon him that something was amiss. The crowd, who was convinced that this was nothing more than another phase in a unique and original performance, roared with laughter and fired their sixguns into the air.

Omally stepped forward. Norman's eyes were starting from their sockets and he was clutching at his throat. The sawdust was settling thickly about him, transforming him into a kind of woodchipped snowman. Omally reached out a hand to brush the sawdust from the struggling man's face and was rewarded by a charge of electrical energy which lifted him from his rented cowboy boots and flung him backwards over the bar counter.

Jim Pooley snatched up a soda siphon and, without thought for the consequences, discharged it fully into the face of the Spirit of the Old West. What followed was later likened by Old Pete to a firework display he had once witnessed at the Crystal Palace when a lad. Sparks flew from Norman's hands and feet, bulbs popped from their holders and criss-crossed the bar like tracer bullets. The crowd took shelter where they could, Young Chips thrust his head into a spitoon, his elderly master lay crouched beneath the piano saying the rosary, the Page Three girls hurriedly ducked away behind the bar counter to where Omally lay unconscious, his face set into an idiot grin. Norman jerked about the room, smoke rising from his shoulders, his arms flailing in the air like the sails of a demented windmill. The final bulb upon his once proud suit gave out with an almighty crack and Norman sank to the floor, where he lay a smouldering ruin.

After a moment or two of painful silence the cowboys rose sheepishly from their makeshift hideouts, patting the dirt from their rented suits and squinting through the cloud of sawdust which filled the room. Pooley came forward upon hesitant rubber-kneed legs and doused down the fallen hero with the remaining contents of the soda siphon. 'Are you all right, Norman?' he asked inanely.

'Oh, bollocks!' moaned the Spirit of the Old West, spitting out a mouthful of sawdust. 'Oh, *bollocks*!'

12

Captain Carson lay draped across an elaborately carved Spanish chair, peeping between his fingers at the preposterous display of exotic foodstuffs heaped upon the gilded tabletop. To think that any one of these rare viands might be purchased anywhere within a mile of the Mission would be to stretch the most elastic of imaginations to its very breaking point. Yet there they were. The Captain covered his eyes again and hoped desperately that they would go away. They did not.

Carrying the tramp's shopping-list, some of which was totally unpronounceable, he had traipsed from shop to shop. It had been almost as if the shopkeepers were lying in wait for him. He had wandered into Uncle Ted's greengrocery to inquire in a doomed voice as to the current availability of Bernese avocados. Uncle Ted had smiled broadly, torn a paper bag from the nail, and asked if he would prefer reds or greens. At every shop it had been the same. When the Captain had demanded an explanation of how these gastronomic delicacies found their way on to the shelves, the shopkeepers had been extremely vague in their replies. Some spoke of consignments arriving by accident, others that it was a new line they were trying out.

After six such encounters in tiny corner-shops which normally complained that they were out of sugar, that the cornflakes were late in again, and that they couldn't get tomato sauce for love nor money, the Captain, his head reeling, had staggered into the High Street off-licence.

'Your usual?' said Tommy Finch, the manager. The Captain sighed gratefully. Could it be possible that here was sanctuary, that this one place had remained free from the tramp's contamination?

'Or,' said Tommy, suddenly, 'could I interest you in a half a dozen bottles of a magnificent vintage claret which arrived here in error this very morning and which is most moderately priced?'

The Captain had cast a fatalistic eye down his list. 'That wouldn't by any chance be Château-Lafite Eighteen twenty-two?'

'That's the one.' Tommy had replied with no hint of surprise.

The Captain rose stiffly from his chair, picked up a can of pickled quails' eggs and gave the label some perusal. As with all the other items he had purchased, and as with everything else which surrounded the mystery tramp, there was something not quite right about it. The label appeared at first sight normal enough, an illustration of the contained foodstuffs, a brand name, a list of ingredients, and a maker's mark; yet the more one looked at it, the more indistinct its features became. The colours seemed to run into one another, the letters were not letters at all but merely rudimentary symbols suggestive of lettering.

The Captain returned the can to the table and shook his head as one in a dream. None of it made any sense. What could the tramp be planning? What had been his motive in inviting the hated Crowley to the Mission? Certainly on his past record alone it could be expected that his motives were nothing if not thoroughly evil. None of it made any sense.

'Is all correct?' said a voice, jarring the Captain from his thoughts. 'There must be no mistake.'

Turning, the Captain peered up at the red-eyed man towering above him. Never had he looked more imposing or more terrible, dressed in an evening suit of the deepest black, a dark cravat about his neck secured at the throat by a sapphire pin. His fingers weighed heavy with rings of gold and his face wore an unreadable expression.

'All is as you ordered,' said the Captain in a querulous voice, 'though as to how, I do not know, nor do I wish to.'

'Good. Our guests will arrive sharp at seven-thirty. They must be received in a manner befitting.'

The Captain chewed ruefully upon his knuckles. 'What would you have me wear for this distinguished gathering?'

The tramp smiled, his mouth a cruel line. 'You may wear the Royal Navy dress uniform which hangs in your wardrobe, the hire company's label cut out from its lining. Pray remember to remove the camphor bags from its pockets.'

The Captain hunched his shoulders and slouched from the room.

*

When he returned an hour later, duly clad, the Captain discovered to his further bewilderment that the food had been laid out in the most exquisite and skilful manner, the claret twinkled in cut-glass decanters, and the delicious smell of cooking filled the air. The Captain shook his befuddled head and consulted his half-hunter. There was just time for a little drop of short. He had lately taken to carrying a hip-flask which he refilled with half-bottles of rum purchased from the off-licence. This seemed the only defence against the tramp, whose intuition of the location of hidden bottles seemed nothing short of telepathic. The two red eyes burned into his every thought, hovering in his consciousness and eating away at his brain like a hideous cancer. The Captain drew deeply upon his flask and drained it to its pewter bottom.

At seven-thirty precisely a black cab drew up outside the Mission. The Captain heard the sound of footsteps crackling up the short path to the Mission door. There were two sharp raps. The Captain rose with difficulty, buttoned up his dress jacket, and shuffled unwillingly towards the front door.

Upon the step stood Councillor Wormwood, wrapped in a threadbare black overcoat, a stained white silk scarf slung about his scrawny neck. He was tall, gaunt, and angular, his skin the colour of a nicotine-stained finger, and his eyes deeply sunk into cavernous black pits. Never had the Captain seen a man who wore the look of death more plainly upon his features. He withdrew a febrile and blue-veined hand from his worn coat pocket and offered the Captain a gilt-edged invitation card. 'Wormwood,' he said in a broken voice. 'I am expected.'

'Please come in,' the Captain replied, making a courteous gesture. The jaundiced spectre allowed himself to be ushered down the corridor and into the dining-room.

The Captain took out the bottle of cheap sherry he kept in reserve for Jehovah's Witnesses.

'I see that I am the first,' said Wormwood, accepting the thimble-sized glass the Captain offered him. 'You have a cosy little nest for yourself here.'

The sound of taxi wheels upon the gravel drew the Captain's attention. 'If you will excuse me,' he said, 'I think I hear the arrival of another guest.' The Councillor inclined his turtle neck and the Captain left the room.

Before the Mission stood Brian Crowley. He was dressed in a

deep-blue velvet suit, which caught the evening light to perfection. A hand-stitched silk dress-shirt with lace ruffles smothered him to the neck, where a large black bow-tie clung to his throat like a vampire bat. His shoes, also hand-made, were of the finest leather; he carried in his hands a pair of kid gloves and an ivory-tipped Malacca-cane. He raised a limp and manicured hand to the Mission's knocker, which receded before his grasp as the Captain swung open the door.

'Mr Crowley,' said the Captain.

'Good evening, Carson,' said the young man, stepping forward. The Captain barred his way. 'Your card, sir?' said the Captain politely.

'Damn you, Carson, you know who I am.'

'We must observe protocol.'

Muttering under his breath Crowley reached into his breast pocket and withdrew a monogrammed morocco wallet. From this he produced the invitation card which he held to the old man's face. 'All right?'

The Captain took the card and bowed graciously. 'Pray come in.' As he followed the effeminate young man down the corridor the Captain smiled to himself; he had quite enjoyed that little confrontation.

Crowley met Councillor Wormwood in the dining-room. The Councillor took the pale white fingers in his yellow claw and shook them without enthusiasm. 'Wormwood,' he said.

Crowley's suspicions had been alerted. Surely this was a dinner exclusively for members of the Mission Trust to celebrate the centenary and the Captain's retirement? Why invite that withered cretin?

It was only now that Crowley became fully aware of the room in which he was standing. Lit only by the two magnificent candelabra upon the loaded table, the rich gildings and embossings upon the furniture glittered like treasure in the tomb of a Pharaoh. Crowley's gaze swept ravenously about the room. He became drawn towards an oil painting which hung in a frame of golden cherubim above a rococo commode. Surely this was a genuine Pinturicchio of his finest period? How could an elderly sea-captain have come by it? Crowley had never credited the grizzled salt with any intelligence whatever, yet recalling his surprise upon receiving the invitation cards, he felt that he had truly misjudged this elder. The young man's eyes glittered with greed.

'Will you take sherry?' the Captain asked. Roused from his covetous reverie, Crowley replied, 'Yes indeed, thank you.'

He accepted his sherry with a display of extraordinary politeness and wondered just how he might avail himself of the Captain's valuable possessions. 'I have been admiring this painting,' he said at length, 'surely it is a Pinturicchio of the Romanesque school?'

The Captain fiddled nervously with the top of a cut-crystal decanter. 'I believe so,' he replied matter-of-factly.

'And the furniture.' Crowley made a sweeping gesture. 'Surely fifteenth-century Spanish Baroque; you have some most exquisite examples.'

'It serves,' said the Captain, studying his broken fingernails. 'Please be seated, gentlemen, place cards have been set out.'

Crowley made a slow perambulation about the table, sherry glass held delicately in his pampered fingers. His eyes wandered over the display of food. 'Why, Captain,' he said in an insinuating voice, 'this is *haute cuisine* to numb the brain of a gourmet. I must confess complete astonishment, I had no idea, I mean, well, most worthy, most worthy.'

The Captain watched Crowley's every movement. While his expression remained bland and self-effacing, his brain boiled with hatred for the effeminate young man. Crowley dipped a hand forward and took up a sweetmeat, pecking it to his nose to savour its fragrance. With a foppish flurry he popped it into his mouth, his small pink tongue darting about his lips. Almost at once his face took on an expression both quizzical and perplexed.

'Extraordinary,' he said, smacking his lips. 'The taste, so subtle, hardly distinguishable upon the palate. It is almost as if one had placed a cube of cold air into one's mouth, most curious.'

'It is an acquired taste,' sneered the Captain.

Wormwood had found his place at the bottom of the table and had seated himself without ceremony. Crowley shrugged his shoulders, licked the ends of his fingers, and sought his seat. 'If you will pardon me, Captain,' he said, 'it would seem that but for our own, the other seven place cards are unlabelled.'

'Possibly an oversight on the part of the caterers,' grumbled the Captain, 'don't let it concern you.' He took his place between the two men and the three sat in silence.

Crowley took out a cocktail cigarette from a gold case and tapped it upon the table. Wormwood wheezed asthmatically into his hand. Drawing a shabby handkerchief from his pocket he dabbed at his sinewy nose.

The Captain sat immobile, wondering what, if anything, was going to happen. Crowley lit his cigarette and looked down at his platinum wristwatch. 'It would seem that your other guests are a trifle late,' said he.

The Captain sniffed and said nothing. Wormwood turned his empty sherry glass between his fingers and shuffled his ill-polished shoes uneasily. Long minutes passed and no sound came to the Captain's ears but for the regular tock tock of the gilded mantel-clock. There was no rumble of an approaching vehicle and no foot-step upon the stairs that might herald the arrival of the red-eyed man. Surely it was not his intention to have the Captain sit here be-tween these two hated individuals all evening? He had nothing to say to them.

Without warning, and silently upon its never-oiled hinge, the hall door swung open. White light streamed into the candlelit room, brighter and brighter it grew, as if a searchlight had been turned upon the opening. The Captain blinked and shielded his eyes. Crowley squinted into the glare. 'Here,' he shouted, 'what's all this?'

In the midst of the now blinding light the silhouette of a tall and boldly-proportioned man gradually became apparent. Well over six foot he stood, and finely muscled as an Olympic athlete. His garb was of the richest crimson, trousers cut impeccably, yet without a crease, a waisted and collarless jacket, lavishly embellished with stitched brocade, a lace cravat about the neck. Upon his head the figure wore a small crimson skullcap.

The face might have been that of a Spanish grandee, tanned and imposing, the nose aquiline, and the mouth a hard and bitter line. The chin was prominent and firmly set. Beneath thick dark eye-brows, two blood-red eyes gleamed menacingly. The room became impossibly cold, the hairs rose upon the Captain's hands and his breath streamed from his mouth as clouds of steam which hovered in the frozen air.

Crowley found his voice. 'Dammit,' he spluttered, his teeth chattering and his face a grey mask of fear. 'What's going on? Who the devil are you?'

Wormwood clutched at his heart with quivering hands and gasped for air.

The crimson figure stood in total silence, his eyes fixed upon the effeminate young man. The Captain had seen that look before and thanked his maritime gods that it was not directed towards him. 'So you would be Crowley?'

An icy hand clasped about the young man's heart. His head nodded up and down like that of an automaton and his lips mouthed the syllables of his own name although no sound came.

'And this is Councillor Wormwood?' The eyes turned upon the unhappy creature who cowered at the table-end.

'Horace Wormwood,' came the trembling reply, 'I was invited.'

'Good.' A broad if sinister smile broke out upon the tall man's face. 'Then all is as it should be. Please be seated, gentlemen.'

The three men, who had risen unconsciously to their feet, reseated themselves, and the warmth of the summer's evening returned to the room. The tall man stepped forward and took his place at the head of the table. To the further horror of those already seated, the hall door swung silently shut and closed into its frame with a resounding crash.

'I hope you will enjoy this modest spread,' said the crimson figure. 'It is but local fare.'

Crowley finally found his voice. He was by nature a predator, and not one to be intimidated by such a theatrical display, no matter how convincing it might appear. It would take more than a few bright lights and a bit of cold air to make him deviate from his calculated scheme. It was clear that the Captain had hired this man, possibly a local actor; there was definitely something familiar about him, and those eyes, certainly tinted contact lenses; nobody could have eyes that colour surely?

'Local fare, you say,' said Crowley merrily. 'It would seem that you have plundered the finest food halls of Christendom and employed one of the world's master chefs to prepare this magnificent feast.'

The tall man in crimson smiled his thinnest of smiles and said, 'I fear that the other guests have declined their invitations and we shall be forced to dine alone, as it were. I also fear that by an unforgivable oversight the caterers have omitted to supply us with either cutlery or serving staff and you will be forced to serve yourselves. Captain, if you would be so kind as to bring in the fish.'

The Captain did as he was bid without hesitation. At the arrival of the fish Crowley clapped his hands together in glee and shouted, 'Magnificent! Magnificent!'

The four men sat about the enormous gilded dining-table, the golden glow of candle flame eerily illuminating their faces whilst casting their shadows about the richly-hung walls in a ragged, wavering, *danse macabre*. Each man was occupied with his own thoughts. Crowley's brain was bursting with a thousand unanswered questions; everything here demanded explanation. His eyes cast about from face to face, and devious plots began to hatch inside his skull. Councillor Wormwood, although a man greatly in favour of connivance and double-dealing, was capable upon this occasion of no such premeditation. He was an old man and felt himself to be pretty well-versed in the ways of the world, but here in this room he knew there was something 'different' going on. There was a dark aura of evil here, and it was evil of the most hideous and malignant variety.

Captain Carson glowered morosely about the table. He really didn't know much about anything any more. All he knew was that he was seated here in a room, which had been exclusively his for the past thirty years, with three men who out of the entire world's population he loathed and hated to a point well starboard of all sanity.

At a gesture from the red-eyed man the three set about the mouthwatering dishes. Crowley was amazed to find that the sweet-meat he had sampled minutes before had now taken on the most delicious and satisfying of tastes. He gurgled his delight and thrust large helpings into his mouth.

Councillor Wormwood pecked at his choosings like the ragged vulture he was, his claws fastening about the leg of some tropical fowl and his hideous yellow teeth tearing the soft white flesh away from the pinkly-cooked bones. The Captain sampled this and that and found all equally to his liking.

As no cutlery had been supplied the three men dug into the finely-dressed displays with their greasy fingers, reducing each dish to a ruination suggestive of the march of soldier ants. The crimson figure at the head of the table left most of the dishes untouched. He dined upon bread, which he broke delicately between his muscular fingers, and drank occasionally from the decanter of claret set at his right elbow.

The hours passed and the gluttony of the three men was slowly satisfied. The Captain loosened the lower buttons of his jacket and broke wind in a loud and embarrassing manner. At length, when it seemed that the undignifed destruction of the table was at an end, the crimson figure spoke. Sweeping his burning eyes over the three men he said, 'Is all to your liking, gentlemen?'

Crowley looked up, his mouth still bulging with food. 'It is all ambrosia,' he mumbled, wiping cream away with the cuff of his lace shirt.

'Mr Wormwood?'

The creature raised its yellow eyes. There was grease upon his cleft chin and he had spilt white sauce on his jacket lapel. 'Most palatable,' said he.

'And Captain?'

The Captain chewed ruefully upon a jellied lark's wing and grunted assent in a surly manner.

Crowley was growing bolder by the minute, and felt it high time that he put one or two of the questions he had stewing in his head. 'Dear sir,' said he. 'May I say how much I have enjoyed this dinner, never in my days have I tasted such claret.' He held up the short crystal glass to the candleflame and contemplated the ruby-red liquid as it ran about the rim. 'To think that anything so exquisite could exist here in Brentford, that such a sanctuary dedicated to life's finer things could be here, it is a veritable joy to the soul.'

The red-eyed man nodded thoughtfully. 'Then you approve?'

'I do, I do, but I must also confess to some puzzlement.'

'Indeed?'

'Well,' and here Crowley paused that he might compose inquisitiveness into a form which might give no offence. 'Well, as to yourself for instance; you are clearly a man of extreme refinement, such is obvious from your carriage, bearing, and manner of speech. If you will pardon my inquiry, might I ask to which part of our sceptred isle you owe your born allegiance?'

'I am broadly-travelled and may call no place truly my home.'

'Then as to your presence in these parts?'

'I am at present a guest of the good Captain.'

'I see.' Crowley turned his eyes briefly towards the elder. His glance was sufficient however to register the look of extreme distaste on the Captain's face.

'Then, sir, as you have the advantage of us, might I inquire your name?'

The red-eyed man sat back in his chair. He took from a golden casket a long green cigar which he held to his ear and turned between thumb and forefinger. Taking up an onyx-handled cigar cutter he sliced away at one end. Satisfied with his handiwork, he placed the cigar between his cruel lips and drew life into it from the candleflame.

'Mr Crowley,' said he, blowing a perfect cube of smoke which hovered in the air a second or two before dissolving into nothingness. 'Mr Crowley, you would not wish to know my name.'

The young man sipped at his wine and smiled coyly. 'Come now,' he crooned, 'you have supplied us with a dinner fit for royalty, yet you decline to identify yourself. It is unfair that we are not permitted to know the name of our most generous and worthy host.'

The red-eyed man drew once more upon his cigar, while the index finger of his left hand traced a runic symbol upon the polished table-top. 'It is to the Captain that you owe your gratitude,' said he. 'He is your host, I am but a guest as yourself.'

'Ha,' the young man crowed, 'I think not. You suit all this a little too well, you sit at the table's head, I feel all this is your doing.'

'My doing?' the other replied. 'And what motive do you think I might have for inviting you to the Mission?'

'That is something I also wish to know. I suspect that no other guests were invited this evening and' – here Crowley leant forward in his seat – 'I demand an explanation.'

'Demand?'

'Yes, demand! Something funny is going on here and I mean to get to the bottom of it.'

'You do?'

'Who are you?' screamed Crowley, growing red in the face. 'Who are you and what are you doing here?'

'What are you doing here, Mr Crowley?'

'Me? I was invited. I came out of respect to the Captain, to celebrate the Mission's centenary, I have a responsible position on the board of trustees, in fact I am a man not without power, you would do well not to bandy words with me!'

'Mr Crowley,' said the crimson figure. 'You are a fool, you have no respect for the Captain, you have only contempt. It was greed that brought you here and it will be greed that will be your ruination.'

'Oh yes?' said Crowley. 'Oh yes?'

'I will tell you why you came here tonight and I will answer your questions. You came here because you knew that not to come would be to draw attention to yourself. It is your plan to have this Mission demolished at the first possible opportunity, and to make your shady and treacherous deals with this corpse here.' Wormwood cowered in his seat as the tall man continued. 'I will never allow a stone of this Mission to be touched without my consent!'

'Your consent?' screeched Crowley. 'Who in the hell do you think you are?'

'Enough!' The red-eyed man pushed back his chair and drew himself to his full height, his eyes blazing, and his shoulders spreading to draw out his massive chest. His hands formed two enormous fists which he brought down on to the table with titanic force, scattering the food and shuddering the candelabra. 'Crowley!' he roared, his voice issuing from his mouth as a gale force of icy wind. 'Crowley, you would know who I am! I am the man to whom fate has led you. From your very birth it was ordained that our paths would finally cross. All things are pre-ordained and no man can escape his fate. You would know who I am? Crowley, I am your Nemesis!'

Crowley hurled his chair aside and rushed for the door, his desperate movements those of a wildly-flapping bird. His hands grasped about the door-handle but found it as solid and unmoveable as if welded to the lock. 'Let me go,' he whimpered, 'I want nothing more of this, let me out.'

The giant in crimson turned his hellish eyes once more upon the young man. 'You have no escape, Crowley,' he said, his voice a low rumble of distant thunder. 'You have no escape, you are already dead, you were dead from the moment you entered this room, dead from the first moment you raised a glass to your mouth, you are dead, Crowley.'

'I'm not dead,' the young man cried, tears welling up in his eyes. 'I'll have the law on you for this, I'm not without influence, I'm . . .' Suddenly he stiffened, as if a strong cord had been tightly drawn about his neck. His eyes stared from their sockets and his tongue burst from his mouth. It was black and dry as the tongue of an old boot. 'You . . . you,' he gagged, tearing at his collar and falling back against the door.

The tall figure loomed above him, a crimson angel of death. 'Dead, Crowley.'

The young man sank slowly to his knees, his eyes rolling horribly until the pupils were lost in his head. A line of green saliva flowed from the corner of his mouth and crept over his shirt. He jerked forward, his manicured nails tearing into the parquet flooring, crackling and snapping as convulsions of raw pain coursed through his body.

Above him, watching the young man's agony with inhuman detachment, stood the crimson giant. Crowley raised a shaking hand, blood flowed from his wounded fingertips, his face was contorted beyond recognition. He bore the look of a grotesque, a gargoyle, the skin grey and parched, the lips blue, bloodless. He raised himself once more to his knees and his mouth opened, the blue lips made a hopeless attempt to shape a final word. Another convulsion tore through his body and flung him doll-like to the floor where he lay, his limbs twisted hideously, his eyes staring at the face of his destroyer, glazed and sightless. Brian Crowley was dead.

The red-eyed man raised his right hand and made a gesture of benediction. With terrifying suddenness he turned upon the Captain, who sat open-mouthed, shaking with terror. 'You will dispose of this rubbish,' he said.

'Rubbish?' The Captain forced the word from his mouth.

The red-eyed man gestured at the twisted body which lay at his feet; then, raising his arm, he pointed across the table. The Captain followed his gaze to where Councillor Wormwood sat. His hands grasped the table-top in a vice-like grip, his eyes were crossed and his head hung back upon his neck like that of a dead fowl in a butcher's window. The skin was no longer yellow, but grey-white and almost iridescent; his mouth lolled hugely open and his upper set had slipped down to give the impression that his teeth were clenched into a sickly grin.

The giant was speaking, issuing instructions, the bodies were to be stripped of all identification, this was to be destroyed by fire, the table was to be cleared, the decanters to be drained and thoroughly washed out. The bodies were to be placed in weighted sacks . . . the voice rolled over the Captain, a dark ocean of words, engulfing and drowning him. He rose to his feet, his hands cupped about his ears that he might hear no more. The words swept into his brain, the black tide washed over him, dragging him down. The Captain fought to breathe, fought to raise his head above the black waters. This was the Mission, his life, the evil must be driven out while any strength remained in his old body. His hands sought to grasp these thoughts, cling to them for dear life.

But the hands were old and the tide strong. Presently the Captain could grip no more, and the poison waters swept over him, covering him without trace.

13

The ambulance roared away from the Flying Swan, its bell ringing cheerfully. Most of the smoke had been fanned away through the Swan's doors and windows, but an insistent smell of electrical burning still hung heavily in the air. After the excitement was over and the ambulance had departed, the cowboys stood about, thumbs in gun-belts, wondering whether that was the night over and they should, out of respect to Norman, saddle up and make for the sunset.

Young Master Robert however, had other ideas. He climbed on to a chair and addressed the crowd. As nobody felt much like talking at that particular moment he was able to make himself heard. 'Partners,' he began, 'partners, a sorry incident has occurred but let us be grateful that the party concerned has not been badly injured. I am assured by the ambulance man that he will be up and about within a couple of days.' There were some half-hearted attempts at a cheer. 'To show the brewery's appreciation of a brave attempt, we are awarding, sadly in his absence, the Best-Dressed Cowboy award, which includes an evening out for two with one of our delightful young ladies here at one of the brewery's eating houses, a bottle of champagne, and twenty small cigars to our good friend Norman, the Spirit of the Old West!'

There was some slightly more enthusiastic cheering at this point, which rose in a deafening crescendo as Young Master Robert continued, 'The next three drinks are on the house!'

Suddenly Norman's unfortunate accident was forgotten, Old Pete set about the ancient piano once more and the Swan emerged again, a phoenix from the ashes of the Old West. Young Master Robert approached Neville behind the bar. 'I am going out to stoke up the barbeque now. I'll get the sausages on and then give you the nod to start leading them in.'

'Leave it to me,' said Neville, 'and I'll see to it that the free drinks are only singles.'

Omally, who had been revived by the aid of mouth-to-mouth resuscitation administered by each of the Page Three girls, overheard this remark and hastily ordered three doubles from Mandy before the part-time barman was able to communicate his instructions. 'Same for me,' said Jim Pooley.

Invigorated by their free drinks the cowboy patrons began to grow ever more rowdy. Old Snakebelly's qualities obviously combined those of Irish potheen, wood alcohol, and methylated spirits. Old Pete had already attempted to blow out a lighted match only to find himself breathing fire and smoke. Small rings from glass bottoms had taken most of the polish from the bar top.

Omally leant across the bar and spoke to Neville. 'You have put on a fine show and no mistake,' said he. 'I had my misgivings about tonight but –' and here he took an enormous swig of Old Snakebelly, draining his glass '– it promises to be a most memorable occasion.'

The part-time barman smiled lopsidedly and polished away at a dazzling pint pot. 'The night is far from over,' he said ominously, 'and are you feeling yourself again, John?'

'Never better,' said Dublin's finest, 'never better.'

''Ere,' said Mandy suddenly, 'That Lone Ranger what stinks of fish keeps pinching my bum.' Neville went over to have words with the unruly lawman. 'Omally,' the Page Three girl said when Neville was out of earshot.

'The same,' said himself.

'Listen.' Mandy made a secretive gesture and the man from the Emerald Isle leant further across the bar, just far enough in fact for a good view down the young lady's cleavage. 'You wanna buy a couple of dozen bottles of this Old Snake whatsit on the cheap?'

Omally grinned. He had not misjudged Mandy from the first moment he'd seen her pocket his pennies. 'What exactly is on the cheap?'

'How does a ten spot sound?'

'It sounds most reasonable, and where are these bottles at present?'

'In the boot of the white M G out the front.'

Omally delved into his moneybelt, and a ten-pound note and a set of car keys changed hands. Winking lewdly, Omally left the bar.

A strange smell of the kind one generally associates with

crematorium chimneys had began to weave its way about the bar. Some thought it was the last relics of the taint left by the Spirit of the Old West, others sensed its subtle difference and began to fan their drinks and cough into their stetsons. Suddenly there was a mighty crash as Neville brought his knobkerry down on the bar top. 'The barbeque is served,' said the part-time barman.

Knowing the rush that would ensue at the announcement of free food, and still wishing to shield his carpet-slippers from critical onlookers, Neville remained behind the bar to watch with some interest the way that one hundred or so cowboys might fit into a six-foot-square patio. Young Master Robert, clad in lurid vinyl apron and tall chef's hat, was going great guns behind the barbeque. Mountains of sizzling sausages and steakettes, and bubbling cauldrons of beans simmered away on the grill, and Sandra stood near at hand proffering paper plates and serviettes printed with the legend, '*A Souvenir of Cowboy Night.*'

The first half-dozen lucky would-be-diners squeezed their way through the Swan's rear door and found themselves jammed up against the blazing barbeque. 'One at a bloody time,' bawled a scorched Ranger, patting at the knees of his trousers. 'Don't push there!' screamed another, as his elbow dipped into a vat of boiling beans.

Order was finally maintained by the skilful wielding of a red-hot toasting fork in the hands of the Young Master. A human chain was eventually set up, and paper plates bearing dollops of beans, a steakette, a sausage, and a roll were passed back along the queue of drunken cowboys.

'More charcoal,' the Young Master cried as a helpful Jim Pooley heaped stack after stack on the flames of the blazing barbeque. 'More sausages, more beans.' Jim dutifully set about the top of a five-gallon drum with a handy garden fork.

Rammed into the corner of the patio and watching the barbeque with expressions of dire suspicion were two Rangers whose abundance of cranial covering identified them to be none other than Hairy Dave and Jungle John, well-known if largely (and wisely), distrusted members of the local building profession.

Jim had watched these two surly individuals from the corner of his eye for the better part of the last half hour and had wondered at their doubtful expressions and occasional bouts of elbow nudging. A sudden sharp report from the base of the brick-built barbeque which slightly preceded their hasty departure from the patio caused Pooley to halt in his can-opening and take stock of the situation.

The barbeque was roaring away like a furnace and the grill had grown red-hot and was slightly sagging in the middle. Young Master Robert was perspiring freely and calling for more charcoal. Jim noticed that his vinyl apron was beginning to run, and that the paint on the Swan's rear door was blistering alarmingly. The heat had grown to such an extent that the remaining cowboys were pressed back against the wall and were shielding their faces and privy parts with paper plates.

'More charcoal,' screamed Young Master Robert.

Pooley's eyes suddenly alighted upon a half-empty bag of cement which lay among a few unused red flettons in the corner of the patio. He recalled a time when, taking a few days' work in order to appease a sadistic official at the Labour Exchange, he had installed a fireplace at a lady's house on the Butts Estate. Knowing little about what happens when bricks and mortar grew hot, and having never heard of fireproof bricks and heat-resistant cement, he had used these very same red flettons and a bag of similarly standard cement. The fire-engine bells still rang clearly in Jim's memory.

There was another loud report from the base of the barbeque and Pooley reached out to make a grab at Young Master Robert's shoulder. 'Come on, come on,' he shouted, trying to make himself heard above the roaring of the fire. 'Get inside.'

'Leave off, will you?' the Young Master shouted back. 'Open those beans.'

Jim was a man who would do most things to protect his fellow man, but he was not one to scoff at self-preservation. 'Run for your life!' bawled Jim, thrusting his way into the suddenly stampeding herd of cowboys who had by now similarly realized that all was not well with the barbeque, and that the all that was not well was of that kind which greatly endangers life and limb.

The mad rush burst in through the Swan's rear-door, carrying it from its hinges and depositing it on the crosslegged form of 'Vindaloo Vic', the manager of the Curry Garden, who had been busily employed in the heaping of sausages and steakettes into a stack of foil containers to be later resold in his establishment as Bombay Duck. He vanished beneath the rented soles of forty-eight trampling cowboy boots.

The merrymakers in the saloon-bar were not long in discerning that something was going very wrong on the patio. As one, they rose to their feet and took flight. Neville found himself suddenly alone in the saloon-bar. 'Now what can this mean?' he asked himself. 'The bar suddenly empty, drinks left untouched upon tables, cigarettes burning in ashtrays, had the Flying Swan become some form of land-locked *Marie Celeste*? Is it the steakettes, perhaps? Is it the Old Snakebelly, stampeding them off to the Thames like lemmings?' Neville's ears became drawn to the sound which was issuing from the direction of the patio and which appeared to be growing second upon second. Something was building up to a deafening crescendo on the back patio and Neville had a pretty good idea what it was. It was Old Moloch itself, the ill-constructed brick barbeque, about to burst asunder.

Before Neville instinctively took the old 'dive for cover' beneath the Swan's counter, he had the impression that a being from another world had entered the bar from the rear passage. This vision, although fleeting and seen only through the part-time barman's good eye, appeared to be clad in a steaming skin-tight vinyl space-suit and wearing the remnants of a chef's hat.

The first explosion was not altogether a large one; it was by no means on the scale of Krakatoa's outburst, and it is doubtful whether it even raised a squiggle upon the seismographs at Greenwich. It was the second one that was definitely the most memorable. Possibly a scientist schooled in such matters could have estimated the exact megatonnage of the thirty cases of Old Snakebelly. However, we must accept, in the untechnical jargon of John Omally who was returning at that moment from the allotment where he had been burying twenty-four bottles of the volatile liquid, that it was one 'bloody big bang'.

The blast ripped through the Swan, overturning the piano, lifting the polished beer-pulls from the counter and propelling them through the front windows like so many silver-tipped torpedoes. The Swiss cheese roof of the gents' toilet was raised from its worm-eaten mountings and liberally distributed over half a dozen back gardens. The crowd of cowboys who had taken cover behind the parked cars in the Ealing Road ducked their heads and covered their ears and faces as shards of smoke-stained glass rained down upon them.

Neville was comparatively unscathed. When he felt it safe he raised his noble head above the counter to peer through shaking fingers at the desolation that had been his pride and joy.

The Swan was wreathed in smoke, but what Neville could see of the basic structure appeared to be intact. As for the cowboy trappings and the pub furniture, little remained that could by any stretch of the imagination be called serviceable. The tables and chairs had joined the patrons in making a rapid move towards the front door, but unlike those lucky personnel their desperate bid for escape had been halted by the front wall, where they lay heaped like the barricades of revolutionary Paris. Sawdust filled the air like a woody snowstorm, and in the middle of the floor, lacking most of his clothes but still bearing upon his head the charred remnants of a chef's hat, lay Young Master Robert. Neville patted away the sawdust from his shoulders and found to his amazement one lone optic full of whisky. This indeed had become a night he would long remember.

The now emboldened cowboys had risen from their shelters and were beating upon the Swan's door. Faces appeared at the glassless windows and inane cries of 'Are you all right?' and 'Is anybody there?' filled the smoky air.

Neville downed his scotch and climbed over the bar to inspect the fallen figure of the Young Master, who was showing some signs of life. The patrons finally broke into the bar and came to a crowded and silent standstill about the prone figure.

'He's all right, ain't he?' said Mandy. 'I mean he's still breathing, ain't he?' Neville nodded. 'Sandra's phoned for an ambulance and the fire brigade.'

A great dark mushroom cloud hung over the Flying Swan. The first brigade, who arrived in record time, on hearing that it was a pub fire, contented themselves with half-heartedly squirting an extinguisher over the blackened yard and salvaging what unbroken bottles of drink remained for immediate consumption. The ambulance driver asked sarcastically whether Neville wanted his home number in case of further calamities that evening.

When the appliances had finally departed, dramatically ringing their bells in the hope of waking any local residents who had slept through the blast, a grim and sorry silence descended upon the Flying Swan. The cowboys drifted away like western ghosts, and the onlookers who had been awakened by the excitement switched out their lights and returned to their beds.

Neville, Pooley, and John Omally were all who remained behind. Neville had brought down a couple of bottles of scotch from the private stock in his wardrobe. The three sat where they could in the ruined bar sipping at their drinks and contemplating the destruction.

'Heads will roll for this,' sighed Neville, 'mine in particular.'

Omally nodded thoughtfully. 'Still,' he said, 'at least we'll get that new bog roof now.'

'Thanks a lot,' said Neville.

'It was a good old do though, wasn't it,' said Jim. 'I don't suppose the brewery would be thinking of following it up at all? I mean maybe Hawaiian Night or a Merrie England festival or something?'

Neville grinned painfully. 'Somehow I doubt it.'

'You must sue that Hairy Dave,' John suggested. 'Him and his hirsute brother are a danger to life and limb.'

Neville opened the second bottle of scotch. 'Come to think of it,' he said, 'I don't recall any specifications for materials coming with that plan from the brewery.'

'Aha!' said John. 'Then all may not be lost.'

'The poor old Swan,' said Pooley. 'What a tragedy.'

'We've had fine times here,' said Omally.

'They'll ruin it you know,' said Neville, 'the brewery. Probably turn it into a discothèque or a steak house or something. There's nothing they like better than getting their hands on a piece of England's heritage and thoroughly crucifying it. It'll be fizzy beer and chicken in a basket, you wait and see.'

'We'll get up a petition,' said Jim. 'Brentonians won't stand for any of that.'

'Won't they though?' Neville nodded towards the broken front windows. 'Look there and what do you see?'

'Nothing, the lights of the flatblocks that's all.'

'Yes, the flatblocks. Fifteen years ago there was a whole community there, small pubs, corner-shops, the pottery, streets full of families that all knew each other.'

Jim nodded sadly. 'All gone now,' said he. The three men sipped silently at their drinks as the air grew heavy with nostalgic reminiscence.

Omally, always the realist, said, 'There's little use in sobbing about the good old days. When my family came over from the old country we moved into one of them little dens where the flats now stand. I can remember them sure enough. No hot water, no bath, outside toilet that froze in the winter, rats, bed-bugs, the children coughing with diphtheria, great old times they were. I'll tell you I cheered when the bulldozer pushed our old house down. Bloody good riddance I said.'

Jim smiled slightly. 'And if I remember rightly the bailiffs were still chasing your lot six months after for five years' back rent.'

Omally laughed heartily. ''Tis true,' said he, ''tis true enough, the daddy took the lot of them back home then, sure he did. Back to the land John, said he, there's a fortune to be made in the land. Mad as a hatter the daddy.'

'Is he still alive your da?' said Neville.

'Oh yes, he's that all right. I read not so long ago in the Dublin press of an old fella at eighty-six being named in a paternity suit by a sixteen-year-old convent girl, that would be the daddy right enough.'

'The Omallys are notable womanizers, that is for certain,' said Jim. 'There is many a well-pleased widow woman hereabouts who will testify to that.'

Omally smiled his winning smile. 'I would thank you to keep your indiscreet remarks to yourself, Jim Pooley,' said he. 'I am a man of the highest principles.'

'Ha,' said Jim as he recalled the spectacle of Omally's moonlit bum going about its hydraulic motions in Archroy's marriage-bed. 'You are an unprincipled bounder, but I am proud to call you friend.'

'You are both good men,' said Neville, a tear unexpectedly forming in his good eye. 'Friendship is a wonderful thing. Whatever the future holds for the Swan, I want you to know that it has always been my pleasure to serve you.'

'Come now,' said Jim, patting the part-time barman on the shoulder. 'There are great days ahead, of this I am certain.'

'Forgive me this sentiment,' said Neville, 'I am drunk.'

'Me also,' said John.

'I am still able to stand and must thus confess my sobriety,' said Jim, refilling his glass with the last of the whisky.

Some time later, two thoroughly drunken Lone Rangers, now somewhat shabby and lacking in hats and masks, were to be found wandering in the direction of the St Mary's Allotment. 'I have a little crop upon my pastures which you will find most satisfying,' the Irish Ranger told his staggering compadre. Jim was desperately hoping that the Irishman was not alluding to some supposed narcotic sproutings from the purloined bean.

The two arrived at the iron gate and stood before that rusting edifice, leaning upon one another for support. 'I've done a little deal,' grinned Omally, pulling at his lower eyelid in an obscene manner, and staggering forward into the silent allotment. It was another fine moonlit night and the old selenic disc sailed above in a cloudless sky. Long jagged shadows cast by bean poles, abandoned wheelbarrows, and heavily-padlocked allotment sheds etched stark patterns across the strangely whitened ground.

Omally's ambling silhouette lurched on ahead and vanished down into the dip before his plot. Jim, who had fallen to the ground upon his companion's sudden departure, climbed shakily to his feet, tightened his bandana against the crisp night air and stumbled after him.

When he reached Omally, he found the Irishman upon all fours grubbing about in the dirt. Happily he was some way from the spot where the magic bean had originally been buried.

'Aha,' said Omally suddenly, lifting a dusty bottle of Old Snakebelly into the moonlight. 'Ripe as ninepence.'

'Good show,' said Jim, collapsing on to his behind with a dull thud. The bottle was speedily uncorked and the two sat drawing upon it turn by turn, at peace with the world, and sharing Jim's last Woodbine. 'It's a great life though, isn't it?' said Jim, wiping the neck of the bottle upon his rented sleeve.

'It's that to be sure.'

Pooley leant back upon his elbows and stared up wistfully towards the moon. 'Sometimes I wonder,' said he.

'I know,' Omally broke in, 'sometimes you wonder if there are folk like us up there wondering if there are folk like them down here.'

'Exactly,' said Jim.

Suddenly, away into the darkness and coming apparently from the direction of the Mission's rear garden-wall, the two wonderers heard a heavy if muffled thump.

'Now what do you wonder that might be?' asked John.

'Truly I have no idea, give me a drag of that Woody.'

Omally passed Jim the cigarette and, taking the bottle, drained away a large portion of its contents. 'Probably a pussycat,' said he.

'Big one though.'

'Archroy told me he once saw a giant feral tom roaming the allotment by night, the size of a tiger he said.'

'Archroy as you well know is greatly subject to flights of fancy.'

'He seemed very sincere at the time, came rushing into the Swan and ordered a large brandy.'

Pooley shifted uncomfortably on his earthy seat, 'I should not wish to end my days as a pussycat's dinner,' said he. Without warning there was a second and slightly louder thump, which was followed almost immediately by the sound of scrambling feet. 'The monster moggy!' said Jim.

Omally threw himself down commando-fashion and crawled to the rim of the dip. Pooley snatched up a fallen farrowing fork and, draining the last of the bottle, stealthily followed him. Sounds of grunting and panting now drifted in their direction and followed by a distant 'squeak-squeak'.

'A giant mouse perhaps?' whispered Jim hoarsely.

'Don't be a damn fool,' Omally replied. 'There's only one thing around here makes a noise like that, my bloody wheelbarrow.'

'Ssh!' said Jim. 'It's coming nearer.' The two lay in silence, squinting lopsidedly into the gloom.

The indistinct form of a man appeared from the shadows. As it drew nearer both Pooley and Omally recognized the dark figure as that of the grizzled-chinned seafarer Captain Carson. He was dressed in a Royal Navy uniform and was pushing with some difficulty Omally's wheelbarrow, which was weighted down heavily by two large and strangely swollen potato sacks.

He was now but ten yards away and the two hidden Rangers caught sight of the Captain's face. It was a thing to inspire horror, the skin deathly-white and glowing hideously in the moon's septic light, the mouth turned down into an attitude of intense hatred, and the eyes glazed and lifeless.

Pooley shuddered and drew his Irish chum down as the wheelbarrow and its zombiesque operator passed them at close quarters. 'Something's not right here,' said John, straightening up upon creaking knee-joints, 'let's follow him.'

Jim was doubtful. 'It's home for me,' he said.

Omally cuffed his cowardly companion. 'That's my damn wheelbarrow,' he said. Ducking low and scurrying from one hiding place to another, the two thoroughly besmutted Rangers followed the ghastly figure with the squeaking wheelbarrow across the allotment.

'He's heading for the river,' said Jim breathlessly, still grasping the farrowing fork. From a little way ahead of them came the sounds of more straining followed by two loud splashes.

'I'd say he was there,' said John. There was a squeak or two, then another loud splash. 'He's dumped my barrow, the bastard!' wailed Omally.

Jim said, 'If you'll pardon me, John, I'll be off about my business.' He turned and blundered into a forest of bean poles.

'Duck, you fool,' whispered John, tripping over the struggling Pooley, 'he's coming back.'

The Captain appeared suddenly from the shadows of the riverside oaks. He surely must have seen the two fallen Rangers, yet his eyes showed no sign of recognition. Forward he came upon wooden legs, moving like a somnambulist, past the Rangers, and back off in the direction of the Mission.

'There's a bean pole stuck up my right trouser,' groaned Jim. 'Help, help, fallen man here!'

'Shut up you bally fool,' said John, flapping his arms and attempting to rise, 'look there.' Pooley raised himself as best he could and stared after John's pointing finger.

Away across the allotment a bright light shone from the Mission. Like a beacon it swept over their heads. For a fleeting moment they saw him, the silhouette of a huge man standing upon the Mission wall, his arms folded and his legs apart. Although the two saw him for only a brief second, the feeling of incontestable grandeur and of malevolent evil was totally overwhelming.

Omally crossed himself with a trembling hand.

Pooley said, 'I think I am going to be sick.'

14

The Flying Swan was closed for three weeks. The sun blazed down day after day, and there were all the makings of a Long Hot Summer. There was never a cloud in the sky, the boating pond in Gunnersbury Park was down a full six inches and the bed of the dried-up canal cracked and hardened into a sun-scorched jigsaw puzzle. As each evening came, the air, rather than growing blessedly cool, seemed to boil, making sleep impossible. Windows were permanently open, butter melted upon grocers' shelves and every kind of cooling apparatus gave up the ghost and ground to a standstill. The residents who nightly tilled their allotment patches watched sadly as their crops shrivelled and died. No amount of daily watering could save them, and the press had announced that water rationing was likely.

When the Swan reopened it was with little ceremony. Nothing much seemed to have changed, some portions of the bar had been half-heartedly repainted, and the gents' toilet had been rebuilt. Neville stood in his usual position, polishing the glasses and occasionally dabbing at his moist brow. It was as if Cowboy Night had never taken place.

The beer pulls had been returned to their places upon the bar, but only three of them were fully functional. 'I put it down to vindictiveness upon the part of the brewery,' he told Omally.

'Good to see you back though,' said the Irishman, pushing the exact money across the counter and indicating his usual.

'That one's still off,' said Neville. 'And the beer's up a penny a pint.'

Omally sighed dismally. 'These are tragic times we live in,' said he. 'A half of light ale then.'

*

Archroy sat alone upon the sun-scorched allotment, his head gleaming like the dome of an Islamic mosque. His discarded wig hung upon the handle of a rake in the fashion of a trophy before the lodge of a great chief. Evil thoughts were brewing in Archroy's polished cranium. It had not been his year at all; first the loss of his cherished automobile, and then the disappearance of his magic beans, the decimation of his tomato crop, and now the aviary. The aviary! Archroy twisted broodingly at the dried stalk of what had been a promising tomato plant and hunched his shoulders in utter despair.

Things could not continue as they were. One of them would have to go, and the accursed aviary looked a pretty permanent affair. Three weeks in the construction and built after the design of Lord Snowdon's famous bird-house, the thing towered in his back garden, overshadowing the kitchen and darkening his bedroom. Its presence had of course inspired the usual jocularity from his workmates, who had dubbed him 'the bird man of Brentford'.

So far the monstrous cage had remained empty, but Archroy grew ever more apprehensive when he contemplated the kind of feathered occupants his wife was planning to house within its lofty environs. He lived in perpetual dread of that knock upon the door which would herald the delivery of a vanload of winged parasites. 'I'll do away with myself,' said Archroy. 'That will show them all I mean business.' He twisted the last crackling fibres from the ruined tomato stalk and threw them into the dust. 'Something dramatic, something spectacular that all the world will take notice of, I'll show them.'

Captain Carson sat huddled under a heavy blanket in the old steamer chair on the Mission's verandah. His eyes stared into the shimmering heat, but saw nothing. At intervals his head bobbed rhythmically, as if in time to some half-forgotten sea shanty. From inside the Mission poured the sounds of industry. For on this afternoon, and in the all-conquering heat which none could escape, great changes were taking place. Timber was being sawn, hammers wielded and chisels manfully employed. The metallic reports of cold chisel upon masonry rang into the super-heated air, the splintering of wormy laths and the creaking of uplifted floorboards. Major reconstruction work was in progress and was being performed apparently with robotic tirelessness.

Hairy Dave swung the five-pound club hammer wildly in the direction of the Victorian marble fireplace. The polished steel of the hammer's head glanced across the polished mantel, raising a shower of sparks and burying itself in the plaster of the wall. Normally such an event would have signalled the summary 'down tools and repair to the alehouse lads', but Dave merely spat upon his palm and withdrew the half-submerged instrument of labour for another attempt. His thickly-bearded brother stood upon a trestle, worrying at a length of picture-rail with a crowbar. Neither man spoke as he went about his desperate business; here was none of the endless banter, cigarette swopping, and merry whistling one associated with these two work-shy reprobates; here was only hard graft, manual labour taken to an extreme and terrifying degree.

The long hot summer's day wore on, drawing itself into a red raw evening, which turned to nightfall with a sunset that would have made the most cynical of men raise his eyes in wonder. Jim Pooley stirred from his hypnotic slumbers upon the Memorial Library bench and rose to his feet, scratching at his stomach and belching loudly. The gnawing within his torso told him that he was in need of sustenance and the evening sky told the ever-alert Jim that day had drawn to a close.

He found his cigarette packet lodged in the lining of his aged tweed jacket. One lone Woody revealed itself. 'Times be hard,' said Jim to no one in particular. He lit his final cigarette and peered up at the sprinkling of stars. 'I wonder,' said he. 'I wonder what Professor Slocombe is up to.'

With the coming of the tropical summer naught had been seen of the learned ancient upon the streets of Brentford. His daily perambulation about the little community's boundaries had ceased. Pooley tried to think when he had last seen the elderly Professor and realised that it was more than a month ago, on the night of his valiant deed.

'The old fellow is probably suffering something wicked with the heat,' he told himself, 'and would be grateful for an evening caller to relieve the tedium of the sultry hours.'

Pleased with the persuasiveness of this reasoning, Pooley drew deeply upon his cigarette, blew a great gust of milk-white smoke into the air, and crossed the carless road towards the Professor's house.

The Butts Estate hovered timelessly in its splendour. The tall Georgian house-fronts gleamed whitely in the moonlight, and the streetlamps threw stark shadows into the walled courtyards and guarded alley entrances.

Hesperus, the first star of evening, winked down as Pooley, hands in pockets, rounded the corner by the Professor's house. The garden gate was ajar and Pooley slipped silently between the ivy-hung walls. A light glowed ahead, coming from the open French windows, and Jim gravitated towards it, thoughts of the Professor's sherry spurring him on.

It was as he reached the open windows that the sounds first reached him. Pooley halted, straining his ears, suddenly alert to a subtle unidentifiable strangeness, a curious rustling from within, a scratching, clawing sound, agitated and frantic.

Pooley reached out a cautious hand towards the net curtain, and as he did so heard the scrabbling sounds increase in urgency and agitation.

There was a sudden movement, firm fingers fastened about his wrist and he was hauled forward with one deft jerk which lifted him from his feet and sent him bowling across the carpet in an untidy tangle of tweed. With a resounding thud, the tumbling Pooley came to rest beneath one of the Professor's ponderous bookcases.

'Mercy!' screamed Jim, covering his head. 'James Pooley here, pacifist and friend to all.'

'Jim, my dear fellow, my apologies.'

Jim peered up warily through his fingers. 'Professor?' said he.

'I am so sorry, I was expecting someone else.'

'Some welcome,' said Jim.

The ancient helped the fallen Pooley to his feet and escorted him to one of the cosy fireside chairs. He poured a glass of scotch, which Pooley took in willing hands.

'That was a nifty blow you dealt me there,' said Jim.

'Dimac,' said the elder. 'A crash course via the mail-order tuition of the notorious Count Dante.'

'I have heard of him,' said Jim, 'deadliest man on earth they say.'

The Professor chewed at his lip. 'Would it were so,' said he, in an ominous tone.

Pooley downed his scotch and cast his eyes about the Professor's study. 'A noise,' he said. 'As I stood at the windows, I heard a noise.'

'Indeed?'

'A scratching sound.' Pooley lifted himself upon his elbows and peered about. All seemed as ever: the clutter of thaumaturgical books, bizarre relics, and brass-cogged machinery. But there in the very centre of the room, set upon a low dais which stood within a chalk-drawn pentagram, was a glass case covered with what appeared to be an altar cloth. 'Hamsters?' said Jim. 'Or gerbils is it? Nasty smelly wee things.'

Pooley rose to investigate but the Professor restrained him with a firm and unyielding hand. Jim marvelled at the ancient's newly-acquired strength. 'Do not look, Jim,' the Professor said, dramatically, 'you would not care for what you saw.'

'Hamsters hold little fear for the Pooleys,' said Jim.

'Tell me,' said the Professor. 'What unlikely adventures have befallen you since our last encounter?'

'Now you are asking,' said Jim, and between frequent re-fillings of scotch he told the chuckling Professor of the excitements and diversions of Cowboy Night at the Flying Swan.

The Professor wiped at his eyes. 'I heard the explosion, of course.' Here the old man became suddenly sober. 'There were other things abroad that night, things which are better not recalled or even hinted at.'

Pooley scratched at his ear. 'Omally and I saw something that night, or thought we did, for we had both consumed a preposterous amount of good old Snakebelly.'

The Professor leant forward in his chair and fixed Jim with a glittering stare. 'What did you see?' he asked in a voice of dire urgency which quite upset the sensitive Pooley.

'Well.' Pooley paused that his glass might be refilled. 'It was a strange e one, this I know.' Jim told his tale as best he could remember, recalling with Gothic intensity the squeaking wheelbarrow and its mysterious cargo, and the awesome figure upon the mission wall.

'And the bright light, had you ever seen anything like it before?'

'Never, nor wish to again.'

The Professor smiled.

'Omally crossed himself,' said Jim. 'And I was taken quite poorly.'

'Ah,' said the Professor. 'It is all becoming clearer by the hour. Now I have a more vivid idea of what we are dealing with.'

'I am glad somebody does,' said Jim, rattling his empty glass upon the arm of the chair. 'It's the wheelbarrow I feel sorry for.'

'Jim,' said the Professor, rising from his seat and crossing slowly to the French windows, where he stood gazing into the darkness. 'Jim, if I were to confide in you my findings, could I rely on your complete discretion?'

'Of course.'

'That is easily said, but this would be a serious vow, no idle chinwagging.' The Professor's tone was of such leaden seriousness that Jim hesitated a moment, wondering whether he would be better not knowing, whatever it was. But as usual his natural curiosity got the upper hand and with the simple words, 'I swear', he irrevocably sealed his fate.

'Come then, I will show you!' The Professor strode to the covered glass case and as he did so the frantic scrabbling arose anew. Jim refilled his glass and rose unsteadily to join his host.

'I should have destroyed them, I know,' said the Professor, a trace of fear entering his voice. 'But I am a man of science, and to feel that one might be standing upon the brink of discovery ...' With a sudden flourish, he tore the embroidered altar cloth from the glass case, revealing to Jim's horrified eyes a sight that would haunt his sleeping hours for years to come.

Within the case, pawing at the glazed walls, were frantically moving creatures: five hideous manlike beings, six to eight inches in height. They were twisted as the gnarled roots of an ancient oak, yet in the 'heads' of them, rudimentary mouths opened and closed. Slime trickled from their ever-moving orifices and down over their shimmering knobbly forms.

Jim drew back in outraged horror and gagged into his hands. The Professor uttered a phrase of Latin and replaced the cloth. The frantic scratchings ceased as rapidly as they had begun.

Pooley staggered back to his chair where he sat, head in hands, sweat running free from his forehead. 'What are they?' he said, his voice almost a sob. 'Why do you have them here?'

'You brought them here. They are Phaseolus Satanicus, and they await their master.'

'I will have nothing of this.' Pooley dragged himself from his seat and staggered to the window. He had come here for a bite to eat, not to be assailed with graveyard nastiness, he would leave the Professor to his horrors. Jim halted in his flight. A strange sensation entered his being, as if voices called to him from the dim past, strange voices speaking in archaic accents hardly recognisable yet urgent, urgent with the fears of unthinkable horrors lurking on the very edges of darkling oblivion.

Pooley stumbled, his hands gripping at the curtain, tearing it from its hooks. Behind him the scrabbling and scratching rose with the awful sounds. As Pooley fell he saw before him, standing in the gloom of the night garden, a massive brooding figure. It was clad in crimson and glowing with a peculiar light. The head was lost in shadows, but beneath the heavy brows two bright red eyes glowed wolfishly.

When Pooley awoke he was lying sprawled across the Professor's *chaise longue*, an icepack upon his head, and the hellish reek of ammonia strong in his nostrils.

'Jim.' A voice came to him out of the darkness. 'Jim.' Pooley brought his eyes into focus and made out the willowy form of the elderly Professor, screwing the cap on a bottle of smelling salts. He offered the half-conscious Jim yet another glass of scotch, which the invalid downed with a practised flick of the wrist. Now fully alert, Pooley jerked his head in the direction of the window. 'Where is he?' he said, tearing the icepack from his forehead. 'I saw him out there.'

The Professor sank into a high-backed Windsor chair. 'Then he did come, I knew he would.'

The first rays of sunlight were falling through the still-open, though now curtainless, French windows. 'Here,' said Pooley 'what time is it?' As if in answer, the ormolu mantel clock struck five times. 'I've been out for hours,' said Jim, holding his head, 'and I do not feel at all well.'

'You had best go home to your bed,' said the Professor. 'Come again tonight and we will speak of these things.'

'No,' said Pooley, taking a Turkish cigarette from the polished humidor. Through force of habit he furtively thrust several more into his top pocket. 'I must know of these things now.'

'As you will.' The Professor smiled darkly and drew a deep breath. 'You will recall the evening when you first came to me with that single bean. You saw my reaction when I first observed it, and when later that night you brought me the other four I knew that my suspicions were justified.'

'Suspicions?'

'That the Dark One was already among us.'

Pooley lit his cigarette and collapsed into an immediate fit of coughing. 'The Dark One?' he spluttered between convulsions. 'Who in the name of the holies is the Dark One?'

The Professor shrugged. 'If I knew exactly who he was, Jim, our task would be simpler. The Dark One has existed since the dawn of time, he may take many forms and live many lives. We are lucky in one respect only, that we have observed his arrival. It is our duty to precipitate his end.'

'I know of no Dark One,' said Jim. 'Although I do remember that several months ago the arrival of a mouldy-looking tramp caused a good degree of speculation within the saloon-bar of the Flying Swan, although in truth I never saw this dismal wanderer myself.'

The Professor nodded. 'You have seen him twice, once upon the allotments and again this very night within my own garden.'

'Nah,' said Pooley. 'That was no tramp I saw.'

'I am certain there is a connection,' said the Professor. 'All the signs are here. I have watched them for months, gathering like a storm about to break. The time, I fear, is close at hand.'

Jim sniffed suspiciously at his Turkish cigarette. 'Are these lads all right?' said he. 'Only they smell somewhat doubtful.'

'You are still a young man, Jim,' said the Professor. 'I cannot expect you to take altogether seriously all that I say, but I swear to you that we are dealing with forces which will not be defeated by simply being ignored.'

Jim glanced distastefully towards the covered glass case. 'You can hardly ignore those,' said he.

'By fire and water only may they be destroyed,' said the Professor. 'By fire and water and the holy word.'

Pooley pulled at his sideburns. 'I'll put a match to the blighters,' he said valiantly.

'It is not as simple as that, it never is. These beans are the symptom, not the cause. To destroy them now would be to throw away the only hope we have of locating the evil force which brought them here.'

'I don't like the sound of this "we" you keep referring to,' said Jim.

'I want you to tell me, Jim, everything you have heard about this tramp. Every rumour, every story, anything that might give us a clue as to his motives, his power, and his weaknesses.'

Pooley's stomach made an unmentionable sound. 'Professor,' said he, 'I would be exceedingly grateful for some breakfast, I have not eaten for twenty-four hours. I am feeling a trifle peckish.'

'Of course.' The Professor rang the bell which summoned his musty servant. Presently a fine breakfast of heated rolls, eggs, bacon, tomatoes, coffee, and toast appeared and Pooley set about it with ravenous zeal.

For the next hour thereafter Jim spoke of all he had heard regarding the mystery tramp, from Neville's first encounter to Norman's terrifying experiences in the Plume Café, and of the welter of theories, conjectures, and speculations which had been rife in the Swan. He spoke of Soap Distant's talk of the Hollow Earth, omitting his own experiences within the mysterious subterranean world, and of Omally's fairy ramblings, and of those folk who held the belief that the tramp was the Wandering Jew.

The old Professor listened intently, occasionally raising his snowy eyebrow or shaking his head until, finally, Jim's tale had run its course. 'Fascinating,' he said at length, 'quite fascinating. And you say that all those who had any personal dealings with this tramp felt an uncanny need to cross themselves?'

'As far as I can make out. But you must understand that a lot of what I have told you was heard second-hand as it were. Nobody around here gives away much if they can possibly help it.'

'So much I know.'

'And so, what is to be done?'

'I think at present there is little we can do. We must be constantly on watch. Report to me with any intelligence, no matter how vague, which comes to hand. I will prepare myself as best I can, both mentally and physically. Our man is close, that is certain. You have seen him. I can sense his nearness and it is likewise with the creatures in the case. Soon he will come for them and when he does so, we must be ready.' Pooley reached out a hand towards the humidor.

'Why don't you have one of the ones in your top pocket?' asked the old Professor, smiling broadly.

15

Pooley sat that lunchtime alone in a corner-seat at the Flying Swan, a half of pale ale growing warm before him. He sighed deeply. All that the Professor had said weighed heavily on his soul, and he wondered what should be done for the best. He thought he should go around to the Mission and confront Captain Carson regarding what Holmes would have referred to as 'the singular affair of the purloined wheelbarrow', which was something he and Omally should really have done the very next day. But the Captain's animosity towards visitors was well-known to all thereabouts, especially to Jim, who had once been round there to scrounge a bed for the night and had been run off with a gaff hook. Anyway, it was Omally's wheelbarrow and if he chose to forget the matter that was up to him.

Maybe, he thought, it would be better for the Professor simply to hand over the bean things to this Dark One, whoever he might be, in the hope that he would depart with them, never to return. But that was no good. Pooley had felt the evil and he knew that the Professor was right. It would not go away by being ignored. Pooley sighed anew. A bead of perspiration rolled down the end of his nose and dropped into his ale.

Archroy entered the Flying Swan. Pooley had not seen him for some weeks; he had been strangely absent from the Cowboy Night fiasco. Jim wondered in which direction his suspicions pointed in the matter of the stolen beans. 'He doesn't know how lucky he is,' he thought.

Archroy, however, looked far from lucky upon this particular occasion. His shoulders drooped and his lopsided hairpiece clung perilously to his shining pate. Pooley watched him from the corner of his eye. He could not recall ever having seen anybody looking so

depressed, and wondered whether the sorry specimen might appreciate a few kind words. For the life of him Jim couldn't think of any.
Archroy looked up from the pouring of his ale and sighted Pooley,
nodded in half-hearted greeting, and sank back into his misery.

Pooley looked up through the pub windows. The flatblocks
quivered mirage-like in the heat and a bedraggled pigeon or two
fluttered away into the shimmering haze. The heat strangled the
bar-room air; everything moved in slow motion. Except Father
Moity, resident priest to St Joan's, Brentford, who unexpectedly
entered the bar at this moment. He strode towards the bar, oblivious
to the battering heat, and ordered a small sherry. Neville poured
this and noted that the priest made no motions towards his pocket
upon accepting same. 'You are far from your cool confessional
upon such a hot day,' said Neville cynically.

'Now, now, Neville,' said the priest, raising his blessing finger in
admonishment. 'I have come to seek out two members of my flock
who seem to have fallen upon stony ground.' Pooley much enjoyed
listening to the young priest, whose endless supply of inaccurate
quotation was a joy to the ear. 'Two prodigal sons who have sold
their birthrights for a mess of porridge.' Pooley chuckled. 'You
know them as Hairy Dave and Jungle John.'

'They're barred!' said Neville with a voice like thunder.

'Barred is it? And what pestilence have they visited upon you on
this occasion?'

'They blew my bloody pub up.'

'Anarchists is it?'

'Bloody maniacs!' said Neville bitterly.

'Raise not thine hand in anger,' said the priest, bringing his
blessing finger once more into play.'How many times shall I forgive
my brother? Seven isn't it? I say unto you seven hundred times
seven, or some such figure.'

'Well they are barred and they stay barred!'

'Tsk, tsk!' said the priest. 'It is because of bars that I find myself
here, a lamb amongst wolves.'

'And how is the bar of your Catholic Club?' asked Neville sarcastically. 'Still doing a roaring trade with its cut-price drinks and
taking the bread of life from the mouths of hardworking publicans?'

'Judge not, lest thyself be judged,' said the priest. 'The bars I
refer to are of the gymnastical variety.'

Keeping fit was an obsession with Father Moity which verged at times upon the manic. He was forever jogging to and fro about the parish; as Pooley watched the young priest he noted the giveaway track-suit bottoms and striped running shoes peeping from beneath his robes of office. He did chin-ups in the vestry, calisthenics in the pulpit, and had developed a system of Tai-Chi exercises to correspond with the ritual movements of the mass. Even as Pooley observed him at the bar, the young priest was flexing his biceps and doing the occasional knees-bend.

None of these things went unnoticed, and the handsome, tanned, and manly figure of the priest raised extraordinary feelings within the breasts of both matronly females and young housewives alike. He had become a focus for their erotic desires. Confession became a nightmare. Even women of well-known and obvious virginity confided to the handsome young priest their nights of passion in the satyric embraces of demonic succubi. Father Moity marvelled at their invention, but more often he covered his ears and allowed his mind to wander. Consequently his penances were likely to be 'three Hail Marys and a hundred press-ups' or 'an Our Father and a work-out on the heavy bag.'

'Gymnasium bars,' the young priest continued, 'for the church hall. I was promised that they would be constructed before the Olympic trials came on the television; I wish to take a few pointers.'

'Well I haven't seen them,' sneered Neville, 'and I have no wish to.'

Father Moity said nothing but peered into his empty sherry glass and then about the bar. 'Jim Pooley,' he said, his eyes alighting upon that very man.

'Father?'

'Jim, my lad.' The priest bounced across the bar and joined Pooley at his table. 'Would you by any chance have seen those two local builders upon your travels?'

'I have not,' said Jim, 'but Father, I would have a few words with you if I may.'

'Certainly.' The priest seated himself, placing the empty sherry glass noisily upon the table. It vastly amused Pooley that even a priest of such Olympian leanings was not averse to a couple of free sherries. Pooley obliged and the young priest thanked him graciously.

'Firstly,' said Jim, in a confidential tone, 'I have been given to understand that Hairy Dave and Jungle John were doing a great deal more construction work for you than a set of gymnasium bars. I heard mention of an entire chapel or the like being built.'

'Did you now?' The young priest seemed genuinely baffled. 'Well I know nothing of that. Chapel, is it?'

'I took it to be R C, because the plans were in Latin.'

The priest laughed heartily. 'Sure you are taking the rise out of me, Jim Pooley, although the joke is well appreciated. The Church has not drawn up its plans in Latin since the fifteenth century.'

Jim shrugged and sniffed at his steaming beer. 'Stranger and stranger,' said he.

'Strange, is it?' said the priest. 'It is indeed strange that those lads downed tools last Thursday night and never returned to be paid for what they had so far accomplished, for those fellows that I could call strange.'

Jim sighed once more. Something was going on in Brentford and it seemed not only he was involved. 'Father,' said Jim with a terrible suddenness, 'what do you know of evil?'

The priest raised his fine dark eyebrows and stared at Pooley in wonder. 'That my son, is a most unexpected question.'

'I mean real evil,' said Pooley, 'not petty getting off the bus without paying evil, or the sin of pride or anger or minor trivial forms of evil, I mean real pure dark evil, the creeping sinister evil which lurks at the corners of men's minds, the low horrible . . .'

The priest broke in upon him. 'Come now,' said he, 'these are not fine things to talk of on a hot summer's day, all things bright and beautiful as they are.'

Pooley studied the honest face of the young priest. What could he know of real evil? Nothing whatever, Jim concluded.

'My son,' said Father Moity, noting well Pooley's disturbed expression, 'what is troubling you?'

Pooley smiled unconvincingly. 'Nothing,' he said, 'just musing I suppose. Of Dave and John, I have seen nothing. Possibly they drink now at the New Inn or Jack Lane's. I should try there if I were you.'

The priest thanked Jim, wished him all of God's blessing for the balance of the day and jogged from the bar.

Pooley returned to his melancholic reverie. When Neville called time at three he left the bar, his half of light ale still steaming in its glass, and shambled out into the glare. He wandered off down Sprite Street and crossed beside his beloved Memorial bench to enter the sweeping tree-lined drive which curved in a graceful arc towards the Butts Estate. He passed within a few yards of the Professor's front door and crunched over the gravel footway before the Seamen's Mission, to emerge through the tiny passageway into the lower end of the High Street near the canal bridge.

As he leant upon the parapet, squinting along the dried-up stretch of ex-waterway into the shimmering distance, Pooley's thoughts were as parched and lifeless as the blistered canal bed. He wondered what had become of Soap Distant. Had he been blasted to dark and timeless oblivion by the flood tide which engulfed him? Or had the rank waters carried him deep into the inner earth where even now he swapped drinking stories with old Rigdenjyepo and the denizens of that sunless domain? He wondered at Archroy's misery, and at what urgent business might have lured Hairy Dave and his hirsute twin from their Friday payment at St Joan's.

Pooley tried to marshal his thoughts into some plan of campaign, but the sun thrashed down relentlessly upon his curly head and made him feel all the more dizzy and desperate. He would repair to the Plume Café for a cup of char, that would invigorate and refresh, that was the thing, the old cup that cheers. Pooley dragged his leathern elbows from the red-hot parapet and plodded off up the High Street.

The door of the Plume was wedged back and a ghastly multi-coloured slash curtain hung across the opening. Pooley thrust the gaudy plastic strips apart and entered the café. The sudden transition from dazzling sunlight to shadowy gloom left him momentarily blind, and he clung to a cheap vinyl chair for support.

Lily Marlene lurked within, fanning her abundant mammaries with a menu card, and cooling her feet in a washbowl of iced water. She noted Pooley's entrance without enthusiasm. 'We still give no credit, Jim Pooley.'

Pooley's eyes adjusted themselves, and he replied cheerfully, if unconvincingly, 'I return from foreign parts, my pockets abulge with golden largesse of great value.'

'It's still sixpence a cup,' the dulcet voice returned, 'or eight pence for a coffee.'

'Tea will be fine,' said Pooley, producing two threepenny bits from his waistcoat pocket.

The grey liquid flowed from the ever-bubbling urn into the chipped white cup, and Pooley bore his steaming prize to a window-table. Other than Jim the café contained but a single customer. His back was turned and his shoulders hunched low over his chosen beverage, but the outline of the closely-cropped head was familiar. Jim realised that he was in close proximity to the semi-mythical entity known as the Other Sam.

Strange rumours abounded regarding this bizarre personage, who was reputed to live the life of a recluse somewhere within an uncharted region of the Royal Botanical Garden at Kew. Exactly who he was or where he came from was uncertain. It was said that he rowed nightly across the Thames in a coracle of ancient design to consort with Vile Tony Watkins, who ran the yellow street-cleaning cart, a grim conveyance which moved mysteriously through the lamplit byways.

Vile Tony was an uncommunicative vindictive, with an ingrained distrust of all humanity, and a dispassionate hatred for anything that walked upon two legs and held its head aloft during the hours of sunlight. Being a deaf-mute he kept his own counsel no matter what should occur.

Pooley had never spoken with the Other Sam, but felt a certain strange comfort in the knowledge of his being. The stories which surrounded him were uniformly weird and fantastical. He was the last of a forgotten race, some said; daylight would kill him, some said, for his eyes had never seen it. Others said that during her pregnancy his mother had observed something which had gravely affected her, and that the midwife upon seeing the child had dropped it in horror, whereupon the tiny creature had scampered from the room and disappeared into the night.

Pooley the realist pooh-poohed such notions, but Pooley the mystic, dreamer, and romantic sensed the aura of pagan mystery which surrounded the crop-headed man.

'Will you not join me at table, James Pooley,' said a voice which weakened Jim's bladder in a manner that formerly only large libations of ale had been able to do. 'I would have words with you.'

Pooley rose from his chair and slowly crossed the mottled linoleum floor of the Plume, wondering whether a leg-job might be preferable to a confrontation that most of Brentford's population would have taken great lengths to avoid.

'Be seated, James.' The face which met Jim's guarded glance was hardly one to inspire horror; it was pale, such as to be expected of one who dwelt in darkness, but it was a face which held an indefinable grandeur, an ancient nobility. 'Your thoughts press heavily upon me, James Pooley,' said the Other Sam.

'I do not know which way to turn,' said Jim. 'Such responsibilities are beyond my scope.'

The Other Sam nodded sagely and Jim knew that he had nothing to fear from the pale-blue eyes and the haunting thoughts which dwelt behind them. 'The evil is among us,' said the Other Sam, 'I will help you as best I may, but my powers are limited and I am no match for such an adversary.'

'Tell me what I should do.'

'The Professor is a man who may be trusted,' said the Other Sam. 'Act upon his instructions to the letter, accept no other advice, although much will be offered, follow your own feelings. The Dark One is vulnerable, he lives a life of fear, even Satan himself can never rest; Truth will be for ever the final victor.'

'But who is he?' said Jim. 'I have been plunged into all this. Outside the sun shines, in offices clerks toil away at their mundane duties, buses rumble towards Ealing Broadway, and I am expected to do battle with the powers of darkness. It all seems a little unfair.'

'You are not alone, James.'

'I feel rather alone.'

The Other Sam smiled wanly; wisdom shone in his ageless blue eyes. Professor Slocombe was a wise and learned man, but here was knowledge not distilled from musty tomes, but born of natural lore. Pooley felt at peace; he was no longer alone, he would cope with whatever lay ahead.

'I have stayed too long already,' said the Other Sam, 'and I must take my leave. I will not be far when you need me again. Take heart, James Pooley, you have more allies than you might imagine.'

With this he rose, a pale ghost who did not belong to the hours of daylight, and drifted out into the sunlit street where he was presently lost from view behind the gasometers.

Pooley took his teacup to his mouth, but the insipid grey liquid had grown cold. 'Cold tea and warm beer,' said Jim, 'and they say an army marches on its stomach.'

16

As August turned into September the residents of Brentford stared from their open windows and marvelled at the endless sunshine. Norman tapped at his thermometer and noted to his despair that it was up another two degrees. 'It's the end of the world for certain,' he said for the umpteenth time. 'I am working at present on an escape ship,' he told Omally. 'I am not going to be caught napping when the continents begin to break up.'

'I wish you luck,' replied Omally. 'I notice that there are no new Fine Arts Publications in your racks.'

'Business has fallen off of late.'

'Oh,' said John, 'must be the heat.'

'I hear,' said Norman, 'that the rising temperatures have started something of a religious revival hereabouts.'

'Oh?' said Omally, thumbing through a dog-eared copy of *Latex Babes*.

'The Church of the Second Coming, or suchlike, seems to be taking the ladies' fancy, although' – and here Norman's thoughts drifted back to his own bitter experiences as a married man – 'one can never expect much common sense from women.'

John's eyes rested upon the full-colour photograph of a voluptuous young female in leather corsets and thigh boots, wielding a riding crop. 'They have their uses,' he said lecherously. 'Can I borrow this magazine?'

'No,' said Norman.

'And where is this Church of the Second Coming then?'

'I've no idea,' said Norman. 'News of it apparently travels by word of mouth. The ladies I have questioned have been loud in their praises for the place but reticent about its location.'

'Oh?' said John. 'I'll bring this back in half an hour.'

'No,' said Norman, 'it is well known that you photostat them at the library and sell the copies in the Swan.'

'Merely satisfying a need,' said John. 'Your prices are too high.'

'Get out of my shop!' said Norman, brandishing a lemonade bottle. Omally made a rapid and undignified departure.

As he tramped up the Ealing Road towards the Flying Swan, John's thoughts turned back towards the Church of the Second Coming. Hard times always brought out the religion in people, and this long hot summer with its rationed water and rising temperatures was enough to set the nervous and susceptible legging it towards the nearest church. There was a good deal of money to be had in that game, and after all one was serving the community by fulfilling a need. Any rewards could be said to be of a just nature. It was a thought, and not a bad one. By the time he reached the Flying Swan his mind was made up. He would seek out the Church of the Second Coming and insinuate himself into a position of responsibility. He would gain respect and prestige, might even become a pillar of the community.

Yes, Omally could feel the call of the mother-church, he was by now completely certain that he had a true vocation. He pushed wide the saloon-bar door and entered the Flying Swan.

'God save all here,' he said, 'and mine's a pint of Large please, Neville.'

The part-time barman did the business and counted Omally's coinage into his hand. 'It's gone up another penny,' he told the Irishman.

Omally smiled pleasantly and produced the coin. 'How are things with your good self, barlord?' he said. 'It is another beautiful day is it not?'

'It is not.'

'Makes one feel good to be alive.'

'It does not.'

'God is in his heaven and all is right . . .'

'Turn it in, Omally.'

'Just remarking upon the splendours of creation.'

'Well, do it elsewhere.'

Omally removed himself to a side-table where Old Pete sat leaning upon his stick, his dog, Young Chips, belly up before him.

'Good day to you Pete,' said John, seating himself. 'It is another beautiful day is it not? I thank God to be alive.'

Old Pete spat in the direction of the cuspidor, which was the last relic of Cowboy Night, having been retained owing to its overwhelming popularity. 'You should take to the wearing of a hat, Omally,' said he. 'The harsh sun has befuddled your brain. I have an old homburg I might sell you.'

'God is in his heaven,' said Omally.

Pete was lining up for another shot at the cuspidor. 'A pox on God,' said the surly old bastard.

It was clear, thought Omally, that the joys of the Church of the Second Coming had not yet made themselves manifest to the barstaff and patrons of the Flying Swan. A more direct approach was in order.

'Don't you ever go to church, Pete?' he enquired.

'Never,' said the ancient. 'I have a straw boater if you don't fancy the homburg.'

'Listen,' said Omally, who was rapidly losing his patience. 'Just because I feel the need to extol the glories of God for once it doesn't follow that I'm heading for a padded cell in St Bernard's.'

'Glories of God?' said Old Pete in a sarcastic tone. 'You are an ungodly womaniser, Omally, with about as much religious inclination as Young Chips here.'

'Ah,' said Omally. 'That may have once been true but I have seen the light. I am mending my ways.'

'I have a very inexpensive cloth cap I might let you have.'

'I don't want a bloody cloth cap.'

'Go down to Father Moity's then.'

'No,' said Omally, 'I need to find a church of a new denomination, one which would offer an honest God-fearing man a chance to be at peace with himself and his maker.' Young Chips made one of those unholy noises he was noted for and his elderly master chuckled maliciously.

'I can see I am wasting my time here,' said John. 'A seeker after truth is not welcome hereabouts, a prophet is without honour in his own land so he is.'

'Listen,' said Old Pete. 'If you really feel the need for something a bit different in the religious line, why don't you go down to the Church of the Second Coming. I hear they have rare old times down there.'

Omally pricked up his ears. All this waste of breath and he might just as well have asked the old fellow straight out. 'Church of the Second Coming?' said he. 'I don't think I've heard of that one.'

'Well, all I know is that two old dears were talking about the place in the supermarket. Seems that there's some sort of New Messiah fellow started up in business, very popular with the ladies he is.'

'And where is this church to be found?'

'Search me,' said Old Pete. 'I didn't overhear that.'

What Omally said next was a phrase in Gaelic which his father had taught him when still a lad for use against the Black and Tans.

'And you,' said Old Pete as Young Chips set about the Irishman's trouser bottoms. He might not have much religious inclination, that dog, but he did speak fluent Gaelic.

Omally shook the mutt free from his ankles and finished his drink at the bar. He began to understand how saints came to get martyred. It wasn't all tea and crumpets with the vicar, this getting into the church. And then a pleasant thought struck him: amongst the many ladies of his acquaintance there must surely be one who had taken up within the new church, and even if there wasn't it would be a pleasure finding out.

Omally took out his little black book and thumbed at the pages Where to start? A for Archroy's missus. He would pay her a visit that very night.

'Another pint please, Neville,' said the Irishman jovially, 'and to hell with the extra penny.'

Archroy stood in his back garden, gazing up at the colossal mesh-covered construction which all but engulfed the entire yard. The deafening chatter of a thousand gaily-coloured birds filled his ears.

Archroy's worst fears had been realized that very morning when the dreaded lorry had arrived, bearing the exotic cargo which now flapped and twittered before him. He had never seen birds quite like them before, nor had he seen such a lorry, black as death and seemingly without windows. And the driver – Archroy shuddered. Where did his wife meet these people?

There must be a thousand of them in there, thought Archroy, peering into the cage. The din was appalling, the neighbours weren't going to like this one. Mrs Murdock appeared at the garden fence, a bundle of limp washing in her arms and a clothes-peg in her mouth. 'Lovely, aren't they?' she mumbled. 'Just what this neighbourhood needs to brighten it up.'

'You *like* them?' Archroy shouted.

Mrs M. nodded enthusiastically. 'Them's lovely.'

Archroy shook his head in wonder; the whole neighbourhood was going mad. It must be the heat.

'I'll bring them out some breadcrumbs,' said Mrs Murdock, oblivious to the row. 'They'll like them.'

'Better tell the bakery to staff up its night shift then,' muttered Archroy. What *did* they eat? He leant forward upon the mesh and squinted at the mass of fluttering feathers. As if in answer to his question a single bird detached itself from the ever-circling throng and swooped down upon him, removing with one deft peck a goodly lump of flesh from his right thumb.

'Damn you!' shrieked Archroy, drawing back in anguish. Blood flowed from the wound and through it he could glimpse the ivory-whiteness of exposed bone. 'Oh my God,' wailed Archroy, coming over faint. 'Oh my God.'

He staggered back into the kitchen and bound the gory thumb with a length of dishcloth. The thumb throbbed like a good 'un, it was definitely a casualty department job. Archroy's mind, alert to the slings and arrows of outrageous fortune which constantly assailed him, could see it all in advance: BRENTONIAN SAVAGED BY BUDGIE. The lads at the wiper-works would have a field day. Archroy groaned in a manner that he had come to perfect of late. Blood began to ooze through the makeshift bandage, Archroy tottered off in the direction of the cottage hospital.

He had no sooner turned the corner into Sprite Street, leaving behind him the kind of trail that bloodhounds love so dearly, when John Omally appeared, pedalling slowly from the direction of the Ealing Road. He dismounted from his iron stallion and leant Marchant against Archroy's fence. With a beaming smile upon his face he strode up the short garden path and rapped upon Archroy's gaily-coloured front door. 'Helloee,' he called through the letter-box.

All was silent within but for a brief rattling flutter, suggestive of a venetian blind being noisily and rapidly drawn up. 'Helloee,' called Omally again. 'Anybody home?' Clearly there was not. 'I'll just have a look around the back,' said John loudly to the deserted street. 'He may be asleep in his deck-chair.'

Omally stealthily edged his way along the side of the house and tested the garden door. It swung soundlessly upon its oiled hinge to reveal the mighty mesh-covered structure. 'By the light of the burning martyrs,' said John.

The cage was partly lost in the shadow of the house and appeared to be empty. Omally prodded at the wire mesh. It was solidly constructed; surely no flock of budgies merited such security? The door was soundly framed in angle-iron, and triple-bolted. Omally slid the first bolt back. It wouldn't hurt to have a swift shufty within. The second bolt shot back with a metallic clang. Omally looked furtively about the gardens; Mrs Murdock's washing hung in a sullen line, dripping into the dust, but there was no sign of any human onlookers.

The third bolt went the way of its fellows, and Omally swung the cage door slowly open. There was not a sound but for the tiny muted explosions of the drips. John stepped nimbly into the cage and peered up into the shadows. All was silent.

Without a second's warning a vast multicoloured mass of squawking violence descended upon him. He was engulfed by a screaming, tearing oblivion of claws and beaks. Sharp horny bills tore at his tweeds and sank greedily into his flesh. Omally howled in pain and battered away at the wildly-flapping horde which bore down upon him. He tore his jacket up over his head and blindly fought his way back to the door of the cage, the demonic creatures ripping at his shirt-tails and sinking their razor-sharp beaks remorselessly into him.

With a superhuman effort born from his infinite reserve of self-preservative energy Omally threw himself through the door, driving it closed behind him and flinging one of the bolts to. He sank to his knees before the cage door, blood flowing from countless wounds. His treasured tweed suit was in ribbons and he clutched between his fingers tufts of his own hair. Bitterly he looked back towards his tormentors, but the feathered fiends had withdrawn once more to their lofty perches high in the shadows. Nothing remained to signify their presence but a few prettily-coloured feathers upon the cage floor.

Omally set a painful course for his rooms. His suit was in such exquisite ruin that there was no hope of restoration. His face had the appearance of one recently engaged in a pitched battle with a rampaging lawnmower. 'Foul feathered bastards,' said John through clenched teeth. He ran a tender hand over his scalp and felt to his horror several large bald patches. 'Feathering their bloody nests with my barnet.' He looked down at his hands as he steered Marchant somewhat erratically towards its destination. They were a mass of tiny V-shaped wounds. 'Carnivorous canaries! What a carve-up!' Archroy would pay dearly for this.

An hour later Omally lay soaking in his bathtub, the water a nasty pink colour. He had affixed small strips of toilet paper to the cuts on his face, and made some attempt to comb his hair forward and up into an extraordinary quiff to cover his bald patches. He drank frequently from a bottle of Old Snakebelly and swore between sips. 'I will set traps upon the allotment,' he said, 'and catch the monster moggy – let's see how those flying piranhas like that up their perches.'

When the bottle was finished Omally felt a little better, but there was still the matter of his suit. What a tragic circumstance. The remnants of his favourite tweed hung upon the bathroom door. He had never seen anything so absolutely destroyed. Fifteen years of constant wear had hardly impinged upon the hardy fabric, but five or so short seconds in that cage of fluttering death had reduced it to ribbons.

'God,' said Omally, 'I bet those lads could strip down an elephant in under a minute, nothing left but four umbrella stands!'

An hour later Omally was out of his tinted bathwater and dressed. Actually he looked pretty natty but for the speckled face and bizarre hairstyle. He had found a pair of cricketer's white flannels, a Fair Isle jumper, and a clean cotton shirt. This had evidently been a Christmas present, as it was wrapped in green paper decorated with holly and foolish fat santas. As to footwear (the winged attackers having even played havoc with his hobnails), he chose a rather dapper pair of black patent dancing pumps he had borrowed from Pooley for some unremembered social function. He slung an old silk cravat about his neck and fastened it with a flourish.

Presently the clock struck seven and Omally wondered whether it might be worth chancing his arm for a swift pedal around to Archroy's. If the bewigged one was there he could always think up some excuse for his visit. But if Archroy's insatiable better-half was home then he should at least be able to charm his way into a bit of compensation for the afternoon's tragic events.

Archroy, as it happened, was not on the night shift. He had suffered the horrors of a tetanus injection, administered at the sneaky end by a sadistic nurse, and had received fourteen stitches in his thumb. The thumb was now liberally swathed in bandages and hidden within the overlarge folds of an impressive-looking sling. This sling now rested upon the bar of the Flying Swan.

'Caught it in the lathe,' he told Neville, but the part-time barman suspected otherwise. 'Honest,' insisted Archroy, 'nearly took my arm off.'

'Looks pretty bad,' said Jim Pooley. 'You'll be in for compensation.'

'Could be hundreds,' said Old Pete.

'Thousands,' said Neville. 'You'll be rich.'

'Mine's a pint then,' said Pooley.

'And mine,' said Old Pete.

Archroy bought another round, there being little else he could do.

'Cut yourself shaving, John?' said Archroy's wife, as she answered the unexpected knock.

'In my eagerness to look my best for you my dear.'

'I like the strides.'

'They are all the rage in Carnaby Street.'

Omally was ushered hastily into the front room, where Archroy's wife pulled the curtains.

'And who might this be?' Omally's eyes had been drawn to a fine oil painting which hung above the fireplace in an ornate gilded frame, looking strangely out of place amid the pink Dralon and mock veneer. It was the portrait of a stern, yet imposing figure of indeterminate years clad in crimson robes and sporting what appeared to be a skullcap. 'Looks very valuable.'

'It is. Will you take tea?'

'I'd prefer something a little stronger if I may.'

'Gin then?'

'Absolutely.'

Archroy's wife poured two large gins and joined Omally upon the quilted pink sofa facing the portrait. Omally found it hard to draw away his eyes as he received his drink. 'There is something familiar about that painting,' he said. 'But I can't quite put my finger on it.'

'It was a present,' said Archroy's wife pleasantly. 'Drink up, John, here's a toast to the future: *Auspicium melioris gevi*.'

Omally raised his glass and from the corner of his eye noticed that Archroy's wife held hers towards the portrait as if in salute. 'Surely that is Latin, is it not?'

'It is?' said Archroy's wife innocently. 'I think it's just a toast or something, don't know where I heard it.'

'It's not important,' said John, sipping his gin. *In vino veritas*, thought he. 'Shall we have one more?' he said, springing to his feet. As Omally decanted two large gins into the dainty glasses, he had a definite feeling that he was being watched – not by Archroy's wife, who sat demurely drawing her skirt up above her knees – but by some alien presence which lurked unseen. It was a most uncomfortable feeling and one which Omally threw off only with difficulty. He returned to the sofa bearing the drinks, his a single and hers a triple.

'To us, 'he said.

'*Ab aeterno, Ab ante, Ab antiquo*,' said Archroy's missus.

'Down the hatch,' said John.

After three more ill-proportioned tipples Archroy's wife began to warm to her unexpected guest in the passionate manner Omally had come to appreciate.

'Shall we go upstairs?' he asked, as the lady of the house began to nibble at his ear and fumble with his Fair Isle.

'Let's do it here,' she purred.

'What, on your new three-piece?'

'Why not?'

Omally kicked off his black patents with practised ease and divested himself of his cricket whites.

'Been shaving your legs as well?' said Archroy's wife, noticing the bloody scars about Omally's ankles.

'Caught myself in the briar patch.'

The pink sofa was solidly constructed and well-padded with the finest foam rubber. It stood the assault upon it uncomplainingly, but something was wrong. Omally felt himself unable to perform with his usual style and finesse, the spark just wasn't there.

Archroy's wife noticed it almost at once. 'Come on man,' she cried, 'up and at it!'

Omally sat upright. 'Someone's watching us,' he said. 'I can feel eyes burning into me.'

'Nonsense, there's nobody here but us.'

Omally made another attempt but it was useless. 'It's that picture,' he said in sudden realization. 'Can't you feel it?'

'I can't feel anything, that's the trouble.'

'Turn its face to the wall, it's putting me off my stroke.'

'No!' Archroy's wife flung herself from the sofa and stood with her back to the portrait, her arms outspread. She appeared ready to take on an army if necessary.

'Steady on,' said Omally. 'I am sorry if I have offended you. 'Hang a dishcloth over it then, I won't touch it.'

'Hang a dishcloth over *him*? Don't be a fool!'

Omally was hurriedly donning his trousers. There was something very wrong here. Archroy's wife looked completely out of her head, and it wasn't just the gin. The woman's possessed, he told himself. Oh damn, he had both feet down the same trouser-leg. He toppled to the floor in a struggling heap. The woman came forward and stood over him, laughing hysterically.

'You are useless,' she taunted, 'you limp fish, you can't do it!'

'I have a prior appointment,' spluttered John, trying to extricate his tangled feet. 'I must be off about my business.'

'You're not a man,' the mad woman continued. '"He" is the only man in Brentford, the only man in the world.'

'Who is?' Omally ceased his vain struggling a moment. All this had a quality of mysterious intrigue. Even though he was at an obvious disadvantage at the feet of a raving lunatic, he would never forgive himself if he missed the opportunity to find out what was going on.

'Who is "He"?'

'He? He is the born again, the second born. He . . .' The woman turned away from Omally and fell to her knees before the portrait. Omally hastily adjusted his legwear and rose shakily to his feet. Clutching his patent shoes, he made for the door. He no longer craved an explanation, all he craved was a large double and the comparative sanity of the Flying Swan. Phrases of broken Latin poured from the mouth of the kneeling woman and Omally fled. He flung open the front door, knocking Archroy who stood, his key raised towards the lock, backwards into the rose bushes. He snatched up the peacefully dozing Marchant and rode off at speed.

As he burst into the saloon-bar Omally's dramatic appearance did not go unnoticed. His cricket whites were now somewhat oily about the ankle regions and his nose had started to bleed.

'Good evening, John,' said Neville. 'Cut yourself shaving?'

'The match finished then?' asked Jim Pooley. 'Run out, were you?'

'Want to change your mind about that hat?' sniggered Old Pete, who apparently had not shifted his position since lunchtime.

'A very large scotch,' said John, ignoring the ribaldry.

'John,' Pooley said in a voice of concern. 'John, what has happened, are we at war?'

Omally shook his head vigorously. 'Oh no,' said he, 'not war.' He shot the large scotch down in one go.

'What then, have you sighted the vanguard of the extraterrestrial strike force?'

'Not those lads.'

'What then? Out with it.'

'Look at me,' said Omally. 'What do you see?'

Jim Pooley stood back. Fingering his chin thoughtfully, he scrutinized the trembling Irishman.

'I give up,' said Jim at length. 'Tell me.'

Omally drew his breath and said, 'I am a man most sorely put upon.'

'So it would appear. But why the fancy dress, it is not cricketers' night at Jack Lane's by any chance?'

'Ha ha,' said John in a voice oddly lacking in humour. He ordered another large scotch and Pooley, who was by now in truth genuinely concerned at his close friend's grave demeanour, actually paid for it. He led the shaken Irishman away from the chuckling throng and the two seated themselves in a shadowy corner.

'I have seen death today,' said Omally in a low and deadly tone. 'And like a fool I went back for a second helping.'

'That would seem an ill-considered move upon your part.'

John peered into his double and then turned his eyes towards his old friend. 'I will tell you all, but this must go no further.'

Inside Pooley groaned dismally. He had become a man of late for whom the shared confidence spelt nothing but doom and desolation. 'Go ahead, then,' he said in a toneless voice.

Omally told his tale, omitting nothing, even his intention towards Archroy's wife. At first Pooley was simply stunned to hear such a candid confession of his colleague's guilty deeds, but as the tale wore on and Omally spoke of the Church of the Second Coming and of the sinister portrait and the Latin babblings, his blood ran cold.

151

'Drink up,' said Jim finally. 'For there is something I must tell you, and I don't think you are going to like it very much.' Slowly, and with much hesitation, Pooley made his confession. He told the Irishman everything, from his first theft of the magic bean to his midnight observation of Omally, and on to all that the Professor had told him regarding the coming of the Dark One and his later meeting with the Other Sam.

Omally sat throughout it all, his mouth hanging open and his glass never quite reaching his lips. When finally he found his voice it was hollow and choked. 'Old friend,' said he. 'We are in big trouble.'

Pooley nodded. 'The biggest,' he said. 'We had better go to the Professor.'

'I agree,' said Omally. 'But we had better have one or two more of these before we go.'

17

When Neville called time at ten-thirty the two men stumbled forth into the street in their accustomed manner. They had spoken greatly during that evening and there had been much speculation and much putting together of two and two. If the Messiah to the Church of the Second Coming was the man in the portrait and the man in the portrait was none other than the dreaded Dark One himself, then he was obviously gaining a very firm foothold hereabouts.

As Omally pushed Marchant forward and Pooley slouched at his side, hands in pockets, the two men began to feel wretchedly vulnerable beneath the moon's unholy light.

'You can almost come to terms with it during the day,' said Pooley. 'But at night, that is another matter.'

'I can feel it,' said John. 'The streets seem no longer familiar, all is now foreign.'

'I know.'

If Marchant knew, he was not letting on. But out of sheer badness he developed an irritating squeak which put the two men in mind of the now sea-going wheelbarrow, and added to their gloom and despondency.

'This lad is heading for the breaker's yard,' said Omally suddenly. Marchant ceased his rear-wheel loquaciousness.

A welcoming glow showed from the Professor's open French windows when presently they arrived. From within came the sound of crackling pages being turned upon the laden desk.

'Professor,' called Jim, tapping upon the pane.

'Come in Jim,' came the cheery reply. 'And bring Omally with you.'

The two men looked at one another, shrugged, and entered the room. Pooley's eyes travelled past the old Professor and settled upon

153

the spot where the bean creatures had been housed. 'Where are they?'

'They have grown somewhat, Jim,' said the Professor. 'I have been forced to lodge them in larger and more secure quarters.' He rang his bell and Gammon appeared as if by magic, bearing a bottle of scotch upon a silver salver.

'Now then,' the Professor said, after what he felt to be a respectable pause, adequate for the settling into armchairs and the tasting of scotch. 'I take it you have something to tell me. I take it further that you have confided all in Mr Omally?' Pooley hung his head. 'It is all for the best, I suppose, it was inevitable that you should. So, now that you know, what are your thoughts on the matter, Omally?'

Omally, caught somewhat off-guard, was hard-pressed for a reply, so he combined a shrug, a twitch, and a brief but scholarly grin, to signify that he had not yet drawn upon his considerable funds of intellect in order to deal fully with the situation.

The Professor, however, read it otherwise. 'You are at a loss,' said he.

'I am,' said John.

'So,' the Professor continued, 'what brings you here?'

Omally looked towards Jim Pooley for support. Jim shrugged. 'You'd better tell him the lot,' said he.

Omally set about the retelling of his day's experiences. When the Irishman had finished, the Professor rose to his feet. Crossing to one of the gargantuan bookcases, he drew forth an old red-bound volume which he laid upon the desk.

'Tell me John,' he said. 'You would recognize the figure in the portrait were you to see his likeness again?'

'I could hardly forget it.'

'I have the theory,' said Professor Slocombe, 'that we are dealing here with some kind of recurring five-hundred-year cycle. I would like you to go through this book and tell me if a facsimile of the portrait you saw exists within.'

Omally sat down in the Professor's chair and began to thumb through the pages. 'It is a very valuable book,' the Professor cautioned, as John's calloused thumb bent back the corner of yet another exquisite page.

'Sorry.'

'Tell me, Professor,' said Jim, 'if we can identify him and even if we can beat on his front door and confront him face to face, what can we do? Omally and I have both seen him, he's getting on for seven feet tall and big with it – I wouldn't fancy taking a swing at him. And anyway, as far as we can swear, he hasn't committed any crime. What do we do?'

'You might try making a citizen's arrest,' said Omally, looking up from his page-turning.

'Back to the books, John,' said the Professor sternly.

'My wrists are beginning to ache,' Omally complained, 'and my eyes are going out of focus looking at all these pictures.'

'Were they sharp, the beaks of those birds?' asked the Professor. John's wrists received a sudden miraculous cure.

'Well,' said Jim to the Professor. 'How do we stop him?'

'If we are dealing with some form of negative theology, then the tried and trusted methods of the positive theology will serve as ever they did.'

'Fire and water and the holy word.'

'The same, I am convinced of it.'

'Got him!' shouted John Omally suddenly, leaping up and banging his finger on the open book. 'It's him, I'm certain, you couldn't mistake him.'

Pooley and the Professor were at Omally's side in an instant, craning over his broad shoulders. The Professor leant forward and ran a trembling hand over the inscription below the etched reproduction of the portrait. 'Are you certain?' he asked, turning upon Omally. 'There must be no mistake. It would be a grave matter indeed if you have identified the wrong man.'

Pooley bent towards the etching. 'No,' said he, 'there is no mistake.'

The Professor turned slowly away from the two men at the desk. 'Gentlemen,' he said solemnly, 'that is a portrait of Rodrigo Borgia, born in Valencia January the first, Fourteen hundred and thirty-one, died in Rome August the eighteenth, Fifteen hundred and three. Rodrigo Borgia – Pope Alexander the Sixth!'

'That is correct,' said a booming voice. 'I am Rodrigo Lenzuoli Borgia and I have come for my children!'

The French windows flew back to the sound of shattering glass and splintering woodwork, and an enormous figure entered the portal. He was easily seven feet in height and he inclined his massive head as he stepped through the casement. He was clad in the rich crimson robes of the papacy and was surrounded by a weirdly-shimmering aura which glittered and glowed about him.

The Professor crossed himself and spoke a phrase of Latin.

'Silence!' The giant raised his hand and the old Professor slumped into his chair as if cataleptic. Pooley and Omally shrank back against the wall and sought the lamaic secrets of invisibility. The mighty figure turned his blood-red glare upon them. Pooley's knees were jelly. Omally's teeth rattled together like castanets.

'I should destroy you now,' said the giant, 'you are but worms that I might crush beneath my heel.'

'Worms,' said Omally, 'that's us, hardly worth the trouble.' He laughed nervously and made a foolish face.

'Ha!' The giant turned away his horrible eyes. 'I have pressing business, you may count yourselves lucky.'

The two men nodded so vigorously that it seemed their heads would detach themselves at any minute from their trembling bodies and topple to the floor.

'Come unto me, my children,' boomed the awful voice, 'come now, there is much work to be done.'

There was a terrible silence. Nothing moved. The two men were transfixed in terror, and the giant in the crimson garb stood motionless, his hands stretched forth towards the study door. Then it came; at first faintly, a distant rattling and thumping upon some hidden door, then a loud report, as if the obstruction had been suddenly demolished. Scratching, dragging sounds of ghastly origin drew nearer and nearer. They stopped the other side of the study door and all became again silent.

The two men stood in quivering anticipation. A mere inch of wood stood between them and the nameless, the unspeakable.

The silence broke as a rain of blows descended upon the study door, the huge brass lock straining against the onslaught. Suddenly, the panels of the elegant Georgian door burst assunder. As gaping holes appeared, the two men caught sight of the malevolent force which battered relentlessly upon them.

The beings were dwarf-like and thickly-set, composed of knobbly root-like growths, a tangle of twisted limbs matted into a sickening parody of human form, dendritic fingers clutching and clawing at the door. Forward the creatures shambled, five in all. They stood clustered in the centre of the room, their gnarled and ghastly limbs a-quiver, and their foul mouths opening and closing and uttering muffled blasphemies.

The giant raised his hand and gestured towards the French windows. The fetid beings shuffled towards the opening, one raising its vile arm defiantly at the two men.

Omally gripped his chum's jacket, his face white and bloodless. Pooley shook uncontrollably, his eyes crossed, and he sank to the floor in a dead faint.

The last of the creatures had left the room and the giant in crimson turned his eyes once more to Omally. 'Irishman,' he said, 'are you a good Catholic?'

Omally nodded.

'Then kneel.'

Omally threw himself to his knees. The giant stepped forward and extended his hand. 'Kiss the papal ring!' Omally's eyes fell upon the large and beautiful ring upon the giant's right hand. 'Kiss the ring!' said Pope Alexander the Sixth.

Omally's head swayed to and fro; the ring came and went as he tried to focus upon it. Although he would have done anything to be free of the evil crimson giant, this was too much. He was not a good Catholic, he knew, but this was supreme blasphemy, one might do a million years in purgatory for this.

'No,' screamed Omally. 'I will not do it.' And with that he too lost consciousness and fell to the floor at the feet of the giant.

A shaft of early sunlight passed through the broken framework of the French windows and fell upon the prone figure of Jim Pooley. Pooley stirred stiffly and uncomfortably in his unnatural sleep, groaned feebly, and flung out his arms. His eyes snapped open, nervously turning on their orbits to the right and left. He flexed his numbed fingers and struggled to his knees. Omally lay a few feet from him, apparently dead.

Pooley pulled himself to his feet and struggled to his chum. 'John,' he shouted, gripping the Irishman by his Fair Isle jumper and shaking him violently, 'John, can you hear me?'

'Away with you, Mrs Granger,' mumbled Omally, 'your husband will be back from his shift.'

'John,' shouted Pooley anew, 'wake up, damn you.'

Omally's eyes opened and he peered up at his friend. 'Bugger you, Pooley,' he said. 'Out of my boudwah!'

157

'Pull yourself together, man.'

Omally's eyes shot to and fro about the room in sudden realization. 'The Professor!' The old man lay draped across his chair, his mouth hung open and his breath came in desperate pants. 'Bring some water, or better still scotch.' Pooley fetched the bottle. Omally dipped in his finger and wiped it about Professor Slocombe's parched lips.

The old man's head slumped forward and his hands came alive, gripping the arms of the chair. His mouth moved and his aged eyes flickered back and forth between the two men. 'W-where is he?' he stuttered. 'Has he gone?' He tried to rise, but the effort was too much and he sank back limply into the chair. 'Give me a drink.'

'What price Dimac?' said Pooley to himself. Omally poured the Professor an enormous scotch and the ancient tossed it back with a single movement. He flung his glass aside and buried his face in his hands. 'My God,' said he, 'I knew he was powerful, but I never realized. His force is beyond comprehension. I set up a mental block but he simply swept it aside. I was helpless!'

Pooley knelt beside the Professor's chair. 'Are you all right, sir?' he asked, placing a hand upon the old man's arm.

'The creatures!' said the Professor, jerking himself upright. 'Has he taken them?'

Pooley gestured towards the broken study door. 'With apparent ease.'

Professor Slocombe climbed to his feet and leant against the fireplace for support. Omally was pouring himself a scotch. 'He will have to be stopped!'

'Oh fine,' said Omally. 'We'll get right to it.'

'I know little of the Catholic faith,' said Pooley. 'Who was Pope Alexander the Sixth?'

'He was not what one would describe as a good egg,' said Omally. 'He was father to Lucretia Borgia, a lady of dubious renown, and of five or so other by-blows along the way. He achieved his papal throne through simony and died, so the fable goes, through mistakenly taking poison intended for Cardinal Adriano de Cornetto, with whom he was dining. He is not well remembered, you could say.'

'A bit of a stinker indeed,' said Pooley, 'but a man of his time.'

The Professor had been silent, but now he raised himself upon his elbows and looked deep into the Irishman's eyes. 'I believe now that my previous proposition was incorrect. The Dark One does not have form; he assumes the form of others by recalling their ambitions and increasing their powers to his own ends. This alien force is capable of acting upon a powerful ego, adding to it and enlarging it until it becomes a power of diabolic magnitude. Alexander the Sixth died before his time, and I suggest that he has returned to carry on where he left off. Only now he is more powerful, he is no longer a mere human, now he can fully realize his ambitions unburdened by the fear of retribution. He thinks himself to be invulnerable. Let us pray that he is not.'

Omally shrugged. 'So what chance do we stand?'

'This is earth and we are alive. Anything that encroaches upon us must by definition be alien. It may appear to have the upper hand, but its unnaturalness puts it at a disadvantage.'

'He didn't look much at a disadvantage.'

'What puzzles me,' said the Professor, 'is why he did not kill us? He knows us to be a threat to him, yet he allowed us to live.'

'Good old him.'

'It is possible,' the old man continued, 'that his powers are limited and that he can only expend a certain amount of energy at one time. Certainly the destruction of the cellar door must have required enormous force, the creatures alone could never have accomplished that. It was reinforced with steel.'

'What about the light which surrounded him?' queried Omally. 'It was blazing when he entered but it had quite dimmed away when at last I set eyes upon his accursed form.'

'What happened after I blacked out?' Pooley asked.

Omally turned away. 'Nothing,' said he in a bland voice, but the violent shaking of his hands did not go unnoticed by Jim or the Professor.

'It looks like another sunny day,' said Jim, changing the subject.

'Will you gentlemen take breakfast with me?' asked the Professor.

There is little need to record the answer to that particular question.

18

As September neared its blazing end, the heat showed no sign of lessening. Now the nights were made terrible by constant electrical storms. Omally had penned Marchant up in his allotment shed, having read of a cyclist struck down one night by the proverbial bolt from the blue.

There could now be no doubt of the location of the Church of the Second Coming. Nightly its grey-faced flock stalked through the tree-lined streets of the Butts Estate en route for its unhallowed portals. Father Moity was going through agonies of self-doubt, as his congregation deserted him in droves.

The Professor stood at his window, watching them pass. He shook his head in sorrow and pulled down the blind. Many had seen the five red monks moving mysteriously through the midnight streets. It was rumoured that they attended at the rites of the new church. The Professor felt the hairs on the nape of his neck rise when he thought of the alien monstrosities which inhabited those saintly crimson robes. He had seen them again only the night before, clustered in a swaying group outside his very garden gate, murmuring amongst themselves.

A streak of lightning had illuminated them for a moment and the Professor had seen the ghastly mottled faces, muddy lustreless masks of horror. He had slammed shut his doors and drawn down the iron screen he had fitted for security. His house was almost in a state of siege now, and he was certain that his every move was closely observed.

Omally had been acting as messenger and delivery boy, freighting quantities of thaumaturgical books which arrived daily in wax-paper packages at Norman's corner-shop. The old man rarely slept now, and his hours were spent committing to memory vast passages of obscure Latin.

'Every day draws us nearer,' he told the struggling Irishman, as Omally manhandled another half-dozen weighty tomes into the study.

'You must surely have half the stock of the British Museum here by now,' said the perspiring John.

'I have almost all I need,' the Professor explained, 'but I have another letter for you to post.'

'Talking of books,' said Omally, 'I have loaned your Dimac training manual to Archroy.'

The Professor smiled briefly. 'And what became of yours?'

'I never owned one,' said Omally. 'It was a rumour put about by Pooley. It kept us out of fights.'

'Well, good luck to Archroy, he has suffered more than most over this affair. I hear that as well as losing his car, his magic beans, and the use of his thumb, he was also unlucky enough to have had his arm broken and his head damaged by a lunatic in a Fair Isle jumper.'

Omally, who now no longer adopted that particular mode of dress, nodded painfully. 'I am grateful that my companions at the Swan have been discreet over that particular matter, and I must thank my good friend Jim for the permanent loan of his second suit.'

The Professor whistled through his teeth. 'Two suits Pooley, a man of means indeed.'

Omally sipped at his drink thoughtfully and knotted his brow. 'Will all this soon be over?' he asked. 'Is there any end in sight?'

The Professor stood at the open French windows, the setting sun casting his elongated shadow back across the room. 'Great forces are at work,' he said in a distant voice, 'and as it is said, "The wheels of God grind slowly but they grind exceedingly small".'

If that was intended as an answer to Omally's question the Irishman failed to understand it, but as the old man's back was turned he took advantage of the fact and poured himself another very large scotch.

'*Woosah!*' An enormous scream, and a startling figure clad in silk kimono, black trousers fastened tightly at the ankles, and grimy plimsolls leapt from the allotment shed, clearing the five-foot bean poles in a single bound to descend with a sickening crash amongst a pile of upturned bell cloches.

'Damn it!' The figure stepped from the wreckage and straightened its wig, then, '*Banzai!*' The figure strutted forward, performed an amazing *Kata*, and drove the fingers of his right hand back through the corrugated wall of his shed.

The figure was Archroy, and he was well on the way to mastering the secrets of the legendary Count Dante. The area around his shed was a mass of tangled wreckage, the wheelbarrow was in splinters, and the watering can was an unrecognizable tangle of zinc.

Archroy strode forward upon elastic limbs and sought things to destroy. The Dimac manual lay open at a marked page labelled *The Art of the Iron Hand.*

'*Aaaroo!*' Archroy leapt into the air and kicked the weather-vane from the top of Omally's shed, returning to the ground upon bouncing feet. He laughed loudly and the sound echoed over the empty dust bowl, bouncing from the Mission wall and disappearing over his head in the direction of the river. 'Iron Hand,' he said, 'I'll show them.'

He had read the Dimac manual from cover to cover and learned it by heart. 'The deadliest form of martial arts known to mankind,' it said, 'whose brutal tearing, rending, maiming, and mutilating techniques have for many years been known only to the high Lamas of Tibet, where, in the snowy wastes of the Himalayas, they have perfected the hidden art of Dimac.' Count Dante had scorned his sacred vow of silence, taken in the lofty halls of the Potala, never to reveal the secret science, and had brought his knowledge and skill back to the West where, for a mere one dollar ninety-eight, these maiming, disfiguring, and crippling techniques could be made available to the simple layman. Archroy felt an undying gratitude to the black-masked Count, the Deadliest Man on Earth, who must surely be living a life of fear lest the secret emissaries from Lhasa catch him up.

Archroy cupped his hand into the Dark Eagle's Claw posture and sent it hurtling through the padlocked door of Omally's shed. The structure burst asunder, toppling to the ground in a mass of twisted wreckage, and exposing the iron frame and sit-up-and-beg handlebars of Marchant.

'Luck indeed,' said Archroy, sniggering mercilessly. He lifted the old black bicycle from the ruins of the allotment hut and stood it against a heap of seed boxes which had escaped his violent attentions.

'You've had it coming for years,' he told Marchant. The bicycle regarded him with silent contempt. 'It's the river for you, my lad.' Marchant's saddle squeaked nervously. 'But first I am going to punish you.'

Archroy gripped the handlebars and wrenched them viciously to one side. 'Remember the time you tripped me up outside the Swan?' Archroy raised his left foot to a point level with his own head, spun around on his right heel, and drove it through Marchant's back wheel, bursting out a dozen spokes, which spiralled into the air to fall some twenty feet away.

Marchant now realized his dire predicament and began to ring his bell frantically. 'Oh no you don't.' Archroy fastened his iron grip about the offending chime and tore it free from its mountings, Crushing its thumb toggle, he flung it high over his shoulder.

The bell cruised upwards into the air and fell in a looping arc directly on to the head of John Omally, who was taking a short-cut across the allotment en route to the post box on the corner of the Ealing Road.

'Ow! Oh! Ouch! Damn!' screamed Omally, clutching at his dented skull and hopping about in pain. He levelled his boot at what he thought must surely be a meteorite and his eyes fell upon the instantly recognizable if somewhat battered form of his own bicycle bell. Omally ceased his desperate hopping and cast his eyes about the allotment. It took hardly two seconds before his distended orbs fixed upon Archroy. The lad was carrying Marchant high and moving in the direction of the river.

Omally leapt upon his toes and legged it towards the would-be destroyer of his two-wheeled companion. 'Hold up there!' he cried, and 'Enough of that! Let loose that velocipede!'

Archroy heard the Irishman's frenzied cries and released his grip. Marchant toppled to the dust in a tangle of flailing spokes. Omally bore down upon Archroy, his face set in grim determination, his fists clenched, and his tweed trouser-bottoms flapping about his ankles like the sails of a two-masted man-o-war. 'What villainy is this?' he screamed as he drew near.

Archroy turned upon him. His hands performed a set of lightning moves which were accompanied by sounds not unlike a fleet of jumbo jets taking off. 'Defend yourself as best you can,' said he.

Omally snatched up the broken shaft of a garden fork, and as the pupil of the legendary Count advanced upon him, a blur of whirling fists, he struck the scoundrel a thunderous blow across the top of the head.

Archroy sank to his knees, covering his head and moaning piteously. Omally raised his cudgel to finish the job. 'No, no!' whimpered Archroy. 'Enough!'

Omally left him huddled in the foetal position and went over to survey the damage done to his trusty iron steed. 'You'll pay for this,' he said bitterly, 'it'll mean a new back wheel, chain set, bell, and a respray.'

Archroy groaned dismally. 'How did you manage to fell me with that damned stick?' he asked. 'I've read the manual from cover to cover.'

Omally grinned. 'I had a feeling that you were not being a hundred per cent honest with me when I lent it to you, so I only gave you Volume One. Volume Two is dedicated to the art of defence.'

'You bastard.'

Omally raised his stick aloft. 'What did you say?'

'Nothing, nothing.'

'And you'll pay for the restoration of my bicycle?'

'Yes, yes.'

Omally caught sight of the heap of splintered wood and warped iron that had once been his second home. 'And my shed?'

'Yes, anything you say.'

'From the ground up, new timbers, and I've always fancied a bit of a porch to sit in at the end of a summer's day.'

'You bas . . .'

'What?' Omally wielded his cudgel menancingly.

'Nothing, nothing, leave it to me.'

'Good, then farewell, all my best to you and please convey my regards to your dear wife.'

Omally strode off in the direction of the post box, leaving the master of the iron fist on the dusty ground, thrashing his arms and legs and cursing between tightly-clenched teeth.

The Professor's letter duly despatched, Omally set his foot towards the Flying Swan. He looked up at the empty sky, blue as the eyes of a Dublin lass. He would really have enjoyed this unusual summer had it not been for the sinister affair he had become involved in. As he approached the Swan he ran into Norman. It was early-closing day and like Omally he was thirsting for a pint of cooling Large and the pleasures of the pot-room. The two men entered the saloon-bar and were met by a most extraordinary spectacle.

Captain Carson, on whom none had laid eyes for several months, stood at the counter, evidently in a state of advanced drunkenness and looking somewhat the worse for wear. He was clad in pyjamas and dressing-gown, and surrounded by what appeared to be his life's possessions in bundles and bags spread about the floor. 'Thirty bloody years,' he swore, 'thirty bloody years serving the troubled and down-at-heel, doing the work that should have won me a Nobel Prize, never a complaint, never a word said against me, and here I am, out on my ear, penniless, banjoed, and broken.'

Omally followed Norman to the polished counter and the lad ordered a brace of Largi. 'What's all this then?' Omally whispered to the part-time barman.

Neville pulled upon the pump handle. 'He's got his marching orders from the Mission. It's been converted into a church now and he's no longer required.'

Omally, who felt somewhat emboldened after his recent en-counter with Archroy, wondered if now might be the time to broach the subject of his wheelbarrow, but the sheer wretchedness the Captain displayed drove any such thoughts from his mind. 'Who kicked him out then, the Mission Trust?'

'No, the new vicar there. Some high Muck-a-Muck it seems.'

High Muck-a-Muck, thought Omally, if only they knew the truth. But the fates must surely be with him, for the Captain must know a good deal about the cuckoo he had harboured within his nest. 'Get him a large rum on me,' said Omally, 'he looks as if he needs it.'

The Captain took the rum in both hands and tossed it back down his open throat. 'God bless you, John Omally,' said he, wiping his mouth on his dressing-gown sleeve. 'You are a good man.'

'I take it that the times are at present against you,' said John.

'Against me? What do you think I'm doing here in my bloody jim-jams, going to a fancy-dress party?'

'It has been known.'

'Listen.' Captain Carson banged his empty glass upon the bar. 'That bastard has driven me from my home, evicted me, me with thirty years serving the troubled and down-at-heel, me who should have won a Nobel bloody Prize for my labours, me who —'

'Yes, yes,' said Omally, 'I can see you are a man sorely put upon, but who has put you in this dire predicament?'

'That bloody Pope geezer, that's who. Came into my Mission as a stinking old tramp and look what he turned out to be.'

Neville pricked up his ears. 'Tramp?' said the part-time barman. 'When was this?'

'About three months ago, called at my door, and I extended him the hospitality that was expected of me. Should have kicked him out on his bloody ear that's what I should have done.'

Neville leant closer to the drunken sea-captain. 'What did he look like?' he asked.

'Oribble, filthy, disreputable, evil creature, ragged as a Cairo cabbie.'

'And is he there now?' Neville continued.

'Well.' The Captain hesitated, swaying somewhat on his slippered feet, and held the bar counter for support. 'You could say he is, but then again he isn't. He was little when he came,' he made a levelling gesture at about chest height, 'small he was, but now, huge, bloody big bastard, bad cess upon him.' His hand soared into the air high over his head, and the eyes of the assembled company travelled with it.

'Aw, get out of here,' said Neville, returning to his glass-polishing. 'No one can grow that big in a few months.'

'I should bloody know,' screamed the Captain, shattering his glass upon the bar counter. 'I should bloody know, I've fed him, cleaned and swept for him, treated him like some holy god all these months. He had me like a ship's rat in a trap, no one can stand against him, but now I'm out, he's kicked me out of my Mission, but I'll finish him, I'll tell all I know, things he's done, things he made me do . . .' Here his voice trailed off and his eyes became glazed.

'Yes?' said Omally, 'What have you done?'

Captain Carson spoke not a word. Neville, who had taken shelter beneath the counter, rose again, wielding his knobkerry. 'Get out!' he shouted. 'You're barred.'

The old man stood unblinking. His mouth was open as if in the formation of a word, but it was a word which never came.

'What's happened to him?' said Neville. 'He's not dead is he?'

Omally walked slowly about the paralyzed figure in the dressing-gown. He snapped his fingers and waved his hands in front of the staring eyes. But the Captain would not move; he was frozen to the spot. Those drinkers who had made vague attempts at private conversation or the perusal of the sporting press during all this, now came slowly forward to view the strange tableau. Suggestions were forthcoming.

'Flick your lighter, that brings them out of it.'

'Bucket of water, that's your man.'

'Ice cube down his neck.'

'Make a grab at his wallet, that will bring him round.'

Omally held an empty wine-glass to the Captain's lips. He turned it between his fingers then held it up to the light. 'He's stopped breathing,' he said. 'This man is dead.'

'Get him out of here,' screamed Neville, climbing over the counter. 'I won't have a stiff in my bar.'

'Quick then,' said Omally, 'give me a hand to carry him out into the sun, maybe we can resuscitate him.'

Omally grasped the Captain under the armpits and Neville made to lift up the slippered feet. What followed was even more bizarre than what had gone before. The old man would not move; it was as if he had been welded to the saloon-bar floor. Omally could not shift the old and crooked shoulders an inch, and Neville let out a sudden 'Oh!' and straightened up, holding his back.

Several men stepped forward and attempted to shake and pull at the Captain, but he would not be moved, not one foot, one inch, one iota.

'Do something,' said Neville in a voice of terror. 'I can't have him standing there forever looking at me, he'll go off in this heat, he'll ruin my trade, it's bad luck to have a stiff in the saloon-bar.'

Omally prodded at the Captain's dressing-gown. 'He appears to be freezing up,' he said. 'The material of his gown here is stiff as a board, you can't even sway it.'

'I don't care!' Neville was beginning to panic. 'He can't stay here, get him out. Get him out!'

Omally returned to the bar and took up his glass, while the crowd closed in about the Captain. 'That is certainly the strangest thing I have ever seen,' he said. 'This might make you famous.' Omally's brain suddenly switched on. There was money in this, that was for sure. He swept back his glass of Large and made for the door, but the part-time barman had anticipated him and stood, knobkerry in hand, blocking the Irishman's exit. 'Oh no you don't,' said he.

Omally began to wheedle. 'Come on Nev,' he said, 'we can't do anything for him now and we certainly can't ignore him. You can't just stick a bar cloth over his head and pretend he's a pile of cheese sandwiches.'

'No publicity,' said Neville, fluttering his hands, 'make me famous? This could ruin me. "Frozen Corpse in Saloon-Bar Scandal", I can see it all.' (So could Omally, but he had phrased the headline a little better). 'They'll say it was the beer, or that I poisoned him or God knows what else. The brewery will be down on me like a ton of red flettons, this is just the excuse they need.'

Omally shrugged. 'All right,' he said, 'I'll say nothing. But that lot,' he gestured over his shoulder, 'I can't vouch for them.'

'Well don't let them out, do something, stop them, get them away from him.'

'Which would you like doing first?'

'The last one.'

'All right.' Omally held his chin between thumb and forefinger, thought for a moment. 'Just back me up on whatever I say.' He took a deep breath and strode into the midst of the throng. 'Nobody touch him,' he shouted, 'for God's sake don't touch him.' The fingers which were inquisitively prodding the Captain withdrew in a hurried rush. 'Who's touched him?' said Omally in alarm. 'Which one of you?'

There was a lot of shuffling and murmuring. 'We've all touched him,' said someone in a guilty voice.

'Oh no!' Omally put his hand to his forehead in a gesture of vast despair.

'What's he got?' someone said. 'Out with it, Omally.'

Omally supported himself on the counter and said gravely, 'It's Reekie's Syndrome . . . the Frozen Death!'

Neville nodded soberly. 'I've heard of it,' he said. 'When I was serving in Burma a fellow caught it, horrible end.'

Someone in the crowd, for there is always one, said, 'That's right, a mate of mine had it.'

Omally struck the counter with his fist. 'What a fool!' he said. 'What a fool, if only I had recognized it sooner.'

'It's contagious then?' somebody asked.

'Contagious?' Omally gave a stage laugh. 'Contagious . . . worse than the Black Death, we'll have to go into quarantine, bar the door Neville.'

Neville strode to the door and threw the brass bolts.

'But how long?' asked a patron whose wife had the dinner on.

Omally looked at Neville. 'Two days?' he asked.

'Twenty-four hours,' said Neville. 'Twelve if the weather keeps up.'

'Still.' Omally grinned. 'You've got to look on the bright side, he's certainly keeping the bar cool, like having the fridge door open.'

'Oh good,' said Neville unenthusiastically. 'Better put up a sign in the window: "The Flying Swan Welcomes You, Relax in the Corpse-Cool Atmosphere of the Saloon-Bar".'

Omally examined the tip of his prodding finger. It had a nasty blister on it, which the Irishman recognized as frostbite. 'If he gets much colder, we should be able to smash him up with a hammer and sweep the pieces into the street.'

The Swan's patrons, some ten in all, who with the addition of Omally, Norman, who had hardly spoken a word since he entered the bar, and Neville, made up a most undesirable figure, were beginning to press themselves against the walls and into obscure corners. Most were examining their fingers and blowing upon them, some had already begun to shiver. Omally knew how easily mass hysteria can begin and he wondered now whether he had been wise in his yarn-spinning. But what had happened to the Captain? Clearly this was no natural ailment, it had to be the work of the villain calling himself Pope Alexander the Sixth. Obviously his power could extend itself over a considerable distance.

Neville had fetched a white tablecloth and covered the Captain with it. There he stood in the very middle of the bar like some dummy in a store window awaiting a change of clothes. 'If you'd let me throw him out none of us would be in this mess,' said Neville.

Omally rattled his glass on the bar. 'I shall have to apply myself to this matter. I am sure that in some way we can save the situation, it is a thirsty business but.'

Neville snatched away the empty glass and refilled it. 'If you can get me out of this,' he said, 'I might be amenable to extending some credit to you in the future.'

Omally raised his swarthy eyebrows. 'I will give this matter my undivided attention,' said he, retiring to a side-table.

Time passed. The corpse, for all his unwelcome presence, did add a pleasantly soothing coolness to the atmosphere within the bar. not that anyone appreciated it. By closing time at three, the bar had become perilously silent. At intervals, one or two of the quarantined patrons would come to the bar, taking great care to avoid the Captain, and order the drinks which they felt were their basic human right. Neville, though a man greatly averse to after-hours drinking, could do little but accede to their demands.

There were a few vain attempts to get a bit of community singing going but Neville nipped that in the bud for fear of beat-wandering policemen. Two stalwarts began a game of darts. There had been a few movements towards the pub telephone, but Neville had vetoed the use of that instrument on the grounds that careless talk cost lives. 'Have you come up with anything yet, John?' he asked, bringing the Irishman another pint.

'I am wondering whether we might saw out the section of floor on which he is standing and despatch him into the cellar, at least then if we can't get rid of him he will be out of the way, and if he remains preserved indefinitely in his icy cocoon he will do wonders for your reserve stock.'

Neville shook his head. 'Absolutely not. I have no wish to confront him every time I go down to change a barrel.'

'All right, it was just a suggestion.'

By nine o'clock the mob, by now extremely drunk and ravenously hungry, began to grow a little surly. There were murmurings that the whole business was a put-up job and that Omally and Neville were in cahoots to con the punters out of their hard-earned pennies. In the corner, a couple of ex-Colditz types were forming an escape committee.

Then, a little after ten, one of the prisoners went over the wall. He had been out in the gents' for more than his allotted two minutes, and when Neville went to investigate, there was no sign of him. 'Legged it across the bog roof,' the part-time barman said breathlessly as he returned to the saloon, 'dropped down into the alley and away.'

'Who was it?' asked Omally.

'Reg Wattis from the Co-op.'

'Don't worry, then.'

'Don't worry? You must be joking.'

'Listen,' said Omally, 'I know his wife and if he tries to give her any excuses about frozen corpses in the Flying Swan he will get very short shrift from that good woman. It occurs to me that we might let them escape. If they talk nobody will believe them anyway.'

'They can always come back here to prove it.'

'Not much chance of that, is there?'

'So what do we do?'

'I suggest that you and I withdraw to your rooms and give them an opportunity to make their getaways.'

'I hope you know what you are doing.' Neville struck the bar counter with his knobkerry. 'Omally and I have some pressing business upstairs,' he announced. 'We will not be long and I am putting you all on your honour not to leave.' Conversation ceased and the eyes of the patrons flickered from Omally to Neville and on to the bolted door and back to Neville again. 'We swear,' they said, amid a flurry of heartcrossing and scoutish saluting.

Omally beckoned to Norman. 'You might as well come too, you overheard everything.' The three men left the bar and trudged up the stairs to Neville's bedroom.

'So what now?' asked the part-time barman.

'We sit it out. Do you still keep that supply of scotch in your wardrobe?'

Neville nodded wearily. 'You don't let much get by you, do you, John?'

Below in the saloon-bar there came the sudden sound of bolts being thrown, followed by a rush of scurrying footsteps. Neville, who had brought out his bottle, replaced the cap. 'Well, we won't be needing this now, will we?'

Omally raised his eyebrows. 'And why not?'

'Well, they've gone, haven't they?'

'Yes. So?'

'So, we go down and dispose of the Captain.'

'Oh, and how do we do that?'

Neville, who had been sitting on the edge of his bed, rose brandishing the whisky bottle. 'So it's treachery is it, Omally?' he roared. 'You had no intention of getting rid of him.'

'Me? No.' Omally wore a quizzical expression, mingled with outraged innocence. 'There is nothing we can do, he is welded to the floor in a most unmovable manner. If I was a man with a leaning towards science fiction I would say that an alien force field surrounded him.'

Neville waggled his bottle at Omally. 'Don't give me any of that rubbish, I demand that you act now, do something.'

'If you will give me a minute or two to explain matters I would greatly appreciate it.'

Neville took out his hunter. 'Two minutes,' said he, 'then I waste this bottle over your head.'

'I deplore such wastage,' said John, 'so I will endeavour to speak quickly.'

'One minute fifty-three seconds,' said Neville.

John composed himself and said, 'As we both observed what happened to the Captain I do not propose to lecture you upon the sheer inexplicable anomaly of it. It was clearly the work of no mortal man, nor was it any natural catastrophe, or at least none that I have ever heard of.'

'It's Reekie's Syndrome,' said Norman.

'Shut up Norman,' said Neville.

'It was caused,' said Omally, 'I believe, to shut the Captain up. He was about to spill the beans over what was going on at the Mission and so he was silenced.'

Neville scratched his Brylcreemed scalp. 'All right,' said he, 'but what do we do about him, we can't let him stay there indefinitely.'

'No, and nor can they. Now, I have listened to certain propositions put forward by Professor Slocombe.'

Neville nodded. 'A good and honourable man.'

'Exactly, and he believes that there has come amongst us of late an individual who can affect the laws of chance and probability to gain his own ends. This individual is presently ensconced in the Seamen's Mission and calls himself Pope Alexander the Sixth. I believe that he is to blame for what happened to the Captain, and I also believe that he cannot afford to be tied into it and will therefore arrange for the disposal of same.'

'You went over your two minutes,' said Neville, 'but if all is as you say, it would go a long way towards explaining certain matters which have been puzzling me for some months now. Have I ever spoken to you of the sixth sense?'

'Many times,' said Omally. 'Many, many times. But if you wish to retell it to me then may I suggest that you do it over a glass or two of scotch?'

'Certainly.'

'And may I also suggest that we keep a watch on the road at all times?'

'I will do it,' said Norman, 'for I have had little to say or do during this entire chapter.'

*

Night fell. Almost at once the sky became a backcloth for a spectacular pyrotechnic exhibition of lightning. The lights of the saloon-bar were extinguished and the frozen Captain stood ghostly and statuesque, covered by his linen cloth. Norman stood at Neville's window staring off down the Ealing Road, and Omally drained the last of the scotch into his glass. Neville held his watch up to what light there was. A bright flash of lightning illuminated the dial. 'It's nearly midnight,' he said. 'How much longer?'

Omally shrugged in the darkness.

The Guinness clock struck a silent twelve below in the bar, and in Neville's room Norman said suddenly, 'Look at that, what is it?'

John and Neville joined him at the window.

'What is it?' said Neville, 'I can't make it out.'

'Down by Jack Lane's,' said Norman. 'You can see it coming towards us.'

From the direction of the river, moving silently upon its eight wheels, came an enormous jet-black lorry. It resembled no vehicle that the three men had ever seen, for it bore no lights, nor did its lustreless bodywork reflect the street-lamps which shone to either side of it. There was no hint of a windscreen, nor cracks that might indicate doors or vents. It looked like a giant mould as it came to a standstill outside the Flying Swan.

Omally craned his neck to look down upon it but the overhang of the gabled roof hid the mysterious vehicle from view. The familiar creak of the saloon-bar door, however, informed the three men that someone had entered the bar. 'Here,' said Neville suddenly, 'what are we doing? Whoever it is down there could be riffling the cash register?'

'Go down then,' said Omally, 'you tell them.'

The part-time barman took a step towards the door then halted. 'Best leave it, eh?'

'I think it would be for the best,' said Omally.

The saloon-bar door creaked again and after a brief pause Norman said from the window, 'It's moving off.' The three men watched as the hellish black lorry crept out once more into the road and disappeared over the railway bridge past the football ground.

Together, the three men descended the stairs. The bar was empty, lit only by the wan light from the street. The lightning had ceased its frenzied dance on the great truck's arrival and the night had become once more clear and silent. In the centre of the floor lay the white linen tablecloth. Neville flicked on the saloon-bar lights. Norman picked up the tablecloth. Holding it out before him he suddenly gave a cry of horror and dropped it to the floor. Omally stooped to retrieve it and held it to the light. Impressed upon the cloth was what appeared to be some kind of negative photographic image. It was clear and brown as a sepia print, and it was the face of Captain Carson.

'There,' said Omally to the part-time barman, 'Now you've something to hang behind your bar. "The Brentford Shroud . . ."'

19

Omally lost little time in conveying news of the previous night's events to Professor Slocombe. The old man sat behind his desk surrounded by a veritable Hadrian's Wall of ancient books. 'Fascinating,' he said at length. 'Fascinating although tragic. You brought with you the tablecloth, I trust?'

'I thought it would be of interest.'

'Very much so.' The Professor accepted the bundle of white linen and spread it over his desk. In the glare of the brass desk lamp the Captain's features stood out, stark and haunting. 'I would never have believed it had I not seen it with my own eyes.'

'It takes a bit of getting used to.'

The old Professor rolled up the tablecloth and returned it to Omally. 'I would like to investigate this at a future date when I have more time upon my hands, but matters at present press urgently upon us.'

'There have been further developments?'

'Yes, many. News has reached me that our adversary is planning some kind of papal coronation in the near future, when I believe he will reach the very zenith of his powers. We must seek to destroy him before this moment comes. Afterwards, I fear there will be little we can do to stop him.'

'So how long do we have?'

'A week, perhaps a little more.'

Omally turned his face towards the French windows. 'So,' said he, 'after all this waiting, the confrontation will be suddenly upon us. I do not relish it, I must admit. I hope you know what you are doing, Professor.'

'I believe that I do John, never fear.'

*

The door to the Seamen's Mission was securely bolted. Great iron hasps had been affixed to its inner side and through these ran a metal rod the thickness of a broom handle, secured to the concrete floor by an enormous padlock. Within the confines of the Mission the air was still and icy-cold. Although long shafts of sunlight penetrated the elaborate stained-glass of the windows and fell in coloured lozenges upon the mosaic floor, they brought no warmth from the outer world. For no warmth whatever could penetrate these icy depths. Here was a tomb of utter darkness and utter cold. Something hovered in the frozen air, something to raise the small hairs upon the neck, something to chill the heart and numb the senses.

And here a face moved from the impenetrable darkness into the light. It was rigid and pale as a corpse, a face cut from timeless marble. The nose aquiline, the nostrils flared, the mouth a cruel slit, and the eyes, set into that face, two hellish blood-red orbs of fire. The face traversed the stream of frozen sunlight and was gone once more into the gloom.

Slow yet certain footsteps crossed the marbled floor, and firm hands gripped a monstrous throne which rose at the end of the pilastered hall. The brooding figure seated himself. Whatever thoughts dwelt within his skull were beyond human comprehension. His being was at one with the sombre surroundings, the gloom, the terrible cold.

And then, from hidden recesses of the darkling hall, there came other figures, walking erect upon two legs yet moving in a way so unlike that of humankind as to touch the very soul with their ghastliness. Forward they came upon dragging feet, to stand swaying, five in all, before their master. Then low they bowed, touching the chill floor with their faces. They murmured softly, imploringly.

The being upon the throne raised a languid hand to silence them. Beneath the hems and cuffs of their embroidered garments, touched upon briefly by the cold sunlight, there showed glimpses of their vile extremities. Here the twisted fibrous claw of a hand, here a gnarled and rootlike leg or ankle; for here were no human worshippers, here were the spawn of the bottomless pit itself, foul and unspeakable creations, sickening vomit of regions beyond thought.

The red-eyed man gazed down upon them. A strange light began to grow around him, increasing in power and clarity. His very being

176

throbbed with a pulsating energy. He raised his mighty hand above his head and brought it down on to the arm of his throne. A voice rose up in his throat, a voice like no other that had ever spoken through Earth's long aeons.

'I will have it,' he said. 'Soon all shall be mine.' The creatures below him squirmed at his feet in an ecstasy of adoration. 'There will be a place for you, my children, my five grand Cardinals of the Holy See, you will know a place in my favour. But now there is much to be done, those who would plot my destruction must be brought to their destiny: the Professor, he must be dragged before me, and the Irishman. Tonight you must go for them. I will tolerate no mistake or you shall know my displeasure. Tonight it must be. And now be gone.'

The writhing creatures drew themselves erect, their heads still bowed in supplication. One by one they shuffled from the great hall, leaving the red-eyed man alone with his unspeakable thoughts.

Atop the Mission roof, and hanging sloth-like by his heels, a lone figure had watched this Gothic fantasy through a chink in the Mission's ventilator. The lone figure was none other than Jim Pooley, Brentford's well-known man of the turf and spy for the forces of mankind, truth, and justice, and he had overheard all of the ghastly speech before he lost his footing and descended to the Mission's row of dustbins in a most undignified and noisy manner.

'Balls,' moaned mankind's saviour, wiping clotted fish-scales from his tweeds, and making a timely if somewhat shop-soiled departure from the Mission's grounds and off across the Butts Estate.

Archroy was working out on Father Moity's horizontal bars. Since the arrival through the post of Book Two and later Book Three of Count Dante's course in the deadly arts of Dimac, the lad had known a renewed vigour, a vibrant rejuvenation of his vital forces. The young priest watched him exercise, marvelling at the fluency of his movements, the ease with which he cleared the vaulting horse at a single bound. All he could do was to clap enthusiastically and applaud the astonishing exhibition of super-human control and discipline.

'You are to be congratulated, Archroy,' said Father Moity. 'I have never seen the like of this.'

'I am only beginning, Father,' Archroy replied. 'Watch this.' He gave out with an enormous scream, threw his hands forward into the posture the Count described as 'The Third Poised Thrust Of Penetrating Death' and leapt from the floor on to a high stanchion atop the gymnasium clock.

'Astonishing.' The young priest clapped his hands again. 'Amazing.'

'It is the mastery of the ancient oriental skills,' Archroy informed him, returning to the deck from his twenty-foot eyrie.

'Bravo, bravo, but tell me my son, to what purpose do you intend that such outstanding gymnastics be put to? It is too late now for the Olympics.'

Archroy skipped before him, blasting holes in the empty air with lightning fists. 'I am a man sorely put upon, Father,' said he.

The priest bowed his head in an attitude of prayer. 'These are sorry times for all of us. Surely if you have problems you might turn to me, to God, to the Church?'

'God isn't doing much for your Church at present.'

The priest drew back in dismay. 'Come now,' said he, 'these are harsh and cruel words, what mean you by them?'

Archroy ceased his exercises and fell into a perfect splits, touched his forehead to his right toe, and rose to his feet. 'You have no congregation left, Father, hadn't you noticed?'

The young priest dropped to his knees. 'I have fallen from grace.'

'You have done nothing of the sort, your flock has been lured away by a callous and evil man. I have taken a lot of stick over the past few months and I have gone to some lengths to find out what is going on hereabouts. My ear has, of late, been pressed against many a partition door and I know what I'm talking about.'

Father Moity rose clumsily to his feet. 'I would know more of this, my son. Let us repair to my quarters for a small sherry.'

'Well, just a small one, Father, I am in training.'

The breathless Pooley staggered in through the Professor's open French windows and flung himself into a fireside chair.

'I take it from your unkempt and dishevelled appearance, Jim, that you bring news of a most urgent nature,' said Professor Slocombe, looking up from his books.

Pooley took a heavy breath. 'You might say that,' he gasped.

'Steady yourself, Jim, you know where the scotch is.'

Pooley decanted himself a large one. 'Not to put too fine a point on the matter, Professor,' said he, 'you and Omally are in big trouble, in fact, the biggest.'

'So, our man is going to make his move then?'

'Tonight he is sending those nasty-looking creatures after you.'

'Well now.' Professor Slocombe crossed to the windows, pulled them shut, and lowered the heavy iron screen. 'We must not be caught napping then, must we?'

'Where is John?' Pooley cast his eyes about the room. 'I thought he was here.'

Professor Slocombe consulted his watch. 'I should imagine that by now the good Omally is propped up against the bar counter of the Flying Swan raising a pint-glass to his lips.'

'I'd better go round and warn him.'

The Professor nodded. 'Bring him back as soon as you can.'

Omally was indeed to be found at the Swan, a pint-glass in his hand and a large wax-paper package at his elbow. 'The Professor,' he would say by way of explanation to the curious who passed him by at close quarters, 'very valuable, very old.'

Pooley entered the saloon-bar. Neville greeted him with a hearty 'Morning Jim, pint of the usual?' and Omally merely nodded a greeting and indicated his parcel. 'The Professor,' he said, 'very valuable, very old.'

Pooley accepted his pint and pushed the exact change across the counter in payment. Neville rang it up in the till. 'No Sale', it said. 'The brewery have been offering me one of these new computerized microchip cash register arrangements,' the part-time time barman told Pooley. 'They do seem to have some obsession about cash registers actually registering the money that is put into them. I can't see it myself.'

'Possibly they would take it kindly if you were to keep accounts,' Pooley suggested, 'it's a common practice among publicans.'

'We always run at a profit,' Neville said in a wounded voice. 'No one could accuse me of dishonesty.'

'Of course not, but breweries are notorious for that sort of thing. Why don't you just accept the new cash register and let Omally give it the same treatment he gave to the jukebox?'

The Irishman grinned wolfishly. A brewer's dray drew up before the Swan, and Neville disappeared down the cellar steps to open the pavement doors. Pooley took Omally aside.

'You had better get around to the Professor's right away,' he said urgently. 'There is a bit of trouble coming your way from the direction of the Mission. Our man Pope Alex is out for your blood.'

'Always the bearer of glad tidings eh, Jim?' said Omally. 'I have to go down there anyway, the Professor's last book has arrived.' Omally gestured to the parcel upon the bar.

'More magic of the ancients?' said Pooley. 'I wonder what this one is all about.'

'More unreadable Latin texts I should expect. That old fellow absorbs knowledge like a sponge. I do not understand where he puts it all, for certain his head is no larger than my own.'

Pooley lifted the package from the counter and shook it gently. 'It is extremely heavy for its size, you are sure that it is a book?'

'I have no reason to doubt it, all the others have been.'

Pooley ran a finger over the glossy surface. 'It's almost like metal, but look here, how is it sealed? There are no flaps and no joint, the book appears to be encased in it rather than packed in it.'

'Indeed, now try and get it open.'

'Better not to, the Professor would not appreciate it.'

'Try anyway, I already have.'

Jim dug his thumbnail into a likely corner of the package and applied a little pressure. The package remained intact. Pooley pressed harder, working his thumbnail to and fro across the edge. 'Nothing,' he said in dismay, 'not even a scratch.'

'Use your pocket knife then, don't let it defeat you.'

Pooley took out his fifteen-function scout knife and selected the most murderous blade. Holding the parcel firmly upon the bar counter he took a vicious stab at it. The blade bent slightly, skidded cleanly off the package, and embedded itself in the counter top.

'You bloody vandal,' screamed Neville, who was entering the saloon-bar door, 'I saw that!'

'I am trying to open this parcel,' Pooley explained, withdrawing his knife and rubbing a bespittled fingertip over the counter's wound.

'Give it to me,' said the part-time barman gruffly, 'I'll open it for you.' He took up the can-opener which hung on a chain from his belt. 'Nothing to parcels if you have the know.'

He scratched the opener roughly down the length of the package. There was not a mark. 'What's this then?' said the part-time barman. 'Trick is it, or some new kind of paper?' He began scratching and scraping with renewed vigour. He laboured at the parcel as one possessed, but succeeded in doing nothing whatever, save taking the nail from his left thumb and totally destroying his opener. 'Bugger,' yelled the part-time barman, 'that was my favourite. Wait here!' He strode from the bar, leaving a fine trail of blood behind him.

'Did he mean that the opener was his favourite or the thumbnail?' wondered Omally.

Neville reappeared behind the bar with a fourteen-inch meat cleaver clutched in a bandaged hand. 'Put it here,' he demanded.

'Now steady on,' said Pooley, 'after all it isn't even our package. You will clearly destroy it with that thing.'

'One good swing,' said Neville, 'just one. I'll merely snip the end, I won't damage the contents, I swear!'

'He's a good man with a cleaver,' said someone, 'he'll open the bugger, never fear.'

Pooley looked to Omally. 'What do you think?'

'Can't hurt. If he damages it we can always say that the Post Office did it in transit.'

'Okay,' said Pooley. 'One swing then, but for God's sake, be careful.'

The parcel was placed upon the bar counter and the spectators withdrew to what they considered to be a safe distance. Neville squared up to the parcel, placed his feet firmly apart, and wiggled his behind in a manner much practised by top pro golfers before applying their wedges to a bunker-bound ball. Spitting on to his palms, he raised the cleaver high above his head and brought it down with a reckless force which would truly have done credit to the Wolf of Kabul wielding the legendary Clicki-Ba.

The patrons let out a collective gasp as the cleaver struck the parcel amidships and rebounded from the part-time barman's grip to go hurtling over their ducking heads like a crossbow bolt and lodge itself up on the hilt in the dartboard.

'Double top,' said Old Pete. 'Give that man a pint.'

Neville stood pale-faced and trembling, regarding the package with horrified eyes. 'Not even bloody dented,' he said in a quivering voice, 'not even bloody scratched.'

Leo Felix, who was making one of his rare appearances at the Swan, thrust his way through the crowd. 'I an' I got me an oxyacetylene cutter back at me work,' said the newly-converted Rastafarian.

'Come on now,' said Pooley, 'this has all got out of hand. Omally, take that package around to the Professor at once!'

The crowd would have none of it. 'Fetch your blowtorch, Leo,' said somebody. Leo left the bar.

Omally picked up the package from the bar counter and made to move in the direction of the door. The mob surrounded him. 'Put that down, mister,' said someone. 'Leave it be till Leo gets back.'

'Come now lads,' said Omally, 'this is madness, mob law in Brentford? Come now.'

'This is going too far,' said Jim, stepping into the fray.

'You do what you want mate,' said a burly navvy, 'but the parcel stays here.'

'This man knows Dimac,' said Pooley, indicating his Irish companion, 'deadliest form of martial art known to mankind and can . . .'

'Instantly disable, mutilate, and kill, his hands and feet being deadly weapons,' chimed the crowd in unison. 'We've heard it.'

'Strike them down, John,' said Pooley, 'give them iron hand.'

'My iron hands are a little rusty at present,' said Omally. 'Archroy is your man for that sort of thing.'

'Did somebody call me?' The voice came from the saloon-bar door, and the crowd, turning as one man, were stunned into absolute silence by what they saw. Framed dramatically by the Swan's doorway, which had always been so excellent for that sort of thing, stood an imposing figure which the startled throng recognized with some difficulty as none other than Archroy.

He had discarded his usual ill-fitting wig for an ornate dark coiffure of oriental inspiration which was secured by elaborately carved ivory pins tipped with jet. He wore a full-length black kimono emblazoned with Chinese characters embroidered richly in gold thread, and walked upon the high wooden shoes much favoured by samurai warlords of the fourteenth Dynasty.

'Blimey,' said Old Pete, 'it's bloody Hirohito.'

Archroy strode forward, scattering the crowd before him. 'Show me the package,' he demanded.

Pooley was amazed to note that Archroy had even adopted a pseudo-Japanese accent. And there was something indefinably different about him, not just the eastern trappings. He had physically changed, that much was certain; broader about the shoulders and narrower at the hip. Through the folds of his silken sleeves muscles seemed to bulge powerfully.

Omally handed him the parcel with an extraordinary display of politeness. 'If you please,' said he, smiling sweetly.

'And it cannot be opened?' The crowd took to shaking its collective head. 'Impregnable,' said somebody.

'Huh!' said Archroy without moving his lips. 'Two men hold it up, one either side.'

Omally shrugged. 'What can happen? Might as well do what he says.' He and Pooley stood several feet apart in the centre of the bar, holding the parcel between them in outstretched hands.

'Better get some assistance,' said Archroy, taking up a stance before the parcel. Several he-men stepped forward and assisted with the gripping and supporting. They made quite an impressive-looking little group really, not unlike one of William Blake's visionary tableaux of struggling heroic figures pressing one upon another in endless titanic conflict. The subtler points of that particular similarity were however lost to most of those present, who merely cleared a path for the lunatic in the kimono.

'When I cry out, hold on as tight as you can,' commanded Archroy.

The grippers, holders, and supporters nodded assent. Archroy took a step back and performed a series of ludicrous sweeping motions with his arms. He took a deep breath and closed his eyes; slowly he drew back his right arm, knotting the fingers of his hand into a fist with a sickening crackle of bones and gristle.

'*Woosah!*' he screamed.

Those who watched him throw the punch say to this day that they never saw his hand move. One moment it was suspended motionless at shoulder height behind him, the next it was similarly motionless but outstretched, fist clenched, at the spot where the parcel had just been.

The two clusters of grippers, holders, and supporters collapsed in opposite directions like two tug-of-war teams suddenly bereft of their rope. There was an almost instantaneous crash, followed by two more. The awe-struck spectators swung in the direction of the crashes. The parcel had travelled across the bar and straight through the outside wall, leaving a perfectly-shaped rectangular hole to mark the point of its departure.

Through this the sun threw a crisp shaft of sunlight which fell in a pleasant golden diamond on to a section of the carpet which had never previously known the joys of solar illumination. Neville looked at the hole, then at Archroy, back to the hole, and back once more to the destroyer of his wall. 'You're barred!' he screamed, searching for his knobkerry. 'You're bloody barred! Vandal! Vandal!'

Archroy was examining his knuckles. 'What's in that parcel?' was all that he could say.

The crowd was making moves towards the door, eager to see what the other two crashes might have been. 'Maybe he's demolished the flatblocks,' said somebody.

Pooley and Omally, intent only upon retrieving the Professor's book, elbowed their way through the push and found themselves the first to emerge into the very daylight which was now beaming so nicely through the neat hole in the Swan's front wall.

'My oh my,' said Omally.

Before them was a vehicle parked at the kerb, a pick-up truck of a type much favoured by used-car dealers. It was one of this doubtful breed of men who sat in the front seat, white-faced and staring. That he should be white-faced was reasonable enough, for sliced through each side of the truck's bodywork was a sharp-edged hole corresponding exactly in shape and size to that of the Professor's parcel. Regarding further this whiteness of face, its sole unusual quality was that the driver of the see-through pick-up was none other than that well-known local Rastaman Leo Felix. The hurtling missile had escaped striking, only by the briefest of inches, the oxygen canister strapped inside his vehicle. Had it struck home there is not much doubt that very little would have remained of Haile Selassie's latest follower.

Pooley and Omally peered through the holes in the hope of lining up on the Professor's parcel. 'It's over there,' said Jim, 'in Mrs Fazackerley's front garden.'

The two men skipped across the carriageway, dodging the traffic which had mercifully escaped the bazooka attack a moment before, and retrieved the parcel.

'Not even a scratch,' said Pooley, examining it. 'Nothing.'

The crowd was now in the street, thronged about Leo's ventilated pick-up, pointing and speculating. Someone was waving a handkerchief before Leo's wildly staring eyes. Neville danced in the doorway of the Swan, ranting and raving, and Archroy stood, calmly regarding his demolition work and wearing a satisfied expression upon his face.

Omally nudged Pooley in the rib area. 'Best make a break for it, eh?'

'Best so.'

The two fled away down the Ealing Road.

20

As they stood puffing and panting in the heat of the Professor's back garden Pooley asked his companion why he thought it was that neither of them ever seemed to be able to visit the old gentleman without arriving in either a harassed or a drunken condition.

'I have no idea whatever,' Omally wheezed. 'It's all go nowadays isn't it?'

'Lunchtime drinking at the Swan is not the peaceful affair it once was.'

The metal shutters were drawn down upon the French windows, and only prolonged knockings, shoutings, and rattlings finally succeeded in eliciting a reply from within. The shutters rose, exposing first carpet-slippered feet, then an expanse of tweed trousering, then a red velvet smoking jacket and quilted waistcoat, and finally the old white head of Professor Slocombe.

He beamed upon them. He spotted the parcel Omally clutched in his perspiring hand. 'Good lad, John,' he said. 'The last book I require, excellent.' Closing and bolting the heavy iron shutters, he took the parcel from Omally's outstretched hand and turned away to his desk. There was a brief rustle of waxen paper and he held the exposed book proudly aloft. 'Excellent, and I see it has withstood the rigours of Post Office despatch unscathed.'

'Don't ask,' said Pooley, as he noticed Omally's mouth opening, 'it is probably better not to know.'

'You look somewhat dishevelled,' said the Professor, noticing for the first time the state of his guests. 'Why is it, do you think, that neither of you ever seems able to visit me without arriving in either a harassed or a drunken condition?'

'We have wondered that ourselves,' said Jim.

'And now,' said the aged host, as the two men slumped before him, sipping scotch and sighing deeply, 'to business, as they say. There are very few hours left for me to school you in all you must know regarding our prospective attackers. I do not expect that their master will take an active part in the proposed assault upon us. That would not be fitting to his dignity. He will despatch his five minions to us, and at least on this score we should be grateful.'

'Extremely,' said Pooley.

'Here's to you, Alex boy,' said Omally, raising his glass.

'I admire your bravado,' the Professor said gravely. 'For my own part I find the situation somewhat alarming. I would have hoped that we could have had a try at him before he has a try at us, if you get my meaning.'

'You are pretty secure here,' said Jim, 'as long as you keep well-bolted up.'

'I have considered several manoeuvres,' said Professor Slocombe. 'Abandoning the house and taking refuge at some undisclosed location, for instance, but this I could not do, for it would mean leaving the books. I considered calling on some help; your friend Archroy I understand has recently mastered certain techniques which I struggled with to a lesser degree.'

'He has?' queried Pooley.

'Most interesting,' said Omally.

'But I do not wish to draw more folk than are strictly necessary into this unfortunate business, so I was left with only one option.'

'Which is?'

'That the three of us should remain on the premises to battle it out.'

Omally said, 'Surely there are other options? Let us put some to a vote.'

'I would gladly stay, but have a pressing engagement elsewhere,' said Jim.

'You should have mentioned it earlier,' the Professor said, a wicked twinkle appearing for a moment in his eye, 'and I would not have closed the shutter. You see, I have set automatic time-locks on all the doors and they will not open for another fifteen hours.' Pooley's face fell. 'You can use the telephone if you wish,' said the Professor brightly.

'I might call a locksmith then?' Jim asked.

'I think not.'

Omally put his hands behind his head and smiled broadly. 'When

I was in the army,' said he, 'I was a happy man; never had to make a decision. It is a pleasure to know those times once more.'

'Oh good old you,' said Jim. 'I have never known the joys of army life and can find little to recommend in that of the trapped rat. I greatly prefer freedom.'

'I am sorry,' said Professor Slocombe, 'to have brought you to this, but it must be the old musketeer philosophy I am afraid: all for one, one for all.'

'This one would have liked a choice in the matter,' said Jim sourly. 'After all, the character at the Mission did not mention me by name.'

'Do you think he would destroy us and let you off scot-free then?'

'I do not believe he thinks of me as much of a threat.'

'Never fear.' The Professor tapped his nose.

'Never fear?' Pooley threw up his hands in a helpless gesture. 'After you with that decanter, John.'

Long hours passed. In the Professor's study the temperature rose alarmingly, and the air became torpid and unbreathable. Jackets were removed and shirt-tails flapped aplenty. The Professor laboured away at his books, as best he could, and when Pooley found the energy he paced the floor like a caged animal. To add to his disgust, Omally had the perfect effrontery to curl up in one of the Professor's armchairs and fall asleep.

The mantelclock struck nine and Pooley tapped at the Victorian barometer which hung beside the marble fireplace. 'Stormy' it read, but the temperature was still in the mid-eighties.

The Professor looked up from his reading. 'Try to relax, Jim,' he said, wiping the perspiration from his deeply-lined forehead.

'Relax? I can hardly draw breath, we will suffocate in here for sure, we are all doomed.'

'Come now, control yourself.' The Professor closed the heavy damask curtains across the iron-shuttered French windows.

'Control myself? Three rats in a trap we are. You've brought us to this. I have no wish to control myself, I prefer to panic.' Pooley began delving amid the curtains and rattling at the iron shutters of the window. 'Let me out,' he shouted, kicking at the lock with his steely toecaps, 'I choose not to end my days here.'

Omally awoke with a start. 'Do turn it in, Jim,' he yawned.

'I'm not turning anything in,' Jim said morosely, 'I'm for panic, what say you?'

'I say that we stand by the Professor. After all we are as much to blame for his plight as he for ours.'

'I have no desire to die,' said Jim, 'I am yet a young man, and a potential millionaire to boot.'

'Pooley, your sixth horse will never come up.'

'Not if I stay here, it won't,' said Pooley petulantly.

The Professor raised his eyes once more from his books. 'I think the time has come for us to discuss this matter fully,' he said. 'We are in a state of siege, panic is a useless and negative commodity which we cannot afford.'

'It's always served me well enough in the past,' Pooley grumbled.

'If we do not stand together,' the Professor continued, 'we shall surely be doomed. Our adversary is a ruthless, cunning individual. In his former incarnation he had the power of life or death over thousands, millions; he was a dictator, a brilliant strategist, he held sway over kingdoms. We are not dealing with some street-corner villain. It is clearly his plan to usurp the papacy, to reclaim his lands and duchies. He sees himself carried aloft through the Vatican City. Ensconced upon the papal throne. Lord High Ruler of the Holy See. This is only the beginning for him.'

'We had best give up,' said Jim, 'all is lost.'

'Bottle job,' said Omally to the Professor, indicating Pooley and making an obscene gesture below the waist. 'His bottle's gone.'

'We can't fight him,' Pooley whined. 'You know how powerful he is.'

'If the Prof says we can, then we can, that's all there is to it. Listen, I'm a Catholic, not a good one, but a Catholic.' Omally opened his shirt and pulled out the army dogtag he still wore about his neck. 'Eight-three-one-oh-two-five-five Private J V Omally, Catholic. I'm not letting that gobshite at the Mission get one over on the Church, I hate him!'

Pooley turned upon his companion. 'What *did* happen after I blacked out that night? What did he say to you?'

Omally replaced his dogtag and rebuttoned his shirt. 'Nothing,' he said, draining his glass.

'All right,' said Pooley, 'as panic is clearly ill-received hereabouts, what do we do?'

The Professor rose from his desk, a book tucked beneath his arm.

'We will fight. I am an old man but I have no intention of dying yet awhiles. We can expect a concentrated attack upon these premises, midnight being the traditional hour for such events. Things might not be as bad as they first appear; although we know that the Dark One can extend his power over a considerable distance, I do not feel that he will wish to do so tonight. His minions greatly fear the wrath of his displeasure, as well they might; they will use every power they possess to succeed in their quest.'

'We are outnumbered,' said Jim.

'But not without power. I consider these beings to be the product of conjuration, therefore they are vulnerable. I intend to use the rites of holy exorcism, and if these fail I have recourse to several other possible methods for their destruction. These beings are not immortal.'

'That is a big weight off my mind,' sneered Jim. 'But listen, the rites of holy exorcism take a while to perform, I do not believe that such time will be made available.'

'Well, with the aid of this volume that Omally has brought to me I believe that I have isolated the key words and phrases which give the rite of exorcism its power. Much of that spoken by the priest is merely padding, theological jargon; if I am correct, the exorcism can be broken down to nothing more than a few lines of ancient Latin and still retain its basic power.'

'Let us hope you are correct.'

'Well,' said the Professor smiling darkly, 'if I am not then the matter will be purely academic.'

'That's it Professor, cheer us up.' Jim Pooley returned to his contemplation of the wallpaper.

The Memorial Library clock struck midnight. The Butts Estate was in darkness, the century-old horse chestnut trees rising like clenched fists against the sky. Beneath them, bowered in the void, the Mission showed no lights. All was silent. Faintly then came sounds, the dragging of feet and the rustling of ancient cloth. A great iron bolt was suddenly drawn up and the aged door creaked ajar. An icy-white shaft of light pierced the darkness, silhouetting the trees and casting their elongated shadows forward through the night. The door swung inwards upon its hinge and now dark forms swayed into the dazzling radiance. Misshapen forms, heavily-robed and in-definite of shape, one by one they issued from the Mission, until five in all they stood before it. Then that heavy panelled door swung closed again, the blinding light was snapped away, and the Butts slept once more in darkness.

But it was no easy sleep, for here moved creatures of nightmare. Slow of foot they laboured across the gravel drive, the ghastly dragging of their feet echoing over the empty estate. Low murmurings accompanied their progress, hoarse whispers and lamenting sobs. For they belonged not here, these spawn of ancient evil, and yet their tasks they must perform.

The slow ungodly procession trailed onward, keeping ever to the shadows beneath the ivy-hung walls. Now they neared the gate to the Professor's garden and stood together, swaying and murmuring.

Within the Professor's study the three men waited tensely. They too had heard the midnight chimes. Pooley stood with his back to the wall, wielding a poker. The Professor himself was on the edge of his chair, book in hand. Omally supported himself upon the fireplace; the decanter was empty and he was dangerously drunk.

Long minutes ticked away upon the mantelclock, its pendulum swung its gilded arc, and the three men held their breath.

Suddenly, there came a rattling upon the window, a repeated and urgent tapping. Pooley shifted the poker from his sweating palm and wiped his hand upon his trousers.

The Professor said, 'Who is there?'

'Is that you, Professor?' came a voice. 'Omally with you? I've brought a crate of beer over. Open up.'

'It's Neville,' said Pooley, breathing a monumental sigh of relief and flinging his poker to the carpeted floor. 'What's he doing here?' Jim crossed the room to throw back the curtains.

The Professor leapt to his feet and barred his way. 'Stop, Jim,' said he in a desperate voice, 'do not open the curtains.'

'But it's Neville, he can pass the drink in through the iron screens. Be reasonable.'

The Professor held up his hand and shook his head. 'Neville?' said he loudly. 'What is the name of your father?'

Pooley turned helplessly to John Omally. 'What sort of question is that, I ask you?'

There was no sound. 'Neville?' called the Professor again, but there was no reply.

'He's gone,' said Jim. 'What I would have given for a cold beer.'

Suddenly the knocking and rattling began again with renewed

vigour, and a voice rang out. 'Help, help, let me in will you, I've got to use the phone.' It was the voice of Old Pete. 'Please open up, you must help me.'

'Something's wrong there,' said Jim, 'open those curtains.'

'My dog,' wailed the voice. 'A bloody lorry's run down Chips. Let me in, I must phone for help.'

'For pity's sake,' said Pooley, 'open the curtains.'

The Professor would have none of it. 'Stand your ground, Jim,' he said sternly. 'Put your hands over your ears if you do not wish to hear it, but make no move towards the curtains.'

'But you've got to do something, let him in.'

The Professor turned to Omally. 'If he makes one step towards those curtains strike him down.'

Jim threw up his arms in defeat.

'Wise up, Pooley,' said Omally. 'Don't you see? Old Pete isn't out there, it's a trick.'

The Professor nodded his old head. 'First temptation through Neville, then an appeal for pity, what next? Threats, I should imagine.'

Pooley had little time to mull over the Professor's words before a deafening voice roared from the garden, 'Open up these windows or I'll smash the bastards down.' This time it was the voice of Count Dante's most accomplished adept in the deadly arts of Dimac. 'Open up in there, I say, or it will be the worse for you!'

Pooley threw himself into a chair. 'If it is all right with you chaps I should prefer to simply panic now and have done with it,' he said.

Archroy's voice slowly faded, still uttering threats, and the three men were left alone once more.

'Do you think that's it then?' Omally asked, tottering to the nearest chair.

The Professor's face was grave. 'I should hardly think so. I suspect that their next attempt to gain entry will be a little less subtle.' In that supposition the Professor was entirely correct.

Omally twitched his nostrils. 'What's that smell?'

The Professor's eyes darted about the room. 'It's smoke, something is burning.'

Pooley pointed helplessly. 'It's coming under the study door. We are ablaze.'

'Ignore it,' said the Professor. 'There is no fire, the doors are shuttered and bolted, nothing could have entered the house unheard.'

'I can see it with my own eyes,' said Pooley. 'Smoke is something I *can* recognize. We'll all be burned alive.'

'I don't see any flames,' said the Professor, 'but if the smoke bothers you so much.' He stepped forward and raised his hands; of the syllables he spoke little can be said and certainly nothing written. The smoke that was gathering thickly now about the room seemed suddenly to suspend itself in space and time, and then, as if a strip of cinema film had been reversed, it regathered and removed itself back through the crack beneath the door, leaving the air clear, although still strangling in the tropical heat.

'That I have seen,' said Pooley, 'but please do not ask me to believe it.'

'A mere parlour trick,' said the Professor, matter-of-factly. 'If our adversaries are no more skilful than this, we shall have little to fear, it is all very elementary stuff.'

'It is all sheer fantasy,' said Jim, pinching himself. 'Shortly I shall awake in my bed remembering nothing of this.'

'The clock has stopped,' said Omally, pointing to the silent timepiece upon the mantelshelf.

The Professor took out his pocket-watch and held it to his ear. 'Bother,' he said, given it a shake, 'I must have mispronounced several of the minor convulotions. Give the pendulum a swing, will you, John?'

Omally rose unsteadily from his chair and reached towards the mantelshelf. The alcohol, however, caused him to misjudge his distance and he toppled forward head first into the fireplace. Turning on to his back in an effort to remove himself from the ashes Omally suddenly let out a terrified scream which echoed about the room, rattling the ornaments and restarting the mantel-clock.

Not three feet above, and apparently wedged into the chimney, a hideous, inhuman face snarled down at him. It was twisted and contorted into an expression of diabolical hatred. A toothless mouth, like that of some vastly-magnified insect, opened and closed, dripping foul green saliva upon him; eyes, two flickering pinpoints of white light; and the entire horrific visage framed in a confusion of crimson cloth. The sobering effect upon Omally was instantaneous. Tearing himself from his ashy repose, he leapt to his feet and fell backwards against the Professor's desk, spilling books, and screaming, 'Up the chimney, up the chimney!'

'I don't think it's Santa,' said Pooley.

Omally was pointing desperately and yelling, 'Light a fire, light a fire!'

Pooley cast about for tinder. 'Where are the logs, Professor, you always have logs?'

The Professor chewed upon his knuckle. 'The shed,' he whispered in a trembling voice.

'We'll have to burn the books then.' Omally turned to the desk and snatched up an armful.

'No, no, not the books.' Professor Slocombe flung himself upon Omally, clawing at his precious tomes.

The broadshouldered Irishman thrust him aside, and Pooley pleaded with the old man. 'There's nothing we can do, we have to stop them.'

Professor Slocombe fell back into his chair and watched in horror as the two men loaded the priceless volumes into the grate and struck fire to them. The ancient books blazed in a crackle of blue flame, and from above them in the chimney there came a frantic scratching and clawing. Strangled cries rent the air and thick black smoke began to fill the room. Now the French windows burst asunder with a splintering of glass and the great curtains billowed in to a blast of icy air. The burning creature's hooded companions beat upon the shuttered metal screen, screeching vile blasphemies in their rasping inhuman voices. There was a crash, and the creature descended into the flames, clawing and writhing in a frenzy of searing agony.

Pooley snatched up his poker and lashed out at it viciously. Omally heaped more books on the fire. The Professor stepped forward, knowing what had to be done.

Slowly raising his hand in benediction, he spoke the magical words of the holy exorcism. The creature groaned and twisted in the flames, its arms flailing at its tormentors. Pooley held it at bay and as the Professor spoke and Omally applied more fuel to the fire, its movements began to slow and presently it crumpled in upon itself to be cremated by the all-consuming flames.

The curtains ceased their billowing and from the garden there came a great wailing and moaning. Pooley cupped his hands over his ears and the Professor stood, book in hand, frozen and corpse-like.

Omally was beating away at the burning books which had fallen from the fireplace on to the carpet. His face was set into a manic grin and he prodded at the remains of the fallen creature with undisguised venom.

The wailing from the garden became fainter, and as it passed into silence the Professor breathed a great sigh and said, 'All the ashes must be gathered and tomorrow cast into the Thames. By fire and by water and the holy writ shall they be destroyed.'

Omally plucked a half-charred volume from the grate. 'I am sorry about the books,' he said, 'but what else could we do?'

'It is no matter, you acted wisely and no doubt saved our lives.' The Professor fingered the ruined binding of the ancient book. 'A pity though, irreplaceable.'

Pooley had unfastened his hands from about his head. 'Are they gone?' he asked inanely.

'Unless they are regrouping for another assault.'

The Professor shook his head. 'I think not, they will be none too eager to return now. But what will happen when they report the loss of their comrade, I shudder to think.'

Omally whistled. 'Our man is not going to be very pleased.'

'We are doomed,' said Pooley once more, 'all doomed.'

'Jim,' said Omally wearily, 'if you say "we are doomed" one more time I am going to set aside the long years of our noble friendship and remodel your beak with the business end of my knuckles.'

'Come now gentlemen,' said the Professor, 'I have a bottle of port which I suggest we now consume before taking a well-earned rest.'

Omally rubbed his hands together. 'That would be excellent.'

Pooley shrugged his shoulders. 'What else can happen?' he asked.

A pink dawn came to Brentford, gilding the rooftops with its sickly hue. Birds that should have by now flown south to winter it in tropical climes sat in silent rows, musing upon the oddness of the season. As the old sun dragged itself into the sky there was all the promise of another fine and cloudless day ahead.

Pooley was the first to awake. He heard the milkfloat clattering over the cobblestones of the Butts, and, rising stiffly, he stumbled to the French windows and drew back the heavy curtains. The sunlight beamed down through the metal screen, laying golden diamonds upon the Professor's carpet and causing Jim to blink wildly whilst performing the ritualistic movements of finding the first fag of the day.

Like all first fags it was a killer. Jim did his best to draw some breath from the fragrant garden between coughs, while he surveyed the damage the night had brought. The French windows had been torn from their hinges once more and their splintered remains littered the small lawn and surrounding flowerbeds. Shards of glass twinkled bright in the morning sunlight.

Pooley's vile coughing awoke Omally who, scratching his nether regions, shambled over to join him. 'A rare mess,' said the Irishman. 'The glaziers will think the Professor a fine man for the wild parties and no mistake.'

Pooley gripped the metal framework of the screen. 'What time does this open?' he asked.

'Nine o'clock, wasn't it?'

The Memorial Library clock struck eight.

'An hour yet then.'

Omally shook the Professor gently awake. The old man stretched his slender limbs to the accompaniment of ghastly bone-cracking sounds. He yawned deeply. 'So we are still alive, then, that is a blessing.'

'Not much left of your windows,' said Jim. 'Might be more economical to wall up the opening.'

The Professor looked at his watch and checked it with the mantelclock. 'Time for breakfast, I think.' He rang the Indian brass bell upon his desk and presently there came a knocking upon the study door, followed by the sound of a key turning in the lock. The door swung open and the decrepit figure of Gammon appeared. 'Breakfast for three, sir,' he said, hefting an oversized butler's tray into view.

'I gave him the night off,' the Professor explained, as the three men sat about the Moorish coffee-table, ravenously devouring the mountainous piles of toast, sausages, eggs, and bacon loaded upon the tray. 'I told him to return at seven and if he found the house intact, to arrange breakfast for three.'

'And what if the house had not been intact?' Omally asked between mouthfuls.

'If the doors were broken in and it was obvious that an entry had been made, I ordered him to set the house ablaze and leave immediately, never to return.'

'And he would have done that?'

'Unquestioningly.'

Omally whistled. 'He is a loyal servant indeed. It would have been my first thought to remove several of the more choice objects – in order to spare them from the blaze, as it were.'

'Gammon has no need for that, I have seen to it that his long years of service will not go unrewarded.'

'You are a strange man, Professor.'

The Professor shook his head. 'On the contrary, my motives are most simple, to advance science and to combat evil.'

'You make it *sound* simple.'

The Professor munched upon a piece of toast. 'I believe in destiny,' he said, 'I believe in the existence of the cosmic masterplan. No man is without a purpose, but few if any find theirs before it is too late. Perhaps I am lucky to believe that I have found mine, possibly not. Possibly ignorance, as they say, is bliss. It is written that "a little knowledge is a dangerous thing, but a great deal of knowledge is a disaster".'

'Probably written by Norman,' said Pooley, pushing another sausage into his mouth.

'A man without talent or ambition is a man most easily pleased. He lives his life with no delusions; other men set his purpose and he is content.'

'That is a depressing thought,' said Omally, 'as that particular definition covers most individuals in this present society.'

'The balance must always be maintained; all have a purpose, be he pauper or king, such it has always been. There could be no giants if there were no dwarves.'

Pooley thought that there probably could be, but he held his counsel as he had no wish to be drawn into an arduous discussion at this time of the day. 'Here,' he said suddenly. 'How did Gammon get in if all the doors were on time-locks?'

Omally raised his eyes suspiciously towards the Professor, but the old man merely chuckled and continued with his breakfasting. Black coffees were drunk and at length Gammon returned to dispose of the tray. At nine o'clock the time-lock upon the metal shuttering snapped open and the Professor raised it. Gammon had swept every ash from the fireplace into a sack, and this the Professor handed to Omally with explicit instructions.

'You must sprinkle it over at least half a mile,' he explained, 'there must be no chance of the particles regrouping. And now I must say farewell to you gentlemen. It is no longer safe for me to remain here. I have other apartments not far from here and I will lodge there. When the moment comes that I need you I will be in contact. Go now and await my call, speak of these matters to no one, and be constantly on your guard. You should be safe during the hours of daylight, but at night go nowhere alone, do not allow yourselves to become separated.'

The two men stepped through the French windows, over the mess of shattered glass, and out towards the Professor's gate. They turned to wave him a cheery farewell but the old man had gone.

21

The people of Brentford had taken to calling them the Siamese Twins. From the moment they had despatched the sinister contents of the sack along the river, John Vincent Omally and James Arbuthnot Pooley were never to be seen apart. The days passed wearily with no call from the Professor. Pooley wondered if the old man might possibly have lost his nerve and decided to do a runner, but Omally, whose faith in the Professor bordered upon the absolute, would have none of that. 'He has seen too much,' he assured Pooley, 'he will not rest till that Pope Alex is driven back into the dark oblivion from whence he came.'

'There is a definite sword of Damocles air to all this,' said Jim. 'I feel that around every corner something is lurking. Every time a telephone rings or a postman appears, I have to make a dash for the gents'.'

'My own bladder has not been altogether reliable of late,' said John dismally.

'Talking of bladders, it would appear to be opening time.'

John nodded. He owned no timepiece, but his biological clock told him to the minute the licensing hours of the country. 'A pint of Large would be favourable.'

Outside the Swan a builder's lorry was parked, and two swarthy individuals of tropical extraction laboured away at the damaged brickwork with mortar and trowel. Neville, his hand still bandaged from his recent encounter with the Professor's unopenable parcel, put down the glass he was polishing and addressed them with a surly, 'What'll it be?'

Omally raised an eyebrow. 'Not still sulking over the hole in the wall, surely, Neville?' he said.

'I am a patient man,' said the part-time barman, 'but I have stood for a lot this year, what with the perils of Cowboy Night and the like. Every time I sit down and catalogue the disasters which have befallen this establishment over recent months, Omally, your name keeps cropping up, regular as the proverbial clockwork.'

'He is a man more sinned against than sinning,' Pooley interjected helpfully.

'Your name comes a close second, Pooley.'

'They're doing a nice job on the front wall,' said Pooley, smiling painfully. 'What did the brewery say?'

'As it happens,' said Neville, 'things didn't work out too badly there. I told them that it was a thunderbolt.'

'A thunderbolt? And they believed it?'

'Yes, indeed, and not only that, they said that due to the evident danger they would give me an increase in salary, but did not think it wise to install the new computerized cash register in case its electronic workings attracted further cosmic assault upon the premises.'

'Bravo,' said Jim, 'so all is well that ends well.' He rubbed his hands together and made a motion towards the beer pulls as if to say 'Merits a couple of free ones then.'

'All is not well,' said Neville coldly, waggling his still bandaged thumb at them. 'Someone could have been killed. I will have no more of it. This is a public house, not a bloody missile-proving station.'

Neville counted the exact number of pennies and halfpennies into the till and rang up 'No Sale'. The Siamese Twins took themselves and their pints off to a side-table. They had little to offer each other by the way of conversation; they had exhausted most subjects, and their enforced closeness had of late caused them generally to witness and experience the same events. Thus they sat, for the most part speechless, oppressed by fears of unexpected telegrams or fluttering pigeon-post.

The bar was far from crowded. Old Pete sat in his regular seat, Young Chips spread out before him, shamming indifference to the unwelcome attention being paid to his hind quarters by a bluebottle. Norman sat at the bar, wearing an extraordinary water-cooled hat of his own design, and a couple of stalwarts braved the heat for a half-hearted game of darts. An electronic Punkahfan installed by the brewery turned upon the ceiling at a dozen revolutions an hour, gently stirring the superheated air. Brentford had fallen once more into apathy. The sun streamed in through the upper windows, and flies buzzed in eccentric spirals above the bar.

Pooley gulped his pint. 'Look at them,' he said. 'The town has come to a standstill. We spend the night matching wits with the forces of darkness while Brentford sleeps on. Seems daft, doesn't it?'

Omally sighed. 'But perhaps this is what we are doing it for? Just so we can sit about in the Swan while the world goes on outside.'

'Possibly,' said Pooley, finishing his pint. 'Another of similar?'

'Ideal.'

Pooley carried the empty glasses to the bar, and as Neville refilled them he did his best to strike up some kind of conversation with the part-time barman. 'So what is new, Neville?' he asked. 'How spins the world in general?'

'Once every twenty-four hours,' came the reply.

'But surely something must be happening?'

'The boating lake at Gunnersbury is dry,' said the part-time barman.

'Fascinating,' said Pooley.

'The temperature is up by another two degrees.'

'Oh good, I am pleased to hear that we can expect some fine weather.'

'They pulled two corpses out of the river at Chiswick, stuck in the mud they were when the water went down.'

'Really?' said Jim. 'Anybody we know?'

'I expect not, only person to go missing from Brentford in the last six months is Soap Distant, but there was only one of him.'

Pooley's face twitched involuntarily; it was certain that sooner or later someone would miss old Soap. 'No one ever did find out what happened to him then?' he asked casually.

'The word goes that he emigrated to Australia to be nearer to his holes in the poles.'

'And nobody has identified the corpses at Chiswick?'

'No,' said Neville, pushing the two pints across the bar top. 'The fish had done a pretty good job on them but they reckon they must have been a pair of drunken gardeners; they found a wheelbarrow stuck in the mud with them.'

Pooley, who had raised his pint to his lips, spluttered wildly, sending beer up his nose.

'Something wrong, Jim?'

'Just went down the wrong way, that's all.'

'Well, before you choke to death, perhaps you wouldn't mind paying for the drinks?'

'Oh yes,' said Jim, wiping a shirt-sleeve across his face, 'sorry about that.'

Omally had overheard every word of the conversation and when the pale-faced Pooley returned with the pints he put a finger to his lips and shook his head. 'Who do you think they were?' Jim whispered.

'I haven't a clue, and there's no way that the Captain is going to tell us. But it's the wheelbarrow I worry about. What if somebody identifies it?' Omally chewed upon his fingers. 'I should have reported it stolen,' he said. 'It's a bit late now.'

'Even if they identify it as yours, there is nothing to tie you into the corpses. We don't know who they were; it is unlikely that you would have killed two complete strangers and then disposed of them in your own wheelbarrow.'

'The English garda have no love for me,' said John, 'they would at least enjoy the interrogation.'

'Anyway,' said Jim, 'whoever the victims were, they must have been killed sometime before being wheeled across the allotment by the Captain and dumped in the river, and we have perfect alibis, we were here at Cowboy Night, everybody saw us.'

'I slipped out to bury a crate of Old Snakebelly,' moaned Omally, 'on the allotment.'

Pooley scratched his head. 'Looks like you'd better give yourself up then. We might go down to the Chiswick nick and steal back your wheelbarrow, or set fire to it or something?'

Omally shook his head. 'Police stations are bad places to break into; this is well-known.'

'I have no other suggestions,' said Jim. 'I can only counsel caution and the maintaining of the now legendary low profile.'

'We might simply make a clean breast of it,' said John.

'We?' said Pooley. 'Where do you get this "we" from? It was your wheelbarrow.'

'I mean we might tell the police about what we saw. It might start an investigation into what is going on in the Mission.'

'I don't think the Professor would appreciate that, it might interfere with his plans. Also the police might claim conspiracy because we didn't come forward earlier.'

Up at the bar Norman, who had quietly been reading a copy of the *Brentford Mercury*, said suddenly, 'Now there's a thing.'

'What's that,' asked Neville.

Norman prodded at his paper. '"WHEELBARROW CLUE IN DOUBLE SLAYING."'

'I was just talking about that to Pooley,' said Neville, gesturing towards Jim's table.

But naught, however, remained to signal that either Jim Pooley or John Omally had ever been there, naught but for two half-consumed pints of Large going warm upon the table and a saloon-bar door which swung quietly to and fro upon its hinge.

Norman's shop was closed for the half-day and a few copies of the midweek *Mercury* still remained in the wire-rack at the front door. Jim took one of these and rattled the letter-box in a perfect impression of a man dropping pennies into it. He and Omally thumbed through the pages.

'Here it is,' said Jim, '"WHEELBARROW CLUE IN DOUBLE SLAYING: Chiswick Police leading an investigation into the matter of the two bodies found on the foreshore upon the fall of the Thames last week believe that they now have a lead regarding the owner of the wheelbarrow discovered at the scene of the crime. Detective Inspector Cyril Barker said in an exclusive interview with the *Brentford Mercury* that he expected to make an early arrest."'

'Is that it?' Omally asked.

'Yes, I can't see the *Mercury*'s ace reporter getting the journalist of the year award for it.'

'But there isn't a photograph of the wheelbarrow?'

'No, either the reporter had no film in his Brownie or the police didn't think it necessary.'

'But "early arrest"? What do you think that means?'

The words were drowned by the scream of a police-car siren. Driven at high speed, the car came through the red lights at the bottom of Ealing Road, roared past them, and screeched to a standstill a hundred yards further on, outside the Flying Swan. A plainclothes detective and three burly constables leapt from the vehicle and swept into the saloon-bar.

The two men did not wait to see what might happen. They looked at each other, dropped the newspaper and fled.

*

There are many pleasures to be had in camping out. The old nights under canvas, the wind in your hair and fresh air in your lungs. An opportunity to get away from it all and commune with nature. Days in sylvan glades watching the sunshine dancing between the leaves and dazzling the eyes. Birdsong swelling at dawn to fill the ears. In harmony with the Arcadian spirits of olden Earth. At night, a time for reverie about the crackling campfire, the sweet smell of mossy peat and pine needles. Ah yes, that is the life.

Omally awoke with a start; something was pressing firmly into his throat and stopping his breath. 'Ow, ooh, get off, get off.' These imprecations were directed towards Jim Pooley, whose oversized boot had come snugly to rest beneath Omally's chin. 'Will you get off I say?'

Pooley jerked himself awake. 'Where am I?' he groaned.

'Where you have been for the last two days, in my bloody allotment shed.'

Pooley groaned anew. 'I was having such a beautiful dream. I can't go on here,' he moaned, 'I can't live out my days a fugitive in an allotment shed, I wish Archroy had never rebuilt it. You must give yourself up, John, claim diminished responsibility, I will gladly back you up on that.'

Omally was not listening, he was peeling a potato. Before him, a monstrous heap of such peelings spoke fluently of the restricted diet upon which the two were at present subsisting. 'It is spud for breakfast,' said he.

Pooley made an obscene noise and clutched at his rumbling stomach. 'We will die from spud poisoning,' he whimpered. 'It is all right for you blokes from across the water, but we Brits need more than just plain spud to survive on.'

'Spud is full of vitamins,' said Omally.

'Full of maggots more like.'

'The spud is the friend of man.'

'I should much prefer an egg.'

'Eggs too have their strong points, but naught can in any way equal for vitamins, carbohydrates, or pure nutritional value, God's chosen food, the spud.'

Pooley made a nasty face. 'Even a sprout I would prefer.'

'Careful there,' said Omally, 'I will have none of that language here.'

'Sorry,' said Pooley, 'it just slipped out.' He patted at his pockets in the hope that a cigarette he had overlooked throughout all of his previous bouts of pocket-patting might have made a miraculous appearance. 'I have no fags again,' he said.

'You've got your pipe,' said Omally, 'and you know where the peelings are. There are some particularly choice ones near the bottom.'

Pooley made another tragic sound. 'We eat them, we smoke them, we sleep on them. About the only thing we don't do is talk to them.'

Omally chuckled. 'I do,' he said. 'These lads are not as dumb as they may look.' He manoeuvred the grimy frying-pan on to the little brick stove he had constructed. 'Barbeque Spud,' he announced, lighting the fire. 'Today, fritters lightly fried in their own juices, turned but once, and seasoned with . . .'

'Seasoned with?'

'Tiny golden flakes . . . of spud!'

'I can't go on!' said Pooley, raising his voice to a new pitch of misery. 'Two days here, wondering who will get us first, the police or that maniac in the Mission. I can't go on, it is all too much.'

'Your fritters are almost done,' said Omally, 'and this morning I have a little treat to go with them.'

'Spudburgers?' queried Pooley. 'Or is it Kentucky fried spud, or spud chop suey?'

'You are warm,' said Omally. 'It is spud gin.' He hefted a dusty bottle into the light. 'I thought I had a few bottles of the stuff left; they were in the bottom of one of the potato sacks, good place to hide them eh?'

Pooley ran a thoughtful hand over his stubbly chin. 'Spud gin, is it good stuff?'

'The best, but seeing as you have this thing against spuds, I shall not offend you by offering you any.'

'It is no offence, I assure you. In fact,' Pooley scooped up a spud fritter and flipped it into his mouth, 'I am growing quite fond of the dear fellows. Ooh, ouch!' He spat out the fritter and fanned his tongue desperately.

'They are better left to cool awhile,' Omally informed him. 'Here, have a swig.' He uncorked the bottle and passed it to Pooley.

Pooley had a swig. 'Not bad,' said he. Omally watched him with interest. Pooley noticed that he was counting under his breath. 'Nine, ten,' said Omally.

'Ye Gods!' croaked Pooley in a strangled voice, clutching at his throat. Sweat was appearing upon his forehead and his eyes were starting to pop.

'Creeps up on you doesn't it?' Omally asked, grinning wickedly and taking a lesser swig from the bottle Pooley had dropped into his wisely outstretched hands.

Pooley's nose had turned a most unpleasant shade of red and his eyes were streaming. 'That definitely has the edge on Old Snakebelly,' he said when finally he found his voice, 'but I feel I have the measure of it now, give me another swig.'

The two men sat awhile in the morning sunlight, sharing the bottle and chewing upon Omally's potato fritters. At length Jim said seriously, 'You know, John, we really cannot keep this up much longer. We are dangerously close to the Mission, and if that character does not get his papal paws upon us, then someone else is bound to observe the smoke from our fire and report our presence to the police.'

Omally nodded sombrely. 'All these things have of course crossed my mind; our imposed isolation here has given us both time for reflection. For myself I am prepared to sit it out and await the Professor's word, what of you?'

Pooley shrugged helplessly. 'What can I say? I am up to my neck in it; I suppose we have little choice.'

Omally passed him the bottle once more and leant back amongst the potato sacks. 'We shall not starve,' said he, 'although I am afraid there is a limit to the things even I can do with a potato.'

Omally had risen to his feet, his right hand shielding his eyes from the sunlight, and he appeared to be gazing off into the distance. 'Now what do you make of that?' he asked in a puzzled voice.

Omally rose to join him. 'Where?' he asked. 'What are you looking at?'

Pooley pointed. 'It's like a swirl of smoke, or a little black cloud.'

Omally shielded his eyes and squinted off into the haze. There was a dark shape twisting and turning in the sky, and as he watched it grew larger and blacker.

'It's locusts,' said Jim, 'a bloody plague of locusts.'

'It's not locusts,' Omally squealed in a terrified voice, 'it's birds, the birds from Archroy's garden. Run for your life!'

Pooley's feet were welded to the ground. 'I can't run,' he whimpered. 'I fear that the potato gin has gone to my legs.'

'Into the shed then.' Omally grabbed his companion by the shoulders and yanked him backwards, slamming the door shut behind them. He was not a moment too soon, as the screeching mass of birds covered the allotment in a whirling feathery cloud, obliterating the sun. The sound was deafening. Horny bills scratched and scraped at the corrugated iron of the small hut, a thousand tiny hooked claws tore at it. Pooley's hands found themselves once more clapped over his ears while Omally beat away at the snapping beaks which forced their way in through the cracks of the door.

'Do something, Jim!' he shouted, his voice swelling above the din, 'if they get in here there won't be enough of you left to send home in a tobacco tin.'

Pooley took to turning about in circles, flapping his hands wildly, and shouting at the top of his voice. It was a technique he had perfected as a lad and it had always served him well when it came to getting his own way.

The birds, however, seemed unconcerned by Pooley's behaviour and, if anything, their assault upon the hut became even more frenzied and violent. There was the sound of splintering wood and Omally saw to his horror that scores of tiny dents were beginning to appear on the corrugated walls. Then suddenly, the attacks ceased. Pooley found himself spinning, flapping, and shouting in absolute silence. The birds had gone.

'The birds have gone,' said Jim, ceasing his foolish gyrations.

'They have not,' Omally replied. 'I fell for a similar trick on my first encounter with them.'

Pooley pressed his eye to a crack in the door. 'I can't see them.'

'They'll be around, on the roof; or around the back.'

'Then should we make a break for it?'

'That I would not advise.'

The two men slumped on the potato sack in the semi-darkness. It was cramped, and with the sun beating down upon the roof, it was also extremely hot.

'We'll die in here for certain,' said Pooley, 'suffocate we will, like rats in a trap.'

'Don't start all that again,' said Omally, raising his fist in the darkness.

Long minutes passed; in the distance the Memorial Library clock struck ten. Several yards away from the shed, Omally's bicycle

Marchant lay in its twisted wreckage, musing upon man's inhumanity to bike and bird's inhumanity to man. Jim struggled out of his jacket and rolled up his sleeves. 'Have you any more of that potato gin?' he asked. 'Only if I am going to die, I should prefer to die as I have lived, drunkenly.'

'Nobody is going to die,' Omally assured him (although to Pooley his voice had a somewhat hollow quality) 'but I would appreciate it if you could be persuaded to channel your enormous intellect towards some means by which we might facilitate our escape.' He pulled another bottle from the potato sack and handed it to his companion.

'You have a lovely turn of phrase, John,' said Jim, drawing the cork from the bottle and taking a large swig. He passed it back to Omally, who took a sip and returned the bottle. 'How does one drive off birds? Such a thing is surely not impossible.'

'A shotgun is the thing,' said Pooley, 'both barrels, small shot.'

'I fear that we will have a long time to wait for a passing gamekeeper,' said John.

'We might tunnel our way out then, possibly dig down, we might even break into one of Soap's underground workings.'

Omally tapped the concrete floor with his hobnails. 'We can forget that I am thinking.'

'A scarecrow then.'

Omally stroked his chin. 'I can't really imagine a scarecrow putting the fear of God into these lads, but if you will give me a few moments I think I have an idea.'

The Memorial Library clock struck the half hour, and within the small hut upon the allotment Jim Pooley stood, wearing nothing but his vest and underpants. 'Don't you ever change your socks?' Omally asked, holding his nose.

Jim regarded him bitterly in the half-darkness. 'Are you sure this is going to work?' he asked.

'Trust me,' said Omally, 'the plan is simplicity itself.'

Pooley chewed upon his lip. 'It doesn't look very much like me,' he said. 'I am hardly that fat.' His remarks were addressed to the life-sized dummy Omally was fashioning from Pooley's garments. He had knotted the sleeves and trouser bottoms and stuffed the thing with potatoes.

'We've got to give it a little weight,' said John. 'How is the head coming?'

'Splendidly, as it happens,' said Jim. 'I like to pride myself that,

208

given a turnip, which I am disgusted to find that you had secreted from me for your own personal consumption, and a penknife, I am able to model a head of such magnificence as to put the legendary Auguste Rodin to shame.' Pooley passed across his sculpted masterpiece and Omally wedged it firmly between the dummy's shoulders. 'Very nice,' he said.

'Very nice if it fools the birds.'

'It will,' said Omally. 'Have some faith in me will you?'

'But what of me?' Pooley complained. 'I shall be forced to run through the streets in my underwear.'

'I have thought of all that, leave it to me. Are the bottles ready?'

Pooley held up two bottles of the potato gin. They had been uncorked, and gin-dampened strips of cloth torn from Jim's shirt-tail thrust into the necks, Molotov cocktail-style.

'Better douse our good friend here,' said Omally. 'We want this to work to maximum effect.' Pooley took up the last bottle and poured it over the dummy. 'Right.' Omally held the dummy with one arm and made the sign of the cross with the other.

'That is very comforting,' said Jim.

'We only get one chance at this, Pooley, don't mess it up, will you?'

Pooley shook his head. 'Not I, but it seems a tragic end to a good suit.'

'I will buy you another,' said Omally.

'What with? You have no money, you are wearing my other suit.'

'You may have my Fair Isle jumper and cricket whites.'

'Bless you,' said Jim Pooley.

Omally edged open the hut door. All was still upon the allotment, the relentless sun beat down upon the parched earth, and in the distance, a train rolled over the viaduct. 'Now as ever,' said Omally firmly; gripping the dummy, he flung it forward with as much strength as he could muster.

There was a great ripple in the sky above the hut and down upon the dummy in a squawking, screaming cascade the birds fell in full feathered fury. Pooley struck his lighter and set flame to the strips of shirt-tail.

'Throw them,' screamed Omally.

Pooley threw them.

There was a double crash, a flash, and a great flaring sheet of flame engulfed the feathered horde. Without looking back Pooley and Omally took once more to their heels and fled.

22

Brentford's Olympic hope and his Irish trainer jogged around the corner into Mafeking Avenue, up the street a short way, down a back alley, and through the gate into the rear yard of Jim Pooley's house. Mrs King next door peered over the washing-line at them. 'People been round here asking for you Jim Pooley,' she said. 'Why are you running about in your underpants?'

'He's in training,' said Omally. 'Who's been round here asking then?'

'You mind your own business, I was talking to Mr Pooley.'

Omally smiled his winning smile. She was a fine-looking woman, he thought; how had he previously failed to make her acquaintance?

'Who has been calling,' asked Jim, 'friends or what?'

'The police were here,' said Mrs King smugly. 'D I Barker, he left his card.' She delved about in her apron pocket and pulled out a damp and crumpled card which had obviously been doing the local rounds.

'What did he want?' Jim asked innocently, accepting the card.

'Didn't say, just said you were to notify them of your return as soon as what you did, if you see what I mean. Mind you, I'm not surprised, you've had this coming for years, Jim Pooley. In and out at all hours, rolling home drunk, making all that noise.'

Pooley ignored her ramblings. 'Anybody else call?'

'An old man with white hair and a black coat.'

'The Professor,' said Omally.

'I wasn't talking to you. Here, what do you think you're looking at?'

Omally's eyes had been wandering up and down Mrs King's tightly-fitting apron. 'I was undressing you with my eyes.'

'Oh yes?'

'Yes, and that safety pin which is holding up your knickers is getting a bit rusty.'

Mrs King snarled furiously at Omally, flung down her washing and stalked off into her house, slamming the back door behind her.

'Was that wise?' Jim asked. 'She'll probably phone the police now.'

'I don't think so,' said John, grinning lewdly. 'I think she quite fancies me.'

Pooley shrugged and rolled his eyes. 'Your technique is to say the least original,' said he.

The two men mounted the back staircase and disappeared in through Pooley's kitchen door. There was little left to wear in Pooley's wardrobe and so he was forced to don the shirt, Fair Isle sweater, and cricketer's whites left by Omally. He passed over the patent-leather pumps, however, preferring to remain in his hobnails.

'A regular dude,' said Omally. Pooley remained unconvinced. 'So what do we do now?' he asked.

'We might begin by a decent if late breakfast. What supplies have you in your larder?'

Pooley found two tins of beans, which he and Omally consumed with relish. 'And now what?' he asked.

'We will just have to wait for the Professor to return.'

'Or the police.'

Omally nodded grimly. 'Or the police.'

The day passed; there was little to do. Omally fiddled with the knobs on Pooley's archaic wireless-set, but raised little but static and what appeared to be a wartime broadcast. By five-thirty the two men were pacing the floor like caged tigers and tempers were becoming dangerously short.

Finally Pooley could stand it no longer. 'I think I will just step out to Jack Lane's for a couple of bottles of light ale.'

Omally looked doubtful. 'We had better not separate,' he said, 'I will come with you.'

'Good man.'

If the atmosphere of the Flying Swan's saloon-bar was timeless, then that of Jack Lane's was even more so. There was a positive sense of the museum about the place. No one could recall a single change being made in the décor since 1928 when Brentford won the FA Cup and Jack Lane retired from the game to take over as landlord. 'The Four Horsemen', as the establishment was more correctly known, although none had used the name within living memory, had become a shrine to Brentford's glorious one and a half hours upon the sacred turf of Wembley.

True, when Jack departed the game to take up the licensed trade, his team lost its finest dribbler and dropped through the various divisions like a two-bob bit in a Woodbine machine. Jack himself became a kind of living monument. The faded photographs of the team he captained showed him standing erect in his broad-striped shirt, his shorts reaching nearly to his ankles, and the leather ball between his feet. A close examination of these blurry mementoes revealed that Jack had changed hardly at all during the preceding fifty-odd years. Proudly he stood, his toothless face smiling, and his bald head nobly reflecting the Wembley sunlight.

Now well over eighty and taking advantage of the fact, Jack held court over his cobwebbed castle, gnomelike and droll and caring nothing for the outside world and the so-called 'changing times'. He had only noticed the Second World War because the noise had woken him up and he had wondered about why so many of his younger patrons had taken to the wearing of uniforms.

When Pooley and Omally sheepishly entered the saloon-bar, the old gnome was perched upon his stool beside the cash drawer, and eyed them with but a passing interest. 'Close that door,' he mumbled, 'you're letting the weather in.'

Pooley looked at Omally, who shrugged. 'He probably still thinks it's winter.'

Pooley was going to say two bottles of pale ale please, but the words would not come. 'Two pints of Large,' he said presently. Omally patted his companion on the back. The sporting ancient climbed down with difficulty from his stool and shuffled over to the pumps. Pooley recalled that it was always advisable to buy two rounds at a time in the Horsemen, as one's thirst could not always survive the wait while Jack methodically pulled his pints.

'Better make that four pints,' said Omally, who harboured similar recollections.

Jack muttered an obscenity beneath his breath and sought two more pint glasses.

'So what's the news then, Jack?' Omally asked cheerfully.

Jack Lane smiled and ran a ragged pullover sleeve across his nose.

'News?' he said. 'I haven't heard of any news, what news should there be?'

Omally shrugged. 'Just wondered, not much of interest ever gets by you.'

'You been barred from the Swan then, Omally?'

'Hardly that, just thought we'd pop in as we were passing. Trade seems a little slack.' He indicated the empty bar.

'It's early yet.' It was well-known to all that Jack's licensing hours were flexible; few entered his establishment until the hostelries they previously frequented were closing up their doors.

'We had a Lascar in last week,' said Jack, struggling over with the first of the four pints. 'Big buck he was. I told him, out of here I said.'

'Fascinating,' said John, 'but nothing else out of the ordinary happened recently then.'

Jack was by now halfway back towards the pumps and as Omally was on his deaf side he did not reply.

'I think we'll be safe enough in here then,' Pooley whispered.

'Might as well settle in then,' said Omally. 'It will take us a goodly number of pints to catch up upon our last few days of abstinence.'

'I will drink to that.'

By around seven, both Pooley and Omally were in an advanced state of drunkenness. They leant upon one another's shoulders, each extolling the other's virtues and expressing his undying friendship. It was a touching thing to behold.

'Buffoons,' muttered Jack Lane.

'I fear that nature is calling me,' said Pooley, 'and in a voice of no uncertain tone.'

'I myself must confess to having overheard her urgent cries,' Omally replied.

The two men lurched up from their chairs and staggered towards the door. Jack Lane's establishment boasted no 'accommodations' and it was therefore necessary to do one's business in the public lavvies next door. The two men stumbled out into the early evening; it seemed unwontedly dark considering the weather, and there was a definite chill in the air. Omally stared up towards the sky, there was something not quite right about it, but he was unable to make out exactly what it was.

Jim swayed in through the ever-open door of the gents' and

sought out the first available cubicle. He relieved himself amid much sighing and heavy breathing. 'A job well done,' he said, pulling the chain.

Suddenly a soft voice spoke his name. 'Who's that?' Pooley said, looking around in surprise. 'John, is that you?'

Evidently it was not, because Pooley could make out the sounds of a similar bout of sighing and gasping from the next cubicle.

'James,' said the voice again; it was coming from a mesh grille beneath the water cistern.

'Good God,' said Pooley, 'I have lost myself and stumbled into a confessional. Father forgive me, for I know not what I do.'

'James, listen to me.' Jim pressed his ear to the grille. 'There is not much time,' whispered the voice. It was the Other Sam!

'Much time? Much time for what?'

'Tonight is to be the night; the two of you must go at once to Professor Slocombe's.'

Pooley groaned dismally. 'I hardly feel up to it,' he complained. 'Couldn't we put if off until tomorrow?'

The Other Sam's voice was both harsh and urgent. 'You must go at once, waste not a moment, go now, and keep together.'

Pooley was about to voice further complaint, but the Other Sam had gone and Omally was rattling at the door. 'John,' said Jim, 'John, you are not going to like what I have just heard.'

The Irishman stood swaying in the doorway, supporting himself upon the doorpost. 'Do not bother to relate your conversation,' he said simply, 'for I have overheard every syllable.'

Pooley dragged himself up to his feet and patted his companion upon the shoulders. 'The fates are against us,' he said, 'we had better go.'

The two men staggered off down Mafeking Avenue, *en route* for the Butts Estate and Professor Slocombe's house. At intervals Omally stopped to stare again at the night sky. 'Something is definitely amiss in the heavens,' he said.

Pooley stumbled on. 'I would gladly offer you my opinion,' he said, 'but I fear that any increased elevation of the head might result in a catalepsy, possibly terminating in death.'

Outside the Memorial Library Pooley stopped and held up his hands. 'Enough,' said he. 'I can go no further.' He collapsed on to his favourite bench, breathing heavily and clutching at his heart.

Omally pulled at his shirt-sleeve. 'Come now, it's only around the corner, and I am sure that there will be time for a glass or three of the Professor's whisky.'

Pooley rose unsteadily. 'We must aid our noble colleague, a fine and learned old gentleman. Come Omally, let us not delay here.'

The Professor's house was shuttered and absolutely silent. As Pooley and Omally stared at the front door the old man's hand appeared, frantically beckoning them to enter.

The Professor bolted the door firmly behind them. The house was in darkness, lit only by the silver candelabra which the old man carried. By the flickering light Pooley could see that his face looked pale, drawn, and deeply-lined. He seemed to have aged terribly since they had seen him last. 'Are you all right, Professor?' Pooley asked in concern.

Professor Slocombe nodded impatiently. 'I will be all right, what of you two? How have things been for you since last we met?'

'Oh, fine,' said Omally. 'We are wanted by the police, we came within inches of being eaten alive – other than that, fine.'

The Professor led them through the ink-dark corridors towards his study. 'The police,' he said, 'how are they involved?'

'They have found my wheelbarrow stuck in the mud at Chiswick, accompanied by two corpses. They raided the Swan and were also at Pooley's asking questions.'

By now the three men had entered the Professor's study and from his candelabra the old man lit an assortment of candles around the room. 'Fear not, John,' he said, seating himself at his desk, 'I have recorded upon paper all that I know regarding this business. It has been witnessed and it is lodged in a safety-deposit box. Should I not survive this night then at least you will be safe upon that account.'

'That is pleasing to my ears,' said John. 'But come now, survive this night, what can you mean by that?'

As Omally filled glasses, Professor Slocombe seated himself at his desk. 'Tonight,' he said, 'the followers of the being who calls himself Pope Alexander the Sixth will gather at the Seaman's Mission to glorify their new Messiah. Tonight he will install himself upon his papal throne and sanctify his "Holy See". The Mission is to be his new Vatican. Tonight will be our last opportunity to stop him. Should we fail then I can see little future for any of us.'

Pooley gulped back his scotch. 'But do you think we alone can stop him?'

'We must try.'

'And at what time will this mockery of the true Church take place?' Omally asked.

'A little after nine. We must lose ourselves amongst the crowd, and once we get inside you must do exactly as I say.'

Pooley refilled the glasses and looked up at the great mantel-clock. It chimed eight-thirty. 'We have half an hour.' He smiled, dropping back into one of the Professor's high-backed fireside chairs.

Omally fingered the neck of the crystal decanter. 'Plenty of time,' said he.

The minutes ticked slowly away. Pooley and Omally fortified themselves until the decanter was spent, and the Professor sat at his desk, scribbling away with a goosefeather quill upon a length of parchment.

Omally watched the old man working. Could he really stand up to this Pope Alex? Omally felt somewhat doubtful. Certainly the Professor was full of good intentions and his knowledge of the esoteric and the occult was profound. But who knows what might be lurking within the Mission? It seemed reasonable to suppose that Pope Alex would not be unguarded. Better a more positive approach then. Something more physical than mere babblings of ancient words. Something more concrete. More concrete?

A smile crossed Omally's face and broadened into a grin of Cheshire cat proportions. Concrete, that was the thing. Or better still, the good old half-brick; always a friend in time of need.

23

The Professor's clock struck nine, and the old man rose unsteadily to his feet. 'We had better go,' he said, 'slip these about your shoulders.' He indicated two mud-brown cloaks draped across a side-table. 'They should help you merge into the crowd.'

Omally raised himself to his feet and swayed over to the table. 'Very pleasing,' he said, casting the cloak about his broad shoulders, 'very ecclesiastical.'

Pooley climbed from his chair and donned his cloak. 'You would make a fine monk, Jim Pooley,' said Omally, chuckling irreverently.

With that the two caped crusaders helped the Professor to extinguish the candles, then followed the old man through the darkened house to the front door. Professor Slocombe eased it open a crack and the three men stared out into the mysterious night.

All across the Butts Estate, grim-faced crowds were moving. They moved with a strange, stiff-legged gait like tailors' dummies removed from their shop windows and grotesquely animated. The eyes of these dummies seemed glazed and sightless, yet stared ever ahead in the direction of the Mission.

Professor Slocombe turned up the astrakhan collar of his elderly coat. 'Come,' he whispered. He ushered Pooley and Omally out through the front door, which he locked with a heavy iron key. Whilst he was thus engaged, his two inebriated colleagues exchanged knowing glances, furtively stooped, and swept up two likely-looking house bricks, which each secreted within the folds of his robes.

Lovingly patting their respective bulges they followed the old Professor down the short path and out into the Butts Estate. The three men slipped in amongst the sombre crowds, doing their best to adopt the stiff-legged gait and lack-lustre stare. Pooley's impersonation was astonishingly convincing, but that was because he was paralytic. Omally stumbled along at his side, occasionally peering up at the sky and muttering to himself.

As the crowd, which was now several hundred strong, neared the Mission, it soberly formed into a single file. The three men could see that the heavily-braced door had been thrown open and that a soft light glowed from within. Pooley fell into line behind the Professor, with the muttering Omally bringing up the rear. As each of the zombiesque walkers crossed the threshold of the Seamen's Mission he or she genuflected and mouthed a short phrase of archaic Latin.

Pooley was pleased to note that the phrase spoken by the Professor as he entered the portal differed substantially from that of the rest. Jim was no scholar of language so he merely mumbled incoherently and hoped that none would notice. Omally was the next to bow his knee, an action which he achieved more through luck than judgment. His knowledge of Latin was extensive, but it was two words of the Gaelic that he chose. 'Pog Mahoun,' said the man from the Emerald Isle, raising two fingers.

There was already a considerable number of people assembled within the Mission, and the three would-be party-poopers could see little above the multitude of heads.

Omally felt the Professor's sinewy hand closing about his arm as the old man drew the Irishman away towards a shadowy corner. Pooley followed them. Here and there he saw a face he recognized, but doll-like, vacant of expression, and seeming to lack some essential ingredient of humanity.

The three men squeezed themselves into a darkened niche at the rear of a large column. The Professor pressed a slender finger to his lips. 'Watch and wait,' he counselled.

Pooley bobbed up and down in the hope of observing what was going on. Tiring of this futile occupation he whispered to Omally, 'Give us a shin up this pillar and I'll have a look around.' Amid a fair amount of puffing and cursing, all performed in muted tones, Pooley was borne aloft.

What he saw sent his brain reeling at the fantastic transformation which had been wrought within the ivy-hung walls of Brentford's Seamen's Mission. The entire building had been gutted, partition-walls, doors, the upper floor, all were gone. Pooley found himself staring into what must surely be a cathedral. Rows of elaborately carved Doric columns soared upwards towards the roof which, once the haunt of nesting wasps and sleeping bats, was now a glistening dome, painted and frescoed in the style of Michaelangelo, depicting mighty biblical scenes.

There was Adam, wide-eyed and innocent, staring into the godly face of his bearded creator; Eve's temptation, with the hideous black serpent entwined about the tree of knowledge; the Flood, ferociously portrayed with roaring skies and smashing waters, Noah's ark pitching, and the man of God raising his hands towards Heaven, there was the fall of the Tower of Babel, the destruction of Sodom and Gomorrah, and countless other scenes depicted so cunningly that the eye might wander forever amongst them.

The great hall was lit by rows of tall wrought-iron torchères of ponderous proportions, and their steady light illuminated the astonishing adornments which lined the walls, the gilded icons and embossed tableaux, the bronze statues of the saints, the silver madonnas, and the rows of heraldic crests, each of which bore the emblazoned figure of a great bull. There was a king's ransom here, that of many kings in fact, in this unlikely setting.

And then Pooley's eyes fell upon the altar. He had seen pictures in library books of the altarpieces of the world's most notable cathedrals, but they paled into insignificance before this. It was magnificence beyond magnificence; opulence and grandeur taken to a point where it surpassed all beauty and became a thing to fear.

A profusion of fatly-bummed cherubim fluttering and fussing in their golden nakedness; row upon row upon row of candles blazing amid the rising gem-covered columns; the traceried woodwork and carved adornments; the proliferation of wondrous beings, half human, half animal, set in attitudes of supplication, gazing ever upwards towards the titanic figure which crested the altarpiece and held in his outstretched arms a hanging tapestry woven in cloth of gold and depicting once again the motif of a great black bull. The banner of the bull. The banner of the Borgias.

Pooley could have spent long hours in reverent contemplation of these wonders had not Omally chosen this particular moment to topple backwards into the darkness, bringing Jim down from his perch and tumbling him to the floor.

'Sorry,' said John. 'Anything to see?'

Pooley shook his befuddled cranium, unable to find words to describe what he had seen. 'You have a look,' he said finally. 'I'll give you a leg up.'

Omally's head rose unsteadily above the crowd, which still flowed unabated through the Mission door. He saw what Pooley had seen. Certainly the glories were undeniable in their magnificence, but there was something more. Omally cocked his head upon one side. The geometry of the entire hall was slightly amiss; it was not immediately noticeable, but the more he looked at it then the more obvious it became.

He squinted up at the great pillars supporting the marvellous domed ceiling. Surely they were slightly out of true? Several seemed more closely-spaced than the others, and the one at the end was not quite perpendicular. And the dome itself, it was not absolutely round, more ovoid, or more accurately it was egg-shaped.

The great golden altar, for all its unworldly spectacle, was definitely crooked, top-heavy. The statuary was similarly lop-sided, some leaning at dangerous angles. The icons seemed to have been nailed into place and the raised dais which filled an enclosed space before the altar was far from level.

Some attempts had obviously been made here to correct the deficiency and Omally noted that a number of red flettons had been wedged under one corner of it. Red flettons!

Omally stifled a great guffaw. So that was it! Old Pope Alex was certainly far from omnipotent if he dwelt under the misconception that present-day jobbing builders could repeat the masterworks wrought by their fifteenth-century counterparts. The thought that the crimson giant at the Mission was actually capable of error set Omally in fine spirits. These fine spirits, however, were soon dispelled by what next occurred.

The door of the Seamen's Mission swung shut with a death-cell finality, and a cry rose up from the throats of the assembled multitude. It was not so much a cry as a howl. Omally hastily returned to floor level and endeavoured to lose himself once and for all amongst the shadows. The howl went up from all corners of the room, animal in nature, atavistic, echoing down centuries, primaeval and cruel.

The howl rose up, filling the great hall, reverberating about the dome and rebounding from the pillars. It rose and rose in pitch, forming into a scream. The hierophants threw back their heads; hands crossed on their chests like a thousand dead Pharoahs, they swayed upon their heels and howled. Pooley tightened the grip upon his ears, Omally rolled his eyes, and the Professor gripped the silver cross he wore about his neck and mumbled his phrases of

Latin. All at once the howl changed, dropped down in tone and formed itself into a low chant.

The Professor pricked up his ears. 'It is a mantra,' he said, although none heard him.

Slowly the syllables formed upon one another, the chant went up time after time, driving itself almost physically at the three men crouched in the darkness behind the column. Omally was staring goggle-eyed and the Professor forced the Irishman's hands up over his ears. 'You must not hear this,' he whispered. 'You must not hear.'

Omally hummed to himself one of his favourite Republican songs, the much-loved standard, 'Kevin Barry'. He was halfway through the now legendary line about the British soldiers torturing the dear lad in order that he might reveal the names of his brave comrades, when he suddenly realized that he was humming alone. Omally unclasped his ears. There was no sound. The awful chanting had stopped, nothing moved, the air was still. Or was it?

It was a low incessant hissing sound, soft yet persistent. Omally raised his eyes once more towards the astonishing ceiling; it was coming from above. He chewed upon his lower lip. This was a sound he recognized, a reassuring natural sound, not a part of the ghastly unnatural cacophony, this was something real.

And then he knew why the sky had seemed so strange to him that evening. The stars were missing, the moon had gone; while he and Pooley had been sitting in Jack Lane's the sky had clouded over. John turned to his companion, who still had his hands desperately clamped about his ears. 'Listen Jim,' he whispered, prising Pooley's hands from his head. 'It is beginning to rain.'

Outside the Mission and all across Brentford great drops were starting to fall. They struck the dust of the streets with muted explosions, spattered upon the rooftops and sizzled in the trees.

At the Flying Swan Neville the part-time barman set aside his polishing cloth and gazed at the front windows in awe as long teardrops of water began to smear the dusty panes. It was gathering in strength now, and any thoughts Brentford's dehydrated populace may have had of dancing in the streets were rapidly smothered as the thunder began to roll ominously across the heavens and lightning tore the sky apart. It was as if at some God-given signal the very floodgates of Heaven had been opened; the rain fell in torrents, a solid sheet of water. The parched ground sucked and gurgled, the allotment lands drew in the lifegiving liquid, and the stretch of dried-up canal bed devoured the downfall greedily. It was a storm such as none living could remember. Old Pete ordered himself another large rum and peered out through the Swan's open doorway with much shaking of his ancient head. Norman leant upon the bar counter. 'Annus Mirabilis,' Old Pete said to the part-time barman. 'The year of wonders.'

At the Seamen's Mission, Pope Alexander the Sixth's congregation paid no heed to the downpour. As the lightning flashed about Brentford, bursting like a million flashbulbs behind the gigantic stained-glass windows above the altarpiece, they stood resolute, unmoving. Pooley and Omally ducked their heads as the thunder crashed deafeningly above. Professor Slocombe stared upwards, an unreadable expression in his pale-blue eyes.

Suddenly the Mission seemed to draw backwards, sideways, forward, simply away, to suck itself into a vacuum beyond the reach of the maelstrom which roared without. It was as if the building had been snatched away into a limbo, a separate dimension insulated totally from all that was real and touchable. The lightning was still visible, flashing behind the stained-glass, but now it seemed unable to pierce the panes, stopping short of them as if held at bay by some invisible barrier. The roaring of the storm could still be heard, but it was muffled as if somebody had closed a padded door.

A great light began to fill the hall. It grew and grew in brightness until every standing figure, every icon, statue, and column became nothing more than a cardboard cut-out, lit dazzlingly from one side and lost in a void of absolute blackness to the other.

Omally shielded his eyes and squinted into the glare. Pooley dragged his cloak over his head, dropping his cherished half-brick to the floor. Professor Slocombe stood transfixed. From the side of the hall, amid the blinding glare, figures were beginning to appear, moving from the realm of dream, or nightmare.

The congregation were shuffling backwards, forming themselves into a great arc stretching from the side-enclosure to the raised dais of the golden altarpiece. The figures were moving forward in a slow methodic rhythm. Omally could make out their silhouettes, sunspots upon the solar disc. There were four shapeless stubby creatures, bearing on their shoulders something enormous upon a kind of chair. Before this procession a lone being moved unsteadily, gaunt and bowed, a golden censer swinging from his clasped hands.

Omally widened his eyes; the figure was that of Captain Carson. He nudged the Professor but the old man put his finger to his lips and whispered, 'I know.'

The Captain was dressed in rough sacking robes, a golden sash knotted about his waist. His head was shaven and his feet were bare. His face was as vacant as those of the congregation.

Behind him trod the four red-clothed and dwarfish figures, the identity of which was well-enough known to the three watchers. Upon the shoulders of these creatures they supported a gilded travesty of the papal throne, carved from a rich red timber of exotic origin, inset with many precious stones. The arms of this throne terminated in large gilded bulls' heads, as did the very crest upon the chair's high back.

The eyes of these bovine spectres were great red rubies, glittering flawlessly in the pulsating light which flowed from the being who lounged on the velvet cushioning of the fabulous chair. He was enormous, a titan; his great hands rested upon the bulls' heads, and one could have passed a copper penny through any one of the rings he wore. He was clad in the richest of crimsons, his gown smothered in jewels. These were woven into cunning arabesques, symbols of cuneiforms, diamonds, spirals, and trapezoids, each complete of itself yet playing an integral part in the overall design. The gown swam in the throbbing light which surrounded the giant and appeared to pass through several dimensions, shrinking, growing, and moving forwards and backwards as if alive. It was belted at the waist by a broad golden cummerbund and heavily-quilted at the sleeves. Over his massive shoulders the giant wore the holy mantle, and upon his head the papal mitre, cloth of gold and set again with priceless gems.

The three men shrank back into the shadows that they might not meet the gaze of the giant as he passed. Never had they seen such a face, surely the very face of death. It was terrible, but it was also magnificent in its perfect control, absolute power, and supreme arrogance. The great hawk of a nose, the prominent chin, the high cheekbones, the broad forehead, and the eyes two flaming red fires of hell.

The throne halted at the dais of the altar. The being who called himself Pope Alexander the Sixth stepped from it on to the platform. The four creatures lowered the great throne chair to the floor and prostrated themselves before their master. Captain Carson stood ghostlike; the censer swinging from his gnarled and tattooed fingers suddenly ceased its movement in mid-swing and hung in the air in defiance of all the laws of gravity.

Outside, great peals of thunder burst overhead, the lightning flashed and fought with the heavens, and the rain smashed deafeningly upon the Mission roof. Within was silence; the flames of the candles upon the torchères stood absolutely still and offered little light.

The giant slowly folded his Herculean arms and gazed down upon his congregation, who stood immobile, heads bowed, before him. He spoke, and his voice echoed cavernously about the great pillars and filled the dome.

'My people,' he said, 'my own people, to you is granted the supreme honour, to you my first chosen, this night you will bear witness to the consecration of the new Holy See. You are my disciples, and I, the born again, the logos, the master, I grant you this honour. You will spread word of my coming across the world, that all might know my power and marvel at my return.'

The words rolled on and on, a litany of terror. In the shadows of the pillar Professor Slocombe closed his hand about his silver crucifix. Omally bared his teeth and fingered his half-brick. Pooley wondered whether there might be a back door open somewhere near at hand.

'For centuries mankind has awaited my return, and now I am here to fulfil the prophecies and to reclaim my throne. You who stand before me are my vessels, into you shall I pour my powers. You will be masters of men, none shall stand before you, through you shall I regain what is rightfully mine.'

Professor Slocombe held his breath; so this was it. There were easily four hundred people in this hall and if each received only a portion of the giant's powers they would be virtually unstoppable.

'Kneel before me,' roared the giant, 'prostrate yourselves before me.' The congregation threw themselves to the floor, pressing their faces down into the cold mosaic. Omally turned his head away.

'Kneel, I say!'

Omally's eyes flashed back to the figure upon the dais; the face was contorted, twisted into a snarl, and the eyes were blazing.

'You will kneel!'

Across the hall, some ten or so yards from the three hidden figures, two men were standing defiantly amid the sea of fallen bodies. Omally had little difficulty in recognizing one of them. This individual was clad in a dark silk kimono, his head covered by an elaborate Japanese wig. His oversized eyebrows had been dyed the very jettest of blacks and were twisted at their extremities into short spikes.

It was Archroy. As Omally watched, the samurai's companion coolly divested himself of his duffle coat to reveal a clerical collar and the vestments of a priest. It was Father Moity.

Omally turned to the Professor, who shrugged helplessly. Pooley whispered, 'This is going to be good, what odds the Chinese then, John?'

'You will kneel before your Master.' The giant knotted his fists and drew himself up to even greater heights.

Archroy curled his lip and Father Moity drew from his raiment a shining crucifix. The congregation were still, their faces pressed to the cold mosaic floor. They would not have dared to rise even if they could. Before the dais the four creatures were shambling to their unearthly feet.

The Professor drew his two cohorts further back into the shadows. 'If the opportunity should arise,' he whispered, 'I trust that you will employ those two poorly-concealed bricks to good advantage.'

Omally winked. Pooley said, 'In for a penny.'

The rain lashed down upon Brentford and Pope Alexander the Sixth raised his massive arm and pointed towards Archroy and the young priest. 'You, I will make an example of,' he roared. 'You will know the exquisite agonies of lingering death.'

Archroy thumbed his nose. 'Balls,' said he.

The giant gestured to his four hooded cardinals. 'Bring them to me, spare only their lives.'

The grotesque creatures turned upon the two men; forward they came upon their twisted legs, murmuring and whispering. They had lost their fifth brother to a son of mankind and yearned only for vengeance upon the entire race. Their beaked mouths opened and closed, dripping vile slime. Closer they came, steering their way amongst the prone figures; slowly they approached the man of the cloth and the student of Count Dante. Archroy watched them come. 'My bloody beans,' he said, nudging the young priest.

Suddenly they were upon him, their clawlike hands reaching out, knobby, crooked appendages, displaying wicked barbs. Father Moity

225

held up his cross and said the words of the rosary. Archroy pivoted upon his heel and swung about, his foot curling through the air in a blurry arc. He struck one of the creatures a devastating blow, sweeping it from its feet and propelling it through the air. It tumbled to the floor several yards away and came to rest beneath one of the great pillars, silent and unmoving. Its unholy brothers slashed at him but Archroy leapt high into the air above their heads, dropping to the floor behind them.

As they turned, the master of Dimac let out a mighty yell and drove forward an iron fist. He struck one of the creatures firmly at neck height. There was a sickening report as the thing's head departed its body, a brief swish as it whirled through the air, and a dull thud as it landed amongst the shadows to the rear of the hall. The decapitated body remained upright a moment, the arms flailing about and clawing at the space its head had occupied, then it toppled backwards, a crumpled heap of red cloth.

The giant upon the dais raised his hands towards the great dome. 'Destroy him!' he screamed. 'Destroy him!'

Archroy stood undaunted, perfect testimony to the confidence-boosting powers of Count Dante's art. As the two demented godless beings fell on him he drew back both his arms and flung them forward in perfect unison. His fists passed clear through the chests of the creatures, emerging from their spines amid a tangle of rootlike fibres and a great tearing of cloth. Archroy shook the now limp forms away from him and turned upon Alexander the Sixth. 'You're next pal,' he said.

Omally stared in awe. This was the Archroy he had struck down upon the allotment? Pooley said, 'That particular blow seems uniformly effective.'

Archroy stood thumbing his nose and flexing his muscles. Clearly it was impossible for him to feel any fear, no matter how appalling his adversary. Father Moity knelt at his side, hands clasped in prayer. Omally's heart went out towards the young priest who, possessing none of Archroy's ripping, tearing, maiming, and mutilating techniques, had come armed only with his faith to face the diabolical power of the crimson giant.

Upon the dais Pope Alexander the Sixth stood, his entire body trembling, throbbing with unimaginable anger. Behind him, through the stained-glass window, the lightning flashed, casting his massive shadow across the great hall. The light about him grew and grew and became a blazing-white inferno, forming itself into a blinding corona. His contours blurred, and naught could be seen of him but for the two red blood-bowls of his eyes.

A strange vibration ran through the air of the Mission. Omally felt the skin of his face being forced back as if by the pressure of increased G-forces. His cheeks seemed to stretch and draw themselves towards his ears, tears flew from his eyes, and he found it impossible to close them. Pooley clung desperately to the great pillar and the frail Professor staggered back against the side-wall. It was as if a hurricane of icy wind had been directed at them. The congregation was beginning to rise, the people shaking their heads like awakened sleepwalkers, and shielding their faces from the glare.

Archroy stood firmly anchored to the floor, his kimono flapping about him. His exotic wig was torn from his head, exposing his alopecia to full effect. Father Moity raised his hand in benediction and uttered the first words of the holy exorcism, but the force struck him, buffeting him backwards and silencing his voice. Folk were tumbling over one another like rag dolls, bowling over the floor, and fluttering against the walls. The door of the Mission burst outwards and crashed into the rain-lashed night, cartwheeling over and over across the Butts Estate. The figure upon the dais came and went amid the corona of light, his arms outstretched and his head thrown back.

And then, amid the icy unstoppable blast, a low rumble penetrated the Mission, issuing up from the very bowels of the Earth. Its reverberations rolled across the floor, quivering the mighty torchères and spilling out the candles. Omally felt the vibrations growing beneath his feet and knew where he had felt them before: that night in Sprite Street when Soap Distant had performed his ill-fated act of inner portal opening. The deluge had raised the level of the Thames, spilling the waters over the lock-gates and down into the dried-up canal. The water was flooding from there into Soap's subterranean labyrinth, which must surely run directly beneath the Mission.

The great ill-constructed columns trembled, and the figure upon the dais looked up, an expression of horror covering his hideous face. For a moment his power faltered, and that moment was all which was required. The congregation, freed of the binding force, began a mad exodus, cramming through the doorway and out across the Butts Estate. Sections of the frescoed ceiling began to fall away. A great crack appeared in the floor near the doorway and shot across the marble mosaic to the foot of the dais. Pope Alexander stepped back and prepared to marshal his power against the ruination of his Vatican.

Father Moity climbed uncertainly to his feet. The floor was shifting beneath him, and portions of it were breaking away and tumbling into the foaming waters which roared beneath. Archroy clutched his clerical companion and the two stood staring towards the figure on the dais.

Pooley and Omally were endeavouring to raise the fallen Professor, who looked near death. 'Don't worry about me,' the old man gasped, 'his defences are down, strike now before it is too late.'

Pooley scrambled off in search of his half-brick, which had been torn away along with his cloak. Omally, who had clutched his throughout, as the drowning man clutches at the proverbial straw, bore it into the light.

Sadly, Omally was no accurate hurler of half-bricks; had he been sober it is possible that his aim would have been greatly improved. As it was his ill-flung projectile looped through the air, missing the crimson figure by several feet and striking one of the torchères, cleaving out a row of the candles. These fell upon one of the woven tapestries, setting it ablaze.

The crimson figure whirled as the flames licked up behind him. Archroy was advancing across the hall, his bald head flashing like a neon sign in the lightning flares. The rain lashed in through the doorway, and the waters beneath roared deafeningly.

The last of the congregation had long since departed. Pope Alexander the Sixth was alone with his tormentors. They would all die for their blasphemy, each in turn: the old man scrambling across the crumbling floor, the young priest kneeling, those two skulking in the shadows, and the maniac in the kimono. He would be the first.

Archroy leapt on to the dais and confronted the glowering giant. 'Come and get your medicine,' he sneered. 'Come and get your –' The words froze in his throat as the giant raised his hand. Archroy became welded to the spot. His face took on an expression of dire perplexity as he strained against the force which surrounded him.

Professor Slocombe had reached Father Moity, and held out his old black book to the priest. 'Read with me,' he said. Pope Alexander turned in satisfaction from the oriental statue upon the dais. He raised his hands aloft and the light reached out from his fingertips and blazed across the hall, striking the two men. But nothing happened. The Professor and the young priest continued to mouth the ancient formula, and although their words were lost in the storm the effect was manifest. Their mouths moved in unison, intoning the spell, syllable upon syllable. Pope Alexander folded his brow and increased his power, the light radiating from his hands flooding the hall. His eyes burned, and his body shuddered and trembled.

Pooley's hands closed about his half-brick.

The giant stiffened, concentrating every last ounce of his energy upon the two men. The corners of the old black book began to smoulder, sweat ran down the face of Father Moity, the Professor's fingernails scorched and crackled. Jim Pooley threw his half-brick.

The missile struck the giant firmly between his flaming eyes. He had channelled his entire energy into attack and had kept little in reserve for his own defence. He stumbled back, his arms flailing, the beams of light criss-crossing the Mission like twin searchlights. And now another figure was moving across the dais. It was Captain Carson, and he clutched two blazing candles.

The giant saw him approaching but it was too late; Captain Carson thrust the candles at the crimson robes, which caught in a gush of fire, enveloping the struggling figure. As he tottered to and fro, striking at himself, his power relaxed, and Archroy, free of the paralysing trance, leapt forward. His foot struck the giant squarely in the chest, buffeting him back into the blazing tapestry which collapsed upon him.

'By fire!' shouted Professor Slocombe, looking up from his book.

Pope Alexander staggered about the dais, an inhuman torch. Above the flames the unnatural light still glowed brightly about him, pulsating and changing colour through the spectrum. Captain Carson was clapping his hands and jumping up and down on his old legs in a delirium of pleasure.

The Professor and the priest continued to read. Pooley emerged from the shadows, and Omally patted him upon the shoulder. 'Nice one,' he said.

Archroy's vindictiveness, however, knew no bounds. He was being given, at long last, a chance to get it all out of his system: his car, his beans, the birdcage, his mad wife, and this staggering inferno before him, who embodied everything he loathed and detested, and who was indeed the cause of all the indignities he had suffered during the last year.

With a cry of something which sounded like Number Thirty-two on the menu of Chan's Chinese Chippy, Archroy leapt at the blazing giant. He struck him another devastating blow; the giant staggered back to the edge of the dais, wildly flapping his arms beneath the blazing tapestry in a vain attempt to remain upright, then fell with a hideous scream down through the gaping crack in the Mission's floor to the torrents beneath.

'By water!'

Archroy slapped his hands together. 'Gotcha!' he chortled. The Professor and the young priest crossed the floor towards the chasm and stood at the brink. 'He will not die,' yelled the old man above the maelstrom, 'we have not yet finished the exorcism.'

Pooley joined the Professor and peered down into the depths. 'He is going down the main drain,' he said, 'we can follow him.'

The flames had by now reached the tracery work of the great altar and were taking hold. Smoke billowed through the Mission and several of the great columns looked dangerously near collapse. 'Out then,' shouted the Professor. 'Lead the way, Jim.'

Pooley looked up towards Captain Carson, who was still dancing a kind of hornpipe upon the dais, the altar flaring about him.

'You'll have to bring him,' cried Jim, 'we can't leave him here.'

The Professor despatched Omally to tackle the task, while he, Jim Pooley, Father Moity, and Archroy tore out into the rain-lashed night. Pooley aided the Professor, although the old man seemed to have summoned up considerable stores of inner strength.

It was almost impossible to see a thing through the driving rain, but as the four ran across the Estate, Pooley suddenly called out, 'There, that grille at the roadside.'

Up through the grating a fierce light burned. As they reached it the old Professor and the young priest shouted down the words of the exorcism. The lightning lit the pages of the old black book to good effect, and as the glow beneath the grating faded and passed on, the four men rushed after it.

Up near Sprite Street Omally caught them up. 'I got him outside,' he panted, 'but he wouldn't leave, said he wanted to see every last inch of the place burn to the ground.'

'There! there!' shouted Pooley, as a glow appeared briefly from a drain-covering up ahead. Professor Slocombe handed his book to Father Moity. 'You must finish it,' he gasped, 'my breath is gone.'

They passed up Sprite Street and turned into Mafeking Avenue, Omally aiding the wheezing ancient as best he could while Pooley, Archroy, and the young priest bounded on ahead, stopping at various drains and reciting the exorcism. As they neared Albany Road, several great red fire-engines screamed around the corner on their way to the blazing Mission.

At the Ealing Road, Archroy, Pooley, and Father Moity stopped. Omally and the Professor caught up with them and the five stood in the downpour. 'We've lost him,' panted Jim. 'The drains all split up along here, he could have gone in any direction, down most probably.'

'Did you finish the exorcism?' the Professor asked, coughing hideously.

The young priest nodded. 'Just before we lost him.'

'Then let us pray that we have been successful.'

Omally looked about him. Before them gleamed the lights of the 'Four Horsemen', for the five bedraggled saviours of society were now standing outside Jack Lane's. 'Well then,' said Omally, 'if that's that, then I think we still have time for a round or two.'

Professor Slocombe smiled broadly. 'It will be a pleasure for me to enjoy a drink at your expense, John,' he said.

'A small sherry,' said Father Moity, 'or perhaps, upon this occasion, a large one.'

As they entered the establishment Pooley felt Archroy's hand upon his shoulders. 'Just a minute, Jim,' said he, 'I would have words with you.'

Jim turned to the waterlogged samurai. The rain had washed the dye from his eyebrows, and they hung, doglike, over his eyes. 'That pair of cricketer's whites you are wearing,' Archroy continued, 'and the unique pattern upon the Fair Isle jumper, surely I have seen these before?'

Jim backed away through the rain. 'Now, now, Archroy,' he said, 'you are making a mistake, I can explain everything.' With these words Jim Pooley took to his heels and fled.

24

By two-thirty the following morning, the storm was over. Along near the Brentford docks all lay silent. The yellow streetlamps reflected in the broad puddles, and a damp pigeon or two cooed in the warehouse eaves. After such a storm the silence had an uneasy quality about it, there was something haunting about the glistening streets, a certain whiteness about the harshly-clouded sky.

About the soft pattering of the leaking gutters and the gurgling of the drains, another sound echoed hollowly along the deserted streets. A heavy iron manhole cover was slowly gyrating on one of the shining pavements. The cover lifted an inch or two and then crashed back into place. Slowly it eased up again and then with a resounding clang fell aside.

A hand appeared from the blackness of the hole beneath. Dreadfully charred and lacking its nails, it scrabbled at the wet pavement, then took hold. An elbow edged from the murky depths, swathed in what had obviously once been the sleeve of a lavish garment, but was now torn and filthy.

After a long moment, the owner of both elbow and hand, a hideous tramp of dreadful aspect and sorry footwear, drew himself up into the street. He dragged the manhole cover back into place and sat upon it, breathing heavily. His head was a mass of burns, while here and there a lank strand of hair clung to the scar-tissue of his skull. Below two hairless eyebrows, a pair of blood-red eyes glittered evilly. He made a feeble attempt to rise but slumped back on to the manhole cover with a dull echoing thud. A faint light glowed about him as he swayed to and fro, steaming slightly.

A faint sound reached his ears, a low hissing. He raised his bloody eyes and cocked his head upon one side. Around the corner of the street came a canary-coloured vehicle. Upon the top of this an orange beacon turned, its light flashing about the deserted roadways. It was the council street-cleaning cart and in the front seat, hidden by the black-tinted windows, sat Vile Tony Watkins.

He saw the tramp squatting upon the manhole cover clad in what appeared to be the remnants of some fancy-dress costume. He saw the faint glow about him, probably a trick of the light, and his hand moved towards the power button of the water jets. The ghastly tramp raised his hand as the cart approached. He stared up into the windscreen and a low cry rose in his throat, a look of horror crossed his hideous face. But the cart was upon him, its occupant laughing silently within his dumb throat. The jets of water bore down upon the tramp and the yellow vehicle passed on into the night.

Vile Tony squinted into the wing mirror to view his handiwork but the street was deserted. Nothing remained but a pool of blood-coloured water, which glowed faintly for a moment or two then faded into the blackness.

From the shadows of a nearby shop doorway, a crop-headed man stared out at the street, a smile upon his lips. He watched the yellow cart disappear around the corner, emerged from the shadows, and stood looking down into the blood-coloured puddle. The toe of his right foot described a runic symbol upon the damp pavement. This too presently faded and the other Sam drew his robes about him, turned upon his heel, and melted away into the night.

EPILOGUE

Spring has come once more to Brentford. Neville the part-time barman draws the brass bolts upon the Swan's doors and stares out into the Ealing Road. Happily, of ill-favoured tramps, the street is bare. Old Pete appears from Norman's papershop, his dog Young Chips at his heels. Pooley is upon his bench, studying the racing papers, and Omally is stirring from his nest, clutching at his hangover and muttering something in Gaelic.

Archroy has left Brentford. The patrons of the Swan got up a whip-round for him and he has gone off to America to challenge Count Dante to life-or-death combat. Sadly, when he reaches New York he will be thwarted, since the legendary Count is nearing eighty and crippled with arthritis.

Professor Slocombe still performs his daily perambulation of the village boundaries, Father Moity rarely has less than a full-house come Sunday mornings, and Norman is currently engaged upon a new project involving the Einstein's unified field theory.

For all Brentford's other citizens, life goes on very much as before. Captain Carson has retired to a cottage beside the sea, the Trust awarding him a small pension. The Mission still stands, partially rebuilt; it is ironic to note that it could never have been demolished, for Crowley's defunct uncle had seen to it that a preservation order had been put on the place.

All in all, nothing has really changed. The events of last year have absorbed themselves into local folklore, and current conversation revolves around the newly-planted crops upon the allotment.

As to what the future may hold, few can say. Those who can are keeping it pretty close to their chests.

THE BRENTFORD TRIANGLE

PROLOGUE

The solitary figure in the saffron robes shielded his eyes from the glare and squinted down the glacier to where the enormous black vessel lay, one-third submerged, in the floor of the valley. Allowing for the portion lost below the icy surface of the frozen lake it was easily some three hundred cubits long, at least fifty wide and another thirty high. It had, overall, the appearance of some fantastic barge with a kind of gabled house mounted upon its deck. Its gopherwood timbers were blackened by a heavy coating of pitch and hardened by the petrification of the glacier which had kept it virtually intact throughout the countless centuries. A great opening yawned in one side; several hundred yards away lay the door which had once filled it, resting upon two huge rocks like some kind of altarpiece.

The solitary figure dropped the butt of his Wild Woodbine, ground it into the snow with the heel of his naked left foot and raised his field glasses. His guides had long since deserted him, fearing in their superstition to set foot upon the ice pastures of the sacred mountain. Now he stood alone, the first man to breast the glacier and view a spectacle which many would gladly have given all to witness.

He whistled shrilly between closed teeth and a faint smile played about his lips. He slapped his hands together, and with his orange robes swirling about him in the bitter winds of the mountain peak, he girded up his loins and strode down the frozen escarpment to survey the ancient wreck at closer quarters.

I

Neville the part-time barman drew back the polished brass bolts and swung open the saloon-bar door of the Flying Swan. Framed in the famous portal, he stood yawning and scratching, a gaunt figure clad in Japanese silk dressing-gown, polka-dot cravat and soiled carpet-slippers. The sun was rising behind the gasometers, and in the distance, along the Ealing Road, the part-time barman could make out the diminutive form of Small Dave the postman beginning his morning rounds. No mail as usual for the Four Horsemen, more bills for Bob the bookie, a small brown parcel for Norman's corner shop, something suspicious in a large plain envelope for Uncle Ted at the greengrocer's, and, could it be –? Neville strained his good eye as Small Dave approached – tunelessly whistling the air to 'Orange Claw Hammer' – a postcard?

The wee postman trod nearer, grinning broadly. As he drew level with the part-time barman he winked lewdly and said, 'Another!' Neville extended a slim white hand to receive the card, but Small Dave held it below his reach. 'It is from Archroy,' announced the malicious postman, who greatly delighted in reading people's mail, 'and bears an Ararat postmark. It says that our lad has discovered . . .' Neville leant hurriedly forward and tore the card from his hand '. . . has discovered the remains of Noah's Ark upon the mountain's peak and is arranging to have it dismantled and brought back to England.'

Neville fixed the little postman with a bitter eye. 'And you could tell all that simply by reading the address?' he snarled.

Small Dave tapped at his nose and winked anew. 'I took the liberty of giving it the once-over,' he explained, 'in case it was bad news. One can never be too careful.'

'One certainly can't!' The part-time barman took a step backwards and slammed the Swan's door with deafening finality upon the dwarfish scrutineer of the Queen's mail. Neville took a deep breath to steady his nerves and turned away from the door. His long strides took him with haste across the threadbare carpet of the saloon-bar.

His first drew him past the pitted dartboard, the chalked scores of the previous night's play faintly aglow in the early light. His second brought him level with the aged shove-halfpenny table, and a third took him past the first of the Swan's eight polished Britannia pub tables. Two more soundless strides and Neville halted involuntarily in his tracks. Before him stood an object so detestable, so loathsome and so mind-stunningly vile that the postman's irritating habits paled into insignificance.

The Captain Laser Alien Attack Machine!

Its lights blinked eternally and a low and sinister hum arose from it, setting the part-time barman's ill-treated teeth on edge. Installed by one of the brewery's cringing catspaws the thing stood, occupying valuable drinking space, and as hated by the Swan's patrons as it was possible for any piece of microchipped circuitry to be hated.

Neville caught sight of his face reflected in the screen and surprised even himself with the ferocity of his expression. He addressed the machine with his regular morning curse, but the monster hummed on regardless, indifferent to the barman's invocation of the dark forces. Neville turned away in disgust and slouched off up the stairs to his rooms. Here in privacy he poured milk upon his cornflakes and perused Archroy's postcard, propped against the marmalade pot.

A rooftop view of Brentford.

It was a great pity that Archroy, in the interests of economy, as he put it, had chosen to take a bundle of local postcards with him when he set off upon his globe-trotting. Rooftop views of Brentford were all very pleasant of course, but they did tend to become a little samey. After all, when one received a card postmarked 'The Potala, Lhasa', or 'The East Pier, Sri Lanka', it wouldn't hurt to see a bit of pictorial representation on the front once in a while. It did tend to take the edge off, having read the exotic details of a Singhalese temple dance, to turn over the card and view the splendours of two gasometers and a water tower.

Neville sighed deeply as he squinted over to the row of identical postcards which now lined his mantelpiece. Certainly, the one view was so commonplace as to be practically invisible, but each of these little cards had been dispatched from some far-flung portion of the great globe. Each had travelled through strange lands, across foreign borders, over continents, finally to return, like little pictorial homing pigeons, to the town of their birth. Certainly there was romance here.

Neville plucked up the card and turned it between his fingers. 'Noah's Ark, eh?' That one took a bit of believing. Each of the postcards had boasted some fabulous deed or another, but this outdid them all.

Noah's Ark? To the pagan Neville it did seem a trifle unlikely. Even if it had existed at all, which Neville considered a matter of grave doubt, the chances of it surviving, even partially intact, down through the long centuries on the peak of Mount Ararat did seem pretty slight. Such things were just silly-season space-fillers for the popular press. The barman recalled reading about that chap up north who claimed to have discovered the bottomless pit in his back garden. He would probably have come clean that it was all a hoax had he not stepped backwards down it while posing for the press photographer.

Noah's Ark indeed! Neville took the card and placed it with its eight identical brothers upon the mantelshelf. Noah's Ark indeed! It couldn't be true. Could it?

2

That same sun, having now risen from behind the gasometers, stretched down a tentative ray towards a rarely washed bedroom window at Number Six Abaddon Street. Passing with some difficulty through the murky pane, it displayed itself upon an inner wall as a pale lozenge of light surrounding a noseless statuette of Our Lady.

This mantelpiece beatification of the blessed Virgin was as usual lost upon the room's tenant. John Vincent Omally was what the textbooks are wont to describe as 'a late riser'. Usually the lozenge of light would move noiselessly across the mantelpiece wall until it reached the cracked mirror, and then reflect itself on to the face of the sleeper, thus awakening him from his restful slumbers. But today, as for some days past, it was to be denied its ritual.

Today it would find but an empty pillow, showing naught of a recumbent head but a slight indentation and a Brylcreem stain. The coverlet was tossed aside and a pair of ragged pyjama strides lay in an athletic splits posture upon the linoleum. A timeworn tweed jacket was missing from its appointed hook behind the door. It was not yet eight of the clock and John Omally was no longer at home to callers. For John Omally had important business elsewhere.

John Omally had gone a-golfing.

'Fore!' The cry echoed across the allotment, struck the wall of the Seamen's Mission and passed back over the head of a curly-headed son of Eire, clad in soiled Fair Isle slipover and rolled-up tweeds. 'Fore and have a care!' Omally swung the aged club, the relic of a former and more refined age, with a vengeance and struck the little white pill a mighty blow. The ball soared some four feet into the clear morning air and fell to earth in the midst of Jim Pooley's radish patch.

Jim stifled a titter and read from a dog-eared exercise book entitled *The Now Official Handbook of Allotment Golf*: 'Unless rendered totally inextricable, by nature of being unreachable, i.e. under more than four feet of water or beyond climbing capability, the player will play the stroke. Should the player, however, endanger the growth of his opponent's radishes he will forfeit the hole.'

Omally scratched his head with a wooden tee and eyed Pooley with some suspicion. 'I don't recall that bit at the end, Jim,' said he. 'May I venture to ask whether the rule applies to runner beans, possibly of the variety which you uprooted from my plot yesterday whilst attempting that trick shot of yours on to the fourth?'

Pooley made a thoughtful face. 'Beans are not specifically mentioned,' he said, carefully examining the note he had so hastily scribbled. 'But if you are making an official request to have them included in the handbook then I think we might stretch a point and pencil them in.'

At this moment the two golfers suddenly threw themselves down commando-fashion into a clump of long grass. An explanation for this extraordinary behaviour was almost immediately forthcoming as the distinctive tuneless whistling of Small Dave signalled the approach of that midget as he took his regular morning short cut through to the Butts Estate.

Allotment Golf had not yet caught the eye either of the allotment holders or the general public, and both Pooley and Omally wished to keep it that way. They would have greatly preferred to golf upon one of the municipal courses, but circumstances had decreed that their photographs now appeared upon every persona-non-grata board throughout the county.

It had all appeared so trivial at the time, the small disagreements, the occasional bout of fisticuffs; hardly police matters one would have thought. Golfers, however, are a clannish bunch with rather a conservative attitude towards sport. The two Brentonians' extraordinary conception of the game had not been appreciated. Their constant rule-bending and wild club-swinging, their numerous bogus claims to the course record, achieved for the most part by omitting to play the more difficult holes, their total disregard for other players' safety, refusing to shout 'Fore', before what Omally described as 'heavy putting', had been too much to bear. The secretary of one course had shown moments of rare tolerance: he had respected Pooley's request to play the holes in reverse order, he had suffered Omally playing in cycling cape and fisherman's waders one particularly wet day, but when Pooley relocated all the tee markers (in order to make the game more interesting) and Omally had dug a second hole upon the third green in order to sink a birdy four, stern measures had been taken. The two potential Ryder Cup winners had been given what the French refer to as 'La Rush de la Bum'.

Thus in a moment of rare inspiration, necessity being, like Frank Zappa, the mother of invention and Jim Pooley being a man of infinite resource when cornered, Allotment Golf had been born.

It had much to recommend it. There was no queuing up to be done, no green fees to pay, no teeing off in front of cynical observers to be suffered; above all, they could invent their own rules as the fancy took them. As originator, Jim took sole charge of the exercise book until every detail was clarified. This, he told Omally, was what is called 'a divine right'. A certain amount of subterfuge was called for, of course; they had no wish to alert any of the other allotment holders to the sport for fear that it might catch on. It had been a moment of rare inspiration indeed on Pooley's part, but one which was to play its part in changing the face of Brentford as we know it for good and all.

'Fore!' Small Dave had departed upon his round and John Omally set to it once more to shift his ball from Pooley's radish patch and belt it heartily towards the fourth hole, which lay cunningly concealed between Old Pete's wheelbarrow and his battered watering-can.

3

Norman was one of those early birds which catch the proverbial worm. Running the down-at-heel corner-tobacconist's at anything remotely resembling a profit was pretty much a full-time occupation. Norman went about it, as he did with everything else, with a will. 'One must remain constantly in the field if one wishes to ladle off the cream which is one's bread and butter,' he constantly explained to his customers. This remark generally met with enough thoughtful head-nodding to offer the shopkeeper the encouragement he needed.

Norman had been up since six, sorting through and numbering up the day's papers. It was Wednesday and the first crop of specialist journals had arrived. There was the *Psychic News* for Lily at the Plume Café. This Norman numbered in large red figures as the new paperboy had the irritating habit of confusing it with *Cycling News* and delivering it to Father Moity at St Joan's. There was the regular welter of sporting mags for Bob the bookie, and a selection of Danish glossies for Uncle Ted the greengrocer. Norman folded a copy of *Muscle Boys* into the widow Cartwright's *Daily Telegraph* and hummed softly to himself. There was a busy day ahead and he intended to take advantage of its each and every minute.

Nick, the big-nosed paperboy, sidled into the shop, chewing gum and smoking what the lads at the Yard refer to as the certain substances. 'Kudos, Norm,' he said.

Norman looked up from his doings and eyed the youth with evident distaste. 'Good morning, Nicholas,' he said, giving his watch minute scrutiny and rattling it against his ear. 'Can that be the time already, or is the old Vacheron Constantine running fast again?'

The paperboy flicked idly through a copy of *Bra-Busting*

Beauties. 'Look at those charlies,' he said, salivating about the gums, 'you'd think you'd gone deaf, eh?'

Norman thrust the bundle of folded papers into the worn canvas bag and pushed it across the worm-eaten counter. 'Away on your toes, lad,' he grunted. 'Time heals all wounds and absence makes the heart grow fonder.'

'Oh, it do,' the lad replied, sweeping up the bag in an eczema-coated fist and bearing it away through the door like the standard of a captured enemy. 'It do that!'

Norman watched him depart in sorrow. There was something decidedly shifty about that boy, but he couldn't quite put his finger on exactly what. The shopkeeper crossed the mottled linoleum floor and turned the CLOSED sign to OPEN. Soon they would arrive, he thought, as he peered through the grimy door-glass: the office girls for their cigarettes and chocolate bars, the revellers of the previous night for their aspirins, the school lads for their comics and penny toffees, the old dears for the pints of milk Reg the Milkman had neglected to leave upon their steps, Old Pete for his half-ounce of tobacco, Pooley and Omally for five Woodbines on their weekly accounts. The same old regular morning faces.

Norman shook his head thoughtfully. It wasn't a bad old life if you didn't weaken, was it? And a trouble shared was definitely a trouble halved, and you had to laugh didn't you?

Retracing his steps to the counter he selected one of the newer brands of bubblegum that the local rep had persuaded him into stocking. Stripping away the wrapper from the stick of Captain Laser Astrogum he thrust the gaudy piece of synthetic sweetmeat into his mouth.

Chewing distractedly he drifted about his shop, flicking without conviction at the dust-filled corners and blowing the falling residue from the faded coverings of the out-of-date chocolate boxes which lined his shelves. Here was the Queen smiling sweetly, if somewhat faintly, at her Coronation. Here two stuffed-looking Scotties peered through the rust from a shortbread biscuit tin, and here was the Pickwickian character still grinning idiotically at that uneatable coughsweet.

Norman drew a bespittled finger across the old tin's surface in an attempt to bring up the brand-name. Did people still eat sweeties like this? he wondered. Or had they ever? He couldn't recall ever having sold any. Out of sudden interest he picked up the old tin and gave it a shake. It was empty, of course. Probably evaporated, he thought.

Norman shrugged once more; he really ought to sling them all out, they served little purpose and could hardly be described as decorative. But he knew he would never part with them. They gave his shop character and were always good for inspiring conversation from the lonely pensioners who happened by, upon some pretext or another, only really wanting a bit of a chat.

Norman thrust his one-feather duster back into its appointed niche and flexed his shoulders as if in an attempt to free himself from the strange melancholia which filled him this morning. Things were going to change in Brentford and there was little good in crying over spilt milk or whistling down the wind.

Upon the counter lay the small brown package which Small Dave had delivered. Norman knew exactly what it contained; the American stamps and spidery Gothic lettering told him well enough. This was the last component he required, the final tiny missing piece of the jigsaw.

This was the make or break. Several years of planning and many many months of hard and exacting work had gone into this, not to mention the small fortune spent upon research, preparation and final construction. This experiment was indeed 'The Big One'. It was a Nobel Prize job this time, and no mistake. Norman had named it 'The Ultimate Quest', and it was indeed a goody.

Certainly, in the past, Norman's little scientific diversions had not been altogether successful. In fact he had become something of a figure of fun because of them. But this time he was sure he had cracked it. The people of Brentford would certainly sit up and take notice of this one. If his calculations, combined with those of a certain Germanic physicist not altogether unknown for his theory of relativity, proved to be correct, then things were going to be very different indeed hereabouts.

Norman patted the tiny brown package. If all was present and correct he would begin the first practical working tests this very early-closing day, then we would see what we would see.

The shop bell rang in a customer. It was Old Pete with his half-terrier Chips as ever upon his heels. 'Morning, Norman,' said the ancient, cheerily, 'a half-ounce of Ships if you will.'

'Grmmph mmmph,' the shopkeeper replied, for the first time becoming aware that the Captain Laser Astrogum had suddenly set hard in his mouth, welding his upper plate to his lower set.

247

'Grmmph mmph?' queried Old Pete, scratching at his snowy head. 'Now what would it be this time? Let me guess? Experimenting with some advanced form of Esperanto is it? Or having a try at ventriloquism?'

Norman clutched at his jaw and grew red about the jowls, his eyes began to roll.

'Ah,' said Old Pete, tapping at his nose. 'I think I am beginning to get the measure of it. Something in mime, isn't it? Now let's have a go, I'm quite good at this, give me a clue now, how many words in the title?'

Norman tore at his welded teeth and bashed at the counter-top with a clenched fist.

'Five words,' said Old Pete. 'No, six, seven? Is it a film or a book?'

Norman lurched from the counter in a most grotesque fashion, grunting and snorting. Old Pete stepped nimbly aside as he blundered past, while Young Chips sought a safe hideyhole.

'It's a poser,' said the Old One, as Norman threw himself about the shop, toppling the magazine stand and spilling out its contents. 'I have it, I have it!' he cried suddenly. 'It is the now legendary Charles Laughton in his famous portrayal of Victor Hugo's *Hunchback of Notre Dame*.'

In heavy congratulations for Norman's excellent impersonation the old man, who still retained a considerable amount of strength in his right arm despite his advancing years, slapped Norman upon the back. The blow loosed the cemented teeth, which flew from the shopkeeper's mouth, tumbled noisily across the linoleum, and finally came to rest in an impenetrable place beneath the counter, where they lay in the darkness grinning ruefully.

'Sanks yous,' spluttered Norman, 'sanks yous, Petes.'

'Credit where credit is due,' the elder replied. 'My tobacco now, if you please.'

Norman staggered to the counter and tore out a one-ounce packet from the tin. 'Ons a houses,' he whistled through his naked gums. 'Ons a houses.'

Old Pete, who was never a man to look a gift impersonator in the mouth, accepted his reward with a hasty display of gratitude and departed the shop at speed. Halfway up the Ealing Road Young Chips unearthed a pristine copy of *Bra-Busting Beauties* from its secret hiding place beneath a beer crate outside the Swan.

'This has all the makings of being a most profitable day,' said the ancient to his furry companion. Young Chips woofed non-committally. Being naturally clairvoyant he sensed something rather to the contrary and therefore wished to reserve judgment for the present.

4

The allotment golfers had come to something of a critical stage in their game. They had by now reached the eighteenth 'green' and Omally had but to sink a nine-foot putt across Reg Watling's furrowed spinach patch to take the match. Betting had been growing steadily during the morning's play and with each increase in financial risk the two men had grown ever more tight-lipped, eagle-eyed, and alert to the slightest infringement of the rules.

Omally spat on his palms and rubbed them together. He stalked slowly about his ball and viewed it from a multiplicity of angles. He scrutinized the lie of the land, tossed a few straws into the air and nodded thoughtfully as they drifted to earth. He licked his finger and held it skyward, he threw himself to the ground and squinted along his putter sniper fashion. 'Right then,' said the broth of a boy. 'It looks like child's play.'

Pooley, who was employing what he referred to as 'the psychology', shook his head slowly. 'That would be at least a three to the sinking I would believe.'

Omally gestured over his shoulder to the water-butt wherein lay Pooley's ball. 'You would be phoning for Jacques Cousteau and his lads, I shouldn't wonder.'

Pooley shrugged. 'That is an easy shot compared to this.'

Omally sniggered. 'Keep your eye on the ball, Jim,' he advised.

Omally's putting technique bore an uncanny resemblance to that practised by seasoned Yorkshire batsmen at the Oval. The putter had a tendency to dig well in on such occasions, sometimes to a depth of some three inches or more, and once beyond digging range. There was generally a fair amount of lift on the ball, although the *Now Official Handbook of Allotment Golf* suggested that any balls putted above shoulder height should be considered as drives and the player penalized accordingly.

Omally squared up his ball whilst Pooley continued to employ 'the psychology'. He coughed repeatedly, rustled sweet papers in his pocket and scuffed his blakey'd heels in the dust. 'Is that a Lurcher or a Dane?' he asked, pointing towards some canine of his own creation.

Omally ignored him. There was big beer money on this shot. John suddenly swung the putter in a blurry arc and struck deeply behind his ball, raising a great clod of earth, which is referred to in golfing circles as a divot. The ball cannonaded across the allotment, with a whine like a doctored tom struck a section of corrugated iron fencing, bowled along Old Pete's herbaceous border, and skidded to a halt a mere inch from the eighteenth hole.

Omally swore briefly, but to the point, flung down his putter and turned his back upon the wanton pill.

'Bad luck,' said Pooley, amid an ill-concealed snigger. By way of consolation, he added, 'It was a brave try. But would you prefer that I pause a moment before sinking my ball, on the off chance that an earth tremor might secure you the match?'

Omally kicked his golf bag over.

'Steady on,' said Pooley.

John turned upon him bitterly, 'Go on then, Jimmy boy,' he sneered, 'let us see you take your shot.'

'You won't like it.'

'Won't I, though?'

Pooley tapped at his nose. 'Care to up the betting a trice?'

Omally stroked his chin. 'From the water-butt in one, that is what you are telling me?' Pooley nodded. 'Unless you, like the Dalai Lama, have mastered the techniques of levitation and telekinesis, which I do not believe, I do not rate your chances.'

'You will kick yourself afterwards.'

Omally spat on to his palm and slapped it into that of his companion. 'All bets are doubled, will that serve you?'

'Adequately.' Pooley strolled over to the water-butt. With the lie of the land, it certainly was in a perfect line for the hole. Just down a slight slope and into the depression where lay the eighteenth.

'I shall play it from here,' said Jim, turning his back upon the target.

Omally stuck his hands into his pockets. 'As you please,' said he.

'I will play it with a mashie if you have no objections.'

'None whatever.' Omally selected the club and handed it to his companion. Pooley leant forward and chalked a small cross at the base of the water-butt. Drawing back, he grasped the club hammerlike in his right fist and with a lewd wink struck the ancient zinc tank a murderous blow.

It was a sizeable hole and the water burst through it with great enthusiasm. Bearing down with the sudden torrent, and evidently much pleased to be free of its watery grave, Pooley's ball bobbed along prettily. It danced down the slight incline, pirouetted about the eighteenth hole, as if taking a final bow, then plunged into it with a sarcastic gurgle.

'My game,' said Pooley rubbing his hands together. 'Best we settle up now, I think.'

Omally struck his companion a devastating blow to the skull. Jim collapsed into a forest of bean poles but rose almost immediately with a great war cry. He leapt upon Omally, catching him around the waist and bearing him towards the now muddy ground. 'Poor loser!' he shouted, grinding his thumb into Omally's right eye.

'Bloody damn cheat,' the other replied, going as ever for the groin.

The two men were more than equally matched, although Omally was by far the dirtier fighter. They bowled over and over in the mud, bringing into play a most extraordinary diversity of unsportsmanlike punches, low kicks and back elbows. They had been tumbling away in like fashion for some ten minutes, doing each other the very minimum amount of damage, yet expending a great deal of energy, when each man suddenly became aware that his antics were being observed.

Some twenty yards or so away, a solitary figure in a grey coverall suit stood silently watching. At the distance it was difficult to make out his features clearly, but they seemed wide and flat and had more than the suggestion of the Orient about them.

The two men rose from the ground, patting away at their clothes. The fight was over, the ref's decision being a draw. They beat a hasty retreat to the doubtful safety of Pooley's allotment shed. Through a knot-hole in the slatted side they squinted at the grey figure. He was as immobile as a shop-window dummy, and stared towards them unblinkingly in a manner which the sensitive Jim found quite upsetting. He was of average height with high cheek-

bones and a slightly tanned complexion and bore a striking resemblance to a young Jack Palance.

Pooley sought about for his tobacco tin. 'I don't like the look of
this,' he said.

Omally, who had liberated Pooley's tin from his pocket during
the fight, was rolling a cigarette behind his back. 'He is probably
some workman chappy,' he suggested, 'or possibly a bus conductor
or site engineer from the gas works.' The hollow tone in Omally's
voice was not lost upon his companion.

'He has more of the look of a municipal worker to me,' said Jim,
shaking his head dismally. 'A park-keeper perhaps, or . . .'

'Don't say it,' said John. 'Some spy from the Council come to
inspect the allotment?'

Pooley clenched his fists. 'This is all too much. Discriminated
against and ostracized from the Council courses, now tracked down
here for further discrimination and ostracization, hounded down
because of our love of the game. It is all too much to bear. Let us
kill him now and bury his body.'

Omally agreed that it was all too much to bear but thought
Pooley's solution a little drastic. 'All may not be lost,' he said. 'He
may have only just arrived and may only have witnessed our slight
disagreement regarding the excellence of your trick shot. He may
not suspect the cause.'

Pooley gestured through a broken window-pane to where his golf
caddy, a converted supermarket trolley, stood bristling with its
assortment of unmatched clubs.

Omally hung his head. 'The game is up,' said he in a leaden tone.

Pooley put his eye once more to the knot-hole. 'He is still there.
Perhaps we could reason with him, or better still offer a bribe.'

Omally thought this sound enough, every man having his price.
'How much have you in your pockets?' he asked.

Pooley smiled grimly. 'We have not yet settled up over the game,
I think that it is for you to approach him, John. Employ your silken
tongue and feel free to invest a portion of my winnings if needs be.
You can always owe me the difference, I consider you to be a man
of honour.'

Omally licked the end of his captured roll-up. 'All right,' he said
nobly, 'I shall go. We shall consider your winnings to be an invest-
ment to secure a further season of uninterrupted play. During this
period I have not the least doubt that if your game continues at its

present standard you will have the opportunity to lighten my pockets continually.'

Pooley opened his mouth to speak but thought better of it. In such matters Omally generally held the verbal edge. 'Go then with my blessings,' he said, 'but kindly leave me my tobacco tin.'

Omally straightened up his regimental necktie, squared his broad and padded shoulders, threw open the hut door, and stepped out into the sunlight. The figure lurking amongst the bean poles watched the Irishman with an inscrutable expression. Omally thrust his hands into his trouser pockets and gazed about the allotment with extreme nonchalance. He yawned, stretched, and then, as if seeing the figure for the first time, flicked at his mop of curly black hair and bid the stranger a hearty 'Good morning there.'

The figure uttered not a word but merely stared on regardless.

'There'll be rain before the evening I shouldn't wonder,' said Omally, who was rarely rattled. 'Won't do the ground any harm though.' As he spoke he slowly strolled in the stranger's direction, covering his approach with the occasional sidestep to scrutinize some flowering bloom. But soon there was less than fifteen yards between them. 'Should get a rare old crop of beans up this year,' said John, stepping nimbly over Old Pete's watering can.

In order that he might reach the Council spy, for by this time Omally felt one hundred per cent certain that this was in fact the lurker's despicable calling, it was necessary for him to pass behind Soap Distant's heavily-bolted corrugated iron shed. Soap himself had vanished away from Brentford under most extraordinary circumstances, but his rental upon the shed was paid up until the turn of the following century and his hut remained untouched and inviolate.

Omally sneaked away behind it. He lost sight of the spy for but a moment, but when he emerged at the spot where the malcontent should have been standing, to John's amazement, not a soul was to be seen.

Pooley came ambling up. 'Where did he go?' he asked. 'I took my eyes off him for a moment and he was gone.'

Omally shook his head. 'There is something not altogether kosher about this, I am thinking.'

'He must have legged it, had it away on his toes.'

Omally scratched at the stubble of his chin. 'Perhaps,' said he,

'perhaps. There is a terrible smell of creosote hereabouts, has anybody been pasting his paintwork?'

'Not to my knowledge.'

Omally shrugged, 'Shall we play another round then?'

Pooley scrutinized his Piaget wristwatch. 'I feel a little unsettled,'
he said. 'Perhaps we should adjourn now to the Swan for a cooling
pint of Large to ease our fractured nerves.'

'That,' said Omally, smacking his hands together, 'is not a bad
idea by any reckoning!'

5

Bitow . . . *Bitow* . . . *Bitow* . . . *Bitow* . . . *Whap* . . . 'What?' The
ungodly sounds echoed across the library-silent saloon-bar of the
Flying Swan, rattling the optics and jarring the patrons from their
contemplation of the racing dailies. Neville the part-time barman
clapped his hands about his ears and swore from between freshly
clenched teeth.

Nicholas Roger Raffles Rathbone, currently serving his time as
local paperlad, stood before the Captain Laser Alien Attack
Machine, his feet at three of the clock and his shoulders painfully
hunched in his bid to defend planet Earth from its never-ending
stream of cosmic cousins ever bent upon conquest, doom, and destruction.

Bitow . . . *Bitow* . . . *Bitow* . . . *Bitow* . . . His right forefinger
rattled away at the neutron bomb release button and a bead of
perspiration formed upon his ample brow. 'Go on my son, go on.'
Little streamers of coloured light, like some residue from a third-
rate firework box, flew up the bluely-tinted video screen to where
the horde of approaching spacecraft, appearing for all the world
like so many stuffed olives, dipped and weaved.

Bitow . . . *Whap* . . . 'What?' Young Nick levelled his cherry-red
boot at the machine, damaging several of his favourite toes.

Neville watched the performance with a face of despair. He too
had made that gesture of defiance with an equal lack of success.

The boy Nick dug deeply into his denim pockets for more small
change, but found only a pound note, whose serial number corre-
sponded exactly with one which had lain not long before in Norman's
secret cashbox beneath his counter. He turned his back momentarily
upon his humming adversary and bounced over to the bar counter.
'Give us change of a quid then, Nev.'

Neville viewed the diminutive figure with the lime-green coiffure. 'I cannot give out change,' he said maliciously. 'You will have to buy a drink.'

'Okay then, a half of shandy and plenty of two-bobs in the change, the Captain awaits.'

Neville drew off a mere trickle of ale into the glass and topped it up from the drips tray. 'We've no lemonade,' he sneered.

'No sweat,' said Nick.

Neville noticed, as he passed the flat half-pint across the gleaming bar top, that the boy's right forefinger drummed out a continual tattoo upon an imaginary neutron bomb release button. Accepting the pound note, he rang up 'No Sale' and scooped out a fistful of pennies and halfpennies and a ten-bob piece. 'Sorry I can't let you have more than a couple of florins,' he told the bouncing boy, 'we are a little down on silver this morning.'

The boy shrugged. 'No sweat.' He was well acquainted with the old adage about a prophet being without honour in his own land, and he made a mental note that he would always in future take his perks in silver before settling in for a lunchtime's cosmic warfare. Without further ado he pocketed his ten-bob piece, swept up his pennies, pushed his half-pint pointedly aside and jogged back to the humming machine.

Pooley and Omally entered the Flying Swan. 'God save all here,' said the Irishman, as more bitowing rent the air, 'and a pox upon the Nipponese and all their hellish works.'

Raffles Rathbone heard not a word of this; he was hunched low, aiding the Captain in his bid to defeat Earth's attackers. His face was contorted into the kind of expression which made Joseph Carey Merrick such a big attraction in the Victorian side-shows. His right forefinger twitched in a localized St Vitus' Dance and his body quivered as if charged with static electricity.

Neville ground his teeth, loosening yet another expensive filling, and tore his eyes away from the loathsome spectacle and towards his approaching patrons. 'What is your pleasure, gentlemen?' he asked.

Pooley hoisted himself on to his favourite stool. 'Two pints of your very best, barlord,' he said. 'My companion is in the chair.'

Making much of his practised wrist action, Neville drew off two pints of the very very best. He eyed Omally with only the merest suspicion as the Irishman paid up without a fuss, guessing accurately that it was some debt of honour. His eyebrows were raised somewhat, however, to the shabby and mudbespattered appearance of the two drinkers. He thought to detect something slightly amiss. 'I think to detect something slightly amiss,' he observed.

John drew deeply upon his pint. 'You find me a puzzled man,' said he with some sincerity.

Pooley nodded, 'I also am puzzled,' he said, tapping his chest.

The part-time barman stood silently a moment, hoping for a little elaboration, but when it became apparent that none was to be forthcoming he picked up a pint glass and began to polish it.

'You have had no luck yet with the disablement of that horror?' said Omally, gesturing over his shoulder towards the video machine.

Neville accelerated his polishing. 'None whatever,' he snarled. 'I have tried the hot soup through the vent, the bent washer in the slot, assault with a deadly weapon. I have tried simply to cut the lead but the thing is welded into the wall.'

'Why not pull the fuse at the mains box?' Pooley asked.

Neville laughed hollowly. 'My first thought. Our friends from the brewery have thought of that. I have pulled every fuse in the place, but it still runs. It works off some separate power supply which doesn't even register on the electric meter. It cannot be switched off. Night and day it runs. I can hear it in my room, humming and humming. I swear that if something is not done soon I will tender my resignation, if only to save my sanity.'

'Steady on,' said Jim.

'Look at it!' Neville commanded. 'It is an obscenity, an abomination, an insult!' He placed one hand over his heart and the other palm downward upon the bar-top. 'Once,' said he, 'once, if you will recall, one could sit in this pub enjoying the converse of good friends well met. Once, in a corner booth, meditate upon such matters as took your fancy. Little, you will remember, and correct me if I am wrong or sinking into melancholy, little broke the harmony of the place but for the whisper of the feathered flight. Once . . .'

'Enough, enough,' said Jim. 'Hold hard now, you are bringing a lump to my throat which is causing some interference to my drinking.'

'I am not a man to panic,' said Neville, which all knew to be a blatant lie. 'But this thing is wearing down my resistance. I cannot take much more, I can tell you.'

Omally noted well the desperation upon the barman's face and felt sure that there was the definite possibility of financial advancement in it. 'You need to play a shrewd game with those mechanical lads,' he said, when he thought the time was right. 'A firm hand is all they understand.'

Neville's eyes strayed towards the jukebox, which had not uttered a sound these ten years, since Omally had applied a firm hand to its workings. It seemed a thing of little menace now compared with the video machine, but Neville could vividly recall the agonies he had gone through at the time. 'You feel that you might meet with such a challenge?' he asked in an even voice.

'Child's play,' said Omally, which made Pooley choke upon his ale.

'Good show.' Neville smiled bravely and pulled two more pints. 'These are on the house,' he said.

Old Pete, whose hearing was as acute as his right arm sound, overheard the last remark. 'Good morning, John, Jim,' he said, rising upon his stick. 'A fine day is it not?'

'It started poorly,' said Omally, 'but it is beginning to perk up. Cheers.'

'Been to the allotment then?' the ancient inquired, placing his empty glass upon the counter and indicating the mud-bespattered condition of the two secret golfers.

'Weeding,' said John, making motions with an ethereal shovel. 'Spring up overnight, those lads.'

Old Pete nodded sagely. 'It is strange,' said he, 'what things spring up upon an allotment patch overnight. Take my humble plot for instance. You'll never guess what I found on it the other day.'

Pooley, who had a kind of intuition regarding these things, kept silent.

'Golf tee,' said Old Pete in a harsh stage whisper.

'Large rum over here,' said Omally, rattling Pete's glass upon the bar.

'How unexpected,' said the wily old bastard. 'Bless you boys, bless you.'

Omally drank a moment in silence. 'Now tell me, Pete,' said he, when the ancient had taken several sips upon his freeman's, 'how spins the world for you at the present hour?'

Old Pete grunted non-committally. 'It is a case of mustn't grumble, I suppose.'

'No news then? Nothing out of the ordinary or untoward on the go?'

'Not that I can think of, did you have anything in mind?'

'No, nothing.' Omally made a breezy gesture. 'It is just, well, to be frank, Pete, it is well known that little, if anything, going on in the Borough ever slips by you, as your present drink will bear testimony to. I just thought that you might have some little snippet of interest up your four-buttoned sleeve.'

'You couldn't be a little more specific?' said Pete, draining his glass. 'So much happens hereabouts, as you know, to keep one's finger upon the pulse is a thirsty business.'

Omally looked towards Pooley, who shrugged. 'Same again please, Neville,' said John to the part-time barman, who had been hovering near at hand, ears waggling.

'All the way round?'

'All the way.'

The honours were done and to Neville's disgust Old Pete drew his benefactors away to the side-table, beneath which his dog Chips lay feigning slumber. The three men seated themselves. 'Would I be right in assuming that you have something on your mind, Omally?' the ancient asked.

'It is but a trivial matter,' Omally lied, 'hardly worth wasting your valuable time with, but I must confess that it causes me some perplexity.'

'Ask on then, John, you are two drinks to credit and I am by no means a hard man to deal with.'

'Then I shall get straight to the point. Have you seen a suspicious-looking character skulking around, on, or near the sacred soil of our allotments?'

Old Pete nodded. 'Of course I have,' he answered, 'both there and elsewhere.'

'Wearing a grey coverall suit, sallow complexion, high cheek-bones?'

'Looks like a young Jack Palance?'

'The very same.'

'I have seen several.'

'Oh dear,' said Pooley, 'more than one?'

'At least four. Take my warning, they have the mark of offi-cialdom upon them. I saw one last week down by the cut, one yesterday on the corner of the Ealing Road, and there is one drinking this very minute in the far corner over by the gents' bog.'

'What?' Omally's head spun in the direction of the gents'. There in the darkened corner stood a sinister figure in a grey uniform. His features were blurry in the dim light, but it was almost certainly the same individual that he and Pooley had spied out on the allotment not half an hour earlier. As Omally watched, the figure turned his back upon them and strode through the door into the gents'.

'All right, Pete,' said Omally turning to the ancient. 'Who is he?'

Old Pete shrugged. 'There you have me, I'm afraid. When first I saw them I took them for Council workers. They had some kind of instruments mounted on a tripod and appeared to be marking the ground. But I never got close enough to question them. They slipped away into side roads or off down alleyways upon my approach. This is the nearest that I have so far come to one of them.'

'But you are sure that there are more than one?' Pooley asked.

'I have seen as many as three of them together at one time. As like as the proverbial peas in a pod. Suspicious, I call it.'

'I shall go and question him.' Omally rose from his chair.

'Best wait till he comes out,' Jim suggested. 'It is hardly sporting to corner a man in the bog.'

'Do it now while you have him cornered,' said Old Pete. 'They are a sly crowd. I never saw that fellow enter the Swan and I was the first man in.'

'That settles it,' said John, drawing up his cuffs. 'I shall have it out with him.' Without further word he crossed the bar and pushed open the door to the gents'.

It closed gently behind him and a long minute passed. Pooley looked up at the Guinness clock and watched the second hand sweeping the dial. 'Do you think he's all right?' he whispered.

Old Pete nodded. 'Omally knows how to handle himself, it is well known that he is a Grand Master in the deadly fighting arts of Dimac.'

'It is much spoken of, certainly,' said Jim with some deliberation. As the second hand passed the twelve for the third time Pooley gripped the table and pulled himself to his feet. 'Something is wrong,' he said.

'He said he was going to have it out with the fellow, don't be so hasty, give him another minute.'

'I don't know, you say you never saw him come in, maybe he has several of his chums in there. I don't like the feel of this.'

Old Pete's dog Chips, who had not liked the feel of this from the word go, retreated silently between the legs of his ancient master. Jim was across the carpet and through the bog doorway in a matter of seconds. Once inside he froze in his tracks, his breath hung in his lungs, uncertain of which way it had been travelling, and his eyes bulged unpleasantly in their sockets. Before him stood John Omally, perspiration running freely down his face in grimy streaks. His tie hung over his shoulder college scarf fashion, and he swayed to and fro upon his heels.

Omally stared at Pooley and Pooley stared at Omally. 'Did he come out?' Omally's voice was a hoarse whisper. Pooley shook his head. 'Then he must still be here then.' Pooley nodded. 'But he's not.'

Pooley was uncertain whether to shake or nod over this. 'There's a terrible smell of creosote in here,' he said. Omally pushed past him and lurched back into the bar leaving Pooley staring about the tiled walls. Above him was an air vent a mere six inches across. The one window was heavily bolted from the inside and the two cubicle doors stood open, exposing twin confessionals, each as empty as the proverbial vessel, but making no noise whatever. There was no conceivable mode of escape, but by the single door which led directly into the bar. Pooley gave his head a final shake, turned slowly upon his heel and numbly followed Omally back into the saloon.

6

As the Memorial Library clock struck one in the distance, Norman finished topping up the battered Woodbine machine outside his corner shop. He locked the crumbling dispenser of coffin nails and pocketed Pooley's two washers, which had made their usual weekly appearance in the cash tray amongst the legitimate coin of the realm.

Norman re-entered his shop and bolted the door behind him, turning the OPEN sign to CLOSED. As he crossed the mottled linoleum he whistled softly to himself; sadly, as he had not yet retrieved his wayward teeth, the air sounded a little obscure. For some reason Norman had never quite got the hang of humming, so he contented himself with a bit of unmelodic finger-popping and what he described as 'a touch of the old Fred and Gingers' as he vanished away through the door behind the counter, and left his shop to gather dust for another Wednesday afternoon.

Norman's kitchenette served him as the traditional shopkeeper's lair, equipped with its obligatory bar-fire and gas-ring. But there, apart from these necessary appliances, all similarities ended. There was much of the alchemist's den about Norman's kitchenette. It was workroom, laboratory, research establishment, testing station and storage place for his somewhat excessive surplus stock of Danish glossies.

At present, the hellishly crowded retreat was base camp and ground control for Norman's latest and most ambitious project to date. Even had some NASA boffin cast his knowledgeable eye over the curious array of electronic hocus-pocus which now filled the tiny room, it was unlikely that he would have fathomed any purpose behind it all. The walls were lined with computer banks bristling with ancient radio valves and constructed from Sun Ray wireless sets and commandeered seedboxes. The floor was a veritable snakehouse of cables. The overall effect was one to set Heath Robinson spinning gaily in his grave.

Norman spat dangerously on his palms and rubbed them together. He picked his way carefully across the floor until he reached a great switchboard, of a type once favoured by Baron von Frankenstein. As Norman squared up before it, however, he had no intention of mouthing the now legendary words, 'We belong dead', but instead lisped a quick 'Here she goes' before doing the business.

With a violent flash and a sparkler fizz, the grotesque apparatus sprang, or, more accurately, lurched, into life. Lights twinkled upon the consoles and valves glowed dimly orange. Little pops and crackles, suggestive of constant electrical malfunction, broke out here and there, accompanied by a thin blue mist and an acrid smell which was music to Norman's nostrils.

The shopkeeper lowered himself on to an odd-legged kitchen chair before his master console and began to unwrap his tiny brown paper parcel. Peeling back the cotton-wool wadding, he exposed an exquisite little piece of circuitry, which he lifted carefully with a pair of philatelist's tweezers and examined through an oversized magnifying glass. It was beautiful, perfect in every degree, the product of craftsmanship and skill well beyond the perception of most folk. Norman whistled through his gums.

'Superbs,' he said. 'Superbs.'

He slotted the tiny thing into a polished housing upon the console and it slipped in with a pleasurable click. The last tiny piece in a large and very complicated jigsaw.

Norman clapped his hands together and rocked back and forwards upon his chair. It was all complete, all ready and waiting for a trial run. He had but to select two suitable areas of land and then, if all his calculations were correct . . . Norman's hand hovered over the console and it trembled not a little. His calculations surely were correct, weren't they?

Norman took down a clipboard and began to make ticks against a long and intricate list, which had been built up over many months, scribbled in variously coloured inks. As his Biro travelled down the paper Norman's memory travelled with it through those long, long months of speculation, theory, planning, and plotting, of begging, borrowing, and building. The sleepless nights, the trepidation and the doubts. Most of all the doubts. What if it all came to nothing, what if it didn't work? He had damn near bankrupted himself over this one. What if the entire concept was a nonsense?

Norman sucked upon the end of his Biro. No, it couldn't be wrong; old Albert E had discontinued his researches on it back in Nineteen hundred and twenty-seven but the essential elements were still sound, it had to be correct. Just because Einstein had bottled out at the last moment didn't mean it couldn't be done.

Norman ticked off the final item on the list. It was all there, all present and correct, all shipshape and Bristol fashion, all just waiting for the off. He had but to choose two areas of land suitable for the test.

His hand did a little more hovering; he, like certain sportsmen in the vicinity, had no wish to draw attention to his project before its completion. Caution was the byword. The two tracts of land, one local and one in the area of the object he sought, would have to be unoccupied at the present time.

The latter was no problem. Norman boldly punched in the coordinates he knew so well, thirty degrees longitude, thirty degrees latitude and the minutiae of minutes. But as to a local site, this presented some difficulties. It was his aim to conduct the final experiment during the hours of darkness, when there would be few folk about to interfere. But for now, a little test run?

Norman snapped his fingers. 'Eurekas,' he whistled, taking up a Brentford street directory and thumbing through the dog-eared pages. The ideal spot. The St Mary's Allotment. The day being hot, all those dedicated tillers of God's good earth would by now be resting their leathern elbows upon the Swan's bar counter and lying about the dimensions of their marrows.

Norman punched in the appropriate coordinates and leant back in his chair, waiting for the power to build up sufficiently for transference to occur. He crossed his fingers, lisped what words he knew of the Latin litany and pressed a blood-red button which had until recently been the property of the local fire brigade.

A low purring rose from the electronic throat of the machinery, accompanied by a pulse-like beating. The lights upon the console sprang into redoubled illumination and the radio valves began to pulsate, expanding and contracting like some vertical crop of transparent onions. The little bulbs blinked in enigmatic sequences, passing back and forwards through the spectrum. Norman clapped his hands together and bobbed up and down in his chair. A thick blue smoke began to fill the room as the humming of the machinery rose several octaves into an ear-splitting whine. A strange pressure made itself felt in the kitchenette as if the gravitational field was being slowly increased.

Norman realized suddenly that he was unable to raise his hands from the console or his feet from the floor, and someone or something was apparently lowering two-hundredweight sacks of cement on to his shoulders. His ears popping sickeningly, he gritted his gums and made a desperate attempt to keep his eyelids up.

The ghastly whining and the terrible pressure increased. The lights grew brighter and brighter and the pulse beat ever faster. The apparatus was beginning to vibrate, window panes tumbled from their dried-putty housings and a crack swept across the ceiling. Beneath closed lids, Norman's eyes were thoroughly crossed. Without grace he left his chair and travelled downwards at great speed towards the linoleum.

All over Brentford electric appliances were beginning to fail: kettles ceased their whistlings, television pictures suddenly shrank to the size of matchboxes, the automated beer pumps at the New Inn trickled to a halt in mid-flow, and at the Swan the lights went out, leaving the rear section of the saloon-bar in darkness and the patrons blindly searching for their pints.

Omally groaned. 'It is the end of mankind as we know it,' he said. 'I should never have got up so early today.'

Pooley, who had had carrots the night before, topped up his pint from the Irishman's glass. 'Steady on, John,' he said in a soothing voice. 'It is a power cut, nothing more. We have been getting them more or less every Wednesday afternoon for months now.'

'But not like this.'

Old Pete's dog Chips set up a dismal howl which was unexpectedly taken up by Neville the part-time barman. 'Look at it! Look at it!' he wailed, pointing invisibly in the darkness. 'Look at the bloody thing!'

Bitow Bitow Bitow Bitow went the Captain Laser Alien Attack Machine, scornfully indifferent to the whims of the Southern Electricity Board, or anyone else for that matter.

In the tiny kitchenette to the rear of the corner shop there was a sharp and deafening twang, and a great bolt of lightning burst forth, charring the walls and upturning the banks of pulsating equipment. There followed a moment or two of very extreme silence. Smoke hung heavily in the air, cables swung to and fro like smouldering leander vines and the general atmosphere of the place had more than the hint of the charnel house about it.

At length, from beneath the fallen wreckage, something stirred. Slowly, and with much coughing, gasping and sighing, a blackened toothless figure rose painfully to his feet. He now lacked not only his upper set but also his eyebrows and sported a fetching, if somewhat bizarre, charcoal forelock. He kicked away the debris and fumbled about amidst the heaps of burned-out valves and twisted gubbins. 'Ahs,' he said, suddenly wielding a smoke-veiled gauge into view, 'success I thinks.'

Something had come through, and by the measurement upon that gauge it was a relatively substantial, goodly few hundredweight of something.

Norman wiped away a few loose eyelashes with a grimy knuckle, satisfied himself that there was no immediate danger of fire and sought his overcoat.

Small Dave had finished his midday deliveries and was taking his usual short cut back from the Butts Estate towards the Flying Swan for a well deserved pint of Large. As he shuffled across the allotment, his size four feet kicking up little dusty explosions, he whistled a plaintive lament, the title of which he had long forgotten. He had not travelled twenty yards down the path, however, when he caught sight of something which made him halt in mid-pace and doubt that sanity which so many had previously doubted in him.

Small Dave took off his cap and wiped it across his eyes. Was this a mirage, he wondered, or was he seeing things? Something overlarge and definitely out of place was grazing amongst his cabbages. It was a foul and scruffy-looking something of bulky proportion and it was emitting dismal grumbling sounds between great munches upon his prizewinning *Pringlea antiscorbutica*.

Dave screwed up his eyes. Could this be the Sasquatch perhaps? Or the Surrey Puma? Possibly it was the giant feral tom, which, legend held, stalked the allotments by night. The postman drew cautiously nearer, keeping even lower to the ground than cruel fate had naturally decreed. Ahead of him the creature's outline became more clearly defined and Small Dave knew that at least he was staring upon a beast of a known genus. Although this gave him little in the way of consolation.

The thing was of the genus *Camelus bactrianus*. It was a camel!

Small Dave's thoughts all became a little confused at this moment. He was never very good when it came to a confrontation with the unexpected. Arriving with a six-inch letter to discover a five-inch letter-box was enough to set him foaming at the mouth. Now, a camel on the allotment, a camel that was eating his precious cabbages, that was a something quite in a class by itself.

Dave's first thought, naturally enough, was that the thing should be driven off without delay. His second was that it was a very large camel and that as a species camels are notoriously malevolent creatures, who do not take kindly to interference during meal times. His third was that they are also valuable and there would no doubt be a handsome reward for anyone who should return a stray.

His fourth, fifth, sixth and seventh thoughts were loosely concerned with circuses, Romany showmen who were apt to snatch dwarves away for side-shows, an old Tod Browning movie he had once seen, and the rising cost of cabbages.

Small Dave's lower lip began to tremble and a look of complete imbecility spread over his gnomish countenance. He dithered a moment or two not knowing what to do, flapped his hands up and down as if in an attempt to gain flight, gave a great cry of despair, took to his heels and finally ran screaming from the allotment.

He had not been gone but a moment or two when a soot-be-smirched head arose from behind a nearby water-butt. Apart from its lack of teeth and eyebrows, it bore a striking resemblance to Sir Lawrence Olivier in his famous portrayal of Othello.

A broad and slightly lunatic smile cleft the blackened face in two and a wicked chuckle rose in the throat of the watcher.

'Success indeeds,' whistled Norman, rubbing his hands together and dancing out from his hiding place. With a quick glance about to assure himself that he was now alone, he skipped over to the cabbage-chewing camel and snatched up its trailing halter line. 'Huts, huts,' he said. 'Imshees yallahs.' With hardly the slightest degree of persuasion and little or no force at all, Norman led the surprisingly docile brute away.

From behind Soap Distant's padlocked shed yet another figure now emerged. This one wore a grey coverall suit, was of average height, with a slightly tanned complexion and high cheek-bones. He looked for all the world like a young Jack Palance. Through oval amber eyes he watched the shopkeeper and his anomalous charge depart. Drawing from a concealed pocket an instrument somewhat resembling a brass divining rod, he traced a runic symbol into the dusty soil of the allotment and then also departed upon light and silent feet.

7

When the lights returned once more to the Flying Swan, a moment or two after the holocaust in Norman's kitchenette, they exposed a frozen tableau of deceit and duplicity, which was a sad indictment upon the state of our society.

Neville stood poised behind the counter, knobkerry at the ready, to defend his optics against any straining hands.

Pooley held Omally's glass above his own, a stupefied expression upon his guilty face. Two professional domino players each had their hands in the spares box. Old Pete's dog was standing, leg raised, to the piano, and a veritable rogues' gallery of similar deeds was exposed the entire length of the bar.

Neville shook his head in disgust. 'You miserable bunch,' was all that he could say.

The only patron who had not shifted his position during the unscheduled blackout was a green-haired youth, who had been so engrossed in his war against the aliens that he had been totally oblivious to the entire event. *Bitow Bitow Bitow Bitow* crackled the machine. *Bitow*, *Bitow* . . . 'Bugger!' The lad restrained a petulant foot and slouched over to the bar counter. 'Where's me drink gone, Nev?' he asked.

The part-time barman shrugged. 'Ask this mutinous crew,' he suggested. Raffles Rathbone turned towards the assembled multitude, but they had by now returned to their previous occupations. Conversations hummed, darts whispered and glasses rose and fell. All was as it had ever been.

'Same again then is it?'

'Why not? Got sixteen thousand, personal high score, got me initials up there three times.'

'Oh goody goody,' sneered Neville. 'Are you sure you only want the half of shandy, I shouldn't crack a bottle of Bollinger, should I?'

'The half will be fine, thank you.' Neville did the honours.

The Swan settled down once more to its lunchtime normality, and such it would no doubt have enjoyed, had it not been for certain distant screams, which were borne upon the light spring breeze to announce the approach of a certain small and disconsolate postman.

'Camels! Camels on the allotment!' The cry reached the Swan shortly before Small Dave.

Omally choked into his beer. 'No more!' he spluttered, crossing himself. Pooley shook his head; it was proving to be a most eventful day and it was early yet. Neville reached once more for his knob-kerry and Raffles Rathbone stood before the video machine, oblivious to the world about him.

Small Dave burst into the Swan, looking very much the worse for wear. He lurched up to the counter and ordered a large scotch. Neville looked down at the distraught postman, and it must be said that the makings of a fine smirk began to form at the edges of his mouth. Turning away he drew off a single for which he accepted double price. Small Dave tossed it back in one gulp as Neville had calculated and ordered another. 'C-C-Camels,' he continued.

Neville drew off a large one this time as a crowd was beginning to gather. 'So, Posty,' he said, pushing the glass across the counter towards the postman's straining hand, 'how goes the day for you then?'

Small Dave made pointing motions towards the general direction of the allotments. His lower lip quivered and he danced about in a state of obvious and acute agitation.

'No more postcards then?' Neville asked.

'C-C-Camels!' howled the midget.

Neville turned to Omally, who had dragged himself up to the bar counter. 'Do you think our postman is trying to tell us something, John?' he asked.

'He is saying camels,' said Jim Pooley helpfully.

'Ah, that is what it is, camels, eh?'

'C-C-Camels!'

'Yes, it is camels for certain,' said Omally.

'He has a lovely way with words,' said Neville, suddenly feeling quite cheerful, 'and a good eye for a picture postcard.

'For God's sake! Camels, don't you understand?' Small Dave was growing increasingly purple and his voice was reaching a dangerous, champagne-glass-splitting kind of a pitch.

'Is he buying or selling, do you think?'

'I hadn't thought to inquire.' Neville squinted down at the postman, who was now down on all fours beating at the carpet. 'He is impersonating, I think.'

Old Pete hobbled up. He had experienced some luck recently over impersonating and wasn't going to miss out on a good thing. 'That's not the way of a camel,' he said authoritatively. 'That's more like a gerbil.'

Small Dave fainted, arms and legs spread flat out on the floor.

'That's a polar bear skin,' said Old Pete, 'and a very good one too!'

Small Dave was unceremoniously hauled up into a waiting chair. A small green bottle was grudgingly taken down from its haunt amongst the Spanish souvenirs behind the bar, uncorked and waggled beneath the midget's upturned nose.

'C-C-Camels!' went Small Dave, coming once more to what there were left of his senses.

'I find that his conversation has become a trifle dull of late,' said Neville.

'I think it might pay to hear him out.' Pooley thrust his way through the throng with a glass of water. The postman spied out his approach. 'What's that for?' he snapped. 'Going to give me a blanket bath, are you?'

Jim coughed politely. 'You are feeling a little better then? I thought perhaps you might like to discuss whatever is troubling you.'

'I should enjoy another scotch to steady myself.'

The crowd departed as one man; they had seen all this kind of stuff many many times before. The ruses and stratagems employed in the cause of the free drink were as numerous as they were varied. The cry of 'Camels', although unique in itself, did not seem particularly meritorious.

'But I saw them, I did, I did,' wailed Small Dave, as he watched the patrons' hurried departure. 'I swear.' He crossed himself above the heart. 'See this wet, see this dry. Come back fellas, come back.'

No one had noticed John Omally quietly slipping away. He had become a man sorely tried of late, what with vanishing Council men and everything. The idea of camels upon the allotment was not one which appealed to him in the slightest. He could almost hear the clicking of tourists' Box Brownies and the flip-flopping of their beach-sandalled feet as they trampled over the golf course. It didn't bear thinking about. If there were rogue camels wandering around the allotment, Omally determined that they should be removed as quickly as possible.

John jogged down Moby Dick Terrace and up towards the allotment gates. Here he halted. All seemed quiet enough. A soft wind gently wrinkled the long grass at the boundary fence. A starling or two pecked away at somebody's recently sown seed and a small grey cat stretched luxuriously upon the roof of Pooley's hut. Nothing unusual here, all peace and tranquillity.

Omally took a few tentative steps forward. He passed the first concealed tee-box and noted with satisfaction that all was as it should be. He crept stealthily in and out between the shanty town of corrugated huts, sometimes springing up and squinting around, eyes shaded like some Indian tracker.

Then a most obvious thought struck him: there were only two entrances to the allotment and any camel would logically have to pass either in or out of these. Therefore any camel would be bound to leave some kind of spoor which could surely be followed.

Omally dropped to his knees upon the path and sought camel prints. He then rose slowly to his feet and patted at the knees of his trousers. What on earth am I doing? he asked himself. Seeking camel tracks upon a Brentford allotment, he answered. Have I become bereft of my senses? He thought it better not to answer that one. And even if I saw a camel track, how would I recognize it as one?

This took a bit of thinking out, but it was eventually reasoned that a camel track would look like no other track Omally had yet seen upon the allotment, and thus be recognized.

Omally shrugged and thrust his hands into his trouser pockets. He wandered slowly about, criss-crossing the pathway and keeping alert for anything untoward. He came very shortly upon the de-cimation of Small Dave's pride and joy. Half-munched cabbages lay strewn in every direction. Something had certainly been having its fill of the tasty veg. Omally stooped to examine a leaf and found to his wonder large and irregular toothmarks upon it.

273

'So,' said he, 'old Posty was not talking through his regulation headgear, something *has* been going on here.'

He scanned the ground but could make out nothing besides very human-looking footprints covering the well-trodden pathway. Some of these led off towards the Butts Estate entrance, but Omally felt disinclined to follow them. His eyes had just alighted upon something rather more interesting. Slightly in front of Soap Distant's padlocked shed, an image glowed faintly in the dirt. Omally strode over to it and peered down. He was certain the thing had not been there earlier.

The Irishman dropped once more to his hands and knees. It had an almost metallic quality to it, as if it had been wrought into the dirt in copper. But as to exactly what it was, that was another matter. Omally drew a tentative finger across its surface but the thing resisted his touch. He rose and raked his heel across it but the image remained inviolate.

John peered up into the sky. It wasn't being projected from above, was it? No, that was nonsense. But surely it had to come off, you couldn't print indelibly on dust. He scuffed at the ground with renewed vigour, raising a fine cloud of dust which slowly cleared to reveal the image glowing up once more, pristine and unscathed.

Omally stooped again and pressed his eye near to the thing. What was it? Obviously a symbol of some sort, or an insignia. There was a vaguely familiar look to it, as if it was something he had half glimpsed upon some occasion but never fully taken in. It had much of the rune about it also.

'So,' said a voice suddenly, 'you are a secret Mohammedan, are you, Omally?' The Irishman rose to confront a grinning Jim Pooley. 'Surely Mecca would be in the other direction?'

Omally dusted down his strides and gestured towards the gleaming symbol. 'Now what would you make of that, lad?' he asked.

Pooley gave the copper coloured image a quick perusal. 'Something buried in the ground?' he suggested.

Omally shook his head, although the thought had never crossed his mind.

'Is it a bench mark then? I've always wondered what those lads look like.'

'Not a bench mark, Jim.'

'It is then perhaps some protective amulet carelessly discarded by some wandering magician?' Although it seemed almost a possibility

Omally gave that suggestion the old thumbs down. 'All right, I give up, what is it?'

'There you have me, but I will show you an interesting thing.' Omally picked up Pooley's spade, which was standing close at hand, raised it high above his head and drove it edgeways on towards the copper symbol with a murderous force. There was a sharp metallic clang as the spade's head glanced against the image, cleared Pooley's terrified face by the merest of inches and whistled off to land safely several plots away.

'Sorry,' said John, examining the stump of spade handle, 'but you no doubt get my drift.'

'You mean you cannot dig it out?' Omally shook his head. 'Right then.' Pooley spat on his palms and rubbed them briskly together.

'Before you start,' said Omally, 'be advised by me that it cannot be either erased, defaced or removed.'

Pooley, who had by now removed his jacket and was rolling up his sleeves, paused a moment and cocked his head on one side. 'It has a familiar look to it,' he said.

John nodded. 'I thought that myself, the thing strikes a chord somewhere along the line.'

Pooley, who needed only a small excuse to avoid physical labour, slipped his jacket back on. He took out a biro and *The Now Official Handbook of Allotment Golf*.

'Best mark it out of bounds,' said Omally.

Pooley shook his head and handed him the book. 'You're good with your hands, John,' he said, 'make a sketch of it on the back. If such a symbol has ever existed, or even does so now, there is one man in Brentford who is bound to know what it is.'

'Ah yes.' Omally smiled broadly and took both book and Biro. 'And that good man is, if I recall, never to be found without a decanter of five-year-old scotch very far from his elbow.'

'Quite so,' said Jim Pooley. 'And as we walk we will speak of many things, of sporting debts and broken spades.'

'And cabbages and camels,' said John Omally.

8

Professor Slocombe sat at his study desk, surrounded by the ever-present clutter of dusty tomes. Behind him twin shafts of sunlight entered the tall French windows and glittered upon his mane of pure white hair, casting a gaunt shadow across the mountain of books on to the exquisite Persian carpet which pelted the floor with clusters of golden roses.

The Professor peered through his ivory-rimmed pince-nez and painstakingly annotated the crackling yellow pages of an ancient book, the Count of St Germaine's treatise upon the transmutation of base metals and the improvement of diamonds. The similarities between his marginal jottings and the hand-inscribed text of the now legendary Count were such as would raise the eyebrows of many a seasoned graphologist.

Had it not been for the fact that the Count of St Germaine had cast his exaggerated shadow in the fashionable places of some three hundred years past, one would have been tempted to assume that both inscriptions were the product of a single hand, the Count's text appearing only the work of a younger and more sprightly individual. But even to suggest such a thing would be to trespass dangerously upon the shores of unreason, although it must be said that Old Pete, one of the Borough's most notable octogenarians, was wont to recall that when he was naught but a tousle-haired sprog, with ringworm and rickets, the Professor was already a gentleman of great age.

Around and about the study, the musty showcases were crowded with a profusion of extraordinary objects, the tall bookshelves bulged with rare volumes and the carved tables stood heavily burdened with brass oraries and silver astrolabes. All these wonders hovered in the half-light, exhibits of a private museum born to the Professor's esoteric taste. Golden, dusty motes hung in the sunlight shafts, and the room held a silence which was all its own. Beyond the French windows, the wonderful garden bloomed throughout every season with a luxuriant display of exotic flora. But beyond the walls existed a changing world for which the Professor had very little time. He trod the boundaries of the Borough each day at sunrise, attended certain local functions, principally the yearly darts tournament at the Flying Swan, and accepted his role as oracle and ornamental hermit to the folk of Brentford.

Omally's hobnails clattered across the cobbled stones of the Butts Estate, Pooley's blakeys offering a light accompaniment, as the two marched purposefully forward.

'No sign of the wandering camel trains then?' asked Jim.

Omally shrugged. 'Something had been giving Dave's cabbage patch quite a seeing to,' he said, 'but I saw no footprints.'

'Neville put the wee lad out, shortly after you'd gone.'

'Good thing too, last thing we need is a camel hunt on the allotment.'

The two men rounded a corner and reached the Professor's garden door. Here they paused a moment before pressing through. Neither man knew exactly why he did this; it was an unconscious action, as natural as blinking, or raising a pint glass to the lips. Omally pushed open the ever-unbolted door and he and Pooley entered the magical garden. The blooms swayed drowsily and enormous bees moved amongst them humming tunes which no man knew the words to.

The Professor turned not his head from his writing, but before his two visitors had come but a step or two towards the open French windows he called out gaily, 'Good afternoon, John, Jim. You are some distance from your watering hole with yet half an hour's drinking time left upon the Guinness clock.'

Pooley scrutinized his Piaget wristwatch, which had stopped. 'We come upon business of the utmost import,' he said, knowing well the Professor's contempt for the mundane, 'and seek your counsel.'

'Enter then. You know where the decanter is.'

After a rather undignified rush and the equally tasteless spectacle of two grown men squeezing together through the open French windows Pooley and Omally availed themselves of the Professor's hospitality. 'You are looking well, sir,' said Jim, now grinning up from a brimming shot-crystal tumbler. 'Are you engaged upon anything interesting in the way of research at present?'

The old man closed his book and smiled up at Pooley. 'The search for the philosopher's stone,' he said simply. 'But what of you fellows? How goes the golfing?'

Omally brought his winning smile into prominence. 'We pursue our sport as best we can, but the Council's henchmen have little love for our technique.'

Professor Slocombe chuckled. 'I have heard tell of your technique,' he said, 'and I suspect that your chances of membership to Gleneagles are pretty slight. I myself recently followed up some reports of UFO sightings above the allotments at night and my investigation disclosed a cache of luminously painted golf balls. Although your techniques are somewhat unorthodox, your enterprise is commendable.' The old man rose from his desk and decanted himself a gold watch. 'So,' he said at length, 'to what do I owe this unexpected pleasure?'

Pooley made free with a little polite coughing and drew out *The Now Official Handbook of Allotment Golf* which he handed to the Professor. The snow-capped ancient raised his bristling eyebrows into a Gothic arch. 'If you seek an impartial judgment over some technicality of the game I will need time to study this document.'

'No, no,' said Jim, 'on the back.'

Professor Slocombe turned over the dog-eared exercise book and his dazzling facial archway elevated itself by another half inch. 'So,' he said, 'you think to test me out, do you, Jim?'

Pooley shook his head vigorously. 'No, sir,' said he, to the accompaniment of much heart crossing. 'No ruse here, I assure you. The thing has us rightly perplexed and that is a fact.'

'As such it would,' said Professor Slocombe. Crossing to one of the massive bookcases, the old man ran a slender finger, which terminated in a tiny girlish nail, along the leathern spines of a row of dusty-looking volumes. Selecting one, bound in a curious yellow hide and bearing a heraldic device and a Latin inscription, he bore it towards his cluttered desk. 'Clear those Lemurian maps aside please, John,' he said, 'and Jim, if you could put that pickled homunculus over on the side table we shall have room to work.'

Pooley laboured without success to shift a small black book roughly the size of a cigarette packet, but clearly of somewhat greater weight. Nudging him aside, the Professor lifted it as if it were a feather and tossed it into one of the leather-backed armchairs. 'Never try to move the books,' he told Jim. 'They are, you might say, protected.'

Jim shrugged hopelessly. He had known the Professor too long to doubt that he possessed certain talents which were somewhat above the everyday run of the mill.

'Now,' said the elder, spreading his book upon the partially cleared desk, 'let us see what we shall see. You have brought me something of a poser this time, but I think I shall be able to satisfy your curiosity. This tome,' he explained, fluttering his hands over the yellow volume, 'is the sole remaining copy of a work by one of the great masters of, shall we say, hidden lore.'

'We shall say it,' said John, 'and leave it at that.'

'The author's name was Cagliostro, and he dedicated his life, amongst other things, to the study of alchemic symbolism and in particular the runic ideogram.'

'Aha,' said Omally, 'so it is a rune then, such I thought it to be.'

'The first I've heard of it,' sniffed Pooley.

'It has the outward appearance of a rune,' the Professor continued, 'but it is a little more complex than that. Your true rune is simply a letter of the runic alphabet. Once one has mastered the system it is fairly easy to decipher the meaning. This, however, is an ideogram or ideograph, which is literally the graphic representation of an idea or ideas through the medium of symbolic characterization.'

'As clear as mud,' said Jim Pooley. 'I should have expected little else.'

'If you will bear with me for a while, I shall endeavour to make it clear to you.' The Professor straightened his ivory-framed spectacles and settled himself down before his book. Pooley turned his empty glass between his fingers. 'Feel at liberty to replenish it whenever you like, Jim,' said the old man without looking up. The pendulum upon the great ormolu mantelclock swung slowly, dividing the day up, and the afternoon began to pass. The Professor sat at his desk, the great book spread before him, his pale, slim hand lightly tracing over the printed text.

Pooley wandered aimlessly about the study, marvelling at how it could be that the more closely he scrutinized the many books the more blurry and indecipherable their titles became. They were indeed, as the Professor put it, 'protected'. At length he rubbed his eyes, shook his head in defeat, and sought other pursuits.

Omally, for his part, finished the decanter of five-year-old scotch and fell into what can accurately be described as a drunken stupor.

At very great length the mantelclock struck five. With opening time at the Swan drawing so perilously close, Pooley ventured to enquire as to whether the Professor was near to a solution.

'Oh, sorry, Jim,' said the old man, looking up, 'I had quite forgotten you were here.'

Pooley curled his lip. It was obvious that the Professor was never to be denied his bit of gamesmanship. 'You have deciphered the symbol then?'

'Why yes, of course. Perhaps you would care to awaken your companion.'

Pooley poked a bespittled finger into the sleeper's ear and Omally awoke with a start.

'Now then,' said Professor Slocombe, closing his book and leaning back in his chair. 'Your symbol is not without interest. It combines two runic characters and an enclosing alchemic symbol. I can tell you what it says, but as to what it means, I confess that at present I am able to offer little in the way of exactitude.'

'We will settle for what it says, then,' said Jim.

'All right.' Professor Slocombe held up Omally's sketch, and traced the lines of the symbol as he spoke. 'We have here the number ten, here the number five and here enclosing all the alchemic C.'

'A five, a ten and a letter C,' said Jim. 'I do not get it.'

'Of course you don't, it is an ideogram: the expression of an idea, if I might be allowed to interpret loosely?' The two men nodded. 'It says, I am "C" the fifth of the ten.'

The two men shook their heads. 'So what does that mean?' asked Omally.

'Search me,' said Professor Slocombe. 'Was there anything else?' Pooley and Omally stared at each other in bewilderment. This was quite unlike the Professor Slocombe they knew. No questions about where the symbol was found, no long and inexplicable monologues upon its history or purpose, in fact the big goodbye.

'There was one other thing,' said the rattled Omally, drawing a crumpled cabbage leaf from his pocket.

'If it is not too much trouble, I wonder if you would be kind enough to settle a small dispute. Would you enlighten us as to what species of voracious quadruped could have wrought this destruction upon Small Dave's cabbage patch?

'His *Pringlea antiscorbutica*?'

'Exactly.' Omally handed the Professor the ruined leaf.

Professor Slocombe swivelled in his chair and held the leaf up to the light, examining it through the lens of a horn-handled magnifying glass. 'Flattened canines, prominent incisors, indicative of the herbivore, by the size and shape I should say that it was obvious.' Swinging back suddenly to Omally he flung him the leaf. 'I have no idea whatever as to how you accomplished that one,' he said. 'I would have said that you acquired a couple of jawbones from Gunnersbury Park Museum but for the saliva stains and the distinctive cross-hatching marks of mastication.'

'So you know what it was then?'

'Of course, it is *Camelus bactrianus*, the common Egyptian Camel.'

There was something very very odd about *Camelus bactrianus*, the common Egyptian Camel. Norman squatted on his haunches in his rented garage upon the Butts Estate and stared up at the brute. There was definitely something very very odd about it. Certainly it was a camel far from home and had been called into its present existence by means which were totally inexplicable, even to the best educated camel this side of the Sahara, but this did not explain its overwhelming oddness. Norman dug a finger into his nose and ruminated upon exactly what that very very oddness might be.

Very shortly it struck him with all the severity of a well-aimed half-brick. When he had been leading the thing away to his secret hideout, it had occurred to him at the time just how easy it had been to move. And he recalled that although he, an eight-stone weakling of the pre-Atlas-course persuasion, had left distinctive tracks, the camel, a beasty of eminently greater bulk, had left not a mark.

And now, there could be little doubt about it, the camel's feet no longer reached the ground. In fact, the creature was floating in open defiance of all the accepted laws of gravity, some eighteen inches above the deck.

'Now that's what I would call odd,' said Norman, startling the hovering ship of the desert and causing it to break wind loudly – a thing which, in itself, might be tolerable in the sandblown reaches of the Sahara, but which was no laughing matter in an eight-by-twelve lock-up garage. 'Ye gods,' mumbled Norman, covering his nose with a soot-stained pullover sleeve.

It was now that he noticed yet another untoward feature about the animal, which, had it been the property of the now legendary

PT Barnum, would no doubt have earned that great showman a fortune rivalling that of Croesus himself: the camel had the appearance of being not quite in focus. Although Norman screwed up his eyes and viewed it from a variety of angles, the zero gravity quadruped remained a mite indistinct and somewhat fuzzy about the edges.

Norman took out an unpaid milk bill and scrawled a couple of dubious equations upon its rear. Weight being the all-important factor of his experiment, it was obvious that his calculations regarding molecular transfer were slightly at fault. He rose from his uncomfortable posture and, the air having cleared a little, picked up a clump of wisely commandeered cabbage leaves and offered them to the camel, now firmly lodged in the rafters. The thing, however, declined this savoury morsel and set up a plaintive crying which sent chills up the back of the scientific shopkeeper.

'Ssh . . . ssh, be quiets, damn yous,' whistled Norman, flapping his arms and searching desperately about for the wherewithal to silence the moaning creature. Something drastic would have to be done, of that there was no doubt. This camel, although living proof of his experiment's success, was also damning evidence against him, and its disclosure to the public at such a time, when he stood poised on the very threshold of a major breakthrough, could only spell doom to his plans in dirty big red letters.

Norman groaned plurally. That must not be allowed to happen. He had had run-ins with the popular press before, and he knew full well the dire consequences. Some way or other he would have to dispose of his hovering charge. Perhaps he could merely await nightfall then drag it outside and allow it to float away upon the wind. Norman shuddered, with his luck the camel would most likely rise to a point just beyond reach and hang there for all the world to see. Or far worse than that, it might sweep upwards into an aircraft's flight-path and cause a major disaster. These thoughts brought no consolation to the worried man.

The camel was still bewailing its lot in excessively loquacious terms and Norman, a man who was rapidly learning the true meaning of the word desperation, tore off his pullover and, having dragged the moaning beastie momentarily to ground level, stuffed the patchworked woolly over its head. A blessed silence descended upon the lock-up, and Norman breathed a twin sigh of relief. Perhaps, he mused, with its obviously unstable molecular structure the camel might simply deteriorate to such a point that a slight draught would waft it away into nothingness.

This seemed a little cruel, as the camel was something of an unwilling victim of circumstance, and Norman was not by nature a cruel or callous man. But considering the eventual good which his great quest would bring to the people of Brentford, the shopkeeper considered the sacrifice to be a small and necessary one.

It will thank me for it in the end, he told himself. To die in so noble a cause. I shall see to it that a memorial is built, the tomb of the unknown camel. We might even organize some kind of yearly festival in its honour. Camel Day, perhaps? Hold it on Plough Monday, incorporate a few morris dancers in Egyptian garb and a maypole or two, make a day of it. Yes, the camel had played its part and it would not go unrewarded.

Anyway, thought Norman, if it doesn't simply evaporate I can always speed the process up with a decent-sized weedkiller bomb.

9

Pooley and Omally sat at a secluded corner-table in the Flying Swan.

'I can't understand the Professor,' said Jim. 'Didn't seem to be himself at all.'

Omally shook his head, 'I don't know,' he replied. 'Appeared to me a clear case of keep-the-golfers-guessing. I suspect that he knows a good deal more than he was letting on to.'

'Not much ever gets by him. He certainly made short work of the cabbage leaf.'

Omally leant back in his seat and cast his arms wide. 'But where are we?' he asked. 'Nowhere at all! We have council men doing the impossible at their every opportunity, we have runic ideograms appearing magically upon the ground and camels working their way through the season's produce. I don't like any of it, it smacks to me of some great conspiracy to confound honest golfers and put them off their game.'

'I suspect that it goes a little deeper than that,' said Jim, 'but I agree that it does nothing to enhance the play. Perhaps we should quit the allotment now. Move on to pastures new. There are several large bombsites down near the docks surrounded by high walls. I know of a secret entrance or two.'

'Never,' said Omally boldly. 'I have had enough of running. If we do not make our stand now, the bastards will eventually drive us into the sea and I care little for the prospect of underwater golf.'

'Cork balls,' said Pooley.

'I beg your pardon?'

Bitow Bitow Bitow Bitow Bitow Whap . . . 'What?' Nicholas Roger Raffles Rathbone turned a full circle upon his heel and drove his reddening fists down on to the console of the Captain Laser Alien Attack Machine. 'You bastard!' he said earnestly. 'You bloody sneaked an extra saucer in there.' He turned towards the bar where Neville stood, his ears protected by cotton-wool balls and his hands feverishly at work with the polished cloth. 'Have you altered this machine?' he cried.

'Get stuffed,' said Neville.

'I know the sequences,' Nick continued unabashed, 'thirty shots, then a big saucer, thirty-eight, then a mother ship. Somebody has tampered with this machine.'

Neville laid down his polishing cloth, plucked the ineffective cotton plugs from his ears and glowered across the bar. 'No one has touched it,' he said, his words forming between two rows of teeth which were showing some signs of wear. 'No one has touched, tampered or tinkered with it. No official brewery representative has ever called to service it. No engineers came to polish its paintwork, change its bulbs or fondle its inner workings, nor even to empty it of the king's ransom it must by now contain. It seemingly never breaks down, nor needs any maintenance, it runs from its own power supply and is a law unto itself. If you have any complaints I suggest that you address them directly to the machine. With any luck it will take exception to your manner and electrocute you!'

'Someone's been tampering,' said Nick, delving into his pockets for more two-bob bits, 'I know the sequences.'

The part-time barman turned away in disgust. 'Jim,' he said, beckoning across the counter towards Pooley, 'might I have a word or two in your ear?'

Pooley hastened from his chair, favouring the possibility of a free drink. 'Your servant, bar lord,' said he.

'Jim,' said Neville, gesturing towards the hunched back of the green-haired youth, 'Jim, has Omally come up with anything yet regarding this abomination? I am at my wits' end. My letter of resignation is folded into the envelope and the stamp is on.'

Jim chewed upon his lip. It was obvious that Neville was speaking with great sincerity. It would be a tragedy indeed if Brentford lost the best part-time barman it ever had. Especially over so trivial a thing as a gambling machine.

'In truth,' lied Jim with great conviction, 'Omally and I have spent the entirety of the afternoon discussing this very matter. We were doing so even when you called me across. We are, I think, nearing a solution.'

'Ah,' said Neville, brightening, 'it is good to know that there are still friends in the camp. Have this one on the house.'

Pooley sank it at a single draught and strolled back to his seated companion.

'I saw that,' said Omally. 'What have you just talked me into?'

'Nothing much,' said Jim nonchalantly. 'It is just that Neville would prefer it if you would break the space machine now rather than later.'

Omally controlled himself quite remarkably. 'But I was of the impression that the thing is indestructable. Do you not feel that this small point might put me at a slight disadvantage?'

Pooley nudged his companion jovially in the rib area. 'Come now,' he said, 'this should provide a little light relief. Take your mind off your worries. What is it that you lads from the old country say? Do it for the crack, that's it, isn't it. The crack, eh?'

'The crack?' Omally shook his head in wonder. As if things weren't bad enough. He scratched at the stubble of his chin, which through the day had grown into what the Navy refer to as a full set, and cast a thoughtful eye towards the video machine. 'I have an idea,' he said, rising from his seat. 'Perhaps a success here might turn the tide of our fortunes. Give me a florin.' Pooley began to pat his pockets. 'Give me the florin,' Omally reiterated. Pooley paid up.

'Now, come Jim,' said the Irishman, 'and we will test the substance of this rogue apparatus.'

Neville the part-time barman watched the silver coin change hands and offered up a silent prayer to the dark and pagan deity of his personal preference.

Nicholas Roger Raffles Rathbone had a pile of not dissimilar coins of the realm stacked upon the chromium roof of the games machine. He was set in for the night.

'Stand aside, laddy,' said Omally in an authoritative tone. 'My friend here wishes to match wits with these extra-terrestrial laddos.'

'No way,' said Nick, turning not a verdant hair, 'I'm halfway through a game here.'

Omally leant down towards the youth and spoke a few words into a pointed, tattooed ear. The scourge of the cosmic commandos stepped aside. 'Be my guest,' he said politely. 'I will explain how it works.'

'That will not be necessary, thank you, off you go then, Jim.'

Pooley shook his head vigorously. 'Not me,' he said, 'these things give out dangerous X-rays. I'm not having my hair fall out and my fingernails drop off. No thank you.'

Omally patted his companion on the shoulder. 'Jim,' said he, 'who was it who set fire to my pop-up toaster?'

Pooley could not see the connection, but he nodded guiltily. 'It was me,' he said.

'And who overwound my alarm clock?'

'Also me.'

'And who fiddled with the tuner on the wireless set which had given me good and trouble-free listening for twenty years?'

Pooley looked away. 'Also me,' he said in a whisper.

'And who borrowed my electric razor and . . .?'

'I didn't know you weren't supposed to use soap when shaving electric,' Pooley complained.

'Who was it?'

'Also me.'

'Then you will understand my reasoning that if there is one man capable of ruining, whether through chance, method or design, any piece of electrical apparatus with only the minimum of tampering then that person is you, James Pooley.'

Jim pushed in the florin and the video screen burst into colour. 'Lift off,' he said.

'You have to use the thrust booster to get optimum lift,' said Raffles Rathbone, prancing on his toes and pointing variously at the throbbing machine. 'Gauge the inclination of the saucers, if you count to three and fire just in front of them you can bring them down. Every third one is worth an extra hundred points, keep to the right and they can't . . .' His voice trailed off as Omally dealt him a severe blow to the skull.

'Silence,' he said, 'Jim knows what he's doing.'

'I don't,' wailed Jim, wildly pressing buttons and joggling the joy stick.

'You're not here to win, Jim, only to break it.'

'Break it?' Raffles Rathbone renewed his frenzied dance. 'Break the machine? Oh, barman, barman, there is sabotage going on here, do something, do something.'

Neville smiled benevolently at the dancing youth. 'There is nothing I can do,' he said. 'All the patrons have a right to play the machine. Don't be so selfish.'

'Selfish? This is a conspiracy, I shall phone the brewery.'

John Omally, a man to whom the word tolerance meant about as much as the rules of backgammon, snatched up the squirming malcontent by his badge-covered lapels and held him high at arms' length. 'We don't want to go threatening the management now do we?' he asked.

'Ooh, I got one,' said Pooley suddenly. 'Blew him right out of the sky. And there goes another, *Bitow*. There's a knack to it you see.'

Omally let the dangling lad fall from his grasp. 'Any sign of damage yet?' he asked.

'I'm damaging their invasion fleet, look that's a hundred points, got the mother ship, you score double for that.'

Omally looked on in wonder. 'Come now, Jim,' he implored, 'try harder, apply a little more force.'

'I am, I am, there, took one straight out, you duck away to the side then, they can't get you there.'

'That's it,' said the fallen Raffles Rathbone. 'Count five from the last saucer across and the scout ship comes straight, down, you can get five hundred for him.'

A look of dire perplexity appeared upon Omally's ruddy face. 'Jim,' he said earnestly, 'what is happening here, Jim?'

'Nice one,' said Raffles Rathbone, 'when you get up to one thousand points you get an extra man. There, you got it.'

'No sweat,' said Jim Pooley.

Omally turned away from the machine and stalked over to the bar. Neville met his approach with a face like thunder. 'What is all this?' the part-time barman demanded. 'Treachery, is it?'

Omally shook his head ferociously, his honour was at stake here. 'Psychology,' he informed Neville.

'Oh, psychology is it, well silly old me, I could have sworn that he was enjoying himself.'

Omally smiled a sickly smile and tapped his nose. 'Leave it to Jim,' he counselled. 'He knows what he's doing. Wins over the machine's confidence, probes its defences, finds the weak spot and *Bitow*!'

'*Bitow*,' said Neville giving the Irishman what is universally known as the old fisheye. '*Bitow* it had better be.'

Omally grinned unconvincingly and ordered another pint.

Bitow Bitow Bitow Bitow Whap . . . 'What?'

'Aha,' yelled Raffles Rathbone, 'forgot to tell you about their strike ships. They got you that time. Care for a game of doubles?'

'Certainly,' said Jim, 'last to ten thousand gets the beer in.'

'You're on,' said the lad.

Omally hid his head in his hands and groaned.

At ten-thirty Neville called time, just to see what might happen. As ever the response was minimal. A few lingering tourists, up to enjoy the tours around the derelict gasworks, upped and had it away in search of their coaches, which had left an hour before. But by the local colour the cry was unheeded as ever. John Omally, whose face was now contorted into an expression which would have put the wind up Rondo Hatton, sat upon his barstool sipping at the fourth pint of Large he had been forced into buying himself during the course of the evening. Jim Pooley had spent the last four solid hours locked in mortal combat with the ever-alert invaders from the outer limits of the cosmic infinite.

For his part, young Nick had never been happier. He had borne the old slings and arrows of outrageous fortune regarding his involvement with the videotic projection of the alien strike force for a goodly while. To be teamed up now with Jim Pooley, a man he had for long admired, gave him a definite feeling of invincibility. Together they would score maximum high points and get the mystery bonus. 'Get that man,' he yelled, dancing like a demented dervish. 'Give that lad some stick . . . nice one.'

Pooley paused at long last to take breath. His neutron bomb release finger had the cramp and he was beginning to suffer withdrawal symptoms from his self-imposed spell of drinklessness.

'I must rest now,' he told Rathbone. 'I heard our good barman calling for the towels up and the habits of a lifetime cannot be set aside in a single evening. I am called to the bar.'

'You are a mean player,' said the boy admiringly. 'It has been a pleasure to do battle with you.'

'You have the edge by virtue of practice,' replied Jim, 'but I'll give you a run for your money tomorrow lunchtime.'

'You're on,' said Raffles Rathbone.

When Jim found his way to the bar counter he was somewhat astonished by the full extent of Omally's hostility.

'What in the name of all the saints, including even those who have recently been given the big "E" by the present papacy, do you think you are up to?' the Irishman asked.

Pooley was unrepentant. 'Psychology?' he suggested.

'Psychology?'

'Yes, you know, win over the machine's confidence, probe its defences, find the weak spot then *Bitow*! Whose round is it?'

'Yours,' said Omally, 'Irrefutably yours.'

'I got fifteen thousand two hundred and one,' said Jim proudly, 'personal high score, take a bit of beating that.'

'Your head likewise.'

'It's in the wrist action,' Pooley continued informatively, 'and you have to know the sequences, once you know the sequences you can go for the high-scoring ships and simply dodge the lower ones. It's simple enough once you've sussed it out.'

'You're mad,' said Omally. 'You were right about the X-rays, they've burned out your brain.'

'Wrist action,' said Pooley, drumming his killing finger on to the bar. 'One, two, three, *Bitow*, move to the left, *Bitow*, *Bitow*, *Bitow*.'

'I will kill you.'

'Tell you what,' said Jim, 'I'll give you a game of doubles tomorrow. Nick will be here and he can give you a few pointers, you'll soon pick it up. Last one to two thousand gets the drinks in, what do you say?'

Omally buried his face in his hands and began to sob plaintively. Pooley finished the Irishman's pint for him. 'You couldn't spare a couple of two-bobs, could you, John?' he asked. 'I just thought I'd get in another game before we go.'

10

Small Dave peeled open a packet of frozen *filet mignon amoureuse* and oozed it into the cankerous baking tray which had served his family for several generations. Turning the enamel oven up to regulo six, he popped the gourmet's nightmare on to a vacant shelf and slammed shut the door. This having been done to his satisfaction, the dwarfish postman slouched over to his sawn-down armchair and flung himself into it. He was not a happy man.

It is a sad fact that those unfortunates amongst us who are born lacking certain vital parts, or possess others to over-abundance, have good cause to bear grievance regarding their lots in life. Those blessed with the lucky humpty back, those who perpetually bump their heads upon the undersides of road bridges, or are capable of walking beneath bar stools without stooping, tend to feel that the gods have dealt with them rather shabbily.

Small Dave was one of this unhappy crew and he played the thing up for all it was worth. He took kindness for pity, the friendly word for the cutting jibe, and spent his days making life miserable for a community which would gladly have taken him as one of its own had he given it half a chance. When it came to having the old chip on the shoulder the little postman was in a class by himself. The arguments that many a famous man had been well below average height and that it wasn't a man's height that mattered, it was what he had in his heart, fell upon very deaf ears. Small Dave had resolved that if it stood taller than four feet and walked about, he hated it.

He was not exactly Mr Popular in Brentford. In fact, in a parish which tolerated almost every kind of eccentricity, he managed to achieve some notoriety.

This pleased his contemporaries, for, after all, they had wasted a lot of breath trying to convince him that you didn't have to be tall to be famous. Now they felt a lot less conscience-stricken about hating the vindictive, grudge-bearing wee bastard.

Small Dave dug his pointed nails into the chair's ragged arms and looked up at the clock. Nearly midnight, nearly time to get this camel business sorted out good and proper. He had been made to look very foolish this day, but he would have his revenge. Rising from his chair and setting flame to his acorn pipe, he paced the threadbare carpet, emitting plumes of sulphurous herbal smoke. At intervals he raised his fists towards heaven and at others he took to bouts of violent hand flapping.

At length the china Alsatian mantelclock struck the witching hour and Small Dave ceased his manic pacing. Striking one diminutive fist into the palm of its opposite number, he lurched from the room as if suddenly dragged forward by the ethereal cord which binds body and soul together. Up the staircase he went at a goodly pace, across a lino-covered landing, and up to the doorway of what agents laughingly refer to as the Master Bedroom.

Here he halted, breathing heavily, further hasty progress rendered impossible by the nature of the room's contents. It was literally filled with books. How the floor of the room was capable of supporting such a load was a matter for debate, but that the room contained what surely would have been sufficient to overstock an average public library was beyond doubt. The books cramming the open doorway formed a seemingly impenetrable barrier.

Small Dave looked furtively around, then withdrew a long key which he wore on a leather thong about his neck. Stooping, he found the hidden keyhole and swung open a tiny concealed door, formed from dummy bookbacks. With a curious vole-like snuffling, he dropped to all fours and scampered into the opening. The door of books swung silently shut behind him, leaving no trace of its presence.

Inside the room of books, Small Dave penetrated a tortuous labyrinth of tiny tunnels which were of his own creating. Deeper and deeper into the books he went, to the room's very core, where he finally emerged into a central chamber. It was a chamber wrought with exact precision into the interior of a perfect pyramid, aligned to the four cardinal points and fashioned from the choicest leather-bound volumes of the entire collection.

Within this extraordinary bower, illuminated by the room's original naked fly-specked bulb, were ranged an array of anomalous objects. A low dais surmounted by a single velvet cushion, a crystal, a milk bottle containing joss sticks, a framed picture of Edgar Allan Poe and a lone sprout under a glass dome.

Small Dave scrambled on to the velvet cushion and closed his eyes. The spines of the books stared down upon him, a multi-coloured leathern brickwork. He knew that he could never remove a single volume, for fear of premature burial, but as he had read every book in the room several times over and had memorized all by heart he had little need ever to consult them. His knowledge of the books transcended mere perusal and absorption of their printed words. He sought the deeper truths, and to do so it was necessary for him to consort with their very author. For if it was strange that such a chamber should exist and that such a collection of books should exist, then it was stranger still that each was the work of one single author: Edgar Allan Poe.

It was certain that if any of the Swan's patrons, who knew only Dave the postman while remaining totally unaware of Dave the mystic, had viewed this outré sanctum, they would have been forced to re-evaluate their views regarding his character. If they had witnessed the man who even now sat upon the dais, hands locked into the lamaic posture of meditation and legs bent painfully into a one-quarter lotus, they would have overwhelmingly agreed that the term vindictive, grudge-bearing wee bastard hardly applied here. Here it was more the case of vindictive, grudge-bearing wee lunatic bastard being a bit nearer the mark.

Small Dave began to whistle a wordless mantra of his own invention. His eyes were tightly closed and he swayed gently back and forth upon his cushion.

He had come to a decision regarding this camel business. He would ask help from the master himself, from the one man who had all the answers, old EAP. After all, had he not invented Dupin, the original consulting detective, and hadn't that original consulting detective been a dwarf like himself? Certainly Poe, who Dave had always noted with satisfaction was a man of less than average height, hadn't actually put it down in black and white, but all the implications were there. Dupin could never have noticed that body stuffed up the chimney in *Murders of the Rue Morgue*, if he hadn't been a little short-changed in the leg department.

Small Dave screwed up his eyes and thought 'Sprout'. It was no easy matter. Ever since he had first become a practising member of the Sacred Order of the Golden Sprout he had experienced quite a problem in coming to terms with the full potential power of that wily veg. His guru, one Reg Fulcanelli, a greengrocer from Chiswick, had spent a great deal of valuable time instructing Dave in the way of the sprout, but the wee lad simply did not seem to be grasping it. 'Know the sprout and know thyself,' Reg had told him, selecting a prime specimen from his window display and holding it up to the light. 'The sprout is all things to all men. And a law unto itself. Blessings be upon it.'

Small Dave had peered around the crowded greengrocery, wondering at the mountain of sprout sacks, the caseloads and boxfuls cramming every corner. 'You have an awful lot here,' he observed.

'You can't have too much of a good thing,' the perfect master had snapped. 'Do you want two pound of self-enlightenment or do you not?'

Small Dave hadn't actually reached the point of self-enlightenment as yet, but Reg had assured him that these things take a good deal of time and a great many sprouts.

Dave contorted his face and rocked ever harder. Ahead of him in the blackness beneath his eyelids the mental image of the sprout became clearer, growing and growing until it appeared the size of the room. Reg had explained that to ascend to the astral, one had to enter the sprout and become at one with it. When one had reached this state of cosmic consciousness all things were possible.

A bead of perspiration rolled down to the end of Dave's upturned nose. He could almost smell the sprout, it was so real, but he did not seem to be getting anywhere with the astral travelling side of it. He took a deep breath and prepared himself for one really hard try.

Downstairs in Small Dave's ancient enamel oven the now unfrozen *filet mignon amoureuse* was beginning to blacken about the edges. Soon the plastic packets of sauce which he had carelessly neglected to remove from the foil container would ignite causing an explosion, not loud, but of sufficient force to spring the worn lock upon the oven's door and spill the burning contents on to the carpet. The flames would take hold upon a pile of *Psychic News* and spread to the length of net curtain which Small Dave had been meaning to put up properly for some weeks.

Small Dave, however, would remain unconscious of this until the conflagration had reached the point which sets schoolboys dancing and causes neighbours from a safe distance to bring out chairs and cheerfully await the arrival of the appliances.

It is interesting to note that, although these things had not as yet actually come to pass, it could be stated with absolute accuracy that they would most certainly occur. That such could be so accurately predicted might in a way, it is to be supposed, argue greatly in favour of such things as precognition and astral projection.

Small Dave would argue in favour of the latter, because by some strange freak of chance, while his physical self sat in a state of complete ignorance regarding its imminent cremation, his astral body now stood upon a mysterious cloudy plane confronting the slightly transparent figure of a man in a Victorian garb with an oversized head and narrow bow tie.

'Mr Poe?' the foggy postman inquired. 'Mr Edgar Allan Poe?'

'Small Dave?' said that famous author. 'You took your time getting here.' He indicated something the ethereal dwarf clutched in his right hand. 'Why the sprout?' he asked.

11

Norman had returned to his kitchenette, leaving his camel snoring peacefully in the eaves of his lock-up garage, its head in a Fair Isle snood. He surveyed the wreckage of his precious equipment and wondered what was to be done. He was going to need a goodly few replacement parts if he ever hoped to restore it. It was going to be another quid or two's worth of postcard ads in all the local news-agents: 'Enthusiast requires old wireless sets/parts, etc., for charity work. Will collect, distance no object.' That had served him pretty well so far. And if the worst came to the worst then he would have to put in a bit more midnight alleyway skulking about the rear of Murray's Electrical in the High Street.

Norman picked his way amongst the tangled wreckage and pondered his lot; it didn't seem to be much of a lot at the present time. It was bound to cost him big bucks no matter how it went, but at least he had the satisfaction of knowing that his theory was at least partially correct. The evil-smelling ship of the desert lodged in his garage testified amply to that. But there was certainly something amiss about his calculations. They would need a bit of rechecking; it was all a matter of weight, all very much a matter of weight.

Norman unearthed his chair and slumped into it. It had been an exhausting day all in all. As he sat, his chin cupped in his hand, his mind wandered slowly back to the moment which had been the source of inspiration for this great and wonderful project. Strange to recount, it had all begun one lunchtime in the saloon-bar of the Flying Swan.

Norman had been listening with little interest to a discussion between Jim Pooley and John Omally, regarding a book Jim had but recently borrowed from the Memorial Library upon the Great Mysteries of the Ancient Past. The conversation had wandered variously about, with Pooley stating that in his opinion Stonehenge was nothing more than scaffolding and that the builders, some megalithic forerunners to Geo. Wimpey and Co., had never actually got around to erecting the building. Doubtless a pub, he considered.

Omally, nodding sagely, added that this was the case with many ancient structures, that their original purposes were sorely misinterpreted by the uninspired scholars of today. The Colosseum, he said, had very much the look of a multi-storey carpark to him, and the Parthenon a cinema. 'Look at the Odeon in Northfields Avenue,' he said, 'the façade is damn near identical.'

Norman was about to make a very obvious remark when Pooley suddenly said, 'It definitely wasn't built as a tomb.'

'What, the Odeon Northfields? No, I don't think so.'

'Not the Odeon, the Great Pyramid at Giza.'

'Oh, that body.' Omally nodded his head. 'Surely I have read somewhere that it was the work of them extra-terrestrial lads who used to carry a lot of weight back in those times.'

Pooley shook his head. 'That I doubt.'

'What then?' Omally asked, draining his glass and replacing it noisily upon the bar counter.

Pooley, who could recognize a captive audience when he saw one queuing up for a one-pint ticket, ordered two more of whatever it was they were drinking at the time and continued. 'It was the ticking of the old Guinness clock up there which solved the thing for me.'

'Oh, you consider the Great Pyramid to have been a pub also?'

'Hardly that.'

'Then might I make so bold as to inquire how such a humble thing as the Guinness clock leads you to solve a riddle which has baffled students of Egyptology for several thousands of years?'

'It is simplicity itself,' said Jim, but of course it was nothing of the sort. 'The ticking of the Guinness clock put me in mind, naturally enough, of Big Ben.'

'Naturally enough.'

'Now as you may have noticed, Big Ben is a very large clock with a pendulum so great that it would easily reach from here, right down the passage and into the gents'.'

Omally whistled. 'As big as that, eh?'

'As big, and this huge clock is kept accurately ticking away by the piles of pennies placed upon that pendulum by the builders of the thing. Am I right?'

'You are,' said Omally agreeably, 'you are indeed.'

'Well then!' said Pooley triumphantly.

'Well then what?'

Pooley sighed; he was clearly speaking to an idiot. 'The Great Pyramid is to the planet Earth what the penny piles are to Big Ben's pendulum. Shall I explain fully?'

'Perhaps you should, Jim, but make it a quick one, eh?'

'Well then, as we are all aware, these ancient Egyptians were a pretty canny bunch. Greatly skilled at plotting the heavens and working things out on the old slide rule. Well, it is my belief that sometime back then some sort of catastrophe, no doubt of a cosmic nature, occurred and pushed the Earth a little off its axis. There is a great deal of evidence to support this, the sudden extinction of the mammoths, the shifting of the Polar caps, all this kind of thing.'

Omally yawned. 'Sorry,' he said.

'Now these Egyptian lads were not to be caught napping and when they realized that impending doom was heading their way they did the only logical thing and took corrective measures.'

'Corrective measures?' The bottom of Omally's glass was already in sight and he could feel the dartboard calling.

'Corrective measures they took,' said Jim, 'by building a kind of counterbalance upon the Earth's surface to keep the thing running on trim. They selected the exact spot which bisects exactly the continents and oceans. They aligned their construction to the four cardinal points and then whammo, or not whammo, as the case may be. There you are, you see, case proven, we have a great deal to thank those ancient sunburned builders for.'

Omally seemed strangely doubtful. 'There has been a lot of building work done about the world since that time,' he said, 'some of which I can personally vouch for. With all that weight being unevenly distributed about the place, I have the feeling that your old pyramid would become somewhat overwhelmed.'

Pooley shook his head. 'The pyramid is an unique structure, it has an exact weight, mass, and density ratio to the planet itself. It is the one construction which will fill the bill exactly. The stones quarried for it were cut to carefully calculated sizes and shapes, each is an integral part interlocking like a Chinese puzzle. The inner chambers are aligned in such a way as to channel certain earth currents to maximum effect. It is much more than simply a big lump of rock. No matter how many other buildings go up all over the world, the pyramid will still maintain its function. To alter the Earth's motion one would have to actually move the Great Pyramid.'

'I'll chalk up then,' said Omally, but the remark was apparently not directed to Jim Pooley.

Norman, however, was entranced. Could there possibly be any conceivable truth behind Pooley's ramblings? It all seemed impossibly far-fetched. But what if it were so? The implications were staggering! If one could actually alter the course of the Earth by moving the Great Pyramid about, then one could wield quite a lot of weight, in more than one sense only. A bit of a tilt northwards and Brentford would enjoy tropical summers, a mite more later in the year and there would be tropical winters too. It was all in the wrist action.

It would be quite a task, though, the Great Pyramid was estimated to weigh upwards of five million, nine hundred and twenty-three thousand, four hundred tons. It would take more than a builder's lorry and a bunch of willing lads on double bubble. Possibly he could bribe coachloads of tourists into each bringing back a bit with them. That would be a lengthy business though.

Norman's gigantic intellect went into overdrive. He had been experimenting for years with a concept based upon Einstein's unified field theory, which was concerned primarily with the invisibilizing and teleportation of solid objects. It was rumoured that the US Navy had made a successful experiment during the war, creating some kind of magnetic camouflage which to all intents and purposes made an entire battle cruiser vanish momentarily. Einstein himself, it was said, had forbidden any further experimentation, due to the disastrous effects visited upon the crew.

Norman had recalled thinking on more than one occasion that Einstein, although an individual given to the rare flash of inspiration, had for the most part been a little too windy by half. Now if the Great Pyramid could be teleported from one site to another it might be very instructive to observe the results . . .

Norman scuffed his feet amongst the wreckage. It had all been so long ago, a lot of peanuts had lodged under the old bridge since then. But he had proved that at least some of it was possible. In fact, the more he thought about it the more he realized that to teleport a live camel from the Nile Delta to the St Mary's allotment, in a matter of seconds, wasn't a bad day's work after all. He was definitely well on his way.

Norman smiled contentedly, picked his way over to the corner sink and, drawing back the undercurtain, took out a bottle of Small Dave's home-made cabbage beer, a crate of which he had taken in payment for an unpaid yearly subscription to *Psychic News*. It was a little on the earthy side and had more than a hint of the wily sprout about it, but it did creep up on you and was always of use if your lighter had run low.

'The ultimate quest,' said Norman, raising the bottle towards the charred ceiling of the war-torn kitchenette.

It had long been a habit of his, one born it is to be believed at a Cowboy Night he had attended some years previously, for Norman to wrench the hard-edged cap from the bottle's neck with his teeth before draining deeply from its glassy throat.

In his enthusiasm he quite forgot the matter of his wayward dentures.

The ensuing scream rattled chimney pots several streets away and caused many of the 'sleeping just' to stir in their slumber and cross themselves fitfully.

12

Elsewhere other early recumbents were stirring to the sound of fire-engine bells and the cheers of an assembled throng of spectators. There was a fair amount of noise and chaos, smoke and flame, when the front bedroom floor at twenty-seven Silver Birch Terrace collapsed, bringing with it a hundred-thousand volumes of Poe and an apparently comatose postman of below average height.

When the firemen, who had been amusing themselves by flooding neighbouring front rooms and washing out carefully-laid gardens, finally finished their work upon Small Dave's house, the ambulance men, who had been grudgingly aroused from their dominoes, moved in to claim the corpse in the interests of medical science. They were more than surprised to find the postman sitting virtually uncharred in the ruins of his living room, legs crossed and bearing a baked sprout in his right hand. He wore a smiling and benign expression upon his elfin face and seemed to be humming something. Shrugging helplessly, they wrapped him up in a red blanket and bundled him into the ambulance.

When the sound of its departing bells had faded, along with those of the appliance, away into the night, the observers of the holocaust drifted away to brew cocoa and prepare for their beds. Eventually just two members of the jolly band remained, one a fellow of Irish extraction and the other a man with a twitching right forefinger.

'What now?' asked John Omally.

'A nocturnal tournament?' Pooley suggested. 'One for the road before we turn in, how does double or quits suit you?'

'Very well, I think you owe me something for the evening of embarrassment you have given me. Care to put an extra wager upon the course record?'

301

Pooley, who considered his sobriety to give him the natural edge, nodded enthusiastically, and the two men wandered off towards the allotment. Omally affected the occasional drunken side-step in the hope of adding weight to Pooley's conviction and causing him to bet a little more recklessly.

It was a clear night. A hunter's moon swam above in the heavens, edging the corrugated sheds with a priceless silver. The course was illuminated to such a degree that there was no need for the employment of the miner's helmets Pooley had improvised for late matches.

The allotment gates were barred and bolted. An officious Council lackey had also seen to it that they were now surmounted by a row of murderous looking barbs and a tangle of barbed wire. Exactly why, nobody could guess. Pooley and Omally were obliged to use their own private entrance.

'A nine-holer or the full eighteen, Jim?'

'The night is yet young and I feel more than equal to the task, remembering that you are already deeply in my debt.' Pooley quietly unlocked his shed and withdrew the two sets of hidden clubs.

Omally tossed a coin. 'Heads,' he said, as the copper coin spun into the night sky.

Had the falling coin actually struck terra firma, as one might naturally have assumed that it would, it is possible that the events which followed might never have occurred. It is possible, but it is unlikely. The coin tumbled towards the allotment dust, until it reached a point about three inches above it, and then an extraordinary thing occurred. The coin suddenly arrested its downward journey and hovered in the air as if now reluctant to return to the planet of its origin.

The two golfers stared at it in dumb disbelief. 'Now that is what I would call a trick' said Jim, when he eventually found his voice. 'You really must teach it to me on some occasion. Wires is it, or magnetism?'

Omally shook his head. 'None of my doing,' he said, crossing his heart solemnly, 'but it has come up heads so I suggest that you tee off first.'

'Not so fast,' Pooley replied. 'The coin has not yet reached the deck, it might have a couple of turns left in it.'

'It has clearly stopped falling,' said John, 'and that is good enough for me. Kindly tee off.'

'I think not,' said Jim, shaking his head slowly and firmly. 'I am not a man to call cheat, but the coin's behaviour leads me to believe that something a little phony is going on here. Kindly toss it again.'

'You want the best out of three then?'

'No, the best out of one. I should like the coin, as the biblical seed itself, to fall upon the stony ground!'

Omally shrugged. 'I confess my own astonishment at the coin's anarchistic behaviour, but I feel deeply insulted that you should even hint at duplicity upon my part. Trust being the bond which cements our long friendship, I suggest that we simply let the matter drop, or in this case hover.'

'Toss the coin again,' said Jim Pooley.

'As you will,' said Omally, who had now determined that he would cheat the second toss come what may. He stooped down and reached out a hand towards the hovering coin. He was rewarded almost instantaneously by a crackle of blue flame which scorched his fingertips and sent him reeling backwards into the shadows as if suddenly hit by a speeding locomotive. 'Ooh, ouch, damn and blast,' came a voice from the darkness.

Pooley sniggered. 'Must be a hotter night than I thought, John,' he said. 'Get a touch of static did you?'

Omally gave out with a brief burst of obscenities.

'Tut tut.' Pooley stretched out a tentative boot to nudge the copper coin aside. This, in the light of Omally's experience, was an ill-considered move upon his part. For his folly he received a similar charge of energy which caught his steel toecap, arched up the back of his leg and hit him squarely in the groin. 'Erg,' he said, which was in technical terms basically accurate. Clutching at his privy parts, he sank to his knees, eyes crossed.

Omally crawled over to his gasping companion's doubled form. 'I take the oath that this is none of my doing,' he said, blowing upon his charred finger-ends.

Pooley said, 'Erg,' once more, which was at least an encouraging sign that life still remained in him.

'Oh no!' said Omally suddenly. 'Not again.' The dust beneath the hovering coin had cleared to reveal the grinning metallic face of yet another runic ideogram. As the two men watched, a faint glow seemed to engulf it; growing steadily, as if somehow charged from beneath, it bathed the symbol in a sharp white light.

But it was no light of Earth. Although the symbol glowed with a dazzling brilliance, the light seemed self-contained and threw no illumination on to the awe-struck faces of the two golfers. Then, with an audible crackle, the light rose in a green column, a clear laser-like shaft, directly into the night sky.

'Erg, erg,' went Jim, gesticulating wildly in many directions. All over the allotments identical columns of light were rising. They soared into the black void of space, and although they dwindled to whitened hairs, there seemed no end to their journeyings.

'Say this isn't happening,' Omally implored.

Pooley could only offer another 'Erg', which was of no comfort whatever. In fact, as a means of communication the word 'Erg' was proving something of a dead loss.

Just then the lights went out. One by one they snapped off, leaving the night as it were untouched, although Pooley and Omally knew very much to the contrary. Pooley at last found a tiny croaking voice which had been hiding at the back of his throat. 'What were they, John?'

Omally shook his head. 'I think that it is possibly God's way of telling us to give up golf.'

Pooley found this explanation doubtful to say the least. 'God, I think, is generally a little more direct about these things. A great man for a thunderbolt is God. But whatever it was, it was the final straw, the allotment has lost its charm for me.'

'I can sympathize.' Omally struggled to his feet and took to dusting down his tweeds with his one good hand. 'With wandering camels, vanishing council spies, symbols and searchlights, there does seem to be an unwonted amount of activity hereabouts of late.'

'I'm for telling the Professor,' said Jim, getting a perfect mental image of a whisky decanter.

Omally had taken to soaking his scorched fingers in a nearby water-butt. 'I think,' said he, 'that the Professor has pressing business of his own. But, as you see, the coin has now reached the ground.' He pointed towards where the rogue penny now lay upon the exposed symbol. 'And even though it is still "heads", in the face of the unfortunate accident which befell you I am willing to concede the toss.'

'Thank you.' Pooley stroked his trouser region gingerly, the old three-piece suite was smarting like a good 'un. 'I have quite gone off golf now, I should prefer a glass or two of nerve tonic rather better.'

'Aha!' Omally tapped his nose. 'I think there might be a bottle or two of such stuff maturing even now in my hut, would you care to step across?'

'I would indeed, but slowly now, I am not feeling at my best.'

The two men wended their way over the allotment, treading warily and taking great lengths to avoid those areas where the strange symbols lay glowing faintly in the moonlight.

Omally's plot was always a matter for discussion and debate amongst his fellow allotment-holders. John tended to steer clear of the general run-of-the-mill, socially acceptable forms of crop and specialize rather in things with unpronounceable Latin names and heady fragrances. Sniffing moggies often emerged from his plot vacant-eyed and staggering.

Pooley stepped carefully across Omally's bed of flowering mandrake and gestured towards a row of towering belladonna. 'You have an unsavoury looking crop on at present,' he said, by way of making conversation.

'Export orders mostly,' John told him. The shed itself had a good deal of the gingerbread cottage about it, with its trelliswork of climbing wolfsbane and its poppy-filled window boxes. Omally unpadlocked the door and picked up a couple of picture postcards from the welcome mat. One of these carried upon its face a rooftop view of Brentford. Omally read this one aloud: 'Encountering difficulties dismantling Ark due to petrified condition, may be forced to bring it down in one piece. Regards to all, Archroy.'

'Do you actually believe any of the stuff he writes?' Pooley asked.

Omally shrugged his broad and padded shoulders. 'Who is to say? He sends these cards to Neville and one or two other prominent Brentonians. I suspect there will shortly be a request for financial assistance with the Ark's transportation. No doubt he will wish to have the money orders forwarded to some post-office box in West Ealing.'

'You are a hard man, John.'

'I am a realist,' said the realist.

Omally's bottles were unearthed and drinks were poured. The two lazed variously upon potato sacks, sharing a Woodbine and musing upon this and that. As the contents of the bottles dwindled, likewise did the musing upon this and that. More and more did this musing spiral inwards, its vagueness and generalities crystallizing with each inward sweep to become definites and absolutes. And thus did these definites and absolutes eventually centre upon the woes and anguishes of interrupted golf tournaments and, in particular, their own.

'It is becoming intolerable,' said Pooley, draining his enamel mug and refilling it immediately.

'Unbearable,' said Omally, doing likewise.

'Something must be done.'

'Absolutely.'

'Something drastic.'

'Quite so.'

'My bottle is empty,' said Jim.

Omally tossed him another.

'Good health to you, John.'

'And to yourself.'

Three hours and as many bottles later the matter was coming very near to being resolved. A vote was being taken and by a show of hands it was carried unanimously. It was agreed that with the aid of two long-handled shovels, each fitted with rubber handgrips as a precautionary measure, the mysterious symbols would be dug from the ground. They would be transported by wheelbarrow, similarly insulated about the handle regions, to the river and therein unceremoniously dumped. With these obstacles to play satisfactorily removed, attention would be turned towards the matter of the council spies. It had not been fully resolved as to the exact course of action to be taken over this, but it was generally agreed that the employment of stout sticks would play a part in it.

The moon had by now run a fair distance along its nightly course, and when the men emerged from Omally's hut the allotment had about it the quality of a haunted place. There was a harsh, collars-up chill in the air and the low moon now cast long and sinister shadows across a deathly-tinted ground. The prospect of digging up a potential minefield held little if any appeal whatsoever.

'Best make a fresh start in the morning,' said Pooley, rubbing his hands briskly together. 'I'm for my cosy nest, bed ways is best ways and all that.'

Omally grasped the retreating Jim firmly by his threadbare collar. 'Not so fast, Pooley,' said he, 'you are not going to bottle out on this now.' Jim thought to detect a lack of conviction in the Irishman's tone. 'I suggest a compromise.'

Pooley hovered on his toes. 'You mean do it in shifts, you dig tonight, I tomorrow, I applaud that.'

'Hardly.' Omally tightened his grip. 'I mean rather that we go round and set markers beside the symbols so we will be able to locate them. Then we both dig tomorrow.'

Pooley thought this not only sound but also far less strenuous. 'That is using the old grey matter,' he told John. 'Now, if you will release your grip, which is causing no little interference to my general welfare about the throat regions, I shall do my best to assist you.'

Now began the inevitable discussion upon the best method of accomplishing the task in hand. Pooley suggested the hardy sprout as a piece of vegetable matter suitable for the job. In the interests of good taste Omally put up the spud as the ideal substitute. The war then waged between bean poles loaded with tinfoil, shredded newspaper laid out in the form of pentagrams and a whole host of objects ranging from the noble and worthy to the positively obscene. Finally, after Pooley had made a suggestion so ludicrous as to bring the naturally short-tempered Irishman within a hair's breath of killing him there and then, Omally put his foot down once and for all.

'Enough, enough,' he shouted. 'We will not mark them at all, we shall merely pace around the allotment and make notes as to each location as we come upon it. That is that.'

If Pooley had worn a hat he would have taken it off to his companion and cast it into the air. 'Brilliant,' he said, shaking his head in admiration. 'How do you do it, John?'

'It is a gift, I believe.'

Pooley pulled out the *Now Official Handbook of Allotment Golf* and handed it to Omally. 'Let us go,' he said. 'The field is yours.'

Now, it is to be remembered that both men had imbibed considerable quantities of potato gin, a drink not noted for its sobering qualities, and that the light was extremely poor. Had it not been for these two facts it is just possible that the job might have been accomplished with some degree of success. As it was, in no time at all, the two men found themselves crossing and recrossing their tracks and scrawling illegible diagrams and unreadable locative descriptions all over the exercise book.

'We have done this one already,' said Pooley, lurching to one side of a glowing symbol. 'I'm sure we've done this one.'

Omally shook his head, 'No, no,' he said, 'it is as clear as clear, look, you can see the way we came.' He tapped at the notebook and as he did so the moon crept away behind a large cloud, leaving them in total darkness. 'Bugger,' said John, 'I cannot seem to find my way.'

'Best call it off then,' said Pooley, 'bad light stops play, nothing more to be done, bed is calling.'

'My hearing is acute,' Omally warned. 'One move and I strike you down.'

'But, John.'

'But nothing.'

The two men stood a moment awaiting the return of the moon. 'What is that?' Omally asked, quite without warning.

'What is what?' Pooley replied sulkily.

Omally gestured invisibly to a point not far distant, where something definitely untoward was occurring. 'That there.'

Pooley peered about in the uncertain light and it did not take him long to see it. 'Right,' said Jim, 'that is definitely me finished. The Pooleys know when their time is up.'

'Keep your gaping gob shut,' whispered Omally hoarsely, as he leapt forward and dragged the quitter to the dust.

Coming from the direction of Soap Distant's abandoned hut a soft red light was growing. The door of the heavily bolted shed was slowly opening, showing a ghostly red glow.

'Would you look at that?' gasped Dublin's finest.

'I should prefer not,' said Pooley, climbing to his feet and preparing for the off.

Omally clutched at his companion, catching him by a ragged trouser cuff. 'Look,' said he, 'now that is a thing.'

From all points of the allotment shadowy forms were moving, figures indistinct and fuzzy about the edges, striding like automata, ever in the direction of the weird red light. 'Ye gods,' whispered Jim as one passed near enough to expose his angular profile, 'the council spies, dozens of them.'

Omally dragged Pooley once more towards terra. 'I would counsel silence,' he whispered, 'and the keeping of the now legendary low profile.'

'I feel sick,' moaned Jim.

The gaunt figures strode ever onwards. Silently they moved amongst the many scattered obstructions upon the allotment soil.

Never a one turned his head from his goal and each walked with a mechanical precision.

Pooley and Omally watched their progress with wide eyes and slack jaws. 'We should follow them,' said John, 'see what they're up to.'

'With the corner up we should.'

'Poltroon. Come on man, let's sort the thing out.'

Pooley sloped his drunken shoulders. 'John,' said he, 'are you honestly suggesting that any good whatsoever will come from following this gang of weirdos? I feel rather that we would be walking straight into a trap. This is only my opinion of course, and it is greatly influenced by the state of blind panic I find myself in at present. There is something altogether wrong about every bit of this. Let us leave the allotment now, depart for ever, never to return. What do you say?'

Omally weighed up the situation. Things did seem a little iffy. They were greatly outnumbered and there was definitely something unnatural about the striding men. Perhaps it would be wiser to run now and ask questions later. But there were a lot of questions that needed asking and now might be the best time to ask them, emboldened as they both were, or he at least, by the surfeit of alcohol pumping about the old arteries. 'Come on, Jim,' he said, encouragingly. 'One quick look at what they're up to, what harm can it do? After the day we've had nothing else can happen to us, can it?'

Pooley thought that it possibly could, and as it turned out Pooley was absolutely correct.

13

Ahead the red light glowed evilly and the spectral figures moved into its aura to become cardboard silhouettes. Pooley and Omally lurched along to the rear of the strange brigade as silently as their inebriate blunderings would allow. None of the queer horde turned a head, although the sounds of their pursuers, as they stumbled amongst corrugated plot dividers and galvanized watering cans, rang loudly across the silent allotments. As the stark figures neared the light they fell into line and strode through the doorway of Soap Distant's hut like so many clockwork soldiers.

When the last of them had entered, the light grew to a blinding intensity then dimmed away to nothingness. 'There,' said Pooley, faltering in his footsteps, 'a trick of the light, nothing more, probably landing lights on a Jumbo or some such. Off to our beds now then, eh?'

Omally prodded him in the loins with the rake he had wisely appropriated in the interests of self-preservation. 'Onward, Pooley,' he ordered. 'We will get to the bottom of this.'

His words, as it happened, could not have been more poorly chosen, but Omally, of course, was not to know that at this time. The two men neared Soap's hut and peered through the open doorway. There was nothing to be seen but sheer, unutterable, unfathomable darkness.

'Lighter,' Omally commanded. Pooley brought out his aged Zippo and sucked at the wick. Omally snatched at the well-worn smoker's friend and as the flame bravely illuminated the hut's interior the two men gave forth with twin whistles of dismay.

The shed was empty: four corrugated walls, a ceiling of slatted asbestos and a concrete floor.

John Omally groaned. Pooley shook his head in wonder. 'These council lads certainly leave the great Houdini with egg on his chin,' he said respectfully. 'How do you suppose they do it?'

'I utterly refuse to believe this,' said Omally, holding the lighter aloft and stepping boldly through the doorway. 'There is no conceivable way they could all have . . .'

He never actually finished the sentence. Pooley's lighter was suddenly extinguished and Omally's words were swallowed up as if sucked into some great and terrible vacuum.

'John?' Pooley found himself alone in the darkness. 'John, this is not funny.' His voice echoed hollowly in the sinister hut.

'Oh dear me,' said Jim Pooley.

The moon slowly withdrew itself from its cloudy lair and shone a broad beam of light through the open doorway. The tiny hut was empty. John Omally had simply ceased to exist. Jim snatched up Omally's discarded rake, prodding ahead of him as he gingerly moved forward. The moon was still shining brightly and now, along the nearby rooftops, the thin red line of dawn was spreading.

'Oh!' The tip of Pooley's prodding rake had of a sudden become strangely fuzzy and ill-defined. Another step forward and Pooley noted to his utter stupefaction that it had vanished altogether into empty air. He withdrew it hastily and ran his finger along its length; it was intact. Jim looked at the rake and then at the empty shed before him, he scratched at his head and then at his chin, he weighed the thing up and tried to make some sense of it.

The shed was obviously not what it at first appeared. An ingenious camouflage indeed. But to camouflage what, and, most importantly, where was John? Obviously somewhere behind the simulated reality of the empty shed lurked another something, and obviously it was a thoroughly unwholesome something which boded ill for unwary golfers.

Pooley approached the doorway once more, and thrust the rake in up to the hilt. He waggled it about and swished it to and fro; it met with no apparent resistance. Jim pulled out the rake and stood a moment rescratching his head. It really was a very clever thing indeed. Possibly that was how these council lads had eluded them before. Probably the one in the Swan's bog had simply switched on some sort of 3-D projector, whipped up an image of an empty cubicle and sat down on the seat for a good sneer whilst Omally got foamy about the jaws. They were probably standing there in the shed even now doing the same.

Pooley took a step backwards. He'd show the buggers! Wielding the rake in as menacing a manner as he could, he took a deep if drunken breath and rushed at the image. 'Ooooooooooh,' went Jim Pooley as the concrete floor of the shed dissolved beneath his feet, plunging him down into the perpetual darkness of the now legendary bottomless pit.

How far Jim fell, and how long his plummet into the nether regions of the great beneath actually took, must remain for ever a matter for conjecture. That his life had plenty of time to flash before his eyes was of little consolation, although it did give an occasion for him to recall that during it he had consumed a very great deal of alcohol. Also, that should he survive this, he had every intention of consuming a great deal more.

Finally, however, after what had been up until then a relatively uneventful if windy fall to oblivion, Pooley's descending form made a painful and quite unexpected contact with a body of ice-cold and seemingly unfathomable water.

'Ow ... ooh!' wailed that unhappiest of men. 'Ow ... ooh and glug.' Pooley surfaced after several desperate and drowning moments, mouthed several very timely and well-expressed obscenities and sank once more into the subterranean depths.

'I forgive all,' he vowed as his head bobbed aloft for a second time. Possibly Jim would have survived for a goodly while bobbing up and down in this fashion. It is more likely, however, that he would have breathed his last as he went down for that famous old third time, had help not arrived from a most unexpected quarter.

'Climb aboard, Jim,' said a voice which struck a strange chord in Pooley's rapidly numbing brain. Jim squinted up from his watery grave to realize for the first time that he was no longer in darkness. Above him he could see the cowled head and shoulders of a man, leaning from what appeared to be a coracle of skin and bark, extending a rugged-looking oar. Without hesitation Pooley clutched at the thing and was unceremoniously hauled aboard. Huddled low in one end of the curious craft lay John Omally, swathed in blankets.

'Nice of you to drop in,' said the Irishman with the rattling teeth. Pooley made some attempts to wring out his tweed lapels, but soon gave up and resigned himself to death by pneumonia.

'Where are we?' he asked, peering about him.

A wan light emanating from some luminescent substance within the very rocks, which swept dome-like and dizzying high above them, illuminated a monstrous cavern. The black waters of the subterranean lake spread away in every direction, losing themselves into a great vastness of absolutely nothing.

It all looked a little worrying.

Jim shuddered, and not from the icy cold which now knotted his every muscle. It was the sheer mind-stunning hugeness of the place, and the fact that it actually existed somewhere deep beneath the roads where he daily set his feet. And those waters, what might lurk in them? It didn't bear thinking about. Jim turned to his saviour.

'You have my thanks, sir,' said he, 'but tell me . . .' His words trailed off as the dark figure turned from the oar he had been carefully slotting into its rowlock and confronted the dripping Brentonian. 'Soap?' said Jim. 'Soap, is that you?'

The boatman slipped back the cowl which covered his head and grinned wolfishly, 'Have I changed so much then, Pooley?' he asked.

Jim surveyed the darkly-clad figure, whose black robes threw the deathlike pallor of his face into ghastly contrast. His hair was peroxide blond and his eyebrows and lashes naught but snowy bristles. Soap was as white as the proverbial sheet. Pooley recalled the ruddy-faced Hollow Earth theorist with the sparkling green eyes who had regaled them with talk of Rigdenjyepo and the denizens of the world beneath. He also recalled only too well that terrible night when Soap had invited him and Omally down into a fantastic tunnel system beneath his house to witness the opening of what Soap believed to be the Portal to Inner Earth.

Pooley and Omally had made a rapid exit from the workings, but Soap had gone through with the thing and opened what turned out to be the stopcocks of the old flood sluices of Brentford Docks. An entire stretch of Grand Union Canal had drained forthwith into Soap's diggings and that had been the last Brentford had seen of the Hollow Earther.

Pooley stared at Soap in disbelief. 'You do appear slightly altered in your appearance,' he said carefully, as he gazed into the latter's eyes, now pink as an albino's, and slightly luminous.

'Five years below can alter any man,' said Soap, readjusting his cowl. 'I have seen things down here that would stagger the senses of the strongest man. I have seen sights which would drive the sanity from your head quicker than shit off a shovel.'

Pooley now also recalled that he and Omally had always been of the opinion that Soap was a dangerous lunatic.

'Yes,' said Jim, 'indeed, ah well then, again my thanks for the old life-saving and now if you would kindly show us the way out of here. I feel that it must be nearing my breakfast time.'

Omally piped up with, 'I have pork in the press if you'd care to come topside with us, Soap me old mate.'

The hooded figure said no more, but sat carefully down and applied himself to the oars. The curious little craft, with its extraordinary crew, slowly edged its way across the pitch-black waters. How Soap could have any idea of which way he was travelling seemed totally beyond conjecture. Hours may have passed, or merely minutes; time did not seem to apply here. Pooley's Piaget wristwatch had now ceased its ticking for good and all and maintained a sullen rusting silence. The high dome of rocks seemed unchanging and Omally wondered on occasions whether they were actually moving at all. Presently, however, a thin line of white appeared upon the horizon.

'Land ho,' said Soap, grinning at his marrow-chilled passengers.

'Would there be any chance of light at the end of the long dark tunnel?' Pooley asked. 'Such as nutrition, or possibly the warming quaff of ale or lick of spirits?'

Soap tapped at his nose in a manner which the two remembered only too well. 'You will be well cared for, you have been long expected.' Upon that doubtful note he withdrew once more into silence and rowed on towards land.

The island, for such it now showed itself to be, was a strange enough place by any reckoning. As Soap beached the craft and ushered the two ashore, Pooley viewed the place with the gravest misgivings. There was a dreadful prehistoric gloom about it; if the black waters were bad enough, this was somehow worse.

The island was a long, rough crescent, covered for the most part with enormous stalagmites. These gave it the appearance of the half-submerged jawbone of some long-dead behemoth. Pooley felt instinctively that to set foot on such a thing was direly wrong and his thoughts were shared by Omally. Yet both were wet, cold, hungry, and demoralized, and with little complaint they numbly followed Soap along the bone-white beach to a craggy outcropping which seemed the highest point of the bleak landfall.

'Would you kindly turn your backs a moment,' Soap asked politely. Pooley eyed his colleague and the blue-faced Irishman shrugged in his blanket shawl. Soap was but a moment in performing whatever action he had in mind, and when the two turned back, a great doorway yawned in the faceless rock revealing a comfortable-looking room of extraordinary size.

'Step inside quickly now, please. I have no wish to expose the entrance any longer than need be. There are eyes everywhere, even here.'

Pooley shook his head in redoubled wonder and the two men scuttled inside, followed by their amiable if enigmatic host. The door swung shut, predictably leaving no trace whatsoever of its existence.

'Now,' said Soap, 'cup of tea, is it?'

A thin smile flickered momentarily upon Omally's arctic boat-race, 'Only Soap Distant could offer a cup of tea at the Earth's core.'

'There have been others,' said Soap, indicating the letters A.S. which were scratched into the stonework of one of the walls. 'But that is another story entirely.'

Pooley cast his eyes about the room. It had all the makings of the average Brentford front sitter: the moquette three-piece, the nylon carpet, the occasional table whose occasion was yet to come, the fitted bookshelves and the television set. But for the hewn rock walls and the obvious lack of windows one might have been fooled into believing that all was suburban mundanity.

'Surely reception hereabouts must be a little ropey?' said Jim, indicating the television.

'Kept purely through nostalgia for my former existence,' said Soap. 'Now, my suggestion of a nice hot cuppa is eliciting very little in the way of positive response. I have some fine Riesling in my cellar, or perhaps some Bordeaux rosé? Shall I open a case or two?'

'That would be the thing,' said Pooley with some enthusiasm, 'events have sorely taxed us of late.'

Soap Distant vanished from the room, away down a flight of hewn rock steps which had not been previously mentioned.

Pooley and Omally sat a moment in silence before the great man of Eire gave voice. 'If I might say so, Jim,' John ventured, 'your suggestion of having it away to our cosy beds and starting afresh on the morrow was one which I really should have picked up on before it went out of fashion.'

315

'I blame nobody,' said the noble Jim, 'but would sincerely ask what in the name of all the holies we are doing in this godforsaken place and how we might facilitate our escape?'

Soap appeared from the cellar, cradling several bottles of wine in his arms. 'The day is yet saved,' he said, beaming hideously. 'The cellar brims with vintage vino of all varieties. I have brought up a selection.'

Omally, who was certain that the day was very far from being saved, rubbed his hands thoughtfully together. 'Why are we here, Soap?' he asked.

'Well now, that is a question and no mistake,' the other replied. 'Some incline towards the theory of a divine creator with reasons of his own for doing things. Others favour the theory of natural selection or hint that we are nothing more than an accident of DNA. I myself have a rather more radical theory.'

'No doubt,' said John sourly, 'but you know perfectly well that is not what I meant. Why are we, that is, Pooley and myself, here, that is, sitting upon this ghastly settee, slowly but surely freezing to death?'

Soap popped the corks from two of the bottles and handed them one apiece to his guests. 'In words of one syllable,' said Soap, 'you are in big schtuck. I think that you might do well to take a sup or two before I fill you in on the details.'

The two sub-zero golfers did not need telling twice, and in a matter of seconds two bottles of vintage Rhine wine had vanished away into the nether regions of two stomachs. 'The floor would seem to be yours,' said Jim wiping his chin. 'Is there any more of this?'

Soap handed over two more bottles and positioned himself in a dignified pose against the stucco fireplace.

'As you will remember,' he said, 'I have spoken to you many times in the past about the family Distant's conviction that an entire world exists here, beneath the Earth's surface, and that it is peopled by superbeings, benign and benevolent, who would bestow the great wealth of their knowledge upon the man from above who came in peace to speak with them.' John and Jim nodded thoughtfully. 'Well, I was wrong.'

'Tough luck,' said Omally. 'Say la vee as the French say.'

'Are you certain?' Pooley asked. Soap had always spoken with such conviction that even though Jim considered him to be three-halfpence short of a shilling, he had half romantically wondered whether his tales might be true.

'I am indeed certain,' said Soap. 'It is the exact opposite. There are dwellers beneath, but far from being benign and benevolent they are foul and evil and intent upon one thing only: to leave this world of darkness and conquer the sun-soaked realm above.' Soap's pink eyes travelled upwards and John and Jim's followed them.

'Now, now,' said Omally, 'I cannot believe all this. Surely if it were so, these fellows would have emerged years ago. They could surely have dug their way out. How did they come to be here in the first place?'

'Ah,' said Soap, giving his nose an annoyingly significant tap. 'That is a tale indeed, and if you have time I will tell it.'

'It would seem,' said John, 'that unless you feel so inclined as to lead us skywards, then we have all the time in the world.'

'Certainly you are a captive audience, but I must impress upon you that this is a very important business, and that your help is sorely needed. I have no wish to return to the surface, my world is here. But neither do I have the wish to see mankind destroyed by these beings, or worse still, driven here to plague me.'

John took off one of his boots and emptied the contents into a nearby aspidistra pot. 'Go on then,' he said, 'let's hear it.'

Soap withdrew a shining disc from an inner pocket and held it towards his guests. 'You recognize this, no doubt?'

Pooley peered at it and nodded. 'The symbol is the same as those on the allotment. You wouldn't happen to know what it means, by any chance?'

'I would, and so would Professor Slocombe.'

'Well, he certainly didn't feel fit to confide in us. "C" the fifth of the ten was all we got for it.'

'I was in the room when he told you,' said Soap. 'The Professor and I have known about the symbols and the plans of the Cereans for some time. We agreed that we should enlist help to assist with their destruction. Men of enterprise, we agreed, men of sterling stuff, good men and true, hearts of oak, valorous men with big . . .'

'Yes, yes,' said Omally, 'naturally you thought of us.'

'Actually no,' said Soap, 'we had hoped that Small Dave might be passing, but as you turned up . . .'

'Thanks a lot,' said Omally.

'I nearly drowned,' said Jim.

'Just my little joke,' said Soap, smiling sweetly. 'The Professor said that you two were his first choice.'

Pooley groaned pathetically, 'It would seem, John,' said he, 'that we have been press-ganged.'

Omally nodded bleakly. 'As running is obviously out of the question, I suggest that we waste no more time. Tell your tale, Soap.'

'Thank you, John, I expected at least a blow or two to the head. I am glad you are taking it so well. What I am about to tell you might seem a little hard to believe, but I can assure you it is all true.'

'No doubt,' said Omally.

'The symbol upon this disc' – Soap held the glittering item aloft – 'means literally what the Professor told you. "I am 'C' the fifth of the ten." It is the insignia of the planet Ceres which was once the tenth planet in our solar system, fifth from the sun. Ceres was the home world to a most advanced race of beings who commuted between the planets much in the way that you or I might take a sixty-five up to Ealing Broadway. Their world was small and their population large. They needed another planet similar to theirs for colonization. Naturally enough their eyes turned towards Earth, a world at that time only sporting a primitive society which offered little opposition to such an advanced race. They sent out scout parties, who were pleased to discover that the simple Earthers hailed them as gods. No doubt the Cereans would be running the place even now had not their warlike natures got the best of them. A great war developed upon Ceres and whilst a considerable number of the lads were here arranging matters to their satisfaction their entire planet was totally destroyed, leaving them marooned.

'The cataclysm was, if you will pardon the expression, somewhat earth-shattering, and the shocks were felt here. A travelling asteroid, the Moon as we now know it, was blown into orbit around the Earth causing absolute devastation. Half of the world was flooded. Those Cereans who survived the holocaust did so by withdrawing here and sealing themselves in. Little remained to ever prove their existence but for legend.

'The Cerean survivors never lost hope, although they were few in number and the centuries which passed saw mankind's development slowly approaching that of their own. Still they remained, waiting and plotting. For they had one thing to wait and plot for.

'Shortly before the planet's destruction the men of Ceres had sent a great strike force out of this solar system to seek other stars and other worlds. The Cereans knew that they would some day return and, finding no Ceres, would put two and two together and revisit the Earth. Thus they have remained, waiting and waiting, preparing for this return. They are doing so still and their time has almost come. Even as I speak the Cerean strike force is streaking across the Cosmos bound for Earth. And they have only one thing upon their minds.'

Soap ceased his fantastic monologue, and Pooley and Omally stared at him dumb and slack-jawed. 'If you don't mind me saying so,' said John at length, 'and please do not construe this as any criticism of yourself or your character, that is the most absurd piece of nonsense I have ever had the misfortune of listening to.'

'I have seen the film of it,' said Pooley, 'dubbed from the original Japanese it was.'

'And the lights upon the allotment,' said Soap, 'what would you take those to be?'

'The work of the council,' said Omally firmly, 'another plot to confound honest golfers.'

Soap burst into a paroxysm of laughter. Tears rolled down his pale cheeks and he clutched at his stomach.

'Come now,' said Pooley, 'it is no laughing matter, those lads have it in for us.'

'Have it in for you?' gasped Soap between convulsions. 'You witness a test run of laser-operated gravitational landing beams, the product of a technology beyond comprehension, and you put it down to the work of Brentford Council?'

'If you will pardon me,' said Pooley, somewhat offended, 'if it is the product of a technology beyond comprehension I hardly feel that we can be blamed for finding it so.'

'Quite,' said Omally.

'And your journey here through the solid concrete floor of an empty allotment shed?'

'I have been meaning to ask somebody about that,' said John.

'It was a hologram,' said Pooley, matter-of-factly.

'Oh, of course, one of those lads.'

'I must apologize for your rapid descent,' Soap explained. 'I had a great deal of trouble in keeping the door open long enough for you both to enter. I was unable, however, to stop the Cereans bringing down the lift.'

'Come now,' said Pooley, who had always been fond of the phrase, 'be fair Soap, all this is a little hard to swallow.'

'Nevertheless, it is true. As true as the fact that you are sitting here, a mile and a half beneath Penge, drinking one-hundred-and-fifty-year-old Rhine wine.'

'Penge?' Pooley shook his head once more. 'Where the hell is Penge?'

'I've never been quite certain myself, but I'm told that it's a very nice place.'

John and Jim finished their second bottles and sat in silence wondering what in the world they were to do next. Omally sat glowering into the carpet. Pooley took off his jacket, which was starting to steam at the shoulders. 'All right,' he said at last, 'say that we do believe you.'

'I don't,' Omally interrupted.

'Yes, well, say that we did. What do you suppose we can do about it? How can we –' he indicated himself and his bedraggled companion '– how can we battle it out with an intergalactic strike force? I myself possess a barlow knife which is good for whittling and Omally has an air pistol. Could you perhaps chip in with a few Sam missiles and the odd thermonuclear device?'

'Sadly no,' said Soap. 'But I am open to any suggestions at this time.'

'I have one to make,' said John Omally bitterly. Pooley covered his ears.

14

Small Dave lay in his hospital bed for some days before the doctors released him. He seemed sound enough physically, a little scorched about the extremities, but nothing more. It was his mental state which put the wind up the hospital staff. The constant talking to himself. Still, there was no law as yet against that sort of thing, and he wasn't a private patient, was he? The doctors consequently turned the dwarf postman out on to the street and left him to fend for himself.

At length he returned to the boarded-up shell which had been his family seat for countless generations. As he stood peering up at the blackened brickwork there was little emotion to be found upon his elfin face. With a mere shrug, a brief display of hand-flapping, and a word or two to an invisible companion, he turned upon his heel and shambled away towards the Ealing Road.

Neville watched him pass from the Swan's doorway. 'Vindictive, grudge-bearing wee bastard,' was all the part-time barman had to say.

As the dwarf receded into the distance, Neville noted to his dismay that a bouncing, striding figure, sporting a lime-green coiffure and a natty line in bondage trousers, was rapidly approaching, his denim pockets bulging with coin of the realm and his trigger finger already a-twitch. It was, in fact, twitching at a rate exactly equivalent to that of the nervous tic the part-time barman had recently developed in his good eye.

'Damn,' said Neville, as Raffles Rathbone offered him a cheery wave. The bouncing boy squeezed past him into the saloon-bar and jogged up to the Captain Laser Alien Attack Machine. 'Good morning to you,' he said, addressing the thing directly. 'Ready for the off?'

With a single movement he tore aside the 'Out of Order' sign Neville had Sellotaped over the video screen and cast it across the floor.

'Broken,' said the part-time barman, without turning from his position in the doorway. 'Coin jammed in the mechanism, won't work.'

Nick eyed the barman's rear quarters with suspicion. 'I'll give it a try, to make sure,' he said slowly.

'Brewery say to leave it, might blow up if anyone tampers with it.'

'Can't see any coin,' said the lad, squinting into the slot.

'I have my orders. Have to wait for the engineer.'

'Really?' Nick's ill-matched eyes flickered between the barman's back and the humming machine. A florin hovered in his hand and a look of indecision wrinkled his brow.

Neville turned suddenly. 'Best leave it, eh?'

The coin was an inch from the slot and the youth's hand was beginning to tremble. A certain electricity entered the air, and with it the distinctive wail of a harmonica, as next door in the rear yard of the Star of Bombay Curry Garden, Archie Karachi performed an apt rendition of 'Do Not Forsake Me Oh My Darling'. It was not that he had any knowledge of the drama enacting itself within the saloon-bar of the Swan, but rather that his son's bar-mitzvah was coming up and he wanted to put on a decent show.

Neville's nervous tic accelerated slightly, but he fixed the boy with a piercing gaze of the type favoured by cobras whilst surveying their four-footed lunch. Nick for his part was not really equal to such a battle of wills. He did his best to look determined, but a bead of perspiration appeared upon his lofty hairline and, taking with it a quantity of green dye, descended towards the bridge of his nose, leaving an unpleasant slug trail behind it.

'Leave it, eh?' said Neville.

'I . . . er.' The boy blew the green bead from the tip of his nose. A minute passed, a long long minute. Nothing moved in the Swan but for a twitching eyelid, and a synchronized right forefinger. Nick's face was now striped, giving him the appearance of a sniper peering through long grass.

Neville's good eye was starting to water. Somebody had to crack.

'I'll have a half of shandy please,' said the boy, breathing a great sigh of relief. Neville smiled broadly and turned towards the pumps.

There was a sudden metallic click, a clunk and then ... *Bitow Bitow Bitow Bitow* went the Captain Laser Alien Attack Machine.

'It's all right,' said Nick sweetly, 'it's mended. You can phone up the brewery and tell them to cancel the engineer.'

Neville ground his teeth sickeningly and clutched at the counter top. He had been so close. So very, very close.

Old Pete entered the Flying Swan, Chips close upon his well-worn heels. 'Good day to you, Neville,' said the ancient. 'A large dark rum if you please.'

Neville did the business, the exact coinage changed hands, and the part-time barman rang up 'No Sale'.

Old Pete eyed the player at the games machine with contempt and unplugged his hearing aid. 'Pardon me whilst I withdraw into a world of silence,' he told Neville.

'Have you seen anything of Pooley and Omally?' the part-time barman asked.

'Pardon?' said Old Pete.

'Pooley and Omally!' shouted Neville. 'Plug the thing in, you old fool!'

Pete refitted his jack plug. 'Haven't seen them,' he said, sipping at his drink.

'It has been more than a week now,' said Neville, with a hint of bitterness in his voice. 'They are supposed to be doing a little bit of work for me. I fear that they have had it away on their toes.'

Old Pete shook his snowy head. 'Perhaps the Four Horsemen has dropped its prices or the Red Lion has got a stripper in.'

Bitow Bitow Bitow Bitow Bitow went the Captain Laser Alien Attack Machine.

Bitow Bitow – Whap – 'What?' Raffles Rathbone turned upon Neville. 'You've been at this again,' he said, curling his lip. 'The sequences have changed again, it's not fair.'

'Get stuffed,' Neville told him.

'But it doesn't give you a fair chance,' whined the young sports-man. 'That's the second time the sequences have changed.' He stalked over to the bar counter. 'Give me a light ale,' he said bravely.

Neville whistled through his ruined teeth. 'A whole half, eh, and no lemonade?'

'Straight,' said the lad.

Old Pete eyed the youth with distaste. Young Chips licked his lips and considered the boy's ankles. Neville poured a half of light and Raffles Rathbone flung a handful of silver across the counter. Neville obligingly short-changed him.

'Anything new with you?' Old Pete asked the barman when the shock-headed hooligan had returned once more to the humming machine.

'Very little,' said Neville. 'I had another postcard from Archroy. Delivered, I hasten to add, by a relief postman of charm and good character, who chooses to deliver a fellow's mail unread.'

Old Pete chuckled. 'Wee Dave still shacked up in the loony ward at the Cottage Hospital then?'

'No, he's out, but happily he has not returned to the round.'

'Vindictive, grudge-bearing wee bastard,' said Old Pete. 'So what of Archroy, how fares the lad upon his travels?'

'He claims to have discovered Noah's Ark upon the peak of Ararat,' said Neville rather proudly. 'His last card said that he has employed a gang of Kurds to work upon chipping the lower portion of the great vessel from the glacial floor. It is tough going by all accounts.'

'It would be.' Old Pete stifled a snigger.

Neville shrugged. 'It is a queer business. I confess that I do not know exactly what to make of it. It would be a rare one if it were true. I can't help feeling that there is a catch in it somewhere and that it will cost me dearly.'

'Well,' said Old Pete, in a tone of great seriousness, 'do not get me wrong, for I am no churchman, but I will tell you a strange thing. During the Hitlerian War I was serving as warden in a refugee centre in South London. One night I got chatting with a young Russian, and he showed me four photographs which he claimed to be of the Ark of Noah.' Neville's good eye widened. 'They were old grainy sepia prints, much travelled and much stained, but he treated them as if they were holy relics. He'd been torpedoed off a troop ship and he claimed that the photos had saved his life. It seems that the folk who live around Ararat have always known of the Ark's existence. Apparently it is visible for only a few short months, once or twice a century, and during this time their holy men make a pilgrimage up the mountainside to scrape off pitch from the hull. This they make into amulets as a protection against drowning.'

Neville was fascinated. 'But how did this fellow come by the photographs?'

Old Pete rattled his empty glass on the counter and feigned deafness. Neville snatched it up from his fist and refilled it. Old Pete continued with his story. 'Told me that his father got them from one of a party of Russians who rediscovered the thing during the time of the Czar.'

'And did you think them genuine?'

'Who can say? They were definitely photographs of some very old and very large vessel half submerged in a glacier. I confess that I never took a lot of notice of them at the time. There was an air raid going on.'

'But what happened to the young Russian?'

'Got blown up!' said Old Pete maliciously. 'Seems that the photographs offered no protection against that kind of thing.'

'You made it all up,' sneered Neville, reaching for a glass and his polishing cloth.

Old Pete took out his shabby-looking wallet and laid it reverently upon the bar. 'And what if I told you that he gave me one of the photographs and that I have been carrying it with me for more than thirty years? What would you say to that, oh doubting Thomas?'

Neville's twitch, which had taken a temporary leave of absence, returned reinvigorated. 'He didn't? You haven't . . .?'

Old Pete swept up his wallet and thrust it back into his pocket. 'Course I bloody haven't!' he said triumphantly. 'You'll believe any damn thing at times, won't you, Neville?'

The part-time barman bit upon a filling. That was twice he had been done down in a single lunchtime and he would have no more of it. Silently he swore a great and terrible oath to his pagan deity, that he would unremittingly bar for life the next person, no matter whom it might be, who tried to get one over on him. To make it more binding he pricked his finger and drew the blood the length of his knobkerry. There was no getting out of a vow like that.

'Give me the same again please, Neville,' said the chuckling ancient.

Norman entered the Flying Swan looking somewhat ashen. Neville hadn't seen him for some time and he marvelled at the shopkeeper's lack of eyebrows and apparently hand-carved wooden teeth. Some new frippery of fashion amongst the shop-keeping fraternity, he supposed.

'Give me one of those,' said Norman, gesturing towards the scotch.

'Closed for stock-taking?' Neville asked. 'Or have the health people been sampling your toffees again?'

'Just pour the drink.' Neville did so.

Norman suddenly stiffened. 'Has Small Dave been in here?' he asked, squinting about the bar.

'No,' said Neville, 'but I think I am about ready for him now.'

'You're not,' moaned Norman, 'take my word for it.' As he had already thrown the scotch down his throat, Neville refilled his glass. 'He was in my place, and there is something not altogether right about him.'

'There never was.'

'This is different.' Norman peered over his shoulder to assure himself that he had not been followed in. 'He knows things.'

'Course he knows things, he's always reading your damned mail and squinting through people's letter-boxes. Vindictive, grudge-bearing wee . . .'

'Yes, I know all that, but listen!' Norman composed himself. Neville took the opportunity to collect payment for the drinks. 'He comes into my shop,' said Norman, 'wants his copy of *Psychic News*. Isn't in, says I. He mutters away to himself for a moment and then, it's third from the bottom of the pile, says he. With the bloody corner up, says I.'

'Well of course you did,' said Neville.

'May I continue?' Neville nodded and Norman drew him closer and spoke in hushed and confidential tones. Old Pete turned up his hearing aid and placed it upon the counter.

'I root through the pile of papers and there it is, plain as plain, third up from the bottom, just like he'd said. Here you go then, says I. Five Woodbine also, says himself. I hand him a packet, he has another mutter then tells me they're stale. Without even opening them! I get in a lather then, but I open up the packet just to be polite, and damn if the things aren't as dry as dust.' Neville looked at Old Pete, who merely shrugged. Young Chips, however, was taking it all in. 'Anyway,' Norman continued, 'he then points to another packet on the shelf and says that he understands that they are all right and so he'll take them. If this wasn't bad enough, as he's leaving the shop, he tells me that my false teeth are going mouldy under the counter.'

'And were they?' asked Old Pete.

Norman drew a furry-looking set of National Healthers from his

326

pocket and tossed them on to the bar top. 'Lost them a week or more back. He couldn't possibly have guessed they were there.'

'Curious,' said Neville, scratching at his greying temples.

'But that's not the worst of it.'

'You mean there's more?'

'Oh yes.' Norman's voice had a disarmingly tremulous pitch to it. 'He said *we* must be off now. *We*, that's what he said. But *we* will be back. With that the shop door opens by itself, he walks out and the thing closes behind him of its own accord.'

'Norman,' said Neville in a calm and even voice, 'Norman, you are barred for life. Kindly get out of my pub and never, ever, ever return.'

15

Professor Slocombe was at his desk, busily at work amongst his books, when two bedraggled and heavily bearded travellers appeared at his French windows. 'Come in, lads,' he said cheerily, 'I am sure I do not need to inform you where I keep the decanter.'

'Do you know how far it is to Penge?' asked John Omally.

'I've never troubled to find out, although they tell me that it's very nice.'

'Oh, very pleasant,' said Pooley, 'but a fair hitch from Brentford.'

'My apologies,' said the old man, when the two men were both seated and clutching at their brimming glasses. 'But you see, I had no wish to force your hands over this matter. I was not altogether certain that if I simply confronted you with the truth you would believe it. Rather, I considered that if matters were simply allowed to run their course, your inquisitiveness would get the better of you and you would involve yourselves. My surmise was accurate, I see.'

'As ever,' said Pooley.

'You quite suit the beards.'

'Soap Distant doesn't own a razor.'

'Apparently he hasn't grown a hair on his face in five years.'

'An interesting man,' said the Professor, 'if a trifle eccentric.'

Omally's attention had become drawn to an elaborate brass device which now stood upon a pedestal in the centre of the Professor's study. 'What is that body?' he asked.

'An orrery,' said the old gentleman. 'I thought it might interest you.'

'Pre-eminently,' said Omally. 'I find little in life more interesting than an orrery.'

Professor Slocombe raised an admonitory eyebrow, but after a moment of brief consideration regarding the deprivations suffered by his guests over the last few days he lowered it again.

'Let me show you,' he said, gesturing towards the instrument. The two men grudgingly rose from their comfy chairs, carefully bearing their glasses.

'It's a mechanical device of great age,' the Professor explained, 'demonstrating the movement of the planets about our Sun and their relative positions to one another during their endless journeys.' He drew their attention to a brazen sphere. 'Here is the Earth,' he said, 'and here the legendary planet Ceres. You can see that its path of orbit lay exactly between those of Mars and Jupiter. Fifth from the Sun. I have no wish to labour this point, but might I explain that although it was a comparatively small world its mass and density were such that its destruction caused a chain reaction in our system which had very serious consequences hereabouts.'

'So we heard.'

The Professor began to hand-crank the amazing piece of machinery and the brass globes pirouetted about the central sphere in a pleasing *danse ronde*.

'Here upon this small date counter you can follow the time-scale of each yearly revolution.'

Pooley and Omally watched the years tick by as the tiny planets spun on their courses.

'Now here,' said the old man, halting the mechanism, 'is where the catastrophe occurred. You will notice the alignment of the planets, almost a straight line from the Earth. With the destruction of Ceres the gravitational effects would have been shattering.'

Pooley noted the date upon the tiny brass counter. 'The time of the biblical Flood,' said he.

'Exactly. I personally subscribe to the theory of Ceres' existence and of its destruction,' said Professor Slocombe. 'It ties up a good many historical loose ends, and I will go further. It is stated in the Bible that after the waters of the great Flood subsided, God set his bow in the heavens as a sign that no such event would occur again. I believe that the popular view that it was the rainbow is incorrect. Rainbows must surely have been observed before the time of the Flood. More likely, I think, that it is to our Moon that the Almighty alluded, the lunar disc's journey describing as it does a bow-like arc in the sky each night.'

'Has a certain ring to it,' Pooley agreed. 'But what puzzles me is to why these Cereans should choose Brentford of all places as a landing site. I take it that by what Soap said regarding gravitational landing beams this is, in fact, the case.'

'Indeed yes, Brentford has been singled out as the target. I thought originally that it was Soap's network of tunnels which had drawn them, but I find that the Cerean tunnel system extends beneath a greater part of the globe. My second thought was that some great centre existed here in the distant past, possibly a previous landing site, but I can find no evidence to support this.'

'What then?'

'I feel it to be the influence of the Brentford Triangle!'

'The Brentford what?' said both men in unison.

The Professor poured a scotch from the crystal decanter and seating himself in a fireside chair did his very best to explain. 'The borough which is Brentford proper,' he said, 'exists within the bounds of a great triangle. The sides of this figure are the Grand Union Canal, the Great West Road and the River Thames. These follow the courses of three major ley lines. As you may know, these are lines of subterranean force which, although never having been fully explained, nevertheless appear to exert an influence upon the surface of the planet. I walk the boundaries of the borough every day and I have dowsed these lines many times. They never move.

'The ancients knew of their existence and aligned their tumuli, barrows, standing stones and circles upon them. Apparently they believed that the power could be tapped. Sadly, down through the centuries man has built across the leys, interrupting their flow and nullifying their power.'

'So,' said Pooley, 'if the power of the leys is lost, why do you attach any significance to this Brentford Triangle business?'

The Professor tapped at his nose, and for the first time both Pooley and Omally realized where Soap Distant had got the habit from. 'Simply because man appears to have lost touch with the leys' power does not mean that other creatures also have. Certain are still susceptible, the most obvious being our feathered friends.'

'Darts?' queried Pooley. The Professor ignored him.

'I have written something of a monograph upon the subject. Migrating birds inevitably take identical routes each year, and these invariably run along the major ley lines of the countrywide system.'

'This all seems a bit iffy,' Omally remarked. 'Are you suggesting that Cereans, like birds, navigate by ley lines?'

'I am suggesting that an advanced civilization such as theirs must surely have discovered them. And here at a time when they were uninterrupted. As the lines appear never to move, they are surely ideal for navigation. The maps of Earth no doubt gather dust in the Cerean ships' computer banks even now. Ready when required.'

'I suppose it is feasible,' Omally conceded. 'But even so, why choose Brentford? Why not Avebury, Glastonbury, Stonehenge or somewhere?'

The Professor rose from his chair and crossed the room to where something rested upon an ornate Victorian easel covered by a green baize cloth. Drawing this aside, he exposed a large mounted map of the district. The lines of the great triangle had been inked in red and stood out clearly.

'Impressive,' said Omally.

'But, as you say, hardly sufficient. It would certainly seem more logical that the Cereans would choose one of the better-known ley centres of this country. No, there is something more here, some inner pattern which I am failing to observe. I am sure it is staring me right in the face, but I cannot find it. Something is shining out like a beacon into space guiding these beings upon their way.'

Pooley and Omally followed the old man over to the map and stood peering over his shoulders. They turned their heads from one side to the other, made as to speak, then reconsidered, traced the courses of the streets, and pointed variously at random. At length they looked at one another and shrugged.

'I cannot see anything,' said Jim, 'just roads and houses, shops and pubs.' With the mention of the latter two pairs of eyes turned simultaneously towards the great ormolu mantel-clock, which obligingly struck five o'clock.

'Nearly opening time,' said Omally. 'I have been a week without a pint of Large. Possibly, Professor, we might continue this discussion over a refreshing bevvy or two?'

The Professor smiled gently and withdrew from his desk a folded map of the neighbourhood. 'You certainly deserve a drink,' he said, 'and here' – he took out a crisp new five-pound note – 'have it on me.'

Pooley accepted both map and fiver. 'Thank you,' he said, 'this is most kind. Will you not join us for one?'

'I think not,' said the old man. 'Study the map though and employ your wits. I ask only one favour: please bring me a pound's worth of silver from the Swan's cash register. From there and nowhere else, do you understand?'

'The motive or the request?'

The old man smiled and tapped again at his nose.

'One question,' said Omally, as he and Jim were turning to leave. 'Suppose by the vaguest of chances we were to discover this pattern, what could we do?'

The Professor shrugged his ancient shoulders. 'No knowledge is ever wasted. You know my methods. I never make a move before acquainting myself with every last piece of relevant information.'

'Yes, but . . .' Jim made a rustling sound with the five-pound note. 'We will be in touch,' said John Omally.

'Good luck,' said the Professor, returning to his desk. 'I shall look forward to hearing from you.'

John and Jim wandered off towards the Flying Swan. 'At least one good thing has come out of all this,' said Jim after a while.

'Then you will kindly enlighten me as to what it is, because it has certainly slipped by me in the heat of the moment.'

'Well,' said Pooley, 'at least now we know that the strangers upon the allotment are not from the council, so we can continue our game.'

'You are wise beyond your years, Jim,' said Omally, dealing his companion a weltering blow to the skull.

16

Neville sat alone at a side table in his favourite darkened corner of the empty saloon-bar. He heard the library clock faintly chiming the hour over towards the Butts Estate and sighed a deep and heartfelt sigh.

This was one of the part-time barman's favourite times, when, the optics replenished, the pumps checked, and the glasses polished, he could sit alone for the short half-hour before opening and reflect upon days gone by and days possibly yet to come.

This afternoon, however, the barman felt oddly ill at ease. Something was going on in the borough, something sinister, and he could smell it. Although whatever it was lurked just out of earshot and beyond his range of vision, Neville knew he could smell it. And what he could smell, he most definitely did not like. It was musty and tomb-like and had the sulphurous odour of the pit to it, and it made him feel awkward and uneasy.

The part-time barman's long thin hand snaked out from the darkness and drew away a tumbler of scotch from the table top. There came a sipping sound, a slight smacking of lips, and another great dismal sigh. Neville leant forward to replace the glass and his nose cleaved through the veil of shadow, a stark white triangle.

He shook his head vigorously in an attempt to free himself of the gloomy feeling which oppressed him. The feeling would not be so easily dislodged, however. Neville took a deep, deep breath, as a drunken man will do under the mistaken belief that it will clear his head. The effort was wasted of course, and the part-time barman slumped away into the darkness taking his scotch with him.

Something was very wrong in Brentford, he just knew it. Some dirty big sword of Damocles was hanging over the place, waiting to drop at any minute. His nose told him so and his nose was never

333

wrong. Certainly the Swan's patrons scoffed and sneered at his extra-nasal perception, but he knew what was what when it came to a good sniff. It was a family gift, his mad Uncle Jimmy had told him when he was but a scrawny sprog. The entire clan possessed it in varying degrees, and had done so since some half-forgotten time, in the pagan past, at the very dawn of mankind. Down through the centuries it came, father to son, father to son, turning up again and again and again. A great and wonderful gift it was, a blessing from the elder gods, which should never be used for personal gain or profit. 'But what exactly is it?' the young Neville had asked his musty-looking relative. 'Search me,' said Uncle Jimmy. 'I'm on your mother's side.'

Neville had total recall when it came to his childhood. He could remember every dismal dreary moment of it, with soul-destroying clarity. He, the gangling lad, always head and shoulders above his classmates and always sniffing. Such children do not have any easy time of it. And with the coming of his teens it got no better. Although highly sexed and eager to make the acquaintance of nubile young ladies, Neville's gaunt, stooping figure, with its slightly effeminate affectations, had attracted the attentions of quite the wrong sort of person. Big fat girls, some sporting cropped heads and tattoos, had sought to smother him with their unsavoury affections. Young fellow-me-lads of the limp-wristed persuasion were forever asking him around for coffee to listen to their Miles Davis records with the lights out. Neville shuddered, grim times.

He had given up all thoughts of being a young buck and a bit of a ladies' man at an early age, and had fallen naturally enough into the role of aesthete. He had dutifully nurtured a six-hair goatee and frayed the bottoms of his jeans. He had done the whole bit: the Aldermaston marches, which he joined for the last half mile to arrive in Trafalgar Square amidst cheering crowds; the long nights in coffee bars discussing Jack Kerouac and René Magritte over cold cups of espresso; the dufflecoats and Jesus boots, the night-school fine arts courses. But he never got his end away.

He had met many a big-breasted girl in a floppy sweater, smelling of joss sticks, who spoke to him of love being free and every experience being sacred. But they always ended up at the art teacher's pad and he back at home with his mum.

He'd never been one of them, and he couldn't blame it all on his nose. He was simply an outsider. That he was an individualist and an original meant little to a lad with stirrings in the groin department.

Neville rose from his seat and padded across the threadbare carpet to the whisky optic. Surely things hadn't been all that bad, had they? Certainly his childhood and years of puberty had not exactly been the stuff of dreams, but there had been moments of joy, moments of pleasure, hadn't there?

Neville's total recall could not totally recall any. Still, things weren't all that bad now. He was the Swan's full-time part-time barman, and it was an office which made him as happy as any he could imagine.

If he had known when he was fifteen that this lay in store for him, he would never have suffered such agonies of self-doubt when he realized that he could not understand a single bit of Bob Dylan's 'Gates of Eden'.

But how had he come to get the job in the first place? It had been a strange enough business by any accounts. Neville remembered the advert in the *Brentford Mercury*: 'Part-time barman required, hours and salary negotiable, apply in person. Flying Swan.'

Now in his late twenties and making a career out of unemployment, Neville had jettisoned the camphor bags and forced himself into his one suit, given his brothel creepers a coat of Kiwi, and wandered down to the Swan to present himself. The acting part-time barman, who shortly afterwards absconded with a month's takings and several cases of scotch, had given him the summary once-over. He asked if he thought he could pull a pint, then hired him on the spot.

As to who the actual tenant of the Flying Swan was, Neville had not the slightest idea. The paint had flaked off the licensee plate outside, and those who swore they knew the man like a brother gave conflicting accounts as to his appearance. Neville had been handed the keys, told to take his wages from the disabled cash register, and left to get on with it. It had been a rare challenge but he had risen to it. He had no knowledge of running a pub but he had learned fast, and the ever-alert locals had only ever caught him the once on any particular dodge. He had single-handedly turned the Swan from a down-at-heel spit and gob saloon to a down-at-heel success. He had organized the trophy-winning darts team, who had now held the local shield for a record five consecutive years. He had supervised the numerous raffles and alehouse events, acted as oracle and

335

confessor to local drunks, and strangely and happily had evolved into an accepted part of the Brentford landscape.

He was at home and he was happy.

Neville's smile broadened slightly, but a grim thought took off its edges. The brewery. Although they had no objection whatsoever to his residency, him being basically honest and the pub now running at a handsome profit, the brewery gave him no rest. They were forever suggesting special events, talking of modernization, and installing things . . . His eyes strayed involuntarily towards the bulky contours of the humming monster which he had now covered with a dust sheet tightly secured with baling wire.

Neville tossed back his scotch and looked up at the Guinness clock; nearly five-thirty, nearly opening time. He squared up his scholar's stoop and took another deep breath. He would just have to pull himself together. Embark upon a course of positive activism. Be polite to his patrons, tolerant of their foibles, and indulgent towards their eccentricities. He would smile and think good thoughts, peace on earth, good will towards men. That kind of thing. He was certain that if he tried very very hard the horrid odour would waft itself away, to be replaced by the honeysuckle fragrance of spring.

From not far away the library clock struck the half-hour, and Neville the part-time barman flicked on the lights, took himself over to the door, and opened up. On the doorstep stood two bearded men.

'Good evening, barlord,' said Jim Pooley.

'God save all here,' said John Omally.

Neville ushered them into the bar without a word. Now was the present and what was to happen happened now and hereafter and it surely couldn't be all bad, could it? The two men, however, seemed to be accompanied by a most extraordinary smell. Neville pinched at his nostrils and managed a somewhat sickly grin. 'Your pleasure, gentlemen?' he asked when he had installed himself behind the jump, and his two patrons had resumed residency of the two bar-stools which had known not the pleasure of their backsides for more than a week. 'What will it be?'

Pooley carefully withdrew from his pocket the five-pound note, which had not left his clammy grip since it had been handed to him, and placed it upon the bar counter.

Neville's eyebrows soared into a Gothic arch. He had hoped that if he thought positively things might turn out okay, but this? This transcended even his wildest expectations. Jim Pooley with a five-pound note?

And it got worse. 'Two pints of Large please, Neville,' said Pooley, smiling almost as hideously as the barman, 'and have one yourself!'

Neville could feel a prickling sensation rising at the back of his neck. Have one yourself? He had read in paperback novels of the phrase being used by patrons of saloon-bars, but he had never actually encountered it in real life. 'Pardon,' said the part-time barman, 'might I have that last bit again.'

'Have one yourself,' Pooley reiterated.

Neville felt at his pulse. Could this really be? Or had he perhaps died and gone to some kind of barman's Valhalla or happy drinking ground? The nervous tic went into overdrive.

Omally, who was growing somewhat thirsty, made the suggestion that if Neville wished to take advantage of Jim's generosity it would be better if he dropped the amateur theatricals and did so at once. Neville hastened to oblige. 'Thank you Jim,' he said. 'I don't know what got into me then. Your kindness is well received, I thank you.'

Still mumbling the phrase 'Have one yourself' under his breath, Neville pulled two pints of the Swan's finest. As he did so he took the opportunity to study the two men, whose eyes were now fastened by invisible chains to the rising liquid. The beards were odd enough in themselves, but that Pooley's shirt appeared to hve shrunk by at least two sizes and that the colour of Omally's regimental tie had run on to his neck were things of exceeding strangeness. Caught in a sudden downpour perhaps? Neville could not remember any rain. The ducking-stool then? Some lynch mob of cuckolded husbands exacting a medieval revenge? That seemed feasible.

The barman passed the two exquisitely drawn pints across the counter and took possession of the magical blue note, which he held to the light as a matter of course. Having waited respectfully whilst Pooley and Omally took the first step towards quenching their long thirst he said at length, 'Well now, gentlemen, we have not had the pleasure of your company for more than a week. You have not been taken with the sickness I hope, nor struck by tragic circumstances.'

Pooley shook his head. 'We have been in Penge,' he said.

'Penge,' said Omally, nodding vigorously.

'Ah,' said Neville thoughtfully. 'I haven't actually been there myself, but I understand that it's very nice.'

337

'Splendid,' said Pooley.

'Very nice indeed,' his colleague agreed. 'You'd love it.'

Neville shrugged and turned away to cash up the traditional 'No Sale' and extract for himself the price of a large scotch. As he did so Pooley remembered the Professor's request.

'Could I have a pound's worth of change while you're at it?' he asked politely.

Neville froze in his tracks. A pound's worth of change? So that was it, eh? The old 'have one yourself, barman' was nothing more than the Judas kiss. Pooley planned to play the video machine. 'You bastard!' screamed Neville, turning upon the drinker.

'Pardon me?' said Jim.

'Pound's worth of change is it? Pound's worth of change? You treacherous dog.'

'Come now,' said Jim, 'steady on.'

'Steady on? Steady on? Have one yourself barman and a pound's worth of change while you're at it! What do you take me for?'

'Seemed a reasonable request to me.' Pooley looked towards Omally, who was covering his drink. 'What is going on, John?' he asked.

Omally, who was certainly never one to be slow on the uptake, explained the situation. 'I think that our good barman here believes that you want the money to play the video machine.'

Pooley, whose mind had been focused upon matters quite removed from video games, suddenly clicked. 'Oh,' he said, 'good idea, make it thirty-bobs' worth, Neville.'

'AAAAAAGH!' went the part-time barman, reaching for his knobkerry.

Pooley saw the hand vanishing below counter level and knew it to be a very bad sign. 'Come now,' he implored, backing away from the bar, 'be reasonable. I haven't played it in a week, I was just getting the hang of it. Look, let's just say the quid's-worth and call it quits.'

Neville brought the cudgel into prominence. 'I've had enough,' he shouted, hefting it in a quivering fist. 'You traitor. Touch the thing and you are barred, barred for life. Already today have I barred one regular, another will do no harm.'

'Who is the unhappy fellow?' asked Omally who, feeling himself to have no part in the present altercation, had not shifted from his seat.

'Norman,' growled Neville. 'Out, barred for life, finished, gone!'
Omally did his best to remain calm. 'Norman?'

'Norman.'

'Norman Hartnell of the corner shop?'

'That Norman, yes.'

'Norman Hartnell, the finest darts player this side of the Thames? Norman the captain of the Swan's darts team? The five times trophy-winning darts team? The very darts team that plays at home for the championship on the twenty-ninth? That Norman you have barred for life?'

What colour had not already drained from Neville's naturally anaemic face took this opportunity to make an exit via his carpet-slipper soles.

'I . . . I . . .' The barman rocked to and fro upon his heels; his good eye slowly ceased its ticking and became glazed, focused apparently upon some point far beyond the walls of the Swan. He had quite forgotten the darts tournament. The most important local sporting event of the entire calendar. Without Norman the team stood little hope of retaining the shield for a sixth year. What had he done? The locals would kill him. They would tar and feather him and ride him out of the town on a rail for this. Darts wasn't just a game in Brentford, it was a religion, and the Flying Swan its high temple. A bead of perspiration appeared in the very centre of Neville's forehead and clung to it in an appropriately religious fashion like some crystal caste mark. 'I . . . I . . . I,' he continued.

Old Pete entered the Swan, Chips as ever upon his heels. Being naturally alert, he spied out the barman's unnatural behaviour almost at once. 'Evening to you, Omally,' he said, nudging the Irishman's arm. 'Haven't missed anything, have I?'

'Sorry?' Omally, although a man rarely rattled, had been severely shaken by the barman's frightful disclosure.

'The mime,' said Old Pete. 'I'm very good at these. Spied out Norman's Quasimodo some days back and won an ounce of tobacco. This one looks quite easy, what's the prize?'

Omally scratched at his whiskers. 'What are you talking about?'

The old loon put his head upon one side and stroked his chin. 'Is it a film or a television programme?' he asked. 'Do I get any clues?'

'It's a book,' said Pooley, taking the opportunity to retrieve his pint before retreating to a safe distance.

'I . . . I . . . I . . .,' went Neville.

'Must be the Bible then,' said Old Pete. 'Not that I've ever read it. Should say by the look of the stick and everything that it's either Moses parting the Red Sea or Samson slaying all those Philippinos with the jawbone of an ass.'

Young Chips, who was of a more metaphysical bent, suspected that it was more likely Lobsang Rampa's *The Third Eye*, with the caste mark and the glassy stare and what was quite obviously some kind of mantra based upon the concept of self-realization; the I.

Neville slowly replaced his knobkerry, and turned to the cash register where he drew out Pooley's change, including amongst it thirty shillings'-worth of florins. Preventing patrons from playing Captain Laser machines did not seem to be of much importance anymore. 'Enjoy your game,' he said, handing the still flinching Jim the money.

Old Pete shook his head. 'Can't abide a poor sport,' he said. 'Guessed it in one, did I? Told you I was good. What about the prize then?' Neville, however, had wandered away to the end of the bar where he now stood polishing an imaginary glass with an in- visible bar cloth. 'What about a drink then?' The ancient turned imploringly towards Pooley and Omally, but the two had taken themselves off to a side table where they now sat muttering over an outspread map. 'I won it fair and square,' said Old Pete to his dog. Chips shrugged, he had a bad feeling about all this and wished as usual to remain non-committal.

Jim Pooley ran his finger up and down the cartographical repre- sentation of Brentford and made a wash-handbasin out of his bottom lip. 'This really is all getting rather dire,' he said. 'Spacemen on the allotment, starships on the attack, and the Flying Swan without a darts captain. Are we dreaming all this or can it really be true?'

Omally fingered his beard and examined the tide marks about his cuff. 'It's true enough,' said he, 'and I think we might do no better than to apply ourselves to the problem in the hope that a solution might be forthcoming.'

'We'll have to do something about Neville.' Pooley peered over his shoulder towards the dejected figure. 'I can't stand seeing him like that.'

'All in good time,' said Omally, giving his nose a tap. 'I am sure I shall be able to effect some compromise which will satisfy both parties and get us one or two freemans into the bargain. For now though the map must be the thing.'

Jim had his doubts but applied himself once more. 'What are we looking for?' he asked very shortly.

Omally took out his Asprey's fountain pen, which by virtue of its quality had withstood its ordeal by water with remarkable aplomb, or la plume, as the French would have it. 'If a pattern exists here I shall have it,' he said boldly. 'When it comes to solving a conundrum, the Omallys take over from where the fellow with the calabash and the deerstalker left off. Kindly turn the map in my direction.'

'Whilst you are solving the Enigmatic Case of the Cerean Cipher,' said Pooley sarcastically, 'I shall be off to the bar for another brace of Large. I am at least getting pleasure from my newly acquired wealth.'

The ordnance survey map had received more than a little attention on his return. 'Looks very nice,' he said. 'I didn't know that there was a streak of William Morris in you, John. Taken to designing wallpaper, is it?'

'Silence,' said Omally. 'If it is here, I will have it.'

Jim sucked at his pint. 'What are all those?' he asked, pointing to a network of squiggles.

'The drainage system of the borough.'

'Very good, and those?'

'All the houses that to my knowledge have recently fitted loft insulation.'

'You are nothing if not thorough. And the curlicues?'

'That is a personal matter; I have left nothing to chance.'

Pooley stifled a snigger. 'You surely don't believe that an alien strikeforce has plotted out the homes of your female conquests as a guideline to their invasion?'

'You can never tell with aliens.'

'Indeed.' Pooley watched the Irishman making crosses along a nearby side-road. 'Might I venture to ask what you are plotting now?'

'Morris Minors,' said Omally.

Jim stroked his beard reflectively. 'John,' he said, 'I think that you are going about this in the wrong way. The Professor suggested that we look for some kind of landmarks, surely?'

'All right then.' Omally handed Jim his cherished pen. 'You are obviously in tune with the Professor's reasoning, you find it.'

Pooley pushed out his lip once more but rose to the challenge. 'Right then,' he said, 'landmarks it is. What do we have?'

'The War Memorial.' Pooley marked a cross. 'The Public Library.' Pooley marked another.

Twenty minutes later the map had the appearance of a spot the ball contest form that had been filled in by a millionaire.

'I've run out,' said Omally.

'So has your pen,' said Jim, handing his friend the now ruined instrument. The two peered over the devastated map. 'One bloody big mess,' said Jim. 'I cannot make out a thing.'

'Certainly the crosses appear a little random.'

'I almost thought we had it with the subscribers to *Angling Times* though.'

'I could do with another drink.'

'We haven't done those yet.'

Omally pressed his hands to his temples. 'There is not enough ink in the country to plot every drinker in Brentford.'

'Go and get them in then.' Pooley handed John one of the Professor's pound notes. 'I'll keep at it.'

Omally was a goodly time at the bar. Croughton the pot-bellied potman, finding himself under the sudden overwhelming strain of handling the bar single-handed while Neville sought divine guidance, had begun to crack and was panicking over the drinks. The Swan now swelled with customers and arguments were breaking out over cloudy beer and short change. Omally, seizing the kind of opportunity which comes only once in a lifetime, argued furiously that he had paid with a fiver; the flustered potman, being in no fit state to argue back, duly doled out the change without a whimper.

Omally pocketed the four well-won oncers, reasoning that the news of such an event might well unbalance the sensitive Pooley's mind and put him at a disadvantage over the map plotting. When he returned to the table bearing the drinks he was somewhat surprised to find that the expression Jim Pooley now wore upon his face mirrored exactly that of Neville the part-time barman. 'Jim?' asked John. 'Jim, are you all right?'

Pooley nodded gently. 'I've found it,' he said in a distant voice. Omally peered over the map. There being no ink left in the pen, Pooley had pierced the points of his speculation through with defunct matchsticks. A pattern stood out clearly and perfectly defined. It was immediately recognizable as the heavenly constellation of Ursa Major, better known to friend and foe alike as The Plough.

'What are they?' Omally asked, squinting at the crucified map.

'It's the pubs,' said Pooley in a quavering voice. 'Every house owned by this brewery.'

Omally marked them off. It was true. All seven of the brewery pubs lay in the positions of the septentriones: the New Inn, the Princess Royal, The Four Horsemen, and the rest. And yes, sure as sure, there it was, there could be no mistake: at the point which marked Polaris, the North Star in Ursa Minor – the Flying Swan. 'God's teeth,' said John Omally.

'Let the buggers land then,' said Jim. 'I am not for destroying every decent drinking-house in Brentford.'

'I am behind you there friend,' said John, 'but what can it mean? The Swan at the very hub, what can it mean?'

'I shudder to think.'

'Roll the map up,' said John, 'we must tell the Professor at once.'

Pooley, who still had upon his person the price of several more pints, was reticent and suggested that perhaps there was no immediate rush. The Professor could hardly have expected them to solve the thing so swiftly. Perhaps a celebration pint or two was called for.

'A sound idea,' said Omally heartily. 'In fact, as you have done so well, I suggest that we dispense with pints and go immediately on to shorts!'

'A fine idea,' said Jim, 'I will get a couple of gold ones in.' Thus saying he rose from his seat and made for the bar. Quite a crush had now developed, and even Pooley's practised elbows were hard put to it to gain him a favourable position. As he stood, waggling his pound note and trying to make himself heard, Jim suddenly felt a most unpleasant chill running up his spine. Pooley, taking this to be some after-effect of his discovery, shuddered briefly and tried to make himself heard. He found to his horror that his voice had suddenly deserted him. And it was then that he noticed for the first time that there was a strong smell of creosote in the air. Pooley clutched at his throat and gagged violently. As he did so a firm and unyielding hand caught his elbow, and held it in a vicelike grip.

Jim turned towards his tormentor and found himself staring into a face which only a mother could love. There was more than a touch of the Orient about it, slightly tanned, the cheekbones high and prominent, and the eyes slightly luminescent. It was a face in fact which bore an uncanny resemblance to a young Jack Palance. The figure was dressed in an immaculate black suit and had about him the feeling of impossible cleanliness.

343

These details Pooley's brain took in, but it was somewhat later before he was actually able to relate them verbally. For the present the awful clone of the legendary Hollywood star was steering the muted Jim through the crowd and towards the Swan's door.

Pooley, realizing that the fate which was in store for him, if not actually worse than death itself, was probably none other than the very same thing, began to struggle for all he was worth. He swung around upon his kidnapper and with deadly accuracy kneed him in the groin. Had he known anything whatever about Cerean anatomy, however, he would have gone immediately for the left armpit. As it was, his blow did little other than damage one of the Cerean's sinuses.

Pooley was nearing the end of the bar counter by now and the Swan's doorway was perilously close. His mouth opened and closed, paying silent tribute to Edvard Munch's most famous painting. The patrons of the Swan, it appeared, cared little for Pooley's plight and paid him not the slightest heed.

At the end of the bar stood Neville, staring into space. Pooley made one single-handed and desperate grab towards his bar apron. Even in a blind panic he knew better than to go for the tie. That being the first thing a drunk ever goes for, and Neville being the professional he was, the part-time barman always wore a clip-on. Pooley caught the apron and the outcome was not a pleasant thing to behold.

Neville's genitalia, which were correctly placed for a man of Earth, were suddenly drawn into violent and painful contact with the tap spout of one of the Swan's finest traditional hand-drawn ales.

'AAAAAAAAAGH!' went Neville the part-time barman, the searing agony suddenly reviving him from his vertical catalepsy.

The sound reberberated about the bar, silencing every conversation and turning every head. Omally, startled by the cry, leapt from his seat, and glimpsed Pooley's dire predicament.

The Cerean tugged once again upon Pooley's elbow, and Jim, who would not have released his grip for all the Lapsang Souchong south of the Yellow River, dragged the barman forward for a second time.

'AAAAAAAAAGH!' the part-time barman reiterated, as his cobblers smote the beer engine anew. All thoughts of darts teams and barred captains were suddenly driven from his head and he howled

344

in pain and did his utmost to free himself of Pooley's maniacal hold.

The Swan's patrons, momentarily stunned by the first cry, were emboldened by the second. Tempers had been growing more and more frayed during the evening and this altercation offered a fine opportunity for giving vent to pent-up emotions. The crowd began to advance upon the threesome, and Omally was in the vanguard. With a Gaelic cry which would surely have put the wind up King Billy himself, Omally made a grab at the Cerean.

The darkly-clad figure shook him off as if he were but a speck of dandruff upon his finely-tailored shoulder. Omally tumbled to the deck, cursing and spitting. Several members of the Swan's drinking élite laid powerful hold upon Pooley, with the result that Neville, who was rapidly giving up all thoughts of potential parenthood, found his good eye crossing once more.

The ensuing *mêlée* was notable for many things, not least the extraordinary display of divided loyalties. One faction was definitely pro-Neville, being firmly of the belief that Pooley had attacked the barman, and that the man in black was attempting to restrain him. Another took it that Neville, whose behaviour that evening had not exactly been exemplary, had gone for Pooley, and that the man in black was one of the brewery's dark forces, assisting in that loyal patron's expulsion from the Swan. A third, which counted but one in its number, and this a son of Eire, was of an entirely different opinion altogether.

It must be stated that other factions existed also. These were formed either from fellows who felt that now was as good a time as any to end some personal vendetta, or from those who by their very natures necessarily misinterpret any given situation. Their participation was notable mainly for its enthusiastic and seemingly indiscriminate violence.

Young Chips, who could smell a nigger in a woodpile even with his nose bandaged, set immediately to work upon the Cerean's ankles.

Pooley had by now, under the welter of blows, lost hold upon Neville's apron, and, as the part-time barman lapsed from consciousness and sank gracefully behind the bar, found himself being borne once more towards the doorway. Towards the very doorway, in fact, where John Omally now stood, brandishing a beer bottle.

'Leave hold,' roared the Irishman. Pooley's mouth opened and

345

closed and a lip reader would have covered his eyes at the obscenity.

The Cerean squared up to the obstacle in his path and raised his left hand to strike. Omally swung his bottle and, it must be reasoned, more from luck than judgment, struck the villain a devastating blow to the left armpit.

As he lost his grip upon Pooley, several of the pro-Neville brigade fell upon the barman's attacker with relish. The Cerean staggered towards Omally, who, having the advantage of fighting upon home territory, stepped nimbly aside and tripped him through the Swan's open doorway and into the street.

Outside, parked close to the kerb, stood an automobile that was a collector's dream. It was ink-black and gleaming, a showroom piece. The handbook had it down as a nineteen-fifty-eight Cadillac Sedan, the deluxe model. In the driving seat sat a man of average height, wearing an immaculate black suit. He bore an uncanny resemblance to a young Jack Palance and favoured a creosote aftershave. It took him but a moment to leave the car and gain the pavement, but by then the chaos of flailing fists which now filled the Swan was spilling into the street.

The pro-Pooley faction, who knew a brewery henchman when they saw one, and who were currently occupied in assaulting the one who was rolling about clutching at his armpit, saw another quarry and wasted little time in taking the opportunity to vent their spleen.

Archie Karachi, who ran the Star of Bombay Curry Garden next door to the Swan, was a man who knew a race riot when he saw one. Thrusting a vindaloo-stained digit into his telephone dial, he rang out a rapid nine, nine, nine. Being also a man of few words, and most of those Hindi, his message was succinct and to the point. 'Bloody big riot in Swan,' he bawled above the ever increasing din, 'many men injured, many dead.'

The blue serge lads of the Brentford nick were not long in responding to this alarm call. With the station grossly over-manned, as befits a district with a low crime rate, what they craved was a bit of real police action. A bit of truncheon-wielding, collarbone-breaking, down to the cells for a bit of summary justice, real police action. Within minutes, several squad cars and a meat wagon were haring along the wrong side of Brentford High Street, through the red lights, and up the down lane of the one-way system, bound for the Flying Swan. Within the wheel-screeching vehicles constables were belting on flak jackets, tinkering with the fittings of their riot shields, and drumming CS gas canisters into their open left palms with increasing vigour.

What had started out as a localized punch-up, had now developed into wholesale slaughter. The numbers involved in the *mêlée* had been swelled significantly by the arrival of a gang of yobbos from the flatblocks opposite. Those crop-headed aficionados of the steely toecap had been met head on by the students of the Brentford Temple of Dimac Martial Arts Society, who had been limbering up for their evening's training schedule with a fifteen-mile run. Neither of these warrior bands having the slightest idea what all the fuss was about, or which was the favourable side to support, had contented themselves with exercising their respective martial skills upon one another. Although this did nothing to ease the situation, to the crowds of onlookers who now lined the opposite pavements and crammed into every available upstairs window, it added that little extra something which makes a really decent riot worthwhile.

With sirens blaring and amber lights flashing, the squad cars slewed to a halt at the rear of a war-torn Cadillac. This development was wildly applauded by the onlookers, many of whom had thought to bring out stools and kitchen chairs, that they might better enjoy the event. As hot-dog men and ice-cream sellers, who have an almost magical knack of appearing at such moments, moved amongst the spectators, the Brentford bobbies went about their business with a will, striking down friend and foe alike. With every concussion inflicted the crowd hoorahed anew and, like the season-ticket holders at the Circus Maximus in days gone by, turned their thumbs towards the pavement.

To the very rear of this scene of massacre, pressed close to the wall of the Flying Swan, two bearded golfing types watched the carnage with expressions of dire perplexity. 'Gather up the map,' said John Omally. 'I feel that we have pressing business elsewhere.'

Easing their way with as little fuss as possible through the Swan's doorway, they passed into the now deserted saloon-bar. Deserted that is, but for a certain part-time barman who now lay painlessly unconscious in the foetal position behind the jump, and an old gentleman and his dog, who were playing dominoes at a side-table.

'Goodnight to you Pooley and Omally,' said Old Pete. 'You will be taking your leave via the rear wall I have no doubt.'

Pooley scooped up the map and stuffed it into an inside pocket.

'Offer my condolences to Neville,' he said. 'I expect that it is too much to hope that he will awake with amnesia.'

'You never can tell,' said the ancient, returning to his game. 'Give my regards to Professor Slocombe.'

17

Professor Slocombe peered over the pen-besmirched, match-riddled map with profound interest. At length he leant back in his chair and stared a goodly while into space.

'Well?' asked John, who had been shifting from one foot to the other for what seemed like an age. 'Has Pooley found it?'

The Professor pulled himself from his chair and crossed the room to one of his bookcases. Easing out an overlarge tome, he returned with it to his desk. 'Undoubtedly,' he said, in a toneless voice. 'If you will pardon my professional pride, I might say I am a little miffed. I have sought the pattern for weeks and you find it in a couple of hours.'

'I think we had the natural edge,' said Omally.

Pooley, whose injured parts were now beginning to pain him like the very devil, lay slumped in an armchair, a hand clasping the neck of the whisky decanter. 'I only hope that it will help,' he said. 'Those lads are on to us, and I escaped death by a mere hairsbreadth this night.'

'We have by no means reached a solution,' said the Professor, in a leaden tone. 'But we are on the way.'

Omally peered over the old man's shoulders as he leafed through his great book. 'What are you looking for now?'

'This book is the Brentford Land Register,' the Professor explained. 'The pubs you have plotted were all built during the last one hundred years. It will be instructive to learn what existed upon the sites prior to their construction.'

'Ah,' said John, 'I think I follow your line of thought.'

'I think my right elbow is fractured,' said Jim Pooley.

The Professor thumbed over several pages. 'Yes,' he said. 'Here we have it. The Four Horsemen, built upon the site of the cattle

349

trough and village hand pump.' He turned several more pages. 'The New Inn, upon this site there has been a coaching house for several hundred years, it has always boasted an excellent cellar and a natural water supply. Built in 1898, the North Star, a significant name you will agree, founded upon Brentford's deepest fresh-water well.' The Professor slammed the book shut. 'I need not continue,' he said, 'I think the point is clearly made.'

'My collarbone is gone in at least three places,' said Jim.

'It can't be the water supply,' said Omally. 'That is ludicrous. Aliens do not steer themselves through space guided by the village waterworks. Anyway, every house in Brentford has water, every house in the country, surely?'

'You fail to grasp it,' said the Professor. 'What we have here is a carefully guided natural watercourse, with the accompanying electrical field which all underground water naturally carries, culminating in a series of node points. The node points channel the ley earth-forces through the system, terminating at the Flying Swan. If you will look upon the map you will see that the Swan is built exactly one third up from the Thames base line of the Brentford Triangle. Exactly the same position as the King's Chamber in the Great Pyramid. A very powerful position indeed.'

'It all appears to me a little over-circuitous,' said Omally. 'Why not simply stick up a row of landing lights? If these Cerean lads have all the wits that you attribute to them, surely they could tamper with the National Grid and form a dirty big cross of lighted areas across half of Britain?'

'Possibly,' the Professor replied, 'they might be able to do that for an hour, possibly for a day, but this pattern has been glowing into space for a hundred years, unnoticed by man and untouched. It is reinforced by the structures built above it, pubs, thriving pubs. This is Brentford; nobody ever knocks down a pub here.'

'True,' said Omally. 'We have little truck with iconoclasts hereabouts.'

'This beacon could go on radiating energy for a thousand years. After all, the Cereans had no idea how long they would have to wait to be rescued.'

'There is definitely evidence of a cracked rib here,' said Pooley, feeling at his chest.

'All is surely lost,' said Omally.

350

'I didn't say it was terminal,' Pooley replied. 'Just a job for a skilled surgeon or two.'

Professor Slocombe stroked his chin. 'At this very moment,' he said, 'somewhere on the outer rim of the galaxy, the Cerean Strike Force is heading towards its homeworld. Finding none, it will inevitably be turning here, guided by the descendants of its stranded forebears. Unless otherwise diverted or destroyed, they will home in upon their landing area, and I do not believe that we can expect any of that "We bring greetings from a distant star" benign cosmic super-race attitude to be very much in evidence upon their arrival. We must work at this thing; I do not believe that it is without solution.'

'My ankle's gone,' grizzled Pooley. 'I shall walk with a limp for the rest of my life.'

'Do put a sock in it, Pooley,' said the Professor.

'But I'm wounded,' said the wounded Pooley. 'Somebody might show a little compassion.'

'I don't think you realize the gravity of the situation.'

'On the contrary,' said Jim, waggling a right wrist which was quite obviously a job for the fracture clinic. 'I've never missed an episode of "The Outer Limits" – true, I've been in the bog during many a title sequence, or slept through the last five minutes, but I know what I'm talking about. None of this smacks to me of sound science fiction. All this sort of stuff does not occur in the shadow of the gasworks. Alien invaders, who we all know to be green in colour and pictured accurately upon the front page of the *Eagle*, do not muck about with council water supplies or conveniently arrange for the location of public drinking-houses. I take this opportunity to voice my opinion and pooh pooh the whole idea. There is a poultice wanting upon these knees and more than one of my fillings has come adrift.'

'An uncle of mine has connections with the Provos,' said Omally. 'If you will sanction the exemption of the Swan, I might arrange for the levelling of every other relevant pub in Brentford.'

Professor Slocombe smiled ruefully. 'That, I think, might be a little too extreme,' he said. 'I am sure that a less drastic solution can be found.'

'Nobody ever listens to me,' said Jim, going into a sulk.

'As I see it,' said Professor Slocombe, 'the Flying Swan is the epicentre of the entire configuration. It has been so aligned as to act as the focal point. The harnessed Earth forces flow through the alignment and culminate therein. There must be something located either within the Swan or beneath it into which the energy flows. Something acting as locative centre or communicating beacon to these beings. As to what it is, I have not the slightest idea.'

'Maybe it's the darts team,' said Pooley. 'We've held the shield for five years. Perhaps your lads have infiltrated the team and are guiding their mates in through a series of pre-planned double tops.'

'You are not being obstructive are you, Jim?' the Professor asked.

'What, me? With the collapsed lung and the damaged cerebral cortex? Perish the thought.' Pooley took up his glass in a grazed fist and refilled it.

'Now we know where it is,' said the Professor, 'it surely cannot be that difficult to find it.'

'But what are we looking for?' asked Omally. 'You find a great triangle, we find the constallation of the Plough.'

'I find it,' said Pooley.

'Pooley finds it,' said Omally, 'one thing leads to another, but we just go around in circles. What are we looking for?'

'I think I can make a reasonable guess,' said Professor Slocombe. 'We are looking for something which is the product of a high technology. Something which utilizes the vast power fed into it and acts as the ultimate homing beacon. It must have been placed in the Swan during the last year or so, for it was only during this time that the Earthbound Cereans gained knowledge of their prodigals' return and wished to announce their own presence.'

Pooley shrugged. 'Product of a high technology, runs off its own power supply and recently installed in the Swan. Can't see anything filling that bill, it would have to be pretty well camouflag . . .' Pooley ceased his discourse in mid-sentence. An image had suddenly appeared in his brain. It was so strong and crystal clear that it blotted out everything else. It was the image of a large bulky-looking object shrouded beneath a groundsheet and secured with baling wire, and it was humming and humming and humming.

'By the light of burning martyrs,' said John Omally. 'It has been staring us in the face for months and we never even twigged.'

'What is it?' the Professor demanded. 'You know, don't you?'

'Oh, yes,' said Jim Pooley. 'We know well enough, but believe me the thing will not be easily tampered with. It will take an electronics expert with the brain of an Einstein to dismantle it, and where are we going to get one of those in Brentford?'

Norman Hartnell was not a happy man. Apart from being barred from the Swan with darts night rapidly approaching, which was the kind of thing that could easily drive a sensitive soul such as himself to the point of suicide, he also was suffering a grave amount of concern over his camel. Still wedged firmly into the eaves of his lock-up garage, and gaining bulk from its hearty consumption of cabbage leaves, the beast still showed no inclination whatever to return to Earth. On top of these two insoluble problems, Small Dave's untimely return to Brentford and his disconcerting perceptions were causing the shopkeeper a good deal of grief. He really would have to get rid of the camel. It was damning evidence by any account, and he also had the definite feeling that Small Dave was on to him. The nasty vindictive grudge-bearing wee bastard seemed to be dogging his every move. If he was ever to transfer the Great Pyramid of Cheops from its present foundations in Egypt to its planned relocation upon the turf of Brentford football ground, he really couldn't have the dwarfish postman blundering in and spoiling everything before the project was completed.

Norman dropped into his kitchen chair and did a bit of heavy thinking. The mantelclock struck eleven, time once more to feed the camel. Norman glanced despairingly about; perhaps he should simply blow the garage up. The trouble was that he was really growing quite attached to the mouldy-looking quadruped.

He'd never been allowed to have a pet when he was a lad, and dogs didn't exactly take to him. But Simon, well, Simon was different; he didn't snap at your ankles or climb on your furniture. True, he didn't exactly do anything other than sleep in the rafters and roar for food when hungry, but there was something about the brute which touched Norman. Possibly it was his helplessness, relying upon him, as it did, for his every requirement. Perhaps it was that he had Simon exclusively to himself, nobody forever patting at him and offering him biscuits. Whatever it was, there was something. Simon was all right. He was cheap to feed, living as he did upon Small Dave's cabbages, and his droppings made excellent manure for the roses. Norman wondered for one bright moment whether a camel might be trained to eat dwarves; shouldn't be but a mouthful or two. Pity camels were exclusively vegetarian.

Norman rose from his chair, drew on his shabby overcoat and put out the kitchen light. Stepping silently through the darkened shop, he put his eye to the door's glass and peered out at the Ealing Road. All seemed quiet, but for the distant sound of police sirens. Small Dave was nowhere to be seen.

The shopkeeper drew the bolt upon the door and slipped out into the night. He scuttled away down Albany Road, keeping wherever possible to the shadows. Down the empty street he hurried, with many a furtive glance to assure himself that he was not being followed.

Young Chips, who was returning from some canine equivalent of a lodge meeting, had been watching the shopkeeper's progress for some moments. Now where is Norman off to, he asked himself, and who is the character in the Victorian garb hard upon his heels? If I wasn't half the dog I believe myself to be, I would be certain that that is none other than the famed American author, Edgar Allan Poe. Scratching distractedly at a verminous ear, the dog lifted his leg at a neighbour's Morris Minor, and had it away for home.

Norman reached the allotment gates and peered around. He had the uncanny feeling that he was being watched, but as there was no one visible he put the thing down to nerves and applied his skeleton key to the lock. A wan moon shone down upon the allotments, and when Norman had had his evil way with Small Dave's already sadly depleted cabbage crop, no living being watched him depart with his swag.

The row of lock-up garages slept in the darkness. As Norman raised the door upon its well-oiled hinges, nothing stirred in the Brentford night. 'Simon,' he said in a soothing tone, 'din dins.'

Having closed the door behind him, he switched on the light, illuminating the tiny lock-up. Simon looked down from his uncomfortable eyrie, and Norman sought some trace of compassion upon the brute's grotesque visage. 'Yum yums,' he said kindly. 'Chow time.'

If camels are capable of displaying emotions, other than the 'go for the groin if cornered' variety, Simon was strangely reticent about putting his about. As he hung in the air, the great ugly-looking beast did little other than to drool a bit and break wind. 'You cheeky boy,' said Norman. 'It's your favourite.'

Behind him, Edgar Allan Poe eased himself through the closed garage door and stood in the shadows watching Norman making a holy show of himself. Simon saw Edgar at once, and Simon did not like the look of Edgar one little bit.

'WAAAAAARK!' went Simon the zero-gravity camel.

'Come, come,' said Norman, flapping his hands, 'there is nothing to get upset about. It's really only cabbage, your favourite.'

'WAAAAAARK!' the disconsolate brute continued.

'Shhh!' said the shopkeeper. 'Calm yourself, please.'

'WAAAAAARK!' Simon set to wriggling vigorously amongst the eaves.

'Stop it, stop it!' Norman frantically waved the cabbage leaves about. 'You'll have the whole neighbourhood up.'

Edgar Allan Poe was fascinated. Times had certainly changed since he had shuffled off the old mortal coil. Small Dave had spent a goodly amount of time impressing upon him the importance of finding a camel. But to think that people actually kept them as pets now, and that they were no longer tethered to the planet of their birth by gravity. That was quite something. 'Stone me,' said Edgar Allan Poe.

John and Jim were taking the long route home. After the incident earlier that evening at the Swan they had no wish to cross the allotment after dark. It was a brisk, cloudless night, and as they slouched along, sharing a late-night Woodbine, they were ill-prepared for the ghastly wailing cries which suddenly reached their ears.

'What is it?' Pooley halted in mid-slouch.

Omally peered up and down the deserted street and over his shoulder to where the allotment fence flanked an area of sinister blackness.

'It is the plaintive cry of the banshee,' said he, crossing himself. 'Back in the old country no man would question that sound. Rather he would steal away to his own dear hovel and sleep with his head in the family Bible and his feet in the fireplace.'

'I have never fully understood the ways of the Irish,' said Jim, also crossing himself just to be on the safe side. 'But I believe them to be a people not without their fair share of common sense, best we have it away on our toes then.'

Another horrific cry rose into the night, raising the small hairs on

355

two ill-washed necks, and causing Pooley's teeth to chatter noisily. This one, however, was followed almost at once by vile but oddly reassuring streams of invective, which could only have arisen from one local and very human throat.

'Could that be who I think it could?' Pooley asked.

'If you mean that very electronics expert with the brain of a veritable Einstein to whom you previously alluded, then I think that it might just be.'

The two men strained their ears for another sound, but none was forthcoming. Slowly, they proceeded along the street, halting outside the row of lock-up garages. 'Would you look at that,' said Omally, pointing to where a line of orange light showed beneath one of the doors. 'Now what would you take that to be?'

'I would take it to be another trap,' said Jim. 'I have recently had a very bad experience through entering sheds without being asked.'

Omally shuddered. The thought of those icy-black subterranean waters was never far from his mind. 'Caution then?' he asked, creeping close to the door and pressing his ear to it.

It was at that exact moment that Edgar Allan Poe, who had been badly shaken by the floating, screaming camel, chose to make his exit from the garage. Passing discreetly through the solid wood of the garage door he slid right into the skulking Omally. For one ghastly moment the two forms, one solid and smelling strongly of drink, the other ectoplasmic and probably incapable of bearing any scent whatever, merged into one.

'Holy Mary, Mother of God!' screamed Omally, clutching at his head. 'The very devil himself has poked his clammy finger into my ear.'

'Who's out there?' Norman spun away from Simon, who was now silent beneath the falcon hood of a potato sack which had been rammed over his head.

'Night watchman,' said Pooley unconvincingly. 'Twelve o'clock and all's well. Goodnight to you, stranger.'

'Pooley, is that you?'

'Norman?'

The garage door rose a couple of feet and Norman's face appeared, peeping through the opening. 'Is Small Dave with you?' asked the persecuted shopkeeper.

'That vindictive grudge-bearing wee bastard? Certainly not.'

Norman crawled out under the door and drew it rapidly down

behind him. 'Just servicing the old Morris Minor,' he said.

'Sounds a bit iffy,' said Omally.

'A bit of gear trouble, nothing more.'

'Let me have a look at it then.' Omally was all smiles. 'I know the old Morris engine like the back of my hand.' He extended this very appendage towards the garage doorhandle, but Norman barred his way.

'Nothing to concern yourself about,' he said, 'nothing I cannot handle.'

'Oh, no trouble, I assure you. Nothing I like better than getting to grips with a monkey wrench and a set of allan keys.'

'No, no,' said Norman, 'I think not, it is growing late now and I have to be up early in the morning.'

'No problem then, I have no a.m. appointments, to me the night is yet young. Leave me the garage key and I will post it through your letter-box as soon as I am done.'

'You are kindness personified,' said Norman, 'but I could not impose upon you in such a fashion. My conscience would not allow it. I will just lock up and then we shall stroll home together.' He stooped to refasten the padlock.

'You'd better switch the light off before you go,' said Jim Pooley.

Norman's hand hovered over the padlock. A look of terrible indecision crossed his face.

'Allow me,' said John Omally, thrusting the shopkeeper aside and taking the handle firmly in two hands. 'I should just like to have a look at this car of yours before we depart.'

'Please don't,' whined the shopkeeper, but it was too late. The door flew upwards and the light from the lock-up garage flooded the street, exposing Norman's secret to the world.

Pooley took a step backwards. 'My God,' was all that he had to say.

Omally, however, was made of sterner stuff. 'Now there we have a thing,' he said, nudging the cowering shopkeeper. 'Now there we have a thing indeed.'

Norman's brain was reeling, but he did his best to affect an attitude of bland composure. 'There, then,' he said, 'satisfied? Now if you don't mind, it is growing late.'

Omally stepped forward into the garage and pointed upwards. 'Norman,' he said, 'there is a camel asleep in your rafters.'

'Camel?' said Norman. 'Camel? I don't see any camel.'

'It is definitely a camel,' said John. 'If it were a dromedary it would have but one hump.'

'You have been drinking, I believe,' said Norman. 'I can assure you that there is nothing here but a Morris Minor with a tetchy gearbox. I have read of folk suffering such hallucinations when they have imbibed too freely. Come, let us depart, we shall speak no more of these things.'

'It's definitely a camel,' said Jim.

'Dear me,' said Norman shaking his head, 'another victim of Bacchus, and so young.'

'Why is it in the rafters?' Pooley asked. 'I was always of the opinion that camels preferred to nest at ground level and in somewhat sunnier climes.'

'Perhaps it is a new strain?' said Omally. 'Perhaps Norman has created some new strain of camel which he is attempting to keep secret from the world? Such a camel would no doubt revolutionize desert travel.'

Norman chewed upon his lip. 'Please be careful where you stand, Omally,' he said. 'Some of the primer on the bonnet is still wet.'

Omally put his arm about the shopkeeper's shoulder. 'Why not just make this easy on yourself?' he asked. 'Although I accept that mentally you are a fearsome adversary, surely you must realize that the game is up? Cease this folly, I beg you.'

'Don't scuff the spare wheel with your hobnails,' said Norman.

Pooley raised his hand to speak. 'If I might make a suggestion,' he said, 'I think that the matter could be easily settled with a little practical demonstration.'

'Yes?' said Norman doubtfully.

'Well, you suggest that Omally and I are suffering some kind of mental aberration regarding this camel.'

'You are.'

'And we say that your Morris Minor is only notable for its complete and utter invisibility.'

'Huh!'

Pooley drew out his pocket lighter and struck fire. 'You rev up your Morris,' he said, 'and I shall toast the feet of my camel.'

'No, no!' Norman leapt into life. 'Not toast his feet, not toast the feet of my Simon.'

'The camel has it,' said Jim Pooley.

Norman sank to his knees and began to sob piteously. Omally suggested that Jim should lower the garage door, and this he did.

'Come, come,' said Omally to the crumpled shopkeeper, 'there is no need for this undignified behaviour. Clearly we have intruded upon some private business. We have no wish to interfere, we are men of discretion, aren't we, Jim?'

'Noted for it.'

'Not men to take advantage of such a situation are we, Jim?'

'Certainly not.'

'Even though this manifestation is clearly of such singularity that any newspaper reporter worthy of his salt would pay handsomely for an exclusive.'

'Say no more,' moaned Norman, between sobs. 'Name your price. I am a poor man but we can possibly come to some arrangement. A higher credit rating, perhaps.'

Omally held up his hand. 'Sir,' he said, 'are you suggesting that I would stoop to blackmail? That I would debase the quality of our long-standing friendship with vile extortion?'

'Such I believe to be the case,' said Norman dismally.

'Well then,' said Omally, rubbing his hands together, 'let us get down to business, I have a proposition to put to you.'

18

After leaving Norman's garage in the early hours of the morning, Pooley found little joy in the comforts of his cosy bed. He had listened with awe and not a little terror to the amazing revelations which Omally had skilfully wrung from the shopkeeper. Although Jim had plaintively reiterated that the Earth-balancing-pyramid theory which Norman had overheard, that lunchtime so long ago, was gleaned from the pages of an old comic book, as usual nobody had listened to him. What small, fitful periods of sleep he had managed were made frightful with dreams of great floating camels, materializing pyramids and invading spacemen.

At around six o'clock Pooley gave the whole thing up as a bad job, dragged on an overcoat, thrust a trilby hat on to his hirsute head, and trudged off round to the Professor's house.

The old man sat as ever at his desk, studying his books, and no doubt preparing himself for the worst. He waved Pooley to an armchair without looking up and said, 'I hope you are not going to tell me that during the few short hours that you have been gone you have solved the thing.'

'Partially,' said Jim without enthusiasm. 'But I think John should take full credit this time.'

The old man shook his head. 'Do you ever feel that we are not altogether the masters of our own destinies?' he asked.

'No,' said Jim. 'Never.'

'And so, what do you have to tell me?'

'You will not like it.'

'Do I ever?'

Pooley eyed the whisky decanter as a source of inspiration but his stomach made an unspeakable sound.

'Would you care to take breakfast with me, Jim?' the Professor asked. 'I generally have a little something at about this time.'

'I would indeed,' said Jim. 'Truly I am as ravenous as Ganesha's rat.'

The Professor tinkled a small Burmese brass bell, and within a few seconds there came a knocking at the study door which announced the arrival of Professor Slocombe's elderly retainer Gammon, bearing an overlarge butler's tray loaded to the gunwhales with breakfast for two.

It was Pooley's turn to shake his head. 'How could he possibly know that I was here?'

Professor Slocombe smiled. 'You ask me to give away my secrets?' he said, somewhat gaily. 'Where would I be if you deny me my mystique?'

'You have mystique enough for twenty,' said Jim.

'Then I will share this one with you, for it is simplicity itself.' He rang the small bell again and Gammon, looking up from the coffee he was pouring into the fine Dresden china cups, said, 'Certainly, sir, two lumps it is.'

'It is a code with the bell-ringing,' said the enlightened Jim.

The Professor nodded his old head. 'You have found me out,' said he. In reality, of course, Pooley had done nothing of the kind.

Gammon departed at a mental command, closing the door behind him. Pooley set about the demolition of the steaming trayload. Between great chewings and swallowings, he did his best to relate to the Professor all that he had seen and heard that night.

Professor Slocombe picked delicately at his morning repast and listened to it all with the greatest interest. When Pooley had finished his long, rambling, and not a little confused monologue, he rose from his chair and took out a Turkish cigarette from the polished humidor. Lighting this with an ember from the grate, he waggled the thing at Pooley, and spoke through a cloud of steely-blue smoke. 'You would not be having one over on me here, would you Pooley?' he asked.

'I swear not.'

'Norman has a camel in his lock-up garage which he teleported from the Nile delta and which openly defies the law of gravity?'

'Not openly. Norman is keeping the matter very much to himself.'

'And he plans to alter the Earth's axis by teleporting the Great Pyramid of Cheops into Brentford football ground?'

'That's about the size of it.'

Professor Slocombe fingered the lobe of his left ear. 'We live in interesting times,' he said.

Pooley shrugged and pushed a remaining portion of buttered toast into his mouth.

'The idea does have a certain charm, though,' said Professor Slocombe. 'I should really have to sit down and work it out with a slide rule. For the moment, however, I feel it would be better if he was dissuaded from going ahead with it. I think we should nip it in the bud.'

'I think John and I can fit that in between engagements,' said Pooley sarcastically. The Professor raised an eyebrow towards him, and he fell back to his toast chewing.

'How near to completion do you believe his project to be?'

Pooley shrugged again. 'Days away, by the manner in which he spoke. Omally, using his usual ingenuity, suggested that he might avail himself of any serviceable components from the Captain Laser machine, once he had successfully disabled it. That idea alone was enough to win him over to the cause. What with thinly-veiled threats of exposure and the assurance that his action would not only save mankind as we know it, but also secure him readmission to the Swan in time for the darts tournament, he was putty in Omally's grubby mitt.'

'It would certainly be nice to clear all this up before darts night,' said the Professor enthusiastically. 'I have booked a table at the Swan, I would not care to miss it for the world.'

'Let us pray that none of us do,' said Pooley. 'Would there be any chance of a little more toast?' Professor Slocombe reached for his small brass bell. 'I know perfectly well that it is not how you do it,' said Jim.

'The toast is on the way,' said Professor Slocombe, smiling broadly.

Neville limped painfully up the stairs to his room, bearing with him the special mid-week edition of the *Brentford Mercury*, which had flopped unexpectedly through the Swan's letter-box. Propping it against the marmalade pot, he lowered himself amid much tooth-grinding on to the gaily-coloured bathing ring, which rested somewhat incongruously upon his dining chair.

As he sipped at his coffee he perused the extraordinary news sheet. BRENTFORD HOLOCAUST! screamed the six-inch banner headline with typically restrained conservatism. '*Many arrests in Battle of Brentford, rival gangs clash in open street warfare.*'

Neville shook his head in wonder at it all. How had the trouble started? It was all a little hazy. That Pooley and Omally were involved, he was certain. He would bar them without further ado.

He groaned dismally and clutched at his tender parts. He surely could not afford to bar any more clients; something desperate was going to have to be done to persuade Norman to return to the fold. And Old Pete; he was sure he had barred him, but he was equally certain that the old reprobate had been in the night before. Perhaps he hadn't. He would bar him again just to be on the safe side.

He perused the long columns of journalistic licence which covered the *Mercury*'s front page. It had been some kind of political rally, so it appeared, the Brownshirts or the League of St George. Apparently these extremists had been drawn into combat with the martial acolytes of the Brentford Temple of Dimac. The police had acted bravely and justly, although greatly outnumbered. There was some talk of decorations at the Palace.

Neville skimmed along the lines of print, seeking to find some reference to the original cause of the incident, but none was forthcoming. The Swan didn't even get a mention, nor did the names of any of the regulars appear amongst the list of arrested villains destined to go up before the beak this very morning. With the arrival of the boys in blue the Swan's stalwarts had either melted away into the night or retired to the tranquillity of the saloon-bar to engage in games of darts and dominoes.

He read the final paragraph. The gallant bobbies had, so it was stated, become involved in a hair-raising car chase through Brentford with a black nineteen-fifties Cadillac which had roared away from the scene of the crime during the height of the disturbances. They had pursued it through the maze of backstreets until unaccountably losing it in a cul-de-sac.

Neville folded the paper and flung it into the fireplace. He would get to the bottom of all this, just as soon as he could get it all clear in his mind. But for now only two things mattered: firstly, that Norman be reinstated as soon as possible in a manner in which neither party would lose face and one which would not anger his pagan deity; and, secondly, that the ice pack which he now wore strapped between his legs got another top-up from the fridge.

*

363

Small Dave sat in the sewage outlet pipe at the old dock, which he now called home. His face wore a manic expression into which it had been moulding itself, a little more permanently, with each passing day. He had given up such niceties as hygiene, and now lived for only one thing.

Dire and unremitting vengeance!

Some way further up the pipe, hovering in the darkness, was a misty figure, visible only to the small postman and to certain members of the animal élite.

Small Dave ground his teeth and spat into the daylight. So Norman had the camel penned up in his garage upon the Butts Estate, did he? He had always suspected the shopkeeper, and now Edgar had confirmed his suspicions.

'We have him,' sneered the dwarf, raising a tiny fist towards the sky. 'Right where we want him.' He grinned towards the spectre, exposing two rows of evil-looking yellow teeth. Edgar Allan Poe shifted uneasily in the darkness. He was not at all happy about any of this. He had made a big mistake in allowing himself to become involved with this diminutive lunatic, and sorely craved to return to the astral plane. Although a grey and foggy realm, which offered little in the way of pleasurable diversion, it was infinitely preferable to this madhouse any day of the week.

Sadly, by the very nature of the laws which govern such matters, he was unable to gain release, other than through the courtesy of the being who had called him into service. The mighty fire which had raged through Small Dave's house, eating up many thousands of copies of his books, had acted as some kind of sacrificial catalyst which now bound him to the material world.

Edgar Allan Poe was thoroughly Earthbound, and he was in a very, very bad mood.

At a little after eleven-thirty John Omally reached the Flying Swan. He would have reached it sooner but for the throng of reporters from the national dailies who had accosted him in the street. With his usual courtesy and willingness to be of assistance he had granted several exclusive interviews on the spot.

Yes, he had been there in the thick of it, braving the rubber bullets and the tear-gas. Yes, he had been the last man standing, by virtue of his mastery in the deadly fighting arts of Dimac. No, he had only saved the lives of three of his companions, not four, as was popularly believed. And no, he was sorry, he could not allow any photographs to be taken, modesty forbidding him to take more than his fair share of credit in saving the day.

Patting at his now heavily burdened pockets, Omally entered the Flying Swan. Neville was at the counter's end, supported upon the gaily-coloured rubber bathing ring which he had Sellotaped to the top of a bar stool. He was studying a picture postcard which boasted a rooftop view of Brentford, but upon Omally's approach he laid this aside and viewed the Irishman with distaste.

'You are not welcome here,' he said in no uncertain terms.

John smiled sweetly. 'Come now,' he said, 'let us not be at odds. You have no axe to grind with me. I come as the bearer of glad tidings. All your troubles are over.'

Neville's good eye widened. 'All my troubles are over?' he roared, but the exertion sent blood rushing to certain areas which were better for the time being left bloodless and kosher. 'I am a ruined man,' he whispered hoarsely, between clenched teeth.

'A regrettable business,' said John. 'If I ever see that fellow in the black suit again, I shall do for him.'

Neville said, 'Hm,' and pulled the Irishman the pint of his prefer-ence.

'Have one yourself,' said John.

Although the deadly phrase burned like a branding iron upon Neville's soul, he was loath to refuse and so drew himself a large medicinal scotch.

'About this being my lucky day then?' he said, when he had carefully re-established himself upon his rubber ring. 'You will pardon my cynicism I hope, but as the bearer of glad tidings you must surely rival the angel of death announcing the first innings score of the battle of Armageddon.'

'Nevertheless,' said Omally, 'if you will hear me out then you will find what I have to say greatly to your advantage.'

Neville sighed deeply and felt at his groin. 'I believe that I am getting old,' he told Omally. 'Do you know that I no longer look forward to Christmas?'

John shook his head. He didn't know that, although he wondered how it might be relevant.

'I haven't had a birthday card in ten years.'

'Sad,' said John.

'At times I wonder whether it is all worthwhile. Whether life is really worth all the pain, disappointment, and misery.' He looked towards Omally with a sad good eye. 'People take advantage of my good nature,' he said.

'No?' said John. 'Do they?'

'They do. I bend over backwards to help people and what do I get?' Omally shook his head. 'Stabs in the back is all I get.' Neville made motions to where his braces, had he worn any, would have crossed. 'Stabs in the back.'

'I really, genuinely, can help you out,' said Omally with conviction. 'I swear it.'

'If only it were so,' moaned Neville. 'If only I could see some ray of hope. Some light at the end of the dark tunnel of life. Some sunbeam dancing upon the bleak rooftop of existence, some . . .'

'All right, all right!' Omally said. 'That's enough, I've been kicked in the cobblers a few times myself, I know how much it hurts. Do you want to know how I can help you out or not?'

'I do,' said Neville wearily.

Omally peered furtively about the bar and gestured the barman closer. 'This is in the strictest confidence,' he whispered. 'Between you and me alone. Should you wish to express your gratitude in some way when the thing is accomplished, then that is a matter between the two of us.'

Neville nodded doubtfully. Whatever it was that Omally was about to say, he knew that it would as usual cost him dearly. 'Say your piece then, John,' he said.

'As I see it,' John continued, 'you have two big problems here. Five, if you wish to number your wounded parts. Firstly, we have the problem of the rapidly approaching darts tournament and the Swan's prospect of certain defeat, should Norman fail to captain the team.' Neville nodded gravely. 'Secondly, we have that.' Omally gestured towards the shrouded video machine, which was even now receiving the attention of a green-haired youth with a large nose and a pair of wire-cutters. Neville bared what was left of his teeth.

'If I was to tell you that I can solve both problems at a single stroke what would you say to me?'

'I would say free beer to you for a year,' said Neville, rising upon his elbows. 'But for now I must say, please get out of my pub and do not return. I am not able to assault you physically at present, but be assured that when I am fully restored to health I shall seek you

366

out. You add insult to my injury and I will have no more of it.'

John tapped at his nose. 'We will let the matter drop for now, as I can see that you are feeling a little under the weather. By the by, might I take the liberty of asking after the postcard.'

'You may,' said Neville, 'and I will give you that small part before you depart. It is from Archroy, he says that he has now removed the Ark of Noah from the peak of Ararat and is in the process of transporting it through Turkey to Istanbul. He hopes to have it here within a week or two.'

'Well, well, well,' said Omally, grinning hugely. 'We do live in interesting times, do we not?'

'Get out of my pub now,' growled Neville with restrained vehemence, 'or truly, despite my incapacitation, I shall visit upon you such a pestilence as was never known by any of your bog-trotting ancestors in all the hard times of Holy Ireland.'

'God save all here,' said Omally.

'Get out and stay out,' said Neville the part-time barman.

19

Professor Slocombe laid aside a scale model of the Great Pyramid and leant back in his chair. 'No,' he said to himself, 'it couldn't be, no, ludicrous, although . . .' He rose from his desk and took himself over to the whisky decanter. 'No,' he said once more, 'out of the question.'

Partly filling an exquisite crystal tumbler, he pressed the prismed top back into the decanter's neck, and sank into one of the leathern fireside chairs. Idly he turned the tumbler between thumb and forefinger, watching the reflected firelight as it danced and twinkled in the clear amber liquid. His eyelids became hooded and heavy, and his old head nodded gently upon his equally aged shoulders. It was evident to the gaunt-faced figure who lurked in the darkness without the French windows, polluting the perfumed garden air with the acrid stench of creosote, that the old man was well set to take a quick forty.

Needless to say, this was far from being the case, and beneath the snowy lashes two glittering blue eyes watched as a flicker of movement close by the great velvet curtains announced the arrival of a most unwelcome guest. It was a flicker of movement and nothing more, for again the room appeared empty, but for an elderly gentleman, now snoring noisily in a fireside chair.

Professor Slocombe watched as the silent figure delved amongst the crowded papers of his desk and ran his hands over the bindings of the precious books. The Cerean, convinced of his invisibility, went about his evil business with a will, but naught was missed by the Professor, to whom the word 'hologram' meant little more than 'electronic party trick'.

At length, however, he could stand the defilement of his property no longer. Rising suddenly from his sham repose he addressed his uninvited visitor in no uncertain terms. 'Replace my papers and get out of my study at once,' said he, 'or know the consequences for your boorish behaviour.'

The Cerean stiffened and turned a startled face towards the Professor. He fingered the dials upon a small black box which hung at his belt.

'You can tinker with that piece of junk until the sun goes dim, but I can assure you that it will not work upon me.'

The Cerean opened his cruel mouth and spoke in an accent which was unlike any other that the Professor had ever heard. 'Who are you?' he asked.

Professor Slocombe smiled wanly. 'I am either your saviour or your nemesis.'

'I think not,' said the Cerean.

'If you are inclined to prolong your visit, might I offer you a drink?' the old man asked courteously.

The Cerean laughed loudly. 'Drink?' said he. 'Drink is the ruination of your species. Who do you think invented it for you in the first place?'

'Hm.' The old man nodded thoughtfully; it would be better to keep that piece of intelligence from Pooley and Omally. They might feel inclined to change sides. 'As you will,' he said blandly. 'May I inquire then why you have come here?'

'I have come to kill you,' said the Cerean, in such an offhand manner that it quite unsettled the Professor's nerves. 'You are proving an annoyance, you and the pink-eyed man beneath. We shall deal with him shortly.'

'That may not be so easy as you might believe.'

The Cerean turned up the palms of his hands. 'You are old and decrepit. A single blow will cut the frail cord of your existence.'

'Appearances can sometimes be deceptive,' said the Professor. 'I for example happen to be a master of Dimac, the deadliest form of martial art known to mankind. My hands and feet are registered with the local constabulary as deadly weapons. They can . . .'

'Rip, maim, mutilate, disfigure and kill with little more than the application of a fingertip's pressure,' said the Cerean. 'I know. Who do you think invented Dimac in the first place?'

'I find your conversation tending towards the repetitious. Kindly take your leave now, I have much to do.'

'Such as plotting the downfall of the Cerean Empire?'

'Amongst other things – I do have more important business.'

The man from Ceres laughed hollowly. 'You have great courage, old man,' said he. 'We of Ceres hold courage and bravery above all other things.'

'I understand that you like a good fight, yes,' said the Professor. 'Although you do not always win. How's the armpit?'

The Cerean clutched at his tender parts. 'Shortly,' he snarled, 'your race will again know the might of Ceres. They will feel the jackboot upon their necks. You, however, will not be here to witness it.'

'I am expecting to enjoy a long and happy retirement,' said Professor Slocombe, noting to his satisfaction and relief that Gammon had now entered the French windows, wielding an antique warming-pan. 'I worry for *you*, though.'

'Do not waste your concern. When the battle fleet arrives and the true masters of Earth once more set foot upon the planet, they will have none to spare for your puny race.'

'Brave talk. When might we expect this happy event?'

'Two days from now. It is a pity you will miss it.'

'Oh, I won't miss it. I have a table booked at the Swan upon that evening. It is the darts tournament. We hold the challenge shield, you know.'

'Of course I know. Who do you think invented darts?'

'Are all your race such blatant liars?'

'Enough talk!' The Cerean pushed past the Professor's desk and crossed the room, to stand glaring, eye to eye with the old man. 'I know not who or what you are,' he said. 'Certainly you are unlike any human I have encountered hereabouts, although long ago I feel that I have met such men as you. But for the present know only this: as a race, you humans fear death, and you are staring yours in the face.'

Professor Slocombe met the Cerean's blazing glare with a cold, unblinking stare. 'I like you not,' he said mildly. 'It was my firm conviction that some compromise might have been reached between our peoples. I strongly disapprove of needless bloodshed, be the blood flowing from human veins or otherwise. There is yet time, if only you could persuade your race to reconsider. Be assured that if you go ahead with your plans you will meet with certain defeat. It is folly to attack Earth. We have been awaiting you for years and we are well prepared.'

'With the corner up, you have,' sneered the Cerean. 'You cannot stand against our battle fleet. We will crush you into submission. Slaves you were and slaves you shall yet become.'

'Is there no compassion then, no spark of what we call humanity?'

The Cerean curled his lip. 'None,' he said.

'Then at least it makes my task a little easier.'

'Prepare for death,' said the man from Ceres.

'Strike the blighter down,' said Professor Slocombe.

Gammon swung the antique warming-pan with a will and struck the Cerean a might blow to the back of the head. A sharp metallic clang announced the departure of a Cerean soul, bound for wherever those lads go to once parted from their unearthly bodies.

'He was surely lying about the darts, wasn't he, sir?' Gammon asked.

'I sincerely hope so,' the Professor replied. 'They might have got a team up.'

20

The editor of the *Brentford Mercury* screwed the cap back on to his fountain pen and wedged the thing behind his right ear. He leant back in his pockmarked swivel chair and gazed up at the fly-specked yellow ceiling of his grimy office. Before him, upon the overloaded desk, was a mountain of reports which, although being the very bread of life to the Fortean Society, could hardly be considered even food for thought to the simple folk of Brentford.

Certainly mystery and intrigue had been known to sell a few papers, but this stuff was silly season sensationalism and it wasn't the silly season for another month or more. The editor reached into his drawer for his bottle of Fleet Street Comfort. Tipping the pencils from a paper cup, he filled it to the brim.

It all seemed to have started with that riot in the Ealing Road. He had been receiving odd little reports prior to this, but they had been mainly of the lights in the sky and rumblings in the earth variety, and merited little consideration. The riot, strange enough in itself in peace-loving Brentford, had turned up the first of a flock of really weird ones, and this verified by the Brentford constabulary.

There was the long black limousine of American manufacture which had roared away from the scene of the crime pursued by two squad cars, and then simply vanished in a most improbable fashion up a cul-de-sac. The boys in blue had made a full-scale search of the area, which backed on to the allotment, but had come up with nothing. The car had simply ceased to exist.

There was this continuing sequence of power cuts the area had been experiencing. The local sub-station had denied any responsibility and their only comment had been that during their duration the entire power supply seemed literally to drain away, as if down a plughole.

If the disappearance of Brentford's electricity was weird, then the sudden appearance last week of a one-inch layer of sand completely blanketing Brentford's football ground was weirder still. The groundsman's claim that it was sabotage upon the part of a rival team seemed unlikely.

And then, of course, there was this lunatic craze for Jack Palance impersonation which was sweeping the borough. It seemed a localized vogue, as he had had no reports of it coming in from outside the area. But there they were in Brentford, lounging on corners or skulking about up alleyways. Nobody knew who they were, what they were up to, or why they did it, but all agreed that, whyever it was, they did it very well.

The editor sighed. What exactly was going on in Brentford? And whatever it was, was it news? He drained his cup and stared for a moment into its murky bottom for inspiration. He would adjourn to the Swan for a couple of pints of liquid lunch, that was the best thing. Get all this ludicrous stuff out of his mind. He flicked through the pages of his appointments diary, which were as ever blank. All except for tomorrow's date and this, surprisingly, was encircled thickly in red ink.

Now what might that be for? The editor drew his pen from behind his ear and scratched at his head with it.

Of course, how could he have forgotten? Tomorrow night was the most important night of Brentford's social calendar. The night which Brentford annually awaited with eagerness and anticipation. Tomorrow night was darts night at the Flying Swan. And it promised to be a night that all present would long remember.

21

Professor Slocombe drew together the great curtains and turned to address the small conclave gathered in his study.

The group, three in number, watched the old man warily. The first, Jim Pooley by name, leant against the marble mantelshelf, fingering the magnificent pair of moustachios he had chosen to cultivate. The second, a man of Irish extraction who had recently sold his razor at a handsome profit, lounged in a fireside chair almost unseen behind a forest of curly black beard. The third, a shopkeeper and a victim of circumstance, toyed nervously with his whisky tumbler and prayed desperately for an opportunity to slip away and feed his camel.

There was one last entity present at this gathering, but he was of ethereal stock and invisible to the naked eye. Edgar Allan Poe was maintaining the lowest of all low profiles.

'I have called you here, gentlemen,' said Professor Slocombe, 'because we have almost run out of time. We must act with some haste if we are to act at all.'

'You have reached a solution then?' asked Jim hopefully.

'Possibly.' The old gentleman made a so-so gesture with a pale right hand. 'Although I am backing a rank outsider.'

'I am not a man to favour long odds myself,' said Omally, 'unless, of course, I have a man on the inside.'

'Quite so. Believe me, I have given this matter a very great deal of thought. I have possibly expended more mental energy upon it than I have ever done upon any other problem. I feel that I might have come up with a solution, but the plan relies on a goodly number of factors working to our favour. It is, as you might reasonably expect, somewhat fraught with peril.'

'Tell us the worst then,' said Omally. 'I think you can call us committed.'

'Thank you, John. In essence it is simplicity itself. This worries me a little, possibly because it lacks any of those conceits of artistic expression which my vanity holds so dearly. It is, in fact, a very dull and uninspired plan.'

'But nevertheless fraught with peril?'

'Sadly yes. Under my instruction, Soap Distant has turned the allotments into a veritable minefield. The explosive used is of my own formulation, and I can vouch for its efficiency. I intend to detonate it as the first craft land. We may not be able to get all of the invading vessels, you understand, but if we can take out one or two of the lead ships then I think that it will give us the edge.'

'But what about the rest of them?' asked Pooley.

'That is where we must trust very much to psychology. These beings have travelled a very long way to return to their homeworld. As you are well aware, it no longer exists. When they discover this, they will logically be asking themselves the big "Why". They are being guided here by the communicating beacon in the Swan, but if the first craft to land are instantly destroyed, then I feel it reasonable to assume that they will draw their own conclusions. They will reason that the men of Earth have evolved into a superior force, which is capable of destroying entire planets, should it so wish. I can only hope that they will hastily take themselves elsewhere. They have a long, long way to call for reinforcements, should any actually exist.'

'I can accept that in theory,' said Omally, 'but with some reservations. There are a goodly number of ifs and buts to it.'

'I accept it wholeheartedly,' said Jim. 'My name has so far gone unmentioned and that suits me well enough.'

'There are one or two little matters to be cleared up,' said Professor Slocombe somewhat pointedly. 'That is where you come in.'

'This would be the fraught with peril side of it I expect,' said Jim dismally.

Professor Slocombe nodded. 'There is the small matter of the communicating beacon in the Swan. It will have to be switched off. We cannot afford to have the Cereans here giving the game away, now can we?'

Jim shook his head gloomily. 'I suppose not,' said he.

'We have only one opportunity to deal with the thing and that is tomorrow night.'

'I have to play in the finals tomorrow night,' Norman complained. 'Omally here promised I would do so.'

'You haven't fulfilled your side of the bargain yet,' said the voice behind the beard. 'The machine still hums, you have done nothing.'

'I haven't had a chance yet. I can't get in there, I'm barred, don't you remember?'

'Steady on now,' said Professor Slocombe, raising a pale hand. 'All can be reconciled.'

'The machine cannot be broken,' said Jim. 'Be assured of it. We are doomed.'

'I can vouch for the fact that it cannot be destroyed from within the Swan,' said the Professor, 'because I have already tried.'

'Come again?' said Pooley.

'Fair dos,' said Professor Slocombe. 'You surely do not believe that I have been idle?' All present shook their heads vigorously. 'My retainer, Gammon, despite his advanced years and decrepit appearance, is a master of disguise. Twice he has visited the Swan with a view to disabling the device. Firstly, he arrived in the guise of a brewery representative come to check the electrics. He assured me that the machine cannot be switched off in any manner whatever and also that Neville has no love whatever for brewery representatives. Later, he returned as an engineer come to service the device prior to switching it off. This time he received a three-course meal on the house, washed down with half a bottle of champagne, but still met with complete failure. Even a diamond-tipped drill could not penetrate the machine's shell.'

'I told you we were doomed,' said Pooley. 'I am for a Jack Palance mask and a dark suit, me.'

Norman shifted uneasily in his chair. 'I really think I must be going,' he said. 'I can't do anything if I cannot get inside the machine. Feel free to contact me at any time, but for now, goodbye.'

'Not so fast,' said Professor Slocombe. 'I have given the matter much thought, and feel that I have found the solution.'

'Can I go anyway?' Norman asked. 'I do have to be up early in the morning.'

'Test-driving your Morris?' Omally asked. The shopkeeper slumped back into his chair.

'We are dealing,' said Professor Slocombe, 'with beings who, although possessed of superior intelligence, are not altogether dissimilar to ourselves. They are of the opinion that we are a rising, but still inferior race. They might have your card marked, Pooley, but I doubt whether they have contemplated open sabotage. Certainly their machine is outwardly protected. But it might have its weakness if attacked from a different direction.'

'How so?' Pooley asked.

'From behind. The thing is faced against the wall of the Swan. My belief is that if we break through from behind we might find little resistance.'

'What, through the wall of Archie Karachi's Curry Garden? I can't see Kali's Curry King giving us the go-ahead on that one.'

'But Archie Karachi is a member of the Swan's darts team. I myself have seen the sign on his door, "Closed For Business All Day Thursday".'

Pooley tweaked the end of a moustachio whose length would have brought a jealous glance from Salvador Dali himself. 'With all the noise in the Swan,' said he, 'nobody is going to pay much attention to a bit of banging next door.'

'My thoughts entirely. We will need a spy on the inside though, just to keep an eye out. Gammon will take care of that side of it. When we have broken through to the machine it will be down to you, Norman, to deal with it appropriately.'

'No problem there,' said the shopkeeper, blowing on his fingertips. 'There is no machine built which I cannot get to grips with.'

'You might find a surprise or two when we open it.'

'Child's play,' said Norman with sudden bravado. He was quite warming to the idea of all this. He had never liked Archie Karachi very much, and the thought of knocking down his kitchen wall held great appeal. Also, if this machine was everything the Professor seemed to think it was, it was bound to contain a few serviceable components. 'Just lead me to it.'

Omally chuckled behind his whiskers. 'Bravo Norman,' said the Professor, smiling profusely. 'Now, if you will pardon me, I suggest that we bring this meeting to a close, I have several loose ends still to tie up.'

The old man took a scrap of paper from his pocket and held it to

377

each man in turn. 'We will meet tomorrow, seven-thirty p.m. sharp at this address. Please do not speak it aloud.'

The three men committed the thing to memory. With the briefest of goodbyes and no hand-shaking, they took their leave.

Professor Slocombe closed the French windows behind them and bolted the shutters. 'Now,' he said, turning upon the silent room, 'will you make yourself known to me of your own accord, Mr Poe, or must I summon you into visibility?'

'I should prefer that we did it the easy way,' said Edgar Allan Poe. 'We have much to speak of.'

22

Neville the part-time barman took up his mail from the mat and thrust it into his dressing-gown pocket. Amongst the bills and circulars were no less than three postcards sporting rooftop views of Brentford, but the barman did not give these even a cursory glance.

He had been up half the night trying to work out a deal with his pagan deity over his ill-considered blood oath, but was still far from certain that the matter would be allowed to rest. It was always a hairy business wheeling and dealing with the Elder Gods of Ancient Earth.

Neville drew the brass bolts and flung the door open to sniff the morning air. It smelt far from promising. He took a deep breath, scratched at his bony ribs, and gave the world a bit of first thing perusal. It had all the makings of a beautiful day but Neville could not find any joy to be had in the twinkling sunlight and precocious bird song.

Like others who had gone before him, Neville the part-time barman was a very worried man. The day he had been dreading had come to pass. All over Brentford, dartsmen were awakening, flexing their sensitive fingers, and preparing themselves for the biggest night of the year. The Swan's team had been growing surlier by the day. Where was Norman? they asked. Why was he not practising with them? Neville's excuses had been wearing thinner than the seat of his trousers. If Norman did not turn up for the tournament the consequences did not bear thinking about.

Neville looked thoughtfully up the road towards the corner shop. Perhaps he should just slip along now and smooth the matter over. Throw himself on Norman's mercy if necessary, promise him anything. Omally had said that the shopkeeper would be present, but was he ever to be trusted?

Neville hovered upon his slippered toes. It would be but the work of a minute. Norman would be numbering up his papers, he could say he just called in for a box of matches, exchange a few niceties, then leave with a casual 'Look forward to seeing you tonight.' Something like that.

Neville took a step forward. At that moment, in the distance, a figure appeared from the shop doorway. Neville's heart rose; it was telepathy surely. The shopkeeper was coming to make his peace. All his troubles were over.

Nicholas Roger Raffles Rathbone hoisted his paperbag into the sunlight. Neville's heart fell. 'Bugger, bugger, bugger,' said the part-time barman, returning to the saloon-bar, and slamming the door behind him.

Parked close to the kerb in a side road opposite to the Swan, and lost for the most part in the shadow of one of the flatblocks, was a long sleek black automobile with high fins. In the front seat of this gleaming motor car sat a man of average height, with a slightly tanned complexion and high cheekbones. He bore an uncanny resemblance to a young Jack Palance, as did his passenger, who lounged in a rear seat, smoking a green cheroot. The two watched the paperboy as he passed within a few feet of their highly polished front bumper and vanished into one of the flatblocks.

No words passed between these two individuals, but the driver glanced a moment into his rear-view mirror, and his passenger acknowledged the reflected eyes with a knowing nod.

The day passed in an agonizing fashion. Pooley and Omally took their lunchtime's pleasure in a neutral drinking house at Kew, where they sat huddled in an anonymous corner, speaking in hushed tones, bitterly bewailing the exorbitant prices, and casting suspicious glances at every opening of the saloon-bar door.

Norman closed up his shop at one and busied himself in his kitchenette. What he did there was strictly his own business, and he had no intention of letting anything, no matter how alien, interfere with his afternoon's work.

In his sewage outlet pipe, Small Dave paced up and down. His hair was combed forward across his forehead and his left hand was thrust into his shirt in a fashion much favoured by a diminutive French dictator of days gone by. As he paced he muttered, and the more he muttered the more apparent it became that he was plotting something which was to cause great ill to any camel owners in Brentford.

At intervals he ceased his frenzied pacing and peered up and down the hideous pipe, as if expecting the arrival of some fellow conspirator. None, however, made an appearance.

Professor Slocombe was not to be found at his desk that afternoon. He had pressing business elsewhere. Whilst the sun shone down upon Brentford and the Brentonians went about whatever business they had, he was conversing earnestly with a pink-eyed man of apparent albino extraction, who had given up such doubtful pleasures to dedicate himself to the search for far greater truths.

Even now, the Professor sat in what was to all appearances a normal Brentford front room, but which was, in fact, situated more than a mile beneath Penge; which I understand is a very nice place, although I have never been there myself.

At a little after three, Neville drew the bolts upon the Swan's door and retired to his chambers. He had been anaesthetizing himself with scotch since eleven and was now feeling less concerned about what was to happen during the coming evening. He was, however, having a great deal of trouble keeping the world in focus. He falteringly set his alarm clock for five and blissfully fell asleep upon his bed.

23

At long last the Memorial Library clock struck a meaningful seven-thirty. The Swan was already a-buzz with conversation. Pints were being pulled a-plenty and team members from the half-dozen pubs competing this year were already limbering up upon the row of dartboards arranged along the saloon-bar wall. The closed sign had long been up upon the Star of Bombay Curry Garden, and within the Swan, Gammon, in the unlikely guise of an Eastern swami, engaged Archie Karachi in fervent debate.

In the back room of number seven Mafeking Avenue four men held a council of war.

'The thing must be performed with all expediency,' said Professor Slocombe. 'We do not want Norman to miss the match. I have, as the colonials would have it, big bucks riding upon this year's competition.'

The shopkeeper grinned. 'Have no fear, Professor,' said he.

'Omally, do you have your tools?' John patted at the bulging plumber's bag he had commandeered during the afternoon from a dozing council worker. 'Then it is off down the alley and fingers crossed.'

Without further ado, the four men passed out into a small back yard and down a dustbin-crowded alleyway towards the rear of the Star of Bombay Curry Garden.

Norman was but a moment at the lock before the four found themselves within the ghastly kitchenette, their noses assailed by the horrendous odours of stale vindaloo and mouldy madras. Kali's face peered down from a garish wall-calendar, registering a look of some foreboding at the prospect of what was to be done to the premises of one of her followers.

'A moment please,' said Professor Slocombe. 'We must be certain that all is secure.'

Within the Swan, Gammon suddenly interrupted his conversation, excused himself momentarily from Archie's company, and thrust a handful of change into the Swan's jukebox. As the thing roared into unstoppable action, Neville, who had taken great pains to arrange for the disabling of that particular piece of pub paraphernalia years before, and had never actually heard it play, marvelled at its sudden return to life. The Professor had left nothing to chance.

'To the wall, John,' said Professor Slocombe.

'Whereabouts?'

'Just there.'

'Fair enough.' Omally swung his seven-pound club hammer and the cold chisel penetrated the gaudy wallpaper. The mouldy plasterwork fell away in great map chunks, and within a minute or two Omally had bared an area of brickwork roughly five feet in height and two in width.

'Better penetrate from the very centre,' the Professor advised. 'Take it easy and we will have a little check-about, in case the thing is booby-trapped.' Omally belted the chisel into the brickwork.

Within the Swan the jukebox was belting out a deafening selection of hits from the early sixties. The sounds of demolition were swallowed up by the cacophony.

'Stop!' said the Professor suddenly.

'What is it?' The words came simultaneously from three death-white faces.

'Changing the record, that's all. You can go on again now.'

Pooley was skulking near to the back door. With every blow to the brickwork his nerve was taking a similar hammering. His hand wavered above the door handle.

'If it goes up, Jim,' said the Professor without looking round, 'it will take most of Brentford with it. You have nowhere to run to.'

'I wasn't running,' said Jim. 'Just keeping an eye on the alleyway, that's all.' He peered over the net curtain into a yard which was a veritable munitions dump of spent curry tins. 'And not without cause. John, stop banging.'

'I'm getting nowhere with all these interruptions,' the Irishman complained. 'Look, I've nearly got this brick out.'

'No, stop, stop!' Pooley ducked down below window level. 'There's one of them out there.'

'Ah,' said Professor Slocombe, 'I had the feeling that they would not be very far from the Swan this night.'

The four men held their breath until they could do it no more. 'Is he still there?' the Professor asked.

Pooley lifted the corner of the net curtain. 'No, he's gone. Be at it, John, get a move on will you?'

'Perhaps you'd rather do the work yourself, Pooley?' said Omally, proffering his tools.

'I am the lookout,' said Pooley haughtily, 'you are the hammerman.'

'Oh, do get a move on,' sighed Norman. 'It's nearly a quarter to eight.'

Omally swung away with a vengeance, raising a fine cloud of brick dust, and dislodging chunks of masonry with every blow. When he had cleared a hole of sufficient size, the Professor stuck his head through and shone about with a small hand torch. 'I see no sign of touch plates or sensory activators. Have it down, John.'

Omally did the business. As Gammon's final selection came to an end and the jukebox switched itself off for another decade, the saboteurs stood before the exposed back plate of the Captain Laser Alien Attack Machine.

Norman opened his tool-box and took out a pair of rubber gloves, which he dusted with talcum powder, and drew over his sensitive digits. Taking up a long slim screwdriver, he teased out the locking screws. As the others crossed their fingers and held their breath, he gently eased away the back plate. The Professor shone his torch in through the crack and nodded. Norman yanked the plate off, exposing the machine's inner workings.

A great gasp went up from the company. 'Holy Mary,' said John Omally, 'would you look at all that lot?'

Norman whistled through his teeth. 'Magic,' said he. Upon the dashboard of a black Cadillac sedan parked in a nearby side-road a green light began to flash furiously.

The shopkeeper leant forward and stared into the machine's innards. 'It is wonderful,' he said. 'Beyond belief.'

'But can you break it up?' Omally demanded.

'Break it up? That would be a crime against God. Look at it, the precision, the design. It is beyond belief, beyond belief.'

'Yes, yes, but can you break it up?'

Norman shook his head, 'Given time, I suppose. But look here, the thing must serve at least a dozen functions. Each of these modules has a separate input and output.'

'Let me give it a welt with my hammer.'

'No, no, just a minute.' Norman traced the circuitry with his screwdriver, whistling all the while. 'Each module is fed by the main power supply, somewhere deep within the Earth, it appears.'

The Professor nodded. 'This is evidently some sort of communications apparatus. There is a signalling device here, obviously for some sort of guidance control. Here is the basic circuitry which powers the games centre. Here is a gravitational field device to draw down orbiting objects on to a preprogrammed landing site. The whole thing is here, complete tracking, guidance, communication and landing controls. There are various other subsidiary components: outward defence modifications, protecting the frontal circuitry, alarm systems, etcetera. Disconnect the guidance, communications, and landing systems, if you please, Norman.'

Norman delved into the works, skilfully removing certain intricate pieces of microcircuitry. 'It occurs to me,' he said, 'speaking purely as a layman, that as a protective measure we might reverse certain sections merely by changing over their positive and negative terminals.'

Professor Slocombe scratched at his snowy head. 'To what end?'

'Well, if this device is guiding the craft in by means of gravitational beams locked into their computer guidance systems, if we were to reverse the polarity, then as they punch in their coordinates on board the ships, the machine will short them out, and possibly destroy the descending craft.'

'Will it work?'

Norman tapped at his nose. 'Take it from me, it won't do them a lot of good. Come to think of it, it might even be possible to cross-link the guidance system with the actual games programme on the video machine. Pot the bastards right out of the sky as they fly in.'

'Can you do it?'

'Can I do it, Professor?' Norman unscrewed a series of terminals and reconnected them accordingly. He also removed a small unobtrusive portion of the contrivance, which appeared of importance only to himself, and secreted it within his toolbox.

'Are you all done?' the Professor asked, when the shopkeeper finally straightened up.

385

'All done,' said Norman, pulling off his gloves and tossing them into his tool-box. 'A piece of cake.'

Professor Slocombe rose upon creaking knees and patted the brick dust from his tweeds. He put a hand upon the shopkeeper's shoulder and said, 'You have done very well, Norman, and we will be for ever in your debt. The night, however, is far from over. In fact it has just begun. Do you think that you might now pull off the double by winning the darts match?'

Norman nodded. He had every intention of pulling off the treble this night. But that was something he was keeping very much to himself.

The Swan was filling at a goodly pace. With seven local teams competing for the cherished shield, business was already becoming brisk. Neville had taken on extra barstaff, but these were of the finger-counting, change-confusing variety, and were already costing him money. The part-time barman was doing all he could, but his good eye wandered forever towards the Swan's door.

When at quarter past eight it swung open to herald the arrival of Omally, Pooley, Professor Slocombe and Norman, the barman breathed an almighty sigh of relief. Omally thrust his way through the crowd and ordered the drinks. 'As promised,' he announced, as the Swan's team enveloped Norman in their midst with a great cheer.

Neville pulled the pints. 'I am grateful, Omally,' said he, 'these are on the house.'

'And will be for a year, as soon as the other little matter is taken care of.'

'The machine?'

'You will have to bear with me just a little longer on that one. Whatever occurs tonight you must stand resolute and take no action.'

Neville's suspicions were immediately aroused. 'What is likely to occur?'

Omally held up his grimy hands. 'The matter is under the control of Professor Slocombe, a man who, I am sure you will agree, can be trusted without question.'

'If all is as you say, then I will turn a blind eye to that despoiler of my loins who has come skulking with you.' Omally grinned handsomely beneath his whiskers. Neville loaded the drinks on to a tray and Omally bore them away to the Professor's reserved table.

A bell rang and the darts tournament began. A hired Master of Ceremonies, acting as adjudicator and positive last word, clad in a glittering tuxedo and sporting an eyebrow-pencil moustache, announced the first game.

First on the oché were the teams from the Four Horsemen and the New Inn. Jack Lane, resident landlord at the Four Horsemen these forty-seven long years, struggled from his wheelchair and flung the very first dart of the evening.

'Double top, Four Horsemen away,' announced the adjudicator in a booming voice.

Outside in the street, two figures who closely resembled a pair of young Jack Palances, and who smelt strongly of creosote, were rapidly approaching the Swan. They walked with automaton precision, and their double footfalls echoed along the deserted Ealing Road.

'Double top,' boomed the adjudicator, 'New Inn away.'

Pooley and Omally sat in their grandstand seats, sipping their ale. 'Your man Jarvis there has a fine overarm swing,' said Omally.

'He is a little too showy for my liking,' Pooley replied. 'I will take five to four on the Horsemen if you're offering it.'

Omally, who had already opened his book and was now accepting bets from all comers, spat on his palm and smacked it down into that of his companion. 'We are away then,' said he.

Bitow bitow bitow went the Captain Laser Alien Attack Machine, suddenly jarring the two men from their appreciation of life's finer things, and causing them to leap from their chairs. Omally craned his neck above the crowd and peered towards the sinister contrivance. Through the swelling throng he could just make out the distinctive lime-green coiffure of Nicholas Roger Raffles Rathbone.

'It is the young ninny,' said John. 'Five to four you have then, I will draw up a page for you.'

Neville was by now moving up and down the bar, taking orders left, right, and centre. The till jangled like a fire alarm, and Croughton the pot-bellied potman was already in a lather.

No one noticed as two men with high cheekbones and immaculate black suits entered the Swan and lost themselves in the crowds. No one, that is, but for a single disembodied soul who lightly tapped the Professor upon the shoulder. 'All right,' said the old man, without drawing his eyes from the match in play. 'Kindly keep me informed.'

The Four Horsemen was faring rather badly. The lads from the New Inn had enlisted the support of one Thomas 'Squires' Trelawny, a flightsmaster from Chiswick. 'Who brought him in?' asked Pooley. 'His name is not on the card.'

'A late entry, I suppose, do I hear a change in the odds?'

'Treacherous to the end, Omally,' said Jim Pooley. 'I will not shorten the odds, who is the next man up?'

'Jack's son, Young Jack.'

Young Jack, who was enjoying his tenth year in retirement, and looked not a day over forty, put his toe to the line and sent his feathered missile upon its unerring course into the treble twenty.

A great cheer went up from the Horsemen's supporters. 'He once got three hundred and one in five darts,' Omally told Jim.

'He is in league with the devil though but.'

'True, that does give him an edge.'

Somehow Young Jack had already managed to score one hundred and eighty-one with three darts, and this pleased the lads from the Four Horsemen no end. To much applause, he concluded his performance by downing a pint of mild in less than four seconds.

'He is wearing very well considering his age,' said Omally.

'You should see the state of his portrait in the attic.'

'I'll get the round in then,' said Professor Slocombe, rising upon his cane.

'Make sure he doesn't charge you for mine,' called Omally, who could see a long and happy year ahead, should the weather hold. With no words spoken the crowd parted before the old man, allowing him immediate access to the bar.

Beneath his table Young Jack made a satanic gesture, but he knew he was well outclassed by the great scholar.

'Same again,' said Professor Slocombe. Neville did the honours. 'All is well with you, I trust, barman?' the old gentleman asked. 'You wear something of a hunted look.'

'I am sorely tried, Professor,' said Neville, 'I can smell disaster, and this very night. The scent is souring my nostrils even now as we speak. It smells like creosote, but I know it to be disaster. If we survive this night I am going to take a very long holiday.'

'You might try Penge, then,' said the old man brightly, 'I understand that it is very nice, although ...' His words were suddenly

388

swallowed up by a battery of *Bitows* from the nearby games machine.

Neville scowled through the crowd at the hunched back of the paperboy. 'Perhaps I will simply slay him now and take my holiday in Dartmoor, they say the air is very healthy thereabouts.'

'Never fear,' said Professor Slocombe, but his eyes too had become fixed upon the green-haired youth. Speaking rapidly into Nick's ear was a man of average height, slightly tanned and with high cheekbones. The Professor couldn't help thinking that he put him in mind of a young Jack Palance. The youth, however, appeared so engrossed in his play as to be oblivious to the urgent chatter of the darkly-clad stranger.

Neville chalked the bill on to the Professor's private account, and the old gentleman freighted his tray back to his table. 'How goes the state of play?' he asked Omally.

'Squires Trelawny is disputing Young Jack's score,' said John, unloading the tray on to the table. 'He is obviously not altogether *au fait* with Jack's technique.'

'Oh dear,' said Pooley pointing towards the dispute. 'Young Jack is not going to like that.'

Trelawny, a temperamental fellow of the limp-wristed brotherhood, frustrated by the apparent wall of indifference his objections ran up against, had poked one of the Horsemen's leading players in the eye with his finger.

'Trelawny is disqualified,' said the adjudicator.

'You what?' Squires turned upon the man in the rented tuxedo and stamped his feet in rage.

'Out, finished,' said the other. 'We brook no violence here.'

'You are all bloody mad,' screamed the disgruntled player, in a high piping voice. The crowd made hooting noises and somebody pinched his bum.

'Out of my way then!' Flinging down his set of Asprey's darts (the expensive ones with the roc-feather flights), he thrust his way through the guffawing crowd and departed the Swan. Young Jack, who numbered among his personal loathings a very special hatred for poofs, made an unnoticeable gesture beneath table level, and as he blustered into the street Trelawny slipped upon an imaginary banana skin and fell heavily to the pavement. As he did so, the front two tyres of his Morris Minor went simultaneously flat.

'This has all the makings of a most eventful evening,' said Jim

Pooley. 'The first eliminator not yet over and blood already drawn.'

The adjudicator wiped away the New Inn's name from the board. With their best player disqualified, morale had suffered a devastating and irrevocable blow, and the New Inn had retired from the competition.

Next up were the North Star and the Princess Royal. The North Star's team never failed to raise eyebrows no matter where they travelled, being five stout brothers of almost identical appearance. They ranged from the youngest, Wee Tam, at five feet five, to the eldest, Big Bob, at six foot two, and had more the look of a set of Russian dolls about them than a darts team. Their presence in public always had a most sobering effect upon the more drunken clientele.

Their opponents, upon the other hand, could not have looked less alike had they set out to do so. They numbered among their incongruous ranks, two garage mechanic ne'er-do-wells, a bearded ex-vicar, a tall lift engineer with small ears, and a clerk of works with large ones. They also boasted the only Chinese player in Brentford. Tommy Lee was the grand master to the Brentford Temple of Dimac and was most highly danned, even amongst very danned people indeed. Few folk in the Borough ever chose to dispute with him over a doubtful throw.

However, Tommy, who had taken the Dimac oath which bound him never to use any of the horrendous, maiming, tearing, crippling and disfiguring techniques unless his back was really up against the wall, was a fair and honest man and very popular locally. He was also the only player known to throw underarm. He fared reasonably well, and as usual it took two strong lads to withdraw his hand-carved ivory darts from the board.

'I'll bet that took the remaining plaster off Archie's back parlour wall,' said Omally. 'By the way, Professor, I hope the man from Bombay is being well-catered for. We wouldn't want him popping next door to grill up a popadum, would we?'

Professor Slocombe tapped his sinuous nose. One or other of the North Star's men was throwing, but it was hard to tell which when they were detached from the set and you couldn't judge them by height.

'One hundred,' bawled the adjudicator.

'What odds are you offering at present upon the North Star?' the Professor asked. Out of professional etiquette John answered him tic-tac fashion. 'I will take your pony on that, then.'

'From your account?'

'Omally, you know I never carry money.'

'The Princess Royal need one hundred and fifty-six,' boomed the adjudicator, taking up the chalks.

The lift engineer, making much of his every movement, stepped on to the oché. There was a ripple amongst the crowd as his first dart entered the treble twenty. A whistle as his second joined it and a great cry of horror as his third skimmed the double eighteen by a hair's breadth. Crimson to the tips of his small and shell-likes, the lift engineer returned to his chair, and the obscurity from which he had momentarily emerged.

'Unfortunate,' said Professor Slocombe, rubbing his hands together, 'I have noticed in matches past that the lift engineer has a tendency to buckle under pressure.'

Omally made a sour face, he had noticed it also, but in the heat of the betting had neglected to note the running order of the players.

'The North Star needs eighty-seven.'

Amidst much cheering, this figure was easily accomplished, with a single nineteen, a double nineteen and a double fifteen.

'I am up already,' said Professor Slocombe to the scowling Irishman.

'And I,' said Pooley.

Now began the usual debate which always marred championship matches. A member of the Princess Royal's team accused the men from the Star of playing out of order. The adjudicator, who had not taken the obvious course of forcing them to sport name tags, found himself at a disadvantage.

Omally, who had spotted the omission early in the game, shook his head towards Professor Slocombe. 'I can see all betting on this one being null and void,' said he.

'I might possibly intervene.'

'That would hardly be sporting now, would it, Professor?'

'You are suggesting that I might have a bias?'

'Perish the thought. It is your round is it not, Jim?'

Pooley, who had been meaning to broach the subject of a loan, set against his potential winnings, began to pat at his pockets. 'You find me financially embarrassed at present,' he said.

'I think not,' said Professor Slocombe. 'I recall asking you for a pound's-worth of change from the Swan's cash register.'

'You did sir, yes.' Pooley shook his head at the Professor's fore-sight and fought his way towards the bar.

Neville faced his customer with a cold good eye. 'Come to kick me in the cobblers again, Pooley?' he asked. 'You are here on sufferance you know, as a guest of Omally and the Professor.'

Jim nodded humbly. 'What can I say?'

'Very little,' said Neville. 'Can you smell creosote?'

Pooley's moustachios shot towards the floor like a dowser's rod. 'Where?' he asked in a tremulous voice.

'Somewhere close,' said Neville. 'Take my word, it bodes no good.'

'Be assured of that.' Pooley loaded the tray and cast a handful of coins on to the counter.

'Keep the change,' he called, retreating fearfully to his table.

'We're up next,' said Omally, upon the shaky Jim's return. 'Will you wager a pound or two upon the home team?'

'Neville smells creosote,' said Jim.

'Take it easy.' Professor Slocombe patted the distraught Pooley's arm. 'I have no doubt that they must suspect something. Be assured that they are being watched.'

The Captain Laser Alien Attack machine rattled out another series of electronic explosions.

Norman stepped on to the mat amidst tumultuous applause. He licked the tips of his darts and nodded towards the adjudicator.

'Swan to throw,' said that man.

Norman's mastery of the game, his style and finesse, were legend in Brentford. Certain supporters who had moved away from the area travelled miles to witness his yearly display of skill. One pink-eyed man, who kept forever to the shadows, had actually travelled from as far afield as Penge.

'One hundred and eighty,' shouted the adjudicator, although his words were lost in the Wembley roar of the crowd.

'It is poetry,' said Omally.

'Perfect mastery,' said Pooley.

'I think it has something to do with the darts,' said Professor Slocombe, 'and possibly the board, which I understand he donated to the Swan.'

'You are not implying some sort of electronic duplicity upon the part of our captain, are you?' Omally asked.

'Would I dare? But you will notice that each time he throws, the

Guinness clock stops. This might be nothing more than coincidence.'

'The whole world holds its breath when Norman throws,' said Omally, further shortening the already impossibly foreshortened odds upon the home team. 'Whose round is it?'

'I will go on to sherry now, if you please,' said the Professor. 'I have no wish to use the Swan's convenience tonight.'

'Quite so,' said John. 'We would all do well to stay in the crowd. Shorts all round then.' Rising from the table, he took up his book, and departed into the crowd.

Old Pete approached Professor Slocombe and greeted the scholar with much hand-wringing. 'My dog Chips tells me that we have a bogey in our midst,' said he.

'And a distinguished one of the literary persuasion,' the elder ancient replied. 'Tell your dog that he has nothing to fear, he is on our side.'

Old Pete nodded and turned the conversation towards the sad decline in the nation's morals and Professor Slocombe's opinion of the post office computer.

Omally found the boy Nick at the bar, ordering a half of light and lime. 'Have this one on me,' he said, handing the boy two florins. 'You are doing a grand job.'

Raffles Rathbone raised a manicured eyebrow. 'Don't tell me you now approve?' he asked.

'Each to his own. I have never been one to deny the pleasures of the flesh. Here, have a couple of games on me and don't miss now, will you?' He dropped several more coins into the boy's outstretched palm.

'I never miss,' Nick replied. 'I have the game mastered.'

'Good boy. Two gold watches and a small sweet sherry please, Neville.'

The part-time barman glared at Omally. 'You are paying for these,' he snarled. 'I still have my suspicions.'

'You can owe me later,' Omally replied, delving into his pockets. 'I am a man of my word.'

'And I mine, eighteen and six please.'

'Do you know something I don't?' Nick asked the Irishman.

'A good many things. Did you have anything specific in mind?'

'About the machine?'

'Nothing. Is something troubling you?'

Nick shook his limey head and turned his prodigious nose once more towards the unoccupied machine. 'I must be going now,' he said, 'the Captain awaits.'

'Buffoon,' said Omally beneath his breath. By the time he returned to the table, the Swan's team had disposed of their adversaries in no uncertain fashion.

'I am sure that I am up by at least two bob on that game,' said Pooley.

'Two and fourpence,' said Professor Slocombe. 'Don't let it go to your head.'

The final eliminating match lay between the Four Horsemen and the Albany Arms, whose team of old stalwarts, each a veteran of Gallipoli, had been faring remarkably well against spirited opposition.

'Albany Arms to throw,' boomed himself.

'Leave me out of this one,' said Pooley. 'Unless God chooses to intervene upon this occasion and dispatch Young Jack into the bottomless pit, I feel it to be a foregone conclusion.'

'I will admit that you would have a wager at least one hundred pounds to win yourself another two and fourpence.'

'Don't you feel that one thousand to one against the Albany is a little cruel?'

'But nevertheless tempting to the outside better.'

'Taking money from children,' said Professor Slocombe. 'How can you live with yourself, John?'

Omally grinned beneath his beard. 'Please do not deny me my livelihood,' said he.

From their first dart onwards, the Albany began to experience inexplicable difficulties with their game. Several of the normally robust geriatrics became suddenly subject to unexpected bouts of incontinence at their moments of throwing. Others mislaid their darts or spilled their beer, one even locked himself in the gents' and refused to come out until the great grinning black goat was removed from in front of the dartboard.

It was remarkable the effect that Young Jack could have upon his team's opponents. The crowd, however, was not impressed. Being responsive only to the finer points of the game and ever alert to such blatant skulduggery, they viewed this degrading spectacle with outrage and turned their backs upon the board.

Young Jack could not have cared less. The Four Horsemen

needed but a double thirteen to take the match and the Albany had yet to get away. The present-day Faust smirked over towards the Professor and made an obscene gesture.

Professor Slocombe shook his head and made clicking noises with his tongue. 'Most unsporting,' said he. 'I shall see to it that none of this occurs in the final.'

Without waiting to watch the inevitable outcome of the game, he rose from his chair and took himself off to where the Swan's team stood in a noisy scrum, ignoring the play.

'He has gone to bless the darts, I suspect,' said Omally. 'In his yearly battle of wits with Young Jack, the Professor leaves nothing to chance.'

'Do you believe it possible?' Pooley asked wistfully. 'That somewhere in this green and pleasant land of ours, this sceptred isle, this jewel set in a silver sea and whatever, that there might somewhere be a little darts team, based possibly in some obscure half-timbered country pub out in the sticks, which actually plays the game for the love of it alone, and without having recourse to some underhand jiggery-pokery?'

'Are you mad?' enquired Omally. 'Or merely drunk?'

Jim shook his head. 'I just wondered how such a game might look. If played by skill alone, I mean.'

'Jolly dull, I should think. Here, take this one-pound note, which you can owe to me, and get in another round.'

Jim watched a moment as Young Jack's hellish black dart cleaved the air, leaving a yellow vapour trail, and thrust its oily nose into the double thirteen. 'I should still like to see it,' he said. 'Just the once.'

'Naïve boy,' sighed Omally, running his pencil down endless columns of figures, and wondering by how many thousands of pounds he was up this particular evening.

Professor Slocombe finished muttering a Latin text over the table of laid-out darts and gave the benediction. 'This will not of course enable you to play any better,' he explained, 'but it will protect your darts from any mysterious deflections which might occur.'

The Swan's team nodded. They had defeated the Four Horsemen in the final five years on the trot now, which was, by way of coincidence, exactly the length of time that the Professor had been acting as honorary President. They took the old man's words strictly at their face value. None of the accidents which marred the play of the Horsemen's other opponents ever befell them, and although few of the team knew anything whatever about the occult, each blessed the day that Norman had suggested the elderly scholar's nomination.

'Be warned now,' Professor Slocombe continued, 'he does appear to be on superb form tonight. Look wherever you like, but avoid his eyes.'

Neville appeared through the crowd bearing a silver tray. On this rested a dozen twinkling champagne saucers and a Georgian silver wine cooler containing a chilled and vintage bottle of Pol Roger.

This little morale-booster was another of the Professor's inspirations.

'Good luck to you all,' said the part-time barman, patting Norman gingerly upon the shoulder. 'Good luck.'

A warlike conclave had formed at the other end of the bar. Young Jack and his demonic cohorts were clustered about Old Jack's wheelchair, speaking in hushed, if heated, tones. Neville sensed that above the smell of creosote, which so strongly assailed his sensitive nostrils, there was a definite whiff of brimstone emanating from the satanic conspirators. The part-time barman shuddered. Why did things always have to be so complicated?

The Swan now swelled with crowds literally to bursting point. It was almost impossible to move amongst the throng, and trayloads of drinks were being passed from the bar counter over the heads of patrons, generally to arrive at their destinations somewhat lighter of load. It was rapidly reaching the 'every man for himself' stage. The atmosphere was electric with anticipation and unbreathable with cigar smoke. The noise was deafening and even the Captain Laser Alien Attack machine rattled mutely, lost amidst the din. Croughton the pot-bellied potman had come down with a severe attack of no bottle and had taken himself off to the rear yard for a quiet fag.

'Ladies and gentlemen,' bellowed the adjudicator at the top of his voice, 'it is my pleasure to announce the final and deciding contest of the evening. The very climax of this evening's sport.' Omally noted that the world 'sport' appeared to stick slightly in the adjudicator's throat. 'The final for the much coveted Brentford District Darts Challenge Trophy Shield.'

Neville, who had taken this cherished item down from its cobwebby perch above the bar and had carefully polished its tarnished surface before secreting it away in a place known only to himself, held it aloft in both hands. A great cheer rang through the Swan.

'Between the present holders, five years' champions, the home team, the Flying Swan.' Another deafening cheer. 'And their challengers from the Four Horsemen.'

Absolute silence, but for the occasional *bitow* in the background.

'Gentlemen, let battle commence.'

The home team, as reigning champions, had call of the toss. As the adjudicator flipped a copper coin high into the unwholesome smoke-filled air, Professor Slocombe, who had taken up station slightly to the rear of Young Jack, whispered, 'The same coin had better come down and it had better not land upon its edge.'

Young Jack leered around at his adversary. 'As honorary President,' said, 'I shall look forward to you personally handing me the shield upon your team's crushing defeat.'

Whether through the action of that fickle thing called fate, or through the influence of some force which the Professor had neglected to make allowance for, unlikely though that might seem, the coin fell tailside up and the Four Horsemen were first upon the oché.

Through merit of his advanced years and the ever-present possibility that he would not survive another championship game through to the end, Old Jack threw first.

Professor Slocombe did not trouble to watch the ancient as he struggled from his wheelchair, assisted by his two aides, and flung his darts. His eyes were glued to the hands of Young Jack, awaiting the slightest movement amongst the dark captain's metaphysical digits.

It was five hundred and one up and a five-game decision and each man playing was determined to give of his all or die in the giving. Old Jack gave a fair account of himself with an ample ton.

Norman took the mat. As he did so, both Pooley and Omally found their eyes wandering involuntarily over the heads of the crowd towards the electric Guinness clock.

Three times Norman threw and three times did those two pairs of eyes observe the fluctuation in the clock's hand.

'He cheats, you know,' whispered Pooley.

'I've heard it rumoured,' Omally replied.

'One hundred and eighty,' boomed the man in the rented tux.

On the outer rim of the solar system, where the planets roll, lax, dark and lifeless, appeared nine small white points of light which were definitely not registered upon any directory of the heavens. They moved upon a level trajectory and travelled at what appeared to be an even and leisurely pace. Given the vast distances which they were covering during the course of each single second, however, this was obviously far from being the case.

Upon the flight deck of the leading Cerean man o' war, the Starship *Sandra*, stood the Captain. One Lombard Omega by name, known to some as Lord of a Thousand Suns, Viceroy of the Galactic Empire and Crown Prince of Sirius, he was a man of average height with high cheekbones and a slightly tanned complexion. He bore an uncanny resemblance to a young Jack Palance and, even when travelling through the outer reaches of the cosmic infinite, smelt strongly of creosote.

'Set a course for home,' he said, affecting a noble stance and pointing proudly into space. 'We have conquered the galaxy and now return in triumph to our homeworld. Ceres, here we come.'

The navigator, who bore a striking resemblance to his Captain, but whose rank merited a far less heavily braided uniform and fewer campaign ribbons, tapped out a series of instructions into a console of advanced design. 'Goodness me,' said he, as the computer guidance system flashed up an unexpected reply to his instructions upon a three-dimensional screen. 'Now there's a funny thing.'

Lombard Omega leant over his shoulder and squinted into the glowing display of nine orbiting worlds. 'Where's the fucking planet gone?' he asked.

'One hundred and forty,' shouted the adjudicator, oblivious to what was going on at the outer edge of the solar system. 'The Horsemen needs ninety-seven.'·

'If they aren't cheating,' said Pooley, 'they are playing a blinder of a game.'

'Oh, they're cheating all right,' Omally replied, 'although I don't think the Professor has worked out quite how yet.'

In truth the Professor had not; he had watched Young Jack like a hawk and was certain that he had observed no hint of trickery. Surely the Horsemen could not be winning by skill alone?

Billy 'Banjoed' Breton, the Horsemen's inebriate reserve, was suddenly up on the oché. The very idea of a team fielding a reserve in a championship match was totally unheard of, the role of reserve being by tradition filled by the pub's resident drunk, who acted more as mascot and comedy relief than player.

A rumble of disbelief and suspicion rolled through the crowd. Two of the Horsemen's team pointed Billy in the direction of the board. 'Over there,' they said. Billy aimed his dart, flight first.

'Young Jack is having a pop at the Professor,' said Omally. 'He is definitely working some kind of a flanker.'

A look of perplexity had crossed Professor Slocombe's face. He cast about for a reason, but none was forthcoming. A gentle tap at his elbow suddenly marshalled his thoughts. 'There is one outside and one by the machine,' said Edgar Allan Poe.

Professor Slocombe nodded.

'May I ask the purpose of the game?'

'It is a challenge match between the hostelry known as the Four Horsemen and our own beloved Flying Swan,' Professor Slocombe replied telepathically.

'Then may I ask why you allow your opponents the edge by having their missiles guided by a spirit form?' A smile broke out upon Professor Slocombe's face which did not go unnoticed by John Omally.

'He's sussed it,' said John.

Professor Slocombe leant close to the ear of Young Jack. 'Have you ever heard me recite the rite of exorcism?' he asked. 'I have it down to something of a fine art.'

Young Jack cast the old man the kind of look which could deflower virgins and cause babies to fill their nappies. 'All right,' said he, 'we will play it straight.'

'That you will never do. But simply chalk that one up and be advised.'

'Forty-seven,' bawled the adjudicator, who was growing hoarse.

'Unlucky,' said Professor Slocombe.

'The Swan need sixty-eight.' The Swan got it with little difficulty.

Lombard Omega ran up and down the flight deck, peering through the plexiglass portholes and waving his fists in the air. 'Where's it gone?' he ranted at intervals. 'Where's it fucking gone?'

His navigator punched all he could into the console and shrugged repeatedly. 'It just isn't there,' he said. 'It's gone, caput, finito, gone.'

'It must be there! It was fucking there when we left it!'

The navigator covered his ears to the obscenity. 'It honestly isn't, now,' he said. 'There's a lot of debris about, though, a veritable asteroid belt.'

'You find something and find it quick,' growled his Commanding Officer, 'or you go down the shit chute into hyperspace.'

The navigator bashed away at the console like a mad thing. 'There's no trace,' he whimpered despairingly, 'the entire system's dead.' He tapped at the macroscopic intensifier. 'Oh no it isn't, look, there's a signal.'

Lombard was at his side in an instant. 'Bring it up then, you wally. Bring the frigging thing up.'

The navigator enlarged the image upon the three-dimensional screen. 'It's on Planet Earth,' he said. 'A triangulation and a ley image, the constellation of the Plough surely, and look there.'

Lombard looked there.

'One third up from the base line of the triangulation, a beacon transmitting a signal. The coordinates of an approach run, that's where they are!'

'Hm.' Lombard stroked his Hollywood chin. 'The bastards have moved closer to the Sun. Wise move, wise bloody move. Take us in then. Earth full steam ahead. Lock into autopilot, the beacon will guide us in. Anybody got a roll-up?'

Omally rolled a cigarette as the Professor joined them at the table. 'You found them out, then?' he asked between licks.

'I don't think we've entirely got the better of him,' the old man replied. 'He's a trick or two up his sleeve yet, I believe.'

'I won't ask what that one turned out to be.'

'The Swan lead by one game to nil,' croaked the adjudicator. 'Second game on, Horsemen to throw.'

As this was a championship match, by local rules, the losing team threw first. Young Jack ran his forked tongue about the tip of his dart. 'Straight and true this time, Professor,' quoth he.

'With the corner up,' the old man replied.

Young Jack flung his darts in such rapid succession that they were nothing more than a triple blur. They each struck the board 'straight and true' within the wired boundaries of the treble twenty, which was nothing more nor less than anybody had expected. The grinning demonologist strode to the board and tore out his darts with a vengeance.

'I should like very much to see the fellow miss once in a while,' Pooley told the Professor. 'Just to give the impression that he isn't infallible.' Professor Slocombe whispered another Latin phrase and Young Jack knocked his pint of mild into his father's lap. 'Thank you,' said Jim, 'I appreciated that.'

Archie Karachi was throwing for the Swan. Dressed this evening in a stunning kaftan, oblivious to the damage wrought upon his kitchen, he was definitely on form. Archie had a most unique manner of play. As a singles man, his techique brought a tear to the eye of many a seasoned player. Scorning the beloved treble twenty, he went instead for bizarre combinations which generally had the chalksman in a panic of fingers and thumbs. On a good night with luck at his elbow he could tear away an apparent two hundred in three throws. Even when chalked up, this still had his opponents believing that he had thrown his shots away. Tonight he threw a stunning combination which had the appearance of being a treble nineteen, a double thirteen and a bullseye, although it was hard to be certain.

The degree of mental arithmetic involved in computing the final total was well beyond the man on the chalks and most of the patrons present. When the five hundred and one was scratched out and two hundred and fifty-seven appeared in its place nobody thought to argue.

'I admire that,' said Professor Slocombe. 'It is a form of negative psychology. I will swear that if the score does not come up in multiples of twenty, nobody can work it out.'

'I can,' said Omally, 'but he is on our side.'

'I can't,' said Pooley. 'He pulls his darts out so quickly I couldn't even see what he scored.'

'Ah,' said Omally, 'here is a man I like to watch.'

The Four Horsemen's most extraordinary player had to be the man Kelly. He was by no means a great dartsman, but for sheer entertainment value he stood alone. It must be understood that the wondrous scores previously recorded are not entirely typical of the play as a whole, and that not each member of the team was a specialist in his field. The high and impossible scores were the preserve of the very few and finest. Amongst each team, the Swan and the Horsemen being no exception, there were also able players, hard triers, and what might be accurately described as the downright desperate.

The man Kelly was one of the latter. When he flung a dart it was very much a case of stand aside lads, and women and children first. The man Kelly was more a fast bowler than a darts player.

The man Kelly bowled a first dart. It wasn't a bad one and it plunged wholeheartedly in the general direction of the board. Somewhere, however, during the course of its journey the lone projectile suddenly remembered that it had pressing business elsewhere. The man Kelly's dart was never seen again.

'A little off centre?' the player asked his fuming and speechless captain.

His second throw was a classic in every sense of the word. Glancing off the board with the sound of a ricocheting rifle bullet it tore back into the assembled crowd, scattering friend and foe alike and striking home through the lobe of Old Pete's right ear.

The crowd engulfed the ancient to offer assistance. 'Don't touch it,' bellowed the old one. 'By God, it has completely cured the rheumatism in my left kneecap.'

Lombard Omega scrutinized the instrument panel and swore between his teeth. 'I can't see this,' he said at length. 'This does not make any fucking sense. I mean, be reasonable, our good world Ceres cannot just vanish away like piss down a cesspit in the twinkling of a bleeding eyelid.'

The navigator whispered a silent prayer to his chosen deity. It was an honour to serve upon the flagship of the Cerean battle fleet, but it was a hard thing indeed to suffer the constant stream of obscenity which poured from his commander's mouth. 'We have been away for a very long time,' he ventured. 'More than six thousand years, Earth time.'

'Earth time? Earth bleeding time? What is Earth time?'

'Well, as target world, it must be considered to be standard solar time.'

Lombard Omega spat on the platinum-coated deck and ground the spittle in with a fibreglass heel. 'This doesn't half get my dander up,' said he.

Standard solar time was approaching ten-fifteen of the p.m. clock, and the Four Horsemen and the Flying Swan now stood even at two games all and one to play for the Shield. Tension, which had been reaching the proverbial breaking-point, had now passed far beyond that, and chaos, panic, and desperation had taken its place. Omally had ground seven Biros into oblivion and his book now resembled some nightmare of Einsteinian cross-calculation.

'I sincerely believe that the ultimate secrets of the universe might well be found within this book,' said Pooley, leafing over the heavily-thumbed pages. For his outspokenness, he received a blow to the skull which sent him reeling. Omally was at present in no mood for the snappy rejoinder.

'For God's sake get another round in,' said Professor Slocombe. Omally left the table.

'Forgive me if you will,' said Pooley, when the Irishman was engaged in pummelling his way through the crowd towards the bar, 'but you do remember that we are under imminent threat of annihilation by these lads from Ceres. I mean, we are still taking it seriously, aren't we?'

Professor Slocombe patted Pooley's arm. 'Good show,' he said. 'I understand your concern. It is always easy to surround oneself with what is safe and comfortable and to ignore the *outré* threats which lurk upon the borderline. Please be assured that we have done everything that can be done.'

'Sorry,' said Jim, 'but strange as it may seem, I do get a little anxious once in a while.'

'Ladies and gentlemen,' croaked the adjudicator in a strangled voice, 'the end is near and we must face the final curtain.' There were some boos and a few cheers. 'The last match is to play, the decider for the Challenge Shield, and I will ask for silence whilst the two teams prepare themselves.'

A respectful hush fell upon the Swan. Even the boy Rathbone ceased his game. However, this was not through his being any respecter of darts tournaments, but rather that his last two-bob bit had run out, and he was forced up to the bar for more change.

'It is the playoff, five hundred and one to gain. By the toss, first darts to the Horsemen, good luck to all, and game on.'

Professor Slocombe's eyes swung towards the Horsemen's team. Something strange seemed to have occurred within their ranks. Old Jack had declined to take his darts and sat sullenly in his wheelchair. The man Kelly was nowhere to be seen, and the other disembodied members of the team had withdrawn to their places of perpetual night and were apparently taking no more interest in the outcome of the game.

Alone stood Young Jack, hollow-eyed and defiant.

'He means to play it alone,' said the Professor. 'I do not believe that it is against the rules.'

'By no means,' said Omally. 'A man can take on a regiment, should he so choose. As a bookmaker I find such a confrontation interesting, to say the least.'

The Swan's patrons found it similarly so and Omally was forced to open book upon his shirt sleeves.

Young Jack took the mat. He gave the Professor never a glance as he threw his stygian arrows. To say that he actually threw them, however, would be to give a false account of the matter, for at one moment the darts were in his hand, and in another, or possibly the same, they were plastered into the darts board. No one saw them leave nor enter, but all agreed that the score was an unbeatable multiple of twenty.

'One hundred and eighty,' came a whispered voice.

Norman stepped to the fore. Although unnoticed by the throng, his darts gave off an electrical discharge which disabled television sets three streets away and spoiled telephonic communications a mile off.

'One hundred and eighty,' came a still small voice, when he had done his business.

Young Jack strode once more into the fray. His eyes shone like a pair of Cortina reversing lamps and a faint yellow fog rose from the corners of his mouth. He turned his head upon its axis and grinned back over his shoulders at the hushed crowd. With hardly a glance towards the board, he flung his darts. The outcome was a matter for the Guinness Book of Records to take up at a later date.

'I don't like this,' said Professor Slocombe. 'I am missing something, but I do not know what it is.'

'We are scoring equal,' said Omally, 'he needs but one unfortunate error.'

'I am loath to intervene, John.'

'It might get desperate, Professor, say a few words in the old tongue, just to be on the safe side.'

'We will wait a bit and see.'

'He is closing for the kill,' said John.

Professor Slocombe shook his head. 'I still cannot see it, he appears to be winning by skill alone.'

'God bless him,' said Pooley.

Omally raised a fist towards his companion. 'We are talking about the Swan's trophy here,' he said, waggling the terror weapon towards Pooley. 'This is no joke.'

'One day,' said Jim calmly, 'I shall turn like the proverbial worm and take a terrible retribution upon you, Omally, for all the blows you have administered to my dear head.'

'*Sssh*,' went at least a dozen patrons. 'Uncle Ted is up.'

Uncle Ted, Brentford's jovial greengrocer, was possibly the most loved man in the entire district. His ready smile and merry wit, his recourse to a thousand cheersome and altruistic *bons mots*, of the 'laugh and the world laughs with you, snore and you sleep alone' variety, brought joy into the lives of even the most manic of depressives. It was said that he could turn a funeral procession into a conga line, and, although there is no evidence to show that he ever took advantage of this particular gift, he was never short of a jocular quip or two as he slipped a few duff sprouts into a customer's carrier-bag.

Omally, who could not find it within himself to trust any man who would actually deal in, let alone handle, a sprout, found the greengrocer nauseous to an extreme degree. 'That smile could make a Samaritan commit suicide,' he said.

Uncle Ted did a little limbering-up knee-work, made flexing motions with his shoulders, and held a wet finger into the air. 'Is the wind behind us?' he asked, amidst much laughter from his supporters. He waved at the smoke-filled air with a beermat. 'Which way's the board then? Anybody got a torch?'

Omally groaned deeply within the folds of his beard. 'Get on with it, you twerp,' he muttered.

Uncle Ted, who for all his inane clowning, was well aware that a wrong move now could cost him his livelihood, took a careful aim whose caution was disguised behind a bout of bum wriggling. His first dart creased into the treble twenty with very little to spare.

'Where did it land then?' he asked, cupping his hand to his forehead and squinting about. His supporters nudged one another, cheered and guffawed. 'What a good lad,' they said. 'Good old Uncle Ted.'

Ted looked towards the board and made a face of surprise upon sighting his dart. 'Who threw that?' he asked.

To cut a long and very tedious story short, Uncle Ted's second dart joined its fellow in the treble twenty, but his third, however, had ideas of its own and fastened its nose into the dreaded single one. The laughter and applause which followed this untimely blunder rang clearly and loudly, but not from any of those present who favoured the home team.

'What a good lad,' said Young Jack. 'Good old Uncle Ted.'

The greengrocer left the Flying Swan that night in disgrace. Some say that like Judas he went forth and hanged himself. Others, who are better informed, say that he moved to Chiswick where he now owns three shops and spends six months of the year abroad.

Omally was leafing frantically through the pages of his book. 'I am in big schtuck here,' he said suddenly, brushing away a bead of perspiration from his brow. 'In my haste to accept bets and my certainty of the Swan's ultimate victory, I have somewhat miscalculated. The fix is in and ruination is staring me in the beard.'

Professor Slocombe took the book from Omally's trembling fingers and examined it with care. 'I spy a little circle of treachery here,' he said.

'The Four Horsemen needs one hundred and forty-one,' gasped the adjudicator.

'I am finished,' said Omally. 'It is back to the old country for me. A boat at the dock and before the night is out.'

Professor Slocombe was staring at the dartboard and shaking his head, his face wearing an unreadable expression. Pooley was ashen and speechless. But for the occasional *bitow* to the rear of the crowd, the Swan was a vacuum of utter silence.

Young Jack squared up to the board as Omally hid his face in his hands and said a number of Hail Marys.

Jack's first dart pierced the treble twenty, his second the double, and his third the single one.

'One hundred and one,' mouthed the adjudicator in a manner which was perfectly understood by all deaf-mutes present.

Omally waved away a later punter proffering a wad of notes. 'Suck, boy,' was all that he could say.

The adjudicator retired to the bar. He would say no more this evening and would, in all probability, make himself known for the rest of his life through the medium of notepad and pencil.

Norman, who had sacked the rest of the team, took the floor. He threw another blinding one hundred and eighty but it really didn't seem to matter any more.

The Four Horsemen needed but a double top to take the Shield, and a child of three, or at a pinch four if he was born in Brentford, could surely have got that, given three darts.

Neville put the towels up and climbed on to the bar counter, knobkerry in hand. There was very likely to be a good deal of death and destruction within another minute or two and he meant to be a survivor at any cost.

Croughton the pot-bellied potman leant back in his beer crate refuge and puffed upon his cigarette. Up above, the night stars glittered eternally, and nothing there presaged the doom and desolation which was about to befall Brentford. 'Oh look,' he said suddenly to himself, as he peered up at the firmament. 'Shooting stars, that's lucky. I shall make a wish on them.'

Upon the allotment a tiny figure moved. He was ill-washed and stubble-chinned and he muttered beneath his breath. At intervals he raised his head and called, 'Edgar.' No reply came, and he continued upon his journey, driven by a compulsion impossible to resist.

'Four Horsemen to throw,' said some drunken good-time Charlie who had no idea of the gravity of the situation. 'The Four Horsemen needs forty.'

Young Jack appeared from the crowd, wielding his dreaded darts. He crossed the floor and approached the Professor. 'You will not enjoy this, St Germaine,' he spat. 'Be advised that I know you for what you are and accept your defeat like the gentleman you are not.'

Professor Slocombe was unmoved, his glittering eyes fixed upon Young Jack. 'If you want this to be sport,' said he, 'then so be it. If however you crave something more, then know that I am equal to the challenge.'

'Do your worst,' sneered Young Jack. 'I am master of you.'

'So be it,' said Professor Slocombe.

Young Jack took the oché. Again his head turned one hundred and eighty degrees upon his neck as he gazed at the crowd. 'The Swan is finished,' he announced. 'Five years have passed and you have grown weak and complacent. Prepare to bow to a superior force. Say goodbye to your trophy, you suckers.'

A murderous rumble rolled through the crowd. There was a great stamping of feet and squaring of shoulders. Ties were being slackened and top buttons undone. Cufflinks were being removed and dropped into inside pockets.

Young Jack raised his dart and lined up for a winner. Neville took a sharper hold upon his knobkerry and patted at his loins to ensure that the cricketer's box he had had the foresight to hire for the occasion was in place.

Omally smote the Professor, 'Save us, old man,' he implored. 'I will apologize later.'

Professor Slocombe rose upon his cane and stared at his adversary.

Young Jack drew back his hand and flung his dart.

The thing creased the air at speed, then suddenly slowed; to the utter dumbfoundment of the crowd, it hung suspended in time and space exactly six feet three inches above the deck and five feet from the board.

Professor Slocombe concentrated his gaze, Young Jack did likewise.

The dart moved forward a couple of inches, then stopped once more and took a twitch backwards.

The crowd were awestruck. Neville's knobkerry hung loose in his hand. Great forces were at work here, great forces that he would rather have no part in. But he was here at the killing, and as part-time barman would do little other than offer support.

Every eye, apart from one ill-matched pair, was upon that dart. Supporters of both Swan and Horsemen alike wrinkled their brows and strained their brains upon that dart. Beads of perspiration appeared a-plenty and fell, ruining many a good pint.

The dart eased forward another six inches. Professor Slocombe turned his stare towards the glowing red eyes of his opponent. The dart retreated.

Young Jack drew a deep breath and the dart edged once more towards its target.

'You wouldn't get this on the telly,' whispered Jim Pooley.

Old Jack suddenly put his wrinkled hands to the wheels of his chair and propelled himself towards the Professor.

'Restrain that man!' yelled Omally.

Pooley lurched from his seat, but, in his haste to halt the wheeling ancient, caught his foot upon a chair leg and tripped. He clutched at the table, overturning it, and blundered into Professor Slocombe, propelling him into the crowd. At this moment of truth the proverbial all hell was let loose.

The night-black dart set forth once more upon its journey and thundered towards the board. Young Jack stood grinning as Pooley upset his infirm father and brought down at least another four people in his desperation. Omally struggled up and struck the nearest man a vicious blow to the skull.

Before the eyes of those stunned patrons who were not yet engaged in the fracas the dart struck the board. As it did so a devastating explosion occurred overhead which shattered the bar optics, brought down great lumps of plaster from the ceiling and upset the part-time barman into the crowd.

'It is God!' shouted Omally, hitting with a will. 'He will stand no more!'

Nicholas Roger Raffles Rathbone fell away from the Captain Laser machine. 'It wasn't me,' he whimpered, 'I didn't do it.'

The lights of the Swan suddenly dimmed as the entire world which was Brentford proper went mad.

'It wasn't me, it wasn't me, I swear it.'

Nobody really cared. Outside something terrific was happening. Possibly it was the prelude to the long-awaited Armageddon, possibly earthquake, or tidal wave. Whatever it was, the darts fans were not going to be caught napping, and the stampede towards the door was all-consuming. A single darkly-clad figure wearing a brand of creosote aftershave was immediately trampled to oblivion beneath the rush.

As the patrons poured into the night the enormity of what had occurred became apparent. Shards of flaming metal were hurtling down upon Brentford. Great sheets of fire were rising from the asphalt of the Ealing Road as the surface met each blazing assault. Several front gardens were ablaze.

Pooley and Omally helped the fallen Professor to his feet. 'It has begun,' said John. 'What do we do?'

'To the machine,' yelled the old man. 'It would appear that Norman has served us right.'

Nicholas Roger Raffles Rathbone stood blankly staring at the screen. 'I didn't do it,' he said repeatedly.

Omally was at his side in an instant. 'Play it,' he roared. 'You are the kiddie, play it.'

Rathbone drew back in horror, 'No,' he shouted. 'Something is wrong. I will have no part of it.'

'Play it!' Omally grabbed at the green hair and drew the stinker close to the machine. 'You are the unbeatable master, play it.'

Nick drew up his head in a gesture of defiance. As he did so, he stumbled upon a chunk of fallen ceiling and fell backwards, leaving Omally clutching a bundle of green hair and what appeared to be an india-rubber face mask. The figure who collapsed to the Swan's floor, now bereft of his disguise, resembled nothing more nor less than a young Jack Palance.

'He's one of them,' screamed Omally, pointing to the fallen Cerean, and dancing up and down dementedly. 'He was never playing the machine, he was signalling with it. Get him, get him!'

Pooley hastened to obey. 'The left armpit, isn't it?' he growled.

The erstwhile paperboy backed away, covering his wedding tackle. 'Not the armpit,' he whimpered. 'Anything but the armpit.'

Professor Slocombe was at the machine. 'How does it work?' he cried. 'How does it work?'

'Leave him, Jim,' yelled Omally, 'play the machine, shoot the bastards down.'

Upon the allotments columns of pure white light were rising into the sky. The door of Soap Distant's hut was wide open and a great glow poured from it, silhouetting dozens of identical figures gliding through the opening.

When the first great explosion occurred, a small dwarf in a soiled postman's suit had flattened himself into a sprout bed, but now he arose to his full height and stared about in horror at the bizarre spectacle.

He danced up and down and flapped his arms, 'Edgar,' he shouted, 'Edgar, help me, help me.' The figures now pouring through the shed doorway were bearing down upon him, and the postman took to his tiny heels and fled. He plunged through the open allotment gates and paused only to assure himself that he still had a tight hold upon the pair of bolt-cutters he had been carrying. Without further ado he continued his journey, bound for a certain lock-up garage upon the Butts Estate, and destiny.

In the Swan, Pooley was at the controls. 'There's eight of them,' he said, 'moving in a V formation.' His finger rattled upon the neutron bomb release button, and tiny beads of yellow light swept upwards towards the bobbing cones at the top of the screen.

'Get them, Jim,' screamed Omally. 'Come on now, you know how it's done.'

'I'm trying, aren't I? Get us a drink for God's sake.'

Neville, who had fallen rather heavily but happily not upon his tender parts, was on all fours in the middle of the floor. 'What the hell is going on?' he gasped. 'Get away from the counter, Omally.'

'We're breaking your machine,' said the breathless Irishman, 'don't knock it.'

'But what was that explosion? My God!' Neville pointed out through the Swan's front windows. 'Half the Ealing Road's on fire. Call the appliances.'

Pooley bashed at the button with his fist and jumped up and down. 'I've got one! I've got one!'

Overhead, but a little less loudly this time, there was another explosion, followed by the sound of faltering engines and a Messerschmitt dive-bomber scream.

Those present at the Swan ducked their heads as something thundered by at close quarters and whistled away into the distance. There was a moment's deadly silence followed by a muted but obviously powerful report.

Another Cerean craft had fallen to Earth upon Brentford; given its point of impact, it was unlikely that Jim Pooley would ever again receive a threatening letter regarding an overdue library book.

'There! There!' Neville was pointing and ranting. 'It is the third world war and we never got the four-minute warning. I am withholding my vote at the next election.'

Small Dave struggled up from the gutter and shrieked with pain. He had been rather nearer to the library's destruction and a sliver of shrapnel from the founder's plaque had caught him in the backside.

'Oh woe, oh woe, oh damn!' he wailed. A less determined man would by now have called it a day and dived for the nearest foxhole, but loathing and hatred overwhelmed the postman, and nothing would turn him from his vendetta. Feeling tenderly at his bleeding bum, he raised the bolt-cutter to the garage lock and applied all his strength. He strained and sweated as he fought with the steel clasp.

Finally, with a sickening crunch the metal gave, and the garage door swung upwards.

Small Dave stood panting in the opening, his features shining pinkly by the light of ten thousand blazing dog-eared library books. Sweat poured from his face as he surveyed the object of his quest. Snorting and wriggling in the eaves of the lock-up garage was Simon. A camel far from home.

'Now that you have it,' said a voice which loosened Small Dave's bowels, 'what are you going to do with it?'

The postman swung upon his blakeys. 'Edgar,' he said, 'where in the holy blazes have you been?'

Norman had been almost the first man out of the Swan. As the explosion rang in his ears he had realized that big trouble was in store and that if he was to take his great quest to its ultimate conclusion, now was going to have to be the time.

Clutching his purloined microcircuit to his bosom he had braved the rain of fire and legged it back to his shop and his workroom. Now, as the explosions came thick and fast from all points of the compass, he fiddled with a screwdriver and slotted the thing into place.

'Power inductor,' he said to himself, 'will channel all the power from miles around directly into the apparatus. Wonderful, wonderful!'

Norman threw the much-loved 'we belong dead' switch and his equipment sprang into life.

In the Swan, the lights momentarily dimmed. 'Another power cut,' groaned Neville. 'All I bloody need, another power cut. Typical it is, bloody typical.'

Pooley thundered away at the machine, watched by the Professor and John Omally, who was feeding the lad with scotch.

'Go to it, Jim,' Omally bashed Pooley repeatedly upon the back. 'You've got them on the run. Here you missed that one, pay attention, will you?'

Pooley laboured away beneath the Irishman's assault. 'Lay off me, John,' he implored. 'They're firing back. Look at that.'

The skyline upon the screen had suddenly been translated into that of the immediate area. The silhouettes of the flatblocks and the gasometer were now clearly visible. As the three men stared in wonder, a shower of sparks descended upon the screen from one of the circling craft and struck the silhouette. Outside, a great roar signalled the demolition of one of the flatblocks.

'Get them, you fool, get them.'

Unnoticed, Raffles Rathbone edged towards the door and slipped through it, having it hastily away upon his toes towards the allotments.

The Swan's lights dimmed once more.

In Norman's kitchenette, lights were flashing, and a haze of smoke was rising from many a dodgy spot weld.

Norman sat at his console, punching coordinates into his computer, an ever-increasing hum informing him that the equipment was warming up nicely.

Clinging to the controls of a not altogether dissimilar console was a swarthy clone of a famous American film star; Lombard Omega had taken the controls.

'Treachery,' he spat, from between his gritted and expensively capped teeth. 'Fucking treachery! Those bastards have drawn us into a trap. Bleeding change of government, I shouldn't wonder. How many ships lost, Mr Navigator?'

The navigator shrank low over his guidance systems. 'Four now, sir,' he said, 'no, make that five.'

'Take us out of autopilot then, I shall fly this frigging ship manually.'

One of the remaining blips vanished from the video screen of the Captain Laser Alien Attack machine.

'Oh dear,' said the Professor. 'It had occurred to me that they might just twig it.'

'There's still another two,' said Omally. 'Get them, get them!'

There was now a good deal of Brentford which was only memory. The New Inn had gone, along with the library, and one of the gasometers was engulfed in flame. A falling craft had cut Uncle Ted's greengrocery business cleanly out of the Ealing Road, which, survivors of the holocaust were later to remark, was about the only good thing to come out of the whole affair. There had miraculously been no loss of life, possibly because Brentford boasts more well-stocked Anderson shelters per square mile than any other district in London, but probably because this is not that kind of book.

Pooley was faltering in his attack. 'My right arm's gone,' moaned he, 'and my bomb release button finger's got the cramp, I can play no more.'

Omally struck his companion the now legendary blow to the skull.

'That does it!' Pooley turned upon Omally. 'When trouble threatens, strike Jim Pooley. I will have no more.'

Pooley threw a suddenly uncramped fist towards Omally's chin. By virtue of its unexpected nature and unerring accuracy, he floored the Irishman for a good deal more than the count of ten.

Professor Slocombe looked down at the unconscious figure beneath the beard. 'If that score is settled, I would appreciate it if you would apply yourself once more to the machine before the other two craft catch wind of what is going on and switch to manual override.'

'Quite so,' said Pooley, spitting upon his palms and stepping once more to the video screen.

Small Dave backed away from Edgar Allan Poe, his tiny hands a flapping blur. 'What is all this?' he demanded. 'I don't like the look of you one bit.'

The Victorian author approached upon silent, transparent feet. 'You conjured me here,' he said, 'and I came willingly, thinking you to be a disciple. But now I find that I am drawn into a position from which I am unable to extricate myself. That I must serve you. That cannot be!'

'So leave it then,' whined Small Dave. 'I meant no offence to you, I only wanted a little assistance.'

'You realize who I am? I am Poe, the master of terror. The greatest novelist ever to live. Poe, the creator of Dupin, the world's original consulting detective. Dupin who was not, I repeat not, a dwarf. You mess me about with your trivial vendettas. I have spoken with Professor Slocombe, there is only one way I can find release. You vindictive grudge-bearing wee bastard!'

Small Dave backed towards the floating camel. Simon was floundering amongst the rafters, bawling now at the top of his voice, loosening slates and splintering woodwork.

'Stay away from me,' shrieked Small Dave.

'Stay away from me!' shrieked Simon in fluent dromedary.

Edgar Allan Poe stalked onwards, his patent leather pumps raising dust upon another plane, but leaving no footprint upon the Earth.

'Stay away from me!'

Simon gave a great lurch and burst out of the rafters of the lock-up garage. As he rose through the shattered opening towards the stars, Edgar Allan Poe lunged forward and, in a single movement, bound the trailing halter line firmly about Small Dave's wrist.

'Oh no!' wailed the dwarf as he was dragged from his feet to follow the wayward camel through the open roof.

Edgar Allan Poe watched them go. 'I will be off now,' he said, and, like Small Dave, he was.

In Norman's kitchenette all sorts of exciting things were happening. Dials were registering overload to all points of the compass, lights were flashing, and buzzers buzzing.

The great brain-hammering hum had reached deafening point and a hideous pressure filled the room, driving Norman's head down between his shoulderblades and bursting every Corona bottle upon his shop shelves. With superhuman effort he thumped down another fist full of switches, clasped his hands across his ears, and sank to the floor.

Every light in Brentford, Chiswick, Hounslow, Ealing, Hanwell, Kew, and, for some reason, Penge went out.

Lombard Omega squinted through a porthole. 'Blackout!' he growled. 'Fucking blackout, the wily sods. Mr Navigator, how many of us left?'

The navigator looked up from his controls. 'We are it,' he said.

What Lombard Omega had to say about that cannot possibly be recorded. It must, however, be clearly stated in his defence that it was one of his ancestors who had invented the Anglo-Saxon tongue.

'Take us in low,' he said. 'We will strafe out the entire area. Stand by at the neutron bomb bays and make ready the Gamma weapon.'

'Not the Gamma weapon?' said all those present.

'The Gamma weapon!'

'Fuck me,' said the navigator.

Pooley, Neville, and Professor Slocombe peered around in the darkness. The only light available flickered through the Swan's front windows from a roaring inferno which had once been much of Brentford.

'What now?' Pooley asked. The Professor shook his head.

'You've done it, you've done it! Crack the champagne.' Neville performed a high-stepping dance before the now darkened and obviously defunct Captain Laser Alien Attack machine.

415

'Free beer for a year,' moaned a voice from the deck.

'For a century,' sang Neville. 'Oh bliss, oh heaven, oh no!'

From the distance came a faint whine of unearthly engines. Something large and deadly was approaching, and all means of confounding its destructive intent had vanished away.

'Oh dear,' said Professor Slocombe, 'anybody want the last rites?'

'Prepare the Gamma weapon,' ordered Lombard Omega.

'Gamma weapon prepared, sir,'

'Take out the entire quadrant, spare not an inch.'

'Not an inch, sir.'

'Fire the Gamma weapon.'

The navigator flinched and touched a lighted panel upon the master console. A broad beam of red raw energy leapt down from beneath the ship and struck home upon the Kew side of the river Thames.

The five-hundred-year-old oaks of the Royal Botanic Gardens took fire and half a millennium of history melted away in a single moment. The beam extended over a wider area and tore into the river. The waters thrashed and boiled, like a witches' cauldron, hissed and frothed beneath the unstoppable power of the deadly Gamma weapon.

And the beam moved forward.

The mother ship ground on over the river, a vast chromium blimp filling a quarter of the sky. Along the length of its mirrored sides, lights glittered and twinkled like oil beads. Above it, great dorsal spines rose sharklike and menacing.

The hideous beam moved up from the churning waters and ripped into the river bank, hewing out a broad and ragged channel into which the old Thames gushed in a billowing flood tide.

Ahead lay the Brentford Quadrant, the Ealing Road, and the Flying Swan.

Brentonians fled from their shelters out into the streets. They shielded their faces against the all-consuming heat and took to their heels. The world was coming to an end and now was not the time to take the old Lot's wife backward glance.

In the Swan the lads cowered in terror as the ghastly rumble of falling masonry and the death-cry of splintering glass drew ever nearer.

Outside, the Ealing Road, crammed with screaming humanity,

pouring and tumbling in a mad lemming dash away from the approaching holocaust. Behind them the blinding red wall of fire pressed on, destroying everything which lay in its path.

Omally was upon his knees. 'Stop it!' he screamed at Professor Slocombe. 'Do something, in the name of our God. Only you can.'

The Professor stood immobile. The cries of terror rang in his ears and stung at his soul. The town he had for so very long cared for and protected was being razed to ashes and he was powerless to stop it. He turned a compassionate face towards the Irishman and tears welled in his eyes. 'What can I do?' he asked, in a choked voice. 'I am truly sorry, John.'

Lombard Omega stared down upon the carnage, with a face of hatred and contempt, 'Run, you bastards!' he shouted, as the antlike figures beneath scattered in all directions. 'I will have every last one of you, look at that, look at that.'

The crew of the mother ship craned their necks to the portholes. Below, the destruction was savage and sickening. The streets were being cleaved apart, the houses and shops, flatblocks and places of worship driven from existence.

More than thirty Morris Minors, some even priceless collectors' models with split windscreens, suicide doors and hand-clap wiper arms, had already been atomized, never again to sneak through the dodgy back street MOT.

Professor Slocombe closed his hands in prayer. As the wall of fire moved relentlessly forward and the buildings fell into twisted ruination, he knew that only a miracle could save Brentford.

'What's that, sir?' asked a Cerean deckhand, pointing through a porthole.

'What's what?'

'That, sir.'

Lombard Omega strained his eyes through the rising smokescreen of burning Brentford. 'Jesus Christ!' he screamed, catching sight of a floating object directly in the ship's path. 'It's a fucking camel! Hard to port! Hard to port!'

'You are at the controls,' the cringing navigator informed his captain.

Lombard swung the wheel and the craft veered sharply to the left, avoiding the drifting mammal by a hair's breadth.

Caught in the slipstream, a certain small postman let fly with a volley of obscenity which would have caused even the ship's captain to blush.

'That was fucking close,' said Lombard Omega, wiping creosote from his brow. 'Those bastards don't miss a trick, do they? Give me more power, Mr Navigator. More power!'

The navigator upped the ante and covered his eyes. A great vibration filled the air. A fearsome pressure driving everything downwards. The flood waters ceased their frenzied rush and hung suspended, as if touched by Moses's staff. The scattering Brentonians tumbled to the pavements, gasping at the super-heated air and clutching at their throats. The Captain Laser Alien Attack machine lurched from its mountings and toppled into the Swan, bringing down the side-wall and exposing the horrors of Archie Karachi's kitchen to Neville, who, borne by the terrible force, vanished backwards over the bar counter, losing the last of his fillings.

As Pooley and Omally struck the fag-scarred carpet, their last glimpse of anything approaching reality was of Professor Slocombe. The old man stood, the hell-fire painting his ancient features, hands raised towards the burning sky now visible through the Swan's shattered roof, his mouth reciting the syllables of a ritual which was old before the dawn of recorded history.

Above came the deadly whine of engines as Lombard Omega and the crew of the Starship *Sandra* moved in for the kill.

'Finish them!' screamed the Captain. 'Finish them!'

The ship rocked and shivered. Needles upon a thousand crystal dials rattled into the danger zone. A low pulsating hum set the Captain's teeth on edge and caused the navigator, who had suddenly found Christianity, to cross himself. 'Finish them!' screamed Lombard.

The ship's engines coughed and faltered. The air about the craft ionized as a vague image of something monstrous swam into view. It wavered, half-formed, and transparent, and then, amid a great maelstrom of tearing elements, became solid.

Lombard Omega stared in horror through the forward port. 'What's that?' he cried drawing up his hands. 'What in the name of F . . .'

His final words, however obscene, must remain unrecorded. For at one moment he was steering his craft through empty air above

Brentford football ground and at the next it was making violent and irreconcilable contact with the capping stone of the Great Pyramid of Cheops.

Whoosh, wham, crash, and *bitow* went the Starship *Sandra* as it lost a goodly amount of its undercarriage and slewed to one side. It plummeted downwards, a screaming ball of fire, narrowly missing the roof of the Flying Swan, cartwheeled over the Piano Museum, and tore down towards the allotments, the last men of Ceres, who were standing around looking rather bemused, a very great deal of carefully-laid explosive, and the few sparse and dismal remnants of a former postman's prize-winning cabbage patch.

There was a moment of terrible silence and then an explosion which rocked the seismographs at Greenwich and had the warlords of a dozen nations reaching towards the panic buttons.

A very great silence then fell upon what was left of the Brentford Triangle.

EPILOGUE

The sun rose the next morning at three a.m.

This came as a great surprise to those folk of Brentford who felt in the mood to enjoy the dawn chorus, but no more so than it did to the peoples of the Nile delta who, somewhat bewildered at the sudden disappearance of their greatest tourist attraction, noticed also that the nights were definitely drawing in a bit.

Had the Memorial Library clock been still extant, it would just have struck the hour when an impossibly long low-loader turned up the Ealing Road, demolishing Brentford's two remaining lampposts, and cracking a hundred paving-stones beneath its many-wheeled assault.

High in the cab, illuminated by the green dashlights and the first rays of the rising sun, sat a bald-headed man in a saffron robe. He puffed upon a Woodbine and stared through the tinted windscreen at the blackened wreckage which had once been the town of his birth.

There had been more than a few changes while he had been away, this was clear. Another council housing project, he assumed, or road-widening scheme, although it appeared a little drastic. He pulled the five-hundred-foot vehicle up through the gears and rolled it over the railway bridge, whose girders groaned beneath the strain. Where had the New Inn gone, and surely the council would not have demolished two of their cherished flatblocks?

The great vehicle's front wheels plunged into a pothole, dislodging the driver's Woodbine into his lap. He would have harsh words to say about all this and no mistake. Here he was, delivering the greatest archaeological discovery in the history of mankind, and they had let the roads go to ruin.

And what in Dante's name was that? Archroy brought the mammoth loader to a shuddering halt. Retrieving his fallen Woodbine, he climbed down from the cab.

In considerable awe he stared up at the vast structure which now stood upon the site formerly occupied by Brentford's football ground. That was the Great Pyramid of Giza or he was a clog-dancing Dutchman.

The man of bronze ground out his cigarette with a naked heel and scratched at his hairless pate. Whatever had been going on around here?

He climbed back into his cab and put the mighty vehicle into gear. He was rapidly losing his temper. Where was the reception committee? Where was the bunting and the Mayor? Had he not written to Neville detailing the time of his arrival? This was all a bit much.

Ahead, in the distance, faint lights showed in a window: the Flying Swan, surely, but candle-lit?

Archroy applied the brakes and brought the low-loader to a stand-still outside the smoke-blackened and shrapnel-pocked drinking house. He fumbled in his dashboard for another packet of cigarettes, but could find nothing but a bundle of picture postcards displaying now inaccurate rooftop views of Brentford.

He climbed down from his cab, slammed shut the door and, kicking rubble to left and right of him, strode across the road to the Swan's doorway. With a single curling backward kick he applied his bare foot to the door, taking it from its hinges and propelling it forwards into the bar.

Four startled men looked up in horror from their drinks at the bar counter. Jim Pooley, John Omally, Professor Slocombe and Neville the part-time barman.

'Archroy?' gasped Neville, squinting towards the terrific figure framed in the Swan's doorway. 'Archroy, is that you?'

Archroy fixed the part-time barman with a baleful eye. 'I have the Ark of Noah outside on my lorry,' he roared. 'I don't suppose that any of you after-hours drinkers would care to step outside and give it the once-over?'

Omally struggled to his feet. 'The Ark of Noah, now, is it?' he said. 'Could I interest you at all in a guided tour around the Great Pyramid of Brentford?'

EAST OF EALING

I

Norman gave his ivory-handled screwdriver a final twist and secured the last screw into the side panel of the slim brass cylinder. Unclamping it from his vice, he lifted it lovingly by its shining axle, and held it towards the dust-smeared glass of the kitchenette window. It was a work of wonder and that was for certain. A mere ten inches in diameter and another one in thickness, the dim light painted a rainbow corona about its varnished circumference.

Norman carried it carefully across to his cluttered kitchen table and, elbowing aside a confusion of soiled crockery, placed it upon the twin bracket mountings which had been bolted through both tablecloth and table. The axle dropped into its mounts with a satisfying click and Norman, hardly daring to breathe, sought out his can of Three-in-One and applied a glistening bead of oil to either end.

If all his calculations, allied to those of a certain Johann Bessler, later known as Orffyreus, who had first demonstrated the prototype as long ago as 1712 in Zittau, East Germany, proved ultimately to be correct, he was even now standing upon the very threshold of yet another earth-shattering scientific breakthrough.

And all it needed was a breath. Norman leaned low over the brazen wheel and blew upon its edge. There was a faint click, followed by another and yet another, and with a beauty, which like all of its strange kind lay firmly within the eye of its beholder, the polished brass wheel began to rotate slowly. Around and around it went, gathering momentum, until at last it reached a steady rate. Norman drew out his pocket-watch and rattled it against his ear. The second hand took to once more sweeping the pitted face of the grandaddy's retirement present. The polished wheel continued to turn; Norman counted beneath his breath and double-checked with his watch. Twenty-six revolutions per minute, exactly as old mad Bressler had predicted. Around and around and around for ever and ever and ever.

A broad, if lopsided, smile travelled where it could over Norman's face. Returning his already failing watch to its fluff-filled waistcoast pocket, he clapped his hands together and did a silly sort of dance right there and then upon the worn lino of the grimy kitchenette.

The wheel spun, its former clicking now a dull purr, and Norman thrust a knuckle to his mouth and chuckled noiselessly. His free hand hovered for a moment above the spinning wheel. If the calculations were indeed correct then virtually nothing, short of out and out destruction, should actually be able to halt the wheel's motion. Tentatively, he tapped a forefinger on to the polished surface. The wheel continued to spin. Gently, he plucked at it with finger and thumb. The wheel showed no signs of easing up. Norman laid firm hold with both hands upon the slim cylinder, his grasp skidded away, and the wheel rolled on and on and on.

This time he had cracked it! This time he had most definitely cracked it! The ultimate source of power. Weighing no more than a couple of pounds, its potential knew no bounds. It could charge up literally anything and, but for the occasional squirt of Three-in-One, needed next to no maintenance. Without the kitchenette, the shop door-bell suddenly rang in a customer and Norman dragged himself away from his spinning masterwork to answer the call of business. As he reached the door he paused a moment and looked back. Twenty-six revolutions per minute, round and around and around, for ever and ever and ever. With a final silent chuckle and a theatrical backways kick, Norman passed through the doorway, leaving his world of magic to emerge into the gloomy reality of his musty corner-shop.

Before the counter stood one James Pooley, betting man, free-thinker, and bachelor of the parish. His hand, which had even then been snaking across towards the peppermint packets, returned itself to the tweedy depths of a bottomless trouser pocket. With a cheery, 'Good morning to you, Norman,' Pooley bade the shopkeeper that very thing.

'Same to yourself, Jim,' said Norman. 'The daily, would it be?'

'The very same, five Woodys and a *Sporting Life*. I think that today I am a little more than usually liable to pull off "The Big One".'

426

'Of course.' Norman deftly drew out a packet of cigarettes and the aforementioned racing paper without for a moment removing his gaze from the approximate location of Pooley's ever-wandering hands. It was not that Jim was by nature a dishonest man, but living daily upon his wits, he dared never let any opportunity, no matter how small, slip by.

'You wear the smile of a man who has already pulled off that ever elusive big fellow,' said Jim, noting well the twisted smirk still firmly plastered across Norman's face.

The shopkeeper passed Jim his life-support apparatus and nodded wildly. 'I have, I have,' said he, amidst a flurry of nose-tapping. 'Although on this occasion, as upon others, I cannot take full credit for it all myself.'

'No matter that. Many a wealthy man owes his success in life to the labours of a deceased relative.' Jim slipped his cigarettes into his breast-pocket and rolled his newspaper. 'So what is it then? Something of a scientific nature I have no doubt.'

'The very same.'

'Might I hazard a guess?'

'Be very pleased to.'

Jim stroked at the stubble of his chin, which he had been meaning to shave off for at least a day or so, and cocked his head upon one side. 'Now, if I am not mistaken,' said he, 'your recent obsession, and I use the word in the kindest possible way, has been with energy. The solar panels upon your roof do not go unnoticed hereabouts and the fact that you possess the only Morris Minor in the neighbourhood which runs upon coke has raised more than the occasional eyebrow. Am I right therefore in assuming that it is towards energy, power, and things of that nature that you have turned your enormous intellect?'

Norman's head bobbed up and down after the fashion of a toy dog in a Cortina rear window.

'Aha, then if I am not mistaken I will hazard a guess that you have rediscovered the long lost secret of perpetual motion.'

Norman clapped his hands together. 'You got it,' he crowed. 'Got it in one. I am glad that I did not lay money upon it. You got it in one.'

'Naturally,' said Jim, blowing on his fingernails. 'But I feel you knew that I would.'

Norman nodded again. 'True,' he said. 'I must admit that I had been somewhat puzzled by the ever-increasing number of little bright patches appearing upon the window of my kitchenette. However, noticing of late that each corresponds exactly in size and shape to the blot of dirt upon the end of your nose, all would seem to be revealed. But what do you think, Jim? The marvel of the age would you say? Feel free to offer criticism; my shoulders although physically bowed are metaphorically broad.'

Jim thrust his rolled-up paper into a jacket pocket. 'If you will pardon me saying this, Norman, I have never myself had a lot of truck with the concept of perpetual motion. You will recall, no doubt, me saying that the chap in Chiswick who gave all those lectures at the Memorial Library propounding the theory of reincarnation has died yet again.'

Norman nodded yet again.

'And you will also recall my brilliant *bon mot* made upon the news of his passing, that the trouble with those fellows is that they are here today and here tomorrow?'

Norman winced.

'Well, such it is with perpetual motion. A fine thing it might be in itself, and a pleasure to the inventor thereof, but to the general public, in particular to the man of limited reason with no care for the higher truth, it presents but one thing only.'

'Which is?'

'Absolute monotony,' said Pooley in a leaden tone. 'All-consuming, soul-destroying, absolute monotony.'

With these few words he turned upon his heel and strode from the shop, leaving Norman to ponder upon not one but two eternal problems. The first being how a man such as Pooley could have the sheer gall to write off the greatest scientific discovery of the age with a few poorly chosen words. And the second, how he had managed, once more, to escape from the shop without having paid for either Woodbines or *Sporting Life*.

'The wheels of God grind slowly,' thought Norman to himself. 'But they do grind at twenty-six revolutions per minute.'

2

Neville the part-time barman flip-flopped across the deserted saloon-bar of the Flying Swan, his monogrammed carpet-slippers raising small clouds of dust from the faded carpet. Rooting with a will, he sought his newspaper which lay upon the pub's welcome mat beneath a pile of final demands, gaudy circulars, and rolled posters advertising the forthcoming Festival of Brentford.

Shaking it free of these postal impediments, Neville unfolded the local tabloid and perused the front page. More good good news. Earthquakes and tidal waves, wars and rumours of wars. Jolly stuff. And on the home front? Well, there was the plague of black fly currently decimating the allotment crops. A rival brewery had just put its beer up a penny a pint and its competition, ever happy to accept a challenge, were hinting at rises of two pence or more.

One particular gem caught the part-time barman's good eye: the local banks, in keeping with a countrywide trend, were investigating the possibility of dispensing with coin of the realm and instigating a single credit card system. That would go down a storm with the locals, thought Neville. Without further ado he consigned the wicked messenger of bad tidings to the wastepaper basket. 'I shall cancel this,' said the part-time barman to himself. 'I shall ask Norman to despatch me something of a more cheerful nature in the future. Possibly the *People's Friend* or *Gardener's Gazette*.'

But on further consideration, even those two periodicals were not exactly devoid of grim tidings nowadays. The *People's Friend*, not content with simply going up three pence, assailed its readers with a fine line in doom prophecy, and the *Gardener's Gazette* dedicated most of its pages to large anatomical diagrams of black·fly. Neville shrugged his dressing-gowned shoulders. Seemed like a nice day though, but. The sun rising majestic as ever from behind the flatblocks and tickling the Swan's upper panes. Always some hope for the future. Although, lately, Neville had been feeling more than a little ill at ease. It was as if some great burden was descending upon him, inch by inch and pound by pound, down on to his bony shoulders. He was hard put to explain the feeling, and there was little point in confiding his unease to the regulars, but he was certain that something altogether wrong was happening and, moreover, that it was happening to him personally.

Leaving his newspaper to confide its black tidings to the fag ends in the wastepaper basket and his mail to gather what dust it wished upon the doormat, Neville the part-time barman flip-flopped away up the Swan's twenty-six stairs to his cornflakes and a cup of the blackest of all black coffees.

In another part of Brentford other things were stirring this Shrove Tuesday morning and what those other things were and what they would later become were matters which would in their turn weigh very heavily indeed upon certain part-time barmen's shoulders.

They all truly began upon a certain section of unreclaimed bombsite along the High Street between the Beehive pub and a rarely used side-turning known as Abaddon Street. And as fate would have it, it was across this very stretch of land that an Irish gentleman of indeterminate years, wearing a well-patched tweed jacket and a flat cap, was even now striding. He was whistling brightly and as it was his wont to do, leading by the perished rubber grip of a pitted handlebar, an elderly sit-up-and-beg bike. This was one John Vincent Omally, and his rattling companion, labouring bravely along, although devoid of front mudguards and rear brake and sorely in need of the healing balm offered by Norman's oil-can, was none other than that prince of pedaldom, Marchant, the wonder bike. Over the rugged strip of land came these two heroic figures, the morning sun tinting their features, treading a well-worn shortcut of their own making. Omally whistling a jaunty tune from the land of his fathers and Marchant offering what accompaniment he could with the occasional bout of melodic bell ringing. God was as ever in Omally's Heaven and all seemed very much all right with the world.

As they came a-striding, a-whistling and a-ringing, small birdies fluttered down on to the crumbling ivy-hung brickwork of the surrounding walls to join them in a rowdy chorus. Beads of dew swung upon dandelion stems and fat-bellied garden spiders fiddled with their diamond-hung webs. It certainly wasn't a bad old life if you had the know of it, and Omally was a man whom it could reasonably be said had that very know. The lad gave a little skip and doffed his hat to the day. Without warning his foot suddenly struck a half-buried object which had certainly not existed upon his previous day's journeyings. To the accompaniment of a great Godless oath which momentarily blotted out the sunlight and raised the twittering birdies into a startled confusion, the great man of Eire plunged suddenly towards the planet of his birth, bringing with him his bicycle and tumbling into a painful, untidy, and quite undignified heap.

'By the blood of the Saints!' swore Omally, attempting to rise but discovering to his horror that Marchant now held him in something resembling an Indian death-lock. 'In the name of all the Holies!' The tangled bike did what it could to get a grip of itself and spun its back wheel, chewing up several of Omally's most highly-prized fingers. 'You stupid beast!' screamed himself, lashing out with an oversized hobnail. 'Have a care will you?' The bike, having long years of acquaintanceship with its master to its credit, considered that this might be the time to keep the now legendary low profile.

Amidst much cursing and a great deal of needless profanity, Omally struggled painfully to his feet and sought the cause of his downfall. Almost at once he spied out the villain, a nubble of polished metal protruding from the dusty path. John was not slow in levelling his size-nine boot at it.

He was someway between mid-swing and full-swing when a mental image of a bygone relative swam into his mind. He had performed a similar action upon a half-buried obstruction during the time of the blitz. The loud report and singular lack of mortal remains paid a posthumous tribute to his lack of forethought. DANGER UNEXPLODED BOMB! screamed a siren in Omally's brain. John lowered his size-nine terror weapon gently to the deck and stooped gingerly towards the earth to examine the object. To his amazement he found himself staring at the proverbial thing of beauty. A mushroom of highly-polished brass surmounted by an enamel crown. There was that indefinable quality of value about it and Omally was not slow to notice the fact. His fingers greedily wore away at its earthy surrounding, exposing a slender, fluted column extending downwards. From even this small portion it was clear that the thing was a rare piece of workmanship; the flutes were cunningly inlaid with mother-of-pearl. Omally climbed to his feet and peered furtively around to assure himself that he was alone with his treasure. That he had struck the motherlode at last was almost a certainty. There was nothing of the doodlebug or Mark Seventeen Blockbuster about this boy, but very much of the antique bedstead of Victoria and Albert proportions.

John rubbed his hands together and chuckled. What was it his old Da had once said? A dead bird never falls out of the nest, that was it. Carefully covering his find with a clump or two of grass, Omally continued upon his way. The birdies had flown and the spiders had it away on their eight ones, but before Omally reached his secret exit in the planked fencing he was whistling once more, and Marchant was doing his level best to keep up with the increasingly more sprightly tune.

3

Jim Pooley sat upon his favourite bench before the Memorial Library, racing paper spread out across his knees, liberated Woodbine aglow between his lips, and Biro perched atop his right ear. Few were the passers-by who even troubled to notice the sitter upon the bench. Fewer still observed the chalk-drawn pentagram encircling that bench, the sprig of hemlock attached to the sitter's lapel, or the bulge of the tarot pack in his waistcoat pocket. Such subtleties were lost to the casual observer, but to the trained eye they would be instantly significant. Jim Pooley was now having a crack at occultism in his neverending quest to pull off the six-horse Super-Yankee.

Jim had tried them all and found each uniformly lacking. The I-Ching he had studied until his eyes crossed. The prophecies of Nostradamus, the dice, the long sticks, the flight paths of birds, and the changes of barometric pressure registered upon the charts of the library entrance hall – each had received his attention as a possible catalyst for the pulling off of the ever-elusive Big One. He had considered selling his soul to the devil but it was on the cards that the Prince of Darkness probably had his name down for con-scription anyway.

Thrusting his hands into his trouser pockets, Jim peered down at his paper. Somewhere, he knew, upon this page were those six horses. Tomorrow, he knew, he would kick himself for not having seen the obvious cosmic connection. Jim concentrated every ounce of his psychic energies upon the page. Presently he was asleep. Blissful were his Morphean slumbers upon this warm spring morning and blissful they would no doubt have remained, at least until opening time at the Swan, had not a deft blow from a size-nine boot struck him upon the sole of the left foot and blasted him into consciousness. The man who could dream winners awoke with a painful start.

'Morning Jim,' said the grinning Omally. 'Having forty winks were we?'

Pooley squinted up at his rude awakener with a bloodshot eye. 'Yoga,' said he. 'Lamaic meditation. I was almost on the brink of a breakthrough and you've spoilt it.'

Omally rested his bicycle upon the library fence and his bum upon the bench. 'Sorry,' said he. 'Please pardon my intrusion upon the contemplation of your navel. You looked to all the world the very picture of a sleeper.'

'Nothing of the sort,' Pooley replied in a wounded tone. 'Do you think that I, like yourself, can afford to fritter away my time in dalliance and idleness? My life is spent in the never-ending search for higher truths.'

'Those which come in six or more figures?'

'None but the very same.'

'And how goes this search?'

'Fraught as ever with pitfalls for the unwary traveller.'

'As does our each,' said the Irish philosopher.

The two men sat awhile upon the library bench. Each would dearly have liked a smoke but out of politeness each waited upon his fellow to make that first selfless gesture of the day. 'I'm dying for a fag,' sighed Jim, at length.

Omally patted his pockets in a professional manner, narrowly avoiding the destruction of five Woodbine he had secreted in his waistcoast pocket. 'I'm out,' he said.

Jim shrugged. 'Why do we always go through this performance?' he asked.

Omally shook his head, 'I have no idea whatever, give us a fag, Jim?'

'Would that I could John, would that I could. But times are up against me at the present.'

Omally shook his head sadly, 'These are troubled times for us all I fear. Take my knee here,' he raised the gored article towards Jim's nose. 'What does that say to you?'

Pooley put his ear to Omally's knee, 'It is not saying much,' he said. 'Is it perhaps trying to tell me that it has a packet of cigarettes in its sock?'

'Not even warm.'

434

'Then you've got me.' Omally sighed. 'Shall we simply smoke our own today, Jim?'

'Good idea.' Pooley reached into his waistcoat pocket and Omally did likewise. Both withdrew identical packets into the sunlight and both opened these in unison. John's displayed five cigarettes. Pooley's was empty. 'Now there's a thing,' said Jim.

'Decoy!' screamed John Omally. Pooley accepted the cigarette in the manner with which it was offered. 'My thanks,' said he. 'I really do have the feeling that today I might just pull off the long-awaited Big One.'

'I have something of the same feeling myself,' his companion replied.

4

The part-time barman finished the last of his toast and patted about his lips with a red gingham napkin. He leaned back in his chair and rested his palms upon his stomach. He felt certain that he was putting on weight. A thin man from birth, tall, gaunt, and scholar-stooped, Neville had never possessed a single ounce of surplus fat. But recently it seemed to him that his jackets were growing ever more tight beneath the armpits, and that the lower button on his waistcoat was becoming increasingly more difficult to secure. 'Most curious,' said Neville, rising from his seat and padding over to the bathroom scales which were now a permanent fixture in the middle of the living-room floor. Climbing aboard, he peered down between his slippered toes. Eleven stone dead, exactly as it had been for the last twenty years. The part-time barman shook his head in wonder, it was all very mysterious. Perhaps the scales were wrong, gummed up with carpet fluff or something. He'd let Norman give them the once-over. Or perhaps it was the dry cleaners? Things never seemed quite right there since that big combine bought old Tom Telford out. Possibly this new lot were having a pop at him. Putting an extra tuck in the seat of his strides every time he put them in for their monthly hose down. Most unsporting that, hitting a lad below the belt.

Neville laughed feebly at his unintended funny, but really this was no laughter matter. Taking out the tape measure, which now never left his person, he stretched it about his waist. All seemed the same. Possibly it was simply a figment of his imagination. Possibly he was going mad. The thought was never far from his mind nowadays. Neville shuddered. He would just have to pull himself together.

Sighing deeply, he shuffled away to the bedroom to dress.

Flinging off his silken dressing-gown he took up the rogue trousers from where they hung in their creases over the chair and yanked them up his legs. With difficulty he buttoned himself into respectability. They were definitely too tight for comfort, there was no point in denying it. Neville stooped for his socks but stopped in horror. The blood drained from his face and his good eye started from its socket; a nasty blue tinge crept about the barman's lips. It was worse than he feared, far worse. His trouser bottoms were swinging about his ankles like flags at half-mast. He wasn't only getting fatter, he was growing taller! Neville slumped back on to his bed, his face a grey mask of despair. It was impossible. Certainly folk could put on weight pretty rapidly, but to suddenly spring up by a good inch and a half over night? That was downright impossible, wasn't it?

Pooley and Omally strolled over the St Mary's Allotments en route to John's hut and the cup that cheers. Jim tapped his racing paper upon his leg and sought inspiration from the old enamel advertising signs along the way which served here and there as plot dividers. None was immediately forthcoming. The two threaded their way between the ranks of bean poles and waxed netting, the corrugated shanties, and zinc watertanks. They walked in single file along a narrow track through a farrowed field of broccoli and one of early flowering sprouts, finally arriving at the wicket fence and pleasant ivy-hung trelliswork that stood before Omally's private plot. John parked his bicycle in its favourite place, took up his daily pinta, turned several keys in as many weighty locks, and within a few short minutes the two men lazed upon a pair of commandeered railway carriage seats, watching the kettle taking up the bubble on the Primus.

'There is a king's ransom, I do hear, to be had out of the antique trade at present,' said John matter-of-factly.

'Oh yes?' Pooley replied without enthusiasm.

'Certainly, the junk of yesterday is proving to be the ob-ja-dart of today and the nestegg of tomorrow.' Omally rose to dump two tea bags into as many enamel mugs and top the fellows up with boiling water. 'A veritable king's ransom, ready for the taking. A man could not go it alone in such a trade, he would need a partner, of course.'

'Of course.'

'A man he could *trust*.' John put much emphasis upon the word as he wrung out the tea bags and added the cream of the milk to his own mug and a splash of the rest to Jim's. 'Yes, he would definitely want a man he could rely on.'

'I am convinced of that,' said Jim, accepting his mug. 'A bit strong, isn't it?'

'Antique bedding is currently the vogue amongst the trendies of Kensington, I understand,' John continued.

'Oh, those bodies.'

'Yes, the fashionable set do be weeping, wailing, and gnashing its expensively-capped teeth for the lack of it.'

Pooley blew on to his tea. 'Strange days,' said he.

John felt that he was obviously not getting his point across in quite the right way. A more direct approach was necessary. 'Jim,' he said in a highly confidential tone. 'What would you say if I was to offer you a chance of a partnership in an enterprise which would involve you in absolutely no financial risk whatever?'

'I would say that there is always a first time for everything, I suppose.'

'What if I was to tell you that at this very moment I know of where there is an extremely valuable antique lying discarded and unwanted which is ours for the taking, what would you say then?'

Jim sipped at his tea. 'I would say to you then, Omally,' he said, without daring to look up, 'dig the bugger out yourself.'

Omally's eyebrows soared towards his flat cap.

Pooley simply pointed to an L-shaped tear in his own left trouser knee. 'I passed along your path not half an hour before you,' he said simply.

'Your lack of enterprise is a thing to inspire disgust.'

'He that diggeth a pit will fall into it. Ecclesiasticus Chapter twenty-seven, verse twenty-six,' said Jim Pooley. 'I am not a religious man as you well know, but I feel that the Scriptures definitely have it sussed on this point. A commendable try though.' Jim took out his cigarette packet from his top pocket and handed the Irishman a tailor-made.

'Thank you,' said Omally.

'Now, if you really have a wish to make a killing today –' John nodded enthusiastically, it was early yet and his brain was only just warming up to the daily challenge, '– I have seen something which has the potential to earn a man more pennies than a thousand buried bedframes. Something which a man can only be expected to witness once in a lifetime. And something of such vast financial potential that if a man was to see it and not take advantage of the experience, he should consider himself a soul lost for ever and beyond all hope.'

'Your words are pure music,' said John Omally. 'Play on, sweet friend, play on.'

As Neville the part-time barman drew the polished brass bolts on the saloon-bar door and stood in the opening, sniffing the air, the clatter of two pairs of hobnail boots and the grating of rear mud-guard upon back wheel announced the approach of a brace of regulars. One of these was a gentleman of Celtic extraction who had recently become convinced that the future lay in perpetual motion and its application to the fifth gear of the common bicycle. Neville installed himself behind the bar counter and closed the hinged counter top.

'God save all here,' said John Omally, pushing open the door.

'Count that double,' said Pooley, following up the rear.

Neville pushed a polished glass beneath the spout of the beer engine and drew upon the enamel pump handle. Before the patrons had hoisted themselves on to their accustomed barstools, two pints of Large stood brimming before them, golden brown and crystal clear. 'Welcome,' said Neville.

'Hello once more,' said Omally. 'Jim is in the chair.' Pooley smiled and pushed the exact amount of pennies and halfpennies across the polished counter top. Neville rang up 'No Sale' and once more all was as it ever had been and hopefully ever would be in Brentford.

'How goes the game then, gentlemen?' Neville asked the patrons, already a third of the way through their pints.

'As ever, cruel to the working man,' said John. 'And how is yourself?'

'To tell you the truth, a little iffy. In your personal opinion, John, how do I look to you?'

'The very picture of health.'

'Not a little puffy?' Neville fingered his middle regions.

'Not at all.'

'No hint of stoutness there? You can be frank with me, I have no fear of criticism.'

Omally shook his head and looked towards Jim. 'You look fine,' said Pooley. 'Are you feeling a bit poorly, then?'

'No, no.' Neville shook his head with vigour. 'It's just that, well . . .' he considered the two drinkers who surveyed him with dubious expressions. 'Oh, nothing at all. I look all right you think? No higher, say, than usual?' Two heads swung to and fro upon their respective necks. 'Best to forget it then, a small matter, do not let it spoil your ale.'

'Have no fear of that,' said John Omally.

The Swan's door opened to admit the entry of an elderly gentleman and his dog. 'Morning, John, Jim,' said Old Pete, sidling up to the bar. 'Large dark rum please, Neville.' Neville took himself off to the optic.

'Morning, Pete,' said Pooley, 'good day, Chips.' The ancient's furry companion woofed non-committally. 'Are you fit?'

'As well as can be expected. And how goes the sport for you? That Big One still lurking up beyond your frayed cuff?'

Pooley made a 'so-so' gesture. 'Inches, but . . .'

Old Pete accepted his drink from Neville and held up the glass to evaluate the exact volume of his measure before grudgingly pushing the correct change across the bar top. 'So,' he continued, addressing himself to Omally, 'and how fare the crops?'

'Blooming,' said Omally. 'I expect a bumper harvest this year. Come the Festival. I expect several firsts and as many seconds in the Show.'

'King Teddies again then, is it?' Revered as the personification of all agricultural knowledge within a radius of an 'nth number of miles, Old Pete had little truck with potato growers.

'Nature's finest food,' said John. 'Was it not the spud which sustained the Joyces, the Wildes, the Behans and the Traynors? Show me a great man and I will show you a spud to his rear.'

'I have little regard for footballers,' said Old Pete. 'If you were any kind of a farmer you would diversify your crops a little. I myself have fostered no fewer than five new varieties of sprout.'

Omally crossed himself and made a disgusted face. 'Don't even speak the word,' said he. 'I cannot be having with that most despicable of all vegetables.'

'The sprout is your man,' intoned the old one. 'Full of iron. A man could live alone upon a desert island all his life if he had nothing more than a few sprout seeds and bit of common sense.'

440

'A pox on all sprouts,' said John, crouching low over his pint. 'May the black fly take the lot of them.'

Pooley was consulting his racing paper. Possibly there was a horse running whose name was an anagram of 'sprout'. Such factors were not to be taken lightly when one was seeking that all elusive cosmic connection. The effort was quite considerable and very shortly Jim, like Dickens's now legendary fat boy, was once more asleep. Neville made to take up the half-finished glass for the washer. With a sudden transformation from Dickens to Edgar Allen Poe, the sleeper awoke. 'Not done here,' said Jim. 'It's Omally's round.' Omally got them in.

'Let us speak no more of horticulture,' said John to Old Pete. 'Your knowledge of the subject is legend hereabouts and I am not up to matching wits with you. Tell me something, do you sleep well of a night?'

'The sleep of the just, nothing else.'

'Then you must indeed have a cosy nest to take your slumbers in.'

'No, nothing much, a mattress upon a rough wooden pallet. It serves as it has since my childhood.'

Omally shook his head in dismay, 'Longevity, as I understand it to be, is very much the part and parcel of good sleeping. Man spends one third of his life in bed. Myself a good deal more. The comfort of the sleeper greatly reflects upon his health and well being.'

'Is that a fact?' said Old Pete. 'I have no complaints.'

'Because you have never experienced greater comfort. Take myself. You would take me for a man of thirty.'

'Never. Forty.'

Omally laughed. 'Always the wag. But truthfully, I attribute my good health to the comfort afforded by my bed. There is a science in these things, and believe me, I have studied this particular science.'

'Never given the matter much thought,' said Old Pete.

'So much I suspected,' said John. 'You, as an elderly gentleman, and by that I mean no offence, must first look after your health. Lying upon an uncomfortable bed can take years off your life.'

'As it happens, my old bed is a bit knackered.'

'Then there you have it.' Omally smacked his hands together.

'You are throwing away your life for a few pennies wisely invested in your own interest.'

'I am a fool to myself,' said Old Pete, who definitely wasn't. 'What are you selling, John?'

Omally tapped at his nose, 'Something very, very special. The proper palatial pit. The very acme of sleeping paraphernalia. Into my possession has come of late a bed which would stagger the senses of the gods. Now had I the accommodation I would truly claim such a prize for my own. But my apartments are small and I know that yours could easily house such a find. What do you say?'

'I'll want to have a look at the bugger first, five-thirty p.m. tonight, here.'

Omally spat upon his palm and smacked it down into the wrinkled appendage of the elder. 'Done,' said he.

'I'd better not be,' said Old Pete.

Omally drew his partner away to a side-table, 'Now that is what you call business,' he told Jim. 'The old bed is not even dug out, yet it is already sold.'

Pooley groaned; he could already feel the blisters upon his palms. 'You are on to a wrong'n there,' he said. 'This venture has to me the smell of doom about it. That is a bomb site *you* will be digging on. There will probably be a corpse asleep in that bed. Should bed it in fact be and not simply a shaft or two of nothing.'

Omally crossed himself at the mention of a corpse. 'Stop with such remarks,' said he. 'There is a day's pay in this and as the digger you deserve half of anything I get.'

'And what about Norman's wheel and the many millions to be made from that?'

'Well, we have no absolute proof that the wheel spins without cessation. This would be a matter for serious scientific investigation. Such things take time.'

'We have no lack of that, surely?'

'I will tell you what,' Omally finished his pint and studied the bottom of his glass. 'I will chance your wheel if you will chance my bedframe.'

Pooley looked doubtful.

'Now be fair,' said John. 'There are degrees of doubt to be weighed up on either side. Firstly, of course you cannot approach Norman, he knows that you are on to him. A third party must act here. Someone with a subtlety of approach. Someone gifted in such matters.'

'Someone such as yourself?'

'Good idea,' said John. 'But time is of the essence, we don't want any opportunists dipping in before us. When we leave here you collect a couple of tools from my plot and whip the bed out and I will go around to Norman's.'

If Pooley had looked doubtful before, it was nought to the way he looked now. 'I do not feel that I am getting the better part of this,' he said slowly.

'Better part?' Omally's face was all outrage. 'We are a business partnership are we not? There are no better parts involved here. Surely you are now sowing seeds of distrust?'

'Who, me? Perish the thought. The fact that I will be labouring away in a minefield digging up a rusty old bedframe while you stand chit-chatting in a cosy corner-shop had not crossed my mind.'

'So?'

Jim folded his brow. 'Whose round is it?'

'Yours, Jim,' said John Omally, 'most definitely yours.'

5

Norman had been dancing gaily through his morning's work. Between customers he had skipped backwards and forwards, turning the enamel door handle and squinting into the gloom to assure himself that all was as it should be. The wheel had been tirelessly spinning for more than four hours now and showed no signs whatever of grinding to a halt. As the Memorial Library clock struck one in the distance he turned his sign to the 'Closed For Lunch' side, bolted up, and pranced away to his sanctum sanctorum. The wheel was an undoubted success and, as such, meant that Phase One of his latest, and in his own humble opinion undeniably greatest, project was complete.

Norman slipped off his shopkeeper's overall and donned a charred leather apron and a pair of welder's goggles. Dusting down his rubber gloves with a tube of baby powder, he drew them over his sensitive fingers and flexed these magical appendages. With a flourish, he dragged aside a length of gingham tablecloth which curtained off a tiny alcove in one corner of the crowded room.

Upon a worm-eaten kitchen chair sat another Norman!

Clad in grey shopkeeper's workcoat, shirt, tie, trousers, and worn brown brogues, he was a waxen effigy of the Madame Tussaud's variety. The scientific shopkeeper chuckled and, reaching out a rubber-clad finger, tickled his *doppelgänger* under the chin. 'Afternoon, Norman,' he said.

The double did not reply, but simply sat staring sightlessly into space. It was as near a perfect representation of its living counterpart as it was possible to be. And so it might well have been considering the long years of Norman's labour. Countless thousands of hours had gone into its every detail. Every joint in its skeletal frame was fully articulated with friction-free bearings of the shopkeeper's

444

own design. The cranial computer banks were loaded to the very gunwhales with all the necessary information, which would enable it to perform the mundane and tiresome duties required of a corner-shopkeeper, whilst its creator could dedicate the entirety of his precious time to the more essential matters of which Phase Three of the project were composed. All it lacked was that essential spark of life, and this now ground away upon the kitchen table at precisely twenty-six revolutions per minute.

Norman chuckled anew and drew his masterpiece erect. Un-buttoning the shirt, he exposed the rubberized chest region which housed the hydraulic unit designed to simulate the motions of breath-ing. Tinkering with his screwdriver, he removed the frontal plate and applied a couple of squirts of Three-in-One to the brace of mountings, identical in shape and size to those which now cradled the ever-spinning wheel. He had sought far and wide for a never-failing power supply, having previously nothing to hand save clumsy mains cables which, even when disguised by poking from trouser bottoms, left his progeny little scope for locomotion. This compact unit would do the job absolutely.

Norman crossed to the table, and with a set of specially fashioned tongs carefully lifted the spinning wheel upon its polished axle-rod. It turned through space gyroscopically, if nothing else it would certainly keep the robot standing upright. With a satisfying click the wheel fell into place, and Norman closed the chest cavity and rebuttoned the shirt, straightening the tie and workcoat lapels. The shopkeeper stepped back to view his mirror image. Perfection. There was a gentle flutter of movement about the chest region, a sudden blinking of eyelids and focusing of eyes, a yawn, a stretch. Clearing its throat with a curiously mechanical coughing sound, the creature spoke.

'Good afternoon, sir,' it said.

Norman clapped his hands together and danced one of his favourite silly dances. 'Wonderful,' he said with glee. 'Wonderful.'

The robot smiled crookedly. 'I am happy that you find all to your satisfaction,' said he.

'Oh, indeed, indeed. How are you then, Norman? Are you well?'

'A bit stiff, sir, as it happens, but I expect that I will wear in. Is there anything in particular you would like doing?'

Norman clapped his hands, 'How about a cup of tea, what do you think?'

'Certainly, sir.' The robot rose unsteadily to its feet, stretched himself again and waggled each foot in turn.

Norman watched in sheer exaltation as his other self performed its first task. The tea was exactly as he would have made it himself. 'You will pardon me if I don't join you, sir,' said the pseudo-shopkeeper, 'but I do not feel at all thirsty.'

At a little after three p.m., Pooley and Omally left the Flying Swan. As the two friends strode off down the Ealing Road, Neville the part-time barman shot home the brass bolts and padded away to his quarters. The floor boards groaned suspiciously beneath his tread but Neville, now buoyed up with a half-bottle of Bells, closed his ears to them.

'Right then,' said Omally, 'to business, it is yet three p.m. and we have not earned a penny.'

'I have missed the bookies,' said Jim. 'I am a hundred thousand pounds down already.'

'The day may yet be saved, positive thinking is your man. To work then.'

Pooley shook his head and departed gloomily down Albany Road, en route for the allotment. Omally squared up his shoulders and entered Norman's corner shop. Behind the counter stood Norman, idly thumbing through a copy of *Wet Girls In The Raw*. Beneath the counter crouched another Norman, chuckling silently into his hands.

'Afternoon, Norman,' said Omally. 'Packet of reds if you please, and a half-ounce of Golden.'

The mechanical confectioner cleared his throat with a curiously mechanical coughing sound. 'Certainly, sir,' said he, turning away to seek out these articles from their niches. Below the counter Norman clicked his tongue in silent displeasure. Above the counter Omally's hand had snaked into the peppermint rack and drew a packet away to his trouser pocket. Norman would have to chalk that one up to experience and punch a few more defence mechanisms into the machine's computer banks. He scribbled a hurried note on to a discarded ice-cream wrapper and awaited developments. He did not have to wait long.

'Stick them on my slate please, Norm,' said Omally.

'Pardon me, sir?'

'On my slate, I'll settle up with you later.'

'I regret, sir, that I cannot allow you to leave the premises without having first paid for the goods. Such is the way with commerce, you understand.' Below the counter, Norman chewed upon his knuckles. This was much better. He patted his creation upon the trouser knee and gave it the old thumbs up. 'Please do not ask for credit, sir,' said the robot, 'as a smack in the mouth so often offends.'

'What?' Omally surveyed the shopkeeper with open horror, this was not the way business was done. Not the way it had been done for the last fifteen years. He did not expect to actually leave the shop without paying, unless, of course, he caught Norman on one of those occasions when he had been testing his home-made sprout beer. But this? Omally pushed back his flat cap and tugged at his curly forelock. Was this simply some new ploy perhaps? Maybe Norman had been reading some American magazine about self-assertion or the like? He would play it along. 'My knees ache something wicked,' he said, changing the subject.

A mystified look appeared upon the robot-Norman's face. 'I am sorry to hear that, sir,' said he, sympathetically.

'It is the cycling I believe,' John continued, 'constantly forcing the pedals round and around and around. I would be lost without the bike of course, as it is my only means of transport, but I do believe that the physical effort required by the cycling is slowly crippling me.'

The robot-Norman shook his head sadly. 'That is a pity,' he sighed.

'Yes, if only there was some alternative to be had for the eternal pedalling. Around and around and around.' Omally's hand made the appropriate movements in the air. 'If you know what I mean.'

The sub-counter Norman nodded, he was already way ahead of him. The duplicate, however, seemed not to have grasped it as yet. 'Could you not possibly trade in the bike for a car or something?' he suggested.

'A car?' Omally looked askance at the shopkeeper. 'A car? How long have you known me, Norman?'

The Irishman did not hear the purring of cogs and the eshing of computer mechanisms as the robot sought out the answer to this question.

'Precisely fifteen years two months and nine days,' he said. 'You were, if I recall, wearing the same cap and trousers.'

'And do you suppose that a man who is still wearing this cap and trousers is the sort of man who could afford to buy a car?'

'I have not given the matter any thought as yet, sir,' said the robot. 'But if you like I will apply myself to it whilst you are paying for your purchases.'

Omally chewed upon his lip; he did not like the smell of this one little bit. 'So how goes the work then?' he asked, changing the subject yet again.

'Business is slack, as ever. The monthly returns are down again.'

'No, not the shop, I mean, your work,' Omally gestured towards the kitchenette door. 'What wonders are germinating in your little den?'

'If you will pardon me, sir,' said the robot, reaching forward, 'it is becoming apparent to me that you have no intention of paying for your purchases, would you kindly hand them back?'

'Norman, are you all right?'

The robot suddenly lunged forward across the counter and grasped Omally by a tweedy lapel.

'Be warned,' said the Irishman. 'I know Dimac.'

Beneath the counter, a sudden terror gripped the heart of the hidden shopkeeper. He had programmed the entirety of *Count Dante's Dimac Manual of Martial Arts* into his creation as a precaution against it being attacked. Omally's statement he knew well enough to be pure bravado, but he doubted that the robot would take it as such.

'Thus and so,' said the duplicate, drawing Omally from his feet, 'and hence.'

With a deft flick of an automated wrist, which the legendary Count catalogued as Move thirty-two A, The Curl of the Dark Dragon's Tail, Omally found himself catapulted through the air in a flailing backward somersault which ended in sprawling confusion amidst a tangle of magazine racks and out of date chocolate-boxes.

'You bastard,' said John, spitting and drawing back his sleeves. Norman cowered in the darkness, covering his ears. The robot climbed nimbly across the counter and stood over the fallen Irishman. 'The tobacco and papers,' said he, extending a hand.

'Come now,' said John, 'be reasonable, what is all this about? You cannot go attacking people over a packet of baccy. Have you gone mad?' Whilst the robot was considering an answer to this question, Omally struck out with a devastating blow to the shopkeeper's groin.

448

There was a sharp metallic clang and a sickening bone-splintering report. 'My God,' groaned John, falling back and gripping at his knee. 'What are you wearing, a bloody cast-iron codpiece?'

The robot was on him in a flash and, whilst Norman cowered in the darkness saying the rosary and praying desperately for the little brass wheel he had so recently set in motion to irrevocably break down, the martial duplicate lifted his struggling prize high above his head and cast him once more across the shop. This time, however, there was little to cushion Omally's fall. He struck the shop's aged front door, carrying it from its hinges, and flew out into the Ealing Road to land across the bonnet of a parked Morris Minor. It is certain that a lesser man would not possibly have survived such an assault, but Omally, momentarily numbed, merely slid down the driver's side of the car bonnet and prepared once more to come up fighting. 'Nuts and noses' his Da always told him, and it was obvious that nuts were at present out of the question.

6

Jim Pooley slouched across the St Mary's Allotments dragging Omally's pickaxe and spade. At intervals he stopped and cursed, he was sure that he had got the worst part of this deal. Omally was probably even now sitting in Norman's kitchenette sipping celery hock and discussing contracts. Somehow John always came out on top and he was left holding the smelly end of the proverbial drain rod. The fates had never favoured the Pooleys. In Jim's considered opinion the fault lay with some neolithic ancestor who had fallen out with God. It had probably been over some quite trivial matter, but as was well known, the Almighty does have an exceedingly long memory and can be wantonly vindictive once you've got his back up. Pooley cursed all his ancestors *en masse* and threw in a few of Omally's just to be on the safe side. He was making more than a three-course meal out of the prospect of a bit of spade work and he knew it. Hopefully, a few digs at the thing and it would simply crumble to dust. At worst, a blow or two from the pickaxe would hasten the action. With all the millions to be made from Norman's wheel a few meagre pennies for a buried bedframe seemed hardly worth the candle.

Pooley slouched through the allotment gates and off up Albany Road, the spade raising a fine shower of sparks along the pavement behind him. He turned into Abaddon Street and confronted the high fence of planking shielding the empty bombsite. With a heartfelt sigh Jim slid aside the hanging board which camouflaged the secret entrance, and climbed through the gap, backwards.

An ill-considered move upon his part. With a sudden strangled cry of horror Pooley vanished away through the gap. Omally's spade spun away from his fingers and tumbled downwards towards oblivion. By the happiest of chances Jim maintained his grip upon the pickaxe, whose head now jammed itself firmly across the gap. Where once there had been well-trodden ground, now there was complete and utter nothing. The bomb-site had simply ceased to exist. Jim was swinging precariously by a pickaxe handle over the sheer edge of a very very large pit indeed. It was the big daddy of them all, and as Jim turned terrified eyes down to squint between his dangling feet, he had the distinct impression that he was staring into the black void of space.

'Help!' wailed Jim Pooley, who was never slow on the uptake when he discovered his life to be in jeopardy. 'Fallen man here, not waving, but drowning ... HELP!' Jim swung desperate feet towards the wall of the chasm, his hobnails scratched and scrabbled at the sheer cliff face but failed to find a purchase. 'Oh woe,' said Jim. 'Oh, help!'

A sickening report above drew Jim's attention. It seemed that the elderly head of Omally's pickaxe was debating as to whether this would be as good a time as any to part company with its similarly aged shaft. 'Oooooooh noooo!' shrieked Jim as he sank a couple of inches nearer to kingdom-come. Pooley closed his eyes and made what preparations he could, given so little time, to meet his Maker. Another loud crack above informed Jim that the pickaxe had made up his mind. The handle snapped away from the shaft and Jim was gone.

Or at least he most definitely would have been, had not a pair of muscular hands caught at his trailing arms and drawn him aloft, rending away his tweedy jacket sleeves from both armpits. A white-faced and gibbering Jim Pooley was dragged out through the gap in the fencing and deposited in a tangled heap upon the pavement.

'You are trespassing,' said a voice somewhere above him. 'These are your jacket sleeves, I believe.'

Jim squinted up painfully from his pavement repose. Above him stood as pleasant a looking angel of deliverance as might be imagined. He was tall and pale, with a shock of black hair combed away behind his ears. His eyes were of darkest jet, as was his immaculate one-piece coverall work suit. He wore a pair of miniscule headphones which he now pushed back from his ears. Jim could hear the tinkling of fairy-like music issuing from them.

'I was passing and I heard your cries,' the young man explained. 'You were trespassing you know.'

Jim climbed gracelessly to his feet and patted the dust from what was left of his jacket. He accepted the sleeves from the young man and stuffed them into a trouser pocket. 'Sorry,' said he. 'I had no idea. My thanks, sir, for saving my life.'

'It is no matter,' said the young man. 'Had you fallen you might have damaged some valuable equipment.'

'Oh, thanks very much.'

'It is no matter. This site has been acquired and excavated for a new complex to be built. Lateinos and Romiith Limited.'

'Oh, those lads.' Pooley blew on to the scorched palms of his hands. The 'Acquired For Lateinos and Romiith' signs had been blossoming upon all manner of vacant plots in Brentford recently, and the black-glazed complexes had been springing up overnight, like dark mushrooms. Exactly who Lateinos and Romiith were, nobody actually knew, but that they were very big in computers was hinted at. 'Don't let the marker posts on your allotment fall down,' folks said, 'or the buggers will stick a unit on it.'

'Well again, my thanks,' said Jim. 'I suppose you didn't see anything of an old bedframe while your lads were doing the excavations?'

'Bedframe?' The young man suddenly looked very suspicious indeed.

'Well, never mind. Listen, if you are ever in the Swan I would be glad to stand you a pint or two. Not only did you save my life but you saved me a good deal of unnecessary labour.' Pooley made as to doff his cap, but it was now many hundreds of feet beneath his reach. Cursing silently at Omally, he said, 'Thank you, then, and farewell.' Snatching up Omally's pickaxe head, he shambled away down Abaddon Street leaving the young man staring after him wearing a more than baffled expression.

Jim thought it best to return Omally's axehead at once to his allotment shed before any more harm could come to it. He also thought it best not to mention the matter of the spade, which having been one of Omally's latest acquisitions was something of a favourite with him. Possibly then, it would be a good idea to slip around to Norman's and stick his nose once more against the kitchenette window.

As Jim came striding over the allotment ground, pickaxe head over shoulder and 'Whistle while you Work' doing that very thing from between his lips, he was more than a little surprised to discover Omally in his shirt-sleeves, bent over the zinc water-butt, dabbing at his tender places. 'John?' said Jim.

Omally looked up fearfully at the sounds of Jim's approach. His right eye appeared to have a Victoria plum growing out of it. 'Jim,' said John.

'You have been in a fight.'

'Astute as ever I see.'

'Outnumbered? How many of them, three, four?'

'Just the one.'

'Not from around these parts then. Circus strongman was it? Sumo wrestler? Surely not . . .' Pooley crossed himself, 'Count Dante himself?'

'Close,' said Omally, feeling at his jaw, which had developed a most alarming click. 'Corner-shopkeeper, actually.'

Pooley hastily secreted the pickaxe head behind his back, turned over a handy bucket, and sat upon it. 'Not Norman? You jest, surely?'

'Look at my shirt-collar.' Omally waggled the frayed relic which now hung over his shoulder, college scarf fashion.

'Aren't they supposed to be sewn on all the way round?'

'I will punish him severely for this.'

'You fancy your chances at a rematch then?'

Omally shook his head painfully and whistled. 'Not I. Certainly the man has been personally schooled in the brutal, maiming, disfiguring art of Dimac by none other than that very Grand Master of the craft to whom you formerly alluded.'

'Gosh,' said Jim.

'I will have him down from a distance when he comes out to take in his milk tomorrow.'

'The half-brick?'

'Nothing less. I feel that we can forget all about ever-spinning wheels for the time being. Still all is not yet lost. How did you fare with the bed?' Omally peered over Jim's shoulder. 'Got it locked away somewhere safe then?'

Pooley scraped his heels in the dust.

'What have you done with the bed, Jim, and where are the sleeves of your jacket?'

'Ah,' said Jim, 'ah now.'

7

Norman sat in his kitchenette, dismally regarding the slim brass wheel spinning once more upon its table-top mountings. Over in the corner alcove his other self sat lifeless and staring, a gaping hole in its chest. Norman swung his leg over the kitchen chair and leaned his arms upon its worm-eaten back. The first run had not been altogether a roaring success. If Omally's bike had not chosen to intervene and trip the robot into the street, there seemed little doubt that it would have killed Omally there and then, merely to retrieve the tobacco from his pocket.

Norman chewed upon his lip. It was a regular Frankenstein's monster, that one. Not what he'd had in mind at all. Placid pseudo-shopkeeper he wanted, not psychotic android on the rampage. He would have to disconnect all the Dimac circuits and pep up the old goodwill-to-mankind modules. Possibly it was simply the case that the robot had been a little over-enthusiastic. After all, it had had his interests at heart. Norman shuddered. Omally had got away with the tobacco, and Hairy Dave had charged him fifty quid to shore up the front of the shop and screw a temporary door into the splintered frame. The robot had not been in service more than a couple of hours and it was already bankrupting him. Fifty quid for a half-ounce of Golden. And what if Omally decided to sue or, more likely, to exact revenge. It didn't bear thinking of. He would have to go round to the Swan later and apologize, stand Omally a few pints of consolation. More expense. The harassed shopkeeper climbed from his chair and sought out a quart of home-made sprout wine from the bottle-rack beneath the sink.

At length the Memorial Library clock chimed five-thirty p.m. in the distance, and upon the Swan's doorstep stood two bedraggled

454

figures who, like Norman, had the drowning of their sorrows very much to the forefronts of their respective minds. Neville the part-time barman drew the polished bolts and swung open the famous door.

'By Magog!' said the pagan barkeep. 'Whatever has happened to you two? Should I call an ambulance?'

Pooley shook his head. 'Merely draw the ales.'

With many a backwards glance, Neville lumbered heavily away to the pumps. 'But what has happened to you both? Your eye, John? And Jim, your sleeves?' Neville pushed two brimming pints across the counter towards the straining hands of his two patrons.

'We were mugged,' said Omally, who was finding it hard to come to terms with the concept of defeat at the hands of a humble shopkeeper.

'Ten of them,' Pooley added. He had once read of a mugger's victim being carried into a pub and revived with free ale.

Neville had also read of it and took up a glass to polish. 'We live in troubled times,' he said profoundly. 'Ten and six please.'

Omally drew his boot away from his bruised ankle and pulled out several pound notes. Neville, who had never before seen the Irishman handling paper money in public, was anxious to see if they were the real McCoy. The wrinkled relic John handed him smelt a bit pony, but it did have a watermark. Neville rang up 'No Sale' and obligingly short-changed his customer. Omally slung the pennies into his trouser pocket without even checking them.

'Mugged then is it?' Neville almost felt guilty. 'Did you best the villains?'

'Did we?' Pooley raised his scorched palm and made chopping movements. 'The blackguards will think twice about molesting the folk of Brentford again I can tell you.'

'I see Norman is having his shopfront done up,' said Old Pete, who had sneaked in hard upon the heels of the two warriors.

Omally spluttered into his beer. 'Is that a fact?' said he.

'Had his shopfront mugged so I hear.'

'Give that gentleman a large dark rum,' said Omally.

The ancient accepted his prize and slunk away to a side-table with much malicious chuckling. Omally grudgingly paid up and joined Pooley, who had taken to hiding in a suitably darkened corner.

'I shan't be able to live with this,' said John, seating himself.

'That old one knows already; it will be all over the parish by morning.'

'But Norman?' said Pooley. 'I still can't quite believe it. Norman wouldn't hurt a spider, and by God his shop gives lodging to enough.'

'A lover of the insect kingdom he may be, but let humankind beware. The shopkeeper has finally lost his marbles. He took it out of me as though violence was going out of fashion.'

Jim sighed. 'This is a day I should certainly choose to forget. We have both paid dearly for our greed.'

John nodded thoughtfully. 'I suppose there are lessons to be learned from it. We have certainly learned ours the hard way.'

'Talking of lessons, I think your homework has just arrived.' Jim pointed over Omally's shoulder to where Norman now stood squinting about the bar.

John sank low in his high-backed chair. 'Has he seen me?' he whispered.

Pooley nodded. 'I'm afraid so, he's coming over.'

'When you hit him go for his beak, ignore the groin.'

'I'm not going to hit him, this is nothing to do with me.'

'Nothing to do with you? You started it, you and your money-making wheel . . .'

'Evening gents,' said Norman.

'Evening to you, old friend,' said Pooley, smiling sweetly.

Omally rummaged in his pockets and brought out a crumpled packet of cigarette papers and a somewhat banjoed half-ounce of tobacco. 'I never smoked it,' he said. 'You can have it back if you still want it.'

Norman held up his hand, which made Omally flinch painfully. 'No, no, I have come to apologize. I really don't know what came over me, to lose my temper like that. I have been working too hard lately, I have a lot of worries. There is no permanent damage done, I trust?'

'I am still in a state of shock.' Omally sensed possibilities. 'Numb all over. I suspect a fracture here and there, though. I'll be off work a good while I shouldn't wonder.'

Norman nodded good-naturedly. Omally would be wanting his pound of flesh, better get it over with in one go. 'Might I buy you a drink?' he asked.

'You might,' said Omally, 'and we will see where it leads. If you

456

could manage one for my companion also it would not go un-appreciated.'

Norman smiled. He wondered whether or not to ask Pooley where the sleeves of his jacket were, but he presupposed the answer to be of a somewhat poignant nature, evoking images of such hardship and tragedy as to morally oblige the asker to purchase many further pints. 'I'll get the round in then,' said Norman, departing to the bar.

'One pint and one half-ounce up,' said John bleakly. 'What profit the day, I ask you?'

'Perk up, John, it can only get better, surely.' Pooley now sighted Old Pete hobbling purposefully towards them. 'Or possibly not.'

'Where's my bed then?' the ancient asked, prodding Omally's bruised shoulderblade with his stick. 'I've brought the money.'

'Money?' John did not recall mentioning a figure. 'How much did you bring?'

'Twenty quid.'

'Twenty quid.' Omally buried his face in his hands.

'It's enough, isn't it? You said it was an antique. I think twenty quid's a fair price if it's a good one. So where's my bed?'

'What bed?' asked Norman, who was bringing up the drinks.

'Omally said he had an antique bedstead to sell me, I want to see it.'

'The muggers took it,' said Jim Pooley helpfully. Omally, who was just coming to terms with a ten pound down payment for an antique bedstead at present being refurbished by mythical up-holsterers, looked up at him in horror. 'Sorry,' said Jim, shrugging innocently.

'What muggers?' asked Norman.

'The ten who blacked his eye, or did you say there were twelve, John?'

'Ah,' said Norman stroking his chin. 'Come to think of it, I did see a gang of bully boys pushing an antique bed along down by the half-acre. Thought it odd at the time. A right evil-looking bunch they were, wouldn't have dared tackle them myself. No fighter me.'

'Bah,' snarled Old Pete. 'You're all bloody mad.' Turning upon his heel, he muttered a few well-chosen obscenities, and shuffled away.

'Thanks,' said Omally when the ancient was beyond earshot. 'I suppose that calls us square.'

457

'Good.' Norman passed the two newly-retired bedsalesmen their pints. 'Then, if you will pardon me, I think I will go and have a word with Old Pete. I have an old brass bed in my lock-up he might be interested in. The money will go somewhere towards meeting the cost of a new shopdoor. So all's well that ends well, eh? Every cloud has a silver lining and a trouble shared is a friend indeed.' With the briefest of goodbyes, Norman left the two stunned drinkers staring after him.

After a short yet very painful silence Omally spoke. 'You and your bloody big mouth,' said he.

Pooley turned up his ruined palms helplessly. 'Still,' he said, 'your reputation is saved at least.'

'You buffoon. There is no reputation worth more than five pounds and the man who is five pounds to credit needs no reputation whatever.'

'Ah well, let's look on the bright side. I think I can say without any fear of contradiction that nothing else can possibly happen to us today.'

It is of some small consequence to note that had Jim been possessed of that rare gift of foresight, even to the degree of a few short hours, he would certainly not have made that particular, ill-considered and totally inaccurate remark.

8

Brentford's only cinema, the Electric Alhambra, had closed its doors upon an indifferent public some fifty years ago. The canny Brentonians had shunned it from the word go, realizing that moving pictures were nothing more than a flash in the pan. Miraculously, the building had remained intact, playing host to a succession of small industries which had sprung up like mushrooms and died like mayflies. The last occupier, a Mr Doveston, Purveyor of Steam-Driven Appliances to the Aristocracy, had weathered it out for a full five years before burning his headed notepaper and vanishing with the smoke.

Now the crumbling edifice, about the size of the average scout hut and still sporting its original mock rococo stuccoed façade, was left once more alone with its memories. The projection room, which had served as governor's office to many a down at heel entrepreneur, now deprived of its desks and filing cabinets, suddenly took to itself once more. With the collapse of some lop-sided partitions, the old and pitted screen made a reappearance. But for the lack of seating and the scattered debris littering the floor, the ancient cinema emerged, a musty phoenix from its fifty-year hibernation.

The 'Sold' notice was up out front and rumour had it that the dreaded Lateinos and Romiith had the place earmarked for re-development. A light evening breeze rattled a corrugated iron shutter upon a glassless window, and something that looked very much like a giant feral tom stole across the floor. In the eaves a bat awoke and whistled something in an unknown dialect.

A gaunt and fragile shadow fell across an expanse of littered linoleum and a pale hand moved into a patch of light. Ghostly fingers drew away a cowled hood, revealing a head of pure white hair, an expanse of pallid forehead, and two eyes which glowed pinkly in the failing light. Surely we have seen this pale hand before? Known the Jason's fleece of snowy hair, and marvelled at the flesh coloured eyes? Can this be he who now dwells beneath, shunning the realm of sunlight and changing seasons? He who tills the subterranean waters in his search for Shamballa and its legendary dwellers in that world of forever night? Yes, there can be no doubt. The name of this seeker after the hidden truths below is well known to the folk of Brentford.

Soap Distant, it is he.

Soap spat his roll-up from between his teeth and ground it to oblivion beneath a boot-heel. He scrutinized the luminous chronometer upon his wrist and said, 'Ten thirty-two. They'll be a while yet.' He paced slowly to and fro, his shadow clattering soundlessly along the corrugated shutters to merge with the blackness as he moved beyond the range of the limited illumination. At length, his chronometer chimed the three-quarter hour, and Soap ceased his pacing. From without came sounds of approaching feet. Harsh footfalls echoing along the deserted street, accompanied by the sounds of foolish giggling and the occasional bout of coughing. 'Pissed again,' said Soap to himself, 'but no matter.'

The inebriated couple, one with a fat eye and the other sleeveless, came to a halt outside the cinema, and Soap could make out snatches of conversation that penetrated the numerous cracks in the wall.

'Who's on then?' asked a voice. 'Where's my opener?'

'William S. Hart,' said another. 'Open it with your teeth.'

'I never could abide that body's hat. I was always an Elmo Lincoln man myself. Christ, there goes a filling. You've got my opener, I remember you borrowing it.'

'I gave it back. Stand aside man, I need a quick jimmy.'

'Not in my doorway!' Soap threw open the shattered glass door to admit a stumbling Jim Pooley, flies gaping.

'By the grave,' said that man.

'By the roadside, but not in my doorway.'

Omally squinted towards the dark void which had suddenly swallowed up his companion. 'Soap?' said he. 'Soap Distant? I know that voice.'

'Come in out of the night, and pick your friend up.'

Omally bumbled in and Soap slammed shut the door upon the Brentford night and, as far as John and Jim were concerned, life as they had once known it.

'Where's the bog?' wailed Pooley, struggling to his feet.

'Stick it out through a crack in the wall and be done.'

Pooley did so.

'How would you two care to make thirty quid for a swift half-hour's work?' Soap asked when Jim had finished his micturition.

Omally was about to say 'Each?' but after his experiences this day he thought better of it. 'I think that we would be very grateful,' he said. 'This has been a bad day for us both, financially.'

'If it is decorating,' said Jim, 'I do not feel that half an hour will be sufficient.'

'It is not decorating, it is a little matter, below.'

'Below . . . ah, well now.' Both Pooley and Omally had in chapters past had very bad experiences 'below'.

'Are you sure this is safe?' queried Omally.

'As houses.'

Pooley was more than doubtful. Sudden chill memories of former times spent beneath the surface of the globe flooded over him in an icy-black tide. 'You can have my half, John,' he said, 'I think I'll get an early night in.'

'It will take the two of you I am afraid.' Soap raised his palms in the gloom. 'It is a simple matter. One man cannot move an object, three men can.'

'Things are rarely as simple as they at first appear,' said Pooley with a wisdom older than his years.

'Come below then.'

With that, a thin line of wan light appeared in the centre of the floor, growing to a pale square illuminating a flight of stairs. Soap led the way down. 'Follow me,' he said gaily.

Pooley sucked upon a knuckle and, like the now legendary musical turn, dilly-dallied on the way. Omally nudged him in the back. 'Thirty quid,' he said.

Soap's newly-hired work-force followed him down the stairway, and above them the trapdoor slammed shut with what is referred to in condemned circles as a 'death-cell finality'. The stairway, as might be imagined, led ever down, its passageway hewn from the living rock. At length it unexpectedly debouched into a pleasant looking sitting-room, furnished with a pale green Waterford settee and matching armchairs, and decorated with Laura Ashley wallpaper. 'Nice, eh?' said Soap as he divested himself of his ankle-length cloak to reveal a natty line in three-piece tweed wear.

'Very,' said John. 'And the Russell Flints?' He pointed to a brace of pictures which hung above the hearth. 'No expense spared.'

'A gift from Professor Slocombe,' said Soap.

Pooley, who had a definite sway on, sank into a comfortable armchair.

'We have a couple of bottles of brown with us,' said John. 'If you have an opener?'

'It's a bit close down here.' Pooley fanned at his brow.

'It was a bit close down that hole today, wasn't it, Jim?' Soap popped the stoppers from the bottles and ignored Pooley's similarly popping eyes.

'How did you know?'

'There's not much that goes on beneath ground level that I don't know something of. Those buggers from Lateinos and Romiith have been making my life a misery lately, sinking their damned foundations every which way about the parish.'

'Progress,' said Pooley in a doomed tone.

'Some say,' said Soap. 'Listen now, let us dispense with brown ale. I have some home-brewed mushroom brandy which I think you might find interesting.'

'That would be a challenge.'

''Tis done then.'

Something over an hour later, three very drunken men were to be found some three miles beneath the surface of planet Earth a-rowing in a leathern coracle over a stretch of ink-black subterranean water.

'Where are we?' asked an Irish surface-dweller.

'Below the very heart of London.'

'I don't recognize it.'

The splish-splash of the oars echoed about the vast cavern, eventually losing itself in the endless silence of the pit.

'How do you know which way we're going?'

Soap pointed to his luminous watch. 'Lodestone,' he said informatively.

'Oh, that lad.'

'There,' said Soap suddenly. 'Dead ahead, land ho.'

Before them in the distance an island loomed and as they drew nearer, the makings of a mausoleum wrought in marble, very much after the style of the Albert Memorial, made itself apparent.

'What is it?' Omally asked. 'King Arthur's tomb, don't tell me.'

Soap tapped at his all but transparent nose. The coracle beached upon the shoreline and Soap stepped out to secure it to a frescoed pillar. The two inebriate sub-earth travellers shrugged and followed the pale man as he strode forward. 'It was never like this for Jerome K Jerome,' said Pooley.

The strange edifice was, if anything, a work of inspiration. Marble pilasters, cunningly wrought with carved tracery-work, soared upwards to dwindle into a high-domed ceiling which glittered with golden mosaic. Above, tapering gothic spires lost themselves in the darkness.

'Here it is,' said Soap. The two wonderers halted in their tracks. In the very centre of this Victorian folly stood something so totally out of place as to take the breath from their lungs. It was a cylinder of bright sparkling metal, but it was of no metal that any man of Earth had yet seen. It glistened with an oily sheen and swam through a spectrum of colours, reflecting mirror-like. A broad panel of what might have been glass, but probably was not, lay set into a section of the cylinder's apparent lid, and it was over this that the three visitors to this sunken marvel craned their necks.

'Strike me down,' said Jim Pooley.

'By Michael and the other lads,' said John Omally.

'Good, eh?' said Soap Distant.

'But who is he?'

Beneath the glazed panel, reclining upon satin cushioning, his head upon a linen pillow, lay the body of a man. He was of indeterminate age, his hair jet-black and combed away behind his ears. He had high cheek-bones and a great hawk of a nose. The face bore an indefinable grandeur, one of ancient aristocracy. From what was immediately visible, he appeared to be wearing a high wing-collared shirt, dark tie affixed with a crested stud, and a silken dressing-gown.

'He seems, almost, well, alive,' said Omally.

Soap pointed towards the gowned chest, and it could be clearly observed that it slowly rose and fell. 'Indubitably,' said he.

'But this thing? Who built it and why?'

'Best thing is to up the lid and ask him.'

Pooley had more than a few doubts upon this score. 'He looks pretty peaceful to me,' he said. 'Best to leave him alone. No business of ours this.'

'I think somehow that it is,' said Soap, and his tone left little doubt that he did.

'This thing doesn't belong,' said Omally. 'It is all wrong. Victorian mausoleum all well and good, but this? This is no product of our age even.'

'Herein lies the mystery,' said Soap. 'Give us a hand then, thirty quid for a quick heave.'

Pooley shook his head so vigorously that it made him more dizzy than he already was. 'I think not, Soap. We are tampering with something which is none of our business. Only sorrow will come out of it, mark my words. "He that diggeth a pit will fall . . ."'

'I know all that,' said Soap. 'Kindly take hold of the top end. I had it giving a little.'

'Not me,' said Jim, folding his arms.

'Jim,' said John. 'Do you know the way back?'

'That way.' Pooley pointed variously about.

'I see. And do you think that Soap will guide us if we do not assist him?'

'Well, I . . .'

'Top end,' said Soap. 'I had it giving a little.'

The three men applied themselves to the lid of the glistening cylinder, and amidst much grunting, puffing, and cursing, there was a sharp click, a sudden rushing of air, and a metallic clang as the object of their efforts tumbled aside to fall upon the marble flooring of the *outré* construction. Three faces appeared once more over the rim of the metal sarcophagus.

The gaunt man lay corpse-like but for his gently-heaving chest; his face was placid and without expression. Then suddenly the eyelids snapped wide, the lips opened to draw in a great gulp of air and the chest rose higher than before. A cry arose from his mouth and three faces ducked away to reappear as a prial of Chads, noses crooked above the coffin's edge. The occupant stretched up his arms and yawned loudly. His eyes flickered wildly about. He snatched at the coffin's side, and drew himself up. He caught sight of the three now-cowering men, and a look of perplexity clouded his face. 'What year is this?' he demanded.

Omally volunteered the information.

'Too early, you have broken the seal.'

'Told you,' said Jim. 'Leave well enough alone I said. But does anybody ever listen to me, do they . . .?'

'Shut up,' said Soap, 'and kindly give me a hand.' With the aid of Omally he helped the bemused-looking man in the dressing-gown

464

up from the steely cylinder and into the upright position. 'Are you feeling yourself now?' The tall man, as now he revealed himself to be, did not reply, but simply stood stretching his limbs and shaking his head. 'Come quickly now,' said Soap. 'We must take him at once to Professor Slocombe.'

The journey back was to say the very least uneventful. The gaunt man in the dressing-gown sat staring into space while Omally, under Soap's direction, applied himself to the oars. Pooley, who had by now given up the ghost, slept soundly; his dreams full of six-horse accumulators coming up at stupendous odds and rocketing him into the super-dooper tax bracket. Of a sudden, these dreams dissolved as Omally dug him firmly in the ribs and said, 'We are going up.'

They made a strange procession through Brentford's night-time streets. The pale ghost of a man, now once more clad in a cloak and hood, leading a striking figure in a silk dressing-gown, and followed by two stumbling, drunken bums. Vile Tony Watkins who ran the Nocturnal Street Cleaning truck watched them pass, and a few swear words of his own invention slipped from between his dumb lips.

As the four men entered the sweeping tree-lined drive which swept into the Butts Estate, one lone light glowed in the distance, shining from Professor Slocombe's ever-open French windows.

The odd party finally paused before the Professor's garden door and Omally pressed his hand to the bolt. Through the open windows all could view the venerable scholar as he bent low over the manuscripts and priceless books. As they drew nearer he set his quill pen aside and turned to greet them.

'So,' said he, rising with difficulty from his leather chair. 'Visitors at such a late hour. And to what do I owe the pleasure?'

'Sorry to interrupt your work,' said Omally, who was now at the vanguard. 'But we have, well, how shall I put it . . .?'

The tall man in the dressing-gown thrust his way past Omally and stood framed in the doorway. A broad smile suddenly broke out upon his bleak countenance. 'Professor,' said he. 'We meet again.'

'My word,' said the other. 'This is a most pleasant if unexpected surprise.'

The tall man stepped forward and wrung the ancient's hand between his own.

'You mean you know who he is?' asked Omally incredulously. Pooley was supporting himself upon the door-frame.

'Have you not been formally introduced?' enquired the Professor. Omally shook his head. 'Then allow me to do the honours. Soap Distant, John Omally, Jim Pooley, gentlemen, it is my pleasure to present Mr Sherlock Holmes, formerly of 221b Baker Street.'

'Your servant,' said that very man.

9

Professor Slocombe closed and bolted the long shutters upon his French windows. When his guests had seated themselves, he moved amongst them, distributing drinks and cigarettes. Sherlock Holmes lounged in a high leather-backed fireside chair and accepted a Turkish cigarette. 'My thanks, Professor,' said he. 'I see that you still favour the same brand.'

The Professor smiled and seated himself. 'I think that we have much to speak of, Sherlock. Your arrival here, although bringing me untold joy at the pleasure of meeting once more a noble friend, is, to say the least, a little perplexing.'

Holmes drew deeply upon his cigarette and blew out a plume of light blue smoke. 'It is a singular business and no mistake.'

Pooley and Omally, who had been shaking their heads in disbelief and generally making with the rumbles of suspicion, gave the thing up and slumped in their seats sipping liquor.

'It all truly began,' said Holmes, 'one foggy November night back in Eighteen-ninety. The previous month had been a successful one for me, having solved the remarkable case of the Naval Treaty and been more than adequately rewarded by Lord Holdhurst. I was experiencing a brief period of inactivity and as you will recall, such spells are no good to me. My soul as ever ached for the thrill of the chase, the challenge of pitting one's wits against some diabolic adversary, the blood coursing through the temples, the rushing of . . .'

'Quite so,' said Professor Slocombe. 'Your enthusiasm for your work is well-recorded. Upon this particular evening, however?'

'Yes, well, Watson and I had, I recall, just partaken of one of Mrs Hudson's most palatable tables of roast beef, and were setting towards consuming the last of a fine bottle of Vamberry's

Port, when there came a violent knocking upon our chambers' door.'

'Probably the raven,' said Omally sarcastically.

'Do you mind?' said Professor Slocombe.

Holmes continued. 'I had heard no rappings upon the front door and knowing that Mrs Hudson was below in the kitchen was put immediately upon my guard. I had many enemies at that time you must understand. I counselled Watson to open the door whilst I remained at my chair, my revolver upon my knee, covered with a napkin.'

'Exciting so far isn't it?' said Pooley, yawning loudly.

'Riveting,' said Omally.

Holmes continued once more. 'The two figures who revealed themselves upon the door's opening were quite unlike any I have before encountered. I pride myself that I can accurately deduce the background and occupation of any man set before me, but those two left me baffled. They were tall and angular with almond-shaped eyes and oriental features. When they spoke I found their accents totally alien. Watson permitted them ingress into our rooms and although they refused both food and drink, saying that such were impossible for them, what they had to say was precise and to the point. They had come from the future, they said, naming a year well in advance of this. The world they came from was vastly different from that I inhabited, but they were adamant in offering few details. They were perplexed by a problem of utmost import which required the deductive reasoning of a mind their century did not possess. They had read in their history books of my humble exploits and felt I was the man to tackle the task. Was I willing?

'As you can imagine, I was more than doubtful and demanded some proof of their claims. What they showed me was more than adequate to convince me that they told no lie.'

'So what are you doing here?' asked Professor Slocombe. 'You should surely be away into the future by now.'

'No,' said Holmes. 'You must understand that their sophisticated equipment enabled them to traverse the fields of time in an instant, but it was not possible for them to take a being from the past forward into the future with them. I would have simply crumbled to dust upon my arrival. They were more subtle than this. They arranged for a secret place to be built for me where I might be placed in suspended animation. They would then travel forward in their time-eliminating conveyance, and unearth and resuscitate me almost on the instant.'

'Ingenious,' said the Professor, turning towards Soap Distant.

'How was I to know?' complained Soap.

'Well,' said the Professor, 'simply consider this a pleasurable stop off along your journey.'

'I think not,' said Holmes. 'Mr Distant here has broken the seal and disabled the means of my travel through time. Unless you happen to know of someone who can reset the apparatus, I would appear to be trapped.'

Professor Slocombe scratched at his head. 'That might present some problems,' said he. 'Although there is always the thought that your visitors are already in the far future discovering your loss and even now are setting back to search for you.'

'Such is, of course, the case, but they might search for a century and not find me.'

'What a load of old rubbish,' said Omally suddenly rising from his seat. 'Come, Jim, let us away to our beds.'

Pooley climbed to his feet. 'Be fair, Professor,' said he. 'This is all a bit too much over the top. I know that the world is always ready and waiting for one more Sherlock Holmes story, but this is pushing credibility to the very limit.'

'Do you doubt who I am?' Holmes rose to his full height and stood glaring at the deuce of Thomases.

'Be fair,' said Pooley, 'this is very far-fetched. You are at the very least extremely fictional in nature.'

'I am as fictional as you,' said Sherlock Holmes.

'Ha,' said Pooley. 'If you are the legendary doyen of detectives, answer me some questions.'

'Proceed.'

'All right then, what are the thirty-nine steps?'

'Wrong story,' said John Omally.

'Ah, well ... In "The Red-Headed League" how did you know Vincent Spaulding was actually John Clay the murderer, thief, forger, and smasher?'

'By the white splash of acid on his forehead and his pierced ears.'

'Who lost his hat and his goose in "The Blue Carbunkle"?'

'Henry Baker.'

'What was the Musgrave Ritual?'

'Who was it? He who is gone. Who shall have it? He who will

469

come. What is the month? Sixth from the first. Where is the sun? Over the oak. What was the shadow? . . .'

'Right, right, under the elm, we know.'

'Who was the Norwood Builder?' Jim asked.

'Jonas Oldacre.'

'And the Three Students?'

'Gilchrist, Danlat Ras and Miles McLaren.'

'And the plumber engaged to Charles Augustus Milverton's housemaid?'

'Myself,' said Holmes.

'Well you could have read them. I always believed that Holmes really did go over the Riechenbach Falls with Professor Moriarty. Those later stories were the work of a stand-in, I thought.'

'Bravo,' said Holmes. 'You are, of course, correct. You must understand that a certain amount of subterfuge was necessary to cover my disappearance. My exploits were chronicled by Doctor Watson, through an arrangement we had with a Mr Conan Doyle. I left it to him to continue with the stories after my supposed death.'

'Hang on,' said Pooley. 'Not that I can make any sense at all out of this, but if you went below under the pretence of dying in the Riechenbach Falls how could you possibly know about the Norwood Builder and the Three Students. That was four years later in *The Return of Sherlock Holmes*.'

'Ah,' said that man.

'Ah, indeed,' said Professor Slocombe. 'And Milverton's plumber?'

'Detective's license?' Holmes suggested.

'I give up,' said John Omally.

'Me also,' said Jim.

10

An inexpensive veneer of sunlight was thinly varnishing the rooftops of Brentford as Norman Hartnell took up the bundle of daily papers from his doorstep and hefted them on to his counter.

The early morning was always Norman's favourite time of the day. The nights were hell, for whilst his body slept upon its Hartnell Mark II Hydrocosipit, his brain went on the rampage, plotting, planning, and formulating, driving him on and on towards more preposterous and unattainable goals. But in the early mornings he could find just a little peace. He could peruse the daily papers as he numbered them up for delivery. He was in the privileged position of ever being the first in the parish to know the news.

On this particular morning, after a very rough night with his capricious cerebellum, Norman sliced away the twine bindings of the paper bundle with his reproduction Sword of Boda paperknife, eager to see what the rest of the world had been up to. As he tore the brown paper covering aside and delved into the top copy a singularly interesting piece met his eye, almost as if it had been simply waiting there to do so: GOVERNMENT GIVES RIGHT-HAND PLAN THE BIG THUMBS UP, he read.

An all-party-sitting last night gave the Lateinos and Romiith scheme for personalized account enumeration the go-ahead. This scheme will eventually make all previous systems of monetary exchange obsolete. Through laser implantation of a personal intromagnetic computer bar code, upon either the forehead or right hand of each individual member of society, it is thought that all crimes involving monetary theft will henceforth be made impossible. Also the need for passports or any other form of identity paper will be eliminated.

Linked with Lateinos and Romiith's master computer now currently in production, the system is expected to be instituted nationally within the next six months.

Norman whistled as he weighed up the concept. It was certainly ingenious: no one could steal your money if you never carried any, or use your banker's card if they found your wallet in the street. With your own personal number printed on your forehead they'd have to cut your head off and pass it across the bank counter to get at your wealth. And with no money there would be no paperwork. No more monthly accounts, the money would pass invisibly, simply at the wave of a light-pen. The more Norman thought about it the more impressed he became. And the more miffed that he hadn't thought of it first.

He scribbled '15 Balfour' on to the first paper and turned it aside without giving the rest of the news even a cursory once-over. As it happened, there was little else but for wars and rumours of wars and a continuance of the black fly plague, so he certainly hadn't missed much.

In the curtained alcove in the kitchenette his duplicate sat staring into space and thinking absolutely nothing whatsoever.

Neville the part-time barman stirred in his pit. He blinked open his good eye and stared up at the ceiling, which unaccountably appeared to have lowered itself by a couple of inches during the night. Drawing back his continental quilt, he set a monumental foot upon the worn Axminster. He yawned, stretched and considered his hands. 'Gross,' he thought. The wrists appeared massive, swelling from his pyjama sleeves to join great five-pound hams with pork sausages glued on to them. Whatever was happening to him was doing it at an accelerated rate of knots. 'It's getting out of control,' said Neville, as to the accompaniment of groaning floorboards, he arose from his bed. He would give up eating, he told himself, live exclusively on scotch, crispbread, and the occasional lime to stave off scurvy.

Neville staggered across the floor; pictures rattled upon the wall in time with his tread, and the entire upper storey of the pub seemed dangerously near to collapse. Why would nobody admit to seeing the state he was in? It had to be part of some enormous conspiracy aimed at ousting him from the Swan. Neville pawed at his swollen skull with a preposterous forefinger. Was that it? Was it the brewery having a go? That nest of vipers? Most horrors which befell him were directly attributable to them. Possibly they were bribing his patrons to ignore his plight? Or possibly they were hypnotizing him while he slept? Neville had read of slimming courses you got on cassettes and played while you were asleep. He'd never quite figured out how you turned the tape recorder on if you were fast a-kip, but it was a thought. He would search his apartments for hidden speakers as soon as he'd had his morning shower.

He struggled to squeeze himself through the bathroom doorway. Whatever it was, he would have to suss it out pretty rapidly or the entire building was going to come down about his ears.

Old Pete ambled along the Ealing Road, his tatty half-terrier, as ever, upon his heels. He had just paid his weekly visit to each of Brentford's two sub-post offices, in order to cash the two pension cheques the post office's errant computer chose weekly to award him. 'God bless the GPO,' the old reprobate had been heard to utter upon more than one occasion.

The ancient shuffled cheerfully along, rattling his stick noisily across Mrs Naylor's front railings in a manner calculated to rudely awaken the insatiable lady librarian from her erotic dreams. Young Chips chuckled to himself and gave the lampposts a bit of first-thing nasal perusal. Norman's new paperboy bustled out of the corner-shop, the heavy bag upon his shoulders, and mounted his bike. Chips momentarily bared his teeth, but it was early yet and he hardly felt up to making the effort.

Pete steered his way between the posts supporting Norman's shopfront and thrust open the temporary door. 'Morning Norman,' said he. The shopkeeper tucked away the copy of *Donkey Capers* he had been ogling and turned to seek out Pete's weekly quota of tobacco.

'How's the bed, Pete?' he asked. 'To your satisfaction I trust?'

'Magic,' said Old Pete.

'I'm so glad. Two ounces of Ships is it?'

'And a copy of the *Mercury*.' Old Pete pushed a crisp fiver across the counter.

'Ever had a credit card, Pete?' Norman rang up the sale on his cash register.

Old Pete shook his head. 'Don't think so. I have a membership card for the British Legion, and a special doo-dad which lets me travel free on the buses, other than that . . .' Old Pete scratched his snow-capped head. 'Had a pack of nudie playing-cards I bought in Cairo during the last lot. What does it do then?'

Norman did his best to explain.

'Oh no,' said Pete. 'Never had one of those. Mind you, I've never had a bank account. You selling them now, then?'

Norman shook his head. 'I was just reading this article. It seems that they are now obsolete. The Government are taking to stamping the numbers on people's heads.'

'Don't talk rubbish,' said Old Pete. 'Here now, what is this?' He pointed to his tin of tobacco.

'What is what?'

'This.' Old Pete indicated a series of little lines imprinted upon the lid. 'They weren't there last week. What are they?'

Norman took the tin and examined it. 'That's the lads,' said he. 'Computer bar coding, it's called. That's what I was trying to explain. All commodities are now being printed with them. They tell you the price and the date you purchased the item and all that sort of thing. You pass a light-pen over them and it logs all the information straight into some master computer. The Government are simply taking the process a logical step further.'

'I don't like the smell of that,' said Old Pete. 'After all, you know when you purchased it and how much it costs, what do you need the lines for?'

Norman shrugged. 'Progress,' he said. 'We must all move with the times you know.'

'You must.' Old Pete snatched back his tobacco. 'For myself, I say a pox on the times. Now don't get me wrong, I have nothing against computers, one in particular there is which I hold in the highest esteem. But for progress in general . . .' Old Pete made the appropriate two-fingered gesture, snatched up his paper, which unbeknown to him bore a not dissimilar set of lines upon it, and shuffled from the shop.

'Daft old fogey,' said Norman to himself; but squinting around, it did occur to him that every item he had ordered during the last few weeks possessed similar markings. No doubt it was all for the common good. There could not possibly be anything sinister at the back of it, surely? No, it was all part of a great masterplan to free society of crime and bring prosperity to all. Norman went off about his business, whistling, 'The Rock Island line is a mighty fine line'.

Jim Pooley was already upon his favourite bench. He had accosted Norman's paperboy and wrung from his clammy grip a copy of the

474

Sporting Life. Yesterday had been a total disaster. His life savings, in the biscuit tin on the mantelpiece, were sadly depleted. In the dubious excitement of the night before, he and Omally had actually forgotten to ask Soap for the thirty quid. Such events were wont to dash any hopes Jim had for the future. He would simply have to pull off The Big One today and that was that.

Pooley scanned the pages in search of inspiration. Almost at once he spied out a little series of lines printed on the lower left-hand corner of the sixth page. 'Aha,' said Jim, 'a code, possibly masonic.' He recalled a discussion he had recently had with Professor Slocombe about what the ancient termed The Science of Numerology. The scholar was convinced that the answer to most if not all of existence could be divined by the study of numerical equivalents. It was all down to breaking the code. The Professor had, of course, said a great deal more at the time, but that was the general gist which Jim managed to take in. No knowledge was ever wasted upon the lad, for as his father, like Omally's, had told him somewhat obscurely when he was a lad, 'a dead bird never falls out of the nest.'

So here was a little offering, possibly a secret code, printed for the benefit of that dark order, The Bookie Brotherhood, who, as any good punter knows, are always tipped the wink in advance. Pooley turned quickly to the front page and his heart jumped for joy. It was true. He had Bob the bookie's *Sporting Life*. Oh, happy day.

'I've cracked it,' said Jim Pooley to the assortment of Brentford wildlife which watched him from the surrounding trees. The squirrels shook their heads and nudged one another. The pigeons turned their beaked faces aside and tittered into their wings. They had seen all this many times before. 'Eighteen lines,' Jim began, 'three groups of six, thick ones and thin ones; now how exactly does this work? Six six six, what might it mean?'

Pooley ran his Biro down the list of runners for the first race, six horses. The first thick line in the first group was number four. It was an outsider, the odds were enormous. Still it was worth a try. If he got it wrong today he could always steal Bob's paper again on the morrow. Jim scribbled the horse's name on to a betting-slip and applied himself to the next race. For the fourth, fifth, and sixth races, he returned to the three groups of lines and selected the second thick bar in each sequence. Satisfied that, even if he was incorrect, he had at least performed this daily task with speed and alacrity, Jim took out his exercise book and made an attempt to calculate his potential winnings. The eventual figure was so large that the last row of noughts flowed off the edge of the page. Pooley folded his betting-slip into his breast-pocket and tucked away his exercise book. 'That will do nicely thank you,' he said, leaning back upon the bench to enjoy the air.

Professor Slocombe sat taking a late breakfast with his Victorian guest. Mr Sherlock Holmes ate sparingly as he studied the day's newspaper. 'I see,' he said at length, as he pushed the tabloid aside, 'that very little has changed since my day.'

'Come now, Holmes,' said the Professor. 'More strides forward have been taken this century than during the previous five.'

'I think not.'

'And what of technological advancement, telecommunications, space travel? We possess sciences now that in your day were undreamed of.'

'And what of poverty, squalor, and cruelty? What of injustice, intolerance, and greed? Has your age of wonder succeeded in abolishing those?'

Professor Slocombe shook his head. 'Sadly, no,' said he.

'Then little has changed. If anything, these horrors have been intensified. Details which I read here would never have been made public knowledge in my time. But if what I see is typical, and such I have no reason to disbelieve, then I am appalled to find that with the resources you now possess, little has been done.'

Professor Slocombe was for once lost for words, and chewed ruefully upon a piece of toast.

'And so I am prompted to ask,' Holmes continued, 'your reason for stranding me in this most dismal age.'

The toast caught in the old man's throat and he collapsed red-faced into a violent fit of coughing.

'Come now,' said Holmes, patting him gently upon the back, 'surely you did not think to deceive me with your display of apparent surprise at my arrival? My favourite cigarettes are in your case and my tobacco in the humidor. You serve me with a Ninety-two Vamberry, by now surely a priceless vintage. I could enumerate another twenty-three such facts regarding the "singular case of the reanimated detective", but I do not believe it to be necessary. Why have you called me here, Professor?'

The scholar took a sip of coffee and dabbed at his lips with a napkin. He rose carefully from his chair and took himself over to the French windows, where he stood, his back to the detective, staring out into his wonderful garden. 'It is a bad business,' he said, without turning.

'I have no doubt of that.'

'I am not altogether certain at present as to what steps can be taken. There is very much I have to know. I cannot face it alone.'

Holmes took out his greasy, black clay pipe from the inner pocket of his dressing-gown and filled it from the Professor's humidor. 'So,' said he, 'once more we are to work together.'

'Let me show you something and then you can decide.' Professor Slocombe lead his gaunt visitor through the study door, along the elegant hall, and up the main staircase. Holmes followed the ancient up several more flights of stairs, noting well the narrow shoulders and fragile hands of the man. The Professor had not aged by a single day since last they met so very long ago.

The two were now nearly amongst the gables of the great house, and the final staircase debouched into an extraordinary room, perfectly round, and some ten or twelve feet in diameter. It was bare of furniture save for a large, circular table with a white marble top which stood at its centre and an assortment of cranks and pulleys which hung above it. The walls were painted the darkest of blacks and there was not a window to be seen. Holmes nodded approvingly, and the Professor said, 'Of course, a camera obscura. This simple device enables me to keep a close eye upon most of the parish without the trouble of leaving my house. Would you be so kind as to close the door?'

Homes did so, and the room plunged into darkness. There was a sharp click, followed by the sound of moving pulleys, and clattering chains. A blurred image appeared upon the table-top, cast down through the system of prisms linked to the uppermost lens mounted upon the Professor's roof. Slowly the image was brought into focus: it was a bird's-eye view of the Memorial Library. Before this, draped across the bench, lay Jim Pooley, evidently fast asleep. The Professor cranked away and the rooftop lens turned, the image upon the table swam up towards the High Street. It passed over Norman's corner-shop and the two observers were momentarily stunned by the sight of the shopkeeper alone in his backyard, apparently breaking up paving-stones with his bare hands.

477

'Most probably Dimac,' Professor Slocombe explained. 'It has come to be something of the vogue in Brentford.'

'I favour Barritso, as you well know,' said Holmes.

'Now,' said Professor Slocombe, as he swung the lens up to its highest mounting and passed the image along the borders of the Brentford Triangle, 'what do you see?'

Holmes cradled his chin in his right hand and watched the moving picture with great interest. 'Some trick of the light, surely?'

'But what do you see?'

Holmes plucked at a neat sideburn. 'I see a faint curtain of light enclosing the parish boundaries.'

'And what do you take it to be?'

Holmes shook his head. 'Some natural phenomenon perhaps? Something akin to the aurora borealis?'

'I think not.' The Professor closed the rooftop aperture and the room fell once more into darkness. Holmes heard the sound of a key turning in a lock, and a thin line of wan light spread into the room from a previously concealed doorway. 'This is a somewhat private chamber,' the Professor whispered as he led the detective through the opening and into a gabled gallery set in the very eaves of the roof. What light there was entered through chinks between the slates. The old man struck flame to an enamelled oil-lamp, and the golden light threw a long and cluttered garret into perspective. It was lined on either side with tall, dark filing cabinets. Bundles of bound documents, some evidently of great age, were stacked upon and about these, or spilled out from half-opened drawers.

'As you can observe, I have been following the course of this particular investigation for a good many years.'

Holmes ran his finger lightly over the waxen paper of a crumbling document exposing a seal imprinted with the date 1703. 'And all this has been amassed to the furtherance of one single goal?'

The Professor nodded. 'It is the product of many lifetimes' work and yet now, with all this behind me, I am still lost for a solution to the matter now closely pressing upon us.'

'But what is it, Professor? What have you found and what do you yet seek? Tell me how I might aid you, you have but to ask.'

'What I have here is evidence. But it is evidence of a most unique nature, for it is evidence of a crime which is yet to be commited; the greatest crime of them all. I have my case together and I can predict fairly accurately as to what will occur and when, but I have yet to come up with a solution as to a way that I might prevent it happening.'

'But what is it?'

'Armageddon. The apocalypse,' said Professor Slocombe. 'The coming of the millennium. Did you think that I would have gone to all this trouble for anything less?'

Sherlock Holmes shook his head slowly. 'I suppose not,' said he.

II

Norman's automaton had finished breaking up the stones and re-surfacing the shopkeeper's backyard. Now he smacked the dust from his duro-flesh palms and returned to the kitchenette to brew up some tea for his living double. Norman watched his approach through the grimy rear window. He was doing very well now, he thought. There were no more signs of violent temperament now that his circuitry had been appropriately readjusted. He would give the creation a couple of days to redecorate the premises then, if all seemed sound, get him back on shop work. Although things had got off to a poor start, Norman was certain that the future looked promising, and that he would soon be able to dedicate all his time to his greatest project yet.

The scientific shopkeeper grinned lop-sidedly and struck up a bit more whistling. He sought about on his shelves for a chocolate bar which was still in date to munch upon. Through the open shop-doorway he spied another whistler. Jim Pooley was striding by at a jaunty pace en route to Bob the bookie. Here Jim would lay on one of the most extraordinary and ill-conceived Super-Yankee accu-mulators ever recorded in the annals of bookmaking history.

Norman gave up his futile search, made a mental observation that when the great day dawned and all his wares were computer-coded he would have no need to bother with such trifles as actually ordering new stock, and repaired to the kitchenette for a cuppa.

Jim Pooley pushed open Bob's armoured-glass door and entered the betting shop. As is well known, to any follower of the sport of kings, the interior of such establishments vary by but the merest detail, be they based upon some busy thoroughfare in John O'Groats or down a back alley in Penge. The betting shop is always instantly recognizable to be the thing of beauty that it is: the grey, fag-scarred linoleum floor, and the ticker-tape welcome of slip stubs; the heavily-barred counter, twelve-inch black and white tellies; the rarely-scrubbed blackboards, displaying hieroglyphics that even the now legendary Champollion would find himself hard-pressed to decipher.

Jim squinted through the blue fog of Havana cigar smoke towards its source. Behind the portcullis, pulling upon his torpedo, sat Bob the bookie.

'In for another hiding?' the millionaire enquired.

Jim smiled and waggled his betting-slip. 'Today is the day,' quoth he.

Bob stifled a yawn and rubbed a newly-purchased diamond ring upon the lapel of his smoking-jacket. The Koh-i-Noor glittered flawlessly in its setting as Jim slid his slip beneath the titanium security bars of the counter fortress. Bob held the crumpled thing at arm's length and examined it with passing interest. 'I have a new pocket calculator,' he told Pooley.

'Personalized for you by Cartiers of Paris, no doubt,' said Jim. 'Wrought in platinum and fashioned into the likeness of a golden calf. Your initials in jade?'

'Something of the sort.'

'I have no wish to see it, but should it give you some small pleasure, I suppose I owe it to you. Times are, I see, as ever against you.'

'It is a hard life.'

'Oh, is it now? To tell you the truth, spending so much of my time, as I do, in the sensual pleasures of unashamed luxury, I rarely have time to notice.'

'It is electric,' Bob continued, 'solar-powered in fact. It will work for a thousand years without maintenance.'

'Handy,' said Jim.

'But nevertheless useless.'

'Oh dear, and why might that be?'

'Well, for all the wondrous ingenuity of its creators, the lads have overlooked one small detail, and have denied it the facility to calculate any sum greater than nine hundred and ninety-nine million, nine hundred and ninety-nine thousand, nine hundred and ninety-nine pounds.'

'The fools,' said Jim.

'My sentiments entirely. Now should your selection,' he waved

481

Pooley's betting-slip sadly before him, 'come up at the predicted odds, I feel that my calculator will find itself many zeros below the mark.'

'Don't worry,' said Pooley sympathetically, 'I have already worked it out in my head. I'll have just the pound on it please, Bob.'

'As you wish, and shall you pay the tax?'

'Oh yes, I have no wish to upset the country's economy. Such is not fair to the Government.'

'As you will then.' Bob pushed Pooley's slip into the machine, and Jim passed him the exact amount in pennies and halfpennies. 'I'll be back around five to settle up,' said he.

Bob nodded and tinkered with his watch. 'Video roulette,' he said. 'The latest thing from Lateinos and Romiith.'

'A pox on those two lads,' said Pooley. 'And good-day.'

Jim folded his betting-slip into his breast-pocket, left the fog-bound bookie, and strolled off along the Ealing Road. He had not gone but fifty yards when he found himself confronted by a most extraordinary little scene. A group of onlookers was gathered in a tight knot about the pavement doors of the Swan's cellar. Pooley craned his head above the assembled throng and was more than a little surprised at what he saw.

Somehow, inexplicably jammed into the four-foot opening, was Neville the part-time barman.

'Someone get me out,' wailed this man, his voice soaring in pitch and volume above that of this rumbling spectators. 'By the gods somebody, please!'

Pooley rubbed at his eyes. This was an impossibility surely? Thin man trapped in fat opening; such things could not be reasonably expected to occur. But strange as strange, here they were doing that very thing. Neville spied out Pooley's face bobbing amongst the sea of others. 'Jim,' he shouted. 'Help me out will you?'

Pooley hastened to oblige. 'Stand back now, ladies and gents,' he said. 'Give the man some air now, please.'

'On your bike, Pooley,' said Old Pete, who had a particularly good place near the front. 'We're not going to miss any of this.'

'Be fair,' Jim pleaded. 'You can see he's in a bad way, give the lad a break.'

'How do you suppose it's done, then?' said Old Pete. 'Mirrors, do you think?'

Pooley shook his head. 'I've really no idea, might it be what they call a shared vision? I've read of such things.'

'Possibly that. When I was in the East, a lad in the regiment took us to see the Indian rope trick. We saw the whole thing. Magician throws up a rope, it hangs in the air, he climbs up then vanishes, then he climbs down, the whole thing.'

'Really?'

'Oh yes, well a bloke with us took pictures and when we got them back, what did they show?'

'Tell me.'

'They showed a mendicant standing beside a coil of rope. Every picture the same. Now what lied, the camera's eye, or our own?'

Neville, whose face had deepened in colour by several shades during the course of this fascinating conversation, let out a great and terrible scream.

'Keep it down, Neville,' said Old Pete. 'Can't you see we are trying to apply ourselves to the situation.'

'Oh, so sorry,' said the bunged-up barman.

'We are doing our best,' Pooley assured him. 'It is just, well, the situation has some rather unique qualities, too hasty a decision could result in disaster.'

'Tell you what,' said Old Pete, 'I'll go through the bar and into the cellar; I'll pull and you push.' Pete scuttled away through the saloon-bar door.

'There,' said Pooley. 'Help is at hand, do not worry.'

'I'm running out of breath,' mumbled the barman. 'I'll die here in full public gaze. The humiliation, the shame. What a way to go.'

'Come on now,' said Jim, doing his best to usher away the crowd which now spilled out into the Ealing Road. 'Be off about your business, please.' He shouted down towards the cellar, 'Pete, are you there?' But there was no reply. 'Now what is he playing at?' asked Pooley. 'I'll slip inside and see if he's all right.' Jim slipped into the bar, leaving the mob to close in about the howling barman. He joined Old Pete up at the bar.

'Took your time, didn't you?' the elder enquired. 'Losing your grip then, is it? Here, have one on the house.' He poured Jim a large whisky from the barman's reserve stock. 'Cheers,' he said.

'Down the hatch,' Pooley replied. 'No offence meant, Neville.'

'So,' Old Pete continued, 'what do you take it to be, publicity stunt do you think?'

Jim shrugged hugely. 'You've got me. I can't see how it works, but he does appear to be wedged in solid.'

'Nah, he's probably up on blocks. No doubt the brewery are planning a Billy Bunter night or some such abomination.'

'Perish the thought.' Jim Pooley crossed himself and tossed back his scotch. 'Any more left in that bottle?' he asked.

Outside, exciting things were about to happen. Leo Felix, Brentford's Rastafarian used-car dealer, had been passing by in his tow-truck; seeing the crowd gathered outside the Swan, the free-ale sign had flashed up in his colourful head. Now, he decided, might be a good time to make his peace with Neville, who had but recently barred him, once more, for life. Even as Pete and Pooley chit-chatted in the bar, Leo, dreadlocks a-dangle, was busily engaged in hooking Neville up to the winch on the back of his truck. 'I and I soon have you back on your feet,' he assured Neville. The part-time barman seemed strangely reticent about accepting this particular offer of help, and while the crowd applauded and offered encouragement, he shrieked and wriggled and invoked the aid of his pagan gods. The way things were going he felt that he would soon be getting the opportunity to address them face to face.

Leo was by now up in his cab. 'Jah, Jah Willing,' he said as he revved the engine and ram-jammed his thumb down on the hoist button. The cheering crowd parted as the hoist took up the slack.

'Ooooooooooh,' went Neville as the improvised harness tightened beneath his armpits.

'Quite mild for the time of year,' said Jim as he poured two more drinks.

'Fair,' said Pete. 'I've seen better.'

Young Chips pricked up his ears as outside the barman's scream rose to a frequency beyond human register. Sickening, bone-crunching sounds were emanating from the barman's middle regions and the cement about the cellar door's metal frame was splitting and shivering. The crowd drew back in sudden alarm; this was no laughing matter. 'Switch your winch off, Leo,' shouted somebody. 'You'll pull him in half.' Leo thumbed the button. He had been meaning to have it fixed for some time. The thing popped out from the dashboard and fell into his upturned palm. 'Haile Selassie!' said Leo Felix.

'   ,' went Neville the part-time barman.

'Back your truck up then for God's sake,' shouted another somebody, 'we'll try and get the cable off him.'

Leo hastened into the driving seat and stuck the customized Bedford into reverse. Gear cogs ground together adding further screams of distress to those already being loudly voiced.

He had been meaning to get the reverse fixed for some time.

With an almighty clunk the gear found its housing, and lodged into it as firmly as a barman in a beer cellar. Leo clawed at the gearstick but it would not shift by an inch. His knackered tow-truck, sick to the worn treads with its constant bad treatment, had chosen this of all times to exact revenge upon its Caribbean tormentor. Tearing his keys from the dash, Leo Felix leapt pale-faced from the cab. The malevolent tow-truck rolled relentlessly backwards, bound for the crowd and the struggling barman.

As the unstoppable vehicle gathered speed, those free to do so hastily took to their heels. Neville stared up, his good eye starting from its socket. The acrid smell of exhaust fumes filled his brain, and a rear number-plate which read N E M 1515 began to engulf his world.

It looked very much like strawberry jam time for Neville the part-time barman. The truck's engine roared like some beast loosed from the bottomless pit, and ground upon its hellish course. With one final despairing gasp Neville passed from consciousness, which as it happened was quite a shame because he missed the very best bit.

As the crowd burst asunder in a screaming panic-torn explosion, a heroic figure leapt into the fray. He plunged through the mass of fleeing humankind and took up a stance between the comatose barman and the roaring instrument of doom. The feet of this titan were firmly rooted upon the pavement and his face was a cold mask of determination. His eyes shone with a strange inner light. With a single sudden lunge forward, he grasped the tailgate of the wheel-screeching vehicle and stopped it dead in its tracks. The tyres squealed upon the pavement, raising black clouds of tread. With superhuman effort Neville's deliverer dragged it up from the ground. The engine whined into overdrive and exhaust smoke enveloped him in a great monoxide cloud of death. Struggling beneath the weight of the possessed vehicle, he bore it aloft, and held it high above his head. The truck rocked and shuddered, howling like a banshee, but in a moment he had done with it.

485

Brentford's St George cast down the mechanical dragon, bursting out its tyres, scrambling its axles, and driving its engine to ruination upon the cold stones of the pavement. As the smoke cleared, small knots of the cowardly crowd stared back in wonder. The hero calmly knotted the slackened hoist cable about his hand and tore it from its mountings. He turned slowly towards Neville and, freeing him from his hangman's harness, stooped and carefully drew him up to pavement level, where he laid him gently to rest.

Before the crowd could arouse itself from its slack-jawed wonderment, engulf the hero, and raise him shoulder-high, Norman silently turned away from the scene of his glory and strode back to his corner-shop.

12

The ambulance bells had long died away into memory when three men came strolling along the Ealing Road. One was bowed and ancient, walking with the aid of a slim ebony cane, a mane of snow-white hair trailing out behind him. Another was tall and gaunt with a great hawk of a nose, clad in an oddly Victorian tweed suit. As to the last, he was Irish and wanted his thirty quid.

As these three approached the Swan, Sherlock Holmes suddenly laid a gentle palm upon the Professor's chest and said, 'Now what do you make of that?'

Professor Slocombe shook his old head. 'Cellar doors ajar, a barman somewhat remiss in his duties?'

'Oh, no,' said Holmes. 'Much more. And what here?'

The elder perused Leo's defunct tow-truck parked at the kerb, its back axle supported by two piles of red flettons. 'Unusual bravado upon the part of the local criminal fraternity?' he suggested.

'I think not.' Holmes drew out his glass and as Omally watched him, with one eye forever straying towards the saloon-bar door, he dropped to all fours and perused the pavement.

'How many entrances to this cellar?' asked Holmes, looking up.

'Just that,' said Omally. 'And a door behind the bar.'

'I see.' Holmes examined the blackened skid marks. 'Interesting,' said he.

'Riveting,' said John. 'Might we step inside now, please?'

Holmes rose to his feet and patted dust from his trouser knees. 'I think so,' he said.

Omally led the way and the three men entered the bar. Pooley, who with Old Pete's aid had long ago finished the bottle of Neville's reserve, rose unsteadily to greet them. Omally eyed him with great suspicion. 'Have you seen Soap this morning?' he asked.

Pooley shook his head. 'You've missed all the excitement.'

'Obviously. Whose round is it?'

'I'll get these,' said Professor Slocombe. 'Holmes?'

'A small sherry,' the detective replied. 'And a small word with Mr Pooley here.'

'Oh yes?' asked the half-drunken Jim.

'The fellow with the beard serving behind the bar is not, I believe, the regular barman.'

Pooley squinted disgustedly towards Croughton the pot-bellied potman, who was now up to his elbows in froth behind the beer engines. 'Certainly not,' said he.

'And the regular barman, a gentleman of some standing in this community, he is not one who would leave the bar during a lunchtime session without a very good reason?'

'Not Neville.'

'So I would be right then in assuming that the fat gentleman who was until recently stuck fast in the cellar doors was this very Neville?'

'You what?' said John Omally. 'What happened here, Jim?'

'I'll do my best to explain,' said Pooley, tumbling backwards from his bar stool. 'But for now I think I need to go to the toilet.'

It was quite some time before Pooley re-emerged looking a little more sober. During the period of his absence Holmes had gleaned all the necessary information from other sources, finished his sherry, and had taken himself off to places elsewhere. Jim relocated his behind upon the bar stool. Looking up at the battered Guinness clock he asked, 'Anybody know what won the one forty-five?'

'Ahriman Boy,' said Old Pete. 'I get Free Radio Brentford on my deaf aid. The commentator was having a coronary by the sound of it.'

Pooley struggled a moment to comprehend this intelligence. Slowly he withdrew his betting-slip and peered between his fingers at his selection. 'By the gods,' said he. 'Did you hear the SP?'

'Sixty-six to one,' Old Pete replied. 'A quid or two there for the outside better.'

Pooley spread his betting-slip before him on the bar counter, 'I am sixty-six quid in the black,' said he.

Omally peered over his shoulder. 'Then order me a pint of froth quickly then, Jimmy boy,' said he. 'I suppose there is no chance that was your only bet of the afternoon?'

'Actually, no,' said Jim. 'I have an accumulator here.'

'A four-horse Yankee?'

'No, a six-horse Super-Yankee.'

'I'll get my own in then.'

'Nobody has any faith in me whatever,' Jim told Professor Slocombe.

'No?' the old man shook his head in wonder. 'Then let me at least get you another drink in. Are you feeling a little better now?'

'A temporary lapse,' said Jim. 'Your man from below puts the wind up me more than a little.'

'The two o'clock's on,' said Old Pete. 'Got one in here, Jim?'

Pooley nodded. 'Lucifer Lad.'

'Want to listen?' Old Pete took out his deaf aid and turned up the volume. The Mickey Mouse voice of the commentator tinkled out the race as three men, at least, knotted their fists and offered up with small sounds of encouragement for the game outsider. Lucifer Lad romped home at sixty-six to one.

'My brain's gone,' said Pooley. 'Can anybody work it out?'

'You don't want to think about it, Jim,' said the Professor. 'Let us just say that it is a goodly sum.'

'How goodly, tell me.'

'Four thousand, three hundred and fifty-six pounds.'

They brought Jim round with the contents of the soda siphon.

'Jim,' said John, drawing him up by the lapels, 'now wake up. What kind of deal have you done with Bob?'

'The six-horse special as ever,' mumbled Pooley. 'Six winners or nothing.'

'You buffoon.' Omally threw up his hands, 'If you'd had another winner you'd get a percentage even with a couple more seconds or thirds. You'd be a thousand pounds in profit now. There is no such thing as a six-horse Super-Yankee, such things are myths. An I T V-seven there is, that bookies laugh at as they fly off to their holidays in the Seychelles. Give me that slip.' Pooley pushed it across the counter. 'Anybody got a paper?' Pooley brought his out. 'Did you pay the tax?' Pooley nodded. 'You bloody buffoon.'

'Tell me again how rich I am,' said Jim. 'Just so I can hear it.' Omally dollied it out on his fingers. By the time he had finished Old Pete said, 'The two-fifteen's on.'

Bob the Bookie was enjoying a most unpleasant lunch at The Bonny

Pit Lad in Chiswick. The tenant of this dire establishment, who, as the result of some major brainstorm, had convinced himself that 'Mining Pubs' were going to be the next big thing, had borrowed a considerable sum from Bob to transform the place from a late Victorian money-spinner to a coalface catastrophe. The pit-props and stuffed ponies, the stark wooden benches and coal-dust floor had proved strangely uninviting to the Chiswick drinking fraternity. Even in those winter months, when lit by the cosy glow of Davy Lamps, there was at least a good fire burning in the hearth.

Bob the bookie had, of course, extended the tenant's credit to the point that he now owned the controlling interest in the place. The plans for the luxury steak-house it was shortly to become were already drawn up and in his safe. As he sat alone in the deserted bar devouring his 'snap', Bob pondered upon what far-flung tropical beach he might park his million-dollar bum at the weekend.

Antoine the Chauffeur entered the bar in a flash of white livery, bearing upon a silver platter the computer print-out of the latest racing update just received through the Lateinos and Romiith in-car teleprinter. The telexed message that Jim Pooley, through merit of his win in the two-fifteen was now two hundred and eighty-four thousand, one hundred and ninety-six pounds up put the definite kibosh on the apple crumble end of Bob's Cornish pasty.

'You bloody buffoon,' went John Omally. 'You'd be rich, you bloody big buffoon.'

'It hasn't changed me,' said Jim. 'I'm still your friend. Lend me a pound and I'll get them in.'

'Are we all aboard for the two-thirty?' asked Old Pete. 'What is your selection, Jim?'

'Seven Seals.' Pooley checked his slip.

'Sixty-six to one,' said Old Pete.

Omally pressed his hands to his temples. 'I just knew he was going to say that,' he groaned.

Exactly how Seven Seals, who had been running a very poor eighteenth, actually managed to catch up and overtake the favourite in the last six furlongs was a matter for experts in that particular field to ponder upon for many moons yet to come.

'You are definitely ahead now,' said John Omally. 'I make that eighteen million, seven hundred and fifty-six thousand, nine hundred and thirty-six pounds at the very last. A tidy sum I would call that.'

'Lend me another quid,' Pooley pleaded. 'I think I'd like to buy a cigar.'

As he steered Bob the bookie's Roller through the crush of lunchtime traffic in the Chiswick High Road, Antoine the Chauffeur leafed through the 'Situations Vacant' column of the *Brentford Mercury*. Bob sat quivering in the back, shaking from head to toe, his knuckles jammed into his mouth. The in-car teleprinter punched out the runners for the two forty-five. There it was, Millennium Choice at sixty-six to one, and the runners coming under starter's orders. Bob punched away at his golden calculator but the thing merely rang up 'No Sale' and switched itself off in disgust.

'Do I get any redundancy money?' Antoine enquired politely.

'They're off,' bawled Old Pete.

The Swan's crowd knotted its fists and shook them in time to Mickey's little voice. Cries of encouragement were obviously out of the question, as to hear anything of the race required a great deal of breath-holding and ear-straining, but the patrons went about this with a will. Their faces like so many gargoyles, veins straining upon temples, and sweat trickling through the Brylcreemed forelocks. They took up the universal stance of punters, legs apart and knees slightly bent, bums protruding, and chins to the fore. They were phantom jockeys to a man, riding upon the commentator's every word. Nerves were cranking themselves into the red sector.

Millennium Choice was laying a not altogether favourable sixth in the six-horse race.

'Come on man!' screamed Omally, who could stand it no longer, his outcry breached the dam and the floodtide hit the valley floor.

'Go on my son! Give him some stick! The whip, man, use the whip! Dig your heels in! Millennium, Millennium, Millennium . . . Millennium . . .' The voices tumbled one upon another rising to a deafening cacophany.

Old Pete snatched up his hearing aid and rammed it back into his ear. If the entire pub had decided to go off its head he felt no reason why he, at least, should be deprived of the result.

Bob the bookie's Roller was jammed up at the Chiswick roundabout but his Lateinos and Romiith Vista Vision portable television was working okay. As Millennium Choice swept past the post a clear six lengths ahead of the field Antoine calmly drew a red circle about a likely vacancy.

Bob looked up towards the flyover soaring away into the distance. I'll have to sell that, he thought.

'Who won it? Who won it?' The Swan's lunchtime crowd engulfed Old Pete. 'Out with it.'

The ancient raised his thumb. 'Your round I think, Jim.'

The crowd erupted and stormed the bar, Croughton the pot-bellied potman took to his heels and fled.

Omally laboured at his exercise book. 'I can't work it out,' said he, tearing out great tufts of hair. 'Professor, please?'

The old man, who had worked it out in his head, wrote one thousand, two hundred and thirty-seven million, nine hundred and fifty-seven thousand, seven hundred and seventy-six pounds.

'I think your day has also come, John,' he said, indicating the vacancy behind the bar counter. Omally thrust his exercise book in front of the golden boy and shinned over the counter to realize his own lifetime's dream. He was a natural at the pumps and the clawing, snapping, human-hydra was rapidly quelled.

'When the sixth horse goes down nobody will ever speak to me again,' the back-patted Jim told the Professor. 'Five offers of marriage I have had already.'

'Perk up,' the scholar replied. 'I know the odds are unthinkable, but I have a feeling just the same.'

Omally stuffed a pint of Large into each of Pooley's outstretched hands. 'What a game this, then?' said he.

'You will hate me also,' Pooley replied dismally.

'Me?' Omally pressed his hands to his heart. 'But I love you, my dearest friend, the brother I never had.'

'You have five brothers.'

'None like you.'

Jim considered his two pints and raised both simultaneously to his lips. It was the kind of feat no man could be expected to perform twice in a lifetime, but he drained the two at a single draught. 'Oh cruel fate,' said he, wiping the merest drip from his chin.

'Tell me, Jim,' Professor Slocombe asked, as a crowd of female kissers took turns at their hero's cheek, 'how did you do it? Was it the product of pure chance or through the study of form? I ask out of professional interest, I can assure you that it will go no further.'

Jim brushed away the barmaid from the New Inn, whose arm had snaked about his waist. 'If you really want to know, it was down to you and your talk of numerology. Find the pattern, you said. Break everything down to its numerological equivalent, you said, and the answer is yours.'

Professor Slocombe nodded enthusiastically, a light shone in his old face. 'Yes, yes,' he cried, 'then you have solved it, you have found the key. Tell me Jim, I must know.'

'It wasn't all that,' Jim replied. 'Get off there woman, those are private places. I simply followed the lines.'

'The lines? What lines?'

Pooley pushed his racing paper towards the Professor, 'Those boys there,' he said. 'Madam, put those hands away.'

Professor Slocombe drew a quivering finger across the row of computer lines, eighteen in all, three groups of six. 'Oh my Lord,' he said slowly. 'Jim, do you realize what you've done?'

'Pulled off The Big One.'

'Very much more than that.' Professor Slocombe thumbed the paper back to its front page. 'I knew it. This is not your paper.'

'I borrowed it,' said Jim guiltily.

'Jim, tear up the slip. I am not joking. You don't understand what you've got yourself into. Tear it up now, I implore you.'

'Leave it out,' Jim Pooley replied.

'I will write you a cheque.' The Professor brought out his cheque-book. 'Name the sum.'

'Is the man jesting?' Pooley turned to Old Pete who was banging his deaf aid on to the bar counter.

'I've gone deaf here,' the other replied.

'Jim,' the Professor implored, 'listen, please.'

'Pete,' said Pooley, 'you old fool, give me that thing.'

Three o'clock was fast approaching upon the Guinness clock.

'Switch her on then,' said somebody, nudging Old Pete upon the arm.

Now, it must be fairly stated that Pete's hearing aid was not one of those microchipped miracle appliances one reads so much of in the popular press. Such articles, one is so informed, although no bigger than a garden pea, can broadcast the sound of a moth

493

breaking wind to the massed appreciation of an entire Wembley cup-tie crowd. No, old Pete's contraption was not one of these. Here instead, you had the valve, the pink Bakelite case, and the now totally expended tungsten carbide battery.

'It's broke,' said Old Pete. 'Caput.'

'It's what?'

'Pardon?' the elder replied. 'You'll have to speak up, my deaf aid's gone.'

'Deaf aid's gone. Deaf aid's gone.' The word spread like marge on a muffin. The panic spread with it.

'Tear up the slip,' the Professor commanded, his words lost in the growing din. Pooley clutched it to his bosom as the threatened firstborn it was. Omally sought Neville's knobkerry as the crowd turned into a mob and sought a beam to throw a rope over. It was lynching time in Brentford. Having seen active service in many a foreign field, Old Pete was well-prepared to go down fighting. He swung his stick with Ninja fury at the first likely skull that loomed towards him. Friend or foe wasn't in it. Fists began to fly. Omally, knobkerry in hand, launched himself from the counter into the middle of the crowd. 'On to the bookie's, Jim,' he shouted as he brought down a dozen rioters.

Sheltering his privy parts and clinging for dear life to his betting-slip, Pooley, in the wake of Professor Slocombe, whom no man present would have dared to strike no matter how dire the circumstances, edged through the *mêlée*.

'He's getting away,' yelled someone, struggling up from beneath the mad Irishman. 'After him, lads.'

The crowd swung in a blurry mass towards the saloon-bar door through which Pooley was now passing with remarkable speed. The tumbling mass burst out after him into the street. Professor Slocombe stepped nimbly aside and took himself off to business elsewhere.

Leo Felix, who had been labouring away with welder's blow-torch in a vain attempt to salvage anything of his defunct tow-truck, stared up, white-faced and dread, as Pooley blundered into him. 'I and I,' squealed the rattled Rastaman, vanishing away beneath a small Mount Zion of bowling bodies. Jim was snatched up by a dozen flailing hands and raised shoulder-high. The stampede turned to a thundering phalanx which lurched forward, bound for Bob the bookie's, bearing at their vanguard their multi-million dollar standard. Jim prepared to make a deal with God for the second time in as many days. When the sixth horse floundered, as surely it must, Mr Popular he was not going to be. 'Father forgive them,' he said.

Antoine turned Bob's Roller into the Ealing Road with an expensive shriek of burning rubber. Ahead, the advancing phalanx filled the street. Antoine yanked hard upon the wheel, but the car appeared to have ideas of its own. It tore forward into the crowd, scattering bodies to left and right. Jim cartwheeled forward and came to rest upon the gleaming bonnet, his nose jammed up against the windscreen. The Roller mounted the pavement, bringing down a lamppost and mercifully dislodging Jim, who slid into the gutter, a gibbering wreck, bereft of yet another jacket sleeve, which now swung to and fro upon a gold-plated windscreen wiper like some captured tribal war trophy.

Antoine leapt from the cab as Pooley's sixth horse kicked betting history into a cocked hat and Bob's Roller plunged onward, bound for the rear of Leo's tow-truck and the paw paw blow-torch which was even now blazing away at the unattended oxy-acetylene gas-bottle beneath it.

'It's been a funny old kind of a day,' said Bob the bookie.

13

The Brentford sun arose the next morning upon a parish which seemed strangely reticent about rising from its collective bed to face the challenge of the day ahead. The Swan in all of its long and colourful history had never known a night like it. Jim had loaded the disabled cash register with more pennies than it could ever hope to hold and announced to all that the drinks were most definitely on him. The parish had not been slow to respond to this selfless gesture, and the word burned like wildfire up the side-streets and back alleys as it generally did when fanned by the wind of a free drink.

Brentford put up the 'Closed for the Night' sign and severed all links with the outside world. The Swan's rival publicans chewed upon their lips for only a short while before leaving their cigars to smoulder in the ashtrays and join in the festivities. The borough council awarded the swaying Jim their highest commendation, the Argentinum Astrum, before drinking itself to collective extinction. With the charred automotive wreckage of Bob's Roller and Leo's tow-truck removed, there had been dancing in the street that night.

For Neville, upon his bed of pain, news never reached him. The Sisters of Mercy who tended to his bed-pan and blanket-baths, hiked up their skirts and joined in the revelry, leaving the metaphysical fat boy to sleep on under his heavy sedation.

For John Omally it was a night he would long remember. As Christ had feasted the five thousand upon half a score of Jewish baps and as many kippers, thus did Omally quench the thirsts of the Brentford multitude. Like the barman of myth, his hand was always there to take up the empty glass and refill it.

For Jim Pooley, morning suddenly appeared out of drunken oblivion beating a loud tattoo of drums upon the inside of his skull. Jim shook his head. An ill-considered move. The tattoo grew louder and more urgent. Jim reopened a pair of blood-red eyes. He found himself staring into the snoring face of Mrs Naylor, Brentford's licentious librarian. 'Gawd,' muttered Jim to himself, 'I did strike it lucky last night.'

The pounding was coming from below, from his front door. It was the relief postman. Jim rose giddily and lurched towards the bedroom door. The words 'never again' could not make it to his lips. 'Shut up,' he whispered as the hammering continued. Jim stumbled down the uncarpeted stairs and caught his bare toe for the umpteenth time upon the tack protruding from the sixth tread. Howling beneath his breath, he toppled into the hall to find himself suddenly swimming in a sea of paper.

The hallway was jam-packed with letters, literally thousands of them, of every way, shape, colour, and form. Telegrams, buff-coloured circulars, and picture postcards.

Pooley rubbed at his eyes as he lay half-submerged in the papery cushion. He was certain that they hadn't been there the night before, but as the later moments of the previous night's revels were blank to his recollection, as attested to by the snoring female above, Jim's certainties were purely subjective in nature.

The banging continued beyond the barricade of the king's mail.

'All right, all right.' Pooley clutched at his temples and fought his way towards the front door. Pushing envelopes to left and right with great difficulty, he opened it.

'Mail,' said a sweating postman, thumbing over his shoulder towards a dozen or so bulging sacks which lay in an unruly line along the pavement. 'Your bloody birthday is it then, pal?'

Pooley shrugged, dislodging an avalanche of letters which momentarily buried him.

'I've been sticking these bastards through your letter-box for the better part of an hour and I can't get anymore through. Do pardon this departure from the norm, but I must insist that you post the rest yourself. I am here on relief from Chiswick as the local bloke hasn't turned in. What is this, some kind of bleeding joke? "Candid Camera", is it, or that "Game for a Laugh" crap?'

Pooley hunched his shoulders beneath the pressing load. 'What are they?' he asked. 'Who has sent them?'

'From those which unaccountably fell open in my hands, they would seem to be begging letters to a man. What did you do then, come up on the bleeding pools?'

'Something like that.' Jim made an attempt to close the door.

The postman's contorted face suddenly sweetened. 'Is that a fact?' he said thoughtfully. 'Then let me be the first to congratulate you.'

'You are not the first,' Jim replied, 'but thanks all the same. Now if you will excuse me.' He fought with the front door but Posty's foot was now firmly in it. Pooley relaxed his grip. 'Your foot is caught,' he observed.

'It must be a wonderful thing to have money,' said the postman, edging forward. 'I have always been a poor man myself, not that I have ever resented the rich their wealth, you understand, but I have often had cause to wonder why fate chose to deal with me and mine in so shabby a way.'

'Really?' said Jim without interest.

'Oh yes. Not that I complain, soldiering on in all weathers, crippled to the fingertips with arthritis, simply so the mail should get through.'

'Very noble.' Jim applied more pressure to the door but it was getting him nowhere.

'And my wife,' the postman continued, 'a holy martyr that woman. If I only had the money to pay for the operation I am certain that she could be relieved of her daily misery.'

'Let us hope so.'

'And my poor blind son, Kevin!'

'Get your bloody foot out of my door.'

Knowing a lost cause when he saw one, the postman withdrew his boot and swung it at the nearest sack. The contents spilled out to flutter away upon the breeze. 'Privileged bastard,' he called after the retreating Pooley. 'Come the revolution, you and your kind will be first up against the wall. Capitalist Pig!'

Pooley slammed fast the door and stood engulfed in the floodtide of mail. He had sent out a few begging letters himself in the past, but now he knew what it felt like to be on the receiving end. Jim Pooley did not like it one little bit. His mail unread and his bed-mate unwoken, Jim left the house that morning by the rear entrance.

Now he sat alone upon the Library bench. The sun had long arisen and all the makings of a great day ahead looked in the offing. Jim sighed mournfully and at intervals studied the palm of his right hand. He was not a happy man. He was a gentleman of substance now and it pained him greatly. The terrible feeling of responsibility, one he had never before experienced, gnawed away at his innards. It was all just too much. The total sum of his wealth was too large even to contemplate and with the passing of the night and the current bank rate it had already grown alarmingly.

Jim made a dismal groaning sound and buried his face in his hands. It was all just too much. He had never owned before what one might actually call 'money' and certainly not what the 'swells' refer to as the current account. He had had an overdraft once but that hadn't proved to be up to much. And the manner in which he had acquired the fortune, also drastically wrong. No betting shop could ever have had that amount of readies waiting under the counter. And even if it had, it would be hardly likely to simply push them across the counter without a life or death struggle at the very least. Guns would have been toted and knee-caps an endangered species. He and Omally had transferred no fewer than twenty-six wheelbarrow loads from there to the bank. It was simply ridiculous.

And the bank? Pooley moaned pitifully. They had taken the entire thing for granted, as if he had been merely bunging in a couple of quid out of his wages. It was almost as if they had been expecting him. Through the bullet-proof glass of the office Pooley had seen the manager sitting at his desk, a pair of minuscule headphones clasped about his ears, nodding his head and popping his fingers.

And as for this, Pooley held up his right hand and examined the palm. The bank had refused to give him either a receipt or a cheque-book. With unveiled condescension they had explained that such methods of personal finance were now obsolete and that for security's sake they must insist upon the new personalized identification system. They had then stamped his right palm with a pattern of eighteen little computer lines in three rows of six. Six six six. Pooley spat on to his palm and rubbed away at the marking; it would not budge. He eased up on the moaning and groaning and took to a bit of soulful sighing. He had become involved in something which was very much bigger than he was. He really should have listened to Professor Slocombe and torn up the slip.

A sudden screeching of white-walled tyres upon tarmac announced the arrival of Antoine with Pooley's new car. Jim distantly recalled a deal he had struck the night before.

'Your carriage awaits,' said the chauffeur of fortune, springing from the automobile and holding open the door.

Jim was entranced. The car, a silver-grey Morris Minor, although of a model some fifteen years out of date, had all the makings of one fresh from the showroom. 'Where did you get it?' he asked, rising from his gloom and strolling over to the automotive gem.

'Purchased with the money you advanced, sir,' Antoine replied politely. 'Has a few tricks under the hood.'

Pooley circled the car approvingly and ran his unsoiled hand along the spanking paintwork. 'Big Boda,' said he. 'It's a corker.'

'And what about the number plates?' Antoine indicated the same, JP 1.

'Double Boda,' said Jim Pooley.

'Would sir care to be taken for a spin?'

'Absolutely.' Jim clapped his hands together and chuckled. Maybe this being wealthy did have its compensations after all. Antoine swung forward the driver's seat and Jim clambered aboard. The chauffeur sat himself down before the wheel and closed the door. 'What is all that?' Pooley asked, spying out the Morris' dashboard; it was far from conventional.

'Customized,' said Antoine. 'By Lateinos and Romiith, who bought out the old Morris patent. This car will do nought to sixty in three point four seconds. It has weather-eye air-conditioning, fuel consumption down to near zero by merit of its improved plasma-drive system. Are you acquainted with quantum mechanics?'

'I get by,' said Jim.

'Solar pod power-retention headlights, under-pinned macro-pleasure full-glide suspension. Sub-lift non-drift gravitational thrust plates . . .'

'Drive please,' said Jim, 'I will tell you when to stop.'

'Where to, sir?' Antoine put the preposterous vehicle into instant overdrive and tore it away at Mach ten.

Pooley slewed back in his seat, cheeks drawn up towards his ears, his face suddenly resembling the now legendary Gwynplaine, of Victor Hugo's *Man who Laughs*. 'Steady on,' winced Jim.

'Gravitational acclimatization auxiliary forward modifications engaged.' Antoine touched a lighted sensor on the dash and Pooley slumped forward. 'A quick tour of the parish, taking in the more desirable residences on the "For Sale" list, would it be, sir?'

'Come again?'

'My previous employers always liked the grand tour.'

'I thought you worked for Bob?'

'Only at lunchtimes, I am a freelance.'

'Very commendable.'

The car screamed into Mafeking Avenue on two wheels, narrowly avoiding Old Pete, who raised two eloquent fingers towards its receding rear end.

'How many clients have you then?'

'Only you,' said Antoine. 'I have attended to all those who came by the big payouts. One after another.'

The Morris roared past the Memorial Park, gathering speed.

'One after another. How many have come up recently then?'

'Twenty-five, although they were never in your league.' The chauffeur cleared his throat with a curiously mechanical coughing sound.

Pooley scratched at his head. He had heard of no recent big winners hereabouts. Jim suddenly smelt the great-grandaddy of all big rats. 'Stop the car,' he demanded.

Antoine crouched low over the computerized controls, his toe edged nearer to the floor, and the modified family saloon performed another impossible feat of acceleration.

'Stop this car!' shouted Jim. 'There is a stitch-up here and I'll have no part of it.'

'Stitch-up?' leered Antoine. Pooley could just make out his face reflected in the driving mirror. It was not a face Jim would wish to recall in his dreams. The chauffeur's normally amiable visage had become contorted into a death-mask of inhuman cruelty. The eyes glowed between hooded slits, the mouth was drawn down, exposing a row of wicked metallic-looking teeth. The face was no longer human, it was atavistic, something beyond and before humanity, compelling and vibrant with dark evil power. The flying Morris cannoned through the short cobbled alleyway between the Police Station and the Beehive and swerved right through the red lights and out into the High Road. It should surely have been forced to a standstill amidst the hubbub of mid-morning traffic, but to Pooley's increasing horror the High Street was empty, the pavements deserted.

'Stop, I say?' screamed Jim. 'I will pay you anything you want, name the sum.' Antoine laughed hideously, the sounds issuing from his throat being those of sharp stones rattled in a tin can. Pooley shook his brain into gear; 'knobble the mad driver', it told him. Climbing forward, Jim lashed out towards the driver's neck. 'AAAAAGH!' went Pooley, as his lunging fingers piled into a barrier of empty air, splintering nails, and dislocating thumbs.

'Safety-shield anti-whiplash modification,' sneered the demonic driver as Pooley sank back into his seat, his wounded hands jammed beneath his armpits. The car swung into a side-road Jim did not clearly remember and thundered on towards ... Jim suddenly stiffened in his seat ... towards the rim of the old quarry. Jim recalled that place well enough, he used to go ferreting there when a lad. The walls were fifty-foot sheer to a man. He was heading for an appointment with none other than good old Nemesis himself. Now was the time to do some pretty nifty fast thinking. Pooley thrust his brain into overdrive. Accelerating Morris, mad driver, two doors only, invisible force-field before. No sun-roof and Nemesis five hundred yards distant. Jim chewed upon his lip, worry beads of perspiration upon his brow. No way out before, above, but possibly ...

The mighty Morris has to its credit many an endearing feature. Ask any driver and he will mention such things as comfort, luxury, fuel economy, or the obvious prestige of ownership. But stand that man in front of his locked car to view the spectacle of his ignition keys dangling in the steering column and he will then address his praise towards the inevitably faulty boot-lock and the detachable rear seat. Pooley had crawled into more than a few Morrises on drunken evenings past when further staggering home looked out of the question. Now he was hardly backward in going that very direction.

Nemesis was yet two hundred and fifty yards to the fore. As the car ploughed on relentlessly towards the yawning chasm ahead, Jim clawed at the rear seat with his maimed fingers. With the kind of superhuman effort which would have done credit to any one of a dozen *Boy's Own Paper* heroes, he plunged into the boot and fought it open.

With one bound he was free.

As the car breasted the rim of the chasm and dashed itself down towards oblivion, Jim tumbled out into the roadway, bowling over and over like a rag doll, to the accompaniment of many a sickening, bone-shattering report. He came to a final dislocated standstill a few short yards from doom. A loud explosion beneath, a column of flame, and a rising black mushroom cloud of oily smoke signalled the sorry end of a fine car. Pooley made a feeble attempt to rise, but to no avail. Every bone in his body seemed broken several times over. His head was pointing the wrong way round for a start. A floodtide of darkness engulfed the fallen hero and Jim lapsed away into a dark oblivion of unconsciousness.

14

John Omally pressed his way through Professor Slocombe's ever-open French windows. The old scholar sat in a fireside chair earnestly conversing with the hawk-nosed man from another time. He waved his hand in familiar fashion towards the whisky decanter.

'So where is lucky Jim?' Sherlock Holmes asked. 'Putting in his bid for the brewery?'

Omally shook his head and his face showed more than just a trace of bitterness. 'I was to meet Jim at the bench. We were planning a Nile cruise.' John flung the bundle of holiday brochures he had acquired the night before into the Professor's fire. 'I missed him. No doubt he is lying even now in the arms of some avaricious female. Oh, cruel fate.'

'Cruel fate indeed,' said Holmes darkly. 'Lucky Jim may not be quite so lucky as he thinks himself to be.'

Omally pinched at the top of his nose. 'We sank a few last night and that is a fact. Jim wisely kept back a wheelbarrow-load for expenses. He was more than generous.'

'So I understand. I regret that we were unable to attend the festivities. Tell me now, would I be right in assuming that Jim was wearing gloves last night?'

Omally nodded. 'Said that the money had given him a rash. I didn't give it a lot of thought, you know what these millionaires are like, walking round in Kleenex boxes and drinking Campbells soup from tins, it's quite regular to those lads.'

Sherlock Holmes leant forward in his seat. 'Might I ask you to show me your hands?'

Omally thrust them hurriedly behind his back.

'As I deduced,' said the great detective. 'Both door and window was it?'

Omally bit at his lip and nodded ruefully. 'Until but a few minutes since.'

Professor Slocombe cast Holmes a questioning glance.

'Purely a matter of deduction,' that man explained. 'Let me see if I can set the scene, as it were. Mr Omally here has seen his dearest friend become a multimillionaire in the matter of an hour and a half. He helps him transport these riches to the bank and the two spend the night in revelry, finally returning to their respective abodes. But our friend cannot sleep, he paces the floor, he is assailed with doubts. Will the money change his companion, will it destroy their long and enduring friendship? Will he turn his back upon him? At last he can stand it no longer, his mind is made up. He will set out at once to his friend's house and knock him up. But this is not to be. He tries to open his door but it will not move. After many vain attempts to secure his freedom he tries the window, this proves similarly unrewarding, the glass cannot even be broken.'

Professor Slocombe looked quizzically towards Omally who was catching flies with his mouth. 'Is this true?' he asked.

'In most respects; it fair put the fear of the Almighty into me I can tell you.'

'We are indeed dealing with mighty forces here,' said Sherlock Holmes, springing to his feet. 'And now I think that should we wish to entertain any hope of saving your friend we had best move with some expediency. Let us pray that the trail is not yet cold.' Without uttering another word he whisked on his tweedy jacket and plunged out through the French windows, followed by Professor Slocombe. Omally shook his head in total disbelief at it all, tossed back his drink, and followed in hot pursuit.

Holmes strode ahead up the sweeping tree-lined drive of the Butts Estate and crossed the road towards the Memorial Library. Before Pooley's bench he halted and threw himself to his hands and knees. 'Aha,' he said, taking up the spent butt of an expensive cigarette. 'He's been here and he walked towards the kerb.' Omally and the Professor looked at one another. Omally shrugged. Holmes scrutinized the roadway. 'He entered a roadster here and was driven off at some speed in that direction.'

'Can you make out the licence plate number?' Omally said cynically.

Holmes looked him up and down coldly. 'I can tell you that he was helped into the car by a gentleman of foreign extraction, who parts his hair on the left side and has his shoes hand-made, size seven and a half.'

Omally's eyes widened. 'Antoine, Bob the bookie's chauffeur.'

'Such was my conclusion. Now, unless you wish to waste more valuable time in fruitless badinage, I would suggest that we make haste. Time is of the essence.'

'Lead on,' said John Omally.

It is a goodly jog from the Memorial Library to the old quarry, but Holmes led the way without faltering once upon his course. Here and there along the route he dropped once more to his knees and examined the road surface. Each time Omally felt certain that he had lost his way, but each time the detective rose again and pointed the way ahead. At length the three men turned into the old quarry road. Ahead in the distance lay the crumpled wreckage which had been Jim Pooley. With a small cry Omally bounded forward and came to a standstill over the disaster area. 'Oh, no,' said he, sinking to his knees. 'Oh no, it wasn't worth this.'

Sherlock Holmes and the Professor slowly approached, the old man supporting himself upon his stick and wheezing terribly. 'Is he . . .?' the words stuck in the Professor's throat.

Omally buried his face in his hands. 'My true friend,' he mumbled, his voice choked by emotion. He slumped back on his knees and stared up at the sky. Tears had formed in his deep-blue eyes and fell over his unshaven cheeks. 'Why?' he shouted up at the firmament. 'Tell me why?'

Holmes came forward and, stooping, turned Pooley's right palm upwards. The eighteen lines glowed darkly in the otherwise brilliant sunlight. 'There is nothing you can do for him now,' he said.

'No!' Omally elbowed the detective's hand away. 'Leave him alone, you are part of this. What the hell is going on here anyway? Why did it happen?'

'Come, John,' said the Professor, laying a slim hand upon the Irishman's shoulder. 'Come away now, there is nothing that can be done.'

Omally looked up bitterly at the old man. 'You knew about this, didn't you?' he said. 'You knew something bad was going on, you should have stopped it. You and your numbers and your magic.'

'Come, John, come please.'

Omally rose slowly to his feet and stared down at Pooley's mortal remains. 'I will kill the man who did this, Jim,' he said slowly and painfully.

Professor Slocombe pressed his hand once more to John's shoulder, and led the stumbling man away.

'All well and bloody good,' came a voice from the grave. 'But who is going to turn my head around for me?'

Omally spun about. 'Jim, you old bastard!'

'Who else would it bloody be? My head, John, if you please? It is most uncomfortable.'

The lads at the Cottage Hospital were nothing if not thorough. Spending their days as they did, playing dominoes and hunt the hypodermic, they were more than willing to face up to the challenge of the bloody spectacle Professor Slocombe presented them with. Having run a light-pen quickly over Pooley's right hand they pronounced him private patient and went about their tasks with a will. Had not the Professor been a member of the Board of Governors, there seemed little doubt that they would have been a great deal more thorough than they were. Most likely to the extremes of an exploratory operation or two, with the removal of Pooley's tonsils as an encore. As it was they prodded and poked, applied iodine, took X-rays, forced him to remove his trousers, turned his head to the right, and made him cough. As an afterthought they inoculated him against tetanus, mumps, whooping cough, and diphtheria. As Doctor Kildare came up on the hospital tele-video they summarily dismissed him with a few kind words, a large bill, and a prescription for Interferon no chemist could ever hope to fill.

'See,' said Omally, as the four men left the hospital, 'all this fuss and not a bone broken.'

Pooley felt doubtfully at his bruised limbs. 'I will not bore you with my opinion of the National Health Service,' said he. 'Nor even waste my time bewailing my lot, as my pleas for sympathy fall forever upon deaf ears.'

At last the four men entered the Professor's study. A large medicinal gold watch was handed at once to the invalid who was placed in a heavily-cushioned chair. 'My thanks,' said Jim, pocketing it away in his throat. The sun danced in upon the carpet and the four weary men lay slumped in various armchairs, each unwilling to be the first to break the tranquil silence. Pooley's limbs creaked and complained to themselves. With a crackling hand he poured himself another drink. Holmes and the Professor exchanged occasional guarded glances, and the old man appeared at times obsessed with the silver pentacle which hung upon his watch-chain. Omally drummed his fingers soundlessly upon the chair's arm and waited for the storm to break; the silence was rapidly becoming close and oppressive.

Finally Jim could stand it no longer. 'All right,' he said, climbing painfully to his feet. 'What is going on? You all know a lot more of this than me.'

'I don't,' said Omally, 'but I am beginning to have my suspicions.'

'So what is it?' Pooley turned to the Professor. 'I have just miraculously survived an attempt upon my life by a lunatic chauffeur. Such should be the cause for some small rejoicing surely. If I was dead, Omally here would already be ordering the beer for the wake.'

Professor Slocombe stepped over to his desk and took up the day's copy of the *Brentford Mercury*. He held the front page towards Jim. 'Have you read this?'

Pooley perused the encircled article with little interest and less comprehension. 'It's about computer lines,' said he. It did not go unnoticed by Holmes and the Professor that his right hand slid unobtrusively away into his trouser pocket.

'It is much more than that,' said the old man. 'It is an essential link in a dark chain of events which, unless severed, will inevitably engirdle us all. To our ultimate destruction.'

'Come now,' said Jim. 'It is just some nonsense about banks and computers, nothing more I assure you.'

Professor Slocombe shook his head, 'Sadly, it is a great deal more than that. It is conclusive proof that all my worst fears are founded and even now the prophecies of the book of Revelation are coming to pass.'

'You jest, surely?'

Professor Slocombe shook his head once more. 'Believe in what I say,' said he. 'We are facing the greatest threat mankind has faced since the deluge. We are facing the final conflict. The apocalypse. Even now the curtains are closing.'

'No.' Jim shook his head violently and not a little painfully. 'All the stuff in that old book is most depressing. Look at me now. I experienced a slight setback, but it was the result of pure spite on Bob's part. Just because I won and he's banged up in hospital a bit scorched. I am battered but wealthy. The gods are smiling upon me.'

'No,' said Professor Slocombe. 'Money will not buy you out of this one, especially money which was never intended for your use.'

Pooley scratched at his head, raising a fine cloud of dust. 'You wouldn't care to enlarge a little on this would you Professor?' he asked. 'You see such news catches me at a rather inopportune moment. John and I are planning a bit of a holiday. Armageddon might interfere with our traveller's cheques.'

Professor Slocombe shook his head once more. Jim was beginning to find the habit mildly annoying. He had millions of pounds knocking about in the bank and was now really looking forward to spending them before they caught the moth. 'Do you really believe yourself to be one favoured of the gods?'

Jim nodded noisily. 'At this time definitely yes.'

'All right then, I will make this short, but by no means sweet. We will speak of these matters again. For now let me read you a verse or two from the Revelation; possibly it will convince you, possibly not.' Definitely not, thought Jim Pooly. The Professor took himself over to his desk where he sat before the large and outspread family Bible. 'I will spare you the preliminaries as it is obvious that you consider your time valuable. I will simply give you the relevant part and allow you to muse upon it.'

'Thanks,' said Jim doubtfully.

'Revelation, Chapter Thirteen,' said Professor Slocombe. 'This speaks of the beast that has risen from the Earth. We will address our attention to verses sixteen, seventeen; and eighteen.' He spoke the final number with a deadly intensity.

'Go ahead then.'

The Professor adjusted his ivory pince-nez and read aloud from the open book:

'16. And he causeth all, both small and great, rich and poor, free and bond to receive a mark in their right hand or in their foreheads.

17. And that no man might buy or sell save that he had the mark or the name of the beast or the number of his name.

18. Here is wisdom. Let he that hath understanding count the number of the beast; for it is the number of a man, and his number is six hundred, three score and six.'

The Professor gently closed the Holy Book and looked up towards Jim

Pooley. The millionaire sat bolt upright in his chair. His eyes were unblinking and stared ever downward towards the open palm of his right hand, where the computer bar code was indelibly printed. Eighteen computer lines. Three rows of six. The number of a man, six hundred, three score and six.

666

The number of the Beast. Things were suddenly beginning to sink in.

'Oh dear,' said John Omally, who was not a man unacquainted with the Scriptures. 'Why did I just know you were going to choose those very verses to be today's text?'

15

At a little after five of the clock, Pooley and Omally left Professor Slocombe's house behind and trudged up the long crescent bound for the Swan. Although the old man had served a fine tea, neither could raise much of an appetite, finding to it more than a hint of the Messianic feast. With rumbling guts and grumbling tongues they mooched along, ignoring the gaily-coloured bunting which fluttered between the great Horse Chestnuts, raised in preparation for the forthcoming Festival of Brentford. Pooley was in full slouch, his chin upon his chest, and his hands thrust deeply into his tweedy trouser pockets. His last suit was in exquisite ruin and lacked a right sleeve, which an over-zealous hospital intern who watched too many Aldo Ray films had cut away from his grazed elbow with a pair of surgical scissors. The thought that he could buy a thousand suits and all of them of the hand-tailored, Saville Row variety, did little to raise his spirits. Jim's right thumbnail worried at his hidden palm.

Omally worried at Marchant's pitted handlebars, the old boy seemed to have developed an irritating pull to the left, which was either something to do with its political leanings or something even more sinister. 'Give it a rest,' growled John as the thing had him in the gutter once more.

After what seemed an age they arrived at the Swan's welcoming portal. And found to their increased horror that it was no longer welcoming. A large plastic sign fastened to the front window announced to the world that THE BUYING OF 'ROUNDS' IS HENCEFORTH FORBIDDEN BY ORDER OF THE BREWERY. ANY CUSTOMER ATTEMPTING TO VIOLATE THIS PRINCIPLE WILL BE BARRED FOR AN INDEFINITE PERIOD.

'By the Saints,' said Omally, turning wobbly at the knees. 'Would you look at that?'

Pooley curled his lip. 'This is too much. I am even to be denied spending my money as I please.' He thrust Omally aside and entered the bar.

The Swan was empty of customers. The only folk present were a pale young man in headphones who stood behind the jump, and two brewery henchmen in drab-coloured overalls, who appeared to be screwing a gleaming contrivance of advanced design on to the bar counter.

'What is the meaning of that notice?' Pooley stormed up to the bar.

The strange young barman watched his furious approach with an untroubled expression. His head moved to and fro to a rhythm only he heard.

'I demand an explanation,' foamed the red-faced Jim.

The young man pushed back his headphones. 'What will it be then, sir?' he asked.

Jim raised his fist. 'That, that bloody notice in the window. What's your game, eh?'

'Oh, that.' The young man was all bland composure. 'Rules and regulations, what can we do?'

'We can tear the bloody thing down for a kick off.'

The young man waggled a finger. 'Naughty, naughty,' said he.

Jim clenched and unclenched his fists. 'Has the world gone mad?' he asked. 'Has the brewery lost its bloody marbles?'

The young man shrugged. 'Since the takeover everything seems to have changed.'

'Takeover, what takeover?'

'Hadn't you heard? Lateinos and Romiith bought the brewery out. An offer too good to refuse I suppose.'

Jim began to flap his hands wildly and spin about in small circles. Omally, who had followed him in, knew this to be a bad sign. Pooley sought men to kill. Two of such were now tinkering at the counter's end. 'Who are they?' Jim ceased his foolish gyrations. 'What are they up to?'

The pale young man smiled wanly. 'Installing a terminal, of course. Under the new system every establishment must have its own terminal, you know.'

'John,' said Jim, 'John, hold me back.' Omally did as he was bidden. 'What, if one might make so bold, is a terminal?' he asked.

'My goodness me,' the pale young man tittered to himself, 'we do live in the dark ages around here, don't we?' He grinned towards the two henchmen, who exchanged knowing glances and sniggered. 'This terminal,' he explained, 'is modular in concept, with a networking capability that is virtually plug-in. It has a one hundred and twenty-eight bit multi-tasking operation, super-advanced W P forms and spread sheet planner; wide area network configuration, multi-key I S A M on shared data bases, L and R six-six-six Asynch emulations, soft fort and bit-mapped graphics.'

'Bit-mapped graphics, eh?'

The young man cleared his throat with a curiously mechanical coughing sound. 'Bit-mapped,' he said slowly. Above his left eyebrow the short row of eighteen vertical lines gave his face a permanently quizzical expression. 'Now, perhaps, sir, you would care to order?'

'Two pints of Large,' said Omally.

'As you wish, sir. Will your irate companion be thinking to order two for himself also, do you think? Once he recovers his senses?'

'We are only just outnumbered,' quoth Pooley. 'Shall we make a fight of it?'

'All in good time, Jim. Now please calm yourself and lend me a couple of quid.' The pale barman raised a tattooed eyebrow. 'Usury is strictly forbidden upon the premises, by order of the brewery.'

'A pox on the brewery,' said John. 'Jim is minding some money for me. Can I have it back please, Jim?'

'Certainly.' Pooley thrust a couple of hundred smackers into Omally's outstretched palm and outstretched his own towards the nearest pint.

The new barman deftly reached across the countertop and caught up Jim's wrist in a vice-like grip. Turning Jim's palm towards the ceiling he drew out a light-wand and ran it across. 'Your credit rating is triple A,' he said. 'Two pints for yourself is it?'

'Make it three,' said Jim bitterly. 'I feel a bit of a thirst coming on.'

'As you please, sir.' The pale young barman replaced his headphones and, nodding to himself, drew off the business.

Bearing their pints away, John and Jim stalked off to a side-table where they dropped into a brace of chairs and sat staring into one another's eyes.

After a somewhat pregnant pause, Jim said, 'I've had enough of all this, John.'

Omally nodded thoughtfully. 'It is not very much to my own liking,' said he, gulping away the nearest pint. 'If you want my considered opinion I feel that we should both do very well to have it away from this district post haste.'

'Look at those bastards.' Jim gestured towards the brewery henchmen who were even now tearing up the Swan's antique carpeting to run a power-line across the floor.

'Rio would be your man,' said John. 'Dusky maidens rolling green cigars upon their bronzed thighs. A train-robber chum of mine has lodgings thereabouts. The climate so they say is ideal for the professional drinking man or the unemployed war criminal.'

Pooley considered his printed palm. 'I can't be having with all this stuff. Things are no longer healthy hereabouts.'

'So let us away.'

Jim chewed upon a thumbnail. 'I think you're right,' said he. 'But what about all this Revelations business? Do you think that the Professor is correct in his theories? If it is the end of the world then it might catch up with us even in Rio.'

Omally downed another pint. 'I have my doubts about the whole thing. Listen, with the old currant bun beaming down and a bottle or two of duty-free on the patio table we can give the matter serious thought. What do you say?'

'I say it's time we had a holiday.'

'Good man. Now the travel agent's in the Ealing Road closes at six, I can be up there in five minutes on the bike and back in another five, I'll book us aboard an aeroplane for first thing tomorrow.'

'Do it then.' Jim dragged out another bundle of banknotes and thrust them at John. 'Go at once. I'll get some bottles to take out, this place is beginning to depress me.'

'Right then, I will be back directly.' Omally left the Swan and mounted up Marchant, who had set himself in for an evening kip. He bumped down the kerb and pedalled furiously up the Ealing Road. Cresting the railway bridge he swept down the other side, legs outspread, past the Mowlem's building. Without warning he suddenly came into contact with a great body of halted traffic. The road was a shambles of stalled automobiles and shouting drivers. Cars were parked at crazy angles across the road, and those at the vanguard lay, their bonnets stove in and steam issuing from their shattered radiators. A blank wall of dark light rose from the street at the junction with the Great West Road. It soared into the sky, an impenetrable barrier blocking all further progress. Omally dragged on his brakes but his iron stallion appeared to have developed ideas of its own. It rocketed him headlong into the boot of a stalled Morris Minor. John sailed forward in a blizzard of whirling banknotes, to tumble down on to the bonnet of the defunct automobile and roll on to the roadway. Cursing and spitting he slowly dragged himself to his feet and stared up at the grim barrier ahead, struck dumb with amazement and disbelief. The curtains, which the Professor had observed for so many weeks through his rooftop viewer, had finally closed upon the borders of the Brentford triangle.

And the parish was now completely sealed off from the outside world.

16

As word spread from house to house that the veil was drawn down, the people of the parish flocked into the streets. They flowed hurriedly towards the borders to stand, their noses pressed against the walls of hard air, staring out into the beyond. The vista, normally so mundane as to be invisible, now assumed a quality of remoteness and unreality. That none might any longer pass into that world made it fairyland and the figures that moved there became exaggerated and larger than life. And though they shouted and coo-eed and smote the barrier with sticks and staves, the world beyond did not see them, nor hear their cries for help. The world beyond simply went on doing that which it had always done – which wasn't very much, although it seemed so now. Although the trapped people watched desperately for some sign which might signal the recognition of their plight by the free folk, who now passed within inches, none came. Their faces never turned and they went about their business as ever they had. To the world outside it seemed that Brentford had simply ceased to exist.

What attempts were made to stir up a bit of healthy rioting were stifled almost as soon as they were begun by the arrival of police snatch squads. Strange pale young men in protective uniforms, sporting minuscule headphones, and carrying small black boxes attached to their belts, moved swiftly into the crowds to bear away the outspoken to waiting meat-wagons. Those who had voiced complaint reappeared hours later passive and uncomplaining, clearing their throats before speech with curiously mechanical coughing sounds. Brentford's ghost people drifted back to haunt their houses and closed their doors behind them.

Days began to pass one upon another, each one the same as the last. Pooley and Omally sat in the Swan bitterly regarding the new barman as he soullessly directed the redecoration of the grand old watering hole. Through the Swan's upper windows, now being double-glazed, the dark walls shimmered. Beyond them the sun shone, but here in Brentford a thin drizzle hissed upon the pavements and trickled down the gutters. Old Pete hobbled in, shaking rain from his cap and muttering under his breath. As he passed his coinage over the counter the young barman tut-tutted and warned him that such cash transactions would soon be impermissible. Old Pete muttered something in reply but it was only the word 'pox' that caught the ears of John and Jim. Pooley lit up a Passing Cloud and drew deeply upon it, he opened his mouth to speak but no word came. Omally read the expression and the open mouth and nodded hopelessly. There was no need for either question or answer, nobody knew what they were going to do next, or even why. When the barman called time six minutes early the two men parted with no words spoken and wandered away into the night. The disappointments and the hopelessness of it all were beginning to take their irrevocable toll.

Pooley lay on his bed, hands cupped behind his head, awake to the sounds of the night. The room was now heaped with a pointless array of useless and expensive articles. The wardrobe overspilled with tailor-made suits, shirts, and shoes. Quadrophonic record players, all lacking plugs, and most not even unpacked from their boxes, lay half-hidden beneath every Frankie Laine record Jim had always promised himself. He had riffled every Brentford store in the vain attempt to spend his wealth. Finding an estate agent with property deeds still for sale he had purchased all available for wallpaper. The things he ordered arrived by the hour, to lie in soaking stacks on the pavement. Jim went about the business with a will but, as with everything now, the task was hopeless. He could never outspend his own wealth. Progress across the cluttered room was made the more precarious for fear of sinking to his doom in the marshland of expensive shagpile carpets heaped one upon another. He should have been sleeping the sleep of the drunk, but no matter how many pints he struggled to down, nowadays he still remained fiercely sober. None of it made the slightest bit of sense to Jim, there seemed no purpose to any last bit of it.

Pooley pressed the time-speak button on his brand new Lateinos and Romiith wristlet watch. 'Eleven forty-five and all is well, Jim,' said the polite little voice. Pooley made an unseemly sound and suggested that all was very far from being that. Professor Slocombe had called him and John to a midnight rendezvous this very night. No doubt the Professor felt the need to impart to them more prophecies of impending doom. Jim did not relish the thought. And to think that he had once considered the old man to be a stimulating conversationalist and source of enlightenment.

He climbed down from the most expensive mattress printed palms could buy and sought out a pair of matching shoes from the undisciplined regiment which stood before him. Having kicked about for several minutes, to Jim's immense chagrin he unearthed one lone matched set, his tired old work-boots. Muttering something about the curse of the Pooleys, Jim drew the wretched articles on to his naked feet. Having recently had a nasty experience in the bathroom with a computerized umbrella which opened automatically upon contact with water, he left the thing rolled up under the bed, and braved the drizzle in a new tweed shooting jacket with matching cap. Neither fitted. Jim shook his head – everything money could buy, but it was all rubbish. The new calfskin waistcoat had looked a bundle in the shop, but no sooner home than the buttons had begun to fall off and the leathery smell vanished away to be replaced by one of plastic. The same smell which permeated everything he had bought. Jim sniffed at the 'tweed' jacket. Yes, even that. Bewailing the millionaire's lot, Pooley slouched on to the Professor's.

Omally was already there, comfortably ensconced in a fireside chair, wearing a natty three-piece whistle Jim had given him, his right hand wrapped about a whisky glass. Professor Slocombe was at his desk amongst his books and Sherlock Holmes was nowhere to be seen.

Upon Jim's noisy entrance, the sole of his right boot having chosen this inopportune moment to part company with its aged leather upper, John and the Professor looked up from their separate reveries and greeted the new arrival. 'Help yourself, Jim,' said the old man. 'I think you will find the fruits of my cellar eminently more stimulating than those of the Swan.'

'Praise be for that,' said Jim Pooley, liberally acquainting himself with the decanter.

'So now,' said the Professor, once Jim had hopped into a comfortable chair and eased off his rogue brogue, 'there are a good many things that I must tell you this evening. Few of which you will find comforting, I fear.'

We're off to a good start, thought Jim, but he kept it to himself.

'As you are both aware, Brentford is now completely surrounded by an impenetrable barrier.' The two men nodded gloomily; they were a long way from Rio and that was a fact. 'And no doubt you have been asking each other why?'

'Never gave it a thought,' said Jim. Omally leaned forward and smote him a painful blow to his naked sole.

'Thank you, John. Now it is my wish to put you both in the picture as far as I am able. It is essential that you understand what we face. Those of us with the power and the will to fight grow fewer by the day. Soon, if the thing is not stopped, there will be none remaining.' Pooley did not like the sound of that very much at all. 'I will start at the very beginning.'

'Do so, sir,' said Jim.

'In the beginning was the word and the word was with God and God was the word . . .'

'Hold hard there,' Pooley interrupted. 'From Genesis to the Revelation is a long haul by any standard. Might we just skip right through to it now?'

'All right, but let me briefly explain. The God of Adam brought something to the world which had not existed before. He brought light. To our perception there is but one God, the true God. But our forefathers believed in an entire pantheon of Elder Gods. These rose and fell with their temples, for how can a god exist when there are none to worship him? It is the balance of equipoise; the harmony of the spheres. Each new and rising god replaces his predecessor when his temple is cast down and his followers no longer believe. Allow me to suggest the possibility that dark and sinister gods existed prior to the word which brought light to our Mother Earth.'

'Sounds pretty iffy so far,' John observed.

'Oh, it gets far worse later on,' the Professor replied. 'This is just the prawn cocktail; by cheese and biscuits you'll be thoroughly sick.'

'I have a strong stomach,' said John, refilling his glass.

'Now,' the old man continued, 'in the beginning of the world we know, our God brought light and created man. Before this time existed only utter cold and utter confusion where reigned the Elder Gods of darkness, unchallenged. With the coming of light and the creation of man they were cast down with their temples. But gods do not die, they sleep and they dream. The old serpent entered

Eden to tempt man back to the darkness; he sowed the seed of doubt in him. Doubt in the power of his Creator. God drove back the serpent but the damage was already done. The serpent never left Eden you see, he slept, and he dreamed, awaiting the time when he would rise again. That time is now upon us. Through the exercise of what man thought to be his own free will he has furthered the aims of the serpent. The prophecies are even now being fulfilled, as testified by your palm there, Jim.' Pooley pocketed his tattooed mit. 'Man has, through the influence of the serpent, given genesis to his own replacement: simply, the thinking machine.'

'I, Robot?' said Omally. 'I've read all that. Machines do not think, they are programmed merely to respond, they answer questions but with the answers that were already fed into them. Computers do not have souls.'

'There now,' said Professor Slocombe, 'you have saved me my old breath. They have no souls. It is man's soul alone which prevents him slipping back into the darkness. The soul cries out to the light, the soul worships the light. Replace man and the temple of the lord of light is cast down. The darkness returns.'

'The whole menu was a bowl of sprouts,' said Omally bitterly. 'I am going to be sick.'

'It all sounds somewhat eclectic,' remarked Jim, surprising even himself. 'I do not pretend to understand much of it.'

'Like the sprout, it takes a bit of swallowing,' the Professor replied. 'What I am trying to say is this: computer science is founded upon the silicon chip. It has long been suggested by scientists that life might exist elsewhere in the universe, life possibly with a silicon base. They do not seem to realize that they have created it here on Earth, at the behest of a hidden master. When man is made subservient to the machine he is no longer in control of his own destiny. Therefore he is no longer the dominant species. The people of Brentford are being replaced one after another by duplicates of themselves. Soulless robots programmed to worship their master. Unless we act quickly, then all we have ever known will be lost.'

Pooley solemnly removed his wristlet watch and cast it into the fire. The plastic crackled amongst the flames, and, to add further horror to a conversation which had already been a far cry from a cosy fireside chat, a shrill voice shrieked out from the flames calling for mercy.

Omally crossed himself. 'I believe,' he said simply.

'Then you will fight with me?'

'I think that we have little choice. Jim?'

Pooley raised his unmarked palm. 'Count me in, I suppose,' said he.

17

The conversation wore long into the night. John and Jim were anxious to know exactly what plans the Professor had formulated, but the old man was obstinately vague in his replies. It was either that he was as yet uncertain as to what had to be done, or that he had already set certain wheels in motion and feared the two men might, out of their eagerness to pitch in for the cause, confound them. Whatever the case, Jim at length returned to his rooms and fell into a most uneasy sleep beset with ghastly dreams of mechanical monsters and bogey men who loomed up from every darkened corner. Omally, as ever, slept the sleep of the just, which was quite unjust of him, considering he had no right to do it.

At around eleven the next morning, the two men met up outside the Flying Swan. Pooley emptied what pennies remained to him into the outspread palm of his fellow. 'He won't take my cash any more, simply runs his damn little wand over my hand. It gives me little pleasure.'

'If there is a word of truth to anything the Professor told us, then at least we have a vague idea what's going on.'

'Vague would be your man, John, this is well out of my league.'

'That is a nice suit you have on there,' Omally observed as Jim strode on before him into the Swan. 'If a little tight across the shoulders perhaps.'

The pale young man in the headphones stood as ever behind the jump. Nothing had been heard of Neville since he had been whisked away in the ambulance. The Sisters of Mercy said that he had been moved to another hospital but seemed uncertain where. The fact that ownership of the brewery had changed hands suggested that Brentford had seen the last of the part-time barman. 'Replacement,' the Professor had said; it was a more than unsettling business. And the thought that duplicates were even now being created to replace each living individual in Brentford was no laughing matter.

'Usual please,' said Jim, extending his palm.

The man in the headset ran his electronic pen across the outstretched appendage and cleared his throat with a curiously mechanical coughing sound. 'Great day for the race,' he said.

'Yours or mine?' muttered Jim beneath his breath.

Omally bought his own. 'It's just not the same any more,' he sighed, as he bore his pint over to the table Jim now occupied. 'I miss the thrill of the chase.'

'I don't think anything is ever going to be the same again,' said Pooley unhappily. 'All is finished here. If only we had legged it away in time we would never be sitting here trapped like rats, waiting to be replaced by piles of diodes.'

John shook his head. 'It is a bad one to be sure. No doubt the walls will expand to finally engulf the whole world, but the Professor never did explain why it all started right here.'

'Well, I suppose it had to start somewhere and Brentford, although worse than some, is, as the world knows, better than most. But it is the unfairness of it that gets my dander up. Me, with money to burn and two dozen High Street shops to burn it in. My God, I'm doing my best, but what about teas at the Ritz and the Concorde flight to the Bahamas? Such things are day to day affairs for lads with my kind of scratch. I can't even buy people drinks. My entire wealth is without purpose.'

'The Professor warned you, Jim, the money wasn't meant for you.'

'This beer is definitely not what it was.' Pooley raised his pint and held it towards the light. Through the clear amber liquid a row of computer lines etched on to the glass twinkled like the slats of a Venetian blind.

'I had been thinking the same,' Omally replied. 'It has a definitely metallic tang to it nowadays.'

An odd figure now entered the Flying Swan. He appeared awkward and ill at ease amongst his surroundings. The stranger wore a wide-brimmed hat of dark material and a similarly-coloured cloak which reached to the floor, exposing only the very tips of his Wellington boots.

'It's Soap,' Omally whispered. 'Now what do you suppose he is doing here?'

'Come to pay us our thirty quid, hopefully,' said Jim, who even in wealth was never too aloof to forget a creditor.

Soap ordered a Guinness, without the head, and paid for the same with a gold nugget which the barman weighed up and committed to the till. The man in black approached the two seated drinkers. 'Good day,' he said.

'Not yet,' said the Omally. 'But you have my full permission to improve upon it should you so wish.'

'Might I take a seat?'

'If you must.'

Soap removed his hat and placed it upon the table. His albino coiffure glowed stunningly even in the dim light of the saloon-bar; the pink eyes wandered between the two men. 'How's tricks?' he asked.

'Oh, going great guns,' Pooley made an airy gesture. 'Just sitting here drinking duff beer, waiting for the end of the world. Ringside seats to boot.'

'Hm.' Soap toyed with the ample brim of his extraordinary hat. 'I'll tell you what though, but. You're better off here than out there.' He thumbed away towards the glistening wall of light which shimmered in the distance beyond the Swan's upper panes. 'It's all hell for sure in that neck of the woods.'

'You mean you've been outside?' Omally raised his ample eyebrows.

'Naturally.' Soap tugged lewdly at his lower eye. 'You know the expression you can't keep a good man down? Well here it's a case of a good man down is worth three in the Butts. Good'n that, eh? One of my own.'

'Bloody marvellous,' said Pooley without conviction. 'So what is going on out there?'

'Bad things.' Soap stared sombrely into his pint. The sharpened, ear-rooting nail of his little finger traced a runic symbol upon the knap of his hatbrim. 'Bad things.' Soap sipped at his pint and drew a slim wrist across his mouth. 'Bloody chaos,' he said simply. 'It makes me sick at heart to see what goes on out there, but the Professor says that I must keep the watch. Although he never says for what.'

'So what have you seen, Soap?'

'They are starving out there.' Soap's pink eyes darted up at his inquisitor.

'You're joking, surely?'

'I am not. Since the institution of the new non-monetary system of exchange the entire country is literally in a state of civil war.'

'Come now,' said Jim. 'What you mean is that a few die-hards are giving two fingers to the printed-palm brigade. Bloody good luck to them I say. I'll arrange to have a couple of million drawn out. You take it with my blessings.'

'Money won't do it,' said Soap. 'Paper currency is illegal. All assets were instantly frozen on the day of the change. Each individual had to hand in his cash to the bank upon his turn for registration. Those who refused to submit to the change found every door closed to them. They could not travel upon buses or trains or buy petrol for their own cars; nor milk from the milkman, nor bread from the bakers. Their friends and neighbours rejected them. Even members of their own families, those who had the mark, refused them. They were ostracized totally from society. Many went straight to the banks but were told that they had missed their opportunity and that was that.'

'And that no man might buy or sell, save he that had the mark or the name of the beast or the number of his name,' said Jim Pooley in a leaden voice.

'The very same.'

'The callous bastards,' said John Omally. 'So what happened then?'

'Exactly what you might expect. Open rebellion on the part of the unmarked. What they could no longer buy they took. There was looting and burning and killing. Much killing. Under the direction of the Government's master computer martial law was imposed. The computer issued a brief edict: all those who do not bear the mark to be shot on sight.'

'Are you making this up, Soap?' Omally leant forward in his seat and waggled his fist threateningly beneath the hollow Earther's all-but-transparent nose. 'Jim and I have both sussed that something pretty pony is going on here. Although we are trapped by a seemingly impenetrable barrier, the shops never run dry. There is always milk and fags, bread and beer, although that is tasting a bit odd of late. It must all be coming in from the outside, although we haven't figured out exactly how as yet. Parachutes in the dead of night we suspect.'

'You're on a wrong'n,' said Soap. 'Nothing gets in or out except me. And there's no food going begging out there either.'

'So how do you account for it then?'

'It is all manufactured right here in the parish.'

'Oh rot,' said Jim. 'Do you see any cows grazing in the Memorial Park, or any hop fields or tobacco plantations? Talk sense, Soap, please. How could any of it be made here?'

'It is all artificially produced. Every last little thing, it's all synthetic. Including your manky beer.' Soap pushed his glass aside. 'I can't tell you how it's done but I can tell you who's doing it.'

'Lateinos and bloody Romiith,' said Omally in a doom-laden voice.

'None other. What do you think the walls are up for anyway?'

'To keep us in,' Jim said gloomily. 'To keep me in and stop me spending my money.'

'Wrong,' said Soap. 'To keep the others out. Those walls were whipped up to protect the master computer complex in Abaddon Street. It is the centre of the whole operation.'

'They got my antique bedstead, the bastards,' snarled Omally, 'and now my beer also. Will it never end?'

'But why is this master complex in Brentford?' Jim asked. 'I'd always pictured Armageddon getting off to its first round in a somewhat more Biblical setting. The gasworks and the flyover just don't seem to fit.'

'You'll have to ask the Professor about that,' said Soap. 'Or possibly your man there.' Soap stretched out a pale hand towards the tall, gaunt spectre wearing long out-moded tweeds and smoking a Turkish cigarette who now stood majestically framed in the Swan's famous portal.

'Gentlemen,' said Mr Sherlock Holmes, gesturing to the three seated figures, two of which were now cowering away and seeking invisibility, 'if I might just prevail upon your aid in a small matter.'

'And there was I utterly convinced that things could get no worse,' said John Omally. 'Oh foolish fellow me.'

18

Sherlock Holmes strode up the Ealing Road, his cigarette billowing smoke about his angular visage. Pooley and Omally plodded behind, and had they chosen to pause a moment and look around they might just have caught sight of the manhole cover which closed upon Soap's retreating form.

'I merely wish you to be close at hand,' said Sherlock Holmes as he marched along. 'Just button your lips and hang loose, got me?'

Pooley, who had recently purchased for the detective an advanced video recorder and the complete series of Basil Rathbone cassettes, thought to detect the hint of an American accent creeping into the Victorian voice. 'Oh, gotcha,' he said.

Outside Norman's corner-shop Holmes drew to a sudden halt. His two followers did likewise and peered without enthusiasm through the spotless plexiglass of the new aluminium-framed door to where Norman stood behind his shining counter. The true shopkeeper was busy in his kitchenette, bent low over a set of indecipherable plans scrawled on to the innards of a cornflake packet. He scarcely heard the shopdoor-bell chime out an electronic fanfare. His double peered up from the countertop computer terminal and surveyed his three potential customers. The Irish one, cowering to the rear, owed, he recalled. Clearing his throat with a curiously mechanical coughing sound, he asked, 'How might we serve you, gentlemen?'

'We?' queried Sherlock Holmes.

'The plurality is used in a purely business sense,' the robot replied. 'We, the interest, which is Norman Hartnell, cornershop, as a small concern, realize the need to extend a personal welcome to the prospective client in these competitive times.'

'Very precise,' said Sherlock Holmes. 'An ounce of Ships, if you please.'

'Certainly, sir.' The robot slipped his hand behind his back and drew out the packet. Omally considered that to be a pretty sneaky move by any reckoning.

'You have redecorated your premises, I see,' said Holmes.

Considering this to be a simple statement of fact which required no reply, the robot offered none.

'And all achieved with the left hand.'

The creation stiffened ever so slightly but retained its composure, although a fleeting look of suspicion crossed its face. Pooley and Omally both stepped back unconsciously.

'I was always given to understand that you were right-handed,' Holmes continued.

'That will be eighteen shillings and sixpence, please, sir.' The robot stretched forward both hands, that he might exhibit no personal preference.

'Put it on my slate, please,' said Sherlock Holmes.

Beneath his breath John Omally began to recite the rosary.

Holmes' deadly phrase clanged amongst the robot's network of inner circuitry and fed out the word 'Dimac' in any one of a dozen known languages. 'Eighteen shillings and sixpence, please,' he said. 'The management regret that . . .'

'So I have been given to understand,' said Holmes. 'If it is not inconvenient, I should like a word or two with the management.'

'I am it.' The robot pressed his hands to the countertop and prepared to spring over. 'Kindly hand me the eighteen shillings and sixpence.'

'I think not,' said Sherlock Holmes. 'Let us not bandy words, please. If the real Norman Hartnell still draws breath then I wish to speak with him. If not, then I am making a citizen's arrest.'

The robot lunged forward across the counter and made a grab at the detective's throat. Holmes stepped nimbly beyond range and drew out his revolver. He pointed it at the space between the robot's eyes, his aim was steady and unshaking. 'Hurry now,' he said, 'my time is valuable.'

The robot stared at the great detective. Its lips were drawn back from its plasticized teeth which glowed an evil yellow. Its eyes blazed hatred and its hands crooked into cruel claws.

'Hold hard or I fire.'

The pseudo-shopkeeper crouched low upon his knees and suddenly leapt upwards. Holmes' finger closed about the trigger, but the inhuman reactions of the creation far outmatched his own. The thing leapt upwards, passing clean through the ceiling of the shop, bringing down an avalanche of lathe and plaster and tumbling timberwork. Holmes staggered backwards, shielding his face from the falling debris. Pooley and Omally adopted the now legendary foetal position. A series of further crashes signalled the departure of the robot through the walls of Norman's back bedroom.

Startled by the sounds of destruction, the shopkeeper burst through his kitchenette door into the now thoroughly ventilated shop. He gazed up at the crude hole yawning above and then down at the faces of the three coughing and spluttering men as they slowly appeared amidst the cloud of dust. 'What ... who ... why ...?' Norman's voice trailed off as Sherlock Holmes rose from the debris, patting plaster from his shoulders, and removing a section of lathing from his hair.

'Mr Hartnell,' he said, 'it is a pleasure to meet you actually in the flesh, as it were.'

Pooley and Omally blinked their eyes towards the gaping ceiling, towards the startled shopkeeper, and finally towards each other. Shaking their dust-covered heads in total disbelief, they followed the detective who was even now ushering the fretful Norman away into his kitchenette. Holmes suggested that Omally might bolt the front door and put up the 'Closed For The Day' sign. This the Irishman did with haste, fearing that he might miss anything of what might be yet to come. When he entered the kitchenette he found Norman squatting upon his odd-legged chair in the centre of the room, surrounded by a clutter of bizarre-looking equipment which was obviously the current fruit of his prodigious scientific brain. Holmes perched behind him upon the kitchen table, a tweedy vulture hovering above his carrion lunch. Without warning he suddenly thrust a long bony finger into Norman's right ear.

'Ooh, ouch, ow, get off me,' squealed the shopkeeper, doubling up.

Holmes examined his fingertip and waggled it beneath his nose. 'I pride myself,' said he, 'that, given a specimen of earwax, I can state the occupation of the donor with such an accuracy that any suggestion of there being any element of chance involved is absolutely confounded.'

'Really?' said Omally studying the ceiling and kicking his heels upon the new lino of the floor.

'Who's your friend?' whined the persecuted shopkeeper.

'Don't ask,' counselled Jim Pooley.

'I will ask the questions, if you don't mind.' Holmes prodded Norman in the ribs with a patent leather toecap.

'I do, as it happens,' said Norman, flinching anew.

'Be that as it may, I believe that you have much to tell us.'

'Bugger off, will you?' Norman cowered in his seat.

'Language,' said Jim. 'Mr H, our companion here, is a house-guest of the Professor's. He can be trusted absolutely, I assure you.'

'I have nothing to say. What is all this about anyway? Can't you see I'm busy redecorating?'

'The shop ceiling seems a bit drastic,' said John.

'Blame the wife,' Norman said sarcastically. 'She said she wanted two rooms knocked into one.'

'I once heard George Robey tell that joke,' said Holmes. 'It was old even then.'

'George Robey?'

'No matter. Now, sir, there are questions that must be answered. How can it be that your duplicate works in your shop yet you still exist? Show me your palms, sir.'

'Show me your palms? Jim, where do you meet these people?' A sudden clout on the back of the head sent the shopkeeper sprawling.

'Here, steady on,' cried Jim. 'There's no need for any of that. Sherlock Holmes never engaged in that kind of practice.'

'Changing times,' the detective pronounced, examining his knuckles.

'Sherlock Holmes?' sneered Norman from the deck. 'Is that who he thinks he is?'

'Your servant, sir,' said Holmes, bowing slightly from the waist.

'Oh yes?' Norman cowered in the corner shielding his privy parts. 'Well if you're Sherlock Holmes then tell me, what are the thirty-nine steps?'

'This is where I came in,' said Jim.

Holmes leant forward and waggled his waxy finger towards Norman. 'Spill the beans, you,' he cried. 'Spill the beans!'

'He's been watching the Basil Rathbone reruns,' Pooley whispered to Omally.

'If you don't mind,' said John, 'I think Jim and I will take our leave now. We are men of peace, and displays of gratuitous violence trouble our sensitivities. Even in the cause of justice and the quest for truth, we find them upsetting.'

Pooley nodded. 'If you are now preparing to wade in with the old rubber truncheon, kindly wait until we have taken our leave.'

'Fellas,' whined the fallen shopkeeper, 'fellas, don't leave me here with this lunatic.'

'Sorry,' said Jim, 'but this is none of our business.'

'If you really wish to make a fight of it, your Dimac should be a match for his Barritso.' Omally pointed to the still prominent lump upon his forehead, which bore a silent if painful testimony to his previous encounter with the martial shopman.

'That wasn't me, John, I swear it.'

'So,' said Sherlock Holmes, 'then spill the beans, buddy.'

'All right, all right, but no more hitting.'

'No more hitting,' said Sherlock Holmes.

Buddy prepared himself to spill all the beans.

19

Old Pete thrust his wrinkled hand beneath the shining plexiglass counter-shield of the sub-post office. The dark young man now serving behind the jump did not remove his minuscule headphones but merely nodded as he passed the electronic light-wand across the ancient's palm. He punched a few details into the computer terminal and awaited the forthcoming readout. Upon its arrival he raised a quizzical eyebrow towards the pensioner and said, 'There appears to be some discrepancy here, sir. I suggest that you come back next week.'

Old Pete glared daggers at the dark young fellow-me-lad behind the tinted screen. 'What damned discrepancy?' he demanded.

The young man sighed tolerantly. 'The computer registers a discrepancy,' he said. 'It states that for the last ten years you have been receiving two pensions each week. Such a thing could not, of course, happen now under the new advanced system. But with the old Giro, well who knows? We shall just have to resubmit the data and await a decision.'

'And how long will that take?'

'Well, computer time is valuable, you are allotted six seconds weekly; we will see what happens when your turn comes around again.'

'And in the meantime?' foamed Old Pete. 'Do you mean that until your filthy electronic box of tricks gives you the go-ahead I am penniless?'

'The word "penniless" no longer applies. It is simply that, pending investigations, your credit is temporarily suspended. You must understand that this is for the public good. We are trying to institute the new system hereabouts in a manner that will cause minimum civil unrest.'

'You'll get maximum civil unrest if I don't get my damned pensions, I mean, pension!' Young Chips growled in agreement and bared his fangs.

'Next customer, please,' the dark young man said.

'Hold hard,' cried Old Pete raising his stick. 'I want to speak to the manager.'

'This branch no longer has a manager, sir, but an operator, fully conversant, I hasten to add, with all current trends in new technology.'

'A pox upon your technology. Who do I see about my pension?'

'Well you might fill in a form which we will forward in due course to Head Office, requesting a manual systems over-ride, although the procedure is somewhat archaic and extremely lengthy.'

'Then I'll go up to your Head Office and speak with them.'

The dark young man laughed malevolently. 'One does not simply go up to Lateinos and Romiiths and speak to them. Whoever heard of such a thing?' He smirked towards his assistant, who tittered behind her hand and turned up her eyes.

'Oh don't they, though?' snarled Old Pete, grinding upon his dentures and rapping his Penang-lawyer upon the plexiglass screen. 'Well, we'll see about that.' With Chips hard on his down-at-heels, the ancient departed the sub-post office, walking for once without the aid of his stick.

Ahead, where once had been only bombsite land, the Lateinos and Romiith building rose above Brentford, a dark and accusing finger pointing towards the enclosed triangle of grey-troubled sky. Sixty-six floors of black lustreless glass, swallowing up the light. Within its cruel and jagged shadow magnolias wilted in their window-boxes and synthetic gold-top became doorstep cheese. It was not a thing of beauty but there was a terrible quality of a joyless for ever about it. High upon the uppermost ramparts, amid the clouds, tiny figures came and went, moving at a furious pace, striving to increase its height. Never had there been a Babel tower more fit for the tumbling, nor a fogey more willing to take on the task.

Old Pete rounded the corner into Abaddon Street and glowered up at the sheer glass monolith. 'Progress,' he spat, rattling his ill-fitting dentures. 'A pox on it all.' His bold stride suddenly became a hobble once more as he passed into the bleak shadow of the imperious building and sought the entrance. A faceless wall met his

533

limited vision. Another painful hundred yards, a further corner, and another blank wall of featureless glass. 'Damned odd,' wheezed the ancient to his dog as he plodded onwards once more. The entrance to the building could only be in the High Street. To Old Pete's utter disgust and still increasing fury, it was not.

He now stood leaning upon his cane beneath the night-black structure, puffing and blowing and cursing loudly whenever he could draw sufficient breath. There was simply no way in or out of the building, not a doorway, not an entrance, not a letter-box or a nameplate, nothing. Young Chips cocked his furry head upon one side and peered up at his ancient master. The old boy suddenly looked very fragile indeed. The snow-capped head shook and shivered, and beneath the frayed cuffs of his one suit, the gnarled and knobby hands with their blue street-maps of veins knotted and reknotted themselves into feeble fists. 'We'll get to the bottom of this,' snarled Old Pete, still undefeated. Once more raising his stick and this time striking at the dead-black wall towering towards infinity. The blow did not elicit a sound and this raised the ancient's fury to cardiac arrest level. Pummelling for all he was worth he retraced his steps and staggered back towards Abaddon Street.

As the aged loon lurched along, raining blows upon the opaque glass, a hidden probe, shielded from his vision, moved with him, scanning his every movement. Digesting and cataloguing the minutiae that made up Old Pete. Through an advanced form of electro-carbon dating it penetrated the bone rings of his skull and accurately calculated his age to five decimal places. Its spectroscopic intensifiers analysed the soil samples beneath his fingernails and generated graphs which were no matters for jest. Fluoroscopes X-rayed his lower gut and ruminated upon the half-digested lunchtime pork pies, which contained no traces of pork whatever. The probe swept into the fabric of his wartime shirt, illuminating a thousand hidden laundry marks and cross-indexed them. It moved down to his underpants and hurriedly retraced its metaphorical footsteps to areas above belt-level. It checked out the tweed of his jacket, measured the angles of the lapels and, through numerous esoteric calculations, tracked down the suit's manufacture to a Wednesday in a long hot summer prior to the Great War. The computer banks gulped it all down and gorged themselves upon the feast of data; gurgled with delight and dug in ever more deeply in search of further toothsome morsels. They entered secretly into his head and chewed upon his brain cells, ravenously seeking the possibility of electron particle variabilities in the codex of his cerebellum.

Within .666 of a second they had done with their main course and were seeking a mangey-looking half-terrier for afters. The read-out which followed, had it been broadcast in standard five-point lettering, would have formed an equation sufficient to engirdle the Earth several times around. Summing up, the computer pronounced Old Pete a harmless loony and no threat to security. It did, however, suggest that certain discrepancies existed regarding multiple payment of pensions in the past and that the data relating to this would require a prolonged period to assess accurately. It refused to comment on Young Chips, offering only a cryptic remark that the wearing of flea collars should be made compulsory.

Old Pete finally gave up his unequal struggle and limped off down the street effing and blinding for all he was worth. Young Chips lifted his furry leg contemptuously on to the dull black-glass wall and skipped off after his master. The Lateinos and Romiith mainframe filed away Old Pete's vitals and beamed a triplicate copy of the now completed programme to the bio-gene constructional workshop, twenty-six storeys below. The probe moved up once more to the building's roof and turned itself to more pressing business. Included amongst a billion or so other tiny matters which required attention was the removal from this plane of existence of a certain local Professor and his unclassifiable house-guest.

The sensory scanner criss-crossed the triangle of streets and houses, prying and probing. The X-ray eye of the great machine penetrated each dwelling, highlighting the plumbing pipes and television tubes. The house-owners were tiny red blotches moving to and fro, going about their business unaware that all was revealed to the voyeurist machine which lurked above their heads. The data whirred into the computer banks, but at intervals the motors flicked and whined as a patch of impenetrable white light appeared on the screen. As the macroscope focused upon the area of disturbance and intensified its gaze, the area revealed itself to be a large house and garden set upon the historic Butts Estate. The data retrieval cross-locators coughed and spluttered, fruitlessly seeking a snippet of relevant information, but none was to be found. The white patch glared on the screen, the missing piece of a great jigsaw. The best the print-out could come up with was 'Insufficient data, scan penetration negative, over-ride and resubmit.'

20

Professor Slocombe rewound the great ormulu mantel-clock and, withdrawing the fretted key from the gilded face, set the pendulum in motion. The sonorous tocking of the magnificent timepiece returned the heartbeat once more to the silent house.

Sherlock Holmes entered the study through the open French windows. 'It has stopped again?' said he.

The Professor nodded sombrely. 'The mechanism has become infected, I believe.'

Holmes slumped into a fireside chair. 'You have had the electricity disconnected, I trust?'

'As we discussed, we will have to be very much upon our guard from now on. I have taken what protective measures I can, but my powers are not inexhaustible, I can feel the pressure upon me even now.'

Holmes slid a pale hand about the decanter's neck and poured himself a small scotch. 'I have just spent a most informative hour with Norman Hartnell. A man of exceptional capability.'

Professor Slocombe smiled ruefully. 'He keeps us all guessing, that is for certain.'

'I discovered the hand of a duplicate replacement at work in his shop and sought to question it.'

Professor Slocombe raised his eyebrows in horror. 'That was a somewhat reckless move upon your part.'

'Perhaps, but when confronted by the gun you gave me, the thing took flight, literally, through the ceiling of the shop. To my astonishment the real Mr Hartnell appears from his quarters. The mechanical double was, in fact, something of his own creation. To spare his time for more important matters, according to himself.'

Professor Slocombe chuckled loudly. 'Bravo, Norman,' he said.

536

'The shopkeeper does have something rather substantial on the go at the present time. It is of the utmost importance that nothing stand in his way.'

Sherlock Holmes shook his head. 'Your corner-shopkeeper produces an all-but-perfect facsimile of himself with no more than a few discarded wireless-set parts and something he calls Meccano and you treat it as if it were an everyday affair.'

'This is Brentford. Norman's ingenuity is not unknown to me.'

'And do you know how his mechanical man is powered?'

'Knowing Norman, it probably has a key in its back or runs upon steam.'

'On the contrary,' said Sherlock Holmes, taking the opportunity to spring from his chair and take up a striking pose against the mantelpiece, 'it runs from a slim brass wheel set into its chest. Your shopkeeper has rediscovered the secret of perpetual motion.'

'Has he, be damned?' The Professor bit upon his lower lip. 'Now that is another matter entirely.'

'Ha,' said Holmes, nodding his head, 'and how would you like me to bring you the automaton, that you might inspect his workings at first hand?'

'Very much. Do you consider that such might be achieved in safety?'

'Certainly, I took the liberty of following the ample trail he left, after my interview with Norman. He is holed up on the allotment.'

'Holed up?'

'Certainly, in Mr Omally's shed. If I can catch him unawares I shall bring him here at gunpoint. Although I must confess to a certain bafflement here. How might it be that an automaton who can leap without effort or apparent harm through ceilings and walls, fears the simple bullet?'

'Ha, yourself!' said Professor Slocombe. 'You have your secrets and I have mine. Go then, with my blessing, but stay upon your guard. Take no unnecessary risks.'

'Natcho,' said Sherlock Holmes, turning as he left to make a gesture which all lovers of the New York television cop genre know to be the 'soul fist'.

'Natcho?' Professor Slocombe shook his old head and returned once more to his work.

21

Having slipped away to Jack Lane's for a pint or three of non-takeover-brewery beer, Pooley and Omally now loped down a bunting bedecked Sprite Street. To either side, front gardens bulged with sections of the home-made floats destined to join the grand carnival procession of this year's Festival which, meaningless as it now appeared, showed every sign of going on regardless. Exactly what the theme of the parade was, neither man very much cared. As they ambled along they muttered away to one another in muted, if urgent, tones.

'As I see it,' mumbled John, 'we have few options left open to us at present. If the end of civilization is approaching there is little, if anything, we can do about it.'

'But what about all my millions?' Jim complained. 'I thought that the holders of the world's wealth always had it up and away on their hand-mades and sailed their luxury yachts into the sunset at the merest mention of impending doom.'

'What, off down the canal you fancy?'

'Well, somewhere, surely? Let us at least go down with Soap and weather it out until the troubles are over.'

'I had considered that, but you will recall that it is very dark down there in his neck of the woods. And darkness would seem to be the keynote of this whole insane concerto.'

'So what do we do then?'

The two stopped on the corner of Abaddon Street and stood a moment, gazing up at the great black monolith towering above them.

'I have been giving this matter a great deal of thought and I think I have come up with an answer.'

'It better be a goody.'

'It is, but not here. Walls have ears as they say. Let us hasten away to a place of privacy and discuss this matter.'

It did not take a child of six to put the necessary two and two together and come up with Omally's suggestion for a likely conspiratorial hideaway. 'My hut,' said John.

The two men strode over the allotments, each alone with his particular thoughts. The first inkling that anything of a more untoward nature than was now the common norm was currently on the go thereabouts hit them like the proverbial bolt from the blue. The sound of gunfire suddenly rattled their eardrums, and the unexpected sight of Omally's corrugated iron roof rising from its mountings and coming rapidly in their direction put new life into their feet.

'Run for your life,' yelled Omally.

'I am already, get out of my way.'

The roof smashed to earth, sparing them by inches. The cause of the shed's destruction tumbled down to bowl over and over between them. Norman's duplicate rose to his feet and glared back towards the ruined hut. Sherlock Holmes appeared at the doorway wielding his gun.

'Not again.' Pooley crawled away on all fours, seeking safety.

'Stop him,' cried Sherlock Holmes.

'With the corner up, pal.'

'Hold hard or I fire.'

Norman's duplicate turned upon his attacker. He snatched up a ten-gallon oil-drum which was harmlessly serving its time as a water-butt and raised it above his head. Holmes stood his ground, feet planted firmly apart, both hands upon his weapon. 'This is a Magnum Forty-four,' he said, 'biggest handgun in the world, and can blow your head clean off your shoulders.'

'He has definitely been watching too many videos,' whispered Omally as he crawled over to Pooley's place of safety.

'Now I know what you're thinking,' Holmes continued, 'you're thinking, in all that commotion did he fire five shots or six, that's what you're thinking, isn't it, punk?'

'I much preferred the Victorian approach,' said Jim Pooley.

Norman's robot stiffened; he was not adverse to watching the occasional Clint Eastwood movie himself on Norman's home-made video.

'Do you know, in all the excitement I'm not really sure myself? So what do you say, punk?'

The mechanical punk, who had seen that particular film six times said, 'It's a fair cop, governor,' and raised its hands.

'Up against the wall and spread'm mother,' cried Sherlock Holmes, causing Sir Arthur Conan Doyle to veritably spin in his grave.

Not too long later, Jim Pooley, John Omally, and Mr Sherlock Holmes, this time accompanied by a near-perfect facsimile of a highly-regarded local shopkeeper, entered the Professor's study. The scholar looked up from his desk and turned about in his chair. 'You made very short work of that,' he said. 'Good afternoon, Norman.'

The mechanical shopkeeper regarded the Professor as if he was guano on a hat-brim. 'You would do well to leave well enough alone,' said he.

Professor Slocombe turned up his palms. 'Please be seated, I have no wish to detain you longer than necessary. I merely seek a few answers to certain pressing questions.'

The duplicate clutched at his chest. 'To take away my life, more likely.'

'No, no, I swear. Please be seated.' Professor Slocombe turned to his other guests. 'Please avail yourselves, gentlemen, Norman and I have much to speak of.'

Holmes held his gun pointing steadily towards the robot's spinning heart. 'You counselled care, Professor,' said he, 'and now it is my turn.'

'A degree of trust must exist, Holmes, kindly put aside your gun.'

Holmes did so. Pooley and Omally fought awhile over the decanter and finally came to an agreement.

'It is of the greatest importance that we speak with each other,' Professor Slocombe told the robot. 'Please believe that I wish you no harm. Will you play straight with me?'

'I will, sir, but have a care for him. The man is clearly mad. Calls himself Sherlock Holmes but knows not a thing of the thirty-nine steps. I would have come to you of my own accord.'

'Really?'

'Oh yes.' The robot cleared his throat with a curiously mechanical coughing sound which sent the wind up Pooley and Omally. 'Things cannot be allowed to continue as they are.'

Professor Slocombe raised his eyebrows. 'You are aware of that?'

'I can hear them talking. They gnaw at my brain but I will not allow them ingress. I am Norman's man and sworn by the bond of birth to protect him.'

'Your loyalty is commendable.'

'I am sworn to serve mankind.'

'From behind a counter,' sneered Omally.

The robot nodded grimly. 'It sounded a little more noble the way I put it, but no matter, there is little enough of mankind now left to serve. The shop doorbell is silent the better part of the day. Trade declines; I rarely punch an order into the terminal, and when I do, the new stocks which finally arrive are further foreshortened. The master computer now runs it all. Mankind is on the wane, the new order prevails, night falls upon Brentford and the world. It is the coming of Ragnorok. Götterdämmerung.'

'Stick the Laurence Olivier circuits into override, you clockwork clown,' said John Vincent Omally, Man of Earth.

'How would you like me to fill your mouth with boot?' the robot enquired.

'Gentlemen, gentlemen,' said Professor Slocombe, 'let us have a little decorum please.'

'Well, he's had my shed down,' Omally complained. 'For one sworn to protect mankind he's about as much use as a nipple on a –'

'Quite so, John. Please be calm, we will achieve nothing by fighting amongst ourselves. We must all pull together.'

'You can pull whatever you want,' said the robot, 'but take it from me, you had better start with your fingers. Unless you can come up with something pretty special, pretty snappish, then you blokes are banjoed, get my meaning, F . . . U . . . C . . .'

'Language, please,' said Professor Slocombe. 'I think we catch your drift. Something pretty special was what I had in mind.'

22

'AAAAOOOOOOOOOAAAAAAAAAAAAOOOOO ... O ... UH?'

Neville the part-time barman awoke after an absence of some eleven chapters. Scorning the tried and tested 'Where am I?' he settled for 'Why have I got a light bulb stuck up my left nostril?' which was at least original. His eyes rolled up towards the ceiling, several inches above his face, and a great hand rose to brush away the obstruction blocking one side of his nose. This bed is a bit high, thought Neville. But then the dreadful memories of his most despicable situation came flooding back in a tidal wave of adipose tissue.

'The fat!' groaned Neville, his voice rumbling up from the depths of his stomach to shiver the ceiling above. 'The terrible fat!' He tried to move his great St Paul's dome of a head, but it seemed to be wedged tightly into an upper corner of the tiny hospital room. Painfully he struggled and shifted until he was able to peer down over the great massed army of himself and gauge some idea of how the land lay. It lay someway distant in the downwards direction. 'OOOOOAAAAAAOOOOOOAAA ... UH,' moaned Neville. 'Worse, much worse.'

A sudden sound distracted him from his misery, somewhere beneath his spreading bulk and slightly to one side, a door appeared to be opening. From his eyrie above the picture-rail Neville watched a minuscule nurse enter the already crowded room.

'And how are we today?' asked this fairy person.

'We?' Neville's voice arose in desperation. 'You mean that there is more than one of me now?'

'No, no.' The tiny nurse held up a pair of doll-like hands. 'You are doing very well, making good progress, great signs of improvement, nothing to fear.'

Neville now noticed to his increasing horror that the midget was brandishing a hypodermic syringe. Which, although perched between her tiddly digits like a Christmas cracker fag-holder, looked none the less as threatening as any of the others he had recently experienced at hind quarters.

'Time for your daily jab, roll over please.'

'Roll over? Are you mad, woman?' Neville wobbled his jowls down at the nurse.

The woman smiled up at him. 'Come on now, sir,' she wheedled. 'We're not going to throw one of our little tantrums now, are we?'

If Neville could have freed one of his feet, possibly the one which was now wedged above the curtain-rail surrounding his bed, he would have happily stamped the tiny nurse to an omelette.

'Come on now, sir, roly-poly.'

'Crunch crunch,' went Neville. 'Fe . . . Fi . . . Fo . . . Fum . . .'

'Don't start all that again, sir. I shall have to call for doctor.'

'Crunch . . . splat.' Neville struggled to free a foot, or anything.

'You leave me no choice, then.' The tiny nurse left the room, slamming the door behind her.

Neville rubbed his nose upon the ceiling. How long had he been here? Days? Months? Years? He really had no idea. What were they doing to him? Pumping him full of drugs to keep him sedated? What? He had known all along that it was a conspiracy, but what were they up to? They had blown him up like a blimp for their own foul ends. Probably for some vile new hormone research designed to increase the bacon yield from porker pigs. It was the Illuminati, or the masons, or the Moonies or some suchlike sinister outfit. Just because he was slightly paranoid, it didn't mean they weren't out to get him.

And far worse even, what was happening at the Swan? That defrocked Matelot Croughton would have his hand in the till up to the armpit. The beer would be flat and the ashtrays full. There was even the possibility of after-hours drinking, Omally would see to that. He was probably even downing pints on credit at this very moment. It was all too much. He must escape, if only to save his reputation. Neville twisted and turned in his confinement, a latterday Alice tormented in a sterilized doll's house.

The door of the room flew open beneath him and the nurse re-entered, accompanied by a pale young doctor in headphones. As Neville watched in fearful anticipation, he withdrew from his belt a small black device bristling with a pair of slim metallic rods. 'We are being naughty again,' he said, clearing his throat with a curiously mechanical coughing sound and arming the mechanism. 'Will we never learn?'

Neville the part-time barman turned up his eyes and gritted his teeth, 'Fe . . . Fi . . . Fo . . .'

The pale young man stepped forward and applied the electrodes to Neville's groin. A mind-rending shock of raw pain tore the captive barman's nerve endings to a million ribbons and he sank once more from consciousness into a blinding red haze of dumb agony.

23

The afflicted sun swung slowly into the Brentford sky, illuminating a parish which seemed already very much on the go. There were now none of the customary morningtide grumblings and complaints which greeted the arrival of each new day. Here were lads leaping to their feet anxious to continue their labours; and their labours as ever centred upon the forthcoming Festival of Brentford. Barefooted children already pranced stiff-leggedly about the maypoles set upon the Butts. The sounds of hammering and nailing echoed in the streets as the great floats were being hobbled into shape in myriad back to backs. The borough was obsessed by the approaching event, but the whys and the wherefores were misty businesses not lightly dwelt upon.

John and Jim slumbered amongst the potato sacks beneath a corrugated iron lean-to, sleeping the blessed sleep of the Bacchanalian. Professor Slocombe toiled with book and abacus, and Sherlock Holmes crept over a distant rooftop, magnifying glass in hand. Norman of the corner shop tinkered with Allen key and soldering iron upon the project of his own conception, and Old Pete with Chips at heel made his way along the Ealing Road, cursing bitterly. Neville slept in a netherworld of force-fed suppressants, dreaming escape and revenge. The old gods slept also, but the morning of the magicians was not far from the dawning.

'Things are certainly not what they used to be in Brentford,' groaned Jim Pooley.

The allotments being something of a parish nature reserve, the over-abundance of hearty birdsong tore the million-dollar bum and his Irish companion grudgingly from the arms of good old munificent Morpheus. Jim emerged from beneath his corrugated iron four-poster and grimaced at the world to be. He shushed at the feathered choristers and counselled silence. 'Before I was rich,' he said, tapping at his skull in the hope of restoring some order, 'before I was rich, I rarely took up a night's lodgings upon the allotments.'

A woebegone face emerged from the lean-to, the sight silencing the birdies in a manner which normally it would have taken a twelve-bore to do. The godforsaken thing that was John Omally was far better kept from the gaze of children or the faint of heart. 'Morning, Jim,' said he.

Pooley caught sight of the facial devastation. 'Put that back for your own sake,' he advised. 'I should not wish to come to close quarters with an article such as that until far starboard of breakfast time.'

Omally's stomach made a repulsive sound. 'Now breakfast would indeed be your man,' he said, taking his ravaged features back into the darkness. The birdsong welled forth anew.

'Shut up,' bawled Pooley, clutching his skull. The birdies put the proverbial sock in it.

'Shall we try the Professor for a slice or two of toast?' Jim asked.

'Definitely not,' a voice called back from the darkness. 'I have no wish to see that good gentleman again. Buy me back my introduction please, Jim. I will owe you.'

'I can lend you a quid, John, but no more.'

'Let us go round and impose upon Norman. He is currently at a disadvantage. A bit of company will do him no harm.'

Pooley rubbed at his forehead and did a bit of hopeless eye focussing. 'All right,' he said, 'but if he starts to part the bacon with his left hand then I am having it away on my toes.'

Omally's face appeared once more in the light. This time it had been translated into the one worn by his normal self.

'You have remarkable powers of recuperation, John,' said Jim.

'I am a Dubliner.'

'But of course.'

The two men tucked in their respective shirt-tails and strolled as best they could over the allotments, through the gates, and off up the Albany Road. A hundred or so yards behind them another Pooley and Omally fell into step and did likewise.

'You were saying last night,' said Jim, as they reached Moby Dick Terrace, 'although I should not broach the subject so early in the morning, something about reaching a decision?'

'Oh yes,' John thrust out his chest and made some attempts to draw in breath. 'My mind is made up, I have the thing figured.'

'And as to this particular plan. Is it kosher and above board or is it the well-intentioned codswallop of the truly banjoed?'

'I had a drink on me, truly. But in no way did it affect my reason.'

Now fifty yards behind, the other Pooley and Omally marched purposefully on in perfect step, their faces staring ever ahead.

'So tell me all about it then, John.'

Omally tapped at his nose. 'All in good time. Let us get some brekky under our belts first.'

As they rounded the corner into Ealing Road they saw Old Pete approaching, cursing and swearing, his daily paper jammed beneath his arm. Young Chips followed, marking the lampposts for his own. The elder hobbled on, and as he caught sight of John and Jim he grunted a half-hearted 'good morning'. As they all but drew level the old man suddenly dropped his paper and raised his stick. He stared past John and Jim and his mouth fell open, bringing the full dental horror of his National Healthers into hideous prominence. 'G . . . gawd,' he stammered, 'now I *have* seen it all.'

John and Jim looked at one another, towards the gesturing ancient, and finally back over their shoulders, following the direction of his confounded gaze. Bearing down upon them at a goodly rate of knots marched their perfect doubles. 'Run for your life!' screamed Omally. Jim was already under starter's orders. The two tore past the befuddled ancient and his similarly bemused pet at an Olympic pace. Their doubles strode on in unison, hard upon the retreating heels.

Old Pete turned to watch the curious quartet dwindle into the distance. He stooped crookedly to retrieve his fallen paper and shook his old head in wonder. 'I am certain that I saw that,' he told Chips. 'Although I am sure it will pass.'

Young Chips made a low gummy sort of growling sound. He had recently bitten a postman's leg and lost several of his favourite teeth for his pains. He just wasn't certain about anything any more.

John and Jim were making admirable time along the Ealing Road. They passed Norman's corner-shop, the Swan, the Princess Vic, and drew level with the football ground. 'Where do we go?' gasped Pooley. 'There's nowhere to run to.'

'Just keep running, we've got to lose them.' John squinted back over his shoulders. Himself and Jim showed no signs of fatigue, if anything they looked more sprightly, as if the exercise was doing them good. 'Run, man, run!'

Round into the maze of back streets behind the football ground went the hunted pair. The doubles came forward at the jog, staring ever ahead. John dragged Pooley into an alleyway. 'Along here and keep it sprightly,' he urged.

The breathless Jim collapsed into a convulsion of coughing, hands upon knees. 'I cannot continue,' he croaked. 'Leave me here to die.'

'And die you surely will. Ahead, man.'

Omally thrust Pooley forward, the sound of approaching footfalls echoing in his ears. Down the dustbin-crowded alley they ran, John overturning as many as he could behind him. The duplicates crashed along, behind, casting the toppled bins effortlessly aside. John and Jim emerged into an obscure side-street neither of them could put a name to. The Lateinos and Romiith computer scan which observed their every movement had it well-catalogued in degrees and minutes to a fearful number of decimal places.

'There has to be some way to dodge them,' gasped Pooley.

'Keep going, damn you.'

The duplicates crashed out into the street behind them.

Across Brentford ran Pooley and Omally, zig-zagging through people's back gardens, up and down fire escapes, in between the trees of the Memorial Park, and ever onwards. Behind them came the pounding of synchronized feet, never letting up for an instant.

'No more,' gulped Jim, when the two had shinned with difficulty over a high wall and dropped down into no safety whatsoever on the other side. 'I am finished.'

The sweat ran freely into Omally's eyes as he tore off his jacket and flung it aside. 'Not me,' said he. 'I'm not giving in to some clockwork copy, not while I still draw breath.'

With a great rending of brick and mortar, a section of the wall collapsed about them as the two duplicates applied their combined force.

'Run, Jim.'

'I'll race you.'

Along the cobbled way towards Old Brentford Docks staggered John and Jim, their last reserves of stamina all but drained away. Their hobnails sparked and clattered upon the cobbles and behind them in perfect unison their soulless pursuers were to be heard click-clacking at an easy pace. John pulled Jim into one of the disused warehouses. As he did so, their infra-red images unaccountably vanished from the screen of the Lateinos and Romiith computer. They ducked away behind a stack of abandoned loading pallets and shrank into the darkness, hearts pounding. From without, the sound of approaching footsteps drew nearer, then suddenly ceased. 'Quiet now,' whispered Omally, ramming his hands over Pooley's convulsing cherry-red face. Jim gasped for breath and sank down on to his bum with a dull thud. Omally ssshed him into silence, his finger upon his lips. The sound of slow, steady footfalls reached their ears. 'Stay quiet.'

The duplicates moved about the building, uncertain of which way to go; they tested the air with their sophisticated nasal sensory apparatus, in the hope of catching the scent of their quarries, but the ozone of the old dock drew the kipper over their tracks. Jim Pooley drew a fistful of sweat from his brow and spattered it on to the dusty floor of the old warehouse. He looked towards John, who shrugged in the darkness. Long, painful minutes passed. Jim folded his jacket across his chest to muffle the sound of his deafening heartbeat. Omally slunk to and fro seeking an exit or a reason or an anything. Outside, the duplicates stealthily encircled the building, sniffing and peering. The Omally gestured to the yawning doorway. The Pooley nodded. The duplicates entered the warehouse. Omally saw their shadows spread across the floor and flattened himself on to the deck. The two came slowly foward, scanning the way before them. Circuits meshed and weaved in their mechanized brains, drawing in the data, and processing it in the twinkling of a plastic eyelid.

From behind the stack of pallets a very foolish voice indeed said suddenly, 'Well, I think we've outrun them, John. Care for a tailor-made?'

Omally's eyes widened in horror as he watched the two heads, one his own and the other that of his dearest friend, swivel upon their frictionless bearings, and swing in the direction of the sound. He gestured towards Jim, whose face could just be seen grinning from behind the stack of pallets. 'Come, come.'

The robot Pooley leapt forward and grasped the obstruction barring his way. He tore the stack apart with a single movement, sending them smashing to all sides.

Jim looked up white and trembling and saw death staring him right between the eyes. 'Help, John,' he squealed, cowering back against the wall. 'Do something.'

Grinning like a gargoyle, the robot slowly withdrew from the pocket of his brand new suit, a small wicked-looking black instrument with two extendable electrodes. With a flick of the thumb he armed the mechanism and sent sparks crackling about the tips of the rods.

Omally floundered about seeking a suitable weapon, his hand closed over a length of iron conduit. 'Up the rebels,' he cried as he flung himself towards Jim's attacker. His own double turned upon him to stand glaring, eye to eye. 'You bastard,' spat Omally, 'come and try your luck.' He swung his cudgel with terrific force but the robot shot out a hand and grasped it, tearing it from his grip and flinging it the length of the warehouse. Omally ducked back as his double delved into its pocket. The smile widened upon its lips as the small black box appeared.

'Hold hard,' a voice echoed about the warehouse. Four pairs of eyes shot in the direction of the sound. A tall, gaunt figure stood crouched in the doorway, silhouetted against the light, legs spread widely apart and hands held forward. 'This is a Magnum Forty-four,' he shouted, 'biggest handgun in the world and can blow your heads clean off your shoulders. What do you say, punks?'

The robot duplicates looked towards their respective quarries, one cowering and covering his nuts, the other standing defiant, thirty-four-function barlow knife now in hand. They turned in unison towards the source of their annoyance.

'Hold hard or I fire,' cried Sherlock Holmes.

The robots stole forward upon synthetic heels.

'Right on.' Holmes' trigger finger tightened. Two shots rang out in rapid succession. The robot Pooley span from his feet in a hazy blur, his head a mass of trailing ribbons and sparking wires. The Omally sank to its knees, foul yellow slime spurting from two over-large holes front and back of its plastic skull. He rose to stumble forward, cruel claws scratching at the air, jerked upright, then slumped to the deck, a rag doll flung carelessly aside. Holmes blew into the barrel of his Forty-four, spun it upon his forefinger, and tucked it away into his shoulder holster. 'Gotcha,' he said.

Omally clicked back the blade of his barlow knife and thrust the thing into his breast pocket. He stepped over to console the gibbering Pooley. 'Thanks yet again,' he said to Sherlock Holmes. 'It seems that we are once more in your debt.'

'No sweat,' the great detective replied. He stooped over the twisted 'corpse' of the false and fallen Pooley and began to turn out its pockets. Jim crept forward and watched in horror as Holmes examined the contents before tossing them aside. A besmutted handkerchief, a leaky ballpoint pen, an initialled gold Cartier lighter, and a packet of Passing Cloud cigarettes.

Pooley patted frantically at his pockets; they'd been picked obviously. To his further horror his patting disclosed an identically besmutted handkerchief, a leaky ballpoint pen, and the same Cartier lighter, which he had not as yet learned how to fill; even the packet of fags. Pooley held out his hands to Sherlock Holmes. The detective took the cigarette packet and shook it open: seventeen cigarettes. He picked up the robot's packet: three gone from the packet of twenty.

'Very thorough. Every last detail absolutely correct,' said Holmes. 'I would hazard a guess that, should we analyse the fluff in your trouser pockets and that of this demon-spawn here, they would match exactly.' Jim shuddered. Holmes completed his search and satisfied himself that he had taken all relevant matters into account. He rose to leave. 'I must away now,' he said. 'The game is afoot.'

'It's costing us an arm and a leg,' said Omally. 'Well, good luck to you at the very least.'

'Your sentiment is appreciated, John, but luck plays no part whatsoever in my investigations.' Holmes tapped at his right temple. 'It all comes from here. The science of deduction, made art.'

'Yes,' said Omally doubtfully. 'Well, be that as it may. My best wishes to you for the success of your mission.'

'Ten-four,' said the detective. 'Up and away.' With these few words he leapt out through the warehouse door and was presently lost from view.

'I still say he's a nutter.' Omally brushed the dust and grime away from the numb and shattered Jim Pooley.

The two electronic cadavers lay spread across the warehouse floor, and it was no pleasant thing to behold your own corpse lying at your very feet. Pocket fluff and all. Omally turned Jim's head away. 'Come on, mate,' said he softly. 'We've had a good innings here, let's not spoil it.'

Jim pointed a dangly hand towards his *doppelgänger*, 'It was me,' he said. 'It was me.'

'Well, it's not any more. Come on, let's get out of here.'

'I shouldn't do it.' A voice from behind froze Omally in his tracks and caused his hand to seek out his barlow knife. 'Don't go outside, I'm telling you.' Omally turned slowly and wearily to face whatever the new threat might be. Across the deserted warehouse floor a head peeped out from a now open manhole. It was Soap Distant. 'Lead roof,' said the pink-eyed man from below. 'The computer scan cannot penetrate it. That's why they couldn't find you.'

Omally peered up into the darkness of the eaves above. 'So that was it.'

'Hurry now,' said Soap. 'Their back-up boys are on the way.'

John did not need telling twice. Thrusting Pooley before him, he made for the manhole and something which loosely-resembled safety. As Jim's head vanished into the darkness below John skipped back to where his duplicate lay. Viewing his own remains, he smiled briefly, and stopped to remove the thing's left boot. Upending this, a bundle of banknotes tumbled out into his hand. 'Very thorough indeed,' said John, pocketing the spoils of war.

24

A half a mile beneath the surface of Planet Earth, Soap Distant offered Omally a cup of tea.

'This time I think I will,' said John. 'Is there any chance of breakfast, Soap?'

'Certainly.' The pink-eyed man applied himself to the frying-pan.

'Are you all right, Jim?' Omally prodded his companion who was staring dumbly into space.

'It was me,' mouthed Jim.

'Well, it isn't now. You're safe.'

'It was me.'

'Sunnyside up,' piped Soap.

'Two on a raft,' Omally replied, 'with all the trimmings.'

Shortly a fine breakfast was in the offing. With the aid of much pushing, prompting, and cuffing, Jim was slowly brought back to the land of the living to enjoy his. For every 'It was me', he received a blow to the head. Somewhat after the fashion of the now legendary Pavlov's pooches he learned the error of his ways. 'Could I have another fried slice?' he asked.

Soap obliged. As he turned the bread in the pan he said, 'The lead you see, the scan cannot penetrate it. They've got an eye in the sky up there watching everybody that's left, but they can't see through the lead. I myself lined the Professor's loft with lead foil. Keeps the buggers out it does.'

Omally wiped his chin. 'Very good, Soap. It is pleasing to hear that some precautions can be taken.'

'Oh yes, no system is infallible. Old Ratinous and Loathesome think they've got it all figured out, but there is always a dodge to be found by the thinking man.'

'Such was once the credo of my karma but I am now experiencing some doubts.'

'Don't,' said Soap. 'We'll beat the blighters yet.'

'You seem very confident.'

Soap dumped the fried slice on to Pooley's plate, and popped a grilled tomato into his mouth. 'Oh yes,' he said between munchings, 'there is not a machine yet that will not fare the worse for a well-placed spanner jammed up its works.'

'Good man,' said Omally, leaning forward to pat his host upon the shoulder. 'I hope you know where to place the spanner.'

'Never fear.' Soap pulled at his lower eye. 'Never fear.'

'See,' said Omally, nudging Pooley in the rib area, 'even with Armageddon staring you in the face there is always a flanker to be pulled.'

'It was me,' said Jim. 'Could I have another grilled sausage do you think, Soap?'

The pink-eyed man laughed heartily. 'Have two,' he cried, 'have three if you wish.'

'Three would be fine,' said Jim. 'I have no wish to appear greedy.'

The three sub-Earthers enjoyed a hearty breakfast washed down with several bottles of Chateau Distant carrot claret. 'I think you might do well to lie low here for a while,' Soap advised his guests. 'Your cards would seem to be well and truly marked at present.'

'What about the spanner?' Omally made turning motions with his hand.

'All in good time, Professor Slocombe has the matter well in hand. He will tell us when the time is right.'

Omally made a sour face. 'Much as I love that old man, I am not altogether sure that his reasoning is quite as clear as it once was.'

Soap flapped his hands wildly. 'Do not say such things. The Professor is an Illuminati. You must trust in all he says.'

'Perhaps,' Omally finished his glass. 'But it is all theories, theories, and there is precious little of what he says that makes any sense to me.'

'I would have thought that as a Catholic yourself, the idea would have held great appeal.'

'What Armageddon? The Twilight of the Gods? Not a lot.'

'No, not that side of it, I mean about the garden.'

'What garden?'

'About the garden being in Brentford. That is the whole point of it all, surely?'

'Soap, in a single sentence you have lost me completely. What are you talking about?'

'Eden, the Garden of Eden. Do you mean he didn't tell you?'

'Hold on, hold on.' Omally held up his hands. 'Go through this again slowly. What are you talking about?'

'The Garden of Eden,' said Soap. 'You know the one, gets a big mention in Genesis.'

'Of course I know. What are you saying?'

Soap shook his head; he was clearly speaking with a half-wit. 'Why do you think the walls have come down about Brentford?'

'To stop me spending my millions,' said Pooley bitterly.

'Hardly that. To protect Eden against the fall of Babylon.'

'I always had Babylon pegged as being a little further south.'

'Not a bit of it,' said Soap. 'Chiswick.'

'Chiswick?'

'Yes. You see, the Professor solved the whole thing years ago, when he reorientated all the old maps. He was under the belief that the entire chronology and location of Biblical events was wildly inaccurate. He spent years piecing it all together before he finally solved the riddle.'

'That Babylon was in Chiswick.'

'Yes, but more importantly, that the Garden of Eden was planted right here. Upon the very spot now enclosed within the Brentford Triangle.'

'Madness,' said Omally, 'nothing more, nothing less.'

'Not a bit of it. He showed me all the reorientated maps. All the events chronicled in the Bible took place right here in England.'

'And Christ?'

'And did those feet in ancient times? Liverpool born, crucified in Edinburgh.'

'Blasphemy,' said Omally, 'heresy also.'

'It is as true as I am sitting here.' Soap crossed his heart with a wet finger. 'All the stories in the Bible are based upon more ancient texts than scholars suppose. The events took place in a more northerly clime. They were transferred to their present incorrect locations upon far later translations of the Holy Word. The dates are thousands of years out. It all happened right here, and, for that matter, it is still happening. I would have thought that matters above make that patently obvious.'

'Blessed Mary,' said John Omally.

'Born in Penge.'

'Where else?'

'Makes you think, though,' said Pooley, freshening his glass. 'After all, we all knew that Brentford was the hub of the universe. This simply confirms it.'

'Exactly,' said Soap. 'And we have always known that God is an Englishman.'

'Steady on,' said John Omally. 'I will swallow a lot but never that. British at a pinch. But English? Never.'

'*Ipso facto*,' said Soap, 'or something like.'

'I will need to give this matter a considerable amount of intense thought,' said John Omally, 'which I believe might necessitate the consumption of a litre or two more of your claret to aid cogitation.'

'Cogitate on me,' said Soap Distant, drawing out a brace of flagons from beneath his chair.

'You are a gentleman, sir.'

25

Norman had the door of his shop well-barred. Trade had fallen off to such an alarming degree that, but for serving Old Pete with his newspaper and tobacco, there seemed no point whatever in opening. Absolute panic, and the fear of his duplicate's return, or possibly the arrival of something far worse, had prompted him this day, upon the ancient's departure, to barricade the premises against the outside world. The counters now stood across the front door, with what few items still remained stacked upon them. Viewing the hole in his ceiling, Norman considered these moves to be little more than token opposition. But even token opposition was surely better than no opposition at all. 'Many hands make light work,' said the shop-keeper, irrelevantly recalling a faith-healing session he had once attended, where a defunct fuse box which had thrown the place into darkness, had been miraculously restored to life.

Norman tottered over the newly-laid linoleum, wielding his screwdriver Excalibur-fashion. He entered the kitchenette. There wasn't a lot of room in there at present. The object of his most recent, all-consuming attention occupied more than a little floor space.

Norman's time machine was a big filler!

There was very much of the electric chair evident in the overall design of the thing. But also a good deal of NASA's mission control and a fair degree of Captain Nemo's Nautilus. A *soupçon* of the pumping station at Kew and Doctor F's laboratory completed the picture. The thing bristled with the banks of twinkling lights Norman always felt were so essential to lend the necessary atmosphere to such a project. Above the driving seat, commandeered from his Morris Minor, a slim brass wheel turned at precisely twenty-six revolutions per minute. From the axle-rods, wires trailed to every compass point like the ribbons of an eccentric electronic maypole, enshrouding the entire contraption, which rested upon a kind of Father Christmas sleigh.

'Now then.' Norman consulted a ludicrous wiring diagram scrawled on to the back of a computer stock control print-out. It was all something to do with E equalling MC^2, the parallax theory, whatever that might be, and the triangulations of Pythagorus. Oh yes, and the space-time continuum, not that that even bore thinking about.

Norman shook his head at the wonder of it all. Scientists always did tend to over-complicate the issues. Professional pride, he supposed. To him science was, and always had been, a pretty straight-forward affair, which required only the minimum of writing down. Once you'd nicked the idea, this time from H G Wells, you simply went down to Kay's Electrical in the High Street and purchased all the component parts. What you couldn't buy you hobbled up out of defunct wirelesses and what was left of the Meccano set. Scientists always made such a big deal out of things and did it all arse about face. Norman was the happy exception to this rule.

Brentford seemed to be in a bit of schtuck at the present, but the shopkeeper considered that once he had the machine on the go he would at least be able to set matters straight once and for all. He always liked to think that he was helping out, and seeing as how nobody had cared to put him in the picture he meant to go it alone. Not being at all silly he had tracked down the root cause of the Parish's ills to the dreaded Lateinos and Romiith concern, and it seemed but a simple thing to him to slip back into the past and make a few subtle changes. Like murdering the bastards where they slept in their cribs for a first off. Then bending the council records so he got that planning permission to do his loft conversion. And he had always wanted to shake the hand of that editor of the *Brentford Mercury* who had run off with his wife. There was quite a lot you could achieve once you'd got time travel licked.

Norman had definitely decided to travel backwards first; the future looked anything but rosy. He dived forward with his screwdriver into an impenetrable-looking network of wires and fuse boxes and twiddled about here and there. The strains of the Rolling Stones' legendary composition 'Time Is On My Side' sprang almost unconsciously to his lips. The whole concept of the enterprise pleased Norman with its every single detail. There was the sheer naked thrill of hurtling into the unknown, allied with the potential power a man might wield once able to traverse the fields of time. Also, and by no means the smallest part of it, was the infinite variety of puns and proverbs that could be drawn from the word 'time'. Such things must never be overlooked. 'Time, gentlemen, please,' said Norman, tittering loudly to himself. He flicked a random selection of likely-looking switches in the hope that he might get some clue as to why he had fitted them. One brought his old Bush Radiogram bucketing into life, 'It's time for old time,' sang a disembodied voice. Norman creased up. He was having the time of his life.

The shopkeeper straightened his back and scratched at his head with the end of his screwdriver. It did all look about finished really. He could always tighten up the odd bolt, or give the gleaming brasswork another polish, but apart from these niceties it looked very much complete. 'And not before time,' chuckled Norman, making nudging notions towards an imaginary companion.

The sounds of sharp tapping suddenly drew his attention. Someone, or something, was knocking upon the barricaded shopdoor. An icy hand clutched at the shopkeeper's heart. Of course, it could be just a customer anxious to pay his newspaper bill? Well, it could be.

The Lateinos and Romiith computer scan monitored Norman's infra-red image as it dithered about in the crowded kitchenette. The sensors gauged the increase in his pulse rate and analysed the sweat particles which broke out on his forehead. It also relayed this information instantly to the shopkeeper's mirror image, which was even now rapping left-handedly upon the door. A cruel smile appeared upon the duplicate's face as it turned and strode purposefully away, bound for the backyard wall.

Norman gnawed upon his knuckles. Now would certainly seem like an ideal time for a bit of test run. He climbed rapidly into the driving seat and fastened his safety belt; as he had no way of telling exactly which way up time was when you travelled through it he did not wish to fall out. Carefully, he swung a pair of great calliper arms, heavily-burdened with switch-boxes and levers, about him, and, turning the ignition key, put the machine into reverse. Lights pulsed and flashed, and the great brazen wheel tumbled on above him, a ring of sparks encircled the machine in a twinkling halo. The sudden crash of brickwork informed the aspiring time traveller that an unwelcome visitor had just entered his backyard. The buzzing and hammering of the mechanism increased at a goodly rate; but to Norman's dismay he did not appear to be going anywhere, either backwards, or forwards, or even upside down. 'Get a move on,' shouted the distraught shopkeeper, thumbing switches and squinting up at the kitchen clock in the hope of a fluctuation. The machine shook and shivered. The lights flashed and the engine roared. The sounds of splintering woodwork as the kitchen door parted company with its hinges were swallowed up in the cacophony.

Norman's fearsome replica stood in the doorway clearing its throat and rubbing its hands together.

Norman flung levers in all directions and waggled the joystick. The creature stalked towards him wearing a most unpleasant expression. It reached down slowly and grasped one of the runners, meaning to up-end the whole caboodle. Norman cowered back in his seat, kicking at any levers which lay beyond his reach. The creature strained at the runner but the thing would not shift. Norman stared up at the great wheel spinning above, its gyroscopic effect was such that the machine could not possible be overturned. The robot, being Norman to its finger ends, twigged this almost instantaneously, and abandoned this futile pursuit to deal with matters more directly. Its hands stretched towards Norman's throat. The wee lad shrank away, burbling for mercy. The demon double clawed towards him, its eyes blazing hatred, and its lips drawn back from gnashing, grinding teeth; the talons were an inch from Norman's throat. Norman unceremoniously wet himself. Not the wisest thing to do when surrounded by so much unearthed electrical apparatus.

'Ooooooooooh!' Norman's voice rose to an operatic soprano as the charge caught him squarely in the nuts, arched up his backbone and shot out through the top of his head, setting his barnet ablaze. A great jolt rocked the machine, sparks cascaded roman candle style from every corner, and the humming and throbbing rose to a deafening crescendo. As if suddenly alert to the possibility of imminent explosion the robot drew back its hands. It dropped them once more to the runner then straightened up and backed towards the door. Norman batted at his cranial bonfire and squinted through the now rising smoke. To his amazement he saw the creature back away through the doorway and the shattered kitchen-door rise magically behind it, to slap back into its mountings, pristine and undamaged. Norman's eyes flew towards the kitchen clock. The second hand was belting round the face like a propeller. It was travelling anti-clockwise. 'Ha ha ha ha ha ha.' Norman clapped his hands together and bounced up and down in his seat, oblivious to his scrambled goolies and smouldering top-knot.

He was travelling back in time!

The second hand was gathering speed, increasing to a blur, followed now by the minute and the hour. The kitchenette began to grow vague and fuzzy and then in a flash it vanished.

The kitchenette door tore from its hinges and crashed down on the linoleum. Norman's duplicate stood horribly framed in the doorway, staring into the fog of smoke which now filled the otherwise empty room. A look of perplexity swept over the robot shopkeeper's face. Data retrieval and logic modification channels whirred and cross-meshed, and finally spelt out absolutely sweet bugger all. Which certainly served them right.

26

Norman held fast to his seat and stared forward into the darkness. Strange lights welled up before him, swung past to either side, and vanished away behind. He experienced no sensation of motion; it was as if he was somehow travelling outside of space and time altogether. He was in limbo. Norman looked at his watch. It had stopped. He scrutinized the date counter he had optimistically screwed on to one of the enclosing calliper arms; a tangle of wires dangled from beneath it. He had forgotten to link the thing up. Where was he, and more importantly when was he? He might have been travelling for an hour or a year or a century. He had no way of telling. He had best put the machine out of gear and cruise to a halt before he slipped back too far. The idea of finding himself trampled on by a dinosaur was most unappealing.

A terrible fear took a grip upon his heart. Exactly what would he find when he stopped? He could wind up in the middle of Rorke's Drift with the Zulus on the attack. Or even in the sea or inside the heart of a mountain. There was no way of telling. Perhaps if he slowed down just a bit he could spy out a safe place to land. Norman's hand hovered over the controls, a look of imbecility folding his face in half. He had pulled off The Big One this time and no mistake, but where was it going to get him? In big big trouble, that was where. Norman did his best to weigh up the pros and cons. Could he get killed in the past before he had even been born? Was such a thing possible? The situation he was now in lent sufficient weight to the conviction that nothing was impossible. The words of the great Jack Vance filled his head, 'In a situation of infinity, every possibility no matter how remote must find physical expression.' He had that sewn into a sampler over his bed.

It was all too much for the shopkeeper and he slumped dejectedly over the controls and grizzled quietly, resigning himself to oblivion. What had he done? What in the name of dear Mother Earth had he done?

'Norman,' a voice called to him from out of the void. 'Norman.'

'Who's that?' Norman squinted into the darkness. 'I know that voice.'

'Norman,' the voice grew louder. 'Halt the apparatus, you will slip beyond reach.'

Norman hammered at the controls; he tore the ignition key from the dashboard, and a sudden rush of air buffeted him back in his seat. Light popped and flashed about him, the machine rattled and shuddered and with a great sigh, daylight spun into view from the end of a long dark tunnel and broke in every direction. Norman shielded his face, closed his eyes and prepared to make what peace he could with his Creator. There was a hefty whack and a moment of terrible silence. Norman flinched and cowered. Warm sunlight tickled his fingers and the sound of birdsong filled his ears. Still not daring to look, Norman sniffed. The sweet scent of flowers, sweeter than any he had previously smelled – or was that now *would* smell? – engulfed him.

He had died, that was it. Died and gone to the good place. Hope always sprang eternal in the wee lad. Norman uncovered his eyes and peered through his fingers. The time machine rested in an Arcadian glade upon a richly-forested hillside, bordering a beautiful valley which swept in gentle rolls down to a picturesque and meandering river. Very nice indeed. This far exceeded his highest hopes of what Heaven might look like. The trip had been well worthwhile after all. Rising high above the hills beyond the river stood a shimmering white fairytale castle, pennants flying in the breeze. It was the stuff of storybooks, of childhood innocence. It was wonderful. Pushing back the calliper arms, Norman unclipped his safety belt and, plucking gingerly at his still damp trouser seat, set his feet upon the lush green carpet of dew-soaked grass. It was paradise; the enchanted glade.

'Norman.' The voice loosened the lad's bowels, but he had nothing left to yield. 'Norman.' An old man was approaching, hobbling upon a cane. He was clothed in a flowing robe of deepest black, embroidered richly with stars and pentacles and magical symbols picked out in silvern thread. Upon his head he wore a tall conical hat of identical craftsmanship. He sported a long white beard and was the very picture of all one might reasonably expect of Merlin the Magician.

Norman peered at the approaching apparition. He knew that face, that stooping gait, as well as he knew anything. A choked voice rose from his throat. 'Professor Slocombe?'

The magician put his long finger to his lips. 'All in good time,' he said. 'Welcome, Norman.'

'Where am I?'

'Why in Camelot, of course. Wherever did you think?'

'I thought, perhaps, well I don't know, still in Brentford maybe.'

Merlin cocked his head on one side. 'Brentford,' he said. 'I like the name, I will see what can be done about that for some future time. But for now we have much to speak of. Will you come with me to yonder castle and take a cup of mead?'

'I think that would be just fine,' said Norman, the once and future shopkeeper of England.

27

Professor Slocombe looked up towards the great ormolu mantelclock and nodded his old head gently in time to the pendulum's swing. 'Good luck, Norman,' he said. Drawing his gaze from the antique timepiece, he turned to stare out through the open French windows. There, in the all-too-near distance, the great black shaft of the Lateinos and Romiith building obscenely scarred the two-hundred-year-old skyline. Its upper reaches were lost high amongst gathering stormclouds. The aura of undiluted evil pressed out from it, seeking to penetrate the very room. The old man shuddered briefly and drew the windows shut. Norman's homemade double laid aside a bound volume of da Vinci, penned in the crooked mirror-Latin of the great man himself, and peered quizzically towards the Professor.

'I know what you are thinking,' the scholar said. 'He is safe thus far, so much is already known to me. But as to the return trip, all depends upon the calculations. It is all in the numbers. We can only offer our prayers.'

'Prayers?'

'They offer some comfort.'

'I wouldn't know,' said the robot, somewhat brusquely. 'Norman did not see fit to log such concepts into my data banks.'

Professor Slocombe watched the mechanical man with unguarded interest. 'I should really like to know exactly what you do feel.'

'I feel texture. I think, therefore I am. Or so I have been informed. Every cloud has a silver lining I was also told, and a trouble shared is a bird in the . . .'

'Yes, indeed. But what causes you to react? How do you arrive at decisions? What motivates you?'

'Impetus. I react as I have been programmed to do. Upon information received, as the boys in blue will have it.'

'Do you believe then that this is how the other duplicates function?'

'Certainly not.' Something approaching pride entered the robot's voice. 'They are merely receivers, created solely to receive and to collect information and perform their tasks. The mainframe of the great computer does all their thinking for them. Clockwork dummies, that's all they are.'

'Interesting,' said Professor Slocombe.

'You spend a great deal of time in idle speculation,' the robot observed, 'considering the gravity of the situation. You seek to detect human emotion in me. I might do the same to you.'

Professor Slocombe chuckled delightedly. 'There are more wheels currently in motion than the one which spins in your chest,' said he. 'Even now, great forces are beginning to stir elsewhere in the parish.'

28

'Fe ... fi ... fo ... fum.' The bloated barman awoke giddily from
another bout of barbiturate-induced slumber and rattled the
window-panes of his hospital prison. The door beneath him opened
and his Promethean tormentor entered the barman-crowded room,
hypodermic at the ready. Neville eyed her with absolute loathing. 'I
smell the blood of an Englishman.'

'We are not going to be naughty again, are we?'

'Be he alive or be he dead.'

'Roly-poly, please, sir.'

'I'll grind his bones to make my bread.'

'I shall have to fetch doctor, then.'

'No!' Neville drew in his breath, filled his cheeks, and blew a
great blast at the clinical harpy. The midget fought at the gale, but
lost her footing and fluttered away through the doorway and out
into the corridor. 'At last,' said Neville to the ceiling against which
his face had been compressed so uncomfortably for so very long.
'At long long last.' He raised a fist the size of a cement sack and
clenched and unclenched the fingers. The sap was beginning to rise
and a great inner strength was rising with it. The power was surging,
driving through his veins; unstoppable and titanic.

At last he realized the truth: his consuming disability had been
nothing more than the painful and grotesque prelude to what was to
come. The time for the settling of scores was fast approaching. The
power of the great Old Ones. The gods of his pagan ancestry born
in the dawn of the light when the world was full of wonder. The
power had returned and it had returned to him. The last of the line.

A broad tight-lipped smile arced up upon the barman's face. His
fingers flexed, and beneath the surgical gown huge muscles rolled
about his body, porpoises swimming in a sack. The Herculean

barman pressed his hands to the ceiling of his most private ward. With a splinter of plastic-cladding, his hands rose, tightening to fists and forcing upwards, unstoppably. Neville rose with them, pouring forth from his prison, rising upon a floodtide of super-human energy. The barman's head and shoulders passed through the ceiling and a low choked cry rose from his throat.

He was ill-prepared for the sight which met his gaze. He had supposed himself to be in the private wing of the Cottage Hospital. The view from the window tending to support this well enough. But not a bit of it. The hospital room and its window view were nothing but a sham, hiding a grim reality. The tiny room was little more than a box, set in some great empty warehouse of a place. It spread away, dimly-lit, acre upon acre of concrete flooring and absolutely nothing. The window view, now seen from above, was a mish-mash of laser lines projected on to a screen. It was a holo-gram.

'Fe . . . fi . . . fo,' said Neville, as he perused his stark sur-roundings. Where was he? He felt like a jack-in-the-box in an empty toy factory. 'Curiouser and curiouser!' Standing erect and kicking aside the make-believe walls of the movie-set hospital room, he stood upon a soundstage vaster by far than any ever envisaged by the now legendary Cecil B himself.

Neville drew in his breath and watched in pride as his great chest rose beneath the gown. This was the dream come true, surely? The impossible dream realized. His gods had at long last decided to smile upon him. He must have performed for them some great service without even realizing it. A million glorious thoughts poured into the barman's head. He would seek out that Trevor Alvy who had bullied him at school; and parade up and down the beach come summer with his shirt actually off. No more heavy sweaters to disguise his bony physique, no more cutting jibes about his round shoulders. He would get a tan. And kick sand in people's faces. Yes, he would definitely do that. He would eject drunks from the bar without having to resort to the sneaky knobkerry from behind. Neville threw himself into a pose, displaying muscles in places where Arnold Schwarzenegger didn't even have places. Conan who? He was quids in here and no mistake. 'Oh joy, oh bliss.' Things were happening about Neville's groin regions which, out of common decency, he did not even dare to dwell upon. The bulging barman paused for a moment or two's reflection. For one thing, it was impossible for him to gauge exactly how high he might be. If the hospital room was life-size, he must surely top the twenty-foot mark. That was no laughing matter. Giants, no matter how well hung they might be, were never exactly the most popular fellows in town. In fact, the more well hung they were, the worse their lot. There was always some would be 'David' about, with a catapult and poor eyesight.

Neville erased such thoughts from his brain with difficulty. If this thing had been done to him, then it had been done with a purpose. There was no accident or casual element of chance evident here. This was something else, something very very special. And he would have to find out the purpose. And to do that, he would first have to make his escape from this great cold dark room at the very hurry-up. Before the chill began to shrink anything. Upon those tireless, finely-muscled legs that Charles Atlas had promised to a dozen generations of sickly youth, Neville took flight and sped away with great leaps and bounds, seeking the exit.

29

A good half-mile beneath the barbarian barman's thundering feet, John Omally opened another bottle of carrot claret and poured himself a large glass. 'Soap,' said he to his host, 'this is good stuff you have here.'

'Nectar,' Jim Pooley agreed. 'Write me down the recipe and I will provide for your old age.'

Soap grinned stupidly. 'You must try the cigars,' he said, rising unsteadily from his horrendous armchair and tottering over to the box.

'Home-grown?'

Soap made a crooked 'O' out of his thumb and forefinger. 'I have a five spot says you cannot identify the blend.'

'Take it out of the money you still owe us,' said Jim.

Soap handed out a brace of lime-green coronas. Omally took his dubiously and rolled it against his ear. 'Not a sprout?' he asked in a fearful voice.

'Heavens no.' Soap crossed his heart. 'Would I do that to you?'

Pooley sniffed his along its length. 'Not spud?'

'Absolutely not. I know Omally stuffs his peelings into his pipe, but even he would draw the line at manufacturing cigars from them.'

'They don't roll,' said John, making the motions.

The two men lit up, and collapsed simultaneously into fits of violent coughing.

'Whatever it is,' wheezed John, tears streaming from his eyes, 'it's good stuff.'

'Perhaps a little sharp.' Jim's face now matched the colour of his cigar.

'Do you give up?'

'Indubitably.'

'Well I shan't tell you anyway.' Soap slumped back into his chair, hands clasped behind his head.

The ruddy hue slowly returned to Jim's face as he got the measure of his smoke. 'How long do you think we are going to have to fiddle about down here?' he asked.

Soap shrugged.

Omally tapped a quarter-inch of snow-white ash into a glass cache pot of the Boda persuasion. 'We can't stay down here indefinitely, Soap,' he said. 'Although your hospitality is greatly appreciated, you must surely realize that we must make some attempts at salvaging something of our former lives. We were quite fond of them.'

Soap waved his hands at the Irishman. 'All in good time, John. The Prof will tip us the wink. For now, have a drink and a smoke and a pleasant chat.'

'I fear we will shortly exhaust all topics of conversation.'

'Not a bit of it, I am a fascinating conversationalist. On most matters I am eloquence personified. My range is almost inexhaustible.'

'And your modesty legend. I know.'

'All right then, what is your opinion of evolution?'

'A nine-aeon wonder.' Omally awaited the applause.

'I have a somewhat revolutionary theory of my own.'

'I do not wish to hear it.'

'I subscribe to the view that the world was created five minutes ago, complete with all records and memories. Although an improbable hypothesis, I think you will find it logically irrefutable.'

'And how long have you held this belief?'

'Hard to say, possibly four and a half minutes.'

'Fol-de-rol.'

'Well, what about politics, then? As an Irishman, you must have some definite views.'

'As an Irishman, I never trouble to give the matter a moment's thought.'

'Religion, then?'

'I subscribe to the view that the world was created five minutes ago. Are you looking for a grazed chin, Soap?'

'Only trying to pass the time with a little pleasant intercourse.'

'Careful,' said Jim.

'Well, I get few callers.'

'Hardly surprising, your address is somewhat obscure even for the A to Z.'

'Would you care to see my mushroom beds?'

'Frankly, no.'

'I spy with my little eye?'

'Stick it in your ear, Soap.'

The three men sat awhile in silence. Jim picked a bit of chive out of his teeth and won five quid from Soap. But other than that there was frankly no excitement to be had whatsoever, which might in its way have been a good thing, for there was a great deal of it in the offing. A sudden bout of urgent knocking rattled Soap Distant's front door.

'Expecting guests?' Omally asked. 'Ladies, I trust. Current affairs have played havoc with my social calendar.'

Soap's face had, within the twinkling of an eye, transformed itself from an amiable countenance into the all-too-familiar mask of cold fear. 'Are either of you tooled up?' he asked inanely.

'I have my barlow knife,' said Omally, rapidly finishing his drink.

'And me my running shoes,' said Jim. 'Where's the back door, Soap?'

Mr Distant dithered in his armchair. 'No one knows of this place,' he whispered hoarsely. The pounding on the door informed him that that statement was patently incorrect.

Omally rose hurriedly from his seat. 'Lead us to the priesthole, Soap, and make it snappy.'

'I'm for that.' Jim leapt up and began smacking at the walls. 'Where's the secret panel, Soap?'

Soap chewed upon his knuckles. 'It's the other me,' he whimpered. 'I knew it had to happen, even here.'

'The odds are in its favour. Kindly show us the way out.'

'There's no other exit.'

'Then find us a place to hide, someone must continue to serve the cause, even if you are indisposed.'

'Yes, fair do's,' Jim agreed, as the pounding rattled ornaments and nerves alike. 'If it's the other you, then he may not know John and I are here. We at least should hide until the bloodshed is over.'

'Oh, thanks very much, pals.'

'We'd do the same for you.'

'Come again?'

'Open up there.' A voice from without brought the ludicrous conversation to a halt.

'It's Sherlock Holmes,' said Omally. 'Let him in.'

Soap hastened to unfasten the front door. 'Close it without delay.' The detective pressed himself inside. 'They are hard upon my heels.'

'How did you know where I lived?' Soap pressed the bolts home.

'No matter. Are you three tooled up?'

Omally shook his head and fell back into his seat. Pooley did likewise. 'Would you care for another splash of carrot, Jim?' Omally waggled the bottle towards Pooley.

'Another would be fine. So how goes the game afoot, Sherlock?'

'A bit iffy as it happens.' Holmes drew out his revolver and flattened himself against the front wall.

Jim rattled his glass against the bottle's neck. 'And you have brought the lads down here after us. Most enterprising.'

'I never really believed in him, you know,' said John, now refreshing his own glass.

'I looked it all up in the library,' Pooley replied. 'The evidence is very much against him. Purely fictitious, I so believe.'

'Wise up,' said Sherlock Holmes. 'These mothers mean business.'

The sounds of terrible ghost train screaming leant weight to his conviction. From beyond, something malevolent was surging forward from the darkness. Pooley covered his ears and crossed his eyes. Omally snatched up a Biba table-lamp and prepared once more to do battle. If the awful screaming was not bad enough, the sounds which accompanied it were sufficient to put the wind up even Saint Anthony himself. Hideous slurpings and suckings, as of some gigantic mollusc, and thrashing sounds, dragging chains and clicking joints. All in all, anything but a Christmas hamper.

Omally turned towards Holmes, who now crouched facing the door, Magnum forty-four poised once more between his outstretched hands. 'What in the name of the Holies is it?' he shouted above the growing din.

'It came at me from a basement opening. I have only seen its like before amongst the work of Hieronymous Bosch.'

This remark meant little to Omally who had always thought a Bosch to be an expensive sports car. But that the something which

573

was approaching was very very nasty and somewhat overlarge seemed on the cards.

As the first concussion shook the front wall, Holmes fired point-blank into the door. A gale-force icy wind swept through the bullet-hole, like a blast from a ruptured gas-pipe. A fetid odour filled the room; the stench of the very pit itself, of all the world's carrion congealed into a single rotting mass. Holmes staggered back into Omally, coughing and gagging. The Irishman fell to his knees, covering his nose, and retching violently. Outside, the thing lashed at the door with redoubled fury. The iron hinges screamed in anguish, echoing those of the satanic emissary of death. Beneath the throbbing door, slim, barbed hooks worked and tore. A yellow haze of brimstone coloured the unbreathable air and the room shook and shivered beneath the hellish assault.

Omally crawled over to Soap Distant, who had wisely assumed the foetal position beneath the table. 'You've got to get us out,' he shouted, tearing away the hands clamped about the albino head. 'There has to be a way.'

'No way.' Soap tore himself from Omally's hold. 'No way.'

Shivers of woodwork flew from the bottom of the door as the evil barbs, now showing porcupine quills and scorpion tails thrashing about them, stripped the Ronseal finish clear down to the filled knot-holes. Omally stumbled to his feet. Sherlock Holmes was standing alone in the whirlwind, a speckled band tied bandana-fashion across his face. A finger in the air. The doyen of dicks was definitely off his trolley, thought John. As if reading his thoughts, Holmes suddenly struck him a weltering blow to the skull. Caught in surprise John hit the deck. Holmes leapt down upon him and pointed frantically through the swirling, cascading stench. 'Fire-place,' he shouted, his voice all but lost amidst the screaming, the hurricane, and the splintering woodwork. 'Up the chimney, get going, quick.'

It took very little time for Omally to cop on. Grabbing the huddled Pooley firmly by the collar, he dragged him towards what was surely the only hope of escape. Holmes stepped over to Soap and booted him in the ribcage. Soap peered up bitterly towards his tormentor, a dizzy blur, lost for the most part in the maelstrom of tearing elements. Holmes stretched deftly forward and hooked a pair of fingers into the sub-Earther's nostrils. 'Lead us out!' he cried, bearing him aloft. Whimpering and howling, but somehow happy for the nose-plugs, Soap staggered forward. Holmes thrust him head first into the fireplace and then, suddenly enlightened, Soap turned towards his persecutor with a nodding, smiling head and gestured upwards. Within a moment he was scrabbling into the darkness above. Omally pressed Jim onwards and followed hard upon his heels. Holmes spun about, revolver in hand, as the door burst from its hinges to spin a million whirling fragments about him. The icy gale tore his tweedy jacket from his shoulders as the thing rolled into the room, a tangle of barbs, quills and spikes, whipping and lashing and screaming, screaming. The great detective held his ground and fired off his revolver again and again into the spinning ball of death as it charged towards him.

The wind and the terror coming from below spurred on the three-man escape committee as it crept higher and higher up the narrow black chimney. Soap's voice called down from above, 'Come on, lads, shouldn't be more than a mile at most.' Pooley mumbled and complained, but Omally, who was tail-end Charlie and in the most vulnerable position, bit him in the ankle. A howl of pain and a sudden acceleration from Jim assured the struggling Irishman that the message was well-received.

The going was far from certain and made ever more perilous by the cramped space and the complete and utter darkness. Stones and grit tumbled down into the climbers' faces. Soap trod upon Jim's hands and Jim out of fairness trod upon John's. Higher and higher up the slim shaft of hope they clambered until at last they could no longer feel the icy wind rushing from below or the awful stench souring their nostrils. They paused a moment, clinging to what they could for dear life, to catch their breath, and cough up what was left of their lungs.

'How much farther, Soap?' Omally wiped at his streaming eyes and strained to support himself whilst delving in his pockets for a fag.

'A goodly way and all of it straight up.'

'There is actually an opening at the top?' Jim ventured. 'I mean I'd just hate to climb all this way and find myself peering out of a ventilation duct in Lateinos and Romiith's basement.'

'Hm. To be quite candid, this digging is one of the great grandaddy's. We shall have to trust to the luck of the Distants.'

'Oh, very comforting. Ooh, ow, ouch!'

'Sorry, Jim. Did I singe your bum?'

'Pass me up that fag, you clumsy oaf.'

'Smoking cigarettes can harm your health,' said Soap. 'Ooh, ow, ouch!'

'Onward, Christian Soldier,' said Jim, withdrawing the lighted fag from Soap's trouser seat.

The three continued their bleak and harrowing journey, now illuminated by the firefly-glow of three burning cigarettes. The first hour was really quite uneventful, other than for the occasional minor avalanche which threatened to plunge them to a most uninviting oblivion. It was several minutes into the second that things took a most depressing turn for the worst.

'I hate to tell you this,' said Soap Distant, 'but I've run out of passage.'

'You've bloody what? Careful there, that's my damn hand you're treading on.'

'Get a move on, Pooley.'

'Shut up, John.'

'Stop the two of you, for God's sake. I can't climb any higher.'

'Then get to one side and let us pass.'

'He means the passage has come to an end, John.'

'Then stand aside and let me kill him.'

'Shut up, I can see daylight.'

'What?'

The three men strained their eyes into the darkness above. In the far distance a dim light showed. A mere pinprick, yet it was some kind of hope, although not a lot.

'Get a move on,' yelled Omally.

'I've told you, something's blocking my way.'

'I just knew it,' said Jim, with the voice of one who just knew it. 'No way up, no way down. Doomed to starve here until we drop away one by one like little shrivelled up . . .'

'Give it a rest, Jim. What's in the way, Soap?'

Soap prodded above. 'Some old grill or grating, rusty as hell.'

'Easy on the descriptions.'

'Solid as a rock also.'

'Doom and desolation of misery, misery.'

'I have plenty of fuel in my lighter, Jim.'

'Sorry, John. Can't you wiggle it loose, Soap?'

'It's bloody rusted in. Can't you hear what I'm saying?'

'Let me get up there then.'

'There's no room, John.'

'Then we'll all just have to push, that's all. Brace yourself, lads, after three. Three!'

Soap wedged his shoulders beneath the obstruction, Jim got a purchase under his bum, with Omally straining from below.

'Heave.'

'AAAGH!'

'OOOOW.'

'Get off there.'

'My God.'

'Again, it's giving.'

'It's not giving, I am.'

'I felt it give.'

'That was my shoulder.'

'Put your back into it.'

'Mind where you're holding.'

'We're there, we're there.'

'Who said that?'

'One more time . . .'

'It's giving . . . It's giving . . . It's gone.'

Soap's head and shoulders battered up through the obstruction, a thin and crumbling iron grid cemented solidly into place through the application of fifty-years pigeon guano. 'You bastards!' Soap's arms were pinned at his sides, his feet lashed out furiously. 'You bastards!'

'Watch where you're kicking,' Pooley complained.

Soap's muffled voice screamed down at them from above. 'You bloody lunatics, I'm stuck in here.'

Now, as you might reasonably expect, a heated debate occurred beneath the struggling Soap, as to what might be the best means of adding the necessary irresistible force to the currently immovable object.

'We must pull him down and give him another charge,' Jim declared.

'Down on top of us so we all fall down the hole?'

'Grease him with goose fat.'

'You wally.'

'Tickle his feet then.'

'And you a millionaire, Jim. I thought you blokes had it all sussed.'

'A hoist, a hoist, my kingdom for a hoist.'

'I'm starting to suffocate, lads,' called Soap, distantly.

Pooley weighed up the situation. 'Doom and desperation,' he concluded.

'Stop everything,' Omally demanded. 'Enough is enough. It is a well-attested fact that the man who can get his head and shoulders through a gap can get the rest of him through also.'

Soap wriggled like a maggot on a number nine hook.

'Stick your head down here, Jim. I want to whisper.'

Soap thrashed and struggled, but his movements were becoming weaker by the moment.

'I can't do that to Soap!'

'It only takes a second. Take my word for it, it will do the trick.'

'But it's not decent.'

'Do it to Soap or I'll do it to you.'

Pooley closed his eyes and gritted his teeth. Reaching up he performed a quick vicious action.

'EEEEEEEEEOOOOOOOOOOOOOOOOW!'

A few moments later three men lay puffing and panting in the entrance to the loading bay at Meeks Boatyard on the bank of the Grand Union Canal. A few feet away a wall of impenetrable turquoise light rose from the water and spread away to either side and ever above.

'Too much to hope that we'd come up on the other side,' sighed Pooley.

Soap Distant, red-faced and clutching at himself, looked daggers at him. 'I'll have you for that,' he said painfully.

Jim smiled sickly. 'What could we do? Look on the bright side, at least we all got out alive.'

'Not all,' said John Omally.

'Eh?'

Omally gestured towards the open manhole through which they had just emerged. 'And then there were three,' he said in a leaden tone.

'Holmes,' cried Pooley. 'In all the excitement . . .' he scrabbled over to the manhole and shouted the detective's name into the void. His voice came back to him again and again, mocking his cries.

'Leave it, Jim.' Omally put his hand to his best friend's shoulder. 'He never had a chance.'

'I didn't think.' Pooley looked up fearfully. 'I didn't think.'

578

'None of us did. We only thought of ourselves and our own.'

'We left him to . . .'

'Yes.'

'The poor bastard.'

'The poor noble bastard. He saved our lives at the expense of his own.'

Pooley climbed slowly to his feet and thrust his hands into his trouser pockets. He looked up to where the Lateinos and Romiith building rose, filling the skyline. 'Oh shit!' he said, kicking at the toppled manhole cover. 'Oh, that's me finished. Those bastards are going to pay for this.'

'Oh yes,' said John Omally. 'They are definitely going to do all of that.'

30

Professor Slocombe withdrew a goose feather quill from the inkwell, and scratched out the fifth day from the June calendar. From beyond the shuttered French windows sounds as of merriment reached him. The Brentford Festival had begun. Throughout the night, the floats had been assembling upon the Butts Estate; lumbering through the darkness, heavy and ponderous. Through a crack in the shutters he had watched their slow progress and viewed their silhouettes, stark against an almost white sky. He had presided over many Festivals past and judged many a float competition, but he had never seen anything such as this. The shapes which rolled onward through the night upon their many wheels were totally alien, even to he who had seen so much. They were the stuff of nightmare, the dreams of the delirious and dying sick. If human hand had wrought these monstrosities, then it was a hand far better stricken from the arm.

A shiver ran up the long spine of the ancient scholar and his mottled hand closed about a crystal tumbler, half-filled upon his desk. Sleep had not touched him in more than a week and could offer nothing to soothe the ache which filled his heart and the very marrow of his bones. The great clock upon the mantelshelf was even now ticking away mankind's final hours. The prophecies were being fulfilled and the helplessness, to one who knew, but was yet unable to act, was beyond human endurance.

Professor Slocombe raked his hand across the desk and tumbled a stack of magazines to the carpeted floor. *Computer Weekly*, *Softwear Review*, *Micro Times*, *Popular Processor:* the poison fruits from the new technology's tree of life. Mankind had finally reached its own level of super incompetence, and made itself obsolete. It had promoted itself into extinction. Uncomprehending, it had made a science out of the thing; established a new order, laid the foundation for a new culture, and ultimately created a god. Or more accurately, aided the reinstatement of one previously superseded. Computer technology had given mankind the opportunity to regress, to cease thinking and in so doing cease to be. Why bother to add? The machine can do it for us. Mankind had been subtly tricked into believing that sophistication was progress. That godhead technology could cure man's ills at the flick of a switch, or if not that, then after a few more years of further sophistication. Man had lost sight of himself. Darkness was soon to triumph over the light, and the real means of confounding it were fading before the Professor's eyes. It was progress. Mankind had made so much progress that it no longer had any hope of survival. The miracle of science had become a chamber of horrors.

Somewhere in the dark tower which pierced the Brentford sky, the bleak temple of technology, the dragon lay curled in its lair. Its moment of release drew nigh, and who was there to plunge the sword of truth into its black heart?

The old man drained his glass and refilled it. He watched the gilded pendulum endlessly carving its arc. Where was Holmes? He was to have returned at daybreak, having followed up certain of his own leads, but he was hours overdue. The Professor had put into his keeping certain documents which he felt might hold an ultimate solution; but where was he now? Crowds were gathering in the street and it was an invitation to disaster to venture out of doors.

The sound of rumbling wheels and wild applause drew his eyes once more towards the shuttered windows. Should they choose now to make an assault upon the house the Professor knew he would be powerless to stop them. If ever there was a time to rally the troops beneath the banner of truth, now was definitely it.

At the present time, the Legion of Light was holed up in an outside privy in Moby Dick Terrace. There was more than just a little of the Lost Patrol about these three particular stalwarts.

'Can you see anything?' asked Jim, as Omally put his eye once more to the door's half-moon.

'I can see a good deal,' the brave Sir Knight replied, 'and to be perfectly frank, I like not a bit of it.'

'Let's have a squint,' said Soap Distant. 'And you keep your hands to yourself, Pooley.'

'They're in my pockets. Have a care where you step, it's crowded in here.'

Soap's pink eye rose to the carved crescent. 'My God,' said he.

'Not mine,' said John Omally.

Beyond the broken trelliswork which topped the garden fence, the great Festival floats were moving in slow procession. The thin dawn light, now tinting their silhouettes, brought them form and solidity. They were vast, towering to fill the streets, extending outwards within inches of the house walls. But what were they? They had something of the look of great bloated sombre reptiles, with scaled flanks and rudimentary limbs. All gill slits and hulking slabby sides. But they were too large, too daunting, too top-heavy. They did not fit. How many of these monstrosities had already passed and how many more were yet to come? The three men skulking in the evil-smelling dunny chose not to make bets.

Soap tore his eye from the hole with difficulty. Already the terrible compulsion to watch each movement of the swaying behemoths had become all but overwhelming. 'What are they?' he gasped, pressing his hands across the hole that he might see no more.

'The work of the Devil.' Omally's voice, coming from the darkness, put the wind up even himself. 'We have to get out of here. At least to the Professor's, then I don't know what.'

'A manhole, two gardens up, leads indirectly into a tunnel to his basement.'

'Oh no.' This voice belonged to Jim Pooley. 'Down again we do not go. I will take my chances above ground.'

'Well, please yourself. Whatever killed Holmes could not pursue us, it was pretty big. The tunnels hereabouts are small. I shall travel below; you do as you see fit.'

'I think we should stick together,' Omally advised.

'Are you sure it's safe, Soap?'

'To tell the absolute truth, I'm not too sure of anything any more.'

'Oh doom, oh desolation. Oooh ooooow!'

'Come on then.' Omally eased open the door, and the three men, one now limping a little and clutching at himself, ducked across the garden and shinned up a dividing fence. Soap's manhole was overgrown with weeds, which seemed promising. The hollow Earther took a slim crooked tool from his belt and, scraping away the undergrowth, flipped off the cover in a professional manner. 'Follow me,' he said, vanishing from sight.

Pooley looked at Omally. 'It's all up and down these days, isn't it?'

'After you, Jim. I should hate you to have cold feet.'

Muttering and complaining, the blighted billionaire clambered into the hole, followed by Omally, who drew the lid back into place.

Three darting images vanished from the screen of the Lateinos and Romiith computer scan, but already the information had been processed and relayed. No less than three Pooleys and a brace of Omallys were already scaling the garden wall. None of them were wearing carnival hats.

'Come on, lads.' Soap's voice urged them on from the darkness. 'And get a move on, something smells a bit iffy down here.' With hands about each other's waists, the most unmusical of all conga lines moved along a few short feet beneath the streets of Brentford. The rumble of the heavy floats and the muffled sounds of chanting, coming faintly to them as the duplicates mouthed to the holophonic images pouring into their brains through their minuscule headphones, were anything but cheering.

Soap suddenly came upon a heavy door blocking his way. 'There now,' said he.

'Where now, exactly?'

'We're there.'

'Good man, Soap. Now open up, let's not waste any time.'

The sounds of Soap fumbling in his pockets preceded a long and dismal groan. 'My keys.'

'Where *are* your keys, Soap?'

'In my desk, I think.'

A piercing white light illuminated the narrow black corridor. It shone directly on to three terrified faces, which had turned instinctively towards it. From about the light source came the flashing of blue sparks as several lethal handsets energized.

'Get out of the way,' said Omally. 'Let me at that lock.' The Irishman squeezed past the pink-eyed man and dropped to his knees. A neat roll of house-breaking implements materialized from a hidden pocket in his waistcoat and were rapidly unfurled.

'John,' said Jim, 'I had no idea.'

'They were the daddy's. Keep out of the light and keep those bastards back somehow.'

The light was moving nearer, spiralling along the wet brick-worked tube of the tunnel. The crackling of the handsets became audible.

'You'll not break it,' gibbered Soap. 'The lock is protected, it cannot be picked.'

'There is no lock which cannot be picked.' Omally flung aside a bundle of metal tags and slotted another sequence into the shaft of the skeleton key.

'You won't open it.'

'Shut up will you?'

'Get away.' For once doing the bold thing, Pooley had crept back up the tunnel towards his attackers. Now he lashed out with his hobnail at the blinding light as it reared up in his face. His boot connected and the beam swung aside, leaving Omally to fumble in the darkness. 'Nice one, Jim,' he spat. 'Now I can't see a bloody thing.'

'Get off me, leave hold.' Clawing hands reached out towards Pooley. In the coruscating blue fire his face twisted and contorted. 'John, protect me for God's sake!'

'Protect me . . .' Omally's brain kicked into gear. He tore his crucifix from about his neck and fumbling for the keyhole thrust it in and turned it sharply to the right. 'We're in, lads,' cried John.

'Go quickly,' said Soap. 'It is up to you now.' With a brisk movement he vanished away as if by magic into the brickwork of the passage.

Omally bundled his way through the doorway. Pooley wrenched himself away from his attackers, leaving them the right sleeve of his cashmere jacket as something to remember him by. The combined weight of two men hurtled the door back into its jambs. Fists rained upon it from without, but they could not penetrate the mantle of protection. Omally winkled out his crucifix and pressed it to his lips. 'And then there were two,' said he, sinking to his bum with a dull thump.

Jim slowly removed his jacket, folding it neatly across his arm. He laid upon the floor and began to leap up and down upon it. 'Bugger, bugger, bugger, bugger,' he went.

Omally watched the performance without comment. They were a strange old breed these millionaire lads and that was a fact. 'When you are done,' he said at length, 'I suggest we go upstairs and break the sad news of Holmes to the old man.'

'Oh bugger,' said Pooley.

'So you said.'

'No, this is another quite separate bugger. I left my fags in the top pocket.'

Professor Slocombe watched the two men plod wearily up the cellar steps, slouch down the side-corridor, and halt before the study door, twin looks of indecision upon their unshaven faces. He opened his eyes. 'Come in, lads,' he called. 'No need to skulk about out here.' Beyond the heavy-panelled door, Omally shrugged. With evasive eyes and shuffling feet, he and Jim sheepishly entered the study. Professor Slocombe indicated the decanter, and Omally grasped it up by the neck and rattled it into a crystal tumbler.

'Easy on the glassware, John.'

Omally, his face like a smacked bottom, looked up at the ancient. 'Sherlock Holmes is dead,' he blurted out.

Professor Slocombe's face was without expression. His eyes widened until they became all but circular. The whites formed two Polo mints about the pupils. The narrow jaw slowly revolved as if he was grinding his teeth upon Omally's words.

'That cannot be,' he said, slowly drawing himself from his desk and turning his back upon his uninvited guests. 'It cannot be.'

Omally poured his drink down his neck and slung another large measure into his glass. 'And mine,' complained Pooley.

The Professor turned upon them. 'How did this happen? Did you see it?' A high tone of fear choked at his voice.

'Not exactly,' Jim replied nervously, 'but believe us, sir, he could not have survived.'

'He saved our lives,' said Omally.

'But you did not actually see?'

'Not exactly, thank God.'

Professor Slocombe smiled ruefully. 'I thought not.'

Omally opened his mouth to speak, but thought better of it. If the old man did not care to accept the truth, then there was no good to be gained through labouring the point. 'All right,' said he carefully, 'we did not actually see it.'

'No,' said the Professor. 'You did not. So let us speak no more of the matter. There is little time left and much which must be done.'

'We are actually somewhat knackered,' said Jim, sinking into a chair. 'We've had a trying day.'

'I am afraid that it is not over yet. Kindly follow me.'

The Professor strode across the room and made towards the

study door. Jim shrugged towards John, who put his finger to his lips and shook his head. 'Come on,' he said. 'We've nothing left to lose have we?' Omally followed the old man into the corridor.

Jim, left alone for a moment, suddenly smiled. He drew from his trouser pocket the ormulu-trimmed Boda hip-flask he had recently purchased and not yet had the opportunity to use, and hastily filled it from the old man's decanter. 'No point in going unarmed,' said he, following up the rear.

The Professor led them up several flights of steps to the room which housed the camera obscura. When Jim had closed the door and plunged them into darkness, he winched the apparatus into action and brought the image of the surrounding area into focus upon the polished marble table-top. The sight which leapt into vision was such as to take the breath from their lungs. Omally crossed himself and took an involuntary step backwards.

The evil travesty which was the Festival procession now filled every road and side-street in view. And the tableaux wrought upon them were now becoming recognizable for the horrors they were. It was as if those earlier floats they had seen were but the blurred and ill-formed shapes of clay, awaiting the hand of the master craftsman to draw form from them. Now the lines were distinct, the contours clearly defined.

'Look there.' Jim pointed to a lighted float which passed close to the Seaman's Mission, a stone's throw from the Professor's door. Depicted there was the form of a giant, clad in robes of crimson and seated upon a great throne, carved with the gilded heads of bulls. Golden banners, each emblazoned with similar motifs, fluttered above and five hooded, stunted figures cowered at his feet in attitudes of supplication. The crimson giant raised and lowered his hand in mechanical benediction, and it appeared that for a moment he raised his eyes, twin blood bowls of fire, towards the men in the rooftop bower, and stared into their very souls.

'Him,' said Omally.

'And there.' Jim pointed vigorously. 'Look at that, look at that.'

As the throned float moved beyond the range of vision, another rose up behind it. Here, a legion of men climbed one upon another, pointing towards the sky. They were identical in appearance, each resembling to a tee the young Jack Palance: the Cereans.

To either side of the floats marched a legion of men, women, and children. Familiar faces, now alien and unknown; their faces wore

determined expressions and each marched in step, raising h
own banner. Each illuminated with eighteen vertical lines, p
three rows of six. The number of the beast, for it is the nun
a man. Professor Slocombe pointed towards the image. Away ᵢₙ the
distance, far greater shapes were looming into view, things so dark
and loathsome, that even there, upon the flat white marble surface,
their ghost images exuded a sense of eldritch horror which stunned
the senses.

'Switch it off,' Omally demanded. 'There is too much madness
here.'

'One more small thing you must see, John.' Professor Slocombe
adjusted the apparatus and the image of the Lateinos and Romiith
building drew a black shroud across the table-top. The old man
cranked the mechanism and enlarged an area at the base of the
building. 'Now look carefuly, did you see that?'

His guests blinked and squinted at the image. 'I saw something,'
said Jim, 'but what?'

'Look harder.'

'Yes, I see it.' It was but a fleeting movement, a single figure
detached himself from the throng, pressed his hand to a section of
the wall and was instantly swallowed up into the building to vanish
without trace.

'I was at a loss to find a means of gaining entry,' the Professor
explained, 'but Holmes reasoned the thing through and deduced
their method.'

'If it's a lock then I shall pick it.'

'Not on this occasion, John. But one of us here has the key in his
hand even now.'

'Oh no,' said Jim, thrusting his tattooed hand into his pocket.
'Not this boy, not in there.'

'You have the right of admission, Jim, right there in the palm of
your hand.'

'No, no, no.' Pooley shook his head vigorously, 'An eight a.m.
appointment with Albert Pierrepoint I should much prefer.'

'In my mind, only one course of action lies open. Unless we can
penetrate the building and apply the proverbial spanner to the computer's works, all will be irretrievably lost. We cannot think to destroy
the dark God himself. But if his temple is cast down and his
worshippers annihilated, then he must withdraw once more, into the
place of forever night from whence he has emerged.' Professor

Slocombe recranked the mechanism and the room fell into darkness.

'Oh doom,' said Jim Pooley. 'Oh doom and desolaoooow! Let go there, John.'

'We must make our move now.' Professor Slocombe's voice echoed in the void. 'There is no more time, come at once.' He opened the door and the wan light from the stairs entered the strange roof chamber.

'But we cannot go outside,' said Omally. 'One step out of this house and goodnight.'

'Have no fear, I have taken the matter into consideration.' Professor Slocombe led the two lost souls back to his study. 'You are not going to like this, John,' said he, as he opened the desk drawer.

'That should create no immediate problem. I have liked nothing thus far.'

'So be it.' Professor Slocombe drew out a number of items, which had very much the appearance of being metallic balaclava helmets, and laid them on the table.

'Superman outfits,' said Pooley, very impressed. 'I should have realized, Professor, you are one of the Justice League of America.'

'Silence, Pooley.'

'Sorry, John.'

'As ludicrous as these items at first must appear, they may well be our salvation. As you are no doubt now aware, the Lateinos and Romiith computer scan cannot penetrate lead. Hopefully, these lead-foil helmets will shield our brain patterns from the machine's detection and allow us to move about unmolested.'

'Size seven and a half,' said Jim. 'But I can fit into a seven at a push.'

'Good man. As an extra precaution, if each of you could slip another piece of foil into your breast pocket then your heartbeat should be similarly concealed. No doubt the infra-red image produced by body heat will still register, but the result should be somewhat confused. "Will not compute", I believe the expression to be.'

'Bravo.' Omally slipped on his helmet without hesitation.

'Very Richard the Lionheart,' chuckled Pooley.

'A fine man,' said Professor Slocombe. 'I knew him well.'

The three men, now decked out in their ludicrous headgear, slipped through the Professor's French windows and out into the garden.

At times one has to swallow quite a lot for a quiet life in Brentford.

Above the wall the titanic floats filled the street. As one by one the balaclava'd goodguys eased their way into the swaying crowd, each held his breath and did a fair bit of praying. Professor Slocombe plucked at Omally's sleeve. 'Follow me.' The marching horde plodded onward. The floats dwarfed both street and sky. Jim peered about him; he was walking in a dream. The men and women to either side of him, each wearing their pair of minuscule headphones, were unreal. And that he knew to be true in every sense of the word. At close hand, the floats appeared shabby and ill-constructed; a mish-mash of texture and hue coming together as if, and no doubt it was exactly thus, programmed to create an overall effect. No hand of man had been at work here. Like all else it was a sick parody, a sham, and nothing more. The bolted wheel near at hand turned in faulty circles grinding the tarmac, untrue. But it was hypnotic, its unreality drew the eye and held it there. 'Come on, Jim.' Omally tugged at Pooley's sleeve. 'You're falling behind again.'

Pooley struggled on. Ahead, the Lateinos and Romiith building dwarfed all beneath its black shadow. The sky was dark with tumbling clouds, strange images weaved and flowed beyond the mysterious glittering walls, shimmering over the roof-tops. Even now something terrible was occurring beyond the boundaries of the borough.

The awful procession turned out of the Butts and up into Moby Dick Terrace. Professor Slocombe drew his followers aside from the throng and the helmeted duo scuttled after him. 'Make haste now.'

The Lateinos and Romiith building filled the eastern skyline. Jim noted with increasing gloom that an entire terrace of houses had gone, overwhelmed by the pitiless structure which reared into the darkling sky.

On a roadside bench ahead an old man sat with his dog.

'Good day, lads,' said Old Pete, as the strangely-clad threesome passed him by at close quarters. 'Fair old do this year, isn't it?'

'Bloody marvellous,' Pooley replied. 'Hope to see you later for one in the Swan if all goes well.'

Old Pete cleared his throat with a curiously mechanical coughing sound. 'Look out for yourself,' said he.

The three men continued their journey at the jog.

'Stop here now,' said Professor Slocombe, as they came finally to the corner of the street. 'I am expecting somebody.'

'A friend I hope.'

'That would be nice,' said Jim, with a little more flippancy than the situation warranted. 'Organizer of the Festival raffle is it? Or chairman of the float committee?'

Omally took what he considered to be one of the last opportunities left to him to welt Jim about the head. 'Oow ouch!' he said, clutching at a throbbing fist. Pooley smiled sweetly. 'How much do you want for the copyright of this helmet?' he asked the Professor.

'Leave it out, you two. Here he comes.'

Along the deserted pavement, weaving with great difficulty, came an all too familiar figure, clad in grey shopkeeper's overall and trilby hat. But what was this that the clone shopkeeper rode upon his precarious journey? Could this be that creaking vestige of a more glorious age, now black and pitted and sorely taken with the rest? Surely we have seen these perished hand-grips before? Marvelled at the coil-spring saddle and oil-bath chainguard? The stymied Sturmey Archer Three-speed and the tungsten-carbide lamp? Yes, there can be no doubt, it is that noted iron stallion, that prince of pedaldom, squeaking and complaining beneath the weight of its alien rider, it can be no other. Let men take note and ladies beware: Marchant the wonder bike, it is he.

'Get off my bleeding bicycle,' yelled John Omally.

Norman the Second leapt down from his borrowed mount with some alacrity. Not, however, with sufficient alertness to avoid the sneaky pedal which had been awaiting its chance to drive in deep. Norman's right trouser cuff vanished into the oil-bath and the automated shopman bit the dust.

'Bastard,' squealed the mechanical man. 'I'll do for you.'

'Nice one, Marchant,' said John, drawing his bike beyond reach. The bicycle rang its bell in greeting and nuzzled its handlebar into its master's waistcoat.

'Bloody pathetic isn't it?' said Jim. 'A boy and his bike, I ask you.'

'Do you think we might apply ourselves to the job in hand?' the Professor asked.

'I like the helmets,' said Norman the Second. 'What is it then, Justice League of America?'

'A running gag I believe,' Jim replied. 'Did you have to bring his bike? That thing depresses me.'

'Easy Jim, if I am going to die, I will do it with Marchant at my side, or at least under my bum.'

'Bloody pathetic.'

'Time to do your party trick, Jim,' said Omally. 'Professor?'

The old man indicated a dimly-lit panel on the bleak wall. 'Just there,' he said.

'I don't know if this is such a good idea,' Jim complained. 'I think the best idea would be to give the place a good leaving alone.'

'Stick your mitt out, Jim.'

The cursed Croesus placed his priceless palm on to the panel. There was a brief swish and a section of the wall shot aside. A very bad smell came from within.

'Quickly now,' said the Professor. 'Keep your hand on the panel until we're all in, Jim.'

A moment later the gap closed upon three men, one robot shopkeeper, and a bike called Marchant.

'Blimey,' said Omally. 'I don't know what I expected, but it wasn't this.'

They stood now in what might have been the lobby and entrance hall of any one of a thousand big business consortiums. The traditional symbols of success and opulence, the marble walls, thick plush carpeting, chromium reception desk, even the rubber plant in its Boda plant-stand, were all there. It was so normal and so very ordinary as to be fearful. For behind this façade, each man knew, lurked a power more evil than anything words were able to express.

'Gentlemen,' said Professor Slocombe, 'we are now in the belly of the beast.'

Omally suddenly clutched at his stomach. 'I think I'm going to chuck up,' he said. 'I can feel something. Something wrong.'

'Hold on.' The Professor laid a calming hand upon Omally's arm. 'Speak the rosary; it will pass.'

Beneath his breath Omally whispered the magical words of the old prayer. Its power was almost instantaneous, and the sick and claustrophobic feeling lifted itself from his shoulders, to alight upon Jim Pooley.

'Blech,' went Jim. Being a man of fewer words and little religious conviction, he threw up over the rubber plant.

'That will please the caretaker,' chuckled Omally.

'Sorry,' said Jim, drawing his shirt-sleeve over the cold sweat on his brow. 'Gippy tummy I think. I must be going cold turkey for the want of a pint.'

'You and me both. Which way, Professor?'

The old man fingered his chin. 'There is no one on the desk, shall we take the lift?'

Norman the Second shook his head, 'I would strongly advise the stairs. A stairway to oblivion is better than no stairway at all I always say. Would you like me to carry your bike, John, or would you prefer to chain it to the rubber plant?'

'I'll carry my own bike, thank you.'

Pooley squinted up at the ragged geometry, spiralling into nothingness above. 'Looks like a long haul,' said he. 'Surely the cellar would be your man, down to the fuse boxes and out with the fuse. I feel that I have done more than my fair share of climbing today.'

'Onward and upward.'

Now there just may be a knack to be had with stairs. Some speak with conviction that the balls of the feet are your man. Others favour shallow breathing or the occupation of the mind upon higher things. Walking up backwards, that one might deceive your legs into thinking they were coming down, has even been suggested. In the course of the next fifteen minutes it must fairly be stated that each of these possible methods and in fact a good many more, ranging from the subtly ingenious to the downright absurd, were employed. And each met with complete and utter failure.

'I'm gone.' Pooley sank to his knees and clutched at his heart.

'Nurse, the oxygen.' Omally dragged himself a stair or more further and collapsed beneath his bike. 'We must give poor Jim a breather,' he said. 'The life of ease has gone to his legs.'

'Are you all right yourself?' Norman the Second enquired.

'Oh yes.' Omally wheezed bronchitically and wiped the sweat from his eyes. 'It is Jim I fear for.'

Professor Slocombe peered down from a landing above. If his ancient limbs were suffering the agonies one would naturally assume them to be, he showed no outward sign. The light of determination burned in his eyes. 'Come on now,' he urged. 'We are nearly there.'

'Nearly there?' groaned Jim. 'Not only can I hear the grim reaper sharpening his scythe, I am beginning to see the sparks.'

'You've enough breath, Jim; lend him your arm, John.'

'Come on, Jim.' Omally shouldered up his bike and aided his sagging companion. 'If we get out of this I will let you buy me a drink.'

'If we get out of this I will buy you a pub.'

'Onward and upward then.'

Another two flights passed beneath them; to John and Jim it was evident that some fiendish builder was steadily increasing the depth of the treads.

'Stop now.'

'With the greatest pleasure.'

Professor Slocombe put his eye to the smoked glass of a partition door. 'Yes,' said he in a whisper. 'We shall trace it from here, I think.'

Norman the Second ran his fingertips about the door's perimeter and nodded. 'Appears safe enough,' he said.

'Then let us see.' Professor Slocombe gestured to Jim. 'You push it, please.'

Pooley shook his head dismally but did as he was bid. The door gave to expose a long dimly-lit corridor.

Omally fanned at his nose. 'It smells like the dead house.'

Professor Slocombe pressed a large gingham handkerchief to his face. 'Will you lead the way, Norman?'

The robot entered the corridor. 'I can feel the vibration of it,' he said, 'but it is some distance away. If I could get to a VDU.'

'Stand alone, clustered, or wide-area network?' Omally asked, sarcastically.

'Super advanced WP and a spread-sheet planner, hopefully,' said Jim.

'Do I take the piss out of your relatives?' Norman the Second asked. 'Stick your palm against this panel will you please?'

'Security round here stinks as bad as the air,' Pooley pressed the panel. A gleaming black door slid noiselessly aside.

'Ah,' said Norman the Second, 'magic.'

The room was nothing more than a cell, happily unoccupied. Black walls, floor and ceiling. A cunningly concealed light source illuminated a centralized computer terminal, bolted to the floor. 'And people have the gall to ask me why I never take employment,' said Omally, parking his bike. 'Imagine this place nine to five.'

The robot faced the console and cracked his nylon knuckles. 'Now,' said he, 'only one small problem. We do not possess the entry code.'

Professor Slocombe handed him a folded sheet of vellum. 'Try this.' The automaton perused the paper and stared up at the old man.

'Don't ask,' said John Omally.

'All right then.' With a blur of digits the robot punched in the locking code. The words 'ENTER ENQUIRY NOW' sprang up upon the now illuminated screen. Norman's hand hovered.

'Ask it for permission to consult the main access body,' said the Professor.

Norman punched away at the keyboard.

PERMISSION DENIED, INFORMATION CLASSIFIED

Professor Slocombe stroked at his chin. 'Ask it for a data report.'

Norman did the business. Rows of lighted figures plonked up on to the monitor. Row upon coloured row, number upon number, little illuminated regiments marching up the screen. 'Magic,' crooned Norman the Second.

'Looks like trig,' said Jim disgustedly. 'Never could abide trig. Woodwork and free periods, but trig definitely not.'

'The music of the spheres,' said Norman the Second.

Professor Slocombe's eyes were glued to the flickering screen. His mouth worked and moved, his head quivered from side to side. As the projected figures darted and weaved, so the old man rose and fell upon his toes.

'Does it mean something to you?' Omally asked.

'Numerology, John. It is as I have tried to explain to you both. Everything, no matter what, can be broken down into its base elements and resolved to a final equation: the numerical equivalent; all of life, each moving cell, each microbe, each network of cascading molecules. That is the purpose of it all. Don't you see?' He pulled Omally nearer to the screen, but John jerked away.

'I'll not have it,' said he. 'It is wrong. Somehow it is indecent. Obscene.'

'No, no, you must understand.' The Professor crouched lower towards the screen, pushing Norman's duplicate aside.

Pooley was jigging from one foot to the other. 'Can't we get a move on. I'm freezing to death here.'

The room had suddenly grown impossibly cold. The men's breath steamed from their faces. Or at least from two of them it did.

Omally grasped Pooley by the wrist, for the first time he realized that the Professor was no longer wearing his helmet, and hadn't been since they had joined him on the landing. 'Oh, Jim,' whispered John, 'bad Boda.'

The 'Professor' stiffened; slowly his head revolved a hundred and eighty degrees upon his neck and stared up at them, sickeningly.

'Learn, last men,' he said, clearing his throat with the curiously mechanical coughing sound John and Jim had learned to fear. 'It is your only salvation. Humble yourselves before your new master.'

'Oh no.' Omally stumbled back and drew out his crucifix. 'Back,' he shouted, holding it before him in a wildly shaking fist. 'Spawn of the pit.'

The Professor's body turned to follow the direction of his face. His eyes had lost their pupils but now glowed from within, two miniature terminal screens, tiny figures twinkling across them in hypnotic succession. 'Behold the power,' said he. 'Know you the number of the beast, for it is the number of a man.'

'By the Cross.'

The thing which dwelt in the Professor's image thrust a hand into its trouser pocket and drew out a small black box with two slim protruding shafts.

'Head for the hills,' yelled Pooley, as the clone touched the nemesis button and the black rods sparkled with electric fire.

Omally flattened himself to the wall as the thing lunged towards him. A great explosion tore the world apart. Shards of glass and splinters of burning circuitry spun in every direction, spattering the walls and the two cowering men; flame and smoke engulfed the room. The Professor's duplicate stood immovable, his synthetic hair ablaze and his clothes in tatters. Norman's double drew a smouldering fist from the shattered terminal screen. He leapt forward, grasping the Professor's *doppelgänger* about the throat, and dragged it backwards. 'Out!' he shouted. 'Run for your lives, lads.'

Pooley and Omally bundled out of the door. John leapt astride Marchant and Pooley clambered on to the handlebars. At very much the hurry-up they took to the retreat.

In absolutely the wrong direction.

Omally's feet flew about and Marchant, realizing the urgency of the situation, made no attempt to ditch its extra rider. With its bell ringing dramatically it cannoned forward up the corridor. Figures appeared before them, dressed in grey uniforms and carrying fire-fighting equipment. Pooley struck aside all he could as the bike ploughed forward. As he cleared a path between several rather sloppy versions of himself, a thought struck him. The great machine for all its dark magic certainly lacked something in the old imagination department. Obviously when idling and stuck for something to do, it just kept turning out the same old thing.

595

'Do you know what this means?' Omally shouted into his ear. Pooley shook his terrified head and lashed out at another robot duplicate of himself.

'It means that I am the last Catholic on Earth.'

'Well, some good came out of it all, then.'

As Omally's hands were busily engaged at the handlebar grips, he could do no more than lean forward and bite Pooley's ear. 'Jim,' he shouted, 'Jim, as the last Catholic, I am Pope! Jim ... I ... am Pope. I am Pope!'

31

Some distance beneath the pedalling pontiff a great cry broke the silence. 'Fe . . . fi . . . fo . . . fum.' Neville the barbarian barman had finally reached a wall. And at long last he had found something he could thump. The thrill of the prospect sent a small shiver up his back which finally lost itself amid acres of straining muscle fibre. Neville ran his hand across the barrier blocking his way; hard and cold as glass. An outside wall surely? The barman pressed his eye to the jet crystal surface and did a bit of squinting. Something vague was moving about on the other side. People in the street? Neville drew back for a shoulder charge, and he would have gone through with it had not a sensible thought unexpectedly entered his head. He wasn't exactly sure which floor, or wherever, he was on. With his track record the movements were likely to be those of roosting rooftop pigeons. It could be a long hard fall to earth. Neville pressed his ear to the wall of black glass. He couldn't hear a damn thing.

Bash out a couple of bore holes to see out through, that would be your man. The barman drew back a fist of fury and hurled it forward at something approaching twice the speed of sound. With a sickening report it struck home. His knotted fist passed clean through the wall, cleaving out a hole the size of a dustbin-lid. 'Gog a Magog!' Neville took an involuntary step backwards. An icy hurricane of fetid wind tore out at him shredding away the last vestiges of his surgical smock and leaving him only his Y-fronts. Neville stood his ground, a great arm drawn over his face to shield his sensitive nostrils from the vile onslaught he had unwittingly unleashed. 'Great mother.' Tears flew from his eyes as he forced himself onward. With his free hand he tore out a great section of the wall, which cartwheeled away in the stinking gale. With heroic effort he charged forward into the not-so-great beyond.

The wind suddenly ceased and he found himself standing in absolute silence and near-darkness. It was very very cold indeed. 'Brr,' said Neville. 'Brass monkey weather.' To the lover of Greek mythology, what next occurred would have been of particular interest. But to a Brentford barman in his present state of undress, the sudden arrival of Cerberus, the multi-headed canine guardian of the underworld, was anything but a comfort.

'Woof, woof, and growl,' went Cerberus, in the plural.

'Nice doggy,' said Neville, covering his privy parts. 'Good boy, there.'

The creature tore at the barman, a blur of slavering mouths and blazing red eyes.

Neville sprang aside and ducked away beneath it as it leapt towards his throat. 'Heel,' he said. 'Sit.'

The thing turned and stood pawing the ground, glowing faintly, its scorpion tail flicking, low growls coming from a multiplicity of throats. By all accounts it made Holmes' Baskerville growler seem pretty silly.

'Grrrrrrrrrrrs,' went Cerberus, squaring up for the kill.

'Grrrrrrrr,' went Neville, who now considered that thumping a multi-headed dog was as good as thumping anything. 'Come and get your Bob Martins.' With a single great bound it was upon him, heads whipping and snapping. Neville caught it at chest height and pummelled it down with flailing fists. It leapt up again and he caught at a scaled throat, crushing his hands about it until the thumbs met. The hell-hound screamed with pain as Neville dragged it from its clawed feet and dashed it to the ground. Roll on chucking-out time, thought the part-time barman. With one head hanging limply but others still on the snap, the fiend was on him once more, ripping and tearing, its foul mouths snapping, brimstone vapour snorting from its nostrils.

The two bowled over again and again, mighty figures locked in titanic conflict. The nightmare creature and the all-but-naked barman. The screams and cries echoed about the void, the echoes doubling and redoubling, adding further horror to a scene which was already fearsome.

Roll over and die for your country Rover, was not in there.

'I'm not doing it, John, and that's the end of the matter.' Pooley clung precariously to his handlebar perch as Pope John the Umpteenth freewheeled down a deserted corridor. 'I am not a Catholic and I utterly refuse to kiss your bloody ring. The thing came out of a Jamboree bag for God's sake.'

'Let me convert you, Jim, come to the Mother Church before it's too late.'

'Let me down from here, I want a drink.'

'Drink?' Omally tugged on the brakes and sent Jim sprawling. 'Drink did I hear you say, my son?'

Pooley looked up bitterly from the deck. 'Popes don't drink,' he said. 'Such is well-known.'

'A new Papal bull,' his Holiness replied.

'All right then, but no ring-kissing, it's positively indecent.' Pooley unearthed the hip-flask and the two plodded on, sharing it turn and turn about.

'It's getting bloody cold,' Pooley observed, patting at his shirt-sleeves. 'And the pong's getting a lot stronger.'

'What do you expect?' Omally passed him back the hip-flask. 'Roses round the door?'

'Are you sure we're going the right way?'

'The passage is going down, isn't it? Would the Pope put you on a wrong 'n?'

'Listen, John, I'm not too sure about this Pope business. I thought you lads had to be elected. White smoke up the chimney or the like?'

'As last Catholic, I have the casting vote. Please don't argue about religious matters with me, Jim. If you let me convert you I'll make you a cardinal.'

'Thanks, but no thanks. God, it stinks down here. Couldn't you issue another Papal bull or something?'

Omally halted the infidel in mid-step. 'Would you look at that?' he said, pointing forward.

Ahead of them loomed a great door. It seemed totally out of context with all they had yet seen. At odds with the bland moder-nistic corridors they had passed down on their abortive journey of escape. It rose like a dark hymn in praise of evil pleasure, and hung in a heavily-carved portico wrought with frescoed reliefs.

Omally parked his bike, and the two men tiptoed forward. The hugeness and richness of the thing filled all vision. It was a work of titanic splendour, the reliefs exquisite, carved into dark pure wood of extreme age.

'Fuck me,' said John Omally, which was quite unbecoming of a Pope. 'Would you look at that holy show?'

'Unholy show, John. That is disgusting.'

'Yes, though, isn't it? And that.' Jim followed Omally's pointing finger. 'You'd need to be double-jointed.'

'There's something inscribed there, John. You know the Latin, what does it say?'

Omally leant forward and perused the inscription, 'Oh,' said he at length, his voice having all the fun of herpes about it, 'that is what it says.'

'Exit does it say?'

Omally turned towards the grinning idiot. 'Give me that hip-flask, you are a fool.'

'And you a Pope. Drink your own.'

'Give me that flask.'

'Well, only a small sip, don't want your judgement becoming impaired.' Pooley began to hiccup.

Omally guzzled more than his fair share. 'It's in there,' he said, wiping his chin and returning the flask to Pooley.

'What is?' Jim shook the flask against his ear and gave the self-made Pope a disparaging look.

'The big It, you damned fool.'

'Then next right turn and on your bike. We don't want to do anything silly now, do we?'

Omally nodded gloomily. 'We must; stick your tattooed mitt up against it.'

'I can think of a million reasons why not.'

'And me. For the Professor, eh Jim?'

'For the Professor, then.' Jim pressed his hand to the door and it moved away before his touch.

Omally took up his bike, and the two men stepped cautiously through the opening.

'Oh, bloody hell,' whispered Jim.

'Yes, all of that.'

They stood now in the vestibule of what was surely a great cathedral. But its size was not tailored to the needs of man. It was the hall of giants. The two stared about them in an attempt to take it in. It was simply too large. The scale of its construction sent the mind reeling. The temperature had dropped another five degrees at least, yet the smell was ripe as a rotten corpse.

'The belly of the beast,' gasped Pooley. 'Let's go back. The utter cold, the feeling, the stench, I can't stand it.'

'No, Jim, look, there it is.'

Ahead, across an endless expanse of shining black marble floor, spread the congregation, row upon regimented row. Countless figures crouched before as many flickering terminal screens, paying obeisance to their dark master. For there, towering towards eternity, rising acre upon vertical acre, spreading away in every direction, was the mainframe of the great computer. Billions of housed microcircuits, jet-black boxes stacked one upon another in a jagged endless wall. Upon giddy stairways and catwalks, minuscule figures moved upon its face, attending to its needs. Feeding it, pampering it with knowledge, gorging its insatiable appetite.

I AM LATEINOS, I AM ROMIITH.

The Latin, the formula, words reduced to their base components, stripped of their flesh, reduced to the charred black dust of their skeletons; to the equations which were the music of the spheres, the grand high opera of all existence. Omally slumped forward on to his knees. 'I see it,' he whispered hoarsely, his eyes starting from his head. 'Now I understand.'

'Then bully for you, John. Come on let's get out, someone will see us.' Pooley fanned at his nose and rubbed at his shirt-sleeves.

'No, no. Don't you understand what it's doing? Why it's here?'

'No. Nor why I should be.'

'It is what the Professor told us.' Omally struck his fist to his temple. 'Numerology; the power lies in the numbers themselves. Can't you see it? This whole madhouse is the product of mathematics. Mankind did not invent mathematics nor discover it. No, the science of mathematics was given to him that he might misuse it to his ruin. That he might eventually create all this.' Omally spread out his arms to encompass the world they now inhabited. 'Don't you understand?'

Jim shook his head. 'Pissed again,' said he. 'And this time as Pope.'

Omally continued, his voice rising in pitch as the revelation struck him like a thunderbolt. 'The machine has now perfected the art. It has mastered the science, it can break anything down to its mathematical equivalent. Once it has the formula it can then rebuild, recreate everything. An entire brand new world built from the ashes of the old, encompassing everything.'

'But all it does is churn out the same old stuff over and over again.'

Omally clambered to his feet and turned upon him. 'Yes, you damn fool, because there is one number it can never find. It found the number of a man, but there is one more number, one more equation which never can be found.'

'Go on then, have your spasm.'

'The soul. That's what the old man was trying to tell us. Don't you see it, Jim?'

'I see that,' said Pooley, pointing away over John's shoulder. 'But I don't believe it.'

Omally turned to catch sight of a gaunt angular figure clad in the shredded remnants of a tweed suit, who was stealing purposefully towards them.

'The Saints be praised.'

'Holmes,' gasped Pooley. 'But how . . .? It cannot be.'

'You can't keep a good man down.'

Sherlock Holmes gestured towards them. 'Come,' he mouthed.

Jim put his hand to Omally's arm. 'What if he starts clearing his throat?'

Omally shrugged helplessly. 'Come on, Jim,' he said, trundling Marchant towards the skulking detective.

Holmes drew them into the shadows. There in the half-light his face seemed drawn and haggard, although a fierce vitality shone in his eyes. 'Then only we three remain.' It was a statement rather than a question. Omally nodded slowly. 'And do you know what must be done?'

'We do not.'

'Then I shall tell you, but quickly, for we have little or no time. We are going to poison it,' said Sherlock Holmes. 'We are going to feed it with death.' The cold determination of his words and the authority with which he spoke to them seemed absolute.

'Poison it?' said Jim. 'But how?'

Holmes drew out a sheaf of papers from his pocket, even in the semi-darkness the Professor's distinctive Gothic penmanship was instantly recognizable. 'Feed it with death. The Professor formulated the final equation. He knew that he might not survive so he entrusted a copy to me. What he began so must we finish.'

'Hear, hear.'

'Computers are the products of diseased minds, but they will

602

react only to precise stimuli. Feed them gibberish and you will not confuse them. But feed them with correctly-coded instructions and they will react and function accordingly, in their own unholy madness. Professor Slocombe formulated the final programme. It will direct the machine to reverse its functions, leading ultimately to its own destruction. This programme will override any failsafe mechanism the machine has. I must, however, gain access to one of the terminals.'

'And how do you propose to do that?' Jim enquired as he slyly drained the last drop from his hip-flask. 'They all seem a little busy at present.'

Sherlock Holmes drew out his gun. 'This is a Forty-four Magnum, biggest . . .'

'Yes, we are well aware of that. It might, however, attract a little too much attention.'

'My own thoughts entirely. I was wondering, therefore, if you two gentlemen might be prevailed upon to create some kind of diversion.'

'Oh yes?' said Pope John. 'What, such as drawing the demonic horde down about our ears whilst you punch figures into a computer terminal?'

Holmes nodded grimly. 'Something like that. I will require at least six clear minutes. I know I am asking a lot.'

'You are asking everything.'

Holmes had no answer to make.

John stared hard into the face of Jim Pooley.

The other shrugged. 'What the heck?' said he.

'What indeed?' Omally climbed on to his bike. 'Room for one more up front.'

Jim smiled broadly and tore off his metallic balaclava. 'Then we won't be needing these any more.'

'No,' said John, removing his own. 'I think not.' Raising his hand in a farewell salute he applied his foot to the pedal. 'Up the Rebels.'

'God for Harry,' chorused Pooley, as the two launched forward across the floor, bound for destiny upon the worn wheels of Marchant the Wonder Bike.

A strange vibration swept up the mainframe of the great computer. The figures moving upon its face stiffened, frozen solid. Diamond-tipped lights began to flicker and flash, forming into sequences, columns, and star-shapes, and pyramids, veering and changing, pulsing faster and faster. A low purr of ominous humming rose in pitch, growing to a siren-screaming crescendo, as the machine's defence system suddenly registered the double image coursing across the floor of its very sanctum sanctorum. A ripple of startled movement spread out from the base, as the terminal operators took in the horror. Their heads rose to face the mainframe, their mouths opened, and the curiously mechanical coughing sounds issued forth, swelling to an atavistic howl.

'Do you think they've tumbled us, John?' Pooley clapped his hands across his ears and Omally sank his head between his shoulders as the two zig-zagged on between the sea of terminals and their shrieking, howling operators. The robots were rising to their feet, stretching out their arms towards their master, their heads thrown back, their mouths opening and closing. They stormed from their seats to pursue the intruders.

At the back of the hall a stealthy figure in shredded tweed slipped into a vacant chair and flexed his long slim fingers.

'Get away there!' Pooley levelled his travelling hobnail towards a shrieking figure looming before them. He caught it a mighty blow to the chest and toppled it down across the face of a terminal, tearing it from its mounts amidst a tangle of sparking wires and scrambled mechanisms.

'Nice one, Jim.'

'Hard to port, John.'

Omally spun a hasty, wheel-screeching left turn, dodging a cluster of straining hands which clawed towards them. They dived off down another line of abandoned terminals, the robots now scrambling over them, faces contorted in hatred, anxious to be done with the last of their sworn enemy. Small black boxes were being drawn into the light, emitting sinister crackles of blue fire. The chase was on in earnest. And there were an awful lot of the blighters, with just two men to the bike.

The figures on the high gantries now ran to and fro in a fever of manic industry. They worked with inhuman energy, tending and caring to their dark master. The lights about them streamed up the dead black face, throbbing in 'V' formations, travelling down again to burst into pentacles and cuneiform. They became a triple-six logo a hundred feet high which reformed into the head of a horned goat, the eyes ringed in blood-red laser fire. Blackpool illuminations it was not.

Holmes laboured away at his terminal, but here and there his trembling fingers faltered and he punched in an incorrect digit. Cursing bitterly, he was forced to erase an entire line and began again.

'You bastard.' A clawed hand tore off Pooley's right shirt-sleeve. 'I'm down to the arm. Let's get out of here, John!'

'Strike that man.' As a foaming psychotic rose up before them, Pooley levelled another flailing boot. The floor was now a hell-house of confusion. The robots were fighting with one another, each desperate to wring the life from Pooley and Omally. The cycling duo thundered on. Omally wore the orange jersey. The tour de Brentford was very much on the go.

'Get a move on, your Popeship, they're closing for the kill.'

John swung away once more, but the road-blocks were up. He skidded about, nearly losing Pooley, who uttered many words of justifiable profanity, and made hurried tracks towards the door. The androids encircled them, black boxes spurting fire. The circle was closing fast and every avenue of escape was blocked as soon as it was entered. Omally drew Marchant to a shivering halt, depositing Pooley on the deck. 'If you know how to fly,' he told his bike, 'now would be the time to impress me.' Sadly, the old battered sit-up-and-beg showed no inclination whatsoever towards sudden levitation. 'Well,' said John, 'one must never ask too much of a bike.'

Pooley rose shakily to his feet. To every side loomed a sea of snarling faces, surrounding them in an unbreakable circle. It was many many faces deep, and none looked amenable to a bloodless surrender. 'Goodbye, John,' said Jim, 'I never knew a better friend.'

'Goodbye, Jim.' Omally pressed his hand into that of his lifelong companion, a tear rose in a clear blue eye. 'We'll go down fighting at least.'

'At the very least.' Pooley raised his fists. 'Beware,' he cried, 'this man knows Dimac, the deadliest martial art known to . . . well, to the two of us anyway.'

The crowd rose up as if drawing its collective sulphurous breath, and fell upon them; cruel hands snatched down, anxious to destroy, to draw out the life. Omally struck where he could but the blows rained down upon him, driving him to his knees. Pooley could manage but one last, two-fingered expression of defiance before he was dashed to the deck. The writhing mob poured forward, thrashing and screaming, and it seemed that nothing less than a very timely miracle could save the dynamic duo now.

A great tremor rushed across the floor of the unholy cathedral. The lynch mob drew back in sudden horror, the black marble surface upon which they stood was being jarred as if by some great force battering up at it. Pooley and Omally cowered as the floor moved beneath them. A great crack tore open, tumbling androids to either side of it. Shards of sparkling marble shot up like some black volcanic eruption. An enormous fist thrust up from the depths. Another followed and, as the crowd backed into a growing circle, crying and pointing, a head and shoulders emerged from the destruction, rising noble and titanic amongst the debris.

'Fe . . . Fi . . . Fo . . . Fum.' As a great section of flooring smashed aside, Neville scrambled up through the opening. He was bloody and scarred, with great wounds upon his arms and legs, but his face bore an old nobility. He was indeed a Titan, a god of olden Earth. Yes, there were giants in the Earth in those days, and also after that. Neville stood, a Hercules in soiled Y-fronts. 'All right,' he cried. 'Who wants a fight then?'

'Not us,' cried Jim Pooley.

'Hello, lads,' said the bulging barman, sighting the cringing twosome, and flexing a selection of chest muscles. 'You appear to be somewhat unfairly outnumbered.'

'A bit of assistance would not go amiss.'

Neville flexed shoulders which had previously only been flexed by the Incredible Hulk, and even then to a minor degree.

'The rest has done him good,' said John. 'He looks well on it.'

Amidst a roar of green flame, Cerberus, the hound of hell, sprang up from the netherworld beneath to confront the barman. Its three heads, one now shredded and dangling, worked and snapped, saliva drooled from fanged jaws, and the stench of brimstone filled the already overloaded air. The scorpion tail flicked and dived. 'Come on, doggy,' called the barman. 'Time for a trip down to the vet's!' The creature launched itself towards him, passing over two terrified human professional cowerers. Neville caught it by a throat and the two crashed back into the crowd.

'On your toes, Jim,' called Omally. 'I see a small ray of light.' Shrinking and flinching, he and Jim edged away.

Neville swung the beast about, bringing down a score of robots. Others snatched at him but he swept them aside. Above, the mainframe pulsed and flashed, the moving lights forming obscene images. Pooley and Omally backed towards it, the exit was thoroughly blocked and the only way seemed like up.

Neville drove his fist through a plasticized face, sending up a cascade of synthetic blood. The hound of hell fell upon him once more but he tore down a lower jaw with a rending of bone and gristle. He was quite coming into his own.

Pooley and Omally gained a first staircase. 'Not more stairs,' gasped Jim.

'Pull the plugs out,' screamed Omally. 'Pull it to pieces. Follow me.' He thundered up the steps on to the first gantry. A vista of housed microcircuits met his gaze. Omally thrust forth his hand and tore out a drawered section, punching the things free. Pooley followed suit. Faces turned from the *mêlée* below, a group of androids detached themselves from the throng. Pooley ran along, drawing out random circuit patterns. Omally followed on, punching them from their housings. They gained the second level. Ahead stood a robot barring their way. 'You duck, I'll hit it.' Omally pressed Jim forward. The robot swung its hand at him but Jim ducked out of reach, grabbing at the knees. Omally drove a fist over his diving back, and the thing lurched off the gantry to fall into the chaos which now reigned below.

Neville stood defiant, taking on all comers. Cerberus with but one head left snarling, snapped at his ankles. A ring of shattered pseudo-corpses surrounded the combatants. John and Jim gained the third level. They were making something of an art out of dispatching the face-workers to whatever fate their microchipped god had in store for them.

'Pull it to pieces, Jimmy boy.'

'I'm pulling, I'm pulling.' Jim ran forward, dragging out segments, Omally came behind, kicking and punching. Microcircuits fell like evil snow upon the ferocious crowd welling beneath. Up another stairway and beyond.

Below them the lights exhibited a jumbled confusion. Great battle waged upon the floor. Neville stood head and shoulders, and a good deal more, above the great ring of his attackers. Blue fire sparkled as they strove to apply their killing weapons to his naked flesh, but Neville snatched out the arms from their silicone sockets and flung them high over his head. Cerberus had barked his last, but from the great chasm yawning in the marble floor other horrors spilled, spinning and thrashing, whirling out of the pit. Barbs and spines, close balls of fur, animals and swollen insects with the heads of infants. A darkness was filling the air, as it were a palpable thing, felt as much as seen. A fog of hard night.

'Bandits at six o'clock,' shouted Pooley. 'Get a move on, John.'

Omally applied his boot to the face of a pursuer as it loomed up from a stairwell. 'Onward and upward, Jimmy.'

The two men struggled in an unreal twilight world. Below, Neville's great warcries and the dull thuds of falling, broken bodies mingled with the unholy screechings of the monstrous obscenities pouring up from the pit. The siren had ceased its banshee wail but voices issued from the computer's mainframe, sighing and gasping from the circuitry, whispering in a thousand tongues, few ever those of man. A hand fastened about Pooley's ankle, drawing him down. Omally turned, sensing rather than seeing his friend's plight. He wrenched out a drawer-load of circuits and swung it like an axe, severing the clinging hand at the wrist. The thing remained in its deathlock about Jim's ankle, but the hero clambered on.

They were by now high upon the computer's great face. The air was thin but sulphurous. John clutched at his chest and strained to draw breath. Pooley leant upon his shoulder, coughing and gasping. 'We're running out of stairs,' he croaked. Above them now was nothing but darkness. They stood engulfed in it, breathing it. The sounds of battle echoed below but nought could now be seen of the conflict. 'You don't happen to see any daylight lurking above?' Jim asked. 'Fast running out of wind this man.'

'I can see sod all. Get off there.' A hand had John by the trouser cuff. He squinted down in horror to see no other face than his own, leering up. Without thought or feeling he tore out another section of circuitry and thrust it down into the snapping mouth which sought his leg. Sparks blistered the visage, and the thing sank away into the darkness.

Pooley clung to a further staircase, his energy, such as it ever was, all but gone. 'About making me a Cardinal?' he gasped.

The Pope followed him up. 'Bless you, my son. Popes and Cardinals first. Press on.'

The two thrust blindly onward; there was nothing left to do but climb. The metals handrails were like ice and their hands were raw from the clinging cold which tore at the flesh. Their attackers poured at them in an unceasing horde. They called to them in voices which were their own, jibing and threatening, crying out explicit details of the fate which they intended for them.

'I'm gone,' said Jim. 'I can climb no more, leave me to die.'

Omally fumbled about with numb and bleeding fingers. 'I will join you,' said he. 'There are no more stairs.' Pressed back against the icy metal of the mainframe the two men stood, alone and trapped. The mob surged up beneath them, swarming over the catwalks and gantries. There was finally nowhere left to run.

'I don't want to die here,' said Pooley, his voice that of pitiful defeat. 'I'm not supposed to be here, amongst all of this. This isn't true, this isn't right.'

Omally clung to the cold hard wall. They were neither of them supposed to be here. They were alone, two men, leaning now as in a time long past, upon the parapet of the canal bridge, above the oiled water of the old Grand Union. They looked down into their own reflections and those of the old stars. The stars always had much to say to drunken men, although none of their counsel and advice was ever heeded upon the cold, cruel, hangover-morning. But the truths lay there. For ordinary men, the truths always lay there upon that very moment before falling over. It was there at that instant a man was truly himself. The truth lay in that netherworld between drunkenness and oblivion, and dwelt where no sober man could ever grasp it. Only the drunken taste reality, and that for an all-too-fleeting moment. Removed from all sensible thought they made their own laws and moulded futures unthinkable at sunrise. Ah yes, John and Jim had tasted the truth upon many many an occasion.

'I see the light,' shouted Omally.

Jim craned his head. Above them a torch beam shone down.

'Get a move on lads,' called a voice. 'You're late as usual.'

'Norman,' called Jim, squinting up at the flashlight. 'Is that you?'

'Sorry, were you expecting someone else?' Norman stretched down an arm towards them. 'A stitch in time never won fair lady you know. Get a move on will you.'

'At the hurry-up.'

Omally shouldered Jim, who took Norman's hand and struggled up through the rooftop opening. The screaming swarm beneath were hard upon the Irishman's heel, he stretched up his hand towards Jim and Pooley leant down, fingers straining to reach. Their fingers met, but with a cry of horror Omally was gone. The screams of the mob welled up and the shouts of Omally as he battered down at the creatures engulfing him were nothing if not ungodly. Their fingers met again and Jim drew him up through the opening.

'That was quite close,' said John, dusting down his trousers. 'But where now?'

Norman's impossible machine was parked near at hand. An icy wind screamed over the rooftop, howling and moaning. 'This way,' cried Norman. With tears flying from their eyes, they followed the shopkeeper. Pooley shielded his face and moved with difficulty, the gale near tearing him from his feet.

The sky above was black and starless. The blank vista of the rooftop seemed to stretch towards impossible extremes in every direction. Beyond, in the vertical seas which girded the borough, strange images burst and sparkled, projecting themselves as if on three vast screens. But the panorama was shrinking, the streets still dimly visible below were diminishing. The building was shuddering beneath them, rising like a lift in a shaft. Its distant edges were becoming ever more distant. The building was duplicating itself. Time had run out, Holmes had not been successful, the Professor's programme had failed.

'The Millennium!' cried Norman, as he forced himself into the driving seat. 'Hurry!'

Pooley clung to the handrail of the time machine. The duplicates were pouring through the roof opening, a screaming mass tumbling towards them through the smashing firmament.

'This helicopter will never fly,' Jim told the shopkeeper.

'You have lost the last of your marbles.'

'All aboard now.' Omally did just that, as the satanic horde engulfed them.

Norman turned the ignition key and engaged reverse.

32

Neville, the new part-time barman, pushed the two brimming pints of Large across the polished counter-top and chalked the difference on to Pooley's slate, a mistake he would soon, through experience, come to rectify. He studied the two men who now sat before him. The sudden change in them was dramatic, it was as if they had aged by twenty years, literally overnight. And the state of them, their clothes hung in ribbons. Evidently they had taken work in the building profession and experienced a hard morning's graft.

The two men stared beyond his crisp right shoulder as if not noticing him. Their eyes seemed glued to the brewery calendar which hung unobtrusively amongst the Spanish souvenirs. Yet there was nothing strange to be seen in it. A simple cardboard rectangle with the brewery's name surmounting an out of register colour print of Constable's 'Haywain' and the hanging tab: June 6 1969. What could they see in it?

As if suddenly aware of the barman's scrutiny, the two men drew themselves away to a side-table, glasses in hand.

Omally studied his pint. 'And so, what do you propose we do now?' he asked.

Pooley sucked beer froth from his upper lip and made smacking sounds. It really did taste better back in those days. He tapped at his nose. 'I have a plan,' said he.

'Oh yes?' Omally's voice lacked enthusiasm.

'Indeed. Don't you understand? We've been given another chance to stop it all. At this moment, the Professor toils amongst his books and Holmes lies sleeping in his mausoleum. Norman chats, no doubt, with Leonardo da Vinci. Or has. I can't be certain exactly how it all works.'

'So what do you intend to do?'

'Down a few more pints for a first off. Drink up, John, you haven't touched yours.'

'I am not thirsty. Don't you understand? We are in an even worse position now than ever we were. We know what is to come, but we can do nothing whatever to stop it. We know that it cannot be stopped.'

'Oh fish,' said Jim Pooley. Delving into his trouser pocket he drew out a bulging drawstring pouch. 'Didn't know I had these, did you?' he asked, weighing it in his hand. 'Pooley's ace in the hole.'

Omally extended his hand but Jim held the thing beyond reach. 'No touching,' he said. 'All mine, but you can have a peep.' He loosened the neck of the pouch and held it tantalizingly apart.

Omally peered forward. 'Diamonds,' he gasped. 'A king's ransom.'

'I should say at the very least. I was going to have some cufflinks made up, but in all the excitement I completely forgot. I have no doubt they are synthetic, but nobody in this day and age is going to know that.'

'So what do you intend to do with them?'

'I am going to become a philanthropist,' said Jim. 'I am going to build a church.'

'A church?'

'A cathedral. And do you know where I'm going to build it?'

Omally nodded slowly. 'On the bombsite.'

'Exactly. No dirty big satanic buildings are going to come springing up from consecrated soil. What do you think, brilliant, eh?'

Omally leant back in his seat, his head nodding rhythmically. 'Brilliant, you almost cracked it.'

'I don't know about almost.'

'I do.' Omally's eyes flickered up towards Jim's. His hand moved towards his trouser pocket wherein rested a small black box, attached to which were a pair of wicked-looking rods. John Omally cleared his throat with a curiously mechanical coughing sound. 'Hand me the diamonds, Jim,' he said in a cold dead voice. 'We have other plans for them.'

Pooley's mouth dropped open in horror. Clasping his diamonds to his bosom, he kicked over the table on to the robot double of his dearest friend and made for the door.

'You're both barred,' screamed Neville, finding his voice, as the sleeveless Jim passed him by at speed, a raging Irishman with a black transitor radio close upon his heels.

As the two pounded off up the Ealing Road they all but collided with a brace of young gentlemen, who were strolling towards the Swan, studying a racing paper.

'Did you see what I just saw? asked Jim Pooley, rubbing at his eyes and squinting off after the rapidly diminishing duo.

John Omally shook his head. 'No,' said he. 'I am certain that I could not. How do you fancy Lucky Number for the three-fifteen?'

'What, out of that new Lateinos and Romiith stable? I wouldn't put my money on that.'